The
Foreign Legion
Novels
Part A

The Collected Novels of P. C. Wren
Volume 3A

Fiction Titles by P. C. Wren

Dew and Mildew. 1912
Father Gregory. 1913
The Snake and Sword. 1914.
Driftwood Spars. 1916
The Wages of Virtue. 1916
The Young Stagers. 1917
Stepsons of France. 1917
Cupid in Africa. 1920
Beau Geste. 1924
Beau Sabreur. 1926
Beau Ideal. 1928
Good Gestes. 1929
Soldiers of Misfortune. 1929
The Mammon of Righteousness. 1930 (U.S. title:
    Mammon)
Mysterious Waye. 1930
Sowing Glory. 1931
Valiant Dust. 1932
Flawed Blades. 1933
Action and Passion. 1933
Port o' Missing Men. 1934
Beggars' Horses. 1934 (U.S. title: The Dark Woman)
Sinbad the Soldier. 1935
Explosion. 1935
Spanish Maine. 1935 (U.S. title: The Desert Heritage)
Bubble Reputation. 1936 (U.S. title: The Cortenay
Treasure)
Fort in the Jungle. 1936
The Man of a Ghost. 1937 (U.S. title: The Spur of Pride)
Worth Wile. 1937 (U.S. title: To the Hilt)
Cardboard Castle. 1938
Rough Shooting. 1938
Paper Prison. 1939 (U.S. Title: The Man the Devil
    Didn't Want)
The Disappearance of General Jason. 1940
Two Feet From Heaven. 1940
The Uniform of Glory. 1941
Odd—But Even So. 1941

The Foreign Legion Novels

Part A

by

Percival Christopher Wren

THE WAGES OF VIRTUE
SOWING GLORY

Edited

by

John L. Espley

Riner Publishing Company
Culpeper Virginia
2017

ISBN
978-0-9990749-0-9

The text of *The Wages of Virtue* is in the Public
Domain since it was originally published in 1916

The text of *Sowing Glory* will be in the Public
Domain as of 1 January 2027 since it was
originally published in 1931

Contents

PREFACE

The Foreign Legion Novels Part A and *The Foreign Legion Novels Part B* by Percival Christopher Wren are the third of a multi-volume series, *The Collected Novels of P. C. Wren.* The purpose of publishing this series is to make the novels written by P. C. Wren more available to the reading public. His novel, *Beau Geste,* is usually recognized by most of the book dealers I have met over the years, but his other works are not so easily remembered.

I have been collecting P. C. Wren for over fifty years, and have been working on a comprehensive bibliography for almost as long. The text of the twenty-eight novels were easily obtained from copies in my own collection. For that collection, I certainly need to thank the hundreds of used book dealers I have purchased items from, and I need to thank some by name: Steven Temple, David Mason, Walt Barrie and, especially, the late Denis McDonnell for the advice and help they have provided over the years.

Mr. John Venmore and Mr. Philip Fairweather, both descendants of the late Mr. Richard Alan Graham-Smith, Wren's stepson, and the executor of Wren's estate, have both been very helpful in providing information about Wren.

As it has been over seventy years since the death of P. C. Wren (November 21, 1941), Wren's works have passed into the public domain in the United Kingdom. In the United States fourteen of the twenty-eight novels are still under copyright. Thanks to information provided by Messrs. Venmore and Fairweather, the heirs to Wren's literary estate, Mr. Danny Adekoya Campbell and Mr. Christopher Oladipo Graham-Smith, were located and permission has been granted to reprint Wren's works.

I also need to acknowledge the help and guidance of my family members: my daughter and son-in-law, Dawn and Andrew; my son and daughter-in-law, Jared and Claudia; and my long-suffering wife, Cathy. Thank you.

In conclusion, I need to thank Percival Christopher Wren for the many years of great enjoyment that his stories have provided. I know that Wren is not a literary or critical success, but, for me, he is one of the great storytellers of the early twentieth century.

John L. Espley
Culpeper, Virginia
July 1, 2017

INTRODUCTION

Percival Christopher Wren is best known as a novelist, publishing twenty-eight novels from 1912 to 1941, the most famous being *Beau Geste* (1924). Wren also published seven short story collections; *Stepsons of France* (1917), *The Young Stagers* (1917), *Good Gestes* (1929), *Flawed Blades* (1933), *Port o' Missing Men* (1934), *Rough Shooting* (1938), and *Odd—But Even So* (1941), containing a total of 116 stories. There were also two omnibus collections, *Stories of the Foreign Legion* (1947) and *Dead Men's Boots* (1949), containing stories taken from *Stepsons of France, Good Gestes, Flawed Blades*, and *Port o' Missing Men*. All 116 short stories can be found in the five volume collection, *The Collected Short Stories of Percival Christopher Wren.*[1]

Wren was a man of mystery in that the more popular biographical statements about him seem to be more fiction than fact. A typical biography places his birth in Devon in 1885, educated at Oxford, and having a career of world traveler, hunter, journalist, tramp, British cavalry trooper, legionary in the French Foreign Legion, assistant director of education in Bombay, and a Justice of the Peace. Most of the above biography, however, has not been verified.

Wren was born Percy Wren on November 1, 1875 in Deptford, a district of South London on the banks of the Thames. He did attend Oxford University, graduating in 1898 with a 3rd class

---

[1] For further information on *The Collected Short Stories of Percival Christopher Wren* see rinerpublishing.wordpress.com

honours in History leading to a Bachelor of Arts degree. He attained his "M.A." in 1901. In those days, a person acquired a "M.A." after a certain number of years (three in Wren's case) and upon payment of a fee.

After leaving Oxford, he married Alice Lucie Shovelier in December 1899 with whom he had a daughter, Estelle Lenore Wren, born in February 1901, and a son, Percival Rupert Christopher Wren, born in February 1904. Percy worked as a teacher at various commercial schools until 1903 when he and his family left England for India.

From 1903 to approximately 1919 Wren was employed as an educator by the Indian Educational Service (I.E.S.). During that time he published a number of educational textbooks, some of which are still in use in Indian schools today. It was during this period that he started using the name Percival C. and Percival Christopher on the textbooks.

From 1905 to 1915, he also served in the Volunteer Corps (Sind and Poona) in India (see the novel *Driftwood Spars*, which has a description of a Volunteer Corps), and was appointed a Captain in the Indian Army Reserve of Officers, the 101st Grenadiers of the Indian Infantry, in November 1914. He probably saw action in the East African campaign of World War I (see the novel *Cupid in Africa*, which takes place in East Africa), and resigned from the Indian Army Reserve of Officers in November 1915.[2]

Wren's first novel, *Dew and Mildew*, was published by Longmans, Green in 1912. His first

---

[2] Most of the biographical information about Wren has been obtained through certificates, documents, and original research at the British Library, Bodleian Library, and the India Office papers. Detailed documentation and sources will be cited in the biographical essay to be included in the forthcoming publication, *An Annotated Bibliography of Percival Christopher Wren.*

novel of the French Foreign Legion, *The Wages of Virtue*, was written in 1913 and published by John Murray in 1916. One of the many questions about Wren is whether he did serve in the French Foreign Legion. Given the chronology of his documented biography it is hard to see where he had time to actually serve in the Legion. Wren himself always maintained that he had served, and his stepson, Richard Alan Graham-Smith, who died in 2006, "strongly maintained that Wren had indeed served in the French Foreign Legion and was always quick to refute those who said otherwise."[3]

*   *   *   *   *   *   *

The series, *The Collected Novels of P. C. Wren*, is intended to include all twenty-eight novels in seven thematic omnibus volumes. The number of physical volumes will be fourteen, with each thematic volume divided into Part A and Part B. The individual titles will not be in Wren's original publication order, but will instead have a connecting theme such as characters or locale. The seven volumes are[4]:

> v. 1 - The Geste Novels
> > Part A:
> > > Beau Geste
> > > Beau Sabreur
> > Part B:
> > > Beau Ideal
> > > Spanish Maine
> v. 2 - The Sinbad Novels
> > Part A:
> > > Action and Passion

---

[3] wikipedia.org/wiki/P._C._Wren
[4] The order of volumes four through seven has been modified since the publication of volume two, *The Sinbad Novels*.

Introduction

Cupid in Africa
Mysterious Waye

*   *   *   *   *   *   *

Volume Three of *The Collected Novels of P. C. Wren, The Foreign Legion Novels*, contains four novels that feature the French Foreign Legion. There are other novels by Wren featuring the Foreign Legion (the three Geste novels, *Spanish Maine, Fort in the Jungle,* and *Valiant Dust*), but they are included in different volumes in *The Collected Novels of P. C. Wren.*

*   *   *   *   *   *   *

The Foreign Legion Novels Part A

The Foreign Legion Novels Part A contains *The Wages of Virtue* (1916), Wren's first novel of the French Foreign Legion, and *Sowing Glory* (1931), a novel supposedly only edited, not written, by Wren.

The Wages of Virtue is the story of Sir Montague Merline and other friends of his in the Legion. Merline (known as John Bull) joined the Legion after recovering from his apparent death in combat in Africa, being only severely wounded and suffering memory loss. When he regained his memory after several years he was told that his wife had married again. In an act of selfless denial he joined the Legion to keep his identity a secret. This theme of a wife remarrying again after her husband's supposed death is also in the novel, *Cardboard Castle* (1938), where the husband is not so noble as Merline.

The majority of the story in *The Wages of Virtue* takes place in the fourteenth year of Merline's enlistment in the Legion and starts with the arrival of a new recruit, an Englishman by the name of Reginald Rupert. The novel is also the story of Carmelita and The Bucking Bronco, the American friend of John Bull (Merline), and Carmelita's boyfriend, the villainous Luigi. There is also the side story of a young woman hiding in the Legion: a pair of Russian fraternal twins. This theme, of a woman disguising herself as a legionnaire, is also the prevalent theme of *Sowing Glory,* the other story in *The Foreign Legion Novels Part A.*

The Wages of Virtue contains several minor characters that also appear in other short stories and novels by Wren: mostly notably, Cigale the Grasshopper, Tant-de-Soif, and Tou-tou Boil-the Cat. Furthermore, John Bull, Bucking Bronco, Reginald Rupert, and Herb Higgins are also featured in a number of short stories in the next Foreign Legion book by Wren: *Stepsons of France* (1917).[5]

The Wages of Virtue, written in 1913, and published in 1916 is the first of Wren's stories to feature the French Foreign Legion. As such, it is of interest since Wren is forever linked to the Legion, most especially for the popularity of *Beau Geste.* If the "written in 1913" is accurate, Wren wrote *The Wages of Virtue* before World War I commenced in July 1914 and before his wife's death in September 1914. Those dates are important since according to The Historical and Information Service of the Foreign Legion it was "their belief that he [Wren] obtained his information [about the Legion] from a legionnaire discharged in 1922."[6]

---

[5] All of the stories from *Stepsons of France* are available in volume one of *The Collected Short Stories of Percival Christopher Wren.*

[6] Windrow, Martin. *Our Friends Beneath the Sands: The Foreign Legion in France's Colonial Conquests 1870-1935.* London, Orion Books, 2011. page 627

Given that Wren entered Oxford in 1894, graduated with a third class degree in 1898, was married in December 1899, and left for India in 1903, it is difficult to see when Wren could have served in the Legion other than before he entered Oxford. It is conceivable, but not likely, that he may have joined the Legion sometime from April 1891 when the census has him living with his family (age 15) to when he entered Oxford in the Fall of 1894. If Wren had not served in the Legion, then the question to be asked is, where did Wren obtain his knowledge of the Legion? While *The Wages of Virtue* and the short stories of *Stepsons of France* are escapist and romantic,

> ". . . Wren's scene-setting is clearly based on detailed knowledge of barracks life at Sidi bel Abbès in the first years of the century. His short stories are set (again, vaguely) in the context of actual campaigns, in Tonkin and Dahomey as well as the Sud-Oranais and Morocco . . ."[7]

What seems most likely is that Wren obtained his knowledge of the Legion from three first person accounts of the Legion published before 1913. These accounts are *A Soldier of the Legion* by George Manington,[8] *In the Foreign Legion* by Erwin Rosen,[9] and *Life in the Legion* by Frederic Martyn.[10]

The Wages of Virtue is Wren's most frequently

---

[7] *Ibid.* page 622.
[8] Manington, George. *A Soldier of the Legion*. London, John Murray, 1907. Electronic version available at www.gutenberg.org/ebooks/53902
[9] Rosen, Erwin. *In the Foreign Legion*. London, Duckworth & Co., 1910. Electronic version available at www.gutenberg.org/ebooks/40479
[10] Martyn, Frederic. *Life in the Legion*. London, Everett & Co., 1911. Electronic version available at archive.org/details/lifeinlegionfrom00martiala

reprinted book after the Geste trilogy: *Beau Geste*, *Beau Sabreur*, and *Beau Ideal*. Until the ready availability of old books due to the explosion of the internet and Print-on-Demand type publications, the last time *The Wages of Virtue* was reprinted was in 1961. The dedication is "To the Charmingest Woman." Since Wren's first wife, Alice Lucie Shovelier, died in 1914, and *The Wages of Virtue* was published in 1916, it is assumed that this person was Wren's to be second wife, Isobel Mountain Graham-Smith, who Wren married in 1927. In November 1924, a silent film version (now lost) was made of *The Wages of Virtue* starring Gloria Swanson.

The second novel in *The Foreign Legion Novels Part A* is *Sowing Glory, The Memoirs of "Mary Ambree" the English Woman-Legionary*, supposedly "Edited by Percival Christopher Wren." It is assumed by most, if not all, critics, reviewers, and librarians, that the "edited" part is a ploy by Wren and his publisher, John Murray. Wren claims, in the Preface,

> "In this book, then, the words are the words of the Editor, but the actual facts, incidents, adventures, memories, descriptions, tales, and stories, are those of 'Mary Ambree'; and the *dramatis personæ* are the living (and the dead) men who were her comrades in the ranks of the French Foreign Legion."[11]

In addition, Wren wrote that an article appeared in the June 19, 1931 issue of the Daily Telegraph about the possibility of a woman

---

[11] page 311, herein.

disguising herself in the Legion.[12] Whatever the truth is, of whether Wren edited Mary Ambree's memoirs, Wren and his publisher certainly went to a lot of trouble to impress people as to truthfulness of the matter.

If it were not for the fantastic ploy of a woman being in the Legion, this book would be one of Wren's most accurate descriptions of the Legion. The book has several descriptions of the Legion and warfare that seemed to "read true". For example, see Wren's description of warfare in Chapter XIV, especially the following:

> I imagine that a man pursued by an elephant would reck but little of an attack by a flea that bit him as he fled. To me, in that hideous hour of agony, Arabs were as fleas, and wounds as flea-bites, while with straining lungs, whooping breath, and bursting heart, I laboured up that awful slope, sideways, on the edges of the soles of my boots, openly and unashamedly using my rifle as an alpenstock, a crutch, and a walking-stick.
>
> I saw the forms of bolting Arabs. . . .
>
> I saw men fall. . . .
>
> I knew that men above me, and not far in front of me, were shooting at point-blank range. . . .
>
> I did not care.
>
> I was past caring for anything, in that dreadful heat, climbing that

---

[12] The existence of such an article appearing in the Daily Telegraph was confirmed by research at the British Library by Mr. Richard Fidczuk in an email received 17 Feb 2017.

mountain of scorching rock; my cracked lips, parched tongue, my whole mouth, like dried bone; my eyeballs bursting in my head; and the knowledge that, with another step, I should vomit my soul up. . . .

And just before I fell, we got the signal to halt.

I dropped to the ground, rolled over that I might rest against my pack and get the sun off my back, and lay gasping like a fish upon a river-bank.

And what . . . *what?*

"*Baïonnettes au canon . . . !* Prepare to charge!"

It was utterly inconceivable. What raving lunatic thought that we . . .

"Come on, *salauds! En avant!* Up with you! *Now* come on . . . *Cha-a-a-arge!*"

And the incredible N.C.O.'s actually sprang up, actually dashed forward . . . and actually expected us to follow them.[13]

For anybody who has been in the military, especially in combat, the above quote sounds accurate.

Other areas of accuracy are the impact of World War I on individuals in Chapter II,[14] and the stories of the "Voulet-Chanoine" affair[15] and the "Battle of Camarón"[16] from the point of view of an old legionnaire.

---

[13]The quote is from pages 507-508 herein.

[14] Pages 328-331, herein.

[15] Pages 458-477, herein. For further information on the Voulet-Chanoine affair, see wikipedia.org/wiki/Voulet-Chanoine_Mission

[16] Pages 405-407, herein. For further information on the Battle of Camarón see wikipedia.org/wiki/Battle_of_Camarón

One of the interesting features of *Sowing Glory* is that almost all of Part 2 is composed of legionnaires telling various stories. These stories are reminiscent of Wren's short stories in *Stepsons of France* (1917), *Good Gestes* (1929), *Flawed Blades* (1933), and *Port o' Missing Men* (1934). There is one incident told towards the end of the book that resembles the Tant de Soif story, "The Return of Odo Klemens", which appeared in *Port o' Missing Men.* Both stories recount attempts by former deserters to recruit legionnaries on guard duty.

Sowing Glory was first published in 1931, initially appearing in serialized form in various newspapers from July of that year. In reverse to what was normal, the American book edition by Stokes was published a month earlier (August 27) than the British edition by Murray (September 23). The book was also published in 1931 by Murray in an Imperial Library edition and by Longmans, Green in Canada. Those were the last English language printings of *Sowing Glory* until this edition.

*   *   *   *   *   *   *

The original spelling, punctuation, and grammar, except for obvious errors, have been preserved as found in the latest editions/printings of the stories during Wren's lifetime (1875-1941). The footnotes, in the novels, are also as found in the original source material.

THE WAGES OF VIRTUE

(Written in the year 1913)

TO
THE CHARMINGEST WOMAN

"Vivandière du régiment,
C'est Catin qu'on me nomme;
Je vends, je donne, je bois gaiment,
Mon vin et mon rogomme;
J'ai le pied leste et l'œil mutin,
Tintin, tintin, tintin, r'lin tintin,
Soldats, voilà Catin!

"Je fus chère à tous nos héros;
Hélas! combien j'en pleure,
Ainsi soldats et généraux
Me comblaient à tout heure
D'amour, de gloire et de butin,
Tintin, tintin, tintin, r'lin tintin
D'amour, de gloire et de butin,
Soldats, voilà Catin!"

BÉRANGER

CONTENTS

PROLOGUE

Lord Huntingten emerged from his little green tent, and strolled over to where Captain Strong, of the Queen's African Rifles, sat in the "drawing-room." The drawing-room was the space under a cedar fir and was furnished with four Roorkee chairs of green canvas and white wood, and a waterproof ground-sheet.

"I do wish the Merlines would roll up," he said. "I want my dinner."

"Not dinner time yet," remarked Captain Strong. "Hungry?"

"No," answered Lord Huntingten almost snappishly. Captain Strong smiled. How old Reggie Huntingten always gave himself away! It was the safe return of Lady Merline that he wanted.

Captain Strong, although a soldier, the conditions of whose life were almost those of perpetual Active Service, was a student—and particularly a student of human nature. Throughout a life of great activity he found, and made, much opportunity for sitting in the stalls of the Theatre of Life and enjoying the Human Comedy. This East African shooting-trip with Lord Huntingten, Sir Montague, and Lady Merline, was affording him great entertainment, inasmuch as Huntingten had fallen in love with Lady Merline and did not know it. Lady Merline was falling in love with Huntingten and knew it only too well, and Merline loved them both. That there would be no sort or kind of "dénouement," in the vulgar sense, Captain Strong was well and gladly aware—for Huntingten was as honourable a man as ever lived, and Lady Merline just as admirable. No saner, wiser, nor better woman had Strong ever met, nor any as well balanced. Had there been any possibility of "developments," trouble, and the usual fiasco of scandal and the Divorce Court, he would have taken an early opportunity of leaving the party and rejoining his company at Mombasa. For Lord Huntingten was his school, Sandhurst and lifelong friend, while Merline was his brother-in-arms and comrade of many an unrecorded, nameless expedition, foray, skirmish, fight and adventure.

"Merline shouldn't keep her out after dusk like this," continued Lord Huntingten. "After all, Africa's Africa and a woman's a woman."

"And Merline's Merline," added Strong with a faint hint of reproof. Lord Huntingten grunted, arose, and strode up and down. A fine upstanding figure of a man in the exceedingly becoming garb of khaki cord riding-breeches, well-cut high boots, brown flannel shirt and broad-brimmed felt hat. Although his hands were small, the arms exposed by the rolled-up shirtsleeves were those of a navvy, or a blacksmith. The face, though tanned and wrinkled, was finely cut and undeniably handsome, with its high-bridged nose, piercing blue eyes, fair silky moustache and prominent chin. If, as we are sometimes informed, impassivity and immobility of countenance are essential to aspirants for such praise as is contained in the term "aristocratic," Lord Huntingten was not what he himself would have described as a "starter," for never did face more honestly portray feeling than did that of Lord Huntingten. As a rule it was wreathed in smiles, and brightly reflected the joyous, sunny nature of its owner. On those rare occasions when he was angered, it was convulsed with rage, and, even before he spoke, all and sundry were well aware that his lordship was angry. When he did speak, they were confirmed in

8

the belief without possibility of error. If he were disappointed or chagrined this expressive countenance fell with such suddenness and celerity that the fact of so great a fall being inaudible came as a surprise to the observant witness. At that moment, as he consulted his watch, the face of this big, generous and lovable man was only too indicative of the fact that his soul was filled with anxiety, resentment and annoyance. Captain Strong, watching him with malicious affection, was reminded of a petulant baby and again of a big naughty boy who, having been stood in the corner for half an hour, firmly believes that the half-hour has long ago expired. Yes, he promised himself much quiet and subtle amusement, interest and instruction from the study of his friends and their actions and reactions during the coming weeks. What would Huntingten do when he realised his condition and position? Run for his life, or grin and bear it? If the former, where would he go? If, living in Mayfair and falling in love with your neighbour's wife, the correct thing is to go and shoot lions in East Africa, is it, conversely, the correct thing to go and live in Mayfair if, shooting lions in East Africa, you fall in love with your neighbour's wife? Captain Strong smiled at his whimsicality, and showed his interesting face at its best. A favourite remark of his was to the effect that the world's a queer place, and life a queer thing. It is doubtful whether he realised exactly how queer an example of the fact was afforded by his being a soldier in the first place, and an African soldier in the second. When he was so obviously and completely cut out for a philosopher and student (with relaxations in the direction of the writing of Ibsenical-Pinerotic plays and Shavo-Wellsian novels), what did he in that galley of strenuous living and strenuous dying? Further, it is interesting to note that among those brave and hardy men, second to none in keenness, resourcefulness and ability, Captain Strong was noted for these qualities.

A huge Swahili orderly of the Queen's African Rifles, clad in a tall yellow tarboosh, a very long blue jersey, khaki shorts, blue puttees and hobnail boots, approached Captain Strong and saluted. He announced that Merline *Bwana* was approaching, and, on Strong's replying that such things did happen, and even with sufficient frequency to render the widest publication of the fact unnecessary, the man informed him that the *macouba Bwana Simba* (the big Lion Master) had given his bearer orders to have the approach of Merline *Bwana* signalled and announced.

Turning to Huntingten, Strong bade that agitated nobleman to be of good cheer, for Merline was safe—his *askaris* were safe—his pony was safe, and it was even reported that all the dogs were safe.

"Three loud cheers," observed his lordship, as his face beamed ruddily, "but, to tell you the truth, it was of *Lady* Merline I was thinking. . . . You never know in Africa, you know. . . ."

Captain Strong smiled.

Sir Montague and Lady Merline rode into camp on their Arab ponies a few minutes later, and there was a bustle of Indian and Swahili "boys" and bearers, about the unlacing of tents, preparing of hot baths, the taking of ponies and guns, and the hurrying up of dinner.

While Sir Montague gave orders concerning the *enyama*[17] for the *safari* servants and porters, whose virtue had merited this addition to their

---

[17] Meat.

posho,[18] Lady Merline entered the "drawing-room," and once again gladdened the heart of Lord Huntingten with her grace and beauty. He struck an attitude, laid his hand upon his heart, and swept the ground with his slouch hat in a most gracefully executed bow. Lady Merline, albeit clad in brief khaki shooting-costume, puttees, tiny hobnail boots, and brown pith helmet, returned the compliment with a Court curtsey.

Their verbal greeting hardly sustained the dignity of the preliminaries.

"How's Bill the Lamb?" quoth the lady.

"How's Margarine?" was the reply.

Their eyes interested Captain Strong more than their words.

(Lady Merline's eyes were famous; and, beautiful as Strong had always realised those wonderful orbs to be, he was strongly inclined to fancy that they looked even deeper, even brighter, even more beautiful when regarding the handsome sunny face of Lord Huntingten.)

Sir Montague Merline joined the group.

"Hallo, Bill! Hallo, Strong!" he remarked. "I say, Strong, what's *marodi,* and what's *gisi* in Somali?"

"Same as *tembo* and *mbogo* in Swahili," was the reply.

"Oh! Elephant and buffalo. Well, that one-eyed Somali blighter with the corrugated forehead, whom Abdul brought in, says there are both—close to Bamania over there—about thirteen miles you know."

"He's a liar then," replied Captain Strong.

"Swears the elephants went on the tiles all night in a *shamba*[19] there, the day before yesterday."

---

[18] Food.
[19] Garden. Cultivation.

"Might go that way, anyhow," put in Lord Huntingten. "Take him with us, and rub his nose in it if there's nothing."

"*You*' re nothing if not lucid, Bill," said Lady Merline. "I'm off to change," and added as she turned away, "I vote we go to Bamania anyhow. There may be lemons, or mangoes, or bananas or something in the *shamba*, if there are no elephants or buffaloes."

"Don't imagine you are going upsetting elephants and teasing buffaloes, young woman," cried "Bill" after her as she went to her tent. "The elephants and buffaloes of these parts are the kind that eat English women, and feeding the animals is forbidden. . . ."

It occurred to Captain Strong, that silent and observant man, that Lady Merline's amusement at this typical specimen of the Huntingten humour was possibly greater than it would have been had he or her husband perpetrated it.

"Dinner in twenty minutes, Monty," said he to Sir Montague Merline and departed to his tent.

"I say, Old Thing, dear," observed Lord Huntingten to the same gentleman, as, with the tip of his little finger, he "wangled" a soda-water bottle with a view to concocting a whiskey-and-soda. "We won't let Marguerite have anything to do with elephant or buffalo, will we?"

"Good Lord, no!" was the reply. "We've promised her one pot at a lion if we can possibly oblige, but that will have to be her limit, and, what's more, you and I will be one each side of her when she does it."

"Yes," agreed the other, and added, "Expect I shall know what nerves are, when it comes off, too."

"Fancy 'nerves' and the *Bwana Simba*," laughed Sir Montague Merline as he held out his glass for the soda. . . . "Here's to Marguerite's first lion," he continued, and the two men solemnly drank the toast.

Sir Montague Merline struck a match for his pipe, the light illuminating his face in the darkness which had fallen in the last few minutes. The first impression one gathered from the face of Captain Sir Montague Merline, of the Queen's African Rifles, was one of unusual gentleness and kindliness. Without being in any way a weak face, it was an essentially friendly and amiable one—a soldierly face without any hint of that fierce, harsh and ruthless expression which is apparently cultivated as part of their stock-in-trade by the professional soldiers of militarist nations. A physiognomist, observing him, would not be surprised to learn of quixotic actions and a reputation for being "such an awful good chap—one of the best-hearted fellers that ever helped a lame dog over a stile." So far as such a thing can be said of any strong and honest man who does his duty, it could be said of Sir Montague Merline that he had no enemies. Contrary to the dictum that "He who has no enemies has no friends" was the fact that Sir Montague Merline's friends were all who knew him. Of these, his best and closest friend was his wife, and it had been reserved for Lord Huntingten unconsciously to apprise her of the fact that she was this and nothing more. Until he had left his yacht at Mombasa a few weeks before, on the invitation of Captain Strong (issued with their cordial consent) to join their projected shooting trip, Lady Merline had fondly imagined that she knew what love was, and had thought herself a thoroughly happy and contented woman. In a few days after his joining the party it seemed that she must have loved him all her life, and that there could not possibly be a gulf of some fifteen years between then and the childish days when he was "Bill the Lamb" and she the unconsidered adjunct of the nursery and schoolroom, generally addressed as "Margarine." Why had he gone wandering about the world all these years? Why had their re-discovery of each other had to be postponed until now? Why couldn't he have been at home when Monty came wooing and . . . When Lady Merline's thoughts reached this point she resolutely switched them off. She was doing a considerable amount of switching off, these last few days, and realised that when Lord Huntingten awoke to the fact that he too must practise this exercise, the shooting trip would have to come to an untimely end. As she crouched over the tiny candle-lit mirror on the *soi-disant* dressing-table in her tent, while hastily changing for dinner that evening, she even considered plausible ways and possible means of terminating the trip when the inevitable day arrived.

She was saved the trouble.

As they sat at dinner a few minutes later, beneath the diamond-studded velvet of the African sky—an excellent dinner of clear soup, sardines, bustard, venison, and tinned fruit—Strong's orderly again appeared in the near distance, saluting and holding two official letters in his hand. These, it appeared, had just been brought by messenger from the railway-station some nineteen miles distant.

Captain Strong was the first to gather their import, and his feeling of annoyance and disappointment was more due to the fact of the interruption of his interesting little drama than to the cancellation of his leave and return to harness.

"Battle, Murder and Sudden Death!" he murmured. "I wish people wouldn't kill people, and cause other people to interfere with the arrangements of people. . . . Our trip's bust."

"What is it?" asked Lady Merline.

"Mutiny and murder down Uganda way," replied her husband, whose letter was a duplicate. "I'm sorry, Huntingten, old chap," he added, turning to his friend. "It's draw stumps and hop it, for Strong and me. We must get to the railway to-morrow—there will be a train through in the afternoon. . . . Better luck next time."

Lord Huntingten looked at Lady Merline, and Lady Merline looked at her plate.

2

Down the narrowest of narrow jungle-paths marched a small party of the Queen's African Rifles. They marched, perforce, in single file, and at their head was their white officer. A wiser man would have marched in the middle, for the leading man was inevitably bound to "get it" if they came upon the enemy, and, albeit brave and warlike men, negroes of the Queen's African Rifles (like other troops) fight better when commanded by an officer. A "point" of a sergeant and two or three men, a couple of hundred yards in front, is all very well, but the wily foe in ambush knows quite enough to take, as it were, the cash and let the credit go—to let the "point" march on, and to wait for the main body.

Captain Sir Montague Merline was well aware of the unwisdom and military inadvisability of heading the long file, but did it, nevertheless. If called upon to defend his conduct, he would have said that what was gained by the alleged wiser course was more than lost, inasmuch as the confidence of the men in so discreet a leader would not be, to say the least of it, enhanced. The little column moved silently and slowly through the horrible place, a stinking swamp, the atmosphere almost unbreatheable, the narrow winding track almost untreadable, the enclosing walls of densest jungle utterly impenetrable—a singularly undesirable spot in which to be attacked by a cunning and blood-thirsty foe of whom this was the "native heath."

Good job the beggars did not run to machine guns, thought Captain Merline; fancy one, well placed and concealed in one of these huge trees, and commanding the track. Stake-pits, poisoned arrows, spiked-log booby-traps, and poisoned needle-pointed snags neatly placed to catch bare knees, and their various other little tricks were quite enough to go on with. What a rotten place for an ambush! The beggars could easily have made a neat clearing a foot or two from the track, and massed a hundred men whose poisoned arrows, guns, and rifles could be presented a few inches from the breasts of passing enemies, without the least fear of discovery. Precautions against that sort of thing were utterly impossible if one were to advance at a higher speed than a mile a day. The only possible way of ensuring against flank attack was to have half the column out in the jungle with axes, hacking their way in line, ahead of the remainder. They couldn't do a mile a day at that rate. That "point" in front was no earthly good, nor would it have been if joined by Daniel Boone, Burnham and Buffalo Bill. The jungle on either side might as well have been a thirty-foot brick wall. Unless the enemy chose to squat in the middle of the track, what could the "point" do in the way of warning?—and the enemy wouldn't do that. Of course, an opposing column might be marching toward them along the same path, but, in that case, except at a sudden bend, the column would see them as soon as the "point."

Confound all bush fighting—messy, chancy work. Anyhow, he'd have ten minutes' halt and send Ibrahim up a tree for a look round.

Captain Merline put his hand to the breast pocket of his khaki flannel shirt for his whistle, with a faint short blast on which he would signal to his "point" to halt. The whistle never reached his lips. A sudden ragged crash of musketry rang out from the dense vegetation on either side, and from surrounding trees which commanded and enfiladed the path. More than half the little force fell at the first discharge, for it is hard to miss a man with a Snider or a Martini-Henry rifle at three yards' range. For a moment there was confusion, and more than one of those soldiers of the Queen, it must be admitted, fired off his rifle at nothing in particular. A burly sergeant, bringing up the rear, thrust his way to the front shouting an order, and the survivors of the first murderous burst of fire crouched down on either side of the track and endeavoured to force their way into the jungle, form a line on either side, and fire volleys to their left, front and right. Having made his way to the head of the column, Sergeant Isa ibn Yakub found his officer shot through the head, chest and thigh.
. . . A glance was sufficient. With a loud click of his tongue he turned away with a look of murderous hate on his ebony face and the lust of slaughter in his rolling yellow eye. He saw a leafy twig fall from a tree that over-hung the path and crouched motionless, staring at the spot. Suddenly he raised his rifle and fired, and gave a hoarse shout of glee as a body fell crashing to the ground. In the same second his tarboosh was spun from his head and the shoulder of his blue jersey torn as by an invisible claw. He too wriggled into the undergrowth and joined the volley-firing, which, sustained long enough and sufficiently generously

and impartially distributed, must assuredly damage a neighbouring foe and hinder his approach. Equally assuredly it must, however, lead to exhaustion of ammunition, and when the volley-firing slackened and died away, it was for this reason. Sergeant Isa ibn Yakub was a man of brains and resource, as well as of dash and courage. Since the enemy had fallen silent too, he would emerge with his men and collect the ammunition from their dead and wounded comrades. He blew a number of short shrill blasts on the whistle which, with the stripes upon his arm, was the proudest of his possessions.

The ammunition was quickly collected and the worthy Sergeant possessed himself of his dead officer's revolver and cartridges. . . . The next step? . . . If he attempted to remove his wounded, his whole effective force would become stretcher-bearers and still be inadequate to the task. If he abandoned his wounded, should he advance or retire? He would rather fight a lion or three Masai than have to answer these conundrums and shoulder these responsibilities. . . . He was relieved of all necessity in the matter of deciding, for the brooding silence was again suddenly broken by ear-piercing and blood-curdling howls and a second sudden fusillade, as, at some given signal, the enemy burst into the track both before and behind the column. Obviously they were skilfully handled and by one versed in the art of jungle war. The survivors of the little force were completely surrounded—and the rest was rather a massacre than a fight. It is useless to endeavour to dive into dense jungle to form a firing line when a determined person with a broad-bladed spear is literally at your heels. Sergeant Isa ibn Yakub did his utmost and fought like the lion-hearted warrior he was. It is some satisfaction to know that the one man who escaped and made his way to the temporary base of the little columns to tell the story of the destruction of this particular force, was Sergeant Isa ibn Yakub.

One month later a Lieutenant was promoted to Captain Sir Montague Merline's post, and, twelve months later, Lord Huntingten married his wife.

Captain Strong of the Queen's African Rifles, home on furlough, was best man at the wedding of the handsome and popular Lord Huntingten with the charming and beautiful Lady Merline.

3

At about the same time as the fashionable London press announced to a more or less interested world the more or less important news that Lady Huntingten had presented her lord and master with a son and heir, a small *safari* swung into a tiny African village and came to a halt. The naked Kavarondo porters flung down their loads with grunts and cluckings, and sat them down, a huddled mass of smelly humanity. From a litter, borne in the middle of the caravan, stepped the leader of the party, one Doctor John Williams, a great (though unknown) surgeon, a medical missionary who gave his life and unusual talents, skill and knowledge to the alleviation of the miseries of black humanity. There are people who have a lot to say about missionaries in Africa, and there are people who have nothing to say about Dr. John Williams because words fail them. They have seen him at work and know what his life is—and also what it might be if he chose to set up in Harley Street.

Doctor John Williams looked around at the village to which Fate brought him for the first time, and beheld the usual scene—a collection of huts built of poles and grass, and a few superior dwelling-places with thatched walls and roofs. A couple of women were pounding grain in a wooden mortar; a small group of others was engaged in a kind of rude basket weaving under the porch of a big hut; a man seated by a small fire had apparently "taken up" poker work, for he was decorating a vase-shaped gourd by means of a red-hot iron; a gang of tiny naked piccaninnies, with incredibly distended stomachs, was playing around a . . .

What?

Dr. John Williams strode over to the spot. A white man, or the ruin of a sort of a white man, was seated on a native stool and leaning against the bole of one of the towering palms that embowered, shaded, concealed and enriched the little village. His hair was very long and grey, his beard and moustache were long and grey, his face was burnt and bronzed, his eyes blue and bright. On his head were the deplorable ruins of a khaki helmet, and, for the rest, he wore the rags and remains of a pair of khaki shorts. Dr. John Williams stood and stared at him in open-mouthed astonishment. He arose and advanced with extended hand. The doctor was too astounded to speak, and the other could not, for he was dumb. In a minute it was obvious to the new-comer that he was more —that he was in some way "wanting."

From the headman of the villagers, who quickly gathered round, he learned that the white man had been with them for "many nights and days and seasons," that he was afflicted of the gods, very wise, and as a little child. Why "very wise" Dr. John Williams failed to discover, or anything more of the man's history, save that he had simply walked into the village from nowhere in particular and had sat under that tree, all day, ever since.

They had given him a hut, milk, corn, cocoanut, and whatever else they had. Also, in addition to this propitiation, they had made a minor god of him, with worship of the milder sorts. Their wisdom and virtue in this particular had been rewarded by him with a period of marked prosperity; and undoubtedly their crops, their cattle, and their married women had benefited by his benevolent presence. . . .

When Doctor John Williams resumed his journey he took the dumb white man with him, and, in due course, reached his own mission, dispensary and wonderful little hospital a few months later. Had he considered that there was any urgency in the case, and the time-factor of any importance, he would have abandoned his sleeping-sickness tour, and gone direct to the hospital to operate upon the skull of his foundling. For this great (and unknown) surgeon, upon examination, had decided that the removal of a bullet which was lodged beneath the scalp and in the solid bone of the top of the man's head was the first, and probably last, step in the direction of the restoration of speech and understanding. Obviously he was in no pain, and he was not mad, but his brain was that of a child whose age was equal to the time which had elapsed since the wound was caused. Probably this had happened about a couple of years ago, for the brain was about equal to that of a two-year-old child. But why had the child not learned to talk? Possibly the fact that he had lived among negroes, since his last return to consciousness, would account for the fact. Had he been shot in the head and recovered among English people (if he were English) he would probably be now talking as fluently as a two-year-old baby. . . .

The first few days after his return to his

headquarters were always exceedingly busy ones for the doctor. The number of things able to "go wrong" in his absence was incredible, and, as he was the only white man resident in a district some ten thousand square miles in area, the accumulation of work and trouble was sufficient to appal most people. But work and trouble were what the good doctor sought and throve on. . . . One piece of good news there was, however, in the tale of calamities. A pencilled note, scribbled on a leaf of a military pocket-book, informed him that his old friend Strong, of the Queen's African Rifles, had passed through his village three weeks earlier, and would again pass through, on his return, in a week's time. Having made a wide détour to see his friend, Strong was very disappointed to learn of his absence, and would return by the same devious route, in the hope of better luck. . . .

Good! A few days of Strong's company would be worth a lot. A visit from any white man was something; from a man of one's own class and kind was a great thing; but from worldly-wise, widely-read, clever old Strong! . . . Excellent! . . .

4

Captain Strong, of the Queen's African Rifles, passed from the strong sunlight into the dark coolness of Doctor John Williams' bungalow side by side with his host, who was still shaking him by the hand, in his joy and affection. Laying his riding-whip and helmet on a table he glanced round, stared, turned as white as a sunburnt man may, ejaculated "Oh, my God!" and seized the doctor's arm. His mouth hung open, his eyes were starting from his head, and it was with shaking hand that he pointed to where, in the doctor's living-room, sat the dumb and weak-witted foundling.

Doctor Williams was astounded and mightily interested.

"What's up, Strong?" he asked.

"B—b—b—but he's *dead!*" stammered Strong with a gasp.

"Not a bit of it, man," was the reply, "he's as alive as you or I. He's dumb, and he's dotty, but he's alive all right. . . . What's wrong with you? You've got a touch of the sun . . ." and then Captain Strong was himself again. If Captain Sir Montague Merline, late of the Queen's African Rifles, were alive, it should not be Jack Strong who would announce the fact. . . .

Monty Merline? . . . Was that vacant-looking person who was rising from a chair and bowing to him, his old pal Merline? . . . Most undoubtedly it was. Besides—there on his wrist and forearm was the wonderfully-tattooed snake. . . .

"How do you do?" he said. The other bowed again, smiled stupidly, and fumbled with the buttons of his coat. . . . Balmy! . . .

Strong turned and dragged his host out of the room.

"Where's he come from?" he asked quickly. "Who is he?"

"Where he came from last," replied the doctor, "is a village called, I believe, Bwogo, about a hundred and twenty miles south-east of here. How he got there I can't tell you. The natives said he just walked up unaccompanied, unwounded, unpursued. He's got a bullet or something in the top of his head and I'm going to lug it out. And then, my boy, with any luck at all, he'll very soon be able to answer you any question you like to put him. Speech and memory will return at the moment the pressure on the brain ceases."

"Will he remember up to the time the bullet hit

him, or since, or both?" asked Strong.

"All his life, up to the moment the bullet hit him, certainly," was the reply. "What happened since will, at first, be remembered as a dream, probably. If I had to prophesy I should say he'd take up his life from the second in which the bullet hit him, and think, for the moment, that he is still where it happened. By-and-by, he'll realise that there's a gap somewhere, and gradually he'll be able to fill it in with events which will seem half nightmare, half real."

"Anyhow, he'll be certain of his identity and personal history and so forth?" asked Strong.

"Absolutely," said the surgeon. "It will be precisely as though he awoke from an ordinary night's rest. . . . It'll be awfully interesting to hear him give an account of himself. . . . All this, of course, if he doesn't die under the operation."

"I hope he will," said Strong.

"What *do* you mean, my dear chap?"

"I hope he'll die under the operation."

"Why?"

"He'll be better dead. . . . And it will be better for three other people that he should be dead. . . . Is he likely to die?"

"I should say it's ten to one he'll pull through all right. . . . What's it all about, Strong?"

"Look here, old chap," was the earnest reply. "If it were anybody else but you I shouldn't know what to say or do. As it's *you*, my course is clear, for you're the last thing in discretion, wisdom and understanding. . . . But don't ask me his name. . . . I know him. . . . Look here, it's like this. His wife's married again. . . . There's a kid. . . . They're well known in Society. . . . Awful business. . . . Ghastly scandal. . . . Shockin' position." Captain Strong took Doctor John Williams by the arm. "Look here, old chap," he said once again. "Need you do this? It isn't as though he was 'conscious,' so to speak, and in pain."

"Yes, I must do it," replied the doctor without hesitation, as the other paused.

"But why?" urged Strong. "I'm absolutely certain that if M——, er—that is—this chap—could have his faculties for a minute he would tell you not to do it. . . . You'll take him from a sort of negative happiness to the most positive and acute unhappiness, and you'll simply blast the lives of his wife and the most excellent chap she's married. . . . She waited a year after this chap 'died' in—er—that last Polar expedition—as was supposed. . . . Think of the poor little kid too. . . . And there's estates and a ti—— so on. . . ."

"No good, Strong. My duty in the matter is perfectly clear, and it is to the sick man, as such."

"Well, you'll do a damned cruel thing . . . er—sorry, old chap, I mean *do* think it over a bit and look at it from the point of view of the unfortunate lady, the second husband, and the child. . . . And of the chap himself. . . . By God! He won't thank you."

"I look at it from the point of view of the doctor and I'm not out for thanks," was the reply.

"Is that your last word, Williams?"

"It is. I have here a man mentally maimed, mangled and suffering. My first and only duty is to heal him, and I shall do it."

"Right O!" replied Strong, who knew that further words would be useless. He knew that his friend's intelligence was clear as crystal and his will as firm, and that he accepted no other guide than his own conscience. . . .

As the three men sat in the moonlight that night, after dinner, Captain Strong was an uncomfortable man. That tragedy must find a place in the human comedy he was well aware. It had its uses like the comic relief—but for human tragedy, undilute, black, harsh, and dreadful, he had no taste. He shivered. The pretty little comedy of Lord Huntingten and Sir Montague and Lady Merline, of two years ago, had greatly amused and deeply interested him. This tragedy of the same three people was unmitigated horror. . . . Poor Lady Merline! He conjured up her beautiful face with the wonderful eyes, the rose-leaf complexion, the glorious hair, the tender, lovely mouth—and saw the life and beauty wiped from it as she read, or heard, the ghastly news . . . bigamy . . . illegitimacy. . . .

The doctor's "bearer" came to take the patient to bed. He was a remarkable man who had started life as a ward-boy in Madras. He it was who had cut the half-witted white man's hair, shaved his beard and dressed him in his master's spare clothes. When the patient was asleep that night, he was going to endeavour to shave the top of his head without waking him, for he was to be operated on, in the morning. . . .

"Yes, I fully understand and I give you my solemn promise, Strong," said the doctor as the two men rose to go in, that night. "The moment the man is sane I will tell him that he is not to tell me his name, nor anything else until he has heard what I have to say. I will then break it to him— using my own discretion as to how and when— that he was reported dead, that his will was proved, that his widow wore mourning for a year and then married again, and had a son a year later. . . . I undertake that he shall not leave this house, *knowing that,* unless he is in the fullest possession of his faculties and able to realise with the utmost clearness *all* the bearings of the case and *all* the consequences following his resumption of identity. And I'll let him hide here for just as long as he cares to conceal himself—if he wishes to remain 'dead' for a time."

"Yes . . . And as I can't possibly stay till he recovers, nor, in fact, over to-morrow without gross dereliction of duty, I will leave a letter for you to give him at the earliest safe moment. . . . I'll tell him that I am the only living soul who knows his name as well as his secret. He'll understand that no one else will know this—from me."

As he sat on the side of his bed that night, Captain Strong remarked unto his soul, "Well— one thing—if I know Monty Merline as well as I think, 'Sir Montague Merline' died two years ago, whatever happens. . . . And yet I can't imagine Monty committing suicide, somehow. He's a chap with a conscience as well as the soul of chivalry. . . . Poor, poor, old Monty Merline! . . ."

CHAPTER I

SOAP AND SIR MONTAGUE MERLINE

Sir Montague Merline, second-class private soldier of the First Battalion of the Foreign Legion of France, paused to straighten his back, to pass his bronzed forearm across his white forehead, and to put his scrap of soap into his mouth—the only safe receptacle for the precious morsel, the tiny cake issued once a month by Madame La République to the Legionary for all his washing purposes. When one's income is precisely one halfpenny a day (paid when it has totalled up to the sum of twopence half-penny), one does not waste much, nor risk the loss of valuable property; and to lay a piece of soap upon the concrete of *Le Cercle d'Enfer* reservoir, is not so much to risk the loss of it as to lose it, when one is surrounded by gentlemen of the Foreign Legion. Let me not be misunderstood, nor supposed to be casting aspersions upon the said gentlemen, but their need for soap is urgent, their income is one halfpenny a day, and soap is of the things with which one may "decorate oneself" without contravening the law of the Legion. To steal is to steal, mark you (and to deserve, and probably to get, a bayonet through the offending hand, pinning it to the bench or table), but to borrow certain specified articles permanently and without permission is merely, in the curious slang of the Legion, "to decorate oneself."

Contrary to what the uninitiated might suppose, *Le Cercle d'Enfer*—the Circle of Hell—is not a dry, but a very wet place, it being, in point of fact, the *lavabo* where the Legionaries of the French Foreign Legion stationed in Algeria at Sidi-bel-Abbès, daily wash their white fatigue uniforms and occasionally their underclothing.

Oh, that *Cercle d'Enfer!* I hated it more than I hated the *peloton des hommes punis, salle de police, cellules,* the "Breakfast of the Legion," the awful heat, monotony, flies, Bedouins; the solitude, hunger, and thirst of outpost stations in the south; I hated it more than I hated *astiquage, la boîte,* the *chaussettes russes,* hospital, the terrible desert marches, sewer-cleaning fatigues, or that villainous and vindictive ruffian of a *cafard*-smitten *caporal* who systematically did his very able best to kill me. Oh, that accursed *Cercle d'Enfer,* and the heart-breaking labour of washing a filthy alfa-fibre suit (stained perhaps with rifle-oil) in cold water, and without soap!

Only the other day, as I lay somnolent in a long chair in the verandah of the Charmingest Woman (she lives in India), I heard the regular *flop, flop, flop* of wet clothes, beaten by a distant *dhobi* upon a slab of stone, and at the same moment I smelt wet concrete as the *mali* watered the maidenhair fern on the steps leading from Her verandah to the garden. Odours call up memories far more distinctly and readily than do other sense-impressions, and the faint smell of wet concrete, aided as it was by the faintly audible sound of wet blows, brought most vividly before my mind's eye a detailed picture of that well-named Temple of Hygiea, the "Circle of Hell." Sleeping, waking, and partly sleeping, partly waking, I saw it all again; saw Sir Montague Merline, who called himself John Bull; saw Hiram Cyrus Milton, known as The Bucking Bronco; saw "Reginald Rupert"; the infamous Luigi Rivoli; the unspeakable Edouard Malvin; the marvellous Mad Grasshopper, whose name no one knew; the truly religious Hans Djoolte; the Russian twins, calling themselves Mikhail and Feodor Kyrilovitch Malekov; the terrible Sergeant-Major Suicide-Maker, and all the rest of them. And finally, waking with an actual and perceptible taste of soap in my mouth, I wished my worst enemy were in the *Cercle d'Enfer*, soapless, and with much rifle-oil, dust, leather marks and wine stains on his once-white uniform —and then I thought of Carmelita and determined to write this book.

For Carmelita deserves a monument (and so does John Bull), however humble. . . . To continue. . . .

Sir Montague Merline did not put his precious morsel of soap into his pocket, for the excellent reason that there was no pocket to the single exiguous garment he was at the moment wearing —a useful piece of material which in its time played many parts, and knew the service of duster, towel, turban, tablecloth, polishing pad, tea-cloth, house-flannel, apron, handkerchief, neckerchief, curtain, serviette, holder, fly-slayer, water-strainer, punkah, and, at the moment, nether garment. Having *cached* his soap and having observed *"Peste!"* as he savoured its flavour, he proceeded to pommel, punch, and slap upon the concrete, the greyish-white tunic and breeches, and the cotton vest and shirt which he had generously soaped before the hungry eyes of numerous soapless but oathful fellow-labourers, who less successfully sought that virtue which, in the Legion, is certainly next to, but far ahead of, mere godliness.

In due course, Sir Montague Merline rinsed his garments in the reservoir, wrung them out, bore them to the nearest clothes-line, hung them out to dry, and sat himself down in their shadow to stare at them unwaveringly until dried by the fierce sun—the ancient enemy, for the moment an unwilling friend. To watch them unwaveringly and intently because he knew that the turning of his head for ten seconds might mean their complete and final disappearance—for, like soap, articles of uniform are on the list of things with which a Legionary may "decorate" himself, if he can, without incurring the odium of public opinion. (He may steal any article of equipment, clothing, kit, accoutrement, or general utility, but his patron saint help him and Le Bon Dieu be merciful to him, if he be caught stealing tobacco, wine, food, or money.)

Becoming aware of the presence of Monsieur le Légionnaire Edouard Malvin, Sir Montague Merline increased the vigilance of his scrutiny of his pendent property, for ce cher Edouard was of pick-pockets the very prince and magician; of those who could steal the teeth from a Jew while he sneezed and would steal the scalp from their grandmamma while she objected.

"Ohé! Jean Boule, lend me thy soap," besought this stout and dapper little Austrian, who for some reason pretended to be a Belgian from the Congo. "This cursed alfa-fibre gets dirtier the more you wash it in this cursed water," and he smiled a greasy and ingratiating grin.

Without for one second averting his steady stare from his clothes, the Englishman slowly removed the soap from his mouth, expectorated, remarked *"Peaudezébie,"*[20] and took no further notice of the quaint figure which stood by his side, clad only in ancient red Zouave breeches and the ingratiating smile.

"Name of a Name! Name of the Name of a Pipe!

---

[20] An emphatic negative.

Name of the Name of a Dirty Little Furry Red Monkey!" observed Monsieur le Légionnaire Edouard Malvin as he turned to slouch away, twirling the dripping grey-white tunic.

"Meaning me?" asked Sir Montague, replacing the soap in its safe repository and preparing to rise.

"But no! But not in the least, old cabbage. Thou hast the *cafard*. Mais oui, tu as le cafard," replied the Belgian and quickened his retreat.

No, the grey Jean Boule, so old, so young, doyen of Légionnaires, so quick, strong, skilful and enduring at *la boxe*, was not the man to cross at any time, and least of all when he had *le cafard*, that terrible Legion madness that all Legionaries know; the madness that drives them to the cells, to gaol, to the Zephyrs, to the firing-party by the open grave; or to desertion and death in the desert. The grey Jean Boule had been a Zephyr of the Penal Battalions once, already, for killing a man, and Monsieur Malvin, although a Legionary of the Foreign Legion, did not wish to die. No, not while Carmelita and Madame la Cantinière lived and loved and sold the good Algiers wine at three-halfpence a bottle. . . . No, bon sang de sort!

M. le Légionnaire Malvin returned to the dense ring of labouring perspiring washers, and edged in behind a gigantic German and a short, broad, burly Alsatian, capitalists as joint proprietors of a fine cake of soap.

Sacré nom de nom de bon Dieu de Dieu de sort! Dull-witted German pigs might leave their soap unguarded for a moment, and, if they did not, might be induced to wring some soapy water from their little pile of washing, upon the obstinately greasy tunic of the good M. Malvin.

Légionnaire Hans Schnitzel, late of Berlin, rinsed his washing in clean water, wrung it, and took it to the nearest drying line. Légionnaire Alphonse Dupont, late of Alsace, placed his soap in the pocket of the dirty white fatigue-uniform which he wore, and which he would wash as soon as he had finished the present job. Immediately, Légionnaire Edouard Malvin transferred the soap from the side pocket of the tunic of the unconscious Légionnaire Alphonse Dupont to that of his own red breeches, and straightway begged the loan of it.

"*Merde!*" replied Dupont. "Nombril de Belzébuth! I will lend it thee *peaudezébie*. Why should I lend thee soap, *vieux dégoutant?* Go decorate thyself, *sale cochon*. Besides 'tis not mine to lend."

"And that is very true," agreed M. Malvin, and sauntered toward Schnitzel, who stood phlegmatically guarding his drying clothes. In his hand was an object which caused the eyebrows of the good M. Malvin to arch and rise, and his mouth to water—nothing less than an actual, real and genuine scrubbing-brush, beautiful in its bristliness. Then righteous anger filled his soul.

"Saligaud!" he hissed. "These pigs of filthy Germans! Soap *and* a brush. Sacripants! Ils me dégoutant à la fin."

As he regarded the stolid German with increasing envy, hatred, malice and all uncharitableness, and cast about in his quick and cunning mind for means of relieving him of the coveted brush, a sudden roar of wrath and grief from his Alsatian partner, Dupont, sent Schnitzel running to join that unfortunate man in fierce and impartial denunciations of his left-hand and right-hand neighbours, who were thieves, pigs, brigands, dogs, Arabs, and utterly *merdant* and *merdable*. Bursting into the fray, Herr Schnitzel found them, in addition, *bloedsinnig* and *dummkopf* in that they could not produce cakes of soap from empty mouths.

As the rage of the bereaved warriors increased, more and more Pomeranian and Alsatian patois invaded the wonderful Legion-French, a French which is not of Paris, nor of anywhere else in the world save La Légion. As Dupont fell upon a laughing Italian with a cry of "Ah! zut! Sacré grimacier," Schnitzel spluttered and roared at a huge slow-moving American who regarded him with a look of pitying but not unkindly contempt. . . .

"Why do the 'eathen rage furious *together* and *imagine* a vain thing?" he enquired in a slow drawl of the excited "furriner," adding "Ain't yew some *schafs-kopf*, sonny!" and, as the big German began to whirl his arms in the windmill fashion peculiar to the non-boxing foreigner who meditates assault and battery, continued—

"Now yew stop *zanking* and playing *versteckens* with me, yew pie-faced Squarehead, and be *schnell* about it, or yew'll git my goat, see? *Vous obtiendrez mon chèvre*, yew perambulating *prachtvoll bierhalle*," and he coolly turned his back upon the infuriated German with a polite, if laborious, "Guten tag, mein Freund."

Mr. Hiram Cyrus Milton (late of Texas, California, the Yukon, and the "main drag" generally of the wild and woolly West) was exceeding proud of his linguistic knowledge and skill. It may be remarked, en passant, that his friends were even prouder of it.

At this moment, le bon Légionnaire Malvin, hovering for opportunity, with a sudden *coup de savate* struck the so-desirable scrubbing-brush from the hand of Herr Schnitzel with a force that seemed like to take the arm from the shoulder with it. Leaping round with a yell of pain, the unfortunate German found himself, as Malvin had calculated, face to face with the mighty Luigi Rivoli, to attack whom was to be brought to death's door through that of the hospital.

Snatching up the brush which was behind Schnitzel when he turned to face Rivoli, le bon M. Malvin lightly departed from the vulgar scuffle in the direction of the drying clothes of Herren Schnitzel and Dupont, the latter, last seen clasping, with more enthusiasm than love, a wiry Italian to his bosom. The luck of M. Malvin was distinctly in, for not only had he the soap and a brush for the easy cleansing of his own uniform, but he had within his grasp a fresh uniform to wear, and another to sell; for the clothing of ce bon Dupont would fit him to a marvel, while that of the pig-dog Schnitzel would fetch good money, the equivalent of several litres of the thick, red Algerian wine, from a certain Spanish Jew, old Haroun Mendoza, of the Sidi-bel-Abbès ghetto.

Yes, the Saints bless and reward the good Dupont for being of the same size as M. Malvin himself, for it is a most serious matter to be short of anything when showing-down kit at kit-inspection, and that thrice accursed Sacré Chien of an *Adjudant* would, as likely as not, have spare white trousers shown-down on the morrow. What can a good Légionnaire do, look you, when he has not the article named for to-morrow's *Adjudant's* inspection, but "decorate himself"? Is it easy, is it reasonable, to buy new white fatigue-uniform on an income of one halfpenny per diem? Sapristi, and Sacré Bleu, and Name of the Name of a Little Brown Dog, a litre of wine costs a penny, and a packet of tobacco three-halfpence, and what is left to a gentleman of the Legion then, on pay-day, out of his twopence-halfpenny, nom d'un pétard? As for ce bon Dupont, he must in his turn "decorate" himself. And if he cannot, but must renew acquaintance with *la boîte* and *le peloton des hommes punis*, why—he must regard things in their true light, be philosophical, and take it easy. Is it not proverbial that "Toutes choses peut on souffrir qu'aise"? And with a purr of pleasure, a positive licking of chops, and a murmur of "Ah! Au tient frais," he deftly whipped the property of the embattled Legionaries from the line, no man saying him nay. For it is not the etiquette of the Legion to interfere with one who, in the absence of its owner, would "decorate" himself with any of those things with which self-decoration is permissible, if not honourable. Indeed, to Sir Montague Merline, sitting close by, and regarding his proceedings with cold impartial eye, M. Malvin observed—

" 'Y a de bon, mon salop! I have heard that le bon Dieu helps those who help themselves. I do but help myself in order to give le bon Dieu the opportunity He doubtless desires. I decorate myself incidentally. Mais oui, and I shall decorate myself this evening with a p'tite ouvrière and to-morrow with une réputation d'ivrogne," and he turned innocently to saunter with his innocent bundle of washing from the *lavabo*, to his *caserne*. Ere he had taken half a dozen steps, the cold and quiet voice of the grey Jean Boule broke in upon the resumed day-dreams of the innocently sauntering M. Malvin.

"Might one aspire to the honour of venturing to detain for a brief interview Monsieur le Légionnaire Edouard Malvin?" said the soft metallic voice.

"But certainly, and without charge, mon gars," replied that gentleman, turning and eyeing the incomprehensible and dangerous Jean Boule, *à coin de l'œil*.

"You seek soap?"

"I do," replied the Austrian "Belgian" promptly. The possession of one cake of soap makes that of another no less desirable.

"Do you seek sorrow also?"

"But no, dear friend. 'J'ai eu toutes les folies.' In this world I seek but wine, woman, and peace. Let me avoid the 'gros bonnets' and lead my happy humble life in peaceful obscurity. A modest violet, I. A wayside flow'ret, a retiring primrose, such as you English love."

"Then, cher Malvin, since you seek soap and not sorrow, let not my little cake of soap disappear from beneath the polishing-rags in my sack. The little brown sack at the head of my cot, cher Malvin. Enfin! I appoint you guardian and custodian of my little cake of soap. But in a most evil hour for le bon M. Malvin would it disappear. Guard it then, cher Malvin. Respect it. Watch over it as you value, and would retain, your health and beauty, M. Malvin. And when *I* have avenged *my* little piece of soap, the true history of the last ten minutes will deeply interest those earnest searchers after truth, Legionaries Schnitzel and Dupont. Depart in peace and enter upon your new office of Guardian of my Soap! Vous devez en être joliment fier."

"Quite a speech, in effect, mon drôle," replied the stout Austrian as he doubtfully fingered his short beard *au poinçon*, and added uneasily, "I am not the only gentleman who 'decorates' himself with soap."

"No? Nor with uniforms. Go in peace, Protector of my Soap."

And smiling wintrily M. Malvin winked, broke into the wholly deplorable ditty of "Pére Dupanloup en chemin de fer," and pursued his innocent path to barracks, whither Sir Montague Merline later followed him, after watching with a contemptuous smile some mixed and messy fighting (beside the apparently dead body of the Legionary Schnitzel) between an Alsatian and an Italian, in which the Italian kicked his opponent in the stomach and partly ate his ear, and the Alsatian used his hands solely for purpose of throttling.

Why couldn't they stand up and fight like gentlemen under Queensberry rules, or, if boxing did not appeal to them, use their sword-bayonets like soldiers and Legionaries—the low rooters, the vulgar, rough-and-tumble gutter-scrappers. . . .

Removing his almost dry washing from the line, Sir Montague Merline marched across to his barrack-block, climbed the three flights of stone stairs, traversed the long corridor of his Company, and entered the big, light, airy room wherein he and twenty-nine other Legionaries (one of whom held the very exalted and important rank of *Caporal)* lived and moved and had their monotonous being.

Spreading his tunic and breeches on the end of the long table he proceeded to "iron" them, first with his hand, secondly with a tin plate, and finally with the edge of his "quart," the drinking-mug which hung at the head of his bed ready for the reception of the early morning *jus,* the strong coffee which most effectively rouses the Legionary from somnolence and most ineffectively sustains him until midday.

Anon, having persuaded himself that the result of his labours was satisfactory, and up to Legion standards of smartness—which are as high as those of the ordinary *piou-piou* of the French line are low—he folded his uniform in elbow-to-finger-tip lengths, placed it with the *paquetage* on the shelf above his bed, and began to dress for his evening walk-out. The Legionary's time is, in theory, his own after 5 p.m., and the most sacred plank in the most sacred platform of all his sacred tradition is his right to promenade himself at eventide and listen to the Legion's glorious band in the Place Sadi Carnot.

Having laid his uniform, belt, bayonet, and képi on his cot, he stepped across to the next but one (the name-card at the head of which bore the astonishing legend "Bucking Bronco, No. 11356. Soldat 1ère Classe"), opened a little sack which hung at the head of it, and took from it the remains of an ancient nail-brush, the joint property of Sir Montague Merline, alias Jean Boule, and Hiram Cyrus Milton, alias Bucking Bronco, late of Texas, California, Yukon, and "the main drag" of the United States of America.

Even as Sir Montague's hand was inserted through the neck of the sack, the huge American (who had been wrongfully accused and rashly attacked by Legionary Hans Schnitzel) entered the barrack-room, caught sight of a figure bending over his rag-sack, and crept on tiptoe towards it, his great gnarled fists clenched, his mouth com-pressed to a straight thin line beneath his huge drooping moustache, and his grey eyes ablaze. Luckily Sir Montague heard the sounds of his stealthy approach, and turned just in time. The American dropped his fists and smiled.

"Say," he drawled, "I thought it was some herring-gutted weevil of a Dago or a Squarehead shenannikin with my precious jools. An' I was jest a'goin' ter plug the skinnamalink some. Say, Johnnie, if yew hadn't swivelled any, I was jest a'goin' ter slug yew, good an' plenty, behind the yeer-'ole."

"Just getting the tooth-nail-button-boot-dandy-brush, Buck," replied Sir Montague. "How are you feeling?"

"I'm feelin' purty mean," was the reply. "A dirty Squarehead of a dod-gasted Dutchy from the Farterland grunted in me eye, an' I thought the shave-tail was fer rough-housin', an' I slugged him one, just ter start 'im gwine. The gosh-dinged piker jest curled up. He jest wilted on the floor."

The Bucking Bronco, in high disgust, expectorated and then chid himself for forgetting that he was no longer on the free soil of America, where a gentleman may spit as he likes and be a gentleman for a' that and a' that.

"I tell yew, Johnnie," he continued, "he got me jingled, the lumberin' lallapaloozer! There he lay *an'* lay—and then some. 'Git up, yew rubberin' rube,' I ses, 'yew'll git moss on your teeth if yew lie so quiet; git up, an' deliver the goods,' I ses, 'I had more guts then yew when I was knee high to a June bug.' Did he arise an' make good? *I* should worry. Nope. Yew take it from Uncle, that bonehead is there yit, an' afore I could make him wise to it thet he didn't git the bulge on Uncle with *thet* bluff, another Squarehead an' a gibberin' Dago put up a dirty kind o' scrap over his body, gougin' and kickin' an' earbitin' an' throttlin', an' a whole bunch o' boobs jined in an' I give it up an' come 'ome." And the Bucking Bronco sat him sadly on his bed and groaned.

"Cheer up, Buck, we'll all soon be dead," replied his comrade, "don't *you* go getting cafard," and he looked anxiously at the angry-lugubrious face of his friend. "What's the *ordre du jour* for walking-out dress to-day?" he added. "Blue tunic and red trousers? Or tunic and white? Or *capote*, or what?"

"It was tunic an' white yesterday," replied the American, "an' I guess it is to-day too."

"It's my night to howl," he added cryptically. "Let's go an' pow-wow Carmelita ef thet fresh gorilla Loojey Rivoli ain't got 'er in 'is pocket. I'll shoot 'im up some day, sure. . . ."

A sudden shouting, tumult, and running below, and cries of "Les bleus! Les bleus!" interrupted the Bronco's monologue and drew the two old soldiers to a window that overlooked the vast, neat, gravelled barrack-square, clean, naked, and bleak to the eye as an ice-floe.

"Strike me peculiar," remarked the Bucking Bronco. "It's another big gang o' tenderfeet."

"A draft of rookies! Come on—they'll all be for our Company in place of those *poumpists*,[21] and there may be something Anglo-Saxon among them," said Legionary John Bull, and the two men hastily flung their capotes over their sketchy attire and hurried from the room, buttoning them as they went.

Like Charity, the Legionary's overcoat covers a multitude of sins—chiefly of omission—and is a most useful garment. It protects him from the cold dawn wind, and keeps him warm by night; it protects him from the cruel African sun, and keeps him cool by day, or at least, if not cool, in the frying-pan degree of heat, which is better than that of the fire. He marches in it without a tunic, and relies upon it to conceal the fact when he has failed to "decorate" himself with underclothing. Its skirts, buttoned back, hamper not his legs, and its capacious pockets have many uses. Its one drawback is that, being double-breasted, it buttons up on either side, a fact which has brought the grey hairs of many an honest Legionary in sorrow to the *cellules*, and given many a brutal and vindictive Sergeant the chance of that cruelty in which his little tyrant soul so revels. For, incredible as it may seem to the lay mind, the ingenious devil

---

[21] Deserters.

whose military mind concocts the *ordres du jour*, changes, by solemn decree, and almost daily, the side upon which the overcoat is to be buttoned up.

Clattering down the long flights of stone stairs, and converging across the barrack-square, the Legionaries came running from all directions, to gaze upon, to chaff, to delude, to sponge upon, and to rob and swindle the "Blues"—the recruits of the *Légion Étrangère*, the embryo *Légionnaires d'Afrique*.

In the incredibly maddeningly dull life of the Legion in peace time, the slightest diversion is a god-send and even the arrival of a batch of recruits a most welcome event. To all, it is a distraction; to some, the hope of the arrival of a fellow-countryman (especially to the few English, Americans, Danes, Greeks, Russians, Norwegians, Swedes, and Poles whom cruel Fate has sent to La Légion). To some, a chance of passing on a part of the brutality and tyranny which they themselves suffer; to some, a chance of getting civilian clothes in which to desert; to others, an opportunity of selling knowledge of the ropes, for litres of canteen wine; to many, a hope of working a successful trick on a bewildered recruit—the time-honoured villainy of stealing his new uniform and pretending to buy him another *sub rosa* from the dishonest quartermaster, whereupon the recruit buys back his own original uniform at the cost of his little all (for invariably the alleged substitute-uniform costs just that sum of money which the poor wretch has brought with him and augmented by the compulsory sale of his civilian kit to the clothes-dealing harpies and thieves who infest the barrack-gates on the arrival of each draft).

As the tiny portal beside the huge barrack-gate was closed and fastened by the Corporal in charge of the squad of "blues" (as the French army calls its recruits[22]), the single file of derelicts halted at the order of the Sergeant of the Guard, who, more in sorrow than in anger, weighed them and found them wanting.

"Sweepings," he summed them up in passing judgment. "Foundlings. Droppings. Crumbs. Tripe. Accidents. Abortions. Cripples. Left by the tide. Blown in by the wind. Born *pékins*.[23] Only one man among them, and he a pig of a Prussian—or perhaps an Englishman. Let us hope he's an Englishman. . . ."

In speaking thus, the worthy Sergeant was behaving with impropriety and contrary to the law and tradition of the Legion. What nouns and adjectives a non-commissioned officer may use wherewith to stigmatise a Legionary, depend wholly and solely upon his taste, fluency and vocabulary. But it is not etiquette to reproach a man with his nationality, however much a matter for reproach that nationality may be.

"Are you an Englishman, most miserable *bleu?*" he suddenly asked of a tall, slim, fair youth, dressed in tweed Norfolk-jacket, and grey flannel trousers, and bearing in every line of feature and form, and in the cut and set of his expensive clothing, the stamp of the man of breeding, birth and position.

"By the especial mercy and grace of God, I am an Englishman, Sergeant, thank you," he replied coolly in good, if slow and careful French.

The Sergeant smiled grimly behind his big moustache. Himself a cashiered Russian officer, and once a gentleman, he could appreciate a gentleman and approve him in the strict privacy of his soul.

---

[22] In the days of the high, tight stock and cravat, the recruit was supposed to be livid and blue in the face until he grew accustomed to them.
[23] Civilians.

"*Slava Bogu!*" he roared. "Vile *bleu!* And now by the especial mercy and grace of the Devil you are a Légionnaire—or will be, if you survive the making. . . ." and added *sotto voce*, "Are you a degraded dog of a broken officer? If so, you can claim to be appointed to the *élèves caporaux* as a non-commissioned officer on probation, if you have a photo of yourself in officer's uniform. Thus you will escape all recruit-drill and live in hope to become, some day, Sergeant, even as I," and the (for a Sergeant of the Legion) decent-hearted fellow smote his vast chest.

"I thank you, Sergeant," was the drawled reply. "You really dazzle me—but *I* am not a degraded dog of a broken officer."

"*Gospodi pomilui!*" roared the incensed Sergeant. "Ne me donnez de la gabatine, pratique!" and, for a second, seemed likely to strike the cool and insolent recruit who dared to bandy words with a Sergeant of the Legion. His eyes bulged, his moustache bristled, and his scarlet face turned purple as he literally showed his teeth.

"Go easy, old chap," spoke a quiet voice, in English, close beside the Englishman. "That fellow can do you to death if you offend him," and the recruit, turning, beheld a grey-moustached, white-haired elderly man, bronzed, lined, and worn-looking—a typical French army *vielle moustache*—an "old sweat" from whose lips the accents of a refined English gentleman came with the utmost incongruity.

The youth's face brightened with interest. Obviously this old dear was a public-school, or 'Varsity man, or, very probably, an *ex*-British officer.

"Good egg," quoth he, extending a hand behind him for a surreptitious shake. "See you anon, what?"

"Yes, you'll all come to the Seventh Company. We are below strength," said Legionary John Bull, in whose weary eyes had shone a new light of interest since they fell upon this compatriot of his own caste and kidney.

A remarkably cool and nonchalant recruit—and surely unique in the history of the Legion's "blues" in showing absolutely no sign of privation, fear, stress, criminality, poverty, depression, anxiety, or bewilderment!

"Now, what'n hell is he doin' in thet bum outfit?" queried the Bucking Bronco of his friend John Bull, who kept as near as possible to the Englishman whom he had warned against ill-timed causticity of humour.

"He's some b'y, thet b'y, but he'd better quit kickin'. He's a way-up white man I opine. What's 'e a'doin' in this joint? He's a gay-cat and a looker. He's a fierce stiff sport. He has sand, some—sure. Yep," and Mr. Hiram Cyrus Milton checked himself only just in time from defiling the immaculate and sacred parade-ground, by "signifying in the usual manner" that he was mentally perturbed, and solaced himself in these circumstances of expectoration-difficulty by observing that the boy was undoubtedly "some" boy, and worthy to have been an American citizen had he been born under a luckier star—or stripe.

"I can't place him, Buck," replied the puzzled John Bull, his quiet voice rendered almost inaudible by the shouts, howls, yells and cries of the seething mob of Legionaries who swarmed round the line of recruits, assailing their bewildered ears in all the tongues of Europe, and some of those of Asia and Africa.

"He doesn't look hungry, and he doesn't look hunted. I suppose he is one of the few who don't come here to escape either starvation, creditors, or the Law. And he doesn't look desperate like the average turned-down lover, ruined gambler, deserted husband, or busted bankrupt. . . . Wonder if he's come here in search of 'Romance'?"

"Wal, ef he's come hyar for his health an' amoosement he'd go to Hell to cool himself, or ter the den of a grizzly b'ar fer gentle stimoolation and recreation. Gee whiz! Didn't he fair git ole Blue-bottle's goat? He sure did git nixt him."

"Bit of a contrast to the rest of the gang, what?" remarked John Bull, and indeed the truth of his remark was very obvious.

"Ain't they a outfit o' dodgasted hoboes an' bindle-stiffs!" agreed his friend.

Straight as a lance, thin, very broad in the shoulders and narrow of waist and hip; apparently as clean and unruffled as when leaving his golf-club pavilion for a round on the links; cool, self-possessed, haughty, aristocratic and clean-cut of feature, this Englishman among the other recruits looked like a Derby winner among a string of equine ruins in a knacker's yard; like a panther among bears—a detached and separated creature, something of different flesh and blood. Breed is a very remarkable thing, even more distinctive than race, and in this little band of derelicts was another Englishman, a Cockney youth who had passed from street-arab and gutter-snipe, *via* Reformatory, to hooligan, coster and soldier. No man in that collection of wreckage from Germany, Spain, Italy, France, and the four corners of Europe looked less like the tall recruit than did this brother Englishman.

To Sir Montague Merline, fallen and shattered star of the high social firmament, the sight of him was as welcome as water in the desert, and he thanked Fate for having brought another English-man to the Legion—and one so debonair, so fine, so handsome, cool and strong.

"There's Blood there," he murmured to himself.

"His shoulders hev bin drilled somewheres, although he's British," added the Bucking one. "Yep. He's one o' the flat-backed push."

"I wonder if he can be a cashiered officer. He's drilled as you say. . . . If he has been broke for something it hasn't marked him much. Nothing hang-dog there," mused Legionary John Bull.

"Nope. He's a blowed-in-the-glass British aristocrat," agreed the large-minded Hiram Cyrus, "and I opine an ex-member of the commishunned ranks o' the British Constitootional Army. He ain't niver bin batterin' the main-stem for light-pieces like them other hoodlums an' toughs an' smoudges. Nope. He ain't never throwed his feet fer a two-bit poke-out. . . . Look at that road-kid next 'im! Ain't he a peach? I should smile! Wonder the medicine-man didn't turn down some o' them chechaquos. . . ."

And, truly, the draft contained some very queer odd lots. By the side of the English gentleman stood a big fat German boy in knicker-bockers and jersey, bare-legged and wearing a pair of button-boots that had belonged to a woman in the days when they still possessed toe-caps. Pale face, pale hair, and pale eyes, conspired to give him an air of terror—the first seeming to have the hue of fright, the second to stand *en brosse* with fear, and the last to bulge like those of a hunted animal.

Presumably M. le Médicin-Major must have been satisfied that the boy was eighteen years of age, but, though tall and robust, he looked nearer fifteen—an illusion strengthened, doubtless, by the knickerbockers, bare calves, and button-boots. If he had enlisted in the Foreign Legion to avoid service in the Fatherland, he had quitted the frying-pan for a furnace seven times heated.

Possibly he hoped to emulate Messieurs Shadrach, Meshach, and Abed-Nego. In point of fact, he was a deserter (driven to the desperate step of fleeing across the French frontier by a typical Prussian non-commissioned officer), and already wishing himself once more *zwei jahriger* in the happy Fatherland.

Already, to his German soul and stomach, the lager-bier of Munich, the sausage, *zwieback*, and *kalte schnitzel* of home, seemed things of the dim and distant past, and unattainable future.

Next to him stood a gnarled and knotted Spaniard, whose face appeared to be carven from his native mahogany, and whose ragged clothing—grimy, oily, blackened—proclaimed him wharfside coal-heaver, dock-rat, and long-shoreman. What did he among the Legion's blues? Was it lack of work, was it slow starvation? Or excess of temper and a quick blow with a coal-shovel upon the head of an enemy in some Marseilles coal-barge—that had brought him to Sidi-bel-Abbès in the sands of Africa?

By his side slouched a dark-faced, blunt-featured Austrian youth, whose evil-looking mouth was unfortunately in no wise concealed by a sparse and straggling moustache, laboriously pinched into two gummed spikes, and whose close-set eyes were not in harmony of focus. His dress appeared to be that of a lower-class clerk, ill-fitting black cloth of lamentable cut, the type of suit that, in its thousands, renders day horrible in European and American cities, and is, alas, spreading to many Asiatic. His linen was filthy, his crinkly hair full of dust, his boots cracked and shapeless. He looked what he was—an absconding Viennese tout who had had a very poor time of it. He proved to be a highly objectionable and despicable scoundrel.

His left-hand neighbour was a weedy, olive-faced youth, wearing a velvet tam-o'-shanter cap, and a brown corduroy suit, of which the baggy, peg-top trousers fitted tightly at the ankles over pearl-buttoned spring-side patent boots. He had long fluffy brown hair, long fluffy brown beard, whiskers, and moustache, long filthy finger nails, and no linen. Apparently a French student of the Sorbonne, or artist from The Quarter, over-whelmed by some terrible cataclysm, some *affaire* of the heart, the pocket, or *l'honneur*.

Beside this gentleman, whose whole appearance was highly offensive to the prejudiced insular eye of the Englishman, stood a typical *Apache*—a horrible-looking creature whose appalling face showed the cunning of the fox, the ferocity of the panther, the cruelty of the wolf, the treachery of the bear, the hate of the serpent, and the rage of the boar. Monsieur l'Apache had evidently chosen the Legion as a preferable alternative to the hulks and the chain-gang—Algeria rather than Noumea. He lived to doubt the wisdom of his choice.

Beside him, and evidently eyeing him askance, stood two youths as extraordinarily similar as were ever twins in this world. Dark, slightly "rat-faced," slender, but decidedly athletic looking.

"Cheer up, *golubtchik*! If one cannot get *vodka* one must drink *kvass*," whispered one.

"All right, Fedia," replied the other. "But I am so hungry and tired. What wouldn't I give for some good hot tea and *blinni!*"

"We're bound to get something of some sort before long—though it won't be *zakuska*. Don't give way on the very threshold now. It is our one chance, or I would not have brought you here, Olichka."

"Ssh!" whispered back the other. "Don't call me that here, Feodor."

49

"Of course not, Mikhail, stout fellow," replied Feodor, and smote his companion on the back.

Regarding them, sharp-eyed, stood the Cockney, an undersized, narrow-chested, but wiry-looking person—a typical East End sparrow; impudent, assertive, thoroughly self-reliant, tenacious, and courageous; of the class that produces admirable specimens of the genus "Tommy."

In curious contrast to his look of *gamin* alertness was that of his neighbour, a most stolid, dull and heavy-looking Dutchman, whose sole conversational effort was the grunt "*Verstaan nie,*" whenever addressed. Like every other member of the draft he appeared "to feel his position" keenly, and distinctly to deplore it. Such expression as his bovine face possessed, suggested that Algerian sun and sands compared unfavourably with Dutch mists and polders, and the barrack-square of the Legion with the fat and comfortable stern of a Scheldt canal boat.

Square-headed, flat-faced Germans, gesticulating Alsatians and Lorraines, fair Swiss, and Belgians, with a sprinkling of Italians, swarthy Spaniards, Austrians and French, made up the remainder of the party, men whose status, age, appearance, bearing, and origins were as diverse as their nationalities, levelled by a common desperate need (of food, or sanctuary, or a fresh start in life), and united by a common filthiness, squalor, and dejection—a gang powerless in the bonds of hunger and fear, delivered bound into the relentless, grinding mills of the Legion.

And thus, distinguished and apart, though in their midst, stood the well-dressed Englishman, apparently calm, incurious, with equal mind; his linen fresh, his face shaven, his clothing uncreased, his air rather that of one who awaits the result of the footman's enquiry as to whether Her

Ladyship is "at home" to him.

More and more, the heart of Sir Montague Merline warmed to this young man of his own race and class, with his square shoulders, flat back, calm bearing, and hard high look. He approved and admired his air and appearance of being a Man, a Gentleman, and a Soldier. Had he a son, it was just such a youth as this he would have him be.

"Any 'Murricans thar?" suddenly bawled the Bucking Bronco.

"Nao," replied the Cockney youth, craning forward. "But I'm Henglish—which is better any d'y in the week, ain't it?"

The eye of the large American travelled slowly and deliberately from the crown of the head to the tip of the toe of the Cockney, and back. He then said nothing—with some eloquence.

"Say, ma honey, yew talk U.S. any?" queried a gigantic Negro, in the uniform of the Legion (presumably recruited in France as a free American citizen of Anglo-Saxon speech), addressing himself to the tall Englishman. "Youse ain't Dago, nor Dutchie, nor French. Cough it up, Bo, right hyar ef youse U.S."

The eyes of the young Englishman narrowed slightly, and his naturally haughty expression appeared to deepen toward one of contempt and disgust. Otherwise he took no notice of the Negro, nor of his question.

Remarking, "Some poah white trash," the Negro turned to the next man with the same query.

Cries in various tongues, such as "Anybody from Spain?" "Anyone from Vienna?" "Any Switzers about?" and similar attempts by the crowding, jostling Legionaries to discover a compatriot, and possibly a "towny," evoked gleams and glances of interest from the haggard, wretched eyes of the "blues," and, occasionally, answering cries from their grim and grimy lips.

A swaggering, strutting Sergeant emerged from the neighbouring regimental offices, roared "*Garde à vous*," brought the recruits to attention, and called the roll. As prophesied by Legionary John Bull, the whole draft was assigned to the Seventh Company, recently depleted by the desertion, en masse, of a *cafard*-smitten German *escouade*, or section, who had gone "on pump," merely to die in the desert at the hands of the Arabs—several horribly tortured, all horribly mangled.

Having called the roll, this Sergeant, not strictly following the example of the Sergeant of the Guard, looked the draft over more in anger than in sorrow.

"Oh, Name of the Name of Beautiful Beelzebub," bawled he, "but what have we here? To *drill* such worm-casts! Quel métier! Quel chien d'un métier! Stand up, stand up, oh sons of Arab mothers and pariah dogs," and then, feigning sudden and unconquerable sickness, he turned upon the Corporal in charge with a roar of—

"March these sacred pigs to their accursed sties."

As the heterogeneous gang stepped off at the word of command, "*En avant. Marche!*" toward the Quarter-master's store of the Seventh Company, it was clear to the experienced eye that the great majority were "Back to the army again," and were either deserters, or men who had already put in their military service in the armies of their own countries.

In the store-room they were endowed by the *Fourrier-Sergent*, to the accompaniment of torrential profanity, with white fatigue-uniforms, nightcaps, rough shirts, harsh towels, and scraps of soap. From the store-room the squad was "personally conducted" by another, and even more terrible, Sergeant to a washing-shed beyond the drill-ground, and bidden to soap and scour itself, and then stand beneath the primitive shower-baths until purged and clean as never before in its unspeakable life.

As they neared the washing-shed, the bare idea of ablutions, or the idea of bare ablutions, appeared to strike consternation, if not positive terror, into the heart of at least one member of the squad, for the young Russian who had been addressed by his twin as Mikhail suddenly seized the other's arm and said with a gasp—

"Oh, Fedichka, how can I? Oh Fedia, Fedia, what shall I do?"

"We must trust in God, and use our wits, Olusha. I will . . ."

But a roar of "Silence, Oh Son of Seven Pigs," from the Sergeant, cut him short as they reached the shed.

"Now strip and scrub your mangy skins, you dogs. Scrape your crawling hides until the floor is thick in hog-bristles and earth, oh Great-grand-sons of Sacred Swine," he further adjured the wretched "blues," with horrible threats and fearful oaths.

"Wash, you mud-caked vermin, wash, for the carcase of the Legionary must be as spotless as the Fame of the Legion, or the honour of its smartest Sergeant—Sergeant Legros," and he tapped his bulging chest lest any Bœotian present should be ignorant of the identity of Sergeant Legros of the Legion.

Walking up and down before the doorless stalls in which the naked recruits washed, Sergeant Legros hurled taunts, gibes, insults, and curses at his charges, stopping from time to time to give special attention to anyone who had the misfortune to acquire his particular regard. Pausing to stare at the tall Englishman in affected disgust at the condition of his brilliant and glowing skin, he enquired—

"Is that a vest, disclosed by scrubbing and the action of water? Or is it your hide, pig?" And was somewhat taken aback by the cool and pleasant reply,

"No, that is not a new, pink silk vest that you see, Sergeant, it really is my own skin—but many thanks for the kind compliment, none the less."

Sergeant Legros eyed the recruit with something dimly and distantly akin to pity. Mad as a March hare, poor wretch, of course—it could not be intentional impudence—and the Sergeant smiled austerely—he would probably die in the cells ere long, if *le cafard* did not send him to the Zephyrs, the firing-platoon, or the Arabs. Mad to begin with! Ho! Ho! What a jest!—and the Sergeant chuckled.

But what was this? Did the good Sergeant's eyes deceive him? Or was there, in the next compartment, a lousy, lazy "blue" pretending to cleanse his foul and sinful carcase without completely stripping? The young Russian, Mikhail, standing with his back to the doorway, was unenthusiastically washing the upper part of his body.

Sergeant Legros stiffened like a pointer, at the sight. Rank disobedience! Flagrant defiance of orders, coupled with the laziest and filthiest indifference to cleanliness! This vile "blue" would put the Legion's clean shirt and canvas fatigue-suit on an indifferently washen body, would he? Let him wait until he was a Legionary, and no longer a recruit—and he should learn something of the powers of the Sergeant Legros.

"Off with those trousers, thou mud-caked flea-bitten scum," he thundered, and then received perhaps the greatest surprise of a surprising life. For, ere the offending recruit could turn, or obey, there danced forth from the next cubicle, with a wild whoop, his exact double, who, naked as he was born, turned agile somersaults and catherine-wheels past the astounded Sergeant, down the front of the bathing-shed, and round the corner.

"Sacré Nom de Nom de Bon Dieu-de-Dieu!" ejaculated Sergeant Legros, and rubbed his eyes. He then displayed a sample of the mental quick-ness of the trained Legionary in darting to the neighbouring corner of the building instead of running down the entire front in the wake of the vanished acrobat.

Dashing along the short side-wall, Sergeant Legros turned the corner and beheld the errant lunatic approaching in the same literally revolu-tionary manner.

On catching sight of the Sergeant, the naked recruit halted, and broke into song and dance, the latter being of that peculiarly violent Cossack variety which constrains the performer to crouch low to earth and fling out his legs, alternately, straight before him.

For the first time in his life, words failed Sergeant Legros. For some moments he could but stand over the dancer and gesticulate and stutter. Rising to his feet with an engaging smile—

"Ça va mieux, mon père?" observed the latter amiably.

Seizing him by arm and neck, the apoplectic Sergeant Legros conducted this weird disciple of Terpsichore back to his cubicle, while his mazed mind fumbled in the treasure-house of his vocab-ulary, and the armoury of his weapons of punish-ment.

Apparently there was method, however, in the

madness of Feodor Kyrilovitch Malekov, for a distinct look of relief and satisfaction crossed his face as, in the midst of a little crowd of open-mouthed, and half-clothed recruits, he caught sight of his brother in complete fatigue-uniform.

Gradually, and very perceptibly the condition of Sergeant Legros improved. His halting recriminations and imprecations became a steady trickle, the trickle a flow, the flow a torrent, and the torrent an overwhelming deluge. By the time he had almost exhausted his vocabulary and himself, he began to see the humorous and interesting aspect of finding two lunatics in one small draft. He would add them to his collection of butts. Possibly one, or both of them, might even come to equal the Mad Grasshopper in that rôle. Fancy more editions of La Cigale—who had provided him with more amusement and opportunities for brutality than any ten sane Legionaries!

"Now, do great and unmerited honour to your vile, low carcases by putting on the fatigue-uniform of the Legion. Gather up your filthy civilian rags, and hasten," he bawled.

And when the, now wondrously metamorphosed, recruits had all dressed in the new canvas uniforms, they were marched to a small side gate in the wall of the barrack-square, and ordered to sell immediately everything they possessed in the shape of civilian clothing, including boots and socks. Civilian clothing is essential to the would-be deserter, and La Légion does not facilitate desertion.

That the unfortunate recruits got the one or two francs they did receive was solely due to the absence of a "combine" among the scoundrelly Arabs, Greeks, Spanish Jews, Negroes, and non-descript rogues who struggled for the cast-off clothing. For the Englishman's expensive suit a franc was offered, and competition advanced this price to four. For the sum of five francs he had to sell clothes, hat, boots, collar, tie, and under-clothing that had recently cost him over fifty times as much. That he felt annoyed, and that, in spite of his apparent nonchalance, his temper was wearing thin, was evidenced by the fact that a big Arab who laid a grimy paw upon his shoulder and snatched at his bundle, received the swift blow of dissuasion—a sudden straight-left in the eye, sending him flying—to the amusement and approval of the sentry whose difficult and arduous task it was to keep the scrambling, yelling thieves of old-clo' dealers from invading the barrack-square, and repentant recruits from quitting it.

When the swindle of the forced sale was complete, and several poor wretches had parted with their all for a few *sous*, the gate was shut and the weary squad marched to the offices of the Seventh Company that each man's name and profession might be entered in the Company Roll, and that he might receive his *matricule* number, the number which would henceforth hide his identity, and save him the trouble of retaining a personality and a name.

To Colour-Sergeant Blanc, the tall English youth, like most Legionaries, gave a *nom d'em-prunt*, two of his own names, Reginald Rupert. He concealed his surname and sullied the crystal truth of fact by stating that his father was the Commander-in-Chief of the Horse Marines of Great Britain and Inspector-General of the Royal Naval Horse Artillery; that he himself was by pro-fession a wild-rabbit-tamer, and by conviction a Plymouth Rock—all of which was duly and solemnly entered in the great tome by M. Blanc, a man taciturn, *très boutonné*, and of no imagina-tion.

Whatever the recruit may choose to say is written down in the Company lists, and should a recruit wax a little humorous, why—the Legion will very soon cure him of any tendency to humour. The Legion asks no questions, answers none, takes the recruit at his own valuation, and quickly readjusts it for him.

Reconducted to the Store-room of the Seventh Company, the batch of recruits, again to the accompaniment of a fusillade of imprecations, and beneath a torrential deluge of insults and oaths, was violently tailored by a number of non-commissioned officers, and a fatigue-party of Légionnaires.

To "Reginald Rupert," at any rate, the badges of rank worn by the non-commissioned officers were mysterious and confusing—as he noted a man with one chevron giving peremptory orders in loud tone and bullying manner to a man who wore two chevrons. It also puzzled him that the fat man, who was evidently the senior official present, was addressed by the others as "*chef*," as though he were a cook. By the time he was fitted out with kit and accoutrement, he had decided that the "chef" (who wore two gold chevrons) was a Sergeant-Major, that the men wearing one gold chevron were Sergeants, and that those wearing two red ones were Corporals; and herein he was entirely correct.

Every man had to fit (rather than be fitted with) a red képi having a brass grenade in front; a double-breasted, dark blue tunic with red facings and green-fringed red epaulettes; a big blue great-coat, or *capote*; baggy red breeches; two pairs of boots; two pairs of linen spats, and a pair of leather gaiters. He also received a long blue woollen cummerbund, a knapsack of the old British pattern, a bag of cleaning materials, belts, straps, cartridge-pouches, haversack, and field flask.

To the fat Sergeant-Major it was a personal insult, and an impudence amounting almost to blasphemy, that a képi, or tunic should not fit the man to whom it was handed. The idea of adapting a ready-made garment to a man appeared less prominent than that of adapting a ready-made man to a garment.

"What!" he roared in Legion French, to the fat German boy who understood not a word of the tirade. "What? Nom d'un pétard! Sacré Dieu! The tunic will not easily button? Then contract thy vile body until it will, thou offspring of a diseased pig and a dead dog. I will fit thee to that tunic, and none other, within the week. Wait! But wait—till thou has eaten the Breakfast of the Legion once or twice, fat sow. . . ."

A gloomy, sardonic Legionary placed a képi upon the crisply curling hair of Reginald Rupert. It was miles too big—a ludicrous extinguisher. The Englishman removed it, and returned it with the remark, "Ça ne marche pas, mon ami."

"*Merde!*" ejaculated the liverish-looking soldier, and called Heaven to witness that he was not to blame if the son of a beetle had a walnut for a head.

Throwing the képi back into the big box he fished out another, banged it on Rupert's head, and was about to bring his open hand down on the top of it, when he caught the cold but blazing eye of the recruit, and noticed the clenched fist and lips. Had the Legionary's right hand descended, the recruit's left hand would have risen with promptitude and force.

"If that is too big, let the sun boil thy brains and bloat thy skull till it fits, and if it be too small, sleep in it," he remarked sourly, and added that thrice-accursed "blues" were creatures of the kind that ate their young, encumbered the earth, polluted the air, loved to *faire Suisse*,[24] and troubled Soldiers of the Legion who might otherwise have been in the Canteen, or at Carmelita's—instead of being the valets of sons of frogs, nameless excrescences. . . .

"Too small," replied Rupert coolly, and flung the cap into the box. "Valet? I should condole with a crocodile that had a clumsy and ignorant yokel like you for a valet," he added, in slow and careful French as he tried on a third cap, which he found more to his liking.

The old Legionary gasped.

"Il m'enmerde!" he murmured, and wiped his brow. He, Jules Duplessis, Soldat 1*ère* Classe, with four years' service and the *médaille militaire*, had been outfaced, brow-beaten, insulted by a miserable "blue." What were the World and La Légion coming to? "*Merde!*"

While trying on his tunic, Rupert saw one of the Russians hand to the other the tunic and trousers which he had tried on. Apparently being as alike as two pins in every respect they had adopted the labour-saving device of one "fitting on" for both.

Having put on the képi, Mikhail bundled up the uniform, struck an attitude with arms akimbo, and inquired of the other—

"Do I look *very* awful in this thing, Fedia?"

"Shut up, you little fool," replied Feodor, with a quick frown. "Try and look more like a *mujik* in *maslianitza*,[25] and less like a young student at private theatricals. You're a Legionary now."

When, at length, the recruits had all been fitted

---

[24] To drink alone; to sulk.
[25] The week before Lent, or "mad week," when all good *mujiks* get drunk—or used to do.

into uniforms, and were ready to depart, they were driven forth with the heart-felt curse and comprehensive anathema of the Sergeant-Major—

"Sweep the room clear of this offal, Corporal," quoth he. "And if thou canst make a Légionnaire's little toe out of the whole draft—thou shalt have the Grand Cross of the Legion of Honour—I promise it."

"*En avant. Marche!*" bawled the Corporal, and the "blues" were led away, up flights of stairs, and along echoing corridors to their future home, their new quarters. A Légionnaire, carrying a huge earthenware jug, encountering them outside the door thereof, gave them their first welcome to the Legion.

"Oh thrice-condemned souls, welcome to Hell," he cried genially, and kicking open the door of a huge room, he liberally sprinkled each passing recruit, murmuring as he did so—

"Le diable vous bénisse."

CHAPTER II

A BARRACK-ROOM OF THE LEGION

The room which Reginald Rupert entered, with
a dozen of his fellow "blues," was long and lofty,
painfully orderly, and spotlessly clean. Fifteen cots
were exactly aligned on each long side, and down
the middle of the floor ran long wooden tables and
benches, scoured and polished to immaculate
whiteness. Above each bed was a shelf on which
was piled a very neat erection of uniforms and kit.
To the eye of Rupert (experienced in barrack-
rooms) there was interesting novelty in the
absence of clothes-boxes, and the presence of
hanging-cupboards suspended over the tables
from the ceiling.

Evidently the French authorities excelled the
English in the art of economising space, as
nothing was on the floor that could be accommo-
dated above it. In the hanging cupboards were tin
plates and cups and various utensils of the
dinner-table.

The Englishman noted that though the Lebel
rifles stood in a rack in a corner of the room, the
long sword-bayonets hung by the pillows of their
owners, each near a tin quart-pot and a small
sack.

On their beds, a few Légionnaires lay sleeping,
or sat laboriously polishing their leatherwork—the
senseless, endless and detested *astiquage* of the
Legion—or cleaning their rifles, bayonets, and
buttons. Whatever else the Légionnaire is, or is
not, he is meticulously clean, neat, and smart,
and when his day's work is done (at four or five

o'clock) he must start a half-day's work in "making *fantasie*"—in preparation for the day's work of the morrow.

Rising from his bed in the corner as the party entered, Legionary John Bull approached the Corporal in charge of the room and suggested that the English recruit should be allotted the bed between his own and that of Légionnaire Bronco, as he was of the same mother-tongue, and would make quicker progress in their hands than in those of foreigners. As the Corporal, agreeing, indicated the second bed from the window, to Rupert, and told him to take possession of it and make his *paquetage* on the shelf above, the Cockney recruit pushed forward:

" 'Ere, I'm Henglish too! I better jine these blokes."

"Qu'est-ce-qu'il dit, Jean Boule?" enquired the Corporal.

On being informed, Corporal Achille Martel allotted the fourth bed, that on the other side of the Bucking Bronco, to Recruit Higgins with an intimation that the sooner he learnt French, and ceased the use of barbarous tongues the better it would be for his welfare. The Corporal then assigned berths to the remaining recruits, each between those of two old soldiers, of whom the right-hand man was to be the new recruit's guide, philosopher and friend, until he, in his turn, became a prideful, full-blown Legionary.

The young Russian who had given his name as Mikhail Kyrilovitch Malekov observed that the card at the head of the cot on his right-hand bore the inscription: "Luigi Rivoli, No. 13874, Soldat 2ième Classe."

As he stood, irresolute, and apparently in great anxiety and perturbation, nervously opening and shutting a cartridge-pouch, his face suddenly brightened as his twin entered the room and intercepted the departing Corporal.

"*Milles pardons*, Monsieur," he said, saluting smartly and respectfully. "But I earnestly and humbly request that you will permit me to inhabit this room in which is my brother. As we reached this door another *sous-officier* took me and the remainder to the next room when twelve had entered here. . . . Alas! My brother was twelfth, and I thirteenth," he added volubly. "Look you, Monsieur, he is my twin, and we have never been separated yet. We shall get on much faster and better, helping each other, and be more credit to you and your room, *petit père*."

"Sacré Dieu, and Name of a Purple Frog! Is this a scurvy and lousy beggar, whining for alms at a mosque door? And am I a God-forsaken and disgusting *pékin* that you address me as 'Monsieur'? Name of a Pipe! Have I no rank? Address me henceforth as Monsieur le Caporal, thou kopeck-worth of Russian."

"Oui, oui; milles pardons, Monsieur le Caporal. But grant me this favour and I and my brother will be your slaves."

"Va t'en, babillard! Rompez, jaseur!" snarled the Corporal.

But the Russian, true to type, was tenacious. Producing a five-franc piece he scratched his nose there-with, and dropping the wheedling and suppliant tone, asked the testy Corporal if he thought it likely Messieurs les Caporaux of the Seventh Company could possibly be induced to drink the health of so insignificant an object as Recruit Feodor Kyrilovitch Malekov.

"Corporals do not drink with Légionnaires," was the answer, "but doubtless Corporal Gilles of the next room will join me in a drink to the health of a worthy and promising 'blue,' " and, removing his képi, he stretched his gigantic frame and yawned hugely as the Russian dexterously, and apparently unnoticed, slipped the coin into the képi. Having casually examined the lining of his képi, Monsieur le Caporal Martel replaced it on his head, and with astounding suddenness and ferocity pounced upon an ugly, tow-haired German, and with a shout of "Out, pig! Out of my beautiful room! Thy face disfigures it," he hunted him forth and bestowed him upon the neighbouring Corporal, M. Auguste Gilles, together with a promise of ten bottles of Madame la Cantinière's best, out of the thirty-and-five which the Russian's five-franc piece would purchase.

In a moment the Russian had opened negotiations with the Spaniard who had taken the bed next but one to that of Mikhail.

Like all educated Russians, Feodor Kyrilovitch was an accomplished linguist, and, while speaking French and English idiomatically, could get along very comfortably in Spanish, Italian, and German.

A very few minutes enabled him to make it clear to the Spaniard that an exchange of beds would do him no harm, and enrich him by a two-franc piece.

"No hay de que, Señor. Gracias, muchas gracias," replied the Spaniard. "En seguida, con se permiso," and transferred himself and his belongings to the berth vacated by the insulted and dispossessed German.

Meanwhile, Reginald Rupert, with soldierly promptitude, lost no time in setting about the brushing and arrangement of his kit, gathering up, as he did so, the pearls of local wisdom that fell from the lips of his kindly mentor, whose name and description he observed to be "Légionnaire John Bull, No. 11867, Soldat 2ième Classe."

Having shown his pupil the best and quickest

way of folding his uniform in elbow-to-finger-tip lengths, and so arranging everything that he could find it in the dark, and array himself *en tenue de campagne d'Afrique* in ten minutes without a light, he invited him to try his own hand at the job.

"Now you try and make that '*paquetage* of the Legion,'" observed the instructor, "and the sooner you learn to make it quickly, the better. As you see, you have no chest for your kit as you had in the British Army, and so you keep your uniform on your shelf, *en paquetage*, for tidiness and smartness, without creases. The Légionnaire is as *chic* and particular as the best trooper of the crackest English cavalry-corps. We look down on the *piou-piou* from a fearful height, and swagger against the *Chasseur d'Afrique* himself. I wish to God we had spurs, but there's no cavalry in the Legion—though there are kinds of Mounted-Rifle Companies on mules, down South. I miss spurs damnably, even after fourteen years of foot-slogging in the Legion. You can't really swagger without spurs—not that the women will look at a Legionary in any case, or the men respect him, save as a fighter. But you can't *swing* without spurs."

"No," agreed Rupert, "I was just thinking I should miss them, and it'll take me some time to get used to a night-cap, a neck-curtained képi, a knapsack, and a steel bayonet-scabbard."

"You'll appreciate the first when you sleep out, and the second when you march, down South. The nights are infernally cold, and the days appallingly hot—and yet sunstroke is unknown in the Legion. Some put it down to wearing the overcoat to march in. The steel scabbard is bad—noisy and heavy. The knapsack is the very devil on the march, but it's the one and only place in the world in which you can keep a photo, letter, book, or scrap of private property, besides spare uniform and small kit. You'll soon learn to pack it, to stow underclothing in the haversack, and to know the place for everything, so that you can get from bed to barrack-square, fully equipped and accoutred in nine minutes from the bugle. . . . And don't, for Heaven's sake, lose anything, for a spiteful N.C.O. can send you to your death in Biribi—that's the Penal Battalion—by running you in two or three times for 'theft of equipment.' Lost kit is regarded as stolen kit, and stolen kit is sold kit (to a court-martial), and the penalty is six months with the Zephyrs. It takes a good man to survive that. . . . If you've got any money, try and keep a little in hand, so that you can always replace missing kit. The fellows here are appalling thieves—of uniform. It is regarded as a right, natural and proper thing to steal uniforms and kit, and yet we'd nearly kill a man who stole money, tobacco, or food. The former would be 'decorating' yourself, the latter disgracing yourself. We've some queer beasts here, but we're a grand regiment."

The disorderly heap of garments having become an exceedingly neat and ingenious little edifice, compact, symmetrical, and stable, Rupert's instructor introduced the subject of that bane of the Legionary's life—the eternal *astiquage*, the senseless and eternal polishing of the black leather straps and large cartridge-pouches.

"This stuff looks as though it had been left here by the Tenth Legion of Julius Cæsar, rather than made for the Foreign Legion," he remarked. "Let's see what we can make of it. Watch me do this belt, and then you can try the cartridge-cases. Don't mind firing off all the questions you've got to ask, meanwhile."

"Thanks. What sort of chaps are they in this room?" asked Rupert, seating himself on the bed

beside his friendly preceptor, and inwardly con-
gratulating himself on his good luck in meeting,
on the threshold of his new career, so congenial
and satisfactory a bunk-mate.

"Very mixed," was the reply. "The fellow on the
other side of your berth is an American, an *ex-*
U.S.A. army man, miner, lumber-jack, tramp,
cow-boy, bruiser, rifle and revolver trick-shooter,
and my very dear friend, one of the whitest men I
ever met, and one of the most amusing. His
French conversation keeps me alive by making me
laugh, and he's learning Italian from a twopenny
dictionary, and a Travellers' Phrase Book, the
better to talk to Carmelita. The next but one is a
Neapolitan who calls himself Luigi Rivoli. He used
to be a champion Strong Man, and music-hall
wrestler, acrobat, and juggler. Did a bit of lion-
taming too, or, at any rate, went about with a
show that had a cageful of mangy performing
lions. He is not really very brave though, but he's
a most extraordinary strong brute. Quite a
millionaire here too, for Carmelita gives him a
whole franc every day of his life."

"What made him enlist then?" asked Rupert,
carefully watching the curious *astiquage* methods,
so different from the pipe-clay to which he was
accustomed.

"This same girl, and she's worth a thousand of
Rivoli. It seems she pretended to turn him down,
and take up with some other chap to punish Rivoli
after some lover's quarrel or other, and our Luigi
in a fit of jealous madness stabbed the other chap
in the back, and then bolted and enlisted in the
Legion, partly to pay her out, but chiefly to save
himself. He was doing a turn at a *café-chantant*
over in Algiers at the time. Of course, Carmelita
flung herself in transports of grief, repentance,
and self-accusation upon Luigi's enormous

bosom, and keeps him in pocket-money while she waits for him. She followed him, and runs a *café* for Légionnaires here in Sidi-bel-Abbès. She gets scores of offers from our Non-coms., and from Frenchmen of the regular army stationed in Sidi, and her *café* is a sort of little Italian club. My friend, the Bucking Bronco, proposes to her once a week, but she remains true to Luigi, whom she intends to marry as soon as he has done his time. The swine's carrying on at the same time with Madame la Cantinière, who is a widow, and whose canteen he would like to marry. Between the two women he has a good time, and, thanks to Carmelita's money, gets all his work done for him. The brute never does a stroke. Pays substitutes for all fatigues and corvées, has his kit and accoutrements polished, and his clothes washed. Spends the balance of Carmelita's money at the Canteen, ingratiating himself with Madame! Keeps up his great strength with extra food too. He *is* a Hercules, and, moreover, seems immune from African fever and *le cafard*, which is probably due to his escaping three-parts of the work done by the average penniless. And he's as nasty as he is strong."

"What's his particular line of nastiness— besides cheating women I mean?" asked Rupert, who already knew only too well how much depends on the character, conduct, manners, and habits of room-mates with whom one is thrown into daily and nightly intimate contact, year after year, without change, relief, or hope of improvement.

"Oh, he's the Ultimate Bounder," replied the other, as he struck a match and began melting a piece of wax with which to rub his leather belt. "He's the Compleat Cad, and the Finished Bully. He's absolute monarch of the rank-and-file of the

Seventh Company by reason of his vast wealth, and vaster strength. Those he does not bribe he intimidates. Remember that the Wages of Virtue here is one halfpenny a day as opposed to the Wages of Sin which is rather worse than death.

"Think of the position of a man who has the income of all in this room put together, in addition to the run of his best girl's own *café*. What with squaring Non-coms., hiring substitutes, and terrorising 'fags,' he hasn't done a stroke, outside parades of course, since he joined—except hazing recruits, and breaking up opponents of his rule."

"How does he fight?" asked Rupert.

"Well, wrestling's his *forte*—and he can break the back of any man he gets his arms round—and the rest's a mixture of boxing, ju-jitsu, and *la savate*, which, as you know, is kicking. Yes, he's a dirty fighter, though it's precious rarely that it comes to what you could call a fight. What I'm waiting for is the most unholy and colossal turn-up that's due to come between him and Buck sooner or later. It's bound to come, and it'll be a scrap worth seeing. Buck has been a professional glove-man among other things, and he holds less conservative views than I do, as to what is permissible against an opponent who kicks, clinches, and butts. . . . No, fighting's apt to be rather a dirty business here, and, short of a proper duel, a case of stand face to face and do all you can with all Nature's weapons, not forgetting your teeth. . . . 'C'est la Légion.' "

"How disgustin'!" murmured the young man. "Will this bird trouble me?"

"He will," answered the other, "but I'll take a hand, and then Buck will too. He hates Luigi like poison, and frequently remarks that he has it in for him when the time comes, and Luigi isn't over anxious to tackle him, though he hankers. Doesn't understand him, nor like the look in his eye. Buck is afraid of angering Carmelita if he 'beats up' Rivoli. . . . Yes, I dare say Buck and I can put the gentle Neapolitan off between us."

Reginald Rupert stiffened.

"I beg that you will in no way interfere," he observed coldly. "I should most strongly resent it."

The heart of the old soldier warmed to the youth, as he contrasted his slim boyish grace with the mighty strength, natural and developed, of the professional Strong Man, Wrestler, and Acrobat—most tricky, cunning, and dangerous of relentless foes.

"You keep clear of Luigi Rivoli as long as you can," he said with a kindly smile. "And at least remember that Buck and I are with you. Personally, I'm no sort of match for our Luigi in a rough-and-tumble nowadays, should he compel one. But he has let me alone since I told him with some definiteness that he would have to defend himself with either lead or steel, if he insisted on trouble between him and me."

"There now," he continued, rising, "now try that for yourself on a cartridge-pouch. . . . First melt the wax a bit, with a match—and don't forget that matches are precious in the Legion as they're so damned dear—and rub it on the leather as I did. Then take this flat block of wood and smooth it over until it's all evenly spread. And then rub hard with the coarse rag for an hour or two, then harder with the fine rag for about half an hour. Next polish with your palm, and then with the wool. Buck and I own a scrap of velvet which you can borrow before Inspection Parades, and big shows—but we don't use it extravagantly of course. . . .

"Well, that's the *astiquage* curse, and the other's washing white kit without soap, and ironing it without an iron. Of course, Madame la République couldn't give us glazed leather, or khaki webbing—nor could she afford to issue one flat-iron to a barrack-room, so that we could iron a white suit in less than a couple of hours. . . . The devil of it is that it's all done in our 'leisure' time when we're supposed to be resting, or recreating. . . . Think of the British 'Tommy' in India with his *dhobi*, his barrack-sweeper, his table-servant, and his *syce*—or his share in them. If we did nothing in the world but our daily polishing, washing and ironing, we should be busy men. However! *'C'est la Legion!'* And one won't live for ever. . . . You won't want any help with the rifle and bayonet, I suppose?"

"No, thanks, I've 'had some,' though I haven't handled a Lebel before," and Reginald Rupert settled down to work while Legionary John Bull proceeded with his toilet.

"Anything else you want to know?" enquired the latter, as he put a final polish upon his gleaming sword-bayonet. "You know enough not to cut your rifle-sling stropping your razor on it. . . . Don't waste your cake of soap making a candle-stick of it. Too rare and precious here."

"Well, thanks very much; the more you tell me, the better for me, if it's not troubling you, Sir."

John Bull paused and looked at the recruit.

"Why do you call me 'Sir'?" he enquired.

"Why? . . . Because you are senior and a Sahib, I suppose," replied the youth.

"Thanks, my boy, but don't. I am just Légionnaire John Bull 11867, Soldier of the Second Class. You'll be a soldier of the First Class, and my senior in a few months, I hope. . . . I suppose you've assumed a *nom de guerre* too," replied the other, making a mental note that the recruit had served in India. He had already observed that he pointed his toes as he walked, and had a general cavalry bearing.

"Yes, I gave part of my own name; I'm 'Reginald Rupert' now. Didn't see why I should give my own. I've only come to have a look round and learn a bit. Very keen on experiences, especially military ones."

"Merciful God!" ejaculated John Bull softly. "Out for experiences! You'll get 'em, here."

"Keen on seein' life, y'know," explained the young man.

"Much more likely to see death," replied the other. "Do you realise that you're in for five years—and that no money, no influence, no diplomatic representations, no extradition can buy, or beg, or drag you out; and that by the end of five years, if alive, you'll be lucky if you're of any use to the Legion, to yourself, or to anyone else? I, personally, have had unusual luck, and am of unusual physique. I re-enlisted twice, partly because at the end of each five years I was turned loose with nothing in the world but a shapeless blue slop suit—partly for other reasons. . . ."

"Oh! I've only come for a year, and shall desert. I told them so plainly at the enlistment bureau, in Paris," was the ingenuous reply.

The old Legionary smiled.

"A good many of our people desert, at least once," he said, "when under the influence of *le cafard*—especially the Germans. Ninety-nine per cent come to one of three ends—death, capture, or surrender. Death with torture at the hands of the Arabs; capture, or ignominious return and surrender after horrible sufferings from thirst, starvation and exposure."

"Yes; I heard the Legion was a grand military school, and a pretty warm thing, and that desertion was a bit of a feat, and no disgrace if you brought it off—so I thought I'd have a year of the one, and then a shot at the other," replied the young man coolly. "Also, I was up against it somewhat, and well—you know—seeking sorrow."

"You've come to the right place for it then," observed Legionary John Bull, sheathing his bayonet with a snap, as the door banged open. . . . "Ah! Enter our friend Luigi," he added as that worthy swaggered into the room with an obsequious retinue, which included le bon Légionnaire Edouard Malvin, looking very smart and dapper in the uniform of Légionnaire Alphonse Dupont of the Eleventh Company.

"Pah! I smell 'blues'! Disgusting! Sickening!" ejaculated Légionnaire Luigi Rivoli in a tremendous voice, and stood staring menacingly from recruit to recruit.

Reginald Rupert, returning his hot, insolent glare with a cold and steady stare, beheld a huge and powerful-looking man with a pale, cruel face, coarsely handsome, wherein the bold, heavily lashed black eyes were set too close together beneath their broad, black, knitted brows, and the little carefully curled black moustache, beneath the little plebeian nose, hid nothing of the over-ripe red lips of an over-small mouth.

"Corpo di Bacco!" he roared in Italian and Legion French. "The place reeks of the stinking 'blues.' Were it not that I now go *en ville* to dine and drink my Chianti wine (none of your filthy Algerian slops for Luigi Rivoli), and to smoke my *sigaro estero* at my *café*, I would fling them all down three flights of stairs," and, like his companions, he commenced stripping off his white uniform. Having bared his truly magnificent arms and chest, he struck an attitude, ostentatiously contracted his huge right biceps, and smote it a resounding smack with the palm of his left hand.

"Aha!" he roared, as all turned to look at him.

"Disgustin' bounder," remarked Reginald Rupert very distinctly, as, with a second shout of "Aha!" Rivoli did the same with the left biceps and right hand, and then bunched the vast *pectoralis major* muscles of his chest.

"Magnifique!" cried Légionnaire Edouard Malvin, who was laying out his patron's uniform from his *paquetage*, preparatory to helping him to dress.

"As thou sayest, my *gallo*, 'C'est magnifique,' " replied Luigi Rivoli, and for five minutes contracted, flexed, and slapped the great muscles of his arms, shoulders, and chest.

"Come hither—thou little bambino Malvin, thou Bad Wine, thou Cattevo Vino Francese, and stand behind me. . . . What of the back? Canst thou see the 'bull's head' as I set the *trapezius*, *rhomboideus*, and *latissimus dorsi* muscles?"

"As clearly as I see your own head, Main de Fer," replied the Austrian in affected astonishment and wonder. "It is the World's Most Wonderful Back! Why, were Maxick and Saldo, Hackenschmidt, the three Saxons, Sandow—yea—Samson and Hercules themselves here, all would be humiliated and envious."

"Aha!" again bawled Rivoli, "thou art right, *piccolo porco*," and, sinking to a squatting position upon his raised heels, he rose and fell like a jack-in-the-box for some time, before rubbing and smiting his huge thighs and calves to the accompaniment of explosive shouts. There-after, he fell upon his hands and toes, and raised and lowered his stiffened body a few dozen times.

The display finished, he enquired with lordly boredom:

"And what are the absurd orders for walking-out dress to-night. Is it blue and red, or blue and white, or overcoats buttoned on the left—or what?"

"Tunic and red, Hercule, and all ready, as you see," replied Malvin, and he proceeded to assist at the toilet of the ex-acrobat, the plutocrat and leader of the rank-and-file of the Seventh Company by virtue of his income of a franc a day, and his phenomenal strength and ferocity.

Turning round that Malvin might buckle his belt and straighten his tunic, the great man's foot touched that of Herbert Higgins (late of Hoxton and the Loyal Whitechapel Regiment) who had been earnestly endeavouring for the past quarter of an hour to follow the instructions of the Bucking Bronco—instructions given in an almost incomprehensible tongue, of choice American and choicer French compact.

Profound disgust, deepening almost to horror, was depicted on the face of the Italian as he bestowed a vicious, hacking kick upon the shin of the offending "blue."

"Body of Bacchus, what is this?" he cried. "Cannot I move without treading in *vidanges?* Get beneath the bed and out of my sight, *cauchemar!*"

But far from retreating as bidden, the undersized Cockney rose promptly to his feet with a surprised and aggrieved look upon his face, hitherto expressive only of puzzled bewilderment.

" 'Ere! 'Oo yer fink you're a kickin' of?" he enquired, adding with dignity, "I dunno' 'oo yer fink you *are*. I'm 'Erb 'Iggins, I am, an' don't yer fergit it."

That Mr. Herbert Higgins stood rubbing his injured shin instead of flying at the throat of the Italian, was due in no wise to personal fear, but to an utter ignorance of the rank, importance, and powers of this "narsty-lookin' furriner." He might be some sort of an officer, and to "dot 'im one" might mean lingering gaol, or sudden death.

Bitterly he regretted his complete ignorance of the French tongue, and the manners and customs of this strange place. Anyhow, he could give the bloke some lip in good old English.

"Bit too 'andy wiv yer feet, ain't yer? Pretty manners, I *don't* fink! 'Manners none, an' customs narsty's' abart your mark, ain't it?"

But ere he could proceed with further flowers of rhetoric, and rush in ignorance upon his fate, the huge hand of the American fell upon his shoulder from behind and pressed him back upon his cot.

"Hello, Loojey dear! Throwin' bouquets to yerself agin, air yew? Gittin' fresh agin, air yew, yew greasy Eye-talian, orgin-grindin', ice-cream-barrer-pushin', back-stabbin', garlic-eatin', street-corner, pink-spangled-tights ackerobat," he observed in his own inimitable vernacular, as he unwound his long blue sash preparatory to dressing for the evening.

"Why don't yew per*chase* a barrel-orgin an' take yure dear pal Malvin along on it? Snakes! I guess I got my stummick full o' yew an' Mon-seer Malvin, some. I wish yew'd kiss yureself good-bye, Loojey. Yew fair git my goat, yew fresh gorilla! *Oui, vous gagnez mon chèvre proprement.*"

"*Qu'est-ce qu'il dit?*" asked Rivoli, his contemptuously curled lips baring his small, even teeth.

"Keskerdee? Why, yep! We uster hev a bunch o' dirty little 'keskerdees' at the ol' Glowin' Star mine, way back in Californey when I was a road-kid. Keskerdees!—so named becos they allus jabbered '*Keskerdee*' when spoke to. We uster use their heads fer cleanin' fryin'-pans. 'Keskerdee' is Eye-talian—a kind o' sorter low French," observed the Bucking Bronco.

It is to be feared that his researches into the ethnological and etymological truths of the European nations were limited and unprofitable, in spite of the fact that (like all other Legionaries of any standing) he spoke fluent Legion French on everyday military matters, and studied Italian phrases for the benefit of Carmelita. The Bucking Bronco's conversational method was to express himself idiomatically in the American tongue, and then translate it literally into the language of the benighted foreigner whom he honoured at the moment.

The Italian eyed the American malevolently, and, for the thousandth time, measured him, considered him, weighed him as an opponent in a boxing-wrestling-kicking match, remembered his uncanny magic skill with rifle and revolver, and, for the thousandth time, postponed the inevitable settlement, misliking his face, his mouth, his eye, and his general manner, air, and bearing.

"Give some abominable 'bleu' the honour of lacing the boots of Luigi Rivoli," he roared, turning with a contemptuous gesture from the American and the Cockney, to his henchman, Malvin. Fixing his eye upon the swarthy, spike-moustached Austrian, who sat at the foot of the bed opposite his own, he added:

"Here, dog, the privilege is thine. *Allez schieb'n los!*[26] and thrust out the unlaced boots that Malvin had pulled on to his feet.

The Austrian, squatting dejected, with his head between his fists, affected not to understand, and made no move.

"*Koom. Adji inna. Balek! fahesh beghla,*"[27] adjured the Italian, airing his Arabic, and insulting his intended victim by addressing him as though he were a native.

The Austrian did not stir.

---

[26] A curious piece of Legion "French" meaning "Be quick."
[27] "Get up. Come here. Take care! You ugly mule."

"Quick," hissed the Italian, and pointed to his boots that there might be no mistake.

The Austrian snarled.

"Bring it to me," said the great man, and, in a second, the recruit was run by the collar of his tunic, his ears, his twisted wrists, his woolly hair, and by a dozen willing hands, to the welcoming arms of the bully.

"Oh, thou deserter from the *Straf Bataillon*,"[28] growled the latter. A sudden grab, a swift twist, and the Austrian was on his face, his elbows meeting and overlapping behind his back, and his arms drawn upward and backward. He shrieked.

A quick jerk and he was on his feet, and then swung from the ground face downward, his wrists behind him in one of Rivoli's big hands, his trouser-ends in the other. Placing his foot in the small of the Austrian's back, the Italian appeared to be about to break the spine of his victim, whose screams were horrible to hear. Dashing him violently to the ground, Rivoli re-seated himself, and thrust forward his right foot. Groaning and gasping, the cowed Austrian knelt to his task, but, fumbling and failing to give satisfaction, received a kick in the face.

Reginald Rupert dropped the cartridge-pouch which he was polishing, and stepped forward, only to find himself thrust back by a sweep of the American's huge arm, which struck him in the chest like an iron bar, and to be seized by Légionnaire John Bull who quietly remarked:

"Mind your own business, recruit. . . . *C'est la Légion!*"

No one noticed that the Russian, Mikhail, was white and trembling, and that his brother came and led him to the other end of the room.

---

[28] Penal battalion.

"Bungler! *Polisson! Coquin!* Lick the soles of my boots and go," cried Rivoli, and, as the lad hesitated, he rose to his feet.

Cringing and shrinking, the wretched "blue" hastened to obey, thrust forth his tongue, and, as the boot was raised, obediently licked the nether surface and the edges of the sole until its owner was satisfied.

"Austria's proper attitude to Italy," growled the bully. "Now lick the other. . . ."

Le Légionnaire Luigi Rivoli might expect prompt obedience henceforth from le Légionnaire Franz Joseph Meyer.

Standing in the ring of amused satellites was the evil-looking *Apache*, a deeply interested spectator of this congenial and enjoyable scene. His hang-dog face caught the eye of the Italian.

"Come hither, thou *blanc-bec*," quoth he. "Come hither and show this *vaurien* how to lace the boots of a gentleman."

The *Apache* obeyed with alacrity, and, performing the task with rapidity and skill, turned to depart.

"A nimble-fingered sharper," observed the Italian, and, rising swiftly, bestowed a shattering kick upon the retreating Frenchman. Recovering his balance after the sudden forward propulsion, the *Apache* wheeled round like lightning, bent double, and flew at his assailant. Courage was his one virtue, and he was the finest exponent of the art of butting in all the purlieus and environs of Montmartre, and had not only laid out many a good bourgeois, but had overcome many a rival, by this preliminary to five minutes' strenuous kicking with heavy boots. If he launched himself— a one-hundred-and-fifty pound projectile—with his hard skull as battering-ram, straight at the stomach of his tormentor, that astounded individual ought to go violently to the ground, doubled up, winded and helpless. A score of tremendous kicks would then teach him that an *Apache* King (and he, none other than Tou-Tou Boil-the-Cat, *doyen* of the heroes of the Rue de Venise, Rue Pirouette, and Rue des Innocents, *caveau*-knight and the beloved of the beauteous Casque d'Or) was not a person lightly to be trifled with.

But if Monsieur Tou-Tou Boil-the-Cat was a *Roi des Apaches*, Luigi Rivoli was an acrobat and juggler, and, to mighty strength, added marvellous poise, quickness and skill.

"*Ça ne marche pas, gobemouche,*" he remarked, and, at the right moment, his knee shot up with tremendous force and crashed into the face of the butting *Apache*. For the first time the famous and terrible attack of the King of the Paris hooligans had failed. When the unfortunate monarch regained his senses, some minutes later, and took stock of his remaining teeth and features, he registered a mental memorandum to the effect that he would move along the lines of caution, rather than valour, in his future dealings with the Légionnaire Luigi Rivoli—until his time came.

"*Je m'en souviendrai,*" said he. . . .

An interesting object-lesson in the effect, upon a certain type of mind, of the methods of the Italian was afforded by the conduct of a Greek recruit, named Dimitropoulos. Stepping forward with ingratiating bows and smiles, as the unfortunate M. Tou-Tou was stretched senseless on the floor, he proclaimed himself to be the best of the *lustroi* of the city of Corinth, and begged for the honour and pleasure of cleaning the boots of Il Signor Luigi Rivoli.

Oh, but yes; a *lustros* of the most distinguished, look you, who had polished the most eminent boots in Greece at ten *leptas* a time. Alas! that he had not all his little implements and sponges, his cloth of velvet, his varnish for the heel. Had he but the tools necessary to the true artist in his profession, the boots of Il Illustrissimo Signor should be then and thenceforth of a brightness dazzling and remarkable.

As he gabbled, the Greek scrubbed at Rivoli's boots with a rag and the palm of his hand. Evidently the retinue of the great man had been augmented by one who would be faithful and true while his patron's strength and money lasted. As, at the head of his band of henchmen and parasites, the latter hero turned to leave the barrack-room with a shout of "*Allons, mes enfants d'Enfer*," he bent his lofty brow upon, cocked his ferocious eye at, and turned his haughty regard toward the remaining recruits, finishing with Reginald Rupert:

"I will teach useful tricks to you little dogs later," he promised. "You shall dance me the *rigolboche*, and the *can-can*," and swaggered out.
. . .

"Nice lad," observed Rupert, looking up from his work—and wondered what the morrow might bring forth. There should be a disappointed Luigi, or a dead Rupert about, if it came to interference and trouble.

"Sure," agreed Légionnaire Bronco, seating himself on the bed beside his beloved John Bull. "He's some stiff, that guy, an' I allow it'll soon be up ter me ter *con*duct our Loojey ter the bone-orchard. He's a plug-ugly. He's a ward-heeler. Land sakes! I wants ter punch our Loojey till Hell pops; an' when it comes ter shootin' I got Loojey skinned a mile—sure thing. *J'ai Loojey écorché un mille.* . . . Nope, there ain't 'nuff real room fer Looje an' me in Algery—not while Carmelita's around.

. . .

"Say, John," he continued, turning to his friend, "she up an' axed me las' night ef he ever went ter the Canteen an' ef Madam lar Canteenair didn't ever git amakin' eyes at her beautiful Looje! Yep! It *is* time Loojey kissed hisself good-bye."

"Oh? What did you tell her?" enquired John Bull. "There is no doubt the swine will marry the Canteen if he can. More profitable than poor little Carmelita's show. He *is* a low stinker, and she's one of the best and prettiest and pluckiest little women who ever lived. . . . She's so *débrouillarde*."

"Wot did I say? Wal, John, wot I ses was— 'Amakin' eyes at yure Loojey, my dear,' I ses, 'Madam lar Canteenair is a woman with horse-sense an' two eyes in 'er 'ead. She wouldn't look twice at a boastin', swankin', fat-slappin', back-stabbin', dime-show ackerobat,' I ses. 'Yure Loojey flaps 'is mouth too much. *Il frappe sa bouche trop*,' I ses. But I didn't tell her as haow 'e's amakin' up ter Madam lar Canteenaire all his possible. She wouldn't believe it of 'im. She wouldn't even believe that 'e *goes* ter the Canteen. I only ses: 'Yure Loojey's a leary lipper so don't say as haow I ain't warned yer, Carmelita honey,' I ses—an' I puts it inter copper-bottomed Frencho langwago also. Yep!"

"What did Carmelita say?" asked John Bull.

"Nix," was the reply. "It passes my com*pre*hension wot she sees in that fat Eye-talian ice-cream trader. Anyhaow, it's up ter Hiram C. Milton ter git upon his hind legs an' *fer*bid the bangs ef she goes fer ter marry a greasy orgin-grinder . . . serposin' he don't git Madam lar Canteenair," and the Bucking Bronco sighed deeply, produced some strong, black Algerian tobacco, and asked High Heaven if he might hope ever again to stuff some real Tareyton Mixture (the best baccy in the world) into his "guley-brooley"—whereby Legionary John Bull understood him to mean his *brûle-gueule,* or short pipe—and relapsed into lethargic and taciturn apathy.

"How would you like a prowl round?" asked John Bull, of Rupert.

"Nothing better, thank you, if you think I could pass the Sergeant of the Guard before being dismissed recruit-drills."

"Oh, that'll be all right if you are correctly dressed. Hop into the tunic and red breeches and we'll try it. You're free until five-thirty to-morrow morning, and can do some more at your kit when we return. We'll go round the barracks and I'll show you the ropes before we stroll round Sidi-bel-Abbès, and admire the wonders of the Rue Prudon, Rue Montagnac, and Rue de Jerusalem. Our band is playing at the Military Club to-night, and the band of the Première Légion Étrangère is the finest band in the whole world—largely Germans and Poles. We are allowed to listen at a respectful distance. We'll look in at the *Village d'Espagnol,* the *Mekerra,* and the *Faubourg des Palmiers* another time, as they're out of bounds. Also the *Village Négre* if you like, but if we're caught there we get a month's hard labour, if not solitary confinement and starvation in the foul and stinking *cellules*—because we're likely to be killed in the *Village Négre.*"

"Let's go there now," suggested Rupert eagerly, as he buttoned his tunic.

"No, my boy. Wait until you know what *cellule* imprisonment really is, before you risk it. You keep out of the *trou* just as long as you can. It's different from the Stone Jug of a British regiment —very. Don't do any *rabiau*[29] until you must. We'll

---

[29] Time spent in prison or in the Penal Battalions—which does not count towards

be virtuous to-night, and when you *must* go out of bounds, go with me. I'll take you to see Carmelita this evening at the Café de la Légion, and we'll look in on Madame la Cantinière, at the Canteen, before the Last Post at nine o'clock. . . . Are you coming, Buck?"

And these three modern musketeers left the *chambrée* of their *caserne* and clattered down the stone stairs to the barrack-square.

---

the five years period of service.

CHAPTER III

CARMELITA ET CIE

"Those boots comfortable?" asked John Bull as they crossed the great parade-ground.

"Wonderfully," replied Rupert. "I could do a march in them straight away. Fine boots too."

"Yes," agreed the other. "That's one thing you can say for the Legion kit, the boots are splendid—probably the best military boots in the world. You'll see why, before long."

"Long marches?"

"Longest done by any unit of human beings. Our ordinary marches would be records for any other infantry, and our forced marches are incredible—absolute world's records. They call us the *'Cavalerie à pied'* in the Service, you know. One of the many ways of killing us is marching us to death, to keep up the impossible standard. Buck, here, is our champion."

"Waal, yew see—I strolled crost Amurrica ten times," apologised the Bronco, "ahittin' the main drag, so I oughter vamoose some. Yep! I can throw me feet *consi*derable."

"I've never been a foot-slogger myself," admitted Rupert, "but I've Mastered a beagle pack, and won a few running pots at school and during my brief 'Varsity career. What are your distances?"

"Our minimum, when marching quietly out of barracks and back, without a halt is forty kilometres under our present Colonel, who is known in the Legion as The Marching Pig, and we do it three or four times a week. On forced marches we do anything that is to be done, inasmuch as it is the unalterable law of the Legion that all forced marches must be done in one march. If the next post were forty miles away or even fifty, and the matter urgent, we should go straight on without a halt, except the usual 'cigarette space,' or five minutes in every hour, until we got there. I assure you I have very often marched as much as six hundred kilometres in fifteen days, and occasionally much more. And we carry the heaviest kit in the world—over a hundred-weight, in full marching order."

"What is a kilometre?" asked the interested Rupert.

"Call it five furlongs."

"Then an ordinary day's march is about thirty miles without a halt, and you may have to do four hundred miles straight off, at the rate of twenty-five consecutive miles a day? Good Lord above us!"

"Yes, my own personal record is five hundred and sixty miles in nineteen days, without a rest day—under the African sun and across sand. . . ."

"I say—what's *this* game?" interrupted Rupert, as the three turned a corner and entered a small square between the rear of the *caserne* of the Fourth Company and the great barrack-wall—a square of which all exits were guarded by sentries with fixed bayonets. Round and round in a ring at a very rapid quick-step ran a dismal procession of suffering men, to the monotonously reiterated order of a Corporal—

"A droit, *droit*. A droit, *droit*. A droit, *droit*."

Their blanched, starved-looking faces, glazed eyes, protruding tongues and doubled-up bodies made them a doleful spectacle. On each man's back was a burden of a hundred pounds of stones. On each man's emaciated face, a look of agony, and on the canvas-clad back of one man, a great stain of wet blood from a raw wound caused by the cutting and rubbing of the stone-laden knapsack. Each man wore a fatigue-uniform, filthy beyond description.

"Why the hell can't they be set ter sutthin' useful—hoein' pertaties, or splittin' rails, or chewin' gum—'stead o' that silly strain-me-heart and break-me-sperrit game on empty stummicks twice a day?" observed the Bucking Bronco.

Every panting, straining, gasping wretch in that pitiable *peloton des hommes punis* looked as though his next minute must be his last, his next staggering step bring him crashing to the ground. What could the dreadful alternative be, the fear of which kept these suffering, starving wretches on their tottering, failing legs? Why would they *not* collapse, in spite of Nature? Fear of the Legion's prison? No, they were all serving periods in the Legion's prison already, and twice spending three hours of each prison-day in this agony. Fear of the Legion's Hospital? Yes, and of the Penal Battalion afterwards.

"What sort of crimes have they committed?" asked Rupert, as they turned with feelings of personal shame from the sickening sight.

"Oh, all sorts, but I'm afraid a good many of them have earned the enmity of some Non-com. As a rule, a man who wants to, can keep out of that sort of thing, but there's a lot of luck in it. One gets run in for a lost strap, a dull button, a speck of rust on rifle or bayonet, or perhaps for being slow at drill, slack in saluting, being out of bounds, or something of that sort. A Sergeant gives him three days' confinement to barracks, and enters it in the *livre de punitions*. Very likely, the Captain, feeling liverish when he examines the book, makes it eight days' imprisonment. That's not so bad, provided the Commander of the Battalion does not think it might be good for discipline for him to double it. And that again is bearable so long as the Colonel does not think the scoundrel had better have a month—and imprisonment, though only called 'Ordinary Arrest,' carries with it this beastly *peloton de chasse*. Still, as I say, a good man and keen soldier can generally keep fairly clear of *salle de police* and *cellule*."

"So Non-coms. can punish off their own bat, in the Legion, can they?" enquired Rupert as they strolled toward the main gate.

"Yes. The N.C.O. is an almighty important bird here, and you have to salute him like an officer. They can give extra corvée, confinement to barracks, and up to eight days' *salle de police*, and give you a pretty bad time while you're doing it, too. In peace time, you know, the N.C.O.s run the Legion absolutely. We hardly see our officers except on marches, or at manœuvres. Splendid soldiers, but they consider their duty is to lead us in battle, not to be bothered with us in peace. The N.C.O.s can do the bothering for them. Of course, we're pretty frequently either demonstrating, or actually fighting on the Southern, or the Moroccan border, and then an officer's job is no sinecure. They are real soldiers—but the weak spot is that they avoid us like poison, in barracks."

"We're mostly foreigners, of course," he continued, "half German, and not very many French, and there's absolutely none of that mutual liking and understanding which is the strength of the British Army. . . . And naturally, in a corps like this, they've *got* to be severe and harsh to the point of cruelty. After all, it's not a girls' school, is it? But take my advice, my boy, and leave the Legion's punishment system of starvation, over-work, and solitary confinement outside your 'experiences' as much as possible. . . ."

"I say—what a ghastly, charnel-house stink," remarked the recipient of this good advice, as the trio passed two iron-roofed buildings, one on each side of the closed main-entrance of the barracks. "I noticed it when I first came in here, but I was to windward of it I suppose. It's the bally limit. Poo-o-oh!"

"Yes, you live in that charming odour all night, if you get *salle de police* for any offence, and all day as well, if you get 'arrest' in the regimental lock-up—except for your two three-hour turns of *peloton des hommes punis*. It's nothing at this distance, but wait until you're on sentry-go in one of those barrack-prisons. There's a legend of a run-away pig that took refuge in one, gave a gasp, and fell dead. . . . Make Dante himself envious if he could go inside. The truth of that Inferno is much stranger than the fiction of his."

"Yep," chimed in the American. "But what gits my goat every time is *cellules*. Yew squats on end in a dark cell fer the whole of yure sentence, an' yew don't go outside it from start to finish, an' thet may be thirty days. Yew gits a quarter-ration o' dry bread an' a double ration of almighty odour. 'Nuff ter raise the roof, but it don't do it. No exercise, no readin', no baccy, no nuthin'. There yew sits and there yew starves, an' lucky ef yew don't go balmy. . . ."

"I hope we get you past the Sergeant of the Guard," interrupted John Bull. "Swank it thick as we go by."

The cold eye of the Sergeant ran over the three Legionaries as they passed through the little side wicket without blazing into wrath over any lack of smartness and *chic* in their appearance.

"One to you," said John Bull, as they found themselves safe in the shadow of the Spahis' barracks outside. "If you had looked too like a recruit he'd have turned you back, on principle. . . ."

To Reginald Rupert the walk was full of interest, in spite of the fact that the half-vulgar, half-picturesque Western-Eastern appearance of the town was no novelty. He had already seen all that Sidi-bel-Abbès could show, and much more, in Algiers, Tangiers, Cairo, Alexandria, Port Said, and Suez. But, with a curious sense of proprietorship, he enjoyed listening to the distant strains of the band—their "own" band. To see thousands of Legionaries, Spahis, Turcos, Chasseurs d'Afrique, Sapeurs, Tirailleurs, Zouaves, and other French soldiery, from their own level, as one of themselves, was what interested him. Here was a new situation, here were new conditions, necessities, dangers, sufferings, relationships. Here, in short, were entirely new experiences. . . .

"This is the Rue Prudon," observed John Bull. "It separates the Military goats on the west, from the Civil sheep on the east. Not that you'll find them at all 'civil' though. . . . Reminds me of a joke I heard our Captain telling the Colonel at dinner one night when I was a Mess Orderly. A new man had taken over the Grand Hotel, and he wrote to the Mess President to say he made a speciality of dinner-parties for Military and *Civilised* officers! Bit rough on the Military, what?"

Having crossed the Rue Prudon rubicon, and invaded the Place de Quinconces with its Palais de Justice and prison, the Promenade Publique with its beautiful trees, and the Rue Montagnac with its shops and life and glitter, the three Legionaries quitted the quarter of electric arc-lights, brilliant cafés, shops, hotels, apéritif-drinking citizens, promenading Frenchwomen, newspaper kiosks, loitering soldiers, shrill hawkers of the *Echo d'Oran*, white-burnoused Arabs (who gazed coldly upon the hated Franswazi, and bowed to officials with stately dignity, arms folded on breast), quick-stepping Chasseurs, scarlet-cloaked Spahis, and swaggering Turcos, crossed the Place Sadi Carnot, and made for the maze of alleys, slums, and courts (the quarter of the Spanish Jews, town Arabs, *hadris*, *adjar*-wearing women, Berbers, Negroes, half-castes, semi-Oriental scum, "white trash," and Legionaries), in one of which was situated Carmelita's Café de la Légion.

§2

La Belle Carmelita, black-haired, red-cheeked, black-eyed, red-lipped, lithe, swift, and graceful, sat at the receipt of custom. Carmelita's Café de la Légion was for the Legion, and had to make its profits out of men whose pay is one halfpenny a day. It is therefore matter for little surprise that it compared unfavourably with Voisin's, the Café de la Paix, the Pré Catalan, Maxim's, the Café Grossenwahn, the Das Prinzess Café, the restaurants of the Place Pigalle, Le Rat Mort, or even Les Noctambules, Le Cabaret de l'Enfer, the Chat Noir, the Elysée Montmartre, and the famous and infamous *caveaux* of Le Quartier—in the eyes of those Legionaries who had tried some, or all, of these places.

However, it had four walls, a floor, and a roof; benches and a large number of tables and chairs, many of which were quite reliable. It had a bar, it had Algerian wine at one penny the bottle, it had *vert-vert* and *tord-boyaud* and *bapédi* and *shum-shum*. It had really good coffee, and really bad cigarettes. It had meals also—but above all, and before all, it had a welcome. A welcome for the Legionary. The man to whose presence the good people of Sidi-bel-Abbès (French petty officials, half-castes, Spanish Jews, Arabs, clerks, workmen, shop-keepers, waiters, and lowest-class bourgeoisie) took exception at the bandstand, in the Gardens, in the Cafés, in the very streets; the man from the contamination of whose touch the very cocottes, the demi-mondaines, the joyless *filles de joie*, even the daughters of the pavement, drew aside the skirts of their dingy finery (for though the Wages of Virtue are a halfpenny a day for the famous Legion, the Wages of Sin are more for the infamous legion); the man at whom even the Goums, the Arab *gens-d'armes* shouted as at a pariah dog, this man, the Soldier of the Legion, had a welcome in Carmelita's Café. There were two women in all the world who would endure to breathe the same air as the sad Sons of the Legion —Madame la Cantinière (official *fille du régiment*) and Carmelita. Is it matter for wonder that the Legion's sons loved them—particularly Carmelita, who, unlike Madame, was under no obligation to shed the light of her countenance upon them? Any man in the Legion might speak to Carmelita provided he spoke as a gentleman should speak to a lady—and did not want to be pinned to her bar by the ears, and the bayonets of his indignant brothers-in-arms—any man who might speak to no other woman in the world outside the Legion. (Madame la Cantinière is inside the Legion, *bien entendu*, and always married to it in the person of one of its sons.) She would meet him as an equal for the sake of her beautiful, wonderful, adored Luigi Rivoli, his brother-in-arms. Perhaps one must be such an outcast that the sight of one causes even painted lips to curl in contemptuous disdain; such a *thing* that one is deterred from entering decent Cafés, decent places of amusement and decent boulevards; so low that one is strictly doomed to the environment of one's prison, or the slums, and to the society of one's fellow dregs, before one can appreciate the attitude of the Sons of the Legion to Carmelita. They revered her as they did not revere the Mother of God, and they, broken and crucified wretches, envied Luigi Rivoli as they did not envy the repentant thief absolved by Her Son.

She, Carmelita, welcomed *them*, Legionaries! It is perhaps comprehensible if not excusable, that the attitude of Madame la Cantinière was wholly different, that she hated Carmelita as a rival, and with single heart, double venom and treble voice, denounced her, her house, her wine, her coffee, and all those *chenapans* and *sacripants* her clients.

"*Merde!*" said Madame la Cantinière, "that which makes the slums of Naples too hot for it, is warm indeed! Naples! Ma foi! Why Monsieur Le Bon Diable himself must be reluctant when his patrol runs in a *prisonnier* from Naples to the nice clean guard-room and *cellules* in his Hell . . . Naples! . . . La! La! . . ." which was unkind and unfair of Madame, since the very worst she knew of Carmelita was the fact that she kept a Café whereat the Legionaries spent their half-pence. It is not (rightly or wrongly) in itself an indictable offence to be a Neapolitan.

So the Legion loved Carmelita, Madame la Cantinière hated her, the Bucking Bronco worshipped her, John Bull admired her, le bon M. Edouard Malvin desired her, and Luigi Rivoli owned her—body, soul and cash-box—what time he sought to do the same for Madame la Cantinière whose body and cash-box were as much larger than those of Carmelita as her soul was smaller.

Between two fools one comes to the ground—sometimes—but Luigi intended to come to a bed of roses, and to have a cash-box beneath it. One of the fools should marry and support him, preferably the richer fool, and meantime, oh the subtlety, the cleverness, the piquancy—of being loved and supported by both while marrying neither! Many a time as he lay on his cot while a henchman polished the great cartridge-pouches (that earned the Legion the sobriquet of "the Leather-Bellies" from the Russians in the Crimea), the belts, the buttons, the boots, and the rifle and bayonet of the noble Luigi, while another washed his fatigue uniforms and under-clothing, that honourable man would chuckle aloud as he saw himself frequently cashing a ten-franc piece of Carmelita's at Madame's Canteen, and receiving change for a twenty-franc piece from the fond, yielding Madame. Ten francs too much, a sigh too many, and a kiss too few—for Madame did not kiss, being, contrary to popular belief with regard to vivandières in general, and the Legion's vivandière in particular, of rigid virtue, oh, but yes, of a respectability profound and colossal— during "vacation." Her present vacation had lasted for three months, and Madame felt it was time to replace le pauvre Etienne Baptiste—cut in small pieces by certain Arab ladies. Madame was a business woman, Madame needed a husband in her business, and Madame had an eye for a fine man. None finer than Luigi Rivoli, and Madame had never tried an Italian. Husbands do not last long in the Legion, and Madame had had three French, one Belgian, and one Swiss (seriatim, *bien entendu*). No, none finer in the whole Legion than Rivoli. None, nom de Dieu! But a foreign husband may be a terrible trial, look you, and an Italian is a foreigner in a sense that a French-speaking Belgian or Swiss is not. No, an Italian is not a Frenchman even though he be a Légionnaire. And there were tales of him and this vile shameless creature from Naples, who decoyed les braves

Légionnaires from their true and lawful Canteen to her noisome den in the foul slums, there to spend their hard-earned sous on her poisonous red-ink wine, her muddy-water coffee, and her—worse things. Yes, that cunning little fox le Légionnaire Edouard Malvin had thrown out hints to Madame about this Neapolitan *ragazza*—but then, ce bon M. Malvin was himself a suitor for Madame's hand—as well as a most remarkable liar and rogue. Perhaps 'twould be as well to accept ce beau Luigi at once, marry him immediately, and see that he spent his evenings helping in the Canteen bar, instead of gallivanting after Neapolitan hussies of the bazaar. Men are but men—and sirens are sirens. What would you? And Luigi so gay and popular. Small blame that he should stray when Madame was unkind or coy. . . . Yes, she would do it, if only to spite this Neapolitan cat. . . . But—he was a foreigner and something of a rogue—and incredibly strong. Still, Madame had tamed more than one recalcitrant husband by knocking the bottom off an empty bottle and stabbing him in the face with it. And however strong one's husband might be, he must, like Sisera, sleep sometimes.

The beautiful Luigi would hate to be awakened with a bottomless bottle, and would not need it more than once. . . . And the business soul of scheming, but amorous Madame, much troubled, still halted between two opinions—while the romantic and simple soul of loving little Carmelita remained steadfast, and troubled but little. Just a little, because the fine *gentilhomme*, Légionnaire Jean Boule, and the great, kind Légionnaire Bouckaing Bronceau, and certain others, seemed somehow *to warn her* against her Luigi; seemed to despise him, and hint at treachery. She did not count the sly Belgian (or Austrian) Edouard

Malvin. The big stupid Americano was jealous, of course, but Il Signor Inglese was not and he was—oh, like a Reverend Father—so gentle and honest and good. But no, her Luigi could not be false, and the next Légionnaire who said a word against him should be forbidden Le Café de la Légion, ill as it could afford to lose even halfpenny custom—what with the rent, taxes, *bakshish* to gens-d'armes, service, cooking, lighting, wine, spirits, coffee, and Luigi's daily dinner, Chianti and franc pocket-money. . . . If only that franc could be increased—but one must eat, or get so thin—and the great Luigi liked not skinny women. What was a franc a day to such a man as Luigi, her Luigi, strongest, finest, handsomest of men?—and but for her he would never have been in this accursed Legion. Save for her aggravating wickedness, he would never have stabbed poor Guiseppe Longigotto and punished her by enlisting. How great and fine a hero of splendid vengeance! A true Neapolitan, yet how magnanimous when punishment was meted! He had forgiven—and forgotten—the dead Guiseppe, and he had forgiven her, and he accepted her miserable franc, dinner and Chianti wine daily. Also he had allowed her—miserable ingrate that she had been to annoy him and make him jealous—to find the money that had mysteriously but materially assisted in procuring the perpetual late-pass that allowed him to remain with her till two in the morning, long after all the other poor Légionnaires had returned to their dreadful barracks. Noble Luigi! Yet there were people who coupled his name with that of wealthy Madame la Cantinière in the barrack yonder.

She had overheard Légionnaires doing it, here in her own Café, though they had instantly and stoutly denied it when accused, and had looked furtive and ashamed. Absurd, jealous wretches, whose heads Luigi could knock together as easily as she could click her castanets. . . .

Almost time that the Légionnaires began to drop in for their litre and their *tasse*—and Carmelita rose and went to the door of the Café de la Légion and looked down the street toward the Place Sadi Carnot. One of three passing Chasseurs d'Afrique made a remark, the import of which was not lost on the Italian girl, though the man spoke in Paris slum argot.

"If Monsieur would but give himself the trouble to step inside and sit down for a moment," said Carmelita in Legion-French, "Monsieur's question shall be answered by Luigi Rivoli of La Legion. Also he will remove Monsieur's pretty uniform and scarlet *ceinturon* and will do for Monsieur what Monsieur's mamma evidently neglected to do for Monsieur when Monsieur was a dirty little boy in the gutter. . . . Monsieur will *not* come in as he suggested? Monsieur will not wait a minute? No? Monsieur is a very wise young gentleman. . . ."

An Arab Spahi swaggered past and leered.

"*Sabeshad zareefeh chattaha*," said he, "*saada atinee.*"

"*Roh! Imshi!*" hissed Carmelita and Carmelita's hand went to her pocket in a significant manner, and Carmelita spat.

A Greek ice-cream seller lingered and ogled.

"*Bros!*" snapped Carmelita with a jerk of her thumb in the direction in which the young person should be going.

A huge Turco, with a vast beard, brought his rolling swagger to a halt at her door and made to enter.

"*Destour!*" said the tiny Carmelita to the giant, pointed to the street and stared him unwaveringly in the eye until, grinning sheepishly, he turned and went.

Carmelita did not like Turcos in general, and detested this one in particular. He was too fond of coming when he knew the Café to be empty of Légionnaires.

An old Spanish Jew paused in his shuffle to ask for a cigarette.

"Varda!" replied Carmelita calmly, with the curious thumb-jerking gesture of negation, distinctive of the uneducated Italian.

A most cosmopolitan young woman, and able to give a little of his own tongue to any dweller in Europe and to most of those in Northern Africa. Not in the least a refined young woman, however, and her many accomplishments not of the drawing-room. Staunch, courageous, infinitely loving, utterly honest, loyal, reliable, and very self-reliant, she was, upon occasion, it is to be feared, more emphatic than delicate in speech, and more uncompromising than ladylike in conduct. She was not *une maîtresse vierge*, and her standards and ideals were not those of the Best Suburbs. You see, Carmelita had begun to earn her own living at the unusually early age of three, and earned it in coppers on a dirty rug, on a dirtier Naples quay, for a decade or so, until at the age of fourteen, or fifteen, she, together with her Mamma, her reputed Papa, her sister and her brother, performed painful acrobatic feats on the edge of the said quay for the delectation of the passengers of the big North German Lloyd and other steamers that tied up thereat for purposes of embarkation and debarkation, and for the reception of coal and the discharge of cargo.

At the age of fifteen, Carmelita, most beautiful of form and coarsely beautiful of face, of perfect health, grace, poise, and carriage, fell desperately in love with the great Signor Carlo Scopinaro, born Luigi Rivoli, a star of her own firmament but of far greater magnitude.

Luigi Rivoli, one of a troupe of acrobats who performed at the Naples Scala, Vésuvie, and Variétés, meditating setting up on his own account as Strong Man, Acrobat, Juggler, Wrestler, Dancer, and Professor of Physical Culture, was, to the humble "tumbler" of the quay, as the be-Knighted Actor-Manager of a West End Theatre to the last joined chorus girl, or walking-lady on his boards. And yet the great Signor Carlo Scopinaro, born Luigi Rivoli, meditating desertion from his troupe and needing an "assistant," deigned to accept the services and whole-souled adoration of the girl who was as much more skilful as she was less powerful than he.

When, in her perfect, ardent, and beautiful love, her reckless and uncounting adoration, she gave herself, mind, body and soul, to her hero and her god, he accepted the little gift "without prejudice"—as the lawyers say. "Without prejudice" to Luigi's future, that is.

During their short engagement at the Scala—terminated by the Troupe's earnest endeavour to assassinate the defaulting and defalcating Luigi, and her family's endeavour to maim Carmelita for setting up on her own account, and deserting her loving "parents"—it was rather the girl whom the public applauded for her wonderful back-somersaults, contortions, hand-walking, catherine-wheels, trapeze-work, and dancing, than the man for his feats with dumb-bells of doubtful solidity, his stereotyped ball-juggling, his chain-breaking, and weight-lifting, his muscle-slapping and *Ha!* shouting, his posturing and grimacing, and his issuing of challenges to wrestle any man in the world for any sum he liked to name, and in any style known to science. And, when engagements at the lower-class halls and cafés of Barcelona,

Marseilles, Toulon, Genoa, Rome, Brindisi, Venice, Trieste, Corinth, Athens, Constantinople, Port Said, Alexandria, Messina, Valetta, Algiers, Oran, Tangiers, or Casa Blanca were obtained, it was always, and obviously, the girl, rather than the man, who decided the proprietor or manager to engage them, and who won the applause of his patrons.

When times were bad, as after Luigi's occasional wrestling defeats and during the bad weeks of Luigi's typhoid, convalescence, and long weakness at Marseilles, it was Carmelita, the humbler and lesser light, who (the Halls being worked out) tried desperately to keep the wolf from the door by returning to the quay-side business, and, for dirty coppers, exhibiting to passengers, coal-trimmers, cargo-workers, porters and loafers, the performances that had been subject of signed contracts and given on fine stages in beautiful music-halls and cafés, to refined and appreciative audiences. Incidentally the girl learned much French (little knowing how useful it was to prove), as well as smatterings of Spanish, Greek, Turkish, English and Arabic.

So Carmelita had "assisted" the great Luigi in the times of his prosperity and had striven to maintain him in eclipse, by quay-side, public-house, workmen's dinner-hour, low café, back-yard, gambling-den, and wine-shop exhibitions of her youthful skill, grace, agility, and beauty—and had failed to make enough by that means. To the end of her life poor Carmelita could never, never forget that terrible time at Marseilles, try as she might to thrust it into the background of her thoughts. For there, ever there, in the background it remained, save when called to cruel prominence by some mischance, or at rare intervals by the noble Luigi himself, when displeased by some failure on the part of Carmelita. A terrible, terrible memory, for Carmelita's nature was essentially virginal, delicate, and of crystal purity. Where she loved she gave all—and Luigi was to Carmelita as much her husband as if they had been married in every church they had passed, in every cathedral they had seen, and by every *padre* they had met. . . .

A terrible, terrible memory. . . . But Luigi's life was at stake and what true woman, asked Carmelita, would not have taken the last step of all (when every other failed) to raise the money necessary for doctors, medicine, delicacies, food, fuel, and lodging? If, by thrusting her right hand into the fire, Carmelita could have burnt away those haunting and corroding Marseilles memories, then into the fire her right hand would have been thrust. Yet, side by side with the self-horror and self-disgust was no remorse nor repentance. If, to-morrow, Luigi's life could only thus again be saved, thus saved should it be, as when at Marseilles he lay convalescent but dying for lack of the money wherewith to buy the delicacies that would save him. . . . Luigi's life always, and at any time, before Carmelita's scruples and shrinkings.

In return, Luigi had been kind to her and had often spoken of matrimony—some day—in spite of what she had done at Marseilles when he was too ill to look after her, and provide her with all she needed. Once even, when they were on the crest of a great wave of prosperity, Luigi had gone so far as to mention her seventeenth birthday as a possibly suitable date for their wedding. That had been a great and glorious time, though all too short, alas! and the sequel to a brilliant scheme devised by that poor dear Guiseppe Longigotto in the interests of his beloved and adored friend Carmelita. Poor Guiseppe! He had deserved as Carmelita was the first to admit, something better, than a stab in the back from Luigi Rivoli, for the idea had been wholly and solely his, until the great Roman sporting Impresario had taken it up and developed it. First there was a tremendous syndicate-engineered campaign of advertisement, which let all Europe know that *Il Famoso e Piu Grande Professore Carlo Scopinaro*, Champion Wrestler of Europe, America and Australia, would shortly meet the Egregious Egyptian, or Conquering Copt, Champion Wrestler of Africa and Asia, in Rome, and wrestle him in the Græco-Roman style, for the World's Championship and ten thousand pounds a side. (Yes actually and authoritatively *diecimila lire sterline.*) From every hoarding in Rome, Venice, Milan, Turin, Genoa, Florence, Naples, Brindisi, and every other town in Italy, huge posters called your attention to the beauties and marvels of the smiling face and mighty form of the great Carlo Scopinaro; to the horrors and terrors of the scowling face and enormous carcase of the dreadful Conquering Copt. (To positively none but Luigi, Guiseppe, and the renowned Roman Impresario was it known that the Conquering Copt was none other than Luigi's old pal, Abdul Hamid, chucker-out at a Port Said music-hall, and most modest and retiring of gentlemen—until this great-ness of Champion Wrestler of Africa and Asia was suddenly thrust upon him, and he was summoned from Port Said to Rome to be coached by Luigi in the arts and graces of realistic stage-wrestling, and particularly in those of life-like and convinc-ing defeat after a long and obviously terrible struggle.) . . . Excitement was splendidly engi-neered, the newspapers of every civilised country and of Germany advertised the epoch-making event, speculated upon its result, and produced interesting articles on such questions as, *"Should* a Colour-Line be drawn in Wrestling?" and, "Is Scopinaro the White Hope?" A self-advertising reverend Nonconformist announced his intention in the English press of proceeding to Rome to create a disturbance at the Match. He got himself frequently interviewed by specimens of the genus, "Our representative," and the important fact that he was a Conscientious Objector to all forms of sport was brought to the notice of the Great British Public.

The struggle was magnificently staged and magnificently acted. Every spectator in the vast theatre, no matter whether he had paid one hundred lire or a paltry fifty centesimi for his seat, felt that he had had his money's worth. In incredibly realistic manner the White Hope of Europe and the Champion of Africa and Asia struck attitudes, cried "Ha!", snatched at each other, stamped, straddled, pushed, pulled, embraced, slapped, jerked, hugged, tugged, lugged, and lifted each other with every appearance of fearful exertion, dauntless courage, fierce determination and unparalleled skill for one crowded hour of glorious life, during which the house went mad, rose at them to a man, and, with tears and imprecations, called upon the Italian to be worthy of his country and upon the Conquering Copt to be damned.

Few scenes in all the troubled history of Rome can have equalled, for excitement, that which ensued when the White Hope finally triumphed, the honour of Europe in general was saved, and that of Italy in particular illuminated with a blaze of glory.

Anyhow, what was solid fact, with no humbug about it, was that Luigi received the renowned Roman Impresario's fervid blessing and five hundred pounds, while the complacent Abdul received blessings equally fervid, though a less enthusiastic cheque. Both gentlemen were then provided by the kind Impresario with single tickets to the most distant spot he could induce them to name.

For Carmelita, the days following that on which her Luigi won the great World's Championship match, were a glorious time of expensive dinners, fine apartments, and beautiful clothes; a time of being café and music-hall patrons instead of performers; of being entertained instead of entertaining. The joy of Carmelita's life while the five hundred pounds lasted was to sit in a stage-box, proud and happy, beside her noble Luigi, and criticise the various "turns" upon the stage. Never an evening performance, nor a matinée did they miss, and Luigi drank a quart of champagne at lunch, and another at dinner. Luigi must keep his strength up, of course, and the soothing influence of innumerable Havana cigars was not denied to his nerves.

And then, just as the five hundred pounds was finished, a wretched Russian (quickly followed by an American, two Russians, a Turk, a Frenchman, and an Englishman) publicly challenged Luigi in the press of Europe, to wrestle for the Championship of the World in any style he liked, for any amount he liked, when and where he liked—and that branch of his profession was closed to Luigi—for these men were giants and terrors, arranging no "crosses," stern fighters, and out for fame, money, genuine sport, and the real Championship.

Then had come a time of poverty, straits, mean shifts and misery, followed by Luigi's job as a "tamer" of tame lions. This post of lion-tamer to a cageful of mangy, weary lions, captive-born, pessimistic, timid and depressed, had been secured by

Guiseppe Longigotto, and handed over to Luigi (on its proving safe and satisfactory), in the interests of Giuseppe's adored and hungry Carmelita. Arrayed in the costume worn by all the Best Lion-tamers, Luigi looked a truly noble figure, as, with flashing eyes and gleaming teeth, he cracked the whip and fired the revolver that induced the bored and disgusted lions to amble round the cage, crouching and cringing in humility and fear. That insignificant little rat, Guiseppe, was far more in the picture, of course, as fiddler to the show, than he was in his original rôle of tamer of the lions. Followed a bad time along the African coast, culminating, at Algiers, in poor Guiseppe's impassioned pleadings that Carmelita would marry him (and, leaving this dreadful life of the road, live with him and his beautiful violin on the banked proceeds of his great Wrestling Championship scheme), Luigi's jealousy, his overbearing airs of proprietorship, his drunken cruelty, his presuming on her love and obedience to him until she sought to give him a fright and teach him a lesson, his killing of the poor, pretty musician, and his flight to Sidi-bel-Abbès. . . .

To Sidi-bel-Abbès also fled Carmelita, and, with the proceeds of Guiseppe's dying gift to her, eked out by promises of many things to many people, such as Jew and Arab lessors and landlords, French dealers, Spanish-Jew jobbers and contractors, and Negro labourers, contrived to open La Café de la Légion, to run it with herself as proprietress, manageress, barmaid, musician, singer, actress, and *danseuse*, and to make it pay to the extent of a daily franc, bottle of Chianti, and a macaroni, polenta, or spaghetti meal for Luigi, and a very meagre living for herself. When in need of something more, Carmelita performed at matinées at the music-hall and at private séances in Arab and other houses, in the intervals of business. When professional dress would have rendered her automatic pistol conspicuous and uncomfortable, Carmelita carried a most serviceable little dagger in her hair. Also she let it be known among her patrons of the Legion that she was going to a certain house, garden, or café at a certain time, and might be there enquired for if unduly delayed. Carmelita knew the seamy side of life in Mediterranean ports, and African littoral and hinterland towns, and took no chances. . . .

And by-and-by her splendid and noble Luigi would marry her, and they would go to America— where that little matter of manslaughter would never crop up and cause trouble—and live happily ever after.

So, faithful, loyal, devoted, Carmelita might be; generous, chaste, and brave, Carmelita might be— but alas! not refined, not genteel, not above telling a Chasseur d'Afrique what she thought of him and his insults; not above spitting at a leering, gesture-making Spahi. No lady. . . .

"Ben venuti, Signori!" cried Carmelita on catching sight of Il Signor Jean Boule and the Bucking Bronco. *"Soyez le bien venu, Monsieur Jean Boule et Monsieur Bronco. Che cosa posso offrirvi?"* and, as they seated themselves at a small round table near the bar, hastened to bring the wine favoured by these favoured customers—the so gentle English Signor, *gentilhomme*, (doubtless once a *milord*, a *nobile*), and the so gentle, foolish Americano, so slow and strong, who looked at her with eyes of love, kind eyes, with a good true love. No *milordino* he, no *piccol Signor* (but nevertheless a good man, a *uomo dabbéne*, most certainly . . .)

Reginald Rupert was duly presented as Légionnaire Rupert, with all formality and ceremony, to the Madamigella Carmelita, who ran her bright, black eye over him, summed him up as another *gentiluomo*, an obvious *gentilhomme*, pitied him, and wondered what he had "done."

Carmelita loved a "gentleman" in the abstract, although she loved Luigi Rivoli in the concrete; adored aristocrats in general, in spite of the fact that she adored Luigi Rivoli in particular. To her experienced and observant young eye, Légionnaire Jean Boule and this young *bleu* were of the same class, the *aristocratico* class of *Inghilterra*; birds of a feather, if not of a nest. They might be father and son, so alike were they in their difference from the rest. So different even from the English-speaking *Americano*, so different from her Luigi. But then, her Luigi was no mere broken aristocrat; he was the World's Champion Wrestler and Strong Man, a great and famous Wild Beast Tamer, and— her Luigi.

"*Buona sera, Signor,*" said Carmelita to Rupert. "*Siete venuto per la via di Francie?*" and then, in Legion-French and Italian, proceeded to comment upon the new recruit's appearance, his *capelli riccioluti* and to enquire whether he used the *calamistro* and *ferro da ricci* to obtain the fine crisp wave in his hair.

Not at all a refined and ladylike maiden, and very, very far from the standards of Surbiton, not to mention Balham.

Reginald Rupert (to whom love and war were the two things worth living for), on understanding the drift of the lady's remarks, proposed forthwith "to cross the bar" and "put out to see" whether he could not give her a personal demonstration of the art of hair-curling, but—

"*Non vi pigliate fastidio,*" said Carmelita. "Don't trouble yourself Signor Azzurro—Monsieur Bleu. And if Signor Luigi Rivoli should enter and see the young Signor on my side of the bar—Luigi's side of the bar—why, one look of his eye would so make the young Signor's hair curl that, for the rest of his life, the *calamistro*, the curling-tongs, would be superfluous."

"Yep," chimed in the Bucking Bronco. "I guess as haow it's about time yure Loojey's bright eyes got closed, my dear, an' I'm goin' ter bung 'em both up one o' these fine days, when I got the cafard. Yure Loojey's a great lady-killer an' recruit-killer, we know, an' he can talk a tin ear on a donkey. I say *Il parlerait une oreille d'étain sur un âne.* Yure Loojey'd make a hen-rabbit git mad an' bark. I say *Votre Loojey causerait une lapine devenir fou et écorcer.* I got it in fer yure Loojey. I say *Je l'ai dans pour votre Loojey. . . .* Comprenny? *Intendete quel che dico?*" and the Bucking Bronco drank off a pint of wine, drew his tiny, well-thumbed French dictionary from one pocket and his "Travellers' Italian Phrase-book" from another, cursed the Tower of Babel, and all foreign tongues, and sought words wherewith to say that it was high time for Luigi Rivoli "to quit beefin' aroun' Madam lar Canteenair, to wipe off his chin considerable, to cease being a sticker, a sucker, and a skinamalink girl-sponging meal-and-money cadger; and to quit tellin' stories made out o' whole cloth,[30] that cut no ice with nobody except Carmelita."

This young lady gathered that, as usual, the poor, silly jealous Americano was belittling and insulting her Luigi, if not actually threatening him. *Him*, who could break any Americano across his knee. With a toss of her head and a contemptuous "Invidioso! Scioccone!" for the Bronco, a flick on the nose with the *krenfell* flower from her ear for Rupert, a blown kiss for *Babbo* Jean Boule,

---

[30] Untrue.

Carmelita flitted away, going from table to table to minister to the mental, moral, and physical needs of her other devoted Légionnaires as they arrived—men of strange and dreadful lives who loved her then and there, who remembered her thereafter and elsewhere, and who sent her letters, curios, pressed flowers and strange presents from the ends of the earth where flies the *tricouleur*, and the Flag of the Legion—in Tonkin, Madagascar, Senegal, Morocco, the Sahara—in every Southern Algerian station wherever the men of the Legion tramped to their death to the strains of the regimental march of "*Tiens, voilà du boudin.*"

"Advise me, Mam'zelle," said a young Frenchman of the Midi, rising to his feet with a flourish of his képi and a sweeping bow, as Carmelita approached the table at which he and three companions sat. "Advise me as to the investment of this wealth, fifty centimes, all at once. Shall it be five glorious green absinthes or five *chopes* of the wine of Algiers?—or shall I warm my soul with burning bapédi . . . ?"

"Four bottles of wine is what you want for André, Raoul, Léon, and yourself," was the reply. "Absinthe is the mamma and the papa and all the ancestors of *le cafard* and you are far too young and tender for bapédi. It mingles not well with mother's milk, that. . . ."

In the extreme corner of the big, badly-lit room, a Legionary sat alone, his back to the company, his head upon his folded arms. Passing near, on her tour of ministration, Carmelita's quick eye and ear perceived that the man was sobbing and weeping bitterly. It might be the poor Grasshopper passing through one of his terrible dark hours, and Carmelita's kind heart melted with pity for the poor soul, smartest of soldiers, and maddest of madmen.

Going over to where he sat apart, Carmelita bent over him, placed her arm around his neck, and stroked his glossy dark hair.

"*Pourquoi faites-vous Suisse, mon pauvre?*" she murmured with a motherly caress. "What is it? Tell Carmelita." The man raised his face from his arms, smiled through his tears and kissed the hand that rested on his shoulder. The handsome and delicate face, the small, well-kept hands, the voice, were those of a man of culture and refinement.

"*I ja nai ka!*—How delightful!" he said. "You will make things right. I am to be made *machi-bugiyo*, governor of the city to-morrow, and I wish to remain a Japanese lady. I do not want to lay aside the *sumagoto* and *samisen* for the *wakizashi* and the *katana*—the lute for the dagger and sword. I don't want to sit on a *tokonoma* in a *yashiki* surrounded by *karo*. . . ."

"No, no, no, mon cher, you shall not indeed. See le bon Dieu and le bon Jean Boule will look after you," said Carmelita, gently stroking his hot forehead and soothing him with little crooning sounds and caresses as though he had really been the child that, in mind and understanding, he was.

John Bull, followed by Rupert, unobtrusively joined Carmelita. Seating himself beside the unhappy man, he took his hands and gazed steadily into his suffused eyes.

"Tell me all about it, Cigale," said he. "You know we can put it right. When has Jean Boule failed to explain and arrange things for you?"

The madman repeated that he dreaded to have to sit on the raised dais of the Palace of a Governor of a City surrounded by officials and advisers.

"I know I should soon be involved in a *kataki-*

uchi with a neighbouring clan, and have to commit hara-kiri if I failed to keep the Mikado's peace. It is terrible. You don't know how I long to remain a lady. I want silk and music and cherry-blossom instead of steel and blood," and again he laid his head upon his arms and continued his low, hopeless sobbing.

Reginald Rupert's face expressed blank astonishment at the sight of the weeping soldier.

"What's up?" he said.

Légionnaire John Bull tapped his forehead.

"Poor chap will behave *more Japonico* for the rest of the day now. I fancy he's been an attaché in Japan. You don't know Japanese by any chance? I have forgotten the little I knew."

Rupert shook his head.

"Look here, Cigale," said John Bull, raising the afflicted man and again fixing the steady, benign gaze upon his eyes, "why are you making all this trouble for yourself? You know I am the Mikado and All-powerful! You have only to appeal to me and the Shogun must release you. Of course you can remain a Japanese lady—and I'll tell you what, ma chère, ma petite fille Japonaise, not only shall you remain a lady, but a lady of the old school and of the days before the accursed Foreign Devils came in to break down ancient customs. I promise it. To-morrow you shall shave off your eyebrows and paint them in two inches above your eyes. I promise it. More. Your teeth shall be lacquered black. Now cease these ungrateful repinings, and be a happy maiden once again. By order of the Mikado!"

Once again the voice and eye, and the gentle wise sympathy and comprehension of ce bon Jean Boule had succeeded and triumphed. The madman, falling at his feet, knelt and bowed three times, his forehead touching the ground, in approved geisha fashion.

"And now you've got to come and lie down, or you won't be fit for the eyebrow-shaving ceremony to-morrow," said Carmelita, and led him to a broad, low divan, which made a cosy, if dirty, corner remote from the bar.

"That's as extraordinary a case as ever I came across," remarked John Bull to Rupert as they rejoined the Bucking Bronco, who was talking to the Cockney and the Russian twins, "as mad as any lunatic in any asylum in the world, and yet as absolutely competent and correct in every detail of soldiering as any soldier in the Legion. He is the Perfect Private Soldier—and a perfect lunatic. Most of the time, off parade that is, he thinks he's a grasshopper, and the rest of the time he thinks he's of some remarkably foreign nationality, such as a Zulu, an Eskimo, or a Chinaman. I should very much like to know his story. He must have travelled pretty widely. He has certainly been an officer in the Belgian Guides (their Officers' Mess is one of the most exclusive and aristocratic in the world, as you know) and he has certainly been a Military Attaché in the East. He is perfectly harmless and a most thorough gentleman, poor soul. . . . Yes, I should greatly like to know his story," and added as he poured out a glass of wine, "but we don't ask men their 'stories' in the Legion. . . ."

Carmelita returned to her high seat by the door of her little room behind the bar—the door upon the outside of which many curious regards had oftentimes been fixed.

Carmelita was troubled. Why did not Luigi come? Were his duties so numerous and onerous nowadays that he had but a bare hour for his late dinner and his bottle of Chianti? Time was, when he arrived as soon after five o'clock as a wash and change of uniform permitted. Time was, when he could spend from early evening to late night in the Café de la Légion, outstaying the latest visitors. And that time was also the time when Madame la Cantinière was not a widow—the days before Madame's husband had been sliced, sawn, snapped, torn, and generally mangled by certain other widows—of certain Arabs—away to the South. This might be coincidence of course, and yet—and yet—several Légionnaires who had no axe to grind and who were not jealous of Luigi's fortune, had undoubtedly coupled his name with that of Madame. . . .

"An' haow did yew find yure little way to our dope-joint hyar?" the Bucking Bronco enquired of Mikhail Kyrilovitch, as he did the honours of Carmelita's "joint" to the three *bleus* who had entered while John Bull was talking to the Grasshopper.

"Well, since you arx, we jest ups an' follers you, old bloke, when yer goes aht wiv these two uvver Henglish coves," replied the Cockney.

The American regarded him with the eye of large and patient tolerance. He preferred the Russians, particularly Mikhail, and rejoiced that they spoke English. It would have been too much to have attempted to add a working knowledge of Russian to his other linguistic stores. Nevertheless, he would, out of compliment to their nationality, produce such words of their strange tongue as he could command. It might serve to make them feel more at home like.

"I'm afraid I can't ask yew moojiks ter hev a little caviare an' wodky, becos' Carmelita is out of it. . . . But there's cawfy in the sammy-var I hev no doubt," he said graciously.

The Russians thanked him, and Feodor pledging him in a glass of absinthe, promised to teach him the art of concocting *lompopo*, while Mikhail quietly sipped his glass of sticky, sweet Algerian wine.

Restless Carmelita joined the group, and her friend Jean Boule introduced the three new patrons.

"Prahd an' honoured, Miss, I'm shore," said the Cockney. " 'Ave a port-an'-lemon or thereabahts?"

But Carmelita was too interested in the startling similarity of the twins to pay attention to the civilities and blandishments of the Cockney, albeit he surreptitiously wetted his fingers with wine and smoothed his smooth and shining "cowlick" or "quiff" (the highly ornamental fringe which, having descended to his eyebrows, turned aspiringly upward).

"*Gemello*," she murmured, turning from Feodor and his cheery greeting to Mikhail, who responded with a graceful little bow, suddenly terminated and changed to a curt nod, like that given by Feodor. As Carmelita continued her direct gaze, a dull flush grew and mantled over his face.

"*Cielo!* But how the boy blushes! Now is it for his own sins, or mine, I wonder?" laughed Carmelita, pointing accusingly at poor Mikhail's suffused face.

"Gawdstreuth! Can't 'e blush," remarked Mr. Higgins.

The dull flush became a vivid, burning blush under Carmelita's pointing finger, and the regard of the amused Legionaries.

"Corpo di Bacco!" laughed the teasing girl. "A blushing Legionary! The dear, sweet, good boy. If only *I* could blush like that. And he brings his blushes to Madame la République's Legion. Well, it is not *porta vasi a Samo!*"[31]

"Never mind, Sonny," said the American

---

[31] Lit., "to carry coals to Newcastle."

soothingly, "there's many a worse stunt than blushin'. I uster use blushes considerable meself—when I was a looker 'bout yure age." He translated.

Carmelita's laughter pealed out again at the idea of the blushing American. Feodor's laughter mingled with Carmelita's, but sounded forced.

"Isn't it funny?" he remarked. "My brother has always been like that, but believe me, Padrona, I could not blush to save my life."

"Si, si," laughed Carmelita. "You have sinned and he has blushed—all your lives, is it not so—le pauvre petit?" and saucily rubbed the side of Mikhail's crimson face with the backs of her fingers—and looked unwontedly thoughtful as he jerked his head away with a look of annoyance.

"La, la, la!" said Carmelita. "Musn't he be teased then? . . ."

"Come, Signora," broke in Feodor again, "you're making him blush worse than ever. Such kindness is absolutely wasted. Now I . . ."

"No, *you* wouldn't blush with shame and fright, no, nor yet with innocence, would you, Signor Feodor? *E un peccato!*" replied the girl, and lightly brushed his cheek as she spoke.

The good Feodor did not blush, but the look of thoughtfulness deepened on Carmelita's face.

To the finer perceptions of John Bull there seemed to be something strained and discomfortable in the atmosphere. Carmelita had fallen silent, Feodor seemed annoyed and anxious, Mikhail frightened and anxious, and Mr. 'Erb 'Iggins of too gibing a humour.

"You are making me positively jealous, Signora Carmelita, and leaving me thirsty," he said, and with a small repentant squeal Carmelita flitted to the bar.

"Would you like a biscuit too, Signor Jean

Boule?" she called, and tossed one across to him as she spoke. John Bull neatly caught the biscuit as it flew somewhat wide. Carmelita, like most women, could not throw straight.

"*Tiro maestro*," she applauded, and launched another at the unprepared Mikhail with a cry of "Catch, *goffo*." Instinctively he "made a lap" and spread out his hands.

"*Esattamente!*" commented Carmelita beneath her breath and apparently lost interest in the little group. . . .

A quartet of Legionaries swaggered into the café and approached the bar—Messieurs Malvin, Borges, Bauer and Hirsch, henchmen and satellites of Luigi Rivoli—and saluted to Carmelita's greeting of "Buona sera, Signori. . . ."

"Bonsoir, M. Malvin," added she to the dapper, low-bowing Austrian, whose evil face, with its close-set ugly eyes, sharp crooked nose, waxed moustache, and heavy jowl, were familiar to her as those of one of Luigi's more intimate followers. "Where is Signor Luigi Rivoli to-night? He has no guard duty?"

"No, mia signora—er—that is—yes," replied Malvin in affected discomfort. "He is—ah—on duty."

"On duty in the Canteen?" asked Carmelita, flushing.

"What do I know of the comings and goings of the great Luigi Rivoli?" answered Malvin. "Doubtless he will fortify himself with a litre of wine at Madame's bar in the Canteen before walking down here."

"Luigi Rivoli drinks no sticky Algerian wine," said Carmelita angrily and her eyes and teeth flashed dangerously. "He drinks Chianti from Home. He never enters her Canteen."

"Ah! So?" murmured Malvin in a non-committal

manner. And then Carmelita's anxiety grew a little greater—greater even than her dislike and distrust of M. Edouard Malvin, and she did what she had never done before. She voiced it to him.

"Look you, Monsieur Malvin, tell me the truth. I will not tell my Luigi that you have accused him to me, or say that you have spoken ill of him behind his back. Tell me the truth. *Is* he in the Canteen? Tell me, cher Monsieur Malvin."

"Have I the double sight, bella Carmelita? How should I know where le Légionnaire Rivoli may be?" fenced the soi-disant Belgian, who desired nothing better than to win the woman from the man—and toward himself. Failing Madame la Cantinière and the Legion's Canteen, what better than Carmelita and the Café de la Légion for a poor hungry and thirsty soldier? If the great Luigi must win the greater prize let the little Malvin win the lesser. To which end let him curry favour with La Belle Carmelita—just as far as such a course of action did not become premature, and lead to a painful interview with an incensed Luigi Rivoli.

"Tell me the truth, cher Monsieur Malvin. Where is my Luigi?" again asked Carmelita pleadingly.

"*Donna e Madonna,*" replied the good M. Malvin, with piteous eyes, broken voice, and protecting hand placed gently over that of Carmelita which lay clenched upon the zinc-covered bar. "What shall I say? Luigi Rivoli is a giant among men—I, a little fat *deboletto,* a *sparutello* whom the great Luigi could kill with one hand. Though I love Carmelita, I fear Luigi. How shall I tell of his doings with that husband-seeking *puttana* of the Canteen; of his serving behind the bar, helping her, taking her money, drinking her wine (wine of Algiers); of his passionate and burning prayers that she will marry him? How can I, his friend, tell of those things? But oh! Carmelita, my poor honest heart is wrung . . ." and le bon Monsieur Malvin paused to hope that his neck also would not be wrung as the result of this moving eloquence.

For a moment Carmelita's eyes blazed and her hands and her little white teeth clenched. Mother of God! If Luigi played her false after all she had done for him, after all she had given him—given *for* him! . . . But no, it was unthinkable. . . . This Malvin was an utter knave and liar, and would fool her for his own ends—the very man *fare un pesce d'Aprile a qualcuno*. He should see how far his tricks succeeded with Carmelita of the Legion, the chosen of Carlo Scopinaro! And yet . . . and yet . . . She would ask Il Signor Jean Boule again. He would never lie. He would neither backbite Luigi Rivoli, nor stand by and see Carmelita deceived. Yes, she would ask Jean Boule, and then if he *too* accused Luigi she would find some means to see and hear for herself. . . . Trust her woman's wit for that. And meantime this serpent of a Malvin . . .

"*Se ne vada!*" she hissed, whirling upon him suddenly, and pointed to the door. Malvin slunk away, by no means anxious to be present at the scene which would certainly follow should Luigi enter before Carmelita's mood had changed. He would endeavour to meet and delay him. . . .

"What do yew say to acontinuin' o' this hyar gin-crawl?" asked the Bucking Bronco of Rupert. "Come and see our other pisen-joint and Madame lar Canten air."

"Anything you like," replied Rupert.

"Let's go out when they do," said Mikhail quickly, in Russian, to Feodor.

"All right, silly Olka," was the whispered reply.

"Silly Fedka, to call me Olka," was the

whispered retort. "You're a pretty *budotchnik*,[32] aren't you?"

"Yus," agreed Mr. 'Erb Higgins, nodding cordially to Rupert, and bursting into appropriate and tuneful song—

"Come where the booze is cheaper,
Come where the pots 'old more,
Come where the boss is a bit of a joss,
Ho! come to the pub next door."

Evidently a sociable and expansive person, easily thawed by a *chope* of cheap wine withal; neither stand-offish nor haughty, for he thrust one friendly arm through that of Jean Boule, and another round the waist of Reginald Rupert. Let it not be supposed that it was under the influence of liquor rather than of sheer, expansive geniality that 'Erb proposed to walk *a braccetto*, as Carmelita observed, with his new-found friends. . . .

As the party filed out of the café, Mikhail Kyrilovitch, who was walking last of the party, felt a hand slip within his arm to detain him. Turning, he beheld Carmelita's earnest little face near his own. In his ear she whispered in French—

"I have your secret, little one—but have no fear. Should anyone else discover it, come to Carmelita," and before the astonished Mikhail could reply she was clearing empty glasses and bottles from their table.

---

[32] Guardian, watchman.

CHAPTER IV

THE CANTEEN OF THE LEGION

From the Canteen, a building in the corner of the barrack-square, proceeded sounds of revelry by night.

"Blimey! Them furriners are singin' 'Gawd save the Queen' like bloomin' Christians," remarked 'Erb as the little party approached the modest Temple of Bacchus.

"No, they are Germans singing '*Heil dir im Sieges-Kranz*,' " replied Feodor Kyrilovitch in English.

"And singing it most uncommonly well," added Legionary John Bull.

"Fancy them 'eathens pinchin' the toon like that," commented 'Erb. "They oughtn't to be allowed. . . . Do they 'old concerts 'ere? I dessay they'd like to 'ear some good Henglish songs. . . ."

Reginald Rupert never forgot his first glimpse of the Canteen of the Legion, though he entered it hundreds of times and spent hundreds of hours beneath its corrugated iron roof. Scores of Legionaries, variously clad in blue and red or white sat on benches at long tables, or lounged at the long zinc-covered bar, behind which were Madame and hundreds of bottles and large wine-glasses.

Madame la Vivandière de la Légion was not of the school of "Cigarette." Rupert failed to visualise her with any clearness as leading a cavalry charge (the *Drapeau* of La France in one hand, a pistol in the other, and her reins in her mouth), inspiring Regiments, advising Generals, softening the cruel hearts of Arabs, or "saving the day" for La Patrie, in the manner of the vivandière of fiction. Madame had a beady eye, a perceptible moustache, a frankly downy chin, two other chins, a more than ample figure, and looked, what she was, a female camp-sutler. Perhaps Madame appeared more Ouidaesque on the march, wearing her official blue uniform as duly constituted and appointed *fille du régiment*. At present she looked . . . However, the bow of Reginald Rupert, together with his smile and honeyed words, were those of Mayfair, as he was introduced by Madame's admired friend ce bon Jean Boule, and he stepped straight into Madame's experienced but capacious heart. Nor was the brightness of the image dulled by the ten-franc piece which he tendered with the request that Madame would supply the party with her most blushful Hippocrene. 'Erb, being introduced, struck an attitude, his hand upon his heart. Madame coughed affectedly.

"Makes a noise like a 'igh-class parlour-maid bein' jilted, don' she?" he observed critically.

Having handed a couple of bottles and a large glass to each member of the party, by way of commencement in liquidating the coin, she returned to her confidential whispering with Monsieur le Légionnaire Luigi Rivoli (who lolled, somewhat drunk, in a corner of the bar) as the group seated itself at the end of a long table near the window.

It being "holiday," that is, pay-day, the Canteen was full, and most of its patrons had contrived to emulate it. A very large number had laid out the whole of their *décompte*—every farthing of two-pence halfpenny—on wine. Others, wiser and more continent, had reserved a halfpenny for tobacco. In one corner of the room an impromptu German glee party was singing with such excellence that the majority of the drinkers were listening to them with obvious appreciation. With hardly a break, and with the greatest impartiality they proceeded from part-song to hymn, from hymn to drinking-song, from drinking-song to sentimental love-ditty. Finally *Ein feste burg ist unser Gott* being succeeded by *Die Wacht am Rhein* and *Deutschland über Alles*, the French element in the room thought that a little French music would be a pleasing corrective, and with one accord, if not in one key, gave a spirited rendering of the Marseillaise, followed by—

> "Tiens, voilà du boudin
> Tiens, voilà du boudin
> Tiens, voilà du boudin
> Pour les Alsaciens, les Suisses, et les Lorraines,
> Four les Belges il n'y en a plus
> Car ce sont des tireurs du flanc . . ." etc.,

immediately succeeded by—

> "As-tu vu la casquette
> La casquette
> Du Père Bougeaud," etc.

As the ditty came to a close a blue-jowled little Parisian—quick, nervous, and alert—sprang on to a table, and with a bottle in one hand, and a glass in the other, burst into the familiar and favour-ite—

> "C'est l'empereur de Danemark
> Qui a dit a sa moitié
> Depuis quelqu' temps je remarque
> Que tu sens b'en fort les pieds . . ." etc.

> "C'est la reine Pomaré
> Qui a pour tout tenue

Au milieu de l'été . . ."

the song being brought to an untimely end by reason of the parties on either side of the singer's table entering into a friendly tug-of-war with his feet as rope-ends. As he fell, amid howls of glee and the crashing of glass, the Bucking Bronco remarked to Rupert—

"Gwine ter be some rough-housin' ter-night ef we're lucky," but ere the mêlée could become general, Madame la Cantinière, descending from her throne behind the bar, bore down upon the rioters and rated them soundly—imbeciles, fools, children, *vauriens*, and *sales cochons* that they were. Madame was well aware of the fact that a conflagration should be dealt with in its earliest stages and before it became general.

"This is really extraordinarily good wine," remarked Rupert to John Bull.

"Yes," replied the latter. "It's every bit as good at three-halfpence a bottle as it is at three-and-six in England, and I'd advise you to stick to it and let absinthe alone. It does one no harm, in reason, and is a great comfort. It's our greatest blessing and our greatest curse. Absinthe is pure curse—and inevitably means 'cafard.' "

"What is this same 'cafard' of which one hears so much?" asked Rupert.

"Well, the word itself means 'beetle,' I believe, and sooner or later the man who drinks absinthe in this climate feels the beetle crawling round and round in his brain. He then does the maddest things and ascribes the impulse to the beetle. He finally goes mad and generally commits murder or suicide, or both. That is one form of *cafard*, and the other is mere fed-upness, a combination of liverish temper, boredom and utter hatred and loathing of the terrible ennui of the life."

"Have you had it?" asked the other.

"Everyone has it at times," was the reply, "especially in the tiny desert-stations where the awful heat, monotony, and lack of employment leave one the choice of drink or madness. If you drink you're certain to go mad, and if you don't drink you're sure to. Of course, men like ourselves—educated, intelligent, and all that—have more chance than the average 'Tommy' type, but it's very dangerous for the highly strung excitable sort. He's apt to go mad and stay mad. We only get fits of it."

"Don't the authorities do anything to amuse and employ the men in desert stations, like we do in India?" enquired the younger man.

"Absolutely nothing. They prohibit the *Village Négre* in every station, compel men to lie on their cots from eleven till four, and do nothing at all to relieve the maddening monotony of drill, sentry-go and punishment. On the other hand, *cafard* is so recognised an institution that punishments for offences committed under its influence are comparatively light. It takes different people differently, and is sometimes comic—though generally tragic."

"I should think you're bound to get something of the sort wherever men lead a very hard and very monotonous life, in great heat," said Rupert.

"Oh yes," agreed John Bull. "After all *le cafard* is not the private and peculiar speciality of the Legion. We get a very great deal of madness of course, but I think it's nearly as much due to predisposition as it is to the hard monotonous life. . . . You see we are a unique collection, and a considerable minority of us must be more or less queer in some way, or they wouldn't be here."

Rupert wondered why the speaker was "here" but refrained from asking.

"Can you classify the recruits at all clearly?" he asked.

"Oh yes," was the reply. "The bulk of them are here simply and solely for a living; hungry men who came here for board and lodging. Thousands of foreigners in France have found themselves down on their uppers, with their last sou gone, fairly on their beam-ends and their room-rent overdue. To such men the Foreign Legion offers a home. Then, again, thousands of soldiers commit some heinous military 'crime' and desert to the Foreign Legion to start afresh. We get most of our Germans and Austrians that way, and not a few French who pretend to be Belgians to avoid awkward questions as to their papers. We get Alsatians by the hundred of course, too. It is their only chance of avoiding service under the hated German. They fight for France, and by their five years' Legion-service earn the right to naturalisation also. There are a good many French, too, who are 'rehabilitating' themselves. Men who have come to grief at home and prefer the Legion to prison. Then there is undoubtedly a wanted-by-the-police class of men who have bolted from all parts of Europe and taken sanctuary here. Yes, I should say the out-of-works, deserters, runaways and Alsatians make up three parts of the Legion."

"And what is the other part?"

"Oh, keen soldiers who have deliberately chosen the Legion for its splendid military training and constant fighting experience—romantics who have read vain imaginings and figments of the female mind like 'Under Two Flags'; and the queerest of Queer Fish, oddments and remnants from the ends of the earth. . . ." A shout of "Ohé, Grasshopper!" caused him to turn.

In the doorway, crouching on his heels, was the man they had left lying on the settee at

Carmelita's. Emitting strange chirruping squeaks, turning his head slowly from left to right, and occasionally brushing it from back to front with the sides of his "forelegs," the Grasshopper approached with long, hopping bounds.

"And that was once an ornament of Chancelleries and Courts," said John Bull, as he rose to his feet. "Poor devil! Got his *cafard* once and for all at Aïn Sefra. There was a big grasshopper or locust in his *gamelle* of soup one day. . . . I suppose he was on the verge at the moment. Anyhow, he burst into tears and has been a grasshopper ever since, except when he's a Jap or something of that sort. . . . He's a grasshopper when he's 'normal' you might say."

Going over to where the man squatted, the old Legionary took him by the arm. "Come and sit on my blade of grass and drink some dew, Cigale," said he.

Smiling up brightly at the face which he always recognised as that of a sympathetic friend, the Grasshopper arose and accompanied John Bull to the end of the long table at which sat the Englishmen, the Russians, and the American. . . .

Yet more wine had made 'Erb yet more expansive, and he kindly filled his glass and placed it before the Grasshopper.

" 'Ere drink that hup, Looney, an' I'll sing yer a song as'll warm the cockles o' yer pore ol' 'eart," he remarked, and suiting the action to the word, rose to his feet and, lifting up his voice, delivered himself mightily of that song not unknown to British barrack-rooms—

"A German orficer crossin' the Rhine
   'E come to a pub, an' this was the sign
  Skibooo, skibooo,
   Skibooo, skiana, skibooo."

The raucous voice and unwonted British accents (for Englishmen are rare in the Legion) attracted some attention, and by the time 'Erb had finished with the German officer and commenced upon " 'Oo's that aknock-in' on the dawer," he was well across the footlights and had the ear and eye of the assembly. Finding himself the cynosure of not only neighbouring but distant eyes, 'Erb mounted the table and "obliged" with a clog-dance and "double-shuffle-breakdown" to the huge delight of an audience ever desiring a new thing. Stimulated by rounds of applause, and by the cheers and laughter which followed the little Parisian's cry of "Vive le goddam biftek Anglais," 'Erb burst into further Barrack-room Ballads unchronicled by, and probably quite unknown to, Mr. Kipling, and did not admit the superior claims of private thirst until he had dealt faithfully with "The Old Monk," "The Doctor's Boy," and the indiscreet adventure of Abraham the Sailor with the Beautiful Miss Taylor. . . .

"Some boy, that *compatriot* o' yourn, John," remarked the Bucking Bronco, "got a reg'lar drorin' room repertory, ain't 'e?" and the soul of 'Erb was proud within him, and he drank another pint of wine.

"Nutthink like a little—*hic*—'armony," he admitted modestly, "fer making a *swarry* sociable an' 'appy. Wot I ses is—*hic*—wot I ses is—*hic*—wot I *ses* is—*hic*. . . ."

"It is *so*, sonny, and that's almighty solemn truth," agreed the Bucking Bronco.

"Wot I ses is—*hic*—" doggedly repeated 'Erb.

"Right again, sonny. . . . He knows what 'e's sayin' all right," observed the American, turning to the Russians.

"Wot I ses is—*hic*—" repeated 'Erb dogmatically.

. . .

" *'Hic jacet!'* Monsieur would say, perhaps?" suggested Feodor.

'Erb turned upon the last speaker with an entirely kindly contempt.

"Don't yer igspose yer *hic*-norance," he advised. "You're a foreiller. You're a neathen. You're a pore *hic*-norant foreiller. Wot I was goin' ter say was . . ." But 'Erb lost the thread of his discourse. "Wisht me donah wos 'ere," he confided sadly to Mikhail Kyrilovitch, wept with his arm about Mikhail's waist, his head upon Mikhail's shoulder, and anon lapsed into dreams. Feodor roused the somnolent 'Erb with the offer of another bottle of wine, and changed places with Mikhail. 'Erb accepted this tribute to the attractiveness of his personality with modesty, and with murmured words, the purport of which appeared to be that Feodor was a discriminating heathen.

As the evening wore on, the heady wine took effect. The fun, which had been fast and furious, grew uproarious. Dozens of different men were singing as many different songs, several were merely howling in sheer joyless glee, many were dancing singly, others in pairs, or in fours; one, endeavouring to clamber on to the bar and execute a *pas seul*, was bodily lifted and thrown half-way down the room by the fighting-drunk Luigi Rivoli. It was noticeable that, as excitement waxed, the use of French waned, as men reverted to their native tongues. It crossed the mind of Rupert that a blindfolded stranger, entering the room, might well imagine himself to be assisting at the building of the Tower of Babel. A neighbouring party of Spaniards dropping their guttural, sibilant Legion-French (with their *ze* for *je*, *zamais* for *jamais*, and *zour* for *jour*) with one accord broke into their liquid Spanish and *Nombre de Dios* took the place of *Nom de Dieu*, as their saturnine faces creased into leathery smiles. Evidently the new recruit who sat in their midst was paying his footing with the few francs that he had brought with him, or obtained for his clothes, for each of the party had four bottles in solemn row before him, and it was not with the clearest of utterance that the recruit solemnly and portentously re-marked, as he drained his last bottle—

"Santissima Maria! Wine is the tomb of memory, but he who sows in sand does not reap fish," the hearing of which moved his neighbour to drop his empty bottles upon the ground with a tear, and a farewell to them—

"Vaya usted con Dios. Adios." He then turned with truculent ferocity and a terrific scowl upon the provider of the feast and growled—"*Sangre de Cristo!* thou peseta-less burro, give me a cigarillo or with the blessing and aid of el Eterno Padre I will cut thy throat with my thumb-nail. Hasten, perro!"

With a grunt of "Cosas d'Espafia," the recruit removed his képi, took a cigarette therefrom and placed it in the steel-trap mouth of his *amigo*, to be rewarded with an incredibly sweet and sunny smile and a "Bueno! Gracias, Senor José. . . ."

Letting his eye roam from this queer band of ex-muleteers, brigands and smugglers to another party who were wading in the wassail, it needed not the loud "Donnerwetters!" and rambling reminiscent monologue of a fat brush-haired youth (on the unspeakable villainies of der Herr Wachtmeister whose wicked *schadenfreude* had sent good men to this *schweinerei* of a Legion, and who was only fit for the military-train or to be decapitated with his own *pallasch*) to label them Germans enjoying a *kommers*. Their stolid, heavy bearing, their business-like and somewhat brutish way of drinking in great gulps and draughts—as though a distended stomach rather than a tickled palate was the serious business of the evening, if not the end and object of life—together with their upturned moustaches, piggish little eyes, and tow-coloured bristles, proclaimed them sons of Kultur.

Rupert could not forbear a smile at the heavy, philosophical gravity with which the speaker, ceasing his monologue, heaved a deep, deep sigh and delivered the weighty dictum that a *schoppen* of the beer of Munich was worth all the wine of Algiers, and the Hofbrauhaus worth all the vineyards and canteens of Africa.

It interested him to notice that among all the nationalities represented, the French were by far the gayest (albeit with a humour somewhat *macabre*) and the Germans the most morose and gloomy. He was to learn later that they provided by far the greatest number of deserters, that they were eternally grumbling, notably bitter and resentful, and devoid of the faintest spark of humour.

His attention was diverted from the Germans by a sudden and horrible caterwauling which arose from a band of Frenchmen who suddenly commenced at the tops of their voices to howl that doleful dirge the "Hymne des Pacifiques." Until they had finished, conversation was impossible.

"Not all foam neither, Miss, please," murmured the sleeping 'Erb in the comparative silence which followed the ending of this devastating chant.

"What's the penalty here for drunkenness?" asked Rupert of John Bull.

"Depends on what you do," was the reply. "There's no penalty for drunkenness, as such, so long as it leads to no sins of omission nor commission. . . . The danger of getting drunk is that it gives such an opportunity to any Non-com. who has a down on you. When he sees his man drunk, he'll follow him and give him some order, or find him some *corvée*, in the hope that the man will disobey or abuse him—possibly strike him. Then it's Biribi for the man, and a good mark, as well as private vengeance, for the zealous Sergeant, who is again noted as a strong disciplinarian. . . . I'm afraid it's undeniably true that nothing helps promotion in the non-commissioned ranks so much as a reputation for savage ferocity and a brutal insatiable love of punishing. A knowledge of German helps too, as more than half the Legion speaks German, but harsh domineering cruelty is the first requisite, and a Non-commissioned Officer's merit is in direct proportion to the number of punishments he inflicts. Our Sergeant-Major, for example, is known as the 'Suicide-maker,' and is said to be very proud of the title. The number of men he has sent to their graves direct, or *via* the Penal Battalions, must be enormous, and, so far as I can see, he has attained his high and exceedingly influential position simply and solely by excelling in the art of inventing crimes and punishing them severely—for he is a dull uneducated peasant without brains or ability. It is this type of Non-com., the monotony, and the poverty, that make the Legion such a hell for anyone who is not dead keen on soldiering for its own sake. . . ."

"I'm very glad you're keen," he added.

"Oh, rather. I'm as keen as mustard," replied Rupert, "and I was utterly fed up with peace-soldiering and poodle-faking. I have done Sand-hurst and had a turn as a trooper in a crack cavalry corps. I wanted to have a look-in at the Northwest Frontier Police in Canada after this, and then the Cape Mounted Rifles. I shan't mind the hardships and monotony here if I can get some active service, and feel I am learning something. I have a few thousand francs, too, at the *Crédit Lyonnais*, so I shan't have to bear the poverty cross."

"A few thousand francs, my dear chap!" observed John Bull, smiling. "Crœsus! A few thousand francs will give you a few hundred fair-weather friends, relief from a few hundred disagreeable corvées, and duties; give you wine, tobacco, food, medicine, books, distractions— almost anything but escape from the Legion's military duties as distinguished from the menial. There is nowhere in the world where money makes so much difference as in the Legion—simply because nowhere is it so rare. If among the blind the one-eyed is king, among Legionaries he who has a franc is a bloated plutocrat. Where else in the world is tenpence the equivalent of the daily wages of twenty men—twenty soldier-labourers? Yes, a few thousand francs will greatly alleviate your lot in the Legion, or expedite your departure when you've had enough—for it's quite hopeless to desert without mufti and money."

"I'll leave some in the bank then, against the time I feel I've had enough. . . . By the way, if you or your friend—er—Mr. Bronco at any time. . . . If I could be of service . . . financially . . ." and he coloured uncomfortably.

To offer money to this grave, handsome gentleman of refined speech and manners was like tipping an Ambassador, or offering the "price of a pot" to your Colonel, or your Grandfather.

"What do you mean by *corvée* and the Legion's menial duties, and soldier-labourers?" he continued hurriedly to change the subject.

"Yesterday," replied Sir Montague Merline coolly, "I was told off as one of a fatigue-party to clean the congested open sewers of the native gaol of Sidi-bel-Abbès. While I and my brothers-in-arms (some of whom had fought for France, like myself, in Tonkin, Senegal, Madagascar, and the Sahara) did the foulest work conceivable, manacled Negro and Arab criminals jeered at us, and bade us strive to give them satisfaction. Having been in India, you'll appreciate the situation. Natives watching white 'sweepers' labouring on their behalf."

"One can hardly believe it," ejaculated Rupert, and his face froze with horror and indignation.

"Yes," continued the other. "I reflected on the dignity of labour, and remembered the beautiful words of John Bright, or John Bunyan, or some other Johnnie about, 'Who sweeps a room as unto God, makes himself and the action fine.' I certainly made myself very dirty. . . . The Legionaries are the labourers, scavengers, gardeners, builders, road-makers, street-cleaners, and general coolies of any place in which they are stationed. They are drafted to the barracks of the Spahis and Turcos—the Native Cavalry and Infantry—to do jobs that the Spahis and Turcos would rather die than touch; and, of course, they're employed for every kind of work to which Government would never dream of setting French regulars. I have myself worked (for a ha'penny a day) at wheeling clay, breaking stones, sawing logs, digging, carrying bricks, hauling trucks, shovelling sand, felling trees, weeding gardens, sweeping streets, grave-digging, and every kind of unskilled manual corvée you can think of—in addition, of course, to the daily routine-work and military training of a soldier of the Legion—which is three times as arduous as that of any other soldier in the world."

"Sa—a—ay, John," drawled the Bucking Bronco, rousing himself at last from the deep brooding reverie into which he had plunged in search of mental images and memories of Carmelita, "give yure noo soul-affinity the other side o' the medal likewise, or yew'll push him off the water-waggon into the absinthe-barrel."

"Well," continued John Bull, "you can honestly say you belong to the most famous, most reckless, most courageous regiment in the world; to the regiment that has fought more battles, won more battles, lost more men and gained more honours, than any in the whole history of war. You belong to the Legion that never retreats, that dies—and of whose deaths no record is kept. . . . It is the last of the real Mercenaries, the Soldiers of Fortune, and if France sent it to-morrow to such a task that five thousand men were wastefully and vainly killed, not a question would be asked in the Chamber, nor the Press: nothing would be said, nothing known outside the War Department. We exist to die for France in the desert, the swamp, or the jungle, by bullet or disease—in Algeria, Morocco, Sahara, the Soudan, West Africa, Madagascar, and Cochin China—in doing what her regular French and Native troops neither could nor would do. We are here to die, and it's the duty of our officers to kill us—more or less usefully. To kill us for France, working or fighting. . . ."

" 'Ear, 'ear, John!" applauded the Bucking Bronco. "Some orator, ain't he?" he observed with pride, turning to Mikhail who had been following the old Legionary with parted lips and shining eyes. "Guess ol' John's some stump-speecher as well as a looker. . . . Go it, ol' section-boss, git on a char," and he smote his beloved John resoundingly upon the back.

John Bull, despite his years and grey hairs, blushed painfully.

"Sorry," he grunted.

"But indeed, Monsieur speaks most interestingly and with eloquence. Pray continue," said Mikhail with diffident earnestness.

John Bull looked still more uncomfortable.

"Do go on," said Rupert.

"Oh, that's all," replied John Bull. . . . "But we are the cheapest labourers, the finest soldiers, the most dangerous, reckless devils ever gathered together. . . . The incredible army—and there's anything from eight to twelve thousand of us in Africa and China, and nobody but the War Minister knows the real number. You're a ha'penny hero now, my boy, and a ha'penny day-labourer, and you're not expected to wear out in less than five years—unless you're killed by the enemy, disease, or the Non-coms."

"Have you ever regretted coming here?" asked Rupert, and could have bitten his tongue as he realised he had asked a personal and prying question.

"Well, I have re-enlisted twice," parried the other, "and that is a pretty good testimonial to La Légion. I have had unlimited experience of active service of all kinds, against enemies of all sorts except Europeans, and I hope to have that— against Germany[33]—before I've done."

"But what about all the Germans in the Legion, in that case?" enquired Rupert.

"Oh, they wouldn't be sent," was the reply. "They'd all go to the Southern Stations, and the Moroccan border, or to Madagascar and Tonkin. Of course, the Alsatians and Lorraines would jump for joy at the chance."

Conversation at this point again became more and more difficult in the increasing din, which was not diminished as 'Erb awoke, yawned, stated that

---

[33] Written in 1913.—AUTHOR.

he had a mouth like the bottom of a parrot's cage, that he was thoroughly blighted, and indeed blasted, produced a large mouth-organ, and rendered "Knocked 'em in the Old Kent Road," with enthusiastic soul and vigorous lungs.

Roused to a pinnacle of joyous enthusiasm and yearning for emulation, not only the little Parisian, but the whole party of Frenchmen leapt upon their table with wild whoops, and commenced to dance, some the *carmagnole*, some the *can-can*, some the cake-walk, and others the *bamboula*, the *chachuqua*, or the "*singe-sur-poele*." Glasses and bottles crashed to the ground, and Legionaries with them. A form broke.

Above the stamping, howling, smashing, and crashing, Madame's shrill screams rang clear, as she mingled imprecations and commands with lamentations that Luigi Rivoli had departed. Pandemonium increased to "*tohuwa-bohu*." Louder wailed the mouth-organ, louder bawled the Frenchmen, louder screamed Madame, loudest of all shrilled the "Lights Out" bugle in the barrack-square—and peace reigned. In a minute the room was empty, silent and dark, as the clock struck nine.

§2

"You'll be awakened by yells of '*Au jus*' from the garde-chambre at about five to-morrow," said John Bull to Rupert as they undressed. "As soon as you have swallowed the coffee he'll pour into your mug from his jug, hop out and sweep under your bed. The room-orderly has got to sweep out the room and be on parade as soon as the rest, and it's impossible unless everybody sweeps under his own bed and leaves the orderly to do the rest."

"What about food?" asked the other, who had

the healthy appetite of his years and health.

"Oh—plain and sufficient," was the answer. "Good soup and bread; hard biscuit twice a week; and wine every other day—monotonous of course. Meals at eleven o'clock and five o'clock only. . . . By the way unless your feet are fairly tough, you'd better wear *chaussettes russes* until they harden—strips of greasy linen bound round, you know. The skin will soon toughen if you pour *bapédi*, or any other strong spirit into your boots, and you can tallow your feet before a long march. Having no socks will seem funny at first, but in time you come to hate the idea of them. Much less cleanly really, and the cause of all blisters."

Rupert looked doubtful, and thought of his silk-sock bills. Even as a trooper he had always kept one silk pair to put on after the bath which followed a long march. (There are few things so refreshing as the vigorous brushing of one's hair and the putting of silk socks on to bathed feet after a heavy day.)

"Good night, and Good Luck in the Legion," added John Bull as he lay down.

"Good night—and thanks awfully, sir, for your kindness," replied Rupert, and vainly endeavoured to compose himself to sleep on his bed which consisted of a straw-stuffed mattress, a straw-stuffed pillow, and two thin raspy blankets. . . .

Mikhail Kyrilovitch sat on his bed whispering with his brother, about the medical examination of recruits which would take place on the morrow.

"Well, we can only hope for the best," said Feodor at last, "and they all say the same thing—that it is generally the merest formality. The Médecin-Major looks at your face and teeth and asks if you are healthy. It's not like what Ivan and I went through in Paris. . . . They wouldn't have two searching medical examinations unless there appeared to be signs of weakness, I should think."

When the room was wrapped in silence and darkness the latter arose.

"Good night, *golubtchik*," he whispered, "and when your heart fails you, remember Marie Spiridinoff—and be thankful you are here rather than There."

Mikhail shuddered.

Anon, every soul in the room was awakened by the uproarious entrance of the great Luigi Rivoli supported by Messieurs Malvin, Borges and Bauer, all very drunk and roaring "*Brigadier vous avez raison*," a song which tailed off into an inane repetition of—

> "Si le Caporal savait ça
> Il dirait 'nom de Dieu,' "

in the midst of which the great man collapsed upon his bed, while, with much hiccupping laughter and foul jokes, his faithful satellites contrived to remove his boots and leave him to sleep the sleep of the just and the drunken. . . .

Anon the Dutch youth, Hans Djoolte, sat up and looked around. All was quiet and apparently everyone was asleep. The conscience of Hans was pricking him—he had said his prayers lying in bed, and that was not the way in which he had been taught to say them by his good Dutch mother, whose very last words, as she died, had been, "Say your prayers each night, my son, wherever you may be."

Hans got out of bed, knelt him down, and said his prayers again. Thenceforward, he always did so as soon as he had undressed, regardless of consequences—which at first were serious. But even the good Luigi Rivoli, in time, grew tired of beating him, particularly when the four English-speaking occupants of the *chambrée* intimated their united disapproval of Luigi's interference. The most startling novelty, by repetition, becomes the most familiar commonplace, and the day, or rather the night, arrived when Hans Djoolte could pray unmolested. . . . Occupants of less favoured *chambrées* came to see the sight. The *escouade* indeed became rather proud of having two authentic lunatics. . . .

CHAPTER V

THE TRIVIAL ROUND

As he had done almost every night for the last twenty-five years, Sir Montague Merline lay awake for some time, thinking of his wife.

Was she happy? Of course she was. Any woman is happy with the man she really loves.

Did she ever think of him? Of course she did. Any woman thinks, at times, of the man in whose arms she has lain. No doubt his photo stood in a silver frame on her desk or piano. Huntingten would not mind that. Nothing petty about Lord Huntingten—and he had been very fond of "good old Merline," "dear old stick-in-the-mud," as he had so often called him.

Of course she was happy. Why shouldn't she be? Although Huntingten was poor as English peers go, there was enough for decent quiet comfort—and Marguerite had never been keen on making a splash. She had not minded poverty as Lady Merline. . . . She was certainly as happy as the day was long, and it would have been the damnedest cruelty and caddishness to have turned up and spoilt things. It would have wrecked her life and Huntingten's too. . . .

Splendid chap, Huntingten—so jolly clever and original, so full of ideas and unconventionality. . . . "How to be Happy though Titled." . . . "How to be a Man though a Peer." . . . "Efforts for the Effete," and Sir Montague smiled as he thought of the eccentric peer's pleasantries.

Yes, she'd be happy enough with that fine brave big sportsman with his sunny face and merry laugh, his gentle and kindly ways, his love of open-air life, games, sport, and all clean strenuous things. Of course she was happy. . . . Did she ever think of him? . . . Were there any more children? . . . (And, as always, at this point, Sir Montague frowned and sighed.)

How he would love a little girl of hers, if she were very, very like her—and how he would hate a boy if he were like Huntingten. No—not hate the boy—hate the idea of her having a boy who was like Huntingten. But how she would love the boy. . . .

What would he not give to see her! Unseen himself, of course. He hoped he would not get *cafard* again, when next stationed in the desert. It had been terrible, unspeakably terrible, to feel that resolution was weakening, and that when it failed altogether, he would desert and go in search of her. . . . Suppose that, with madman's cunning, and with madman's strength, he should be successful in an attempt to reach Tunis—the only possible way for a deserter without money—and should live to reach her, or to be recognised and proclaimed as the lost Sir Montague Merline. Her life in ruins and her children illegitimate—nameless bastards. . . . It was a horribly disturbing thought, that under the influence of *cafard* his mind might lose all ideas and memories and wishes except the one great longing to see her again, to clasp her in his arms again, to have and to hold. . . . Well—he had a lot to be thankful for. So long as Cyrus Hiram Milton was his bunk-mate it was not likely to happen. Cyrus would see that he did not desert, penniless and mad, into the desert. And now this English boy had come—a man with the same training, tastes, habits, haunts and *clichés* as himself. Doubtless they had numbers of common acquaintances. But he must be wary when on that ground. Possibly the boy knew Lord and Lady Huntingten. . . . After all it's a very small world, and especially the world of English Society, clubs, Services, and sport. . . . This boy would be a real *companion*, such as dear old Cyrus could never be, best of friends as he was. He would make a hobby of the boy, look after him, live his happy past again in talking of London, Sandhurst, Paris, racing, golf, theatres, clubs, and all the lost things whose memories they had in common. The boy might perhaps have been at Winchester too. . . . Thank Heaven he had come! It would make all the difference when *cafard* conditions arose again. Of course he'd get promoted *Soldat première classe* before long though, and then *Caporal*. Corporals may not walk and talk with private soldiers. Yes—the boy would rise and leave him behind. Just his luck. . . . Might he not venture to accept promotion now—after all these years, and rise step by step with him? No, better not. Thin end of the wedge. Once he allowed himself to be *Soldat première classe* he'd be accepting promotion to *Caporal* and *Sergent* before he knew it. The temptation to go on to *Chef* and *Adjudant* would be overwhelming, and when offered a commission (and the return to the life of an officer and gentleman) would be utterly irresistible. Then would come the very thing to prevent which he had buried himself alive in this hell of a Legion—recognition and then the public scandal of his wife's innocent bigamy, and her children's illegitimacy. As an officer he would meet foreign officers and visitors to Algeria. His portrait might get into the papers. He might have to go to Paris, or Marseilles, and run risks of being recognised. No—better to put away temptation and take no chance of the evil thing. Poor little Marguerite! Think of the cruel shattering blow to her. It would kill her to give up Huntingten in addition to knowing her children to be nameless, unable to inherit title or estates. . . . No— unthinkable! Do the thing properly or not at all. . . . But it was hell to be a second-class soldier all the time, and never be exempt from liability to sentry-duty, guards, fatigues, filthy corvées and punishment at the hands of Non-coms. seeking to acquire merit by discovering demerit. . . . And he could have had a commission straight away, when he got his bit of *ferblanterie*[34] in Tonkin and again in Dahomey. They knew he could speak German and had been an officer. . . . It had been a sore temptation—but, thank God, he had conquered it and not run the greatly enhanced risk of discovery. He ought really to have committed suicide directly he learned that she was married. No business to be alive—let alone grumbling about promotion. Moreover, if any living soul on this earth discovered that he was alive he must not only die, but let his wife have proof that he really *was* dead, this time. Then she and Huntingten could re-marry as the first ceremony was null and void, and the children be legitimatised. . . . Of course there would be more children—they loved each other so. . . .

As things were, his being alive did the Huntingtens no harm. It was the *knowledge* of his existence that would do the injury—both legal and personal. . . . No harm, so long as it wasn't known. They were quite innocent in the sight of le bon Dieu, and so long as neither they, nor anyone else, knew—nothing mattered so far as they were concerned. . . .

But fourteen years as a second-class soldier of the Legion! . . . And what was he to do at the end

---

[34] Lit., tin-ware (medals and decorations).

of the fifteenth? They would not re-enlist him. He would get a pension of five hundred francs a year—twenty pounds a year—and he had got the cash "bonus" given him when he won the *médaille militaire*. Where could he hide again? Perhaps he could get a job as employed-pensioner of the Legion—such as sexton at the graveyard or assistant-cook, or Officers'-Mess servant? . . . Otherwise he'd find himself one fine morning at the barracks-gates, dressed in a suit of blue sacking from the Quartermaster's store, fitting him where it touched him; a big flat tam-o'-shanter sort of cap; a rough shirt, and a blue cravat "to wind twice round the neck"; a pair of socks (for the first time in fifteen years), and a decent pair of boots. He'd have his papers, a free pass to any part of France he liked to name, a franc a day for the journey thereto, and his week's pay.

And what good would the papers and pass be to him—who dared not leave the shelter of the all-concealing Legion? . . . Surely it would be safe for him to return to England, or at any rate to go to France or some other part of Europe? Why not to America or the Colonies? No, nowhere was safe, and nothing was certain. Besides, how was he to get there? His pass would take him to any part of France, and nowhere else. A fine thing—to hide in the Legion for fifteen years, actually to survive fifteen years of a second-class soldier's life in the Legion, and then to risk rendering it all useless! One breath of rumour—and Marguerite's life was spoilt. . . . Discovery—and it was ruined, just when her children (if she had any more) were on the threshold of their careers. . . . Well, life in the Legion was remarkably uncertain, and there still remained a year in which all problems might be finally solved by bullet, disease, or death in some other of the many forms in which it visited the stepsons of France. . . . Where was old Strong now? . . .

Legionary John Bull fell asleep.

Meanwhile, a few inches from him, Reginald Rupert had found himself unusually and unpleasantly wakeful. It had been a remarkably full and tiring day, and as crowded with new experiences as the keenest experience-seeker could desire. . . . He was very glad he had come. This was going to be a good toughening *man's* life, and real soldiering. He would not have missed it for anything. It would hold a worthy place in the list of things which he had done and been, the list that, by the end of his life, he hoped would be a long and very varied one. By the time "the governor" died (and he trusted that might not happen for another forty years) he hoped to have been in many armies and Frontier Police forces, to have been a sailor, a cowboy, a big-game hunter, a trapper, an explorer and prospector, a gold-miner, a war correspondent, a gum-digger, and many other things in many parts of the world, in addition to his present record of Public-school, Sandhurst, 'Varsity man, British officer, trooper, and French Légionnaire. He hoped to continue to turn up in any part of the world where there was a war.

What Reginald, like his father, loathed and feared was Modern Society life, and in fact all modern civilised life as it had presented itself to his eyes—with its incredibly false standards, values and ideals, its shoddy shams and vulgar pretences, its fat indulgences, slothfulness and folly.

To him, as to his father (whose curious mental kink he had inherited), the world seemed a dreadful place in which drab, dull folk followed drab, dull pursuits for drab, dull ends. People who lived for pleasure were so occupied and exhausted in its pursuit that they got no pleasure. People who worked were so closely occupied in earning their living that they never lived. He did not know which class he disliked more—the men who lived their weary lives at clubs, grandstands, country-house parties, Ranelagh and Hurlingham, the Riviera, the moors, and the Yacht Squadron; or those who lived dull laborious days in offices, growing flabby and grey in pursuit of the slippery shekel.

The human animal seemed to him to have become as adventurous, gallant, picturesque and gay as the mole, the toad, and the slug. An old tomcat on a backyard fence seemed to him to be a more independent, care-free, self-respecting and gentlemanly person than his owner, a man who, all God's wide world before him, was, for a few monthly metal discs, content to sit in a stuffy hole and copy hieroglyphics from nine till six—that another man might the quicker amass many dirty metal discs and a double chin. To Reginald, the men of even his own class seemed travesties and parodies of a noble original, in that they were content to lead the dreadful lives they did—killing tame birds, knocking little balls about the place, watching other people ride races, rushing around in motors, sailing sunny seas in luxury and safety, seeing foreign lands only from their best hotels, poodle-faking and philandering, doing everything but anything—pampered, soft, useless; each a most exact and careful copy of his neighbour. Reginald loved, and excelled at, every form of sport, and had been prominent in the playing-fields at Winchester, Sandhurst and Oxford, but he could not live by sport alone, and to him it had always been a means and not an end, a means to health, strength, skill and hardihood—the which were to be applied—not to *more* games—but to the fuller living of life. The seeds of his father's teaching had fallen on most receptive and fertile soil, and their fruit ripened not the slower by reason of the fact that his father was his friend, confidant, hero and model. . . . He could see him now as he straddled mightily on the rug before the library fire, in his pink and cords, his spurred tops splashed with mud, and grey on the inner sides with the sweat of his horse. . . .

"Brown-paper prisons for poor men, and pink-silk cages for rich—that's Life nowadays, my boy, unless you're careful. . . . Get hold of Life, don't let Life get hold of you. Take the family motto for your guidance in actual fact. *'Be all, see all.'* Try to carry it out as far as humanly possible. *Live* Life and live it in the World. Don't live a thousandth part of Life in a millionth part of the World, as all our neighbours do. When you succeed me here and marry and settle down, be able to say you've seen everything, done everything, been everything. . . . Be a gentleman, of course, but one can be a man as well as being a gentleman—gentility is of the heart and conduct and manners—not of position and wealth and rank. What's the good of seeing one little glimpse of life out of one little window—whether it's a soldier's window (which is the best of windows), or a sailor's, or a lawyer's, parson's, merchant's, scholar's, sportsman's, landowner's, politician's, or any other. . . . And go upwards and downwards too, my boy. Tramps, ostlers, costermongers and soldiers are a dam' sight more interestin' than kings—and a heap more human. A chap who's only moved in one plane of society isn't educated—not worth listening to . . ." and much more to the same effect— and Rupert smiled to himself as he thought of how his father had advised him not to "waste" more than a year at Sandhurst, another at Oxford, and another in an Officers' Mess, before setting forth to see real life, and real men living it hard and to the full, in the capitals and the corners of the earth.

"How the dear old boy must have worshipped mother—to have married and settled down, at forty," he reflected, "and what a beauty she must have been. She's lovely now," and again his rather hard face softened into a smile as he thought of the interview in which he told her of his intention to "chuck" his commission and go and do things and see things. Little had he known that she had fully anticipated and daily expected the declaration which he feared would be a "terrible blow" to her. . . . Did she expect him to be anything else than the son of his father and his eccentric and adventurous House?

"I wouldn't have you be anything but a chip of the old block, my darling boy. You're of age and your old mother isn't going to be a millstone round your neck, like she's been round your father's. Only one woman can have the right to be that, and you will give her the right when you marry her. . . . Your family really ought not to marry."

"Mother, Mother!" he had protested, "and 'bring up our children to do the same,' I suppose?"

She had been bravely gay when he went, albeit a little damp of eye and red of nose. . . . Really he was a lucky chap to have such a mother. She was one in a thousand and he must faithfully do his utmost to keep his promise and go home once a year or thereabouts—also "to take care of his nails, not crop his hair, change damp socks, and wear wool next his skin. . . ." Want a bit of doin' in the Legion, what! Good job the poor darling couldn't see Luigi Rivoli breaking up recruits, or Sergeant Legros superintending the ablutions of her Reginald. What *would* she think of this galley and his fellow galley-slaves—of 'Erb, the *Apache*, Carmelita, the Grasshopper, and the drunkards of the Canteen? The Bucking Bronco would amuse her, and she'd certainly be interested in John Bull, poor old chap. . . . What could his story be, and why was he here? Was there a woman in it? . . . Probably. He didn't look the sort of chap who'd "done something." Poor devil! . . . Yes, her big warm heart would certainly have a corner for John Bull. Had she not been well brought up by her husband and son in the matter of seeing a swan in every goose they brought home? Yes, he'd repay John Bull's kindness to the full when he left the Legion. He should come straight to Elham Old Hall and his mother should have the chance, which she would love, of thanking and, in some measure, repaying the good chap. He wouldn't tell him exactly who they were and what they were, lest he should pretend that fifteen years of Legion life had spoilt him for *la vie de château*, and refuse to visit them. . . . He'd like to know his story. What *could* be the cause of a man like him leading this ha'penny-a-day life for fourteen years? Talk of paper prisons and silken cages—this was a prison of red-hot stone. Fancy *this* the setting for the best years of your life, and he sat up and looked round the moonlit room.

Next to him lay the Bucking Bronco, snoring heavily, his moustache looking huge and black in the moonlight that made his face appear pale and fine. . . . A strong and not unkindly face, with its great jutting chin and square heavy jaw.

'Erb lay on the neighbouring cot, his hands clasped above his head as he slept the sleep of the just and innocent, for whom a night of peaceful slumber is the meet reward of a well-spent day. His pinched and cunning little face was trans-figured by the moonlight, and the sleeping Herbert

Higgins looked less the vulgar, street-bred gutter-snipe than did the waking " 'Erbiggins" of the day.

Beyond him lay the mighty bulk of Luigi Rivoli, breathing stertorously in drunken slumber as he sprawled, limb-scattered, on his face, fully dressed, save for his boots. . . .

What an utter swine and cad—reflected Reginald—and what would happen when he selected him for his attentions? Of course, the Neapolitan had ten times his strength and twice his weight—but there would have to be a fight—or a moral victory for the recruit. He would obey no behests of Luigi Rivoli, nor accept any insults nor injuries tamely. He would land the cad one of the best, and take the consequences, however humiliating or painful. And he'd do it every time too, until he were finally incapacitated, or Luigi Rivoli weary of the game. Evidently the brute had some sort of respect for the big American and for John Bull. He should learn to have some for "Reginald Rupert," too, or the latter would die in the attempt to teach it. The prospect was not alluring though, and the Austrian and the *Apache* had received sharp and painful lessons on the folly of defying or attacking Luigi Rivoli. Still—experiences, dangers, difficulties and real, raw, primitive life were what his family sought—and here were some of them. Yes, he was ready for Il Signor Luigi Rivoli. . . .

In the next bed lay the Russian, Mikhail. Queer, shy chap. What a voice, and what a complexion for a recruit of the Foreign Legion! How extraordinarily alike he and his brother were, and yet there was a great difference between their respective voices and facial expressions. . . . Another queer story there. They looked like students. . . . Probably involved in some silly Nihilist games and had to bolt for their lives from the Russian police or from Nihilist confederates, or both. It was nice to see how the manlier brother looked after the other. He seemed to be in a perpetual state of concern and anxiety about him.

Beyond the Russian recruit lay the mad Legionary known as the Grasshopper. What a pathetic creature—an ex-officer of one of the most aristocratic corps in Europe. In fact he must be a nobleman or he could not have been in the Guides. Must be of an ancient family moreover. Besides, he was so very obviously of *ceux qui ont pris la peine de naître*. What could his story be? Fancy the man being a really first-class soldier on parade, manœuvres, march, or battle-field, and an obvious lunatic at the same time. . . . Poor devil! . . .

Next to him was the other Russian, and then Edouard Malvin, the nasty-looking cad who appeared to be Rivoli's chief toady. His neighbour was the fat and dull-looking Dutch lad (who was to display such unusual and enviable moral courage). . . .

Footsteps resounded without, and the Room-Corporal entered with a clatter. Turning down his blanket, as though expecting to find something beneath it, he disclosed some bottles, a few packets of tobacco and cigarettes, and a little heap of coins.

"Bonheur de Dieu vrai!" he ejaculated. " 'Y'a de bon!" and examined the packets for any indication of their orientation. " 'Les deux Russes,' " he read, and broke into a guinguette song. Monsieur le Caporal loved wine and was *un ramasseur de sous*. These Russians were really worthy and sensible recruits, and, though they should escape none of their duties, they should be regarded with a tolerant and non-malicious eye by Monsieur le Caporal. No undue share of corvées should be theirs. . . . No harm in their complimenting their good Caporal and winning his approval—but, on the other hand, no bribery and corruption. Mais non—c'est tout autre chose!

As the Corporal disrobed, the Grasshopper rose from his cot, crouched, and hopped towards him.

The Corporal evinced no surprise.

"Monsieur le Caporal," quoth the Grasshopper. "How can a Cigale steer a gunboat? . . . I ask you. . . . How can I possibly dip the ensign from peak to taffrail, cat the anchor or shoot the sun, by the pale glimmer of the binnacle light? . . . And I have, for cargo, the Cestus of Aphrodite. . . ."

"And *I* have, for cargo, seven bottles of good red wine—beneath my Cestus of Corporal—so I can't tell you, Grasshopper," was the reply. . . . "Va t'en! . . . You go and ask Monsieur le bon Diable—and tell him his old *ami* Caporal Achille Martel sent you. . . . Go on—*allez schieb' los*—and let me sleep. . . ."

The Grasshopper hopped to the door and out into the corridor. . . .

Rupert fell asleep. . . .

As John Bull had prophesied, he was awakened by yells of "*Au jus! Au jus! Au jus!*" from the garde-chambre, the room-orderly on duty, as he went from cot to cot with a huge jug.

Each sleepy soul roused himself sufficiently to hold out the tin mug which hung at the head of his bed, and to receive a half-pint or so of the "gravy"—which proved to be really excellent coffee. For his own part, Rupert would have been glad of the addition of a little milk and sugar, but he had swallowed too much milkless and sugarless tea (from a basin) in the British Army, to be concerned about such a trifle. . . .

"Good morning. Put on the white trousers and come downstairs with me," said John Bull, as he also swallowed his coffee. "Be quick, or you won't get a chance at the lavatory. There's washing accommodation for six men when sixty want it. . . . Come on."

As he hurried from the room, Rupert noticed that Corporal Martel lay comfortably in bed while the rest hurriedly dressed. From time to time he mechanically shouted: "Levez-vous, mes enfants. . . ." "Levez-vous, assassins. . . ." "Levez-vous, scélérats. . . ."

After each of his shouts came, in antistrophe, the anxious yell of the garde-chambre (who had to sweep the room before parade) of "Balayez audessous vos lits!"

Returning from his hasty and primitive wash, Rupert noticed that the Austrian recruit was lacing Rivoli's boots, while the *Apache*, grimacing horribly behind his back, brushed the Neapolitan down, Malvin superintending their labours.

"Shove on the white tunic and blue sash," said John Bull to his protégé—"and you'll want knapsack, cartridge-belt, bayonet and rifle. . . . Bye-bye! I must be off. You'll have recruit-drills separate from us for some time. . . . See you later. . . ."

§2

Légionnaire Reginald Rupert soon found that French drill methods of training differed but little from English, though perhaps more thorough and systematically progressive, and undoubtedly better calculated to develop initiative.

It did not take the Corporal-Instructor long to single him out as an unusually keen and intelligent recruit, and Rupert was himself surprised at the pleasure he derived from being placed as Number One of the *escouade* of recruits, after a few days. His knowledge of French helped him considerably, of course, and on that first morning he had obeyed the Corporal's roar of "*Sac à terre*," "*A gauche*," "*A droit*," "*En avant, marche*," "*Pas gymnastique*," or "*Formez les faisceaux*," before the majority of the others had translated them. He also excelled in the eating of the "Breakfast of the Legion," which is nothing more nor less than a terribly punishing run, in quick time, round and round the parade-ground. By the time the Corporal called a halt, Rupert, who was a fine runner, in the pink of condition, was beginning to feel that he had about shot his bolt, while, with one or two exceptions, the rest of the squad were in a state of real distress, gasping, groaning, and coughing, with protruding eyeballs and faces white, green, or blue. During the brief "cigarette halt," he gazed round with some amusement at the prostrate forms of his exhausted comrades.

The Russian, Feodor, seemed to be in pretty well as good condition as himself—in striking contrast to Mikhail, whose state was pitiable, as he knelt doubled up, drawing his breath in terrible gasps, and holding his side as though suffering agonies from "stitch."

'Erb was in better case, but he lay panting as though his little chest would burst.

"Gawdstrewth, matey," he grunted to M. Tou-tou Boil-the-Cat, "I ain't run so much since I last see a copper."

The *Apache*, green-faced and blue-lipped, showed his teeth in a vicious snarl, by way of reply. Absinthe and black cigarettes are a poor training-diet.

The fat Dutch lad, Hans Djoolte, appeared to be *in extremis* and likely to disappear in a pool of perspiration. The gnarled-looking Spaniard drew his breath with noisy whoops, and stout Germans, Alsatians, Belgians and Frenchmen gave the impression of persons just rescued from drowning or suffocation by smoke. Having finished his cigarette, the Corporal ran to the far side of the parade-ground, raised his hand with a shout, and cried, "*A moi.*"

"Well run, *bleu*," he observed to Rupert, who arrived first.

Before the "breakfast" half-hour was over, he was thoroughly tired, and more than a little sorry for some of the others. M. Tou-tou Boil-the-Cat was violently sick; the plump Dutchman was soaked from head to foot; many a good, stout Hans, Fritz and Carl wished he had never been born; and Mikhail Kyrilovitch distinguished himself by falling flat in a dead faint, to the contemptuous and outspoken disgust of the Corporal.

It was indeed a kill-or-cure training, and, in some cases, bade fair to kill before it cured. One drill-manœuvre interested Rupert by its novelty and yet by its suggestion of the old Roman *testudo*. On the order "*A genoux*," all had to fall on their knees and every man of the squad, not in the front rank, to thrust his head well under the knapsack of the man in front of him. Since, under service conditions, knapsacks would be stuffed with spare uniforms and underclothing, and covered with tent-canvas, blanket, spare boots, fuel or a cooking-pot, excellent head-cover was thus provided against shrapnel and shell-fragments, and from bullets from some of such rifles as are used by the Chinese, African, Madagascan, and Arab foes of the Legion. Interested or not, it was with unfeigned thankfulness that, at about eleven o'clock, Rupert found himself marching back to barracks and heard the "*Rompez*" command of dismissal outside the *caserne* of his Company. Hurrying up to the *chambrée* he put his Lebel in the rack, his knapsack and belts on the shelf above his bed, and lay down to get that amount of rest without which he felt he could not face breakfast.

"Hallo, Rupert! Had a gruelling?" enquired John Bull, entering and throwing off his accoutrements. "They make you earn your little bit of corn, don't they? You feel it less day by day though, and soon find you can do it without turning a hair. Not much chance of a chap with weak lungs or heart surviving the 'Breakfast of the Legion,' for long. You see the point of the training when you begin the desert marches."

"Quite looking forward to it," said Rupert.

"It's better looking back on it, on the whole," rejoined the other grimly. . . . "Feel like breakfast?" he added in French, remembering that the more his young friend spoke in that tongue the better.

"Oh, I'm all right. What'll it be?"

"Well, not *bec-fins* and *pêche Melba* exactly. Say a mug of bread-soup, containing potato and vegetables and a scrap of meat. Sort of Irish stew."

"*Arlequins* at two sous the plate, first, for me, please," put in M. Tou-tou Boil-the-Cat, whose small compact frame seemed to have recovered its normal elasticity and vigour.

As he spoke, the voice of a kitchen-orderly was raised below in a long-drawn howl of "*Soupe! A la Soupe!*" Turning with one accord to the *garde-chambre* the Legionaries bawled "*Soupe!*" as one man, and like an arrow from a bow, the room-orderly sped forth, to return a minute later bearing the soup-kettle and a basket of loaves of grey bread. Tin plates and utensils were snatched from the hanging-cupboards, and mugs from their hooks on the wall and the Legionaries seated themselves on the benches that ran down either side of the long table.

" 'Fraid you'll have to stand out, Rupert, being

a recruit," said John Bull. "There's only room for twenty at this table."

"Of course. Thanks," was the reply, and the speaker betook himself to his bed, and sat him down with his mug and crust.

With cheerful sociability, 'Erb had already seated himself at table, and was beating a loud tattoo with mug and plate as he awaited the administrations of the soup-laden Ganymede.

Suddenly the expansive and genial smile faded on 'Erb's happy face, as he felt himself seized by the scruff of his neck and the seat of his trousers, and raised four feet in the air. . . . For a second he hovered, descended a foot and was then shot through the air with appalling violence to some distant corner of the earth. Fortunately for 'Erb, that corner contained a bed and he landed fairly on it. . . . The Legionary Herbert Higgins in the innocence of his ignorance had occupied the Seats of the Mighty, had sat him down in the place of Luigi Rivoli—and Luigi had removed the insect.

"Gawd love us!" said 'Erb. " 'Oo'd a' thought it?" as he realised that he was still in barracks and had only travelled from the table to a cot, a distance of some six feet. . . .

Mikhail Kyrilovitch lay stretched on his bed, too exhausted to eat. It interested and rather touched Rupert to see how tenderly the other Russian half raised him from the bed, coaxed him with soup and, failing, produced a bottle of wine from behind the *paquetage* on his shelf, and induced him to drink a little. . . .

"Potato fatigue after this, Rupert," said John Bull as he came over to the recruit, and offered him a cigarette. "Ghastly stuff you'll find this black Algerian tobacco, but one gets used to it. It's funny, but when I get a taste of any of the tobaccos from Home, I find my palate so ruined that I don't enjoy it. Seems acrid and strong though it's infinitely milder. . . ."

The Kitchen-Corporal thrust his head in at the door of the *chambrée*, roared *"Aux palates"* and vanished. Trooping down to the kitchen, the whole Company stood in a ring and solemnly peeled potatoes. Here, at any rate, Mikhail Kyrilovitch distinguished himself among the recruits, for not only was his the first potato to fall peeled into the bucket, but his peel was the thinnest, his output the greatest. Standing next to him, Rupert noticed how tiny were his hands and wrists, and how delicate his nails.

"Apparently this is part of regular routine and not a corvée," he remarked.

"Mais oui, Monsieur," replied Mikhail primly.

"Great tip to get cunning at dodging extra fatigues when you're a soldier," continued Rupert.

"Mais oui, Monsieur," replied Mikhail primly.

"Expect they'll catch us wretched recruits on that lay until we get artful."

"Mais oui, Monsieur," replied Mikhail primly.

What a funny shy lad he was, with his eternal "Mais oui, Monsieur" . . . Perhaps that was all the French he knew! . . .

"Do you think the medical-examination will be very—er—searching, Monsieur?" asked Mikhail.

So he did know French after all. What was he trembling about now?

"Shouldn't think so. Why? You're all right, aren't you? You wouldn't have passed the doctor when you enlisted, otherwise."

"Non, Monsieur."

"Where did you enlist?"

"At Paris, Monsieur."

"So did I; Rue St. Dominique. Little fat cove in red breeches and a white tunic. I suppose you had the same chap?"

"Er—oui, Monsieur."

"I suppose he overhauled you very thoroughly? . . . Wasn't it infernally cold standing stark naked in that beastly room while he punched you about?"

"Oh!—er—oui, Monsieur. Oh, please let us . . . Er—wasn't that running dreadful this morning?" . . .

"I say, Monsieur Rupaire, do you think we shall have the same 'breakfast' every morning?" put in Feodor Kyrilovitch. "It'll be the death of my brother here, if we do. He never was a runner."

" 'Fraid so, during recruits' course," replied Rupert, and added: "I noticed a great difference between you and your brother."

"Oh, it's only just in that respect," was the reply. "I've always been better winded than he. . . . Illness when he was a kid. . . . Lungs not over strong. . . ."

Even as he had prophesied, an Orderly-Sergeant swooped down upon them as the potato-fatigue finished, and, while the old Legionaries somehow melted into thin air and vanished like the baseless fabric of a vision, the recruits were captured and commandeered for a barrack-scavenging corvée which kept them hard at work until it was time to fall in for "theory."

This Rupert discovered to be instruction in recognition of badges of rank, and, later, in every sort and kind of rule and regulation; in musketry, tactics, training and the principles and theory of drill, entrenchment, scouting, skirmishing, and every other branch of military education.

At two o'clock, drill began again, and lasted until four, at which hour Monsieur le Médicin-Major held the medical examination, the idea of which seemed so disturbing to Mikhail Kyrilovitch. It proved to be the merest formality—a glance, a question, a caution against excess, and the recruits were passed and certified as *bon pour le service* at the rate of twenty to the quarter-hour. They were, moreover, free for the remainder of the day (provided they escaped all victim-hunting Non-coms., in search of corvée-parties) with the exception of such hours as might be necessary for labours of *astiquage* and the *lavabo*.

On returning to the *chambrée*, Rupert found his friend John Bull awaiting him.

"Well, Rupert," he cried cheerily, "what sort of a day have you had? Tired? We'll get 'soupe' again shortly. I'll take you to the *lavabo* afterwards, and show you the ropes. Got to have your white kit, arms and accoutrements all *klim-bim*, as the Germans say, before you dress and go out, or else you'll have to do it in the dark."

"Yes, thanks," replied Rupert. "I'll get straight first. I hate 'spit and polish' after Lights Out. What'll the next meal be?"

"Same as this morning—the eternal 'soupe.' The only variety in food is when dog-biscuit replaces bread. . . . Nothing to grumble at really, except the infernal monotony. Quantity is all right —in fact some fellows save up a lot of bread and biscuit and sell it in the town. (Eight days *salle de police* if you're caught.) But sometimes you feel you could eat anything in the wide world except Legion 'soupe,' bread and biscuit. . . ."

After the second and last meal of the day, at about five o'clock, Rupert was introduced to the *lavabo* and its ways—particularly its ways in the matter of disappearing soap and vanishing "washing"—and, his first essay in laundry-work concluded, returned with Legionary John Bull and the Bucking Bronco for an hour or two of leather-polishing, accoutrement-cleaning and "ironing" without an iron.

The room began to fill and was soon a scene of more or less silent industry. On his bed, the great Luigi Rivoli lay magnificently asleep, while, on neighbouring cots and benches, his weapons, accoutrements, boots and uniform received the attentions of Messieurs Malvin, Meyer, Tou-tou Boil-the-Cat, Dimitropoulos, Borges, Bauer, Hirsch, and others, his henchmen.

Anon the great man awoke, yawned cavernously, ejaculated *"Dannazione"* and sat up. One gathered that the condition of his mouth was not all that it might be, and that his head ached. Even he was not exempt from the penalties incurred by lesser men, and even he had to recognise the fact that a next-morning follows an evening-before. Certain denizens of the *chambrée* felt, and looked, uneasy, but were reassured by the reflection that there was still a stock of *bleus* unchastened, and available for the great man's needs and diversion. Rising, he roared *"Oho!"*, smacked and flexed his muscles according to his evening ritual, and announced that a recruit might be permitted to fetch him water.

Feodor Kyrilovitch unobtrusively changed places with his brother Mikhail, whose bed was next to that of the bully.

"Here, dog," roared the Neapolitan, and brought his "quart" down with a right resounding blow upon the bare head of Feodor. Without a word the Russian took the mug and hurried to the nearest lavatory. Returning he handed it respectfully to Rivoli, and pointing into it said in broken Italian—

"There would appear to be a mark on the bottom of the Signor's cup."

The great man looked—and smiled graciously as he recognised a gold twenty-franc piece. "A thoroughly intelligent recruit," he added, turning to Malvin, who nodded and smiled drily. It entered the mind of le bon Légionnaire Malvin that this recruit should also give an exhibition of his intelligence to le bon Légionnaire Malvin.

"Where's that fat pig from Olanda who can only whine *'Verstaan nie'* when he is spoken to?" enquired Rivoli, looking round. "Let me see if I can 'Verstaan' him how to put my boots on smartly."

But, fortunately for himself, the Dutch recruit, Hans Djoolte, was not present.

"Not there?" thundered the great man, on being informed. "How dare the fat calf be not there? Let it be known that I desire all the recruits of this room to be on duty from 'Soupe' till six, or later, in case I should want them. Let them all parade before me now."

Some sheepishly grinning, some with looks of alarm, some under strong protest, all the recruits with one exception, "fell in" at the foot of the Italian's bed. Some were dismissed as they came up; the two Russians, as having paid their footing very handsomely; the *Apache*, and Franz Josef Meyer, as having been properly broken to bit and curb; the Greek, as a declared admirer and slave; and one or two others who had already wisely propitiated, or, to their sorrow, encountered less pleasantly, the uncrowned king of the Seventh Company. The remainder received tasks, admonitions and warnings, the which were received variously, but without open defiance.

The attitude of le Légionnaire 'Erbiggins was characteristic. Realising that he had not a ghost of a chance of success against a man of twice his weight and thrice his strength, he took the leggings which were given him to clean and returned a stream of nervous English, of which the pungent insults and vile language accorded but ill with the bland innocence of his face, and the deferential acquiescence of his manner.

"Ain't yew goin' ter jine the merry throng?" asked the Bucking Bronco of Reginald Rupert, upon hearing that recruit reply to Malvin's order to join the line, with a recommendation that Malvin should go to the devil.

"I am not," replied Rupert.

"Wal, I guess we'll back yew up, sonny," said the American with an approving smile.

"I shall be glad if you will in no way interfere," returned the Englishman.

"Gee-whillikins!" commented the Bucking Bronco.

John Bull looked anxious. "He's the strongest man I have ever seen," he remarked, "besides being a professional wrestler and acrobat."

Malvin again approached, grinning maliciously.

"Il Signor Luigi Rivoli would be sorry to have to come and fetch you, English pig," said he. "Sorry for you, that is. Do you wish to find yourself *au grabat*,[35] you scurvy, mangy, lousy cur of a recruit? . . . What reply shall I take Il Signor Luigi Rivoli?"

"*That!*" replied the Englishman, and therewith smote the fat Austrian a most tremendous smack across his heavy blue jowl with the open hand, sending him staggering several yards. Without paying further attention to the great man's ambassador, he strode in the direction of the great man himself, with blazing eyes and clenched jaw.

"You want me, do you?" he shouted at the astonished Luigi, who was rising open-mouthed from his bed; and, putting the whole weight of his body behind the blow, drove most skilfully and scientifically straight at the point of his jaw.

It must be confessed that the Italian was taken unawares, and in the very act of getting up, so

---

[35] On a sick bed.

that his hands were down, and he was neither standing nor sitting.

He was down and out, and lay across his bed stunned and motionless.

Into the perfect silence of the *chambrée* fell the voice of the Bucking Bronco. Solemnly he counted from one to ten, and then with a shout of *"OUT!"* threw his képi to the roof and roared *"Hurrah!"* repeatedly.

"Il ira loin," remarked Monsieur Tou-tou Boil-the-Cat, viewing Rupert's handiwork with experienced, professional eye.

Exclamatory oaths went up in all the languages of Europe.

"Il a fait de bon boulet," remarked a grinning grey-beard known as "Tant-de-Soif" to the astounded and almost awe-stricken crowd.

But le Légionnaire Jean Boule looked ahead.

"You've made two bad enemies, my boy, I'm afraid. . . . What about when he comes round?"

"I'll give him some more, if I can," replied Rupert. "Don't interfere, anyhow."

"Shake, sonny," said the Bucking Bronco solemnly. "An' look at hyar. Let's interfere, to the extent o' makin' thet cunning coyote fight down in the squar'. . . . Yew won't hev no chance—so don't opine yew will—but yew'll hev' more chance than yew will right hyar. . . . Yew want space when you rough-houses with Loojey. Once he gits a holt on yew—yure monica's up. Savvy?"

"Thanks," replied the Englishman. "Right-ho! If he won't fight downstairs, tell him he can take the three of us."

"Fower, matey. Us fower Henglishmen agin' 'im an' 'is 'ole bleedin' gang," put in 'Erb. " 'E's a bloke as wants takin' dahn a peg. . . . Too free wiv' hisself. . . . Chucks 'is weight abaht too much. . . . An' I'll tell yer wot, Cocky. Keep a heye on that

165

cove as you giv' a smack in the chops."

"Sure thing," agreed the Bucking Bronco, and turned to the Belgian who stood ruefully holding his face and looking as venomous as a broken-backed cobra, added: "Yew look at hyar, Mounseer Malvin, my lad. Don't yew git handlin' yure Rosalie[36] any dark night. Yew try ter *zigouiller*[37] my pal Rupert, an' I'll draw yure innards up through yure mouth till yew look like half a pound of dumplin' on the end of half a yard of macaroni. Twiggez vous? *Je tirerai vos gueutes à travers votre bouche jusqu' à vous resemblez un demi-livre de pouding au bout d'un demi-yard de macaroni.* . . . Got it? . . ."

Rivoli twitched, stirred, and groaned. It was interesting to note that none of his clients and henchmen offered any assistance. The sceptre of the great man swayed in his hand. Were he beaten, those whom he ruled by fear, rather than by bribery, would fall upon him like a pack of wolves. The hands of Monsieur Tou-tou Boil-the-Cat twitched and he licked his lips.

"*Je m'en souviendrai,*" he murmured.

Rivoli sat up.

"Donna e Madonna!" he said. "Corpo di Bacco!" and gazed around. "What has happened? . . ." and then he remembered. "A minute," he said. "Wait but a minute—and then bring him to me."

Obedience and acquiescence awoke in the bosoms of his supporters. The great Luigi was alive and on his throne again. The Greek passed him a mug of water.

"Yes, wait but a moment, and then just hand him to me. . . . One of you might go over to the hospital and say a bed will be wanted shortly," he

---

[36] Bayonet.
[37] To bayonet.

added. "And another of you might look up old Jules Latour down at the cemetery and tell him to start another grave."

"You're coming to *me*, for a change, Rivoli," cut in Rupert contemptuously. "You're going to fight me down below. There's going to be a ring, and fair play. Will you come now, or will you wait till to-morrow? I can wait if you feel shaken."

"Plug the ugly skunk while he's rattled, Bub," advised the American, and turning to the Italian added, "Sure thing, Loojey. Ef yew ain't hed enuff yew kin tote downstairs and hev' a five-bunch frame-up with the b'y. Ef yew start rough-housin' up hyar, I'll take a hand too. I would anyhaow, only the b'y wants yew all to himself. . . . Greedy young punk."

"I will kill him and eat him *now*," said the Italian rising magnificently. Apparently his splendid constitution and physique had triumphed completely, and it was as though the blow had not been struck.

"Come on, b'ys," yelped the American, "an' ef thet Dago don't fight as square as he knows haow, I'll pull his lower jaw off his face."

In a moment the room was empty, except for Mikhail Kyrilovitch, who sat on the edge of his brother's bed and shuddered.

Clattering down the stairs and gathering numbers as it went, the party made for the broad space, or passage, between high walls near the back entrance of the Company's *caserne*, a safe and secluded spot for fights. As they went along, John Bull gave good advice to his young friend.

"Remember he's a wrestler and a *savate* man," he said, "and that public opinion here recognises the use of both in a fight—so you can expect him to clinch and kick as well as butt."

"Right-o!" said Rupert.

A large ring was formed by the rapidly growing crowd of spectators, a ring, into the middle of which the Bucking Bronco stepped to declare that he would rearrange the features, as well as the ideas, of any supporter of Luigi Rivoli who in any way interfered with the fight.

The two combatants stripped to the waist and faced each other. It was a pleasant surprise to John Bull to notice that his friend looked bigger "peeled," than he did when dressed. (It is a good test of muscular development.) Obviously the youth was in the pink of condition and had systematically developed his muscles. But for the presence of Rivoli, the arms and torso of the Englishman would have evoked admiring comments. As it was, the gigantic figure of the Italian dwarfed him, for he looked what he was—a professional Strong Man whose stock-in-trade was his enormous muscles and their mighty strength. . . . It was not so much a contrast between David and Goliath as between Apollo and Hercules.

The Italian assumed his favourite wrestling attitude with open hands advanced; the Englishman, the position of boxing.

The two faced each other amidst the perfect silence of the large throng.

As, to the credit of human nature, is always the case, the sentiment of the crowd was in favour of the weaker party. No one supposed for a moment that the recruit would win, but he was a "dark horse," and English—of a nation proverbially dogged and addicted to la boxe. . . . He might perhaps be merely maimed and not killed. . . . For a full minute the antagonists hung motionless, eyeing each other warily. Suddenly the Italian swiftly advanced his left foot and made a lightning grab with his left hand at the Englishman's neck. The latter ducked; the great arm swung, harmless, above his head, and two sharp smacks rang out like pistol-shots as the Englishman planted a left and right with terrific force upon the Italian's ribs. Rivoli's gasp was almost as audible as the blows. He sprang back, breathing heavily.

John Bull moistened his lips and thanked God. Rupert circled round his opponent, sparring for an opening. Slowly . . . slowly . . . almost imperceptibly, the Italian's head and shoulders bent further and further back. What the devil was he doing?—wondered the Englishman—getting his head out of danger? Certainly his jaw was handsomely swollen. . . . Anyhow he was exposing his mark, the spot where the ribs divide. If he could get a "right" in there, with all his weight and strength, Il Signor Luigi Rivoli would have to look to himself in the ensuing seconds. Rupert made a spring. As he did so, the Italian's body turned sideways and leant over until almost parallel with the ground, as his right knee drew up to his chest and his right foot shot out with the force of a horse's kick. It caught the advancing Englishman squarely on the mouth, and sent him flying head over heels like a shot rabbit. The Italian darted forward—and so did the Bucking Bronco.

"Assez!" he shouted. "Let him get up." At this point his Legion French failed him, and he added in his own vernacular, "Ef yew think yu're gwine ter kick him while he's down, yew've got another think comin', Loojey Rivoli," and barred his path.

John Bull raised Rupert's head on to his knee. He was senseless and bleeding from mouth and nose.

Pushing his way through the ring, came 'Erb, a mug of water in one hand, a towel in the other. Filling his mouth with water, he ejected a fine spray over Rupert's face and chest, and then, taking the towel by two corners of a long side, flapped it mightily over the prostrate man.

The latter opened his eyes, sat up, and spat out a tooth.

"Damned kicking cad," he remarked, on collecting his scattered wits and faculties.

"No Queensberry rules here, old chap," said John Bull.

"You do the sime fer 'im, matey. Kick 'is bleedin' faice in. . . . W'y carn't 'e fight like a man, the dirty furriner?" and turning from his ministrations to where the great Luigi received the congratulations of his admiring supporters, he bawled with the full strength of his lungs: "Yah! you dirty furriner!" and crowned the taunt by putting his fingers to his nose and emitting a bellowing *Boo-oo-oo!* of incredibly bull-like realism. "If I wasn't yer second, matey, I'd go an' kick 'im in the stummick naow, I would," he muttered, resuming his labour of love.

Rupert struggled to his feet.

"Give me the mug," he said to 'Erb, and washed out his mouth. "How long 'time' is observed on these occasions?" he asked of John Bull.

"Oh, nothing's regular," was the reply. " 'Rounds' end when you fall apart, and 'time' ends when both are ready. . . . You aren't going for him again, are you?"

"I'm going for him as long as I can stand and see," was the answer. 'Erb patted him on the back.

"Blimey! You're a White Man, matey," he commended. "S'welp me, you are!"

"Seconds out of the ring," bawled the Bucking Bronco, and unceremoniously shoved back all who delayed.

A look of incredulity spread over the face of the Italian. Could it be possible that the fool did not know that he was utterly beaten and abolished? . . . He tenderly felt his jaw and aching ribs. . . .

It was true. The Englishman advanced upon him, the light of battle in his eyes, and fierce determination expressed in the frown upon his white face. His mouth bore no expression—it was merely a mess.

A cheer went up from the spectators.

A recruit asking for it *twice*, from Luigi Rivoli!

That famous man, though by no means anxious, was slightly perplexed. There was something here to which he was not accustomed. It was the first time in his experience that this had happened. Few men had defied and faced him once—none had done it twice. This, in itself was bad, and in the nature of a faint blow to his prestige. . . . He had tried a grapple—with unfortunate results; he had tried a kick—most successfully, and he would try another in a moment. Lest his opponent should be warily expecting it, he would now administer a battering-ram butt. He crouched forward, extending his open hands as though to grapple, and, suddenly ducking his head, flung himself forward, intending to drive the breath from his enemy's body and seize him by the throat ere he recovered.

Lightly and swiftly the Englishman side-stepped and, as he did so, smote the Italian with all his strength full upon the ear—a blow which caused that organ to swell hugely, and to "sing" for hours. Rivoli staggered sideways and fell. The Englishman stood back and waited. Rivoli arose as quickly as he fell, and, with a roar of rage, charged straight at the Englishman, who drove straight at his face, left and right, cutting his knuckles to the bone. Heavy and true as were the blows, they could not avail to stop that twenty-stone projectile, and, in a second, the Italian's arms were round him. One mighty hug and heave, and his whole body, clasped as in a vice to that of the Italian, was bent over backward in a bow.

"Thet's torn it," groaned the American, and dashed his képi upon the ground. "Fer two damns I'd . . ."

John Bull laid a restraining hand upon his arm.

"Go it, Rupert," bawled 'Erb, dancing in a frenzy of excitement. "Git 'is froat. . . . Swing up yer knee. . . . Kick 'im."

"Shut up," snapped John Bull. "He's not a hooligan. . . ."

One of Rupert's arms was imprisoned in those of the Italian. True to his training and standards, he played the game as he had learnt it, and kept his free right hand from his opponent's throat. With his failing strength he rained short-arm blows on the Italian's face, until it was turned sideways and crushed against his neck and shoulder.

John Bull mistook the bully's action.

"If you bite his throat, I'll shoot you, Rivoli," he shouted, and applauding cheers followed the threat.

The muscles of Rivoli's back and arms tightened and bunched as he strained with all his strength. Slowly but surely he bent further over, drawing the Englishman's body closer and closer in his embrace.

To John Bull, the seconds seemed years. Complete silence reigned. Rupert's blows weakened and became feeble. They ceased. Rivoli bent over further. As Rupert's right arm fell to his side, the Italian seized it from behind. His victim was now absolutely powerless and motionless. John Bull was reminded of a boa-constrictor which he had once seen crush a deer. Suddenly the Italian's left arm was withdrawn, his right arm continuing to imprison Rupert's left while his right hand retained his grip of the other. Thrusting his left hand beneath the Englishman's chin he put all his colossal strength into one great effort—pushing the head back until it seemed that the neck must break, and at the same time contracting his great right arm and bending himself almost double. He then raised his opponent and dashed him to the ground. . . .

Reginald Rupert recovered consciousness in the Legion's Hospital.

A skilful, if somewhat brutal, surgeon soon decided that his back was not broken but only badly sprained.

On leaving hospital, a fortnight later, he did eight days *salle de police* by way of convalescence.

On return to duty, he found himself something of a hero in the Seventh Company, and decidedly the hero of the recruits of his *chambrée*.

Disregarding the earnest entreaties of John Bull and the reiterated advice of the Bucking Bronco, and of the almost worshipping 'Erb—he awaited Luigi Rivoli on the evening after his release and challenged him to fight.

The great man burst into explosive laughter—laughter almost too explosive to be wholly genuine.

"Fight you, whelp! *Fight* you, whelp!" he scoffed. "*Why* should I fight you? Pah! Out of my sight—I have something else to do."

"Oh have you? Well, don't forget that I have nothing else to do, any time you feel like fighting. See?" replied the Englishman.

The Italian again roared with laughter, and Rupert with beating heart and well-concealed sense of mighty relief, returned to his cot to work.

It was noticeable that Il Signor Luigi Rivoli invariably had something else to do, so far as Rupert was concerned, and molested him no more.

CHAPTER VI

LE CAFARD AND OTHER THINGS

For Légionnaire Reginald Rupert the days slipped past with incredible rapidity, and, at the end of six months, this adaptable and exceedingly keen young man felt himself to be an old and seasoned Legionary, for whom the Depôt held little more in the way of instruction and experience.

His thoughts began to turn to Foreign Service. When would he be able to volunteer for a draft going to Tonkin, Madagascar, Senegal, or some other place of scenes and experiences entirely different from those of Algeria? When would he see some active service—that which he had come so far to see, and for which he had undergone these hardships and privations?

Deeply interested as he was in all things military, and anxious as he was to learn and become the Compleat Soldier, he found himself beginning to grow very weary of the trivial round, the common task, of life in the Depôt. Once he knew his drill as an Infantryman, he began to feel that the proportion of training and instruction to that of corvée and fatigues was small. He had not travelled all the way to Algiers to handle broom and wheelbarrow, and perform non-military labours at a wage of a halfpenny per day. Of course, one took the rough with the smooth and shrugged one's shoulders with the inevitable "Que voulez-vous? C'est la Légion," but, none the less, he had had enough, and more than enough, of Depôt life.

He sometimes thought of going to the *Adjudant-*

Major, offering to provide proofs that he had been a British officer, and claiming to be placed in the class of *angehende corporale* (as he called the *élèves Caporaux* or probationary Corporals) with a view to promotion and a wider and different sphere of action.

There were reasons against this course, however. It would, very probably, only result in his being stuck in the Depôt permanently, as a Corporal-Instructor—the more so as he spoke German. Also, it was neither quite worth while, nor quite playing the game, as he did not intend to spend more than a year in the Legion and was looking forward to his attempt at desertion as his first real Great Adventure.

He had heard horrible stories of the fate of most of those who go "on pump," as, for no discoverable reason, the Legionary calls desertion. In every barrack-room there hung unspeakably ghastly photographs of the mangled bodies of Legionaries who had fallen into the hands of the Arabs and been tortured by their women. He had himself seen wretched deserters dragged back by Goums,[38] a mass of rags, filth, blood and bruises; their manacled hands fastened to the end of a rope attached to an Arab's saddle. Inasmuch as the captor got twenty-five francs for returning a deserter, alive or dead, he merely tied the wounded, or starved and half-dead wretch to the end of a rope and galloped with him to the nearest outpost or barracks. When the Roumi[39] could no longer run, he was quite welcome to fall and be dragged.

Rupert had also gathered a fairly accurate idea of the conditions of life—if "life" it can be called—

---

[38] Arab gens d'armes.
[39] White man.

in the Penal Battalions.

Yes, on the whole, desertion from the Legion would be something in the nature of an adventure, when one considered the difficulties, risks, and dangers, which militated against success, and the nature of the punishment which attended upon failure. No wonder that desertion was regarded by all and sundry as being a feat of courage, skill and endurance to which attached no slightest stigma of disgrace! One gathered that most men "made the promenade" at some time or other—generally under the influence of *le cafard* in some terrible Southern desert-station, and were dealt with more or less leniently (provided they lost no articles of their kit) in view of the fact that successful desertion from such places was utterly impossible, and only attempted by them "while of unsound mind." Only once or twice, in the whole history of the Legion, had a man got clear away, obtained a camel, and, by some miracle of luck, courage and endurance, escaped death at the hands of the Arabs, thirst, hunger, and sunstroke, to reach the Moroccan border and take service with the Moors —who are the natural and hereditary enemies of the Touaregs and Bedouins.

Yes, he had begun to feel that he had certainly come to the end of a period of instruction and experience, and was in need of change to fresh fields and pastures new. Vegetating formed no part of his programme of life, which was far too short, in any case, for all there was to see and to do. . . .

Sitting one night on his cot, and talking to the man for whom he now had a very genuine and warm affection, he remarked—

"Don't you get fed up with Depôt life, Bull?"

"I have been fed up with life, Depôt and otherwise, for over twenty years," was the reply.   . . .

"Don't forget that life here in Sidi is a great deal better than life in a desert station in the South. It *is* supportable anyhow; there—it simply isn't; and those who don't desert and die, go mad and die. The exceptions, who do neither, deteriorate horribly, and come away very different men. . . . Make the most of Sidi, my boy, while you are here, and remember that foreign service, when in Tonkin, Madagascar, or Western Africa, inevitably means fever and dysentery, and generally broken health for life. . . . Moreover, Algeria is the only part of the French colonial possessions in which the climate lets one enjoy one's pipe."

That very night, shortly after the *caserne* had fallen silent and still, its inmates wrapped in the heavy sleep of the thoroughly weary, an alarm-bugle sounded in the barrack-square, and, a minute later, non-commissioned officers hurried from room to room, bawling, *"Aux armes! Aux armes! Aux armes!"* at the top of their voices.

Rupert sat up in his bed, as Corporal Achille Martel began to shout, *"Levez-vous donc. Levez-vous! Faites le sac! Faites le sac! En tenue de Campagne d'Afrique."*

" 'Ooray!" shrilled 'Erb. "Oo-bloomin'-ray."

"Buck up, Rupert," said John Bull. "We've got to be on the barrack-square in full 'African field equipment' in ten minutes."

The *chambrée* became the scene of feverish activity, as well as of delirious excitement and joy. In spite of it being the small hours of the morning, every man howled or whistled his own favourite song, without a sign of that liverish grumpiness which generally accompanies early-morning effort. The great Luigi's slaves worked at double pressure since they had to equip their lord and master as well as themselves. Feodor Kyrilovitch appeared to pack his own knapsack with one hand and that of

Mikhail with the other, while he whispered words of cheer and encouragement. The Dutch boy, Hans Djoolte, having finished his work, knelt down beside his bed and engaged in prayer. Speculation was rife as to whether France had declared war on Morocco, or whether the Arabs were in rebellion, for the hundredth time, and lighting the torch of destruction all along the Algerian border.

In ten minutes from the blowing of the alarm-bugle, the Battalion was on parade in the barrack-square, every man fully equipped and laden like a beast of burden. One thought filled every mind as the ammunition boxes were brought from the magazine and prised open. *What would the cardboard packets contain?* A few seconds after the first packet had been torn open by the first man to whom one was tossed, the news had spread throughout the Battalion.

Ball-Cartridge!

The Deity in that moment received the heartfelt fervid thanks of almost every man in the barrack-square, for ball-cartridge meant active service—in any case, a blessed thing, whatever might result— the blessing of death, of promotion, of decorations, of wounds and discharge from the Legion. The blessing of change to begin with.

There was one exception however. When Caporal Achille Martel "told off" Légionnaire Mikhail Kyrilovitch for orderly-duty to the *Adjudant Vaguemestre*,[40] duty which would keep him behind in barracks, that Legionary certainly contrived to conceal any disappointment that he may have felt.

A few minutes later the Legion's magnificent band struck up the Legion's march of "*Tiens, voilà*

---

[40] The postmaster.

du boudin," and the Battalion swung out of the gate, past the barracks of the Spahis, through the quiet sleeping streets into the main road, and so out of the town to which many of them never returned.

In the third row of fours of the Seventh Company marched the Bucking Bronco, John Bull, Reginald Rupert, and Herbert Higgins. In the row in front of them, Luigi Rivoli, Edouard Malvin, the Grasshopper, and Feodor Kyrilovitch. In the front row old Tant-de-Soif, Franz Josef Meyer, Tou-tou Boil-the-Cat, and Hans Djoolte. In front of them marched the four drummers. At the head of the Company rode Captain d'Armentières, beside whom walked Lieutenant Roberte.

Marching "at ease," the men discussed the probabilities and possibilities of the expedition. All the signs and tokens to be read by experienced soldier-eyes, were those of a long march and active service.

"It'll be a case of 'best foot foremost' a few hours hence, Rupert, I fancy," remarked John Bull. "I shouldn't be surprised if we put up thirty miles on end, with no halt but the 'cigarette spaces.'"

"Sure thing," agreed the Bucking Bronco. "I got a hunch we're gwine ter throw our feet some, to-day. We wouldn't hev' hiked off like this with sharp ammunition and made our get-away in quarter of an hour ef little Johnnie hadn't wanted the doctor. Well, I'm sorry fer the b'ys as ain't good mushers . . . Guess we shan't pound our ears[41] before we wants tew, this trip."

Marching along the excellent sandy road through the cool of the night, under a glorious moon, with the blood of youth, and health, and

---

[41] Sleep.

strength coursing like fire through his veins, it was difficult for Rupert to realise that, within a few hours, he would be wearily dragging one foot after the other, his rifle weighing a hundred-weight, his pack weighing a ton, his mouth a lime-kiln, his body one awful ache. He had had some pretty gruelling marches before, but this was the first time that the Battalion had gone out on a night alarm with ball-cartridge, and every indication of it being the "real thing."

On tramped the Legion.

Anon there was a whistle, a cry of *Halt!* and there was a few minutes' rest. Men lit cigarettes; some sat down; several fumbled at straps and endeavoured to ease packs by shifting them. Malvin made his master lie down after removing his pack altogether. It is a pack well worth removing—that of the Legion—save when seconds are too precious to be thus spent, and you consider it the wiser plan to fall flat and lie from the word *"Halt!"* to the word *"Fall in!"* The knapsack of black canvas is heavy with two full uniforms, underclothing, cleaning materials and sundries. Weighty tent-canvas and blankets are rolled round it, tent-supports are fastened at the side, firewood, a cooking-pot, drinking-mug and spare boots go on top.

Attached to his belt the Legionary carries a sword-bayonet with a steel scabbard, four hundred rounds of ammunition in his cartridge-pouches, an entrenching tool, and his "sac." Add his rifle and water-bottle, and you have the most heavily laden soldier in the world. He does not carry his overcoat—he wears it, and is perhaps unique in considering a heavy overcoat to be correct desert wear. Under his overcoat he has only a canvas shirt and white linen trousers (when *en tenue de campagne d'Afrique*), tucked into leather gaiters. Round his waist, his blue sash—four yards of woollen cloth—acts as an excellent cholera-belt and body-support. The linen neck-cloth, or *couvrenuque*, buttoned on to the white cover of his képi, protects his neck and ears, and, to some extent, his face, and prevents sunstroke. . . .

The Battalion marched on through the glorious dawn, gaily singing "*Le sac, ma foi, toujours au dos,*" and the old favourite marching songs "*Brigadier*," "*L'Empereur de Danmark*," "*Père Bugeaud*," and "*Tiens voilà du boudin*." Occasionally a German would lift up his splendid voice and soon more than half the battalion would be singing—

"Trinken wir noch ein Tröpfchen
Aus dem kleinen Henkeltöpfchen."

or *Die Wacht am Rhein* or the pathetic *Morgenlied*.

At the second halt, when some eight miles had been covered, there were few signs of fatigue, and more men remained standing than sat down. As the long column waited by the side of the road, a small cavalcade from the direction of Sidi-bel-Abbès overtook it. At the head rode a white-haired, white-moustached officer on whose breast sparkled and shone that rare and glorious decoration, the Grand Cross of the Legion of Honour.

"That's the Commander-in-Chief in Algeria," said John Bull to Rupert. "That settles it: we're out for business this time, and I fancy you'll see some Arab-fighting before you are much older. . . . Feet going to be all right, do you think?"

"Fine," replied Rupert. "My boots are half full of tallow, and I've got a small bottle of bapédi in my sack. . . ."

On tramped the Legion.

The day grew hot and packs grew heavy. The

Battalion undeniably and unashamedly slouched. Many men leant heavily forward against their straps, while some bent almost double, like coal-heavers carrying sacks of coal. Rifles changed frequently from right hand to left. There was no singing now. The only sound that came from dry-lipped, sticky mouths was an occasional bitter curse. Rupert began to wonder if his shoulder straps had not turned to wires. His arms felt numb, and the heavy weights, hung about his shoulders and waist, caused a feeling of constriction about the heart and lungs. He realised that he quite understood how people felt when they fainted. . . .

By the seventh halt, some forty kilometres, or twenty-seven miles lay behind the Battalion. At the word *Halt!* every man had thrown himself at full length on the sand, and very few wasted precious moments of the inexorably exact five minutes of the rest-period in removing knapsacks. Hardly a man spoke; none smoked.

On tramped the Legion.

Gone was all pretence of smartness and devil-may-care humour—that queer *macabre* and bitter humour of the Legion. Men slouched and staggered, and dragged their feet in utter hopeless weariness. Backs rounded more and more, heads sank lower, and those who limped almost outnumbered those who did not. A light push would have sent any man stumbling to the ground.

As the whistle blew for the next halt, the Legion sank to the ground with a groan, as though it would never rise again. As the whistle blew for the advance the Legion staggered to its feet as one man. . . . Oh, the Legion marches! Is not its motto, *"March or Die"*? The latter it may do, the former it must. The Legion has its orders and its destination, and it marches. If it did not reach its destination at the appointed time, it would be because it had died in getting there.

On tramped the Legion.

With horrible pains in its blistered shoulders, its raw-rubbed backs, its protesting, aching legs and blistered heels and toes, the Legion staggered on, a silent pitiable mass of suffering. Up and down the entire length of the Battalion rode its Colonel, "the Marching Pig." Every few yards he bawled with brazen throat and leathern lungs: "March or die, my children! March or die!" And the Legion clearly understood that it must march or it must die. To stagger from the ranks and fall was to die of thirst and starvation, or beneath the *flissa* of the Arab.

Legionary Rupert blessed those "Breakfasts of the Legion" and the hard training which achieved and maintained the hard condition of the Legionary. Sick, giddy, and worn-out as he felt, he knew he could keep going at least as long as the average, and by the time the average man had reached the uttermost end of his tether, the end of their march must be reached. After all, though they were Legionaries whose motto was "March or Die," they were only human beings—and to all human effort and endeavour there is a limit. He glanced at his comrades. The Bucking Bronco swung along erect, his rifle held across his shoulder by the muzzle, and his belt, with all its impedimenta, swinging from his right hand. He stared straight ahead and, with vacant mind and tireless iron body, "threw his feet."

Beside him, John Bull looked very white and worn and old. He leant heavily against the pull of his straps and marched with his chest bare. On Rupert's left, 'Erb, having unbuttoned and un- buckled everything unbuttonable and unbuck- leable, slouched along, a picture of slack unsoldierliness and of dauntless dogged endurance. Suddenly throwing up his head he screamed from parched lips, "Aw we dahn 'earted?" and, having painfully swallowed, answered his own strident question with a long-drawn, contemptuous "Ne—a—ow." Captain d'Armentières, who knew England and the English, looked round with a smile. . . . "Bon garçon," he nodded.

On the right of the second row of fours marched Luigi Rivoli, in better case than most, as the bulk of his kit was now impartially distributed among Malvin, Meyer, Tou-tou and Tant-de-Soif. (The power of money in the Legion is utterly incredible.) Feodor Kyrilovitch was carrying the Grasshopper's rifle—and that made a mighty difference toward the end of a thirty-mile march.

At the end of the next halt, the Grasshopper declared that he could not get up. . . . At the command, "Fall in!" the unfortunate man did not stir.

"Kind God! What *shall* I do?" he groaned. It was his first failure as a soldier.

"Come on, my lad," said John Bull sharply. "Here, pull off his kit," he added and unfastened the Belgian's belt. Between them they pulled him to his feet and dragged him to his place in the ranks. John Bull took his pack, the Bucking Bronco his belt and its appurtenances, and Feodor his rifle. His eyes were closed and he sank to the ground.

"Here," said Rupert to 'Erb. "Get in his place and let him march in yours beside me. We'll hold him up."

"Give us yer rifle, matey," replied 'Erb, and left Rupert with hands free to assist the Grasshopper.

With his right arm round the Belgian's waist, he helped him along, while John Bull insisted on having the poor fellow's right hand on his left shoulder.

On tramped the Legion.

Before long, almost the whole weight of the Grasshopper's body was on Rupert's right arm and John Bull's left shoulder.

"Stick to it, my son," said the latter from time to time, "we are sure to stop at the fifty-kilometre stone."

The Belgian seemed to be semiconscious, and did not reply. His feet began to drag, and occasionally his two comrades bore his full weight for a few paces. Every few yards Feodor looked anxiously round. These four, in their anxiety for their weaker brother, forgot their own raw thighs, labouring lungs, inflamed eyes, numbed arms and agonising feet.

Just as the Colonel rode by, the Grasshopper's feet ceased to move, and dragged lifeless along the ground.

Rupert stumbled and the three fell in a heap, beneath the Colonel's eye.

"*Sacré Baptême!*" he swore—the oath he only used when a Legionary fell out on the march— "March or die, accursed pigs."

Rupert and John Bull staggered to their feet, but the Grasshopper lay apparently lifeless. The Colonel swore again, and shouted an order. The Grasshopper was dragged to the side of the road, and a baggage-cart drove up. A tent-pole was thrust through its sides and tied securely. To this pole the Belgian was lashed, the pole passing across the upper part of his back and under his arms, which were pulled over it and tied together. If he could keep his feet, well and good. If he could not, he would hang from the pole by his arms (as an athlete hangs from a parallel-bar in a gymnasium, before revolving round and round it).

On tramped the Legion.

Before long, the Grasshopper's feet dragged in the dust as he drooped inanimate, and then hung in the rope which lashed him to the pole.

At the fifty-fifth kilometre, thirty-five miles from Sidi-bel-Abbès, the command to halt was followed by the thrice-blessed God-sent order:

"*Campez!*"

Almost before the words, "*Formez les faisceaux*" were out of the Company-Commanders' mouths, the men had piled arms. Nor was the order "*Sac à terre*" obeyed in any grudging spirit. In an incredibly short space of time the jointed tent-poles and canvas had been removed from the knapsacks. Corporals of sections had stepped forward, holding the tent-poles above their heads, marking each Company's tent-line, and a city of small white tents had come into being on the face of the desert. A few minutes later, cooking-trenches had been dug, camp-fires lighted and water, containing meat and macaroni, put on to boil.

A busy and profitable hour followed for Madame la Cantinière, who, even as her cart stopped, had set out her folding tables, benches and bar for the sale of her Algerian wine. Her first customer was the great Luigi, who, thanks to Carmelita's money, could sit and drink while his employees did his work. The fly in the worthy man's ointment was the fact that his Italian dinner and Italian wine were thirty-five miles behind him at Carmelita's café. Like ordinary men, he must, to-night and for many a night to come, content himself with the monotonous and meagre fare of common Legionaries. However—better half a sofa than no bed; and he was easily prime favourite with Madame. . . . This would be an excellent chance for consolidating his position with her, winning her for his bride, and apprising Carmelita, from afar, of the fact that he was now respectably settled in life. Thus would a disagreeable scene be avoided and, on the return of the Battalion to Sidi-bel-Abbès, he would give the Café de la Légion a wide berth. . . . Could he perhaps *sell* his rights and goodwill in the café and Carmelita to some Legionary of means? One or two of his own *chambrée* seemed to have money—the Englishman; the Russians. . . . Better still, sell out to Malvin, Toutou, Meyer, or some other penniless toady and *make him pay a weekly percentage* of what he screwed out of Carmelita. Excellent! And if the scoundrel did not get him enough, he would supplant him with a more competent lessee. . . . Meanwhile, to storm Madame's experienced and undecided heart. Anyhow, if she wouldn't have Luigi she shouldn't have anyone else. . . .

There was, that evening, exceeding little noise and movement, and "the stir and tread of armed camps." As soon as they had fed—and, in many cases, before they had fed—the soldiers lay on their blankets, their heads on their knapsacks and their overcoats over their bodies.

Scarcely, as it seemed to Rupert, had they closed their eyes, when it was time to rise and resume their weary march. At one o'clock in the morning, the Battalion fell in, and each man got his two litres of water and strict orders to keep one quarter of it for to-morrow's cooking purposes. If he contributed no water to the cooking-cauldron he got no cooked food.

On tramped the Legion.

Day after day, day after day, it marched, and, on the twelfth day from Sidi-bel-Abbès, had covered nearly three hundred and fifty miles. Well might the Legion be known in the Nineteenth Division as the *Cavalerie à pied.*

§2

Life for the Seventh Company of the First Battalion of the Legion in Aïnargoula was, as John Bull had promised Rupert, simply hell. Not even the relief of desert warfare had broken the cruel monotony of desert marches and life in desert stations—stations consisting of red-hot barracks, and the inevitable filthy and sordid *Village Négre*. Men lived—and sometimes died—in a state of unbearable irritation and morose savageness. Fights were frequent, suicide not infrequent, and murders not unknown. *Cafard* reigned supreme. The punishment-cells were overcrowded night and day, and abortive desertions occurred with extraordinary frequency.

The discontent and sense of wasted time, which had begun to oppress Rupert at Sidi-bel-Abbès, increased tenfold. To him and to the Bucking Bronco (who daily swore that he would desert that night, and tramp to Sidi-bel-Abbès to see Carmelita) John Bull proved a friend in need. Each afternoon, during that terrible time between eleven and three, when the incredible heat of the barrack-room made it impossible for any work to be done, and the men, by strict rule, were compelled to lie about on their cots, it was John Bull who found his friends something else to think about than their own sufferings and miseries.

A faithful coadjutor was 'Erb, who, with his mouth-organ and Jew's-harp, probably saved the reason, or the life, of more than one man. 'Erb seemed to feel the heat less than bigger men, and he would sit cross-legged upon his mattress, evoking tuneful strains from his beloved instruments when far stronger men could only lie panting like distressed dogs. Undoubtedly the three Englishmen and the American exercised a restraining and beneficial influence, inasmuch as they interfered as one man (following the lead of John Bull, the oldest soldier in the room) whenever a quarrel reached the point of blows, in their presence. . . . Under those conditions of life and temper a blow is commonly but the prelude to swift homicide.

One terrible afternoon, as the Legionaries lay on their beds, almost naked, in that stinking oven, the suddenness of these tragedies was manifested. It was too hot to play *bloquette* or *foutrou*, too hot to sing, too hot to smoke, too hot to do anything, and the hot bed positively burnt one's bare back. The Bucking Bronco lay gasping, his huge chest rising and falling with painful rapidity. John Bull was showing Rupert a wonderfully and beautifully Japanese-tattooed serpent which wound twice round his wrist and ran up the inner side of his white forearm, its head and expanded hood filling the hollow of his elbow. Rupert, who would have liked to copy it, was wondering how its brilliant colours had been achieved and had remained undimmed for over thirty-five years, as John Bull said was the case, it having been done at Nagasaki when he was a midshipman on the *Narcissus*. It was too hot even for 'Erb to make music and he lay fanning himself with an ancient copy of the *Echo d'Oran*. It was too hot to sleep, save in one or two cases, and these men groaned, moaned and rolled their heads as they snored. It was too hot to quarrel—almost. But not quite. Suddenly the swift *zweeep* of a bayonet being snatched from its steel scabbard hissed through the room, and all eyes turned to where Legionary Franz Josef Meyer flashed his bayonet from his sheath and, almost in the same movement, drove it up through the throat of the Greek, Dimitropoulos, and into his brain.

"Take that, you scum of the Levant," he said, and then stared, wide-eyed and open-mouthed, at his handiwork. There had been bad blood between the men for some time, and for days the Austrian had accused the Greek of stealing a piece of his wax. Some taunt of the dead man had completed the work of *le cafard.* . . .

That night Meyer escaped from the cells—and his body, three days later, was delivered up in return for the twenty-five francs paid for a live or dead deserter. It would perhaps be more accurate to say that parts of his body were brought in—sufficient, at any rate, for identification.

He had fallen into the hands of the Arabs.

To give the Arabs their due, however, they saved the situation. Just when Legionary John Bull had begun to give up hope, and nightly to dread what the morrow might bring forth for his friends and himself, the Arabs attacked the post. The strain on the over-stretched cord was released and men who, in another day, would have been temporarily or permanently raving madmen, were saved.

The attack was easily beaten off and without loss to the Legionaries, firing from loopholes and behind stone walls.

On the morrow, a reconnaissance toward the nearest oasis discovered their camp and, on the next day, a tiny punitive column set forth from Aïnargoula—the Legionaries as happy, to use Rupert's too appropriate simile, as sand-boys. Like everybody else, he was in the highest spirits. Gone was the dark shadow of *le cafard* and the feeling that, unless something happened, he would become a homicidal maniac and run amuck.

Here was the "real thing." Here was that for which he had been so long and so drastically trained—desert warfare. He thrilled from head to foot with excitement, and wondered whether the day would bring forth one of the famous and terrible Arab cavalry charges, and whether he would have his first experience of taking part in the mad and fearful joy of a bayonet charge. Anyhow, there was a chance of either or both.

The Company marched on at its quickest, alternating five minutes of swift marching with five minutes of the *pas gymnastique*, the long, loping stride which is the "double" of the Legion.

Far ahead marched a small advance-guard; behind followed a rear-guard, and, well out on either side, marched the flankers. Where a sandy ridge ran parallel with the course of the Company, the flankers advanced along the crest of it, that they might watch the country which lay beyond. This did not avail them much, for, invariably, such a ridge was paralleled by a similar one at no great distance. To have rendered the little Company absolutely secure against sudden surprise-attack on either flank, would have necessitated sending out the majority of the force for miles on either side. Rupert, ever keen and deeply interested in military matters, talked of this with John Bull, who agreed with him that, considerable as the danger of such an attack was, it could not be eliminated.

"Anyhow," concluded he, "we generally get something like at least five hundred yards' margin and if the Arabs can cut us up while we have that—they deserve to. Still, it's tricky country I admit, with all these *wadis* and folds in the ground, as well as rocks and ridges."

On marched the Company, and reached an area of rolling sand-hills, and loose heavy sand under foot.

The day grew terribly hot and the going terribly heavy. As usual, all pretence and semblance of smart marching had been abandoned, and the men marched in whatever posture, attitude or style seemed to them best. . . .

. . . It came with the suddenness of a thunder-clap on a fine day, at a moment when practically everything but the miseries of marching through loose sand in the hottest part of one of the hottest days of the year had faded from the minds of the straining, labouring men.

A sudden shout, followed by the firing of half a dozen shots, brought the column automatically to a halt and drew all eyes to the right.

From a wide shallow *wadi*, or a fold in the ground, among the sand-hills a few hundred yards away, an avalanche of *haik* and *djellab*-clad men on swift horses suddenly materialised and swept down like a whirlwind on the little force. Behind them, followed a far bigger mass of camel-riders howling *"Ul-Ul-Ullah-Akbar!"* as they came. Almost before the column had halted, a couple of barks from Lieutenant Roberte turned the Company to the right in two ranks, the front rank kneeling, the rear rank standing close up behind it, with bayo-nets fixed and magazines charged . . . Having fired their warning shots, the flankers were running for their lives to join the main body. The Company watched and waited in grave silence. It was Lieutenant Roberte's intention that, when the Arabs broke and fled before the Company's withering blast of lead, they should leave the maximum number of "souvenirs" behind them. His was the courage and nerve that is tempered and enhanced by imperturbable coolness. He would let the charging foe gallop to the very margin of safety for his Legionaries. To turn them back at fifty yards would be much more profitable than to do it at five hundred.

Trembling with excitement and the thrilling

desire for violent action, Rupert knelt between John Bull and the Bucking Bronco, scarcely able to await the orders to fire and charge. Before any order came he saw a sight that for a moment sickened and shook him, a sight which remained before his eyes for many days. Corporal Auguste Gilles, who was commanding the flankers, either too weary or too ill to continue his sprint for comparative safety, turned and faced the thundering rush of the oncoming Arab *harka*, close behind him. Kneeling by a prickly pear or cactus bush he threw up his rifle and emptied his magazine into the swiftly rushing ranks that were almost upon him. As he fired his last shot, an Arab, riding ahead of the rest, lowered his lance and, with a cry of "*Kelb ibn kelb*,"[42] bent over towards him. Springing to his feet the Corporal gamely charged with his bayonet. There can be only one end to such a combat when the horseman knows his weapon. The Corporal was sent flying into the cactus, impaled upon the Arab's lance, and, as it was withdrawn as the horseman swept by, the horrified Rupert saw his comrade stagger to his feet and totter forward—tethered to the cactus by his own entrails. Happily, a second later, the sweep of an Arab *flissa* almost severed his head from his shoulders. . . .

The Company stood firm and silent as a rock, the shining bayonets still and level. Just as it seemed to Rupert that it must be swept away and every man share the fate of that mangled lump of clay in front (for there is no more nerve-shaking spectacle than cavalry charging down upon you like a living avalanche or flood) one word rang out from Lieutenant Roberte.

When the crashing rattle (like mingled, tearing

---

[42] Dog—and son of a dog.

thunder and the wild hammer of hail upon a corrugated iron roof), ceased as magazines were emptied almost simultaneously, the Arabs were in flight at top speed, leaving two-thirds of their number on the plain; and upon the fleeing *harka* the Company made very pretty shooting—for the Legion shoots as well as it marches.

When the "Cease Fire" whistle had blown, Rupert remarked to John Bull—

"No chance for a bayonet charge, then?" to which the old soldier replied—

"No, my son, that is a pleasure to which the Arab does not treat us, unless we surprise his sleeping *douar* at dawn. . . ."

The Arabs having disappeared beyond the horizon, the Company camped and bivouacked on the battle-field, resuming its march at midnight. As Lieutenant Roberte feared and expected, the oasis which was surrounded and attacked at dawn, was found to be empty.

The Company marched back to Aïnargoula and, a few days later, returned to Sidi-bel-Abbès.

CHAPTER VII

THE SHEEP IN WOLF'S CLOTHING

Légionnaire John Bull sat on the edge of his cot at the hour of *astiquage*. Though his body was in the *chambrée* of the Seventh Company, his mind, as usual, was in England, and his thoughts, as usual, played around the woman whom he knew as Marguerite, and the world as Lady Huntingten.

What *could* he do next year when his third and last period of Legion service expired? Where could he possibly hide in such inviolable anonymity that there was no possible chance of any rumour arising that the dead Sir Montague Merline was in the land of the living? . . . How had it happened that he had survived the wounds and disease that he had suffered in Tonkin, Madagascar, Dahomey, and the Sahara—the stake-trap pit into which he had fallen at Nha-Nam—the bullet in his neck from the Malagasy rifle—the hack from the *coupe-coupe* which had split his collar-bone in that ghastly West African jungle—the lance-thrust that had torn his arm from elbow to shoulder at Elsefra?

It was an absolute and undeniable fact that the man who desired to die in battle could never do it; while he who had everything to live for, was among the first to fall. If they went South again to-morrow and were cut up in a sudden Arab *razzia*, he would be the sole survivor. But if a letter arrived on the previous day, stating that Lord Huntingten was dead leaving no children, and that Lady Huntingten had just heard of his survival and longed for his return—would he survive that fight? Most certainly not.

What to do at the end of the fifteenth year of his service? His face had been far too well known among the class of people who passed through Marseilles to India and elsewhere—who winter on the Riviera, who golf at Biarritz, who recuperate at Vichy or Aix, who go to Paris in the Spring; and who, in short, are to be found in various parts of France at various times of the year—for him to dream of using the Legion's free pass to any part of France. The risk might be infinitesimal, but it existed, and he would run no risk of ruining Marguerite's life, after more than twenty-five years.

She must be over forty-five now. . . . Had time dealt kindly with her? Was she as beautiful as ever? Sure to be. Marguerite was of the type that would ripen, mature, and improve until well on into middle life. Who was the eminent man who said that a woman was not interesting until she was forty? . . .

What would he not give for a sight of Marguerite? It would be easy enough, next year. Only next year—and it was a thousand to one, a million to one, against anyone recognising him if he were well disguised and thoroughly careful. Just one sight of Marguerite—after more than twenty-five years! Had he not made sacrifices enough? Might he not take *that* much reward for half a lifetime of life in death—a lifetime in which his body dragged wretchedly and wearily along among the dregs of the earth, while his mind haunted the home of his wife, a home in which another man was lord and master. Was it much to ask—one glimpse of his wife after twenty-seven years of renunciation?

"Miserable, selfish cur!" he murmured aloud as he melted a piece of wax in the flame of a match. "You would risk the happiness of your wife, your

old friend, and their children—all absolutely innocent of wrong—for the sake of a minute's self-
indulgence. . . . Be ashamed of yourself, you
whining weakling. . . ."

It had become a habit of Légionnaire John Bull
to talk to himself aloud, when alone—a habit he
endeavoured to check as he had recently, on more
than one occasion, found himself talking aloud in
the company of others.

Having finished the polishing of his leatherwork, he took his Lebel rifle from the rack and
commenced to clean it. As he threw open the
chamber, he paused, the bolt in his right hand,
the rifle balanced in his left. Someone was running with great speed along the corridor toward
the room. What was up? Was it a case of *Faites le
sac?* Would the head of an excited and delighted
Legionary be thrust in at the door with a yell of—
"*Aux armes! Faites le sac*"?

The door burst open and in rushed Mikhail
Kyrilovitch, bare-headed, coatless, with staring
eyes and blanched cheeks.

"Save me, save me, Monsieur," he shrieked,
rushing towards the old Legionary. "Save me—*I
am a woman.* . . ."

"Good God!" ejaculated Legionary John Bull,
involuntarily glancing from the face to the flat
chest of the speaker.

"I am a girl," sobbed the *soi-disant* Mikhail. . . .
"I am a girl. . . . And that loathsome beast Luigi
Rivoli has found me out. . . . He's coming. . . . He
chased me. . . . What shall I do? What *shall* I do?
Poor Feodor. . . ."

As Légionnaire Luigi Rivoli entered the room,
panting slightly with his unwonted exertions, the
girl crouched behind John Bull, her face in her
hands, her body shaken by deep sobs. It had all
happened so quickly that John Bull found himself

standing with his gun balanced, still in the attitude into which he had frozen on hearing the running feet without.

So it had come, had it—and he was to try conclusions with Luigi Rivoli at last? Well, it should be no inconclusive rough-and-tumble. Perhaps this was the solution of his problem, and might settle, once and for all, the question of his future?

"Ho-ho! Ho-ho!" roared the Neapolitan, "she's your girl, is she, you *aristocratico Inglese?* Ho-ho! You are *faisant Suisse* are you? Ho-ho! Your own private girl in the very *chambrée!* Corpo di Bacco! You shall learn the penalty for breaking the Legion's first law of share-and-share-alike. Get out of my way, *cane Inglese.*"

John Bull closed the breech of his rifle, and pointed the weapon at Rivoli's broad breast.

"Stand back," he said quietly. "Stand back, you foul-mouthed scum of Naples, or I'll blow your dirty little soul out of your greasy carcase." He raised his voice slightly. "Stand back, you dog, do you hear?" he added, advancing slightly towards his opponent.

Luigi Rivoli gave ground. The rifle might be loaded. You never knew with these cursed, quiet Northerners, with their cold, pale eyes. . . . The rifle might be loaded. . . . Rivoli was well aware that every Legionary makes it his business to steal a cartridge sooner or later, and keeps it by him for emergencies, be they of suicide, murder, self-defence, or desertion. . . . The Englishman had been standing in the attitude of one who loads a rifle at the moment of his entrance. Perhaps his girl had told him of the discovery and assault, and he had been loading the rifle to avenge her.

"Listen to me, Luigi Rivoli," said John Bull, still holding the rifle within a foot of the Italian's breast. "Listen, and I'll tell you what you are. Then

I will tell the Section what you are, when they come in. . . . Then I will tell the whole Company. . . . Then I will stand on a table in the Canteen and shout it, night after night. . . . This is what you are. You are a coward. A *coward*, d'you hear? —a miserable, shrinking, frightened coward, who dare not fight. . . ."

"Fight! *Iddio! Fight!* Put down that rifle and I'll tear you limb from limb. Come down into the square and I will break your back. Come down now—and fight for the girl."

". . . A trembling, frightened *coward* who dare not fight, and who calls punching, and hugging and kicking 'fighting.' I challenge you to fight, Luigi Rivoli, with rifles—at one hundred yards and no cover; or with revolvers, at ten paces; or with swords of any sort or kind—if it's only sword-bayonets. Will you fight, or will you be known as *Rivoli the Coward* throughout both Battalions of the Legion?"

Rivoli half-crouched for a spring, and straightway the rifle sprang to the Englishman's shoulder, as his eyes blazed and his fingers fell round the trigger. Rivoli recoiled.

"I don't want to shoot you, unarmed, Coward," he said quietly. "I am going to shoot you, or stab you, or slash you, in fair fight—or else you shall kneel and be christened *Rivoli the Coward* on the barrack square. . . . I've had enough of you, and so has everybody—unless it's your gang of pimps. . . . Now go. Go on—get out. . . . Go on—before I lose patience. Clear out—and make up your mind whether you will fight or be christened."

"Oh, I'll fight you—you mangy old cur. You are brave enough with a loaded rifle, eh? Mother of Christ! I'll send you where the birds won't trouble you. . . . Shoot me in the back as I go, Brave Man with a Gun"—and Luigi Rivoli departed, in a state of horrid doubt and perturbation. . . . This cursed Englishman meant what he said. . . .

Legionary John Bull lowered his rifle with a laugh, and became aware of the fact that the Russian girl was hugging his leg in a way which would have effectually hampered him in the event of a struggle, and which made him feel supremely ridiculous.

"Get up, *petite*," he said bending over her, as she lay moaning and weeping. "It's all right—he's gone. He won't trouble you again, for I am going to kill him. Come and lie on your bed and tell me all about it. . . . We must make up our minds as to what will be the best thing to do. . . . Rivoli will tell everybody."

He helped the girl to her feet, partly led and partly carried her to her bed, and laid her on it.

Holding his lean brown hand between her little ones, in a voice broken and choked with sobs, she told him something of her story—a sad little story all too common.

The listener gathered that the two were children of a prominent revolutionary who had disappeared into Siberia, after what they considered a travesty of a trial. They had been students at the University of Moscow, and had followed in their father's political footsteps from the age of sixteen. Their youth and inexperience, their fanatical enthusiasm, and their unselfish courage, had, in a few years, brought them to a point at which they must choose between death or the horrors of prison and Siberia on the one hand, and immediate flight, and most complete and utter evanishment on the other. When his beloved twin sister had been chosen by the Society as an "instrument," Feodor's heart had failed him. He had disobeyed the orders of the Central Committee; he had coerced the girl; he had made disclosures.

They had escaped to Paris. Before long it had been a question as to whether they were in more imminent and terrible danger from the secret agents of the Russian police or from those of the Nihilists. The sight of the notice, *"Bureau de recruitment. Engagements volontaires,"* over the door of a dirty little house in the Rue St. Dominique had suggested the Légion Étrangère, and a possible means of escape and five years' safety.

But the Medical Examination? . . .

Accompanied by a fellow-fugitive who was on his way to America, Feodor had gone to the Bureau and they had enlisted, passed the doctor, and received railway-passes to Marseilles, made out in the names of Feodor and Mikhail Kyrilovitch; sustenance money; and orders to proceed by the night train from the Gare de Lyons and report at Fort St. Jean in the morning, if not met at the station by a Sergeant of the Legion. Their compatriot had handed his travelling warrant to the girl (dressed in a suit of Feodor's) and had seen the twins off at the Gare de Lyons with his blessing. . . .

Monsieur Jean Boule knew the rest, and but for this hateful, bestial Luigi Rivoli, all might have been well, for she was very strong, and had meant to be very brave. Now, what should she do; what *should* she do? . . . And what would poor Feodor say when he came in from corvée and found that she had let herself get caught like this at last? . . . What could they do?

And indeed, Sir Montague Merline did not know what a lady could do when discovered in a *chambrée* of a *caserne* of the French Foreign Legion in Sidi-bel-Abbès. He did not know in the least. There was first the attitude of the authorities to consider, and then that of the men. Would a Court Martial hold that, having behaved as a man, she should be treated as one, and kept to her bargain, or sent to join the Zephyrs? Would they imprison her for fraud? Would they repatriate her? Would they communicate with the Russian police? Or would they just fling her out of the barrack-gate and let her go? There was probably no precedent, whatever, to go upon.

And supposing the matter were hushed up in the *chambrée*, and the authorities never knew—would life be livable for the girl? Could he, and Rupert, the Bucking Bronco, Herbert Higgins, Feodor, and perhaps one or two of the more decent foreigners, such as Hans Djoolte, and old Tant-de-Soif, ensure her a decent life, free from molestation and annoyance? No, it couldn't be done. Life would be rendered utterly impossible for her by gross animals of the type of Rivoli, Malvin, the *Apache*, Hirsch, Bauer, Borges, and the rest of Rivoli's sycophants. It was sufficiently ghastly, and almost unthinkable, to imagine a woman in that sink when nobody dreamed she was anything but what she seemed. How could one contemplate a woman, who was *known* to be a woman, living her life, waking and sleeping, in such a situation? The more devotedly her bodyguard shielded and protected her, the more venomously determined would the others be to annoy, insult and injure her in a thousand different ways. It would be insupportable, impossible. . . . But of course it could not be kept from the authorities for a week. What was to be done?

As he did his utmost to soothe the weeping girl, clumsily patting her back, stroking her hands, and murmuring words of comfort and promises of protection, Merline longed for the arrival of Rupert. He wanted to take counsel with another English gentleman as to the best thing to be done for this unfortunate woman. He dared not leave her weeping there alone. Anybody might enter at any moment. Rivoli might return with the choicest scoundrels of his gang. . . . Why did not the Bucking Bronco turn up? When he and Rupert arrived there would be an accession of brawn and of brains that would be truly welcome.

Curiously enough, Sir Montague Merline's insular Englishness had survived fourteen years of life in a cosmopolitan society, speaking a foreign tongue in a foreign land, with such indestructible sturdiness that it was upon the Anglo-Saxon party that he mentally relied in this strait. He had absolutely forgotten that it was the girl's own brother who was her natural protector, and upon whom lay the onus of discovering the solution of this insoluble problem and extricating the girl from her terrible position.

What could he do? It was all very well to say that the three Englishmen and the American would protect her, that night, by forming a sentry-group and watching in turn—but how long could that go on? It would be all over the barracks to-morrow, and known to the authorities a few hours later. Oh, if he could only do her up in a parcel and post her to Marguerite with just a line, "*Please take care of this poor girl.—Monty.*" Marguerite would keep her safe enough. . . . But thinking nonsense wasn't helping. He would load his rifle in earnest, and settle scores with Luigi Rivoli, once and for all, if he returned with a gang to back him. Incidentally, that would settle his own fate, for it would mean a Court Martial at Oran followed by a firing-party, or penal servitude in the Zephyrs, and, at his age, that would only be a slower death.

All very well for him and Rivoli, but what of the girl? . . . What ghastly danger it must have been that drove them to such a dreadful expedient. Truly the Legion was a net for queer fish. Poor, plucky little soul, what could he do for her?

Never since he wore the two stars[43] of a British Captain had he longed, as he did at that moment, for power and authority. If only he were a Captain again, Captain of the Seventh Company, the girl should go straight to his wife, or some other woman. Suddenly he rose to his feet, his face illuminated by the brilliance of the idea which had suddenly entered his mind.

"*Carmelita!*" he almost shouted to the empty room. He bent over the crying girl again, and shook her gently by the shoulder.

"I have it, little one," he said. "Thank God! Yes—it's a chance. I believe I have a plan. Carmelita! Let's get out of this at once, straight to the Café de la Legion. Carmelita has a heart of gold. . . ."

The girl half sat up. "She may be a kind girl—but she's Luigi Rivoli's mistress," she said. "She would do anything he ordered."

"Carmelita considers herself Rivoli's wife," replied the Englishman, "and so she would be, if he were not the biggest blackguard unhung. Very well, he can hardly go to the woman who is practically his wife and say, 'Hand over the woman you are hiding.'"

"When a woman loves a man she obeys him," said the girl, and added with innocent naïveté, "And I will obey you, Monsieur Jean Boule. . . . Anyhow, it *is* a hope—in a position which is hopeless."

"Get into walking-out kit quickly," urged the old soldier, "and see the Sergeant of the Guard has no excuse for turning you back. The sooner we're away the better. . . . I wish Rupert and the Bronco would roll up. . . . If you can get to

---

[43] Since increased to three, of course.

Carmelita's unseen, and change back into a girl, you could either hide with Carmelita for a time, or simply desert in feminine apparel."

"And Feodor?" asked the Russian. "Will they shoot him? I can't leave . . ."

"Bother Feodor," was the quick reply. "One soldier is not responsible because another deserts. Let's get you safe to Carmelita's, and then I'll find Feodor and tell him all about it."

Hiram Cyrus Milton, entering the room bare-footed and without noise, was not a little surprised to behold a young soldier fling his arms about the neck of the eminently staid and respectable Legionary John Bull, with a cry of—

"Oh, may God reward you, kind good Monsieur."

"Strike me blue and balmy," ejaculated the Bucking Bronco. "Ain't these gosh-dinged furrin-ers a bunch o' boobs? Say, John, air yew his long-lost che-ild? It's a cinch. Where's that dod-gasted boy 'Erb fer slow music on the jewzarp? . . . Or is the lalapaloozer only a-smellin' the roses on yure damask cheek?"

"Change quickly, *petite*," said John Bull to the girl as he pushed her from him, and turned to the American.

"Come here, Buck," said he, taking the big man's arm and leading him to the window.

"Don't say as haow yure sins hev' come home to roost, John? Did yew reckernise the puling infant by the di'mond coronite on the locket, or by the strawberry-mark in the middle of its back? Or was his name wrote on the tail of his little shirt? Put me next to it, John. Make me wise to the secret mystery of this 'ere drarmer."

The Bucking Bronco was getting more than a little jealous.

"I will, if you will give me a chance," replied

John Bull curtly. "Buck, that boy's a girl. Rivoli has found her out and acted as you might expect. I suppose he spotted her in the wash-house or somewhere. She rushed to me for protection, and the game's up. I am going to take her to Carmelita."

The big American stared at his friend with open mouth.

"Yew git me jingled, John," he said slowly. "Thet little looker a *gal?* Is this a story made out of whole cloth,[44] John?"

"Get hold of it, Buck, quickly," was the reply. "The two Russians are political refugees. Their number was up, in Russia, and they bolted to Paris. Same in Paris—and they made a dash for here. Out of the frying-pan into the fire. This one's a girl. Luigi Rivoli knows, and it will be all over the barracks before to-night. She rushed straight to me, and I am going to see her through. If you can think of anything better than taking her to Carmelita, say so."

"I'll swipe the head off'n Mister Lousy Loojey Rivoli," growled the American. "God smite me ef I don't. Thet's torn it, thet has. . . . The damned yaller-dog Dago. . . . Thet puts the lid on Mister Loojey Rivoli, thet does."

"*I'm* going to deal with Rivoli, Buck," said John Bull.

"He'd crush yew with a b'ar's hug, sonny; he'd bust in yure ribs, an' break yure back, an' then chuck yew down and dance on yew."

"He won't get the chance, Buck; it's not going to be a gutter-scrap. When he chased the girl in here I challenged him to fight with bullet or steel, and told him I'd brand him all over the shop till he was known as 'Rivoli the Coward,' or fought a fair

---

[44] Untrue.

and square duel. . . . Let's get the girl out of this, and then we'll put Master Luigi Rivoli in his place once and for all."

"Shake!" said the Bucking Bronco, extending a huge hand.

"Seen Rupert lately?" asked the Englishman.

"Yep," replied the other. "He's a-settin' on end a-rubberin' at his pants in the lavabo."

"Good! Go and fetch him quick, Buck."

The American sped from the room without glancing at the girl, returning a minute or two later with Rupert. The two men hurried to their respective cots and swiftly changed from fatigue-dress into blue and red.

"If Carmelita turns us down, let's all three desert and take the girl with us," said Rupert to John Bull. "I have plenty of money to buy mufti, disguises, and railway tickets. She would go as a woman of course. We could be a party of tourists. Yes, that's it, English tourists. Old Mendoza would fit us out—at a price."

"Thanks," was the reply. "We'll get her out somehow. . . . She'd stand a far better chance alone though, probably. If suspicion fell on one of us they'd arrest the lot."

"Say," put in the American. "Ef she can do the boy stunt, I reckon as haow her brother oughter be able ter do the gal stunt ekally well. Ef Carmelita takes her in, and fits her out with two of everything, her brother could skedaddle and jine her, and put on the remainder of the two-of-every-thing; then they ups and goes on pump as the Twin Sisters Golightly, a-tourin' of the Crowned Heads of Yurrup, otherwise, as The Twin Roosian Bally-Gals Skiporfski. . . ."

"Smart idea," agreed Rupert. "I hope Carmelita takes her in. What the devil shall we do with her if she won't? She can't very well spend the night here after Luigi has put it about. . . . And what's her position with regard to the authorities? Is it a case of Court Martial or toss for her in the Officers' Mess, or what?"

"Don't know, I'm sure. Haven't the faintest idea," replied John Bull. "If only Carmelita turns up trumps. . . ."

"Seenyoreena Carmelita is the whitest little woman as ever lived," growled the American. "She's a blowed-in-the-glass heart-o'-gold. Yew can put yure shirt on Carmelita. . . . Yew know what I mean—yure bottom dollar. . . . Ef it wasn't fer that filthy Eye-talian sarpint, she'd jump at the chance of giving this Roosian gal her last crust. . . . I don't care John whether you shoot him up or nit. I'm gwine ter slug him till Hell pops. Let him fight his dirtiest an' damnedest—I'll see him and raise him every time, the double-dealin' gorilla. . . ."

"I am ready, Monsieur," said the girl Olga to John Bull. "But I do not want you, Monsieur, nor these other gentlemen, to make trouble for your-selves on my account. . . . I have brought this on myself, and there is no reason why you . . ."

"Oh, shucks! Come on, little gal," broke in the Bucking Bronco. "We'll see yew through. We ain't Loojeys. . . ."

"Of course, we will. We shall be only too delighted," agreed Rupert. "Don't you worry."

"Pull yourself together and swagger all you can," advised John Bull. "It might ruin everything if the Sergeant of the Guard took it into his head to turn you back. I wonder if we had better go through in a gang, or let you go first? If we are all together there is less likelihood of excessive scrutiny of any one of us, but on the other hand it may be remembered that you were last seen with us three, and that might hamper our future

usefulness. . . . Just as well Feodor isn't here. . . .
Tell you what, you and I will go out together, and
I'll use my wits to divert attention from you if we
are stopped. The others can come a few minutes
later, or as soon as someone else has passed."

"That's it," agreed Rupert; "come on."

With beating hearts, the old soldier and the
young girl approached the little side door by the
huge barrack-gates. Close by it stood the Sergeant
of the Guard. Their anxiety increased as they
realised that it was none other than Sergeant
Legros, one of the most officious, domineering and
brutal of the Legion's N.C.O.'s. Luck was against
them. He would take a positive delight in standing
by that door the whole evening and in turning
back every single man whose appearance gave him
the slightest opportunity for fault-finding, as well
as a good many whose appearance did not.

As they drew near and saluted smartly, the
little piggish eyes of Sergeant Legros took in every
detail of their uniform. The girl felt the blood
draining from her cheeks. What if they had made
a mistake? What if red trousers and blue tunic
should be wrong, and the *ordre du jour* should be
white trousers and blue tunic or capote? What if
she had a button undone or her bayonet on the
wrong side? What if Sergeant Legros should see,
or imagine a speck upon her tunic? . . . Had she
been under his evil gaze for hours? Was the side of
the Guard House miles in length? . . . Thank God,
they were through the gate and free. Free for the
moment, and if the good God were merciful she
was free for ever from the horrors and fears of that
terrible place. Could anything worse befall her?
Yes, there were worse places for a girl than a
barrack-room of the French Foreign Legion. There
was a Russian prison—there was the dark prison-
van and warder—there was the journey to Siberia

—there was Siberia itself. Yes, there were worse places than that she had just left—until her secret was discovered. A thousand times worse. And she thought of her friend, that poor girl who had been less fortunate than she. Poor, poor Marie! Would she herself be sent back to Russia to share Marie's fate, if these brave Englishmen and Carmelita failed to save her? What would become of Feodor? . . . Did this noble Englishman, with the gentle face, love this girl Carmelita? . . . Might not Carmelita's house be a very trap if the loathsome Italian brute owned its owner? . . .

"Let's stroll slowly now, my dear," said John Bull, "and let the others overtake us. The more the merrier, if we should run into Rivoli and his gang, or if he is already at Carmelita's. I don't think he will be. I fancy he puts in the first part of his evening with Madame la Cantinière, and goes down to Carmelita's later for his dinner. . . . If he should be there I don't quite see what line he can take in front of Carmelita. He could hardly molest you in front of the woman whom he pretends he is going to marry, and I don't see on what grounds he could raise any objection to her befriending you. . . . It's a deuced awkward position—for the fact that I intend to kill Rivoli, if I can, hardly gives me a claim on Carmelita. She loves the very ground the brute treads on, you know, and it would take me, or anybody else, a precious long time to persuade her that the man who rid the world of Luigi Rivoli would be her very best friend. . . . He's the most noxious and poisonous reptile I have ever come across, and I believe she is one of the best of good little women. . . . It *is* a hole we're in. We've got to see Carmelita swindled and then jilted and broken-hearted; or we've got to bring the blackest grief upon her by saving her from Rivoli."

"Do *you* love her too, Monsieur?" asked Olga.

"Good Heavens, no!" laughed the Englishman. "But I have a very great liking and regard for her, and so has my friend Rupert. It is poor old Buck who loves her, and I am really sorry for him. It's bad enough to love a woman and be unable to win her, but it must be awful to see her in the power of a man whom you know to be an utter black-guard. . . . Queer thing, Life. . . . I suppose there is some purpose in it. . . . Here they come," he added, looking round.

"Who's gwine ter intervoo Carmelita, and put her wise to the sitooation?" asked the Bucking Bronco as he and Rupert joined the others. "Guess yew'd better, John. Yew know more Eye-talian and French than we do, an', what's more, Carmelita wouldn't think there was any *'harry-air ponsey'*— or is it *'double-intender'*—ef the young woman is interdooced, as sich, by yew."

"All right," replied John Bull. "I'll do my best— and we must all weigh in with our entreaties if I fail."

"Yew'll do it, John. I puts my shirt on Carmelita every time. . . ."

Le Café de la Légion was swept and garnished, and Carmelita sat in her *sedia pieghevole*[45] behind her bar, awaiting her evening guests.

It was a sadder-looking, thinner, somewhat older-looking Carmelita than she who had welcomed Rupert and his fellow *bleus* on the occasion of their first visit to her café. Carmelita's little doubt had grown, and worry was bordering upon anxiety—for Luigi Rivoli was Carmelita's life, and Carmelita was not only a woman, but an Italian woman, and a Neapolitan at that. Far better than life she loved Luigi Rivoli, and only next to him did she love her own self-respect and

---

[45] Deck-chair.

virtue. As has been said before, Carmelita considered herself a married woman. Partly owing to her equivocal position, partly to an innate purity of mind, Carmelita had a present passion for "respectability" such as had never troubled her before.

And Luigi was causing her grief and anxiety, doubt and care, and fear. For long she had fought it off, and had stoutly refused to confess it even to herself, but day by day and night by night, the persistent attack had worn down her defences of Hope and Faith until at length she stood face to face with the relentless and insidious assailant and recognised it for what it was—Fear. It had come to that, and Carmelita now frankly admitted to herself that she had fears for the faith, honesty and love of the man whom she regarded as her husband and knew to be the father of the so hoped-for *bambino*. . . .

Could it be possible that the man for whom she had lived, and for whom she would at any time have died, her own Luigi, who, but for her, would be in a Marseilles graveyard, her own husband— was laying siege to fat and ugly Madame la Cantinière, because her business was a more profitable one than Carmelita's? It could not be. Men were not devils. Men did not repay women like that. Not even ordinary men, far less her Luigi. Of course not—and besides, there was the Great Secret.

For the thousandth time Carmelita found reassurance, comfort and cheer in the thought of the Great Secret, and its inevitable effect upon Luigi when he knew it. What would he say when he realised that there might be another Luigi Rivoli, for, of course, it would be a boy—a boy who would grow up another giant among men, another Samson, another Hercules, another winner of a

World's Championship.

What would he do in the transports of his joy? How his face would shine! How heartily he would agree with her when she pointed out that it would be as well for them to marry now before the *bambino* came. No more procrastination now. What a wedding it should be, and what a feast they would give the brave *soldati!* Il Signor Jean Boule should have the seat of honour, and the Signor Americano should come, and Signor Rupert, and Signor 'Erbiggin, and the poor Grasshopper, and the two Russi (ah! what of that Russian girl, what would be her fate? It was wonderful how she kept up the deception. Poor, poor little soul, what a life—the constant fear, the watchfulness and anxiety. Fancy eating and drinking, walking, talking and working, dressing and undressing, waking and sleeping among those men—some of them such dreadful men). Yes, it should be a wedding to remember, without stint of food or drink—*un pranzo di tre portate* with *i maccheroni* and *la frittate d'uova* and the best of *couscous*, and there should be *vino Italiano*—they would welcome a change from the eternal *vino Algerino*. . . .

Four Legionaries entered, and Carmelita rose with a smile to greet them. There was no one she would sooner see than Il Signor Jean Boule and his friends—since it was not Luigi who entered.

"*Che cosa posso offrirve?*" she asked. (Although Carmelita spoke Legion French fluently one noticed that she always welcomed one in Italian, and always counted in that language.)

"I want a quiet talk with you, carissima Carmelita," said John Bull. "We are in great trouble, and we want your help."

"I am glad," replied Carmelita. "Not glad that you are in trouble, but glad you have come to me."

"It is about Mikhail Kyrilovitch," said the

Englishman.

"I thought it was," said Carmelita.

"Don't think me mad, Carmelita," continued John Bull, "but listen. Mikhail Kyrilovitch is a *girl*."

"Don't think me mad, Signor Jean Boule," mimicked Carmelita, "but listen. I have known Mikhail Kyrilovitch was a girl from the first evening that she came here."

The Englishman's blue eyes opened widely in surprise, as he stared at the girl. "How?" he asked.

"Oh, in a dozen ways," laughed Carmelita. "Hands, voice, manner. I stroked her cheek, it was as soft as my own, while her twin brother's was like sand-paper. When she went to catch a biscuit she made a 'lap,' as one does who wears a skirt, instead of bringing her knees together as a man does. . . . And what can I do for Mademoiselle Mikhail?"

"You can save her, Carmelita, from I don't know what dangers and horrors. She has been found out, and what her fate would be at the tender mercies of the authorities on the one hand, and of the men on the other, one does not like to think. The very least that could happen to her is to be turned into the streets of Sidi-bel-Abbès."

"Do the officers know yet?" asked Carmelita. "Who does know? Who found her out?"

"Luigi Rivoli found her out," replied John Bull.

"And sent her to me?" asked Carmelita. "I *am* glad he . . ."

"He did not send her to you," interrupted the Englishman gravely.

"What did he do?" asked Carmelita quickly.

"I will tell you what he did, Carmelita, as kindly as I can. . . . He forgot he was a soldier, Carmelita; he forgot he was an honest man; he forgot he was your—er—*fidanzato*, your *sposo*, Carmelita. . . ."

Carmelita went very white.

"Tell me, Signor," she said quickly. "Did you have to protect this Russian wretch from Luigi?"

"I did," was the reply. "Why do you speak contemptuously of the girl? She is as innocent as—as innocent as you are, Carmelita."

"I hate her," hissed Carmelita. . . . "Did Luigi kiss her? What happened? Did he . . . ?"

The Englishman put his hand over Carmelita's little clenched fist as it lay on the bar.

"Listen, little one," he said. "You are one of the best, kindest and bravest women I have known. I am certain you are going to be worthy of yourself now. So is Rupert, so is Monsieur Bronco. He has been blaming us bitterly when we have even for a moment wondered whether you would save this girl. He is worth a thousand Rivolis, and loves you a thousand times better than Rivoli ever could. Don't disappoint him and us, Carmelita. Don't disappoint us *in yourself*, I mean. . . . What has the girl done that you should hate her?"

"Did Luigi kiss her?" again asked Carmelita.

"He did not," was the reply. "He behaved . . ."

"And he could not, of course, while she was with me, could he?" said Carmelita.

"Exactly," smiled the Englishman. "Take her in now, little woman, and lend her some clothes until we can get some things bought or made for her."

"Clothes cost francs, Signor Jean," was the practical reply of the girl, who had grown up in a hard school. "I can give her food and shelter, and I can lend her my things, but I have no francs for clothes."

"Rupert will find whatever is necessary for her clothes and board and lodging, and for her ticket too. She shan't be with you long, cara Carmelita, nor in Sidi-bel-Abbès."

Carmelita passed from behind the bar and

went over to the table at which sat Rupert, the American, and the girl Olga. Putting her arm around the neck of the last, Carmelita kissed her on the cheek.

"Come, little one," she said. "Come to my bed and sleep. You shall be as safe as if in the Chapel of the Mother of God," and, as the girl burst into tears, led her away.

John Bull joined his friends as the two women disappeared through the door leading to Carmelita's room.

"Well, thank God for that," he said as he sat down, and wiped his forehead. "What's the next step?"

"Find the other little Roosian guy, an' put him wise to what's happened to sissy, I guess," replied the American.

"Yes," agreed Rupert. "It's up to him to carry on now, with any sort or kind of help that we can give him. . . . Where did he go after parade, I wonder?"

"The gal got copped for a wheel-barrer corvée—they was goin' scavengin' round the officers' houses and gardens I think—an' he took her place. . . . He'd be back by dark an' start washin' hisself," opined the American.

"Better get back at once then," said John Bull.

"I feel a most awful cad," he added.

"What on earth for?" asked Rupert.

"About Carmelita," was the reply. "I've got her help under false pretences. If I had told her that I was going to fight a serious duel with her precious Luigi, she'd never have taken that girl in. If I don't fight him now, he'll make my life utterly unlivable. . . . I wish to God Carmelita could be brought to see him as he is and to understand that the moment the Canteen will have him, he is done with the Café. . . . I wish Madame la Cantinière would take him and settle the matter. Since it has got to come, the sooner the better. I should really enjoy my fight with him if he had turned Carmelita down, and she regarded me as her avenger instead of as the destroyer of her happiness."

"One wouldn't worry about Madame la Cantinière's feelings if one destroyed her young man or her latest husband, I suppose?" queried Rupert with a smile.

"Nope," replied the American. "Nit. Not a damn. Nary a worry. You could beat him up, or you could shoot him up, and lay your last red cent that Madam lar Canteenair would jest say, '*Mong Jew! C'est la Légion*' and look aroun' fer his doo and lorful successor. . . . Let's vamoose, b'ys, an' rubber aroun' fer the other Roosian chechaquo."

The three Legionaries quitted le Café de la Légion and made their way back to their *caserne*.

"I'll look in the *chambrée*," said John Bull as they entered the barrack-square. "You go to the lavabo, Rupert, and you see if he is in the Canteen, Buck. Whoever finds him had better advise him to let Luigi Rivoli alone, and make his plans for going on pump. Tell him I think his best line would be to see Carmelita and arrange for him and his sister to get dresses alike, and clear out boldly by train to Oran, as girls. After that, they know their own business best, but I should recommend England as about the safest place for them."

"By Jove! I could give him a letter to my mother," put in Rupert. "Good idea. My people would love to help them—especially as they could tell them all about me."

"Gee-whiz! Thet's a brainy notion," agreed the Bucking Bronco. "Let 'em skin out and make tracks for yure Old-Folk-at-Home. It's a cinch."

Legionary John Bull found Legionary Feodor Kyrilovitch sitting on his cot polishing "Rosalie," as the soldier of France terms his bayonet. Several other Legionaries were engaged in *astiquage* and accoutrement cleaning. For the thousandth time, the English gentleman realised that one of the most irksome and maddening of the hardships and disabilities of the common soldier's life is its utter lack of privacy.

"Bonsoir, cher Boule," remarked Feodor Kyrilovitch, looking up as the English approached. "Have you seen my brother? He appears to have come in and changed and gone out without me."

Evidently the boy was anxious.

"Your brother is at Carmelita's," replied John Bull, and added: "Come over to my bed and sit beside me with your back to the room. I want to speak to you."

"Don't be alarmed," he continued as they seated themselves. "Your brother is absolutely all right."

The Russian gazed anxiously at the kindly face of the man whom he had instinctively liked and trusted from the first.

"Your brother is quite all right," continued the Englishman, "but I am afraid you will have to change your plans."

"Change our plans, Monsieur Boule?"

"Yes," replied the older man, as he laid his hand on Feodor's knee with a reassuring smile. "You will have to change your plans, for Mikhail can be Mikhail no longer."

The Russian bowed his head upon his hands with a groan.

"My poor little Olusha," he whispered.

"Courage, mon brave," said John Bull, patting him on the back. "We have a plan for you. As soon as your sister was discovered, we took her to Carmelita, with whom she will be quite safe for a while. Our idea is that she and Carmelita make and buy women's clothes for both of you, and that you escape as sisters. Since she made such a splendid boy, you ought to be able to become a fairly convincing girl. Légionnaire Mikhail Kyrilovitch will be looked for as a man—probably in uniform. By the time the hue and cry is over, and he is forgotten, everything will be ready for both of you, then one night you slip into Carmelita's café and, next day, two café-chantant girls who have been visiting Carmelita, walk coolly to the station and take train for Oran. . . . Rivoli can't tell on them and still keep in with Carmelita. He'll have to help—or pretend to."

Feodor Kyrilovitch was himself again—a cool and level-headed conspirator, accustomed to weighing chances, taking risks and facing dangers.

"Thanks, mon ami," he said. "I believe I owe you my sister's salvation. . . . There will be difficulties, and there are risks—but it is a plan."

"Seems fairly hopeful," replied the other. "Anyhow, we could think of nothing better."

"We might get to Oran," mused Feodor; "but where we can go from there, God knows. We daren't go to Paris again, and I doubt if we have a hundred and fifty roubles between us. . . . And we dare not write to friends in Russia."

"We've thought of that too, my boy," interrupted the Englishman. "My friend Rupert has money in the Credit Lyonnais, here in the town. He says he will be only too delighted to lend you enough to get you to England, and write a letter for you to take to his people. He says his mother will welcome you with open arms as coming from him. . . . From what he has said to me about her at different times, I imagine her to be one of the best—and the best of Englishwomen are the best of women, let me tell you."

"And the best of Englishmen are the best of men," replied Feodor, seizing the old Legionary's hand and kissing it fervently—to the latter gentleman's consternation and utter discomfort.

"Don't be an ass," he replied in English. . . . "Clear out now, and go and have a talk with Carmelita. You can trust her absolutely. Give her what money you've got, and she'll poke around in the ghetto for clothes. She'll know lots of the Spanish Jew dealers and cheap *couturières*, if old Mendoza hasn't what she wants. Meanwhile, Rupert will draw some money from the *banque*."

The Russian rose to his feet.

"But how can I thank you, Monsieur? How can I repay Monsieur Rupert for his kindness?"

"Don't thank me, and repay Rupert by visiting his mother and waxing eloquent over his marvellous condition of health, happiness and prosperity. Tell her he is having a lovely time in a lovely place with lovely people."

"You joke, Monsieur, how *can* I repay you all?"

"Well, I'll tell you, my son—by getting your sister clear of this hell and safe into England."

The Russian struck himself violently on the forehead and turned away.

A minute later Rupert entered the *chambrée*.

"He's not in the lavabo," he announced.

"No, it's all right. I found him here. He has just gone down to Carmelita's. . . . Let's go over to the Canteen, I want to meet the gentle Luigi Rivoli there."

On the stairs they encountered the Bucking Bronco, who was told that Feodor had been found and informed.

"Our Loojey's in the road-house," he announced, "layin' off ter Madam. . . . I wish she'd deliver the goods ef she's gwine ter. Then we could git next our Loojey without raisin' hell with

Carmelita."

"Is the Canteen fairly full?" asked John Bull.

"Some!" replied the Bucking Bronco.

"Then I'm going over to seek sorrow," said the other.

"Yure not goin' ter git fresh, an' slug the piker any, air yew, John?" enquired the American anxiously.

"No, Buck," was the reply. "I'm only going to make an interestin' announcement," and, turning to Rupert, he advised him not to identify himself with any proceedings which might ensue.

"You are hardly complimentary, Bull," commented Rupert resentfully. . . .

As the three entered the Canteen, which was rapidly filling up, they caught sight of Rivoli lolling against the bar in his accustomed corner, and whispering confidentially to Madame, during her intervals of leisure. Pushing his way through the throng John Bull, closely followed by his two friends, approached the Neapolitan. His back was towards them. The American, whose face wore an ugly look, touched Rivoli with his foot.

"Makin' yure sweet self agreeable as usual, Loojey, my dear?" he enquired, and proceeded with the difficult task of making himself both sarcastic and intelligible in the French language. The Italian wheeled round with a scowl at the sound of the voice he hated.

John Bull stepped forward.

"I have come for your answer, Rivoli," he said quietly. "I wish to know when and with what weapons you would prefer to fight me. Personally, I don't care in the least what they are, so long as they're fatal."

A ring of interested listeners gathered round. The Neapolitan laughed contemptuously.

"Weapons!" he growled. "A *fico* for weapons. I'll

twist your neck and break your back, if you trouble me again."

"Very good," replied the Englishman. "Now listen, bully. We have had a little more than enough of you. You take advantage of your strength to terrorise men who are not street acrobats, and professional weight-lifters. Now *I* am going to take advantage of this, to terrorise *you*," and he produced a small revolver from his pocket. "Now choose. Try your blackguard-rush games and get a bullet through your skull, or fight me like a man with any weapon you prefer."

An approving cheer broke from the quickly increasing audience. The Italian moistened his lips and glared round.

"Mais oui," observed Madame with cool impartiality, "but that is a fair offer."

As though stung by her remark, the Italian threw himself into wrestling attitude and extended his arms. John Bull moved only to extend his pistol-arm, and Luigi Rivoli recoiled. Strangling men who could not wrestle was one thing, being shot was quite another. The thrice-accursed English dog had got him nicely cornered. To raise a hand to him was to die—better to face his enemy, himself armed than unarmed. Better still to catch him unarmed and stamp the life out of him. He must temporise.

"Ho-ho, Brave Little Man with a Pistol," he sneered. "Behold the English hero who fears the bare hands of no man—while he has a revolver in his own."

"You miss the point, Rivoli," was the reply. "I want nothing to do with you bare-handed. I want you to choose any weapon you like to name," and turning to the deeply interested crowd he raised his voice a little:

"Gentlemen of the Legion," he said, "I challenge

le Légionnaire Luigi Rivoli of the Seventh Company of the First Battalion of La Légion Étrangère to fight me with whatever weapon he prefers. We can use our rifles; he can have the choice of the revolvers belonging to me and my friend le Légionnaire Bouckaing Bronceau; we can use our sword-bayonets; we can get sabres from the Spahis; or it can be a rifle-and-bayonet fight. He can choose time, place, and weapon—and, if he will not fight, let him be known as *Rivoli the Coward* as long as he pollutes our glorious Regiment."

Ringing and repeated cheers greeted the longest public speech that Sir Montague Merline had ever made.

A bitter sneer was frozen on Rivoli's white face.

"*Galamatias!*" he laughed contemptuously, but the laugh rang a little uncertain.

Madame la Cantinière was charmed. She felt she was falling in love with ce brave Jean Boule *au grand galop*. This was a far finer man, and a far more suitable husband for a hard-working Cantinière than that lump of a Rivoli, with his pockets always *pleine de vide* and his mouth always full of *langue vert*. A trifle on the elderly side perhaps, but aristocrat *au bout des ongles*. Yes, decidedly grey as to the hair, but then, how nice to be an old man's darling!—and Madame simpered, bridled and tried to blush.

"Speak up thou, Rivoli," she cried sharply. "Do not stand there like a *blanc bec* before a Sergeant-Major. Speak, *bécasse*—or speak not again to me."

The Neapolitan darted a glance of hatred at her.

"Peace, fat sow," he hissed, and added unwisely —"You wag your beard too much."

In that moment vanished for ever all possibility of Madame's trying an Italian husband. "Sow" may be a term of endearment, but no gentleman alludes to beards in the presence of a lady whose chin does not betray her sex.

Turning to his enemy, Rivoli struck an attitude and pointed to the door.

"Go, dig your grave *ci-devant*," he said portentously, "and I will kill you beside it, within the week."

"Thanks," replied the Englishman, and invited his friends to join him in a litre. . . .

The barracks of the First Battalion of the Foreign Legion hummed and buzzed that night, from end to end, in a ferment of excitement over the two tremendous items of most thrilling and exciting news, to wit, that there was among them a sheep in wolf's clothing—a girl in uniform—and, secondly, that there was a duel toward, a duel in which no less a person than the great Luigi Rivoli was involved.

Cherchez la femme was the game of the evening; and the catch-word of the wits on encountering any bearded and grisled *ancien* in corridor, *chambrée*, canteen, or stair-case, was—

"Art *thou* the girl, petite?"

The wrinkled old grey-beard, Tant-de-Soif, was christened Bébé Fifinette, provided with a skirt improvised from a blanket, and subjected to indignities.

CHAPTER VIII

THE TEMPTATION OF SIR MONTAGUE MERLINE

Il Signor Luigi Rivoli strode forth from the Canteen in an unpleasant frame of mind.

"Curse the Englishman!" he growled. "Curse that hag behind the bar. Curse that Russian *ragazza*. Curse that thrice-damned American. . . ."

In fact—curse everybody and everything. And among them, Il Signor Luigi Rivoli cursed Carmelita for not making a bigger financial success of her Café venture, and saving a Neapolitan gentleman from the undignified and humiliating position of having to lay siege to a cursed fat French *bitche*, to get a decent living. . . . What a fool he'd been that evening! He had lost ground badly with Madame, and he had lost prestige badly with the Legionaries. He must regain both as quickly as possible. . . . That accursed English devil must meet with an accident within the week. It would not be the first time by hundreds that a Légionnaire had been stabbed in the back for his sash and bayonet in the *Village Négre* and alleys of the Ghetto. . . . A little job for Edouard Malvin, or Tou-tou Boil-the-Cat. Yes, a knife in the back would settle the Englishman's hash quite effectually, and it would be the simplest thing in the world to leave his body in one of those places to which Legionaries are forbidden to go—for the very reason that they are likely to remain in them for ever. . . . Curse that old cow of the Canteen! Had he offended her beyond hope of reconciliation? The Holy Saints forbid, for the woman was positively wealthy. Well, he must bring the whole battery of his blandishments to bear and make one mighty effort to win her fortune, hand and heart—in fact, he would give her an ultimatum and settle things, one way or the other, for Carmelita was beginning to show distinct signs of restiveness. Curse Carmelita! He was getting very weary of her airs and jealousies—a franc a day did not pay for it all. As soon as things were happily settled with Madame he would be able to sell his rights and goodwill in Carmelita and her Café. But one must not be precipitate. There must be no untimely killing of geese that laid golden eggs. Carmelita must be kept quiet until Madame's affair was settled. 'Twas but a clumsy fool that would lose both the substance and the shadow—both the Canteen and the Café. If Madame returned an emphatic and final *No*, to his ultimatum, the Café must suffice until something better turned up. Luigi Rivoli and an unaugmented halfpenny a day would be ill partners, and agree but indifferently. . . .

Revolving these things in his heart, the gentle Luigi became conscious of a less exalted organ, and bethought him of dinner, Chianti, and his cigar. He turned in the direction of the Café de la Légion, his usual excellent appetite perhaps a trifle dulled and blunted by uncomfortable thoughts as to what might happen should this grey English dog survive the week, in spite of the attentions of Messieurs Malvin, Tou-tou, et Cie. The choice between facing the rifle or revolver of the Company marksman, or of being branded for ever as *Rivoli the Coward* was an unpleasant one. . . . Should he choose steel and have a dagger-fight with sword-bayonets? No, he absolutely hated cold steel, and his mighty strength would be almost as useless to him as in a shooting-duel. Suppose he selected sword-bayonets, to be used as daggers—held his in his left hand, seized his enemy's right wrist, broke his arm, and then made a wrestle of it after all? He could strangle him or break his back with ease. And suppose he missed his snatch at the Englishman's wrist? The devil's bayonet would be through his throat in a second! . . . But why these vain and discomforting imaginings? Ten francs would buy a hundred bravos in the *Village Négre* and slums, if Malvin failed him. . . .

He turned into Carmelita's alley and entered the Café.

Carmelita, whose eyes had rarely left the door throughout the evening, saw him as he entered, and her face lit up as does a lantern when the wick is kindled. Here was her noble and beautiful Luigi. Away with all wicked doubts and fears. Even the good Jean Boule was prejudiced against her Luigi. She would now hear his version of the discovery of the Russian girl. How amused he would be to know that she had guessed Mikhail's secret long ago.

Rivoli passed behind the bar. Carmelita held open the door of her room, and having closed it behind him, turned and flung her arms round his neck.

"Marito amato!" she murmured as she kissed him again and again. How could she entertain these doubts of her Luigi in his absence? She was a wicked, wicked girl, and undeserving of her fortune in having so glorious a mate. She decided to utter no reproaches and ask no questions concerning the discovery of the Russian girl. She would just tell him that she had taken her in and that she counted on his help in keeping the girl's secret and getting her away.

"Beloved and beautiful Luigi of my heart," she said, as she placed a steaming dish of macaroni before him, "I want your help once more. That poor, foolish, little Mikhail Kyrilovitch has come and told me he is in trouble, and begged my help. Fancy his thinking he could lead the life that my Luigi leads—that of a soldier of France's fiercest Regiment. Poor little fool. . . . Guess where he is at this moment, Luigi."

With his mouth full, the noble Luigi intimated that he knew not, cared not, and desired not to know.

"I will tell my lord," murmured Carmelita, bending over his lordship's huge and brawny shoulder, and kissing the tip of the ear into which she whispered, "He is in my bed."

Luigi had to think quickly. How much had the Russian girl told of what had happened in the wash-house? Nothing, or Carmelita would not be in this frame of mind. What did Carmelita know? Did she know that *he* knew? He sprang to his feet with an oath, and a well-assumed glare of ferocity. He raised his fist above his head, and by holding his breath, contrived to induce a dark flush and raise the veins upon his forehead.

"In your bed, *puttana*?" he hissed. (Carmelita was overjoyed, Luigi was angered and jealous. Where there is jealousy, there is love! Of course, Luigi loved her as he had always done. How dared she doubt it? Throwing her arms around his neck with a happy laugh, she reassured her ruffled mate until he permitted himself to calm down and resume his interrupted meal. Jean Boule had lied to her! Luigi knew nothing! . . .) She went to the bar.

Curse this Russian anarchist! But for her he would not have been in danger of losing Madame, nor of finding a violent death. Curse Carmelita, the stupid fool, for harbouring her. What should he do? What could he say? If he thwarted

Carmelita's plan, she would think he desired the Russian wench for himself, and fly into a rage. She would be a very fiend from hell if she were jealous! A pretty pass he would be brought to if both Canteen and Café were closed to him! He had better walk warily here, until he had ascertained the exact amount of damage he had done by his most unwise allusion to Madame's whiskers. (Never tell a cross-eyed man he squints.) But he must get even with this Russian she-devil who had thwarted him in the lavatory, struck him across the face, humiliated him before the Englishman, ruined his prestige with his comrades and Madame, and brought him to the brink of an abyss of danger. . . . He had an idea. . . . When Carmelita came into the room again from the bar, she should have the shock of her life, and the Russian *puttana*, another. Also the over-clever Jean Boule should learn that the race is not always to the slow, nor the battle to the weak. . . . Carmelita entered. Picking up his képi, he extended his arms, and with a smile of lofty sadness, bade her come and kiss him while she might. . . .

While she might! Carmelita turned pale, and Doubt again reared its horrid head. Was this his way of beginning some tale concerning separation? Some tale in which Madame la Cantinière's name would appear sooner or later? By the Blessed Virgin and the Holy Bambino, she would tear the eyes from Luigi Rivoli's head, before they should look on that French *meretrice* as his wife.

"While I may? Why do you say that, Luigi?" she asked in a dead voice.

The ruffian felt uncomfortable as he watched those great, black eyes blazing in the pinched, blanched face, and realised that there were depths in Carmelita that he had not sounded—and would be ill-advised to sound. What a devil she looked!

Luigi Rivoli would do well to eat no food to which Carmelita had had access, when once she knew the truth. Luigi Rivoli would do well to watch warily, and move quickly, should Carmelita's hand go to the dagger in her garter when he told her that he was thinking of settling in life. In fact it was a question whether his life would be safe, so long as Carmelita was in Sidi-bel-Abbès, and he was the husband of Madame! Another idea! *Madre de Dios!* A brilliant one. Denounce Carmelita for aiding and abetting a deserter! Two birds with one stone—Carmelita jailed and deported, and the Russian recaptured—Luigi Rivoli rid of a danger from the one, and gratified by a vengeance on the other! As these thoughts flashed through the Italian's evil mind, he maintained his pose, and gently and sadly shook his head.

"While you may, indeed, my Carmelita," he murmured, and produced the first of his brilliant ideas. "While you may. Do not think I reproach you, Carmelita, for you have acted but in accordance with the dictates of your warm young heart in taking in this girl. How were *you* to know that this would involve me in a duel to the death with the finest shot in the Nineteenth Division, the most famous marksman in the army of Africa?"

"What?" gasped Carmelita.

"What I say, my poor girl," was the reply, uttered with calm dignity. "Your English friend, this Jean Boule, who fears to meet me face to face, and man to man, with Nature's weapons, has forced a quarrel on me over this Russian girl. He challenged me in the Canteen this night, and I, who could break him like a dried stick, must stand up to be shot by him, like a dog. . . . I do not blame *you*, Carmelita. How were you to know? . . ."

Carmelita suddenly sat down.

"I do not understand," she whispered and sat agape.

"The Englishman owns this girl. . . ."

"He brought her here," Carmelita interrupted, nodding her head.

"Ha! I guessed it. . . . Yes, he owns her, and when I discovered the shameless *puttana's* sex he drew a pistol on *me*, an innocent, unarmed man. . . . Did he tell you it was I who found the shameful hussy out? What could I do against him empty-handed? . . . And now I must fight him— and he can put a bullet where he will. . . . So kiss me, while you may, Carmelita."

With a low cry the girl sprang into his arms.

"My love! My love! My husband!" she wailed, and Luigi hoped that she would release her clasp from about his neck in time for him to avoid suffocation. . . . Curse all women—they were the cause of nine-tenths of the sorrows of mankind. But one could not do without them. . . . Suddenly Carmelita started back, and clapped her hands with a cry of glee. "The Holy Virgin be praised! I have it! I have it! Unless Légionnaire Jean Boule confesses his fault and begs my Luigi's pardon— out into the gutter goes his Russian mistress," and Carmelita pirouetted with joy. . . . Thank God! Thank God! Here was a solution, and she embraced her lover again and again. Luigi's face was wreathed in smiles. *Excellente!* That would do the trick admirably, and the thrice-accursed, and ten-times-too-clever English *aristocratico* should publicly apologise, if he wished to save his mistress. . . . Yes, that would be very much pleasanter than a mere stab-in-the-back revenge, as well as safer. There is always some slight risk, even in Sidi-bel-Abbès, about arranging a murder, and blackmail is always unpleasant—for the black- mailed. Ho-ho! Ho-ho! Only to think of the cold and haughty Englishman publicly apologising and begging Luigi, of his mercifulness, to cancel the duel. *Corpo di Bacco*, he should do it on his knees. "Rivoli the Coward," forsooth, and what of "Jean Boule the Coward," after this? . . . Yes; Jean Boule defeated, the Russian girl denounced when clear of Carmelita's Café, if Madame proved unkind, and denounced in the Café together with Carmelita if Madame accepted him. He himself need not appear personally in the matter at all. And when Carmelita was jailed or deported, and the Russian girl sent to Biribi, or turned into a *figlia del reggimento*, the Englishman should still get it in the back one dark night—and Signor Luigi Rivoli would wax fat behind Madame's bar, until his five years' service was completed and he could live happy ever after, upon the earnings of Madame. . . .

Stroking her hair, he smiled superior upon Carmelita.

"A clever thought, my little one," he murmured, "and bravely meant, but your Luigi's days are numbered. Would that proud, cold *aristocratico* eat the words he shouted before half the Company? No! He will leave the girl to shift for herself."

Carmelita's face fell.

"Do not say so," she begged. "No! No! He would not do that. You know how these English treat women. You know the sort of man this Jean Boule is," and for a moment, involuntarily, Carmelita contrasted her Luigi with Il Signor Jean Boule in the matter of their chivalry and honour, and ere she could thrust the thought from her mind, she had realised the comparison to be unfavourable to her lover.

"Luigi," she said, "I feel it in my heart that, since the Englishman has said that he will save his mistress, he will do it at any cost whatsoever to himself. . . . Go, dearest Luigi, go now, and I will send to him, and say I must see him at once. He will surely come, thinking that I send on behalf of this Russian fool."

And with a last vehement embrace and burning kiss, she thrust him before her into the bar and watched him out of the Café.

Le Légionnaire Jean Boule was not among the score or so of Legionaries who sat drinking at the little tables, nor were either of his friends. Whom could she send? Was that funny English *ribaldo*, Légionnaire Erbiggin, there? . . . No. . . . Ah!— There sat the poor Grasshopper. He would do. She made her way with laugh and jest and badinage to where he sat, *faisant Suisse* as usual.

"Bonsoir, cher Monsieur Cigale," she said. "Would you do me a kindness?"

The Grasshopper rose, thrust his hands up the sleeves of his tunic as far as his elbows, bowed three times, and then knelt upon the ground and smote it thrice with his forehead. Rising he poured forth a torrent of some language entirely unknown to Carmelita.

"Speak French or Italian, cher Monsieur Cigale," she said.

"A thousand pardons, Signora," replied the Grasshopper. "But you will admit it is not usual for a Mandarin of the Highest Button to speak French. I was saying that the true kindness would be your allowing me to do you a kindness. May I doom your *wonk*[46] of an enemy to the death of the Thousand Cuts?"

"Not this evening, dear Mandarin, thank you," replied Carmelita; "but you can carry a message of the highest military importance. It is well known that you are a soldier of soldiers, and have never

[46] Chinese pariah dog.

yet failed in any military duty."

The Mandarin bowed thrice.

"Will you go straight and find le Légionnaire Jean Boule of your Company, and tell him to come to me at once. Say Carmelita sent you and tell him you have the countersign: 'Our Ally, Russia, is in danger!' "

"I am honoured and I fly," was the reply. "I will send no official of the Yamen, but go myself. Should the Po Sing, they of the Hundred Names, the ὁι πολλοι, beset my path I will cry, 'Sha! Sha!— Kill! Kill!—and scatter them before me. Should the *kwei tzu*, the Head Dragon from Hell, or the Military Police (and they are *tung yen* you know— of the same race and tarred with the same brush) impede me, they too shall die the death of the Wire Net," and the Grasshopper placed his képi on his head.

Carmelita knew that John Bull would be with her that evening, and that the risk of eight days' *salle de police*, for being out after tattoo, would not deter him.

In a fever of anxiety, impatience, hope and fear, Carmelita paced up and down behind her bar, like a panther in its cage. One thought shone brightly on the troubled turmoil of her soul. Luigi loved her still; Luigi so loved her that he had been ready to strike her dead as the tide of jealousy surged in his soul. That was the sort of love that Carmelita understood. Let him take her by the throat until she choked—let him seize her by the hair and drag her round the room—let him stab her in the breast, so it be for jealousy. Better Luigi's knife in Carmelita's throat than Luigi's lips on Madame's face. Thank God! Luigi had suffered those pangs— on hearing of a Russian boy in her room—that she herself had suffered on hearing Malvin and the rest couple Luigi's name with Madame's. Thank

God! that Luigi knew jealousy even as she did herself. Where there is jealousy, there is love. . . .

And then Carmelita struck her forehead with her clenched fists and laid her head upon her folded arms with a piteous groan. Luigi had been acting. Luigi had *pretended* that jealousy of the Russian. Luigi knew Mikhail Kyrilovitch was a girl—he had fooled her, and once again doubt raised its cruel head in Carmelita's poor distracted mind. "Oh Luigi! Luigi!" she sobbed beneath her breath. And then again a ray of comfort—the *bambino*. Merciful Mother of God grant that it might be true, and that her bright and golden hopes were based on more solid foundation than themselves. Why had she not told him that evening? But no, she was glad she hadn't. She would keep the wonderful secret until such moment as it really seemed to her that it should be produced as the gossamer fairy chain, weightless but unbreakable, that should bind them together, then and forever, in its indissoluble bonds. Yes, she must force herself to believe devoutly and implicitly in the glorious and beautiful secret, and she must treasure it up as long as possible and whisper it in Luigi's ear if it should ever seem that, for a moment, her Luigi strayed from the path of justice and honesty to his unwedded wife.

Faith again triumphed over Doubt.

These others were jealous of her Luigi, or mistook his natural and beautiful politeness to Madame, for overtures and love-making. Could not her Luigi converse with, and smile upon, Madame la Cantinière without setting all their idle and malicious tongues clacking and wagging? As for this Russian wretch, Luigi had given her no more thought than to the dust beneath his feet, and she should go forth into the gutter, in Carmelita's night-shift, before her protector should injure a hair of Luigi's head. She was surprised at Jean Boule, but there—men were all alike, all except her Luigi, that is. How deceived she had been in the kindly old Englishman! . . . Fancy coming to her with their cock-and-bull story. . . .

The voice of the man of whom she was thinking broke in upon her reverie.

"What is it, little one? Nothing wrong about Olga?"

"Come in here, Signor Jean Boule," said Carmelita, and led the way into her room.

The Englishman involuntarily glanced round the little sanctum into which no man save Luigi Rivoli had been known to penetrate, and noted the clean tablecloth, the vase with its bunch of krenfell and oleander flowers, the tiny, tidy dressing table, the dilapidated chest of drawers, bright oleographs, cheap rug, crucifix and plaster Madonna—a room still suggestive of Italy.

Turning, Carmelita faced the Englishman and pointed an accusing finger at his face, her great black eyes staring hard and straight into the narrowed blue ones.

"Signor Jean Boule," she said, "you have played a trick on me; you have deceived me; you have killed my faith in Englishmen—yes, in all men—except my Luigi. Why did you bring your mistress to me and beg my help while you knew you meant to kill my husband, because he had found you out? Oh, Monsieur Jean Boule—but you have hurt me so. And I had thought you like a father—so good a man, yes, like a holy padre, a *prête*. Oh, Signor Jean Boule, are you like those others, loving wickedly, killing wickedly? Are there *no* good honest men—except my Luigi? . . ."

The Englishman shifted uncomfortably from foot to foot, twisting his képi in his fingers, a picture of embarrassment and misery. How could he persuade this girl that the man was a double-dealing, villainous blackguard? And if he could do so, why should he? Why destroy her faith and her happiness together? If this hound failed in his attempt upon the celibacy of Madame, he would very possibly marry the girl, and, in his own interests, treat her decently. Apparently he had kept her love for years—why should she not go on worshipping the man she believed her lover to be, until the end? But no, it was absurd. How should Luigi Rivoli ever treat a woman decently? Sooner or later he was certain to desert her. What would Carmelita's life be when Luigi Rivoli had the complete disposal of it? Sooner or later she must know what he was, and better sooner than later. A thousand times better that she should find him out now, while there was a risk of his marrying her. . . . It would be a really good deed to save Carmelita from the clutches of Luigi Rivoli. Stepping toward her, he laid his hands upon the girl's shoulders and gazed into her eyes with that look which he was wont to fasten upon the Grasshopper to soothe and influence him.

"Listen to me, Carmelita," he said, "and be perfectly sure that every word I say to you is absolutely true. . . . I did not know that Mikhail Kyrilovitch was a woman more than half an hour before you did. I only knew it when she rushed to me for protection from Luigi Rivoli, who had discovered her and behaved to her like the foul beast he is. I have challenged him to fight me in the only way in which it is possible for me to fight him, and I mean to kill him. I am going to kill him partly for your sake, partly for my own, and partly for that of every wretched recruit and decent man in the Company."

Carmelita drew back.

"Coward!" she hissed. "You only dare face my

Luigi with a gun in your hand."

"I am not a coward, Carmelita. It is Rivoli who is the coward. He is by far the strongest man in the Regiment, and is a professional wrestler. He trades on this to bully and terrorise all who do not become his servants. He is a brutal ruffian, and he is a coward, for he would do anything rather than meet me in fair fight. He is only a *risquetout* where there are no weapons and the odds are a hundred to one in his favour. . . . If I hear one more word about my trading on my marksmanship, he shall fight me with revolvers across a handkerchief. Besides, I have told him he can choose any weapon in the world."

"And now hear *me*," replied Carmelita, "and I would say it if it were my last word. Either you take all that back and apologise to my Luigi, or out into the night goes this Russian girl," and she pointed with the dramatic gesture of the excited Southerner to the *bassourab*-cloth which screened off the little inner chamber which was just big enough to hold Carmelita's bed.

The Englishman started.

"You don't mean that, Carmelita!" he asked anxiously.

The girl laughed bitterly, cruelly.

"Do you think a thousand Russians would weigh with me against one hair of my husband's head?" she answered. "Give me your solemn promise now and here, or I will do more than throw her out, I will denounce her. I will give her to the Turcos and Spahis. I will have her dragged to the Village Négre."

"Hush! Carmelita. I am ashamed of you. Are you mad?" said John Bull sternly.

"I am sorry," was the reply. "Yes, I *am* mad, Signor Jean Boule. I am being driven mad by this horrible plot against my Luigi. Why are you all his enemies? It is because you are jealous of him and because you fear him—but you shall not hurt him. This, at least, I say and mean: Take the Russian girl away with you now, or promise me you will never fight my husband with lead or steel."

"I cannot promise it, Carmelita. I have challenged Rivoli publicly and must fight him. To draw out now would brand me as a coward, would make him twice the bully he is, and would be a cruelty to you. . . . You ask too much, you ask an impossibility. I must make some other plan for Olga Kyrilovitch."

Carmelita staggered, and stared open-mouthed. She could not believe her ears.

"What?" she gasped.

"The girl must go elsewhere," repeated the Englishman. Carmelita appeared to be about to faint. Could he mean it? Was it possible? Was her brilliant plan failing?

"Will you lend the girl some clothes?" asked John Bull.

"Most certainly will I not," she whispered.

"Then please go and tell her to dress again in uniform," was the answer, as he pointed to the uniform lying folded on a chair.

"And will you ruin her chance of escape, Signor Jean Boule?" asked Carmelita. "Is *that* how Englishmen treat women who throw themselves on their mercy? Do you put your own vengeance before her safety and honour and life?"

"No, Carmelita, I do not," answered the man. "I am in a terrible position, and am going to choose the lesser of two evils. It is better that I take the girl away and help her brother to desert with her, than let Rivoli wreck your life, break your heart, and doubly regain the bully's prestige and power to make weaker comrades' lives a misery and a burden. He, at any rate, shall be the cause of no more suicides."

Carmelita flung herself upon the hideous horsehair couch and burst into a torrent of hysterical tears. What could she say to this hard, cold man? What could she do? What *could* she do?

John Bull, suffering acutely as he had ever suffered in his life, stood silent, and wondered how far the wish was father to the thought that, in this ghastly dilemma, it was his duty to stand firm in his attitude toward Rivoli. For once, the thing he longed to do was the right thing to do, and the course which he would loathe to follow was the wrong course for him to pursue. Olga Kyrilovitch had brought her fate upon herself, and he had no more responsibility to her than the common duty of lending a helping hand to a neighbour in trouble. Had there been no other consideration, he would have helped her to the utmost of his power, without counting cost or risk. When it came to a clear choice between saving Carmelita, protecting recruits, making a stand for self-respect and decency, and redeeming his own word and honour and reputation on the one hand, and, on the other hand, helping this rash and lawless Russian girl, there could be no hesitation.

Carmelita sprang to her feet.

"I will denounce her," she cried. "I will throw open those shutters and scream and scream until there is a crowd, and they shall have her in her nightdress. *Now* will you spare my husband?"

"You'll do nothing of the kind," answered John Bull calmly. "You know you would regret it all the days of your life. Is this Italian hospitality, womanliness, and honour? Be ashamed of yourself, to talk so. Be fair. Be just. Who needs protection most—your bully, or this wretched girl?" and here Legionary John Bull showed more than his wonted wisdom in dealing with women. Stepping up to

Carmelita he seized her by the shoulders and shook her somewhat sharply, saying as he did so, "And understand once and for all, little fool, I keep my promise to Luigi Rivoli—whatever you do."

In return for her shaking, the surprising Carmelita smiled up into the old soldier's face, and clasped her hands behind his head.

"Monsieur Jean Boule," she said, "I think I would have loved my father like I love you—but how you try to hide the soft, kind heart with the hard, cruel face!" and Carmelita gave John Bull the first kiss he had received for over a quarter of a century.

He pushed her from him roughly. Carmelita was glad. This was a thousand times better than that glacial immobility. This meant that he was moved.

"Save Olga's life, Babbo," she whispered coaxingly. "Save Olga and make me happy. Don't ruin two women for fear men should not think you brave. Who doubts the courage of the man who wears the *médaille?* The man who had the courage to challenge Luigi Rivoli can have the courage to withdraw it if it suits him."

"The man who killed Luigi Rivoli would be your best friend, Carmelita," was the reply, "and Olga Kyrilovitch must be saved in some other way. I must keep my word. It is due to others as well as to myself that I do so."

The two regarded each other without realising that it was across an abyss of immeasurable width and unfathomable depth. He was a man, she was a woman; he a Northerner, she a Southerner. To him honour came first; and without love there could be, she thought, neither honour nor happiness nor life itself.

How should these two understand each other, these two whose souls spoke languages differing as widely as those spoken by their tongues? The woman understood and appreciated the rectitude and honour of the man as little as he realised and fathomed the depth and overwhelming intensity of her love and devotion.

Carmelita now made a great mistake and took a false step—a mistake which turned to her advantage and a false step which led whither she so yearned to go. For Luigi's sake she played the temptress. In defence of her virtue let it be said that, as once before, she believed that her Luigi's life was actually at stake; in defence of her judgment, let it be remembered that she had grown up in a hard school, and had reason to believe that no man does something for nothing where a woman is concerned. She advanced with her bewitching smile, took the Englishman's face between her hands, drew his head down and kissed him upon the lips.

The Englishman blushed as he returned her kiss, and laughed to find himself blushing as the thought struck him that he might have had a daughter older than Carmelita. The girl misunderstood the kiss and smile. Alas! all men were alike in one thing and the best were like the worst. She put her lips to his ear and whispered. . . .

John Bull drew back. Placing his hands upon the girl's shoulders, he gazed into her eyes. Carmelita blushed painfully, and dropped her eyes before the man's searching stare. She heaved a sobbing sigh. Yes, all alike, all had their price— and any pretty woman could pay it. All alike—even grey-haired, kind old Babbo Jean Boule, who looked as though he might be her grandfather.

She felt his hand beneath her chin, raising her face to his. Again he gazed into her eyes and slowly shook his head.

"And is this what men and Life have taught

you, Carmelita?" he said. . . .

A horrid fear gripped Carmelita's heart. Could she be wrong? Could she have offered herself in vain? Could this man's pride and hatred be so great that the bribe was not enough?

"And you would do this—*you*, Carmelita; for that filthy blackguard?"

"I would do *any*thing for my Luigi. Sell me his life and I will pay you now, the highest price a woman can. Kiss me on the lips, dear Monsieur Jean, and I will trust you to keep your part of the bargain—never to fight nor attack my Luigi with a weapon in your hand. Kiss me! Kiss me!"

The Englishman drew the pleading girl to him and kissed her on the forehead. She flung her arms around his neck in a transport of joy and relief.

"You will sell me my Luigi's life?" she cried. "Oh praise and thanks to the Mother of God. You *will?*"

"I will *give* you your Luigi's life," said Sir Montague Merline, and went out.

CHAPTER IX

THE CAFÉ AND THE CANTEEN

As the door closed behind the departing John Bull, the heavy *purdah* between the sitting-room and the tiny side-chamber or alcove in which was Carmelita's bed, was pushed aside, and Olga Kyrilovitch, barefooted and dressed in night attire belonging to Carmelita, entered the room. On the sofa lay Carmelita sobbing, her hands pressed over her eyes.

Looking more boy-like than ever, with her short hair, the Russian girl advanced noiselessly and shook Carmelita sharply by the shoulder.

"You fool," she hissed between clenched teeth. "You stupid fool. You blind, stubborn, hopeless *fool!*" Carmelita sat up. This was language she could understand, and a situation with which she could deal.

"Yes?" she replied without resentment, "and why?"

"Those two men. . . . Compare them. . . . I heard every word—I could not help it. I could not come out—I should not have been safe, even with you here, with that vile, filthy Italian in the room, nor could I come, for shame, like this, while the Englishman was here. . . . *Why did you let him say he does not love me?*" and the girl burst into tears. Carmelita stared.

"Oho! you love him, do you?" quoth she. . . . "Then if you know what love is, why do you abuse the man *I* love?"

The girl raised her impassioned tear-stained face to Carmelita's.

"Will nothing persuade you, little fool?" she cried, "that that Italian beast no more loves you than—than Jean Boule loves me—that he is playing with you, that he is battening on you, and that, the moment the fat Canteen woman accepts him, he will marry her and you will see him no more? Why should Jean Boule lie to you? Why should the American? Why should I?—Ask any Legionary in Sidi."

Carmelita clenched her little fist and appeared to be about to strike the Russian girl.

"Stop!" continued Olga, and pointed to the uniform which lay folded on the chair. "See! Prove your courage and prove us all liars if you can. Put on that uniform, disguise yourself, and go to the Canteen any night in the week. If your Rivoli is not there behind the bar, hand-in-glove with Madame, turn me into the street—or leave me at the mercy of your Rivoli. There now. . . ."

"*I will*," said Carmelita, and then screamed and laughed, laughed and screamed, as her over-wrought nerves and brain gave way in a fit of hysterics.

When she recovered, Olga Kyrilovitch discovered that the seed which she had sown had taken root, and that it was Carmelita's unalterable intention to pay a visit to the Canteen on the very next evening.

"For my Luigi's own sake I will spy upon him," she said, "and to prove all his vile accusers wrong. When I have done it I will confess to him with tears and throw myself at his feet. He shall do as he likes with me. . . . But he will understand that it was only to disprove these lies that I did it, and not because I for one moment doubted him."

But doubt him Carmelita did. As soon as her decision was taken and announced, she allowed Olga to talk on as she pleased, and insensibly came to realise that at the bottom of her heart she knew John Bull to be incapable of deceiving her. Why should he? Why should all the Legionaries, except Rivoli's own hirelings, take up the same attitude towards him? Why should there be no man to speak well of him save such men as Borges, Hirsch, Bauer, Malvin, and the others, all of whom carried their vileness in their faces? As her doubts and fears increased, so did her wrath and excitement, until she strode up and down the little room like a caged pantheress, and Olga feared for her sanity and her own safety. And then again, Love would triumph, and she would beat her breast and wildly reproach herself for her lack of faith, and overwhelm Olga with a deluge of vituperation and accusation.

At length came the relief of quiet weeping, and, having whispered to Olga her Great Secret, or rather her hopes of having one to tell, she sobbed herself to sleep on the girl's shoulder, to dream of the most wonderful of *bambinos*.

Meanwhile, John Bull spent one of the wretchedest evenings of a wretched life. Returning to his *chambrée* to find himself hailed and acclaimed "hero," he commenced at once, with his usual uncompromising directness and simplicity, to inform all and sundry, who mentioned the subject, that there would be no duel. It hurt him most of all to see the face of his friend Rupert fall and harden, as he informed him that he could not fight Rivoli after all. On his explaining the position to him, Reginald Rupert, decidedly shocked, remarked—

"*Your* business, of course," and privately wondered whether *les beaux yeux* of Carmelita, or of Olga, had shed the light in which his friend had come to see things so differently. Surely, Carmelita's best friend would be the person who saved her from Rivoli; and, if it were really Olga whom Bull were considering, there were more ways of killing a cat than choking it with melted butter. Anyhow, he didn't envy John Bull, nor yet the weaker vessels of the Seventh Company. What would John Bull do, if, on hearing of his change of mind, Rivoli simply took him and put him across his knee? Would his promise to Carmelita sustain him through that or similar indignities? After all, a challenge is a challenge; and some people would consider that the prior engagement to Rivoli could not in honour be cancelled afterwards by an engagement with Carmelita or anybody else.

No. To the young mind of Rupert this was not "the clean potato," and he was disappointed in his friend. As they undressed, in silence, an idea struck him, and he turned to that gentleman.

"I say, look here, Bull, old chap," quoth he. "You'll of course do as you think best in the matter, and so shall I. I'm going to challenge Rivoli myself. I shall follow your admirable example and challenge him publicly, and I shall add point to it by wasting a litre of wine on his face, which I shall also smack with what violence I may. I am not Company Marksman like you, but, as Rivoli knows, I am a First Class shot. I shall say I have been brooding over his breaking my back, and now want to fight him on even terms."

A look of pain crossed the face of the old soldier.

"Rupert," he said, rising and laying his hand on his friend's shoulder, "you'll do nothing of the kind. . . . Not, that is, if you value my friendship in the least, or have the slightest regard for me. Do you not understand that I have given Carmelita my word that I will neither fight Rivoli with a weapon in my hand, nor attack him with one? Would she not instantly and naturally suppose that I had got you to do it *for* me? . . . Would anything persuade her to the contrary?"

"Is he to go unpunished then? Is he to ride roughshod over us all? He'll be ten times worse than before. You know he'll ascribe your withdrawal to cowardice—and so will everybody else," was the reply.

"They will," agreed John Bull.

"What's to be done then?"

"I don't know, but I'll tell you what is *not* to be done. No friend of mine is to challenge Rivoli to a duel."

The Bucking Bronco entered.

"Say, John," he drawled, "I jest bin and beat up Mister Mounseer Malvin, I hev'. 'Yure flappin' yure mouth tew much,' I ses. '*Vous frappez votre bouche trop*,' I ses. 'Yew come off it, me lad,' I ses. 'Yew jes' wipe off yure chin some. *Effacez votre menton*,' I ses. Then I slugs him a little one."

"What was it all about, Buck?" enquired Rupert.

"Do yew know what the little greasy tin-horn of a hobo was waggin' his chin about? Sed as haow yew was *a-climbin' down and a-takin' back the challenge to our Loojey!* I told him ef he didn't wipe off his chin and put some putty on his gas-escape I'd do five-spot in Biribi fer him. 'Yes, Mounseer Malvin,' I ses when I'd slugged him, 'I'll git the *as de pique*[47] on my collar for yew!' . . . '*It's true*,' he snivelled. '*It's true*,' and lays on the groun' so as I shan't slug him agin. So I comes away—not seein' why I should do the two-step on nuthin' at the end of a rope for a dod-gasted little bed-bug like Mounseer Malvin."

"It *is* true, Buck," replied John Bull.

"Well then, I wisht I'd stayed and plugged him

---

[47] Mark of the Zephyrs.

some more," was the remarkable reply.

"Rivoli told Carmelita about the duel, and I've promised her I'd let him go," continued John Bull.

"Then yure a gosh-dinged fool, John," said the Bucking Bronco. "Yew ain't to be trusted where wimmin's about. It would hev' bin the best day's work yew ever done fer Carmelita ef you'd let daylight through thet plug-ugly old bluff. He'll lie ter her from Revelley to Taps[48] until old Mother Canteen takes him into her shebang fer good—and then as like as not, he'll put Carmelita up at auction. . . . There'll be no holding our Loojey now, John. I should smile. Anybody as thinks our Loojey'll make it easy fer yew has got another think comin'. It's a cinch. He'll give yew a dandy time, John. What's a-bitin' yew anyway?"

"Carmelita," was the reply.

"I allow the right stunt fer eny pal o' Carmelita's is ter fill our Loojey up with lead as you perposed ter do. . . . Look at here, John. *I'll* do it. I could hit all Loojey's buttons with my little gun, one after the other, at thirty yards—and I'd done it long ago, but I know'd it meant the frozen mit fer mine from Carmelita, and I wasn't man enuff ter kill him fer Carmelita's good and make my name mud to her fer keeps."

"Same thing now, Buck," was the answer. "Challenge Luigi, and you can never set foot in the Café de la Légion again. If you killed him—it would be Carmelita's duty in life to find you and stab you."

"Sure thing, John—an' what about yew? Ef our Looj was to be 'Rivoli the Coward' ef he wouldn't fight, who's to be 'coward' now? . . . Yew've bitten off more'n yew can chew."

---

[48] Last Post. So called (in the American Army) because it is the signal to leave the Canteen and turn off the beer-taps.

"Anyhow, Buck, if you're any friend of mine—you'll let Rivoli alone. *Qui facit per alium facit per se*, and that's Dutch for 'I might as well kill Rivoli with my own hand as kill him through yours.'"

The Bucking Bronco broke into song—

"But serpose an' serpose,
   Yure Hightaliand lad shouldn't die?
   Nor the bagpipes shouldn't play o'er him
   Ef I punched him in the eye?"

chanted he, as he placed his beloved "gun"—an automatic pistol—under his pillow. "I'll beat him up, Johnnie. Fer Carmelita's sake I ain't shot him up, an' fer her sake and yourn I won't shoot him up now, but the very first time as he flaps his mouth about this yer dool, I'll beat him up—and there'll be *some* fight," and the Bucking Bronco dived into his "flea-bag."

The next day the news spread throughout the *caserne* of the First Battalion of the Legion that the promised treat was off, the duel between the famous Luigi Rivoli and the Englishman, John Bull, would not take place, the latter, in spite of the publicity and virulence of his challenge, having apologised.

The news was ill received. In the first place the promise of a brilliant break in the monotony of Depôt life was broken. In the second place, the undisputed reign of a despotic and brutal tyrant would continue and grow yet heavier and more insupportable; while, in the third place, it was not in accordance with the traditions of the Legion that a man should fiercely challenge another in public, and afterwards apologise and withdraw. Italian shares boomed and shot sky-high, while John Bulls became a drug in the market.

That evening the Bucking Bronco, for the first

time in his life, received a message from Carmelita, a message which raised him to the seventh
heaven of expectation and hope, while the san-
guine blood coursed merrily through his veins.

Carmelita wanted him. At five o'clock without
fail, Carmelita would expect him at the Café. She
needed his help and relied upon him for it. . . .
Gee-whillikins! She should have it.

At half-past five that evening, the Bucking
Bronco entered le Café de la Légion and stared in
amazement at seeing a strange Legionary behind
Carmelita's bar. He was a small, slight man in
correct walking-out dress—a blue tunic, red
breeches and white spats. His képi was pulled well
down over a small, intelligent face, the most
marked features of which were very broad black
eyebrows, and a biggish dark moustache. The
broad chin-strap of the képi was down, and
pressed the man's chin up under the large
moustache beneath which the strap passed. The
soldier had a squint and the Bucking Bronco had
always experienced a dislike and distrust of people
so afflicted.

"An' what'n Hell are *yew* a-doin' thar, yew
swivel-eyed tough?" he enquired, and repeated his
enquiry in Legion French.

The Legionary laughed—a ringing peal which
was distinctly familiar.

"Don't yew git fresh with me, Bo, or I'll come
roun' thar an' improve yure squint till you can see
in each ear-'ole," said the American, trying to
"place" the man.

Again the incongruous tinkling peal rang out
and the Bucking Bronco received the shock of his
life as Carmelita's voice issued through the big
moustache. Words failed him as he devoured the
girl with his eyes.

"Dear Monsieur Bouckaing Bronceau," said

she. "Will you walk out to-night with the youngest recruit in the Legion?"

The Bronco still stared agape.

"I am in trouble," continued Carmelita, "and I turn to you for help."

The light of hope shone in the American's eyes.

"Holy Poker!" said he. "God bless yure sweet eyes, fer sayin' so, Carmelita. But why *me*? Have yew found yure Loojey out, at last? Why me?"

"I turn to you for help, Monsieur Bronco," said the girl, "because you have told me a hundred times that you love me. Love gives. It is not always asking, asking, asking. Now give me your help. I want to get at the truth. I want to clear a good and honest man from a web of lies. Take me to the Canteen with you to-night. They say my Luigi goes there to see Madame la Cantinière. They say he flirts and drinks with her, that he helps her there, and serves behind her bar. They even dare to say that he asks her to marry him. . . ."

"It's true," interrupted the Bucking Bronco.

"Very well—then take me there now. My Luigi has sworn to me a hundred times that he never sets foot in Madame's Canteen, that he would not touch her filthy Algerian wine—my Luigi who drinks only the best Chianti from Home. Take me there and prove your lies. Take me now, and either you and your friends, or else Luigi Rivoli, shall never cross my threshold again." Carmelita's voice was rising, tears were starting to her eyes, and her bosom rose and fell as no man's ever did.

"Easy, honey," said the big American. "Ef yure gwine ter carry on right here, what'll you do in the Canteen when yew see yure Loojey right thar doin' bar-tender fer the woman he's a-doin' his damned-est to marry?"

"*Do?*" answered Carmelita in a low tense voice. "Do? I would be cold as ice. I would be still and hard as one of the statues in my own Naples. All Hell would be in my breast, but a Hell of frozen fire do you understand, and I would creep away. Like a silent spirit I would creep away—but I would be a spirit of vengeance. To Monsieur Jean Boule would I go and I would say, 'Kill him! Kill him! For the love of God and the Holy Virgin and the Blessed Bambino, *kill* him—and let me come and stamp upon his face.' That is what I would say, Monsieur Bronco."

The American covered the girl's small brown hand with his huge paw.

"Carmelita, honey," he whispered. "Don't go, little gel—don't go. May I be struck blind and balmy right hyar, right naow, ef I tell you a word of a lie. Every night of his life he's thar, afore he comes down hyar with lies on his lips to yew. Don't go. Take my word fer it, an' John Bull's word, and young Rupert's word. They're White Men, honey, they wouldn't lie ter yew. Believe what we tell yew, and give ole John Bull back his promise, an' let him shoot-up this low-lifer rattle-snake. . . ."

"I will see with my own eyes," said Carmelita—adding with sound feminine logic, "and if he's not there to-night, I'll know that you have all lied to me, and that he never was there—and never, never, never again shall one of you enter my house, or my Legionaries shall nail you by the ears to the wall with their bayonets. . . . Shame on me, to doubt my Luigi for a moment."

The American gave way.

"Come on then, little gel," he said. "P'raps it's fer the best."

§2

Entering the Canteen that evening for his

modest litre, 'Erb caught sight of his good friend, the Bucking Bronco, seated beside a Legionary whom 'Erb did not know. The American beckoned and 'Erb emitted a joyous sound to be heard more often in the Ratcliffe Highway than in the wilds of Algeria. Apparently his pal's companion was, or had been, in funds, for his head reposed upon his folded arms.

"Wotto, Bucko!" exclaimed the genial 'Erb. "We a-goin' to ketch this pore bloke's complaint? Luv-vus! Wish I got enuff to git as ill as wot 'e is."

"Sit down t'other side of him, 'Erb," responded the American. "We may hev' to help the gay-cat to bed. He's got a jag. Tight as a tick—an' lef me in the lurch with two-francs' worth to drink up."

"Bless 'is 'eart," exclaimed 'Erb. "I dunno wev-ver 'e's a-drinkin' to drahn sorrer or wevver he's a-drinkin' to keep up 'is 'igh sperrits—but he shan't say as 'ow 'Erb 'Iggins didn't stand by 'im to the larst—the larst boll' I mean," and 'Erb filled the large glass which the American reached from the bar.

" 'Ere's 'ow, Cocky," he shouted in the ear of the apparently drunken man, giving him a sharp nudge in the ribs with his elbow.

The drunken man gasped at the blow, gave a realistic hiccough and murmured: "A votre santé, Monsieur."

"Carn't the pore feller swaller a little more, Buck?" enquired 'Erb with great concern. "Fency two francs—an' he's 'ad ter giv' up! . . . Never mind, Ole Cock," he roared again in the ear of the drunkard, "p'raps you'll be able ter go ahtside in a minnit an' git it orf yer chest. Then yer kin start afresh. See? . . . 'Ope hon, 'ope hever. . . . 'Sides," he added, as a cheering afterthought, "It'll tiste as good a-comin' up as wot it did a-goin' dahn." He then blew vinously into his mouth-organ and settled down for a really happy evening.

A knot of Legionaries, friends of Rivoli, stood at the bar talking with Madame.

"Here he comes," said one of them, leaning with his back against the bar. "Ask him."

Luigi Rivoli strode up, casting to right and left the proud glances of the consciously Great.

"Bonsoir, ma belle," quoth he to Madame. "And how is the Soul of the Soul of Luigi Rivoli?"

The drunken man, sitting between the Bucking Bronco and le Légionnaire 'Erbiggin, moved his head. He lay with the right side of it upon his folded arms and his flushed face toward the bar. His eyes were apparently closed in sottish slumber.

Madame la Cantinière fixed Rivoli with a cold and beady eye. (She "wagged her beard" too much, did she? Oho!)

"And since when have I been the Soul of the Soul of Luigi Rivoli?" she enquired.

"Can you ask it, My Own?" was the reply. "Did not the virgin fortress of my heart capitulate to the trumpet of your voice when first its musical call rang o'er its unsealed walls?"

"Pouf!" replied Madame, bridling. . . . (What a way he had with him, and what a fine figure of a man he was, but *"beards"* quotha!) Raising the flap of the zinc-covered bar, Luigi, as usual, passed within and poured himself a bumper of wine. Raising the glass—

"To the brightest eyes and sweetest face that I ever looked upon," he toasted, and drank.

Madame simpered. Her wrath had, to some extent, evaporated. . . . Not that she would ever *dream* of marrying him. No! that "beard" would be ever between them. No! No! He had dished himself finally. He had, as it were, hanged himself in that beard as did Absalom in the branches of a tree.

The price he should pay for that insult was the value of her Canteen and income. There was balm and satisfaction in the thought. Still—until his successor were chosen, or rather, the successor of the late-lamented, so cruelly, if skilfully, carved by those *sacrépans* and *galopins* of Arabs—the assistance of the big man as waiter and chucker-out should certainly not be refused. By no means.

"And what is this tale I hear of you and le Légionnaire Jean Boule?" enquired Madame. "They say that the Neapolitan trollop of Le Café de la Légion (*sous ce nom-là!*) has begged your life of him."

The drunken man slowly opened his eyes and Rivoli put down his glass with a fierce frown.

"And who invented that paltry, silly lie?" he asked, and laughed scornfully. Madame pointed a fat forefinger at the Bucking Bronco who leant, head on fist, regarding Rivoli with a sardonic smile.

"Sure thing, Loojey. I'm spreadin' the glad joyous tidin's, as haow yure precious life has been saved, all over the whole caboodle," and proceeded to translate.

"Oh, is *that* the plot?" replied the Italian. "Is *that* the best lie the gang of you could hatch? Corpo di Bacco! It's a poor one. Couldn't the lot of you think of a likelier tale than that?"

The Bucking Bronco opined as haow thar was nuthin' like the trewth.

"Look you," said the Italian to Madame, and the assembled loungers. "This grey English cur—pot-valiant—comes yapping at me, being in his cups, and challenges me, *me*, Luigi Rivoli, to fight. I say: 'Go dig your grave, dog,' and he goes. I have not seen him since, but on all hands I hear that he has arranged with this strumpet of the Café to say that she has begged my life of him," and Luigi

Rivoli roared with laughter at the idea. "Now listen you, and spread this truth abroad. . . . Madame will excuse me," and he turned with his stage bow to Madame. . . . "I am no plaster saint, I am a Légionnaire. Sometimes I go to this Café—I admit it," and again turning to Madame, he laid his hand upon his heart. "Madame," he appealed, "I have no home, no wife, no fireside to which to be faithful. . . . And as I honestly admit I visit this Café. The girl is glad of my custom and possibly a little honoured—of that I would say nothing. . . . Accidents will happen to the bravest and most skilful of men in duels. The girl begged me not to fight. 'You are my best customer,' said she, 'and the handsomest of all my patrons,' and carried on as such wenches do, when trade is threatened. 'Peace, woman,' said I, 'trouble me not, or I go to Zuleika across the way.' . . . She then took another line. 'Look you, Signor,' said she, 'this old fool, Boule, comes to me when he has money; and he drinks here every night. Spare his miserable carcase for what I make out of it,' and with a laugh I gave the girl my franc and half-promise. . . . Still, what is one's word to a wanton? I may shoot the dog yet, if he and his friends be not careful how they lie."

The drunken man had turned his face on to his arms. No one but the American and 'Erb noticed that his body was shaken convulsively. Perhaps with drunken laughter?

"Tole yer so, Cocky," bawled 'Erb in his ear. "You'll be sick as David's sow in a minnit, 'an' we'll all git blue-blind, paralytic drunk,' " and rising to his feet 'Erb lifted up his voice in song to the effect that—

"White wings they never grow whiskers,
They kerry me cheerily over the sea

To ye Banks and Braes o' Bonny Doon
Where we drew 'is club money this
    mornin'.
Witin' to 'ear the verdick on the boy in the
    prisoner's dock
When Levi may I menshun drew my perlite
    attenshun
To the tick of 'is grandfarver's clock.
Ninety years wivaht stumblin', Tick, Tick,
    Tick,—
Ninety years wivaht grumblin', gently does
    the trick,
When it stopped short, never to go agine
Till the ole man died.
An' ef yer wants ter know the time, git yer
    'air cut."

For the moment 'Erb was the centre of interest, though not half a dozen men in the room understood the words of what the vast majority supposed to be a wild lament or dirge.

John Bull entered the Canteen, and 'Erb was forgotten. All near the counter, save the drunken man, watched his approach. He strode straight up to the bar, his eyes fixed on Rivoli.

"I wish to withdraw my challenge to you," he said in a clear voice. "I am not going to fight you after all."

"*But, Mother of God, you are!*" whispered the drunken man.

"Oho!" roared Rivoli. "Oho!" and exploded with laughter. "Sober to-night are you, English boaster? And how do you know that I will not fight you, *flaneur?*"

"That rests with you, of course," was the reply.

"Oho, it does, does it, Monsieur Coup Manqué? And suppose I decide *not* to fight you, but to punish you as little barking dogs should be punished? By the Wounds of God you shall learn a lesson, little cur. . . ."

The drunken man moved, as though to spring to his feet, but the big American's arm flung round him pressed him down, as he lurched his huge body drunkenly against him, pinning him to the table.

" 'Ere," expostulated 'Erb. " 'E wants ter be sick, I tell yer. Free country ain't it, if 'e *is* a bloomin' Legendary. . . . Might as well be a bleed'n drummerdary if 'e carn't be sick w'en 'e wants to. . . . 'Ope 'e ain't got seven stummicks, eny'ow," he added as an afterthought, and again applied himself to the business of the evening.

John Bull turned, without a word, and left the Canteen. The knot about the bar broke up and Luigi was alone with Madame save for two drunken men and one who was doing his best to achieve that blissful state.

"Have you forgiven me, Beloved of my Soul?" asked Rivoli of Madame, as she mopped the zinc surface of the bar.

"No," snapped Madame. "I have not."

"Then do it now, my Queen," he implored. "Forgive me, and then do one other thing."

"What is that?" enquired Madame.

"Marry me," replied Rivoli, seizing Madame's pudgy fist.

The eyes of the drunken man were on him, and the American watching, thought of the eyes of the snake that lies with broken back watching its slayer. There was death and the hate of Hell in them, and while he shuddered, his heart sang with hope.

"Marry me, Véronique," he repeated. "Have pity on me and end this suspense. See you, I grow thin," and he raised his mighty arms in a pathetic gesture.

Madame glanced at the poor man's stomach. There was no noticeable *maigreur*.

"And what of the Neapolitan hussy and your goings on in the Café de la Légion?" she asked.

"To Hell with the *putain*," he almost shouted. "I am like other men—and I have been to her dive like the rest. Marry me and save me from this loose irregular soldier's life. Do you think I would stray from *thee*, Beloved, if thou wert mine?"

"Not twice," said Madame.

"Then away with this jealousy," replied the ardent Luigi. "Let me announce our nuptials here and now, and call upon my comrades-in-arms to drink long life and happiness to my beauteous bride—whom they all so chastely love and revere. Come, little Star of my Soul! Come, carissima, and I will most solemnly swear upon the Holy Cross that never, never, never again will I darken the doors of the *casse-croûte* of that girl of the Bazaar. I swear it, Véronique—so help me God and all the Holy Saints—your husband will die before he will set foot in Carmelita's brothel."

"Come," said the drunken man, with a little piteous moan. "Could you carry me out, Signor? I am going to faint."

The Bucking Bronco gathered Carmelita up in his arms and strode toward the door.

" 'Ere 'old on," ejaculated 'Erb. " 'Arf a mo'! I'll tike 'is 'oofs. . . ."

"Stay whar yew are, 'Erb," said the American sternly, over his shoulder.

"Right-o, ole bloke," agreed 'Erb, always willing to oblige. "Right-o! Shove 'im in 'is kip[49] while I 'soop 'is bare.' "[50]

Outside, the Bucking Bronco set Carmelita

---

[49] Bed.
[50] Drink his beer.

down upon a bench in a dark corner and chafed her hands as he peered anxiously into her face.

"Pull yureself together, honey," he urged. "Don't yew give way yit. Yew've gotter walk past the Guard ef I carries yew all the rest of the way."

The broken-hearted girl could only moan. The American racked his brains for a solution of the difficulty and wished John Bull and Rupert were with him. It would be utterly hopeless to approach the gate with the girl in his arms. What would happen if he could not get her out that night? Suddenly the girl rose to her feet. Pride had come to her rescue.

"Come, Monsieur Bronco," she said in a dead, emotionless voice. "Let me get home," and began to walk like an automaton. Slipping his arm through hers, the American guided and supported her, and in time, Carmelita awoke from a terrible dream to find herself at home. The Russian girl, in some clothing and a wrap of Carmelita's, admitted them at the back door.

"Get her some brandy," said the Bucking Bronco.

"Shall I open the Caffy and serve fer yew, Carmelita, ma gel?" he asked.

Before he could translate his question into Legion French, Carmelita had understood, partly from his gestures. She shook her head.

Olga Kyrilovitch looked a mute question at the American. He nodded slightly. Carmelita caught the unspoken communication between the two.

"Yes," she said, turning to Olga, "you were right. . . . They were all right. And I was wrong. . . . He is the basest, meanest scoundrel who ever betrayed a woman. I do not realise it yet—I am stunned. . . . And I am punished too. I shall die or go mad when I understand. . . . And I want to be alone. Go now, dear Signor Orso Americano, and take my love and this message to Signor Jean Boule. *I kiss his boots in humility and apology, and if he will kill this Rivoli for me I will be his slave for life.*"

"Let *me* kill him fer yew, Carmelita," begged the American as he turned to go, and then paused as his face lit up with the brightness of an idea. "No," he said. "Almighty God! I got another think come. I'll come an' see yew to-morrow, Carmelita—and make yew a *pro*posal about Mounseer Loojey as'll do yew good." At the door he beckoned to the Russian girl.

"Look at hyar, Miss Mikhail," he whispered. "Stand by her like a man to-night. Nuss her, and coddle her and soothe her. You see she don't do herself no harm. Yew hev' her safe and in her right mind in the mornin'—an' we'll git yew and yure brother outer Sidi or my name ain't Hyram Cyrus Milton."

§3

That night was one of the most unforgettable of all the memorable nights through which Olga Kyrilovitch ever lived in the course of her adventurous career. For it was the only night during which she was shut up with a violent and dangerous homicidal maniac. In addition to fighting for her own life, the girl had, at times, to fight for that of her assailant, and she deserved well of the Bucking Bronco. Nature at length asserted herself and Carmelita collapsed. She slept, and awoke in the middle of the next day as sane as a person can be, every fibre of whose being yearns and tingles with one fierce obsession. Even to the experienced Russian girl, the wildness of the Neapolitan revenge-passion was an alarming revelation.

"Though I starve or go mad, I cannot eat nor sleep till I have spat on his dead face," were the only words she answered to Olga's entreaty that she would take food. But she busied herself about her daily tasks with pinched white face, pinched white lips, and cavernous black brooding eyes.

"Rivoli's next meal here will be his last," thought Olga Kyrilovitch, and shuddered.

Terrible and unfathomable as was Carmelita's agony of mind, she insisted on carrying out the programme for the escape of the two Russians fixed for that day, and Olga salved a feeling of selfishness by assuring herself that anything which took the girl's thoughts from her own tragedy was for her good.

That afternoon, Feodor Kyrilovitch made his unobtrusive exit from the Legion and was admitted by his sister at the back door of the Café. In his pocket was a letter enclosed in a blank envelope. On an inner envelope was the following name and address: *"Lady Huntingten, Elham Old Hall, Elham, Kent, England."*

By the five-thirty train two flighty females—one blonde, the other brunette—were seen off from the little Sidi-bel-Abbès station of the Western Algerian Railway, which runs from Tlemcen to Oran, by Mademoiselle Carmelita of the Café de la Légion. Their conversation and playful badinage with the guard of Légionnaires, which is always on duty at the platform gate, were frivolous and unedifying. Sergeant Boulanger, as gallant to women as he was ferocious to men, vowed to his admired Carmelita that it broke his heart to announce that he feared he could not allow her two friends to proceed on their journey until—Carmelita's white face seemed to go a little whiter—they had both given him a chaste salute. On hearing this, one of the girls fled squealing to the train, while the other, with very real blushes and unfeigned reluctance, submitted her face to partial burial beneath the vast moustache of the amorous Sergeant. . . . As the ramshackle little train crawled out of the station, this girl said to the one who had fled: "You *were* a sneak to bolt like that, Feodor," and received the somewhat cryptic reply—

"My dear Olga, and where should we both be now if his lips had felt the bristles around mine? . . . You don't suppose that a double shave, twice over, makes a man's face like a girl's, do you? . . ."

These two young females found Lady Huntington all, and more than all, her son had prophesied. When Feodor and Olga Kyrilovitch left the hospitable roof of Elham Old Hall, she parried their protestations of gratitude with the statement that she was fully repaid and over-paid, for anything she had been able to do for them, by the pleasure of talking with friends of her son, friends who had actually been with him but a few days before, and who so fully bore out the statements contained in his letter to the effect that he was in splendid health and having a splendid time.

On returning to her Café, Carmelita found the Bucking Bronco, John Bull, Reginald Rupert, 'Erbiggins, and several other Légionnaires awaiting admittance. Having opened her bar and mechanically ministered to her customers' needs, the unsmiling, broken-looking Carmelita, all of whose vitality and energy seemed concentrated in her burning eyes, beckoned to the American and led him into her room. Gripping his wrist with her cold hand, and almost shaking him in her too-long suppressed frenzy:

"Have you told Jean Boule?" she asked. "When will he kill him? Where? Quick, tell me! I must be there. I must see him do it. . . . Oh! He will die too quickly. . . . It is too good a death for such a reptile. . . . It is no punishment. . . . Why should he not suffer some thousandth part of what *I* suffer?"

"Look at hyar, Carmelita, honey," interrupted the American, putting his arm round the little heaving shoulders as he mentally translated what he must first say in his own tongue. "Thet's jest whar the swine would git the bulge on yew. Why shouldn't he git a glimpse o' sufferin', sech as I had ter sit an' see yew git, las' night? . . . An' I gits it in the think-box las' night, right hyar. Listen, ma honey. *I'm gwine ter beat him up*, right naow, right hyar, in yure Caffy—an' before yure very eyes. In front of all his bullies an' all the guys he's beat up, I'll hev' him on his knees a-blubberin' an' a-prayin' fer mercy. . . . Then he shall lick yure boots, little gel, same as he makes recruits lick his. Then he shall grovel on the ground an' beg an' pray yew to marry him, and at that insult yew shall ask me to put him across my knee and irritate his pants with my belt—an' then throw him neck and crop, tail over tip, in the gutter! Ter-morrer John Bull smacks his face on the barrack-square an' tells him he was only playin' with him about lettin' him off that dool."

When Carmelita clearly understood the purport of this remarkable speech she put her arms around the Bucking Bronco's neck.

"Dear Signor Orso Americano," she whispered. "Humiliate him to the dust before his comrades, bring him grovelling to my feet, begging me to marry him—and I will be your wife. . . . Blind, blind, unnameable *fool* that I have been—to think this dog a god and you a rough barbarian. . . . Forgive me, Signor. . . . I could kill myself."

The Bucking Bronco folded the woman in his arms. Suddenly she struggled free, thrust him from her, and, falling into a chair, buried her face in her arms and burst into tears. Standing over her the Bucking Bronco awkwardly patted her back with his huge hand.

"Do yew good, ma gel," he murmured over and over again. "Nuth'n like a good cry for a woman. . . . Git it over naow, and by'n-by show a smilin' face an' a proud one fer Loojey Rivoli to see fer the las' time."

"The *bambino*," wailed the girl. "The *bambino*."

"*What?*" exclaimed the Bucking Bronco.

Rising, the girl looked the man in the face and painfully but bravely stammered out what had been her so-wonderful Secret, and the hope of her life.

The Bucking Bronco again folded Carmelita in his arms.

CHAPTER X

THE WAGES OF SIN

It was soon evident that the word had been passed round that there would be "something doing" at the Café de la Légion that evening. Never before had its hospitable roof covered so large an assembly of guests. Though it was not exactly what could be called "a packed house," it was far from being a selected gathering of the special friends of Il Signor Luigi Rivoli. To Legionaries John Bull, Reginald Rupert and 'Erb 'Iggins it was obvious that the Bucking Bronco had been at some pains to arrange that the spectators of whatever might befall that evening, were men who would witness the undoing of Luigi Rivoli—should that occur—with considerable equanimity. Scarcely a man there but had felt at some time the weight of his brutal fist and the indignity of helpless obedience to his tyrannous behest. Of one thing they were sure—whatever they might, or might not behold, they would see a Homeric fight, a struggle that would become historic in the annals of la Légion. The atmosphere was electric with suppressed excitement and a sense of pleasurable expectation.

In a group by the bar, lounged the Bucking Bronco and the three Englishmen with a few of their more immediate intimates, chiefly Frenchmen, and members of their *escouade*. Carmelita, a brilliant spot of colour glowing on either cheek, busied herself about her duties, flitting like a butterfly from table to table. Never had she appeared more light-hearted, gay, and *insouciante*.

267

But to John Bull, who watched her anxiously, it was clear that her gaiety was feverish and hectic, her laughter forced and hysterical.

"Reckon 'e's got an earthly, matey?" asked 'Erb of Rupert. " 'E'll 'ave ter scrag an' kick, same as Rivoli, if 'e don't want ter be counted aht."

"I'd give a hundred pounds to see him win, anyhow," was the reply. "I expect he'll fight the brute with his own weapons. He'll go in for what he calls 'rough-housing' I hope. . . . No good following Amateur Boxing Association rules if you're fighting a bear, or a Zulu, or a Fuzzy-wuzzy, or Luigi Rivoli. . . ."

And that was precisely the intention of the American, whose fighting had been learnt in a very rough and varied school. When earning his living as a professional boxer, he had given referees no more than the average amount of trouble; and in the ring, against a clean fighter, had put up a clean fight. A tricky opponent, resorting to fouls, had always found him able to respond with very satisfying tricks of his own—"and then some." But the Bucking Bronco had also done much mixed fighting as a hobo[51] with husky and adequate bulls[52] in many of the towns of the free and glorious United States of America, when guilty of having no visible means of support; with exasperated and homicidal shacks[53] on most of that proud country's railways, when "holding her down," and frustrating their endeavours to make him "hit the grit"; with terrible and dangerous lumber-jacks in timber camps when the rye whiskey was in and all sense and decency were out; with cow-punchers and ranchers, with miners, with Bowery toughs, and assorted des-

---

[51] Tramp, a rough.
[52] Policemen.
[53] Train conductors.

peradoes.

To-night, when he stood face to face with Luigi Rivoli, he intended to do precisely what his opponent would do, to use all Nature's weapons and every device, trick, shift and artifice that his unusually wide experience had taught him.

He knew, and fully admitted, that, tremendously powerful and tough as he himself was, Rivoli was far stronger. Not only was the Italian a born Strong Man, but he had spent his life in developing his muscles, and it was probable that there were very few more finely developed athletes on the face of the earth. Moreover, he was a far younger man, far better fed (thanks to Carmelita), and a trained professional wrestler. Not only were his muscles of marvellous development, they were also trained and educated to an equally marvellous quickness, skill and poise. Add to this the fact that the man was no mean exponent of the arts of *la savate* and *la boxe*, utterly devoid of any scruples of honour and fair-play, and infused with a bitter hatred of the American—and small blame accrues to the latter for his determination to meet the Italian on his own ground.

As he stood leaning against the bar, his elbows on it and his face toward the big room, it would have required a very close observer to note any signs of the fact that he was about to fight for his life, and, far more important, for Carmelita, against an opponent in whose favour the odds were heavy. His hard strong face was calm, the eyes level and steady, and, more significant, the hands and fingers quiet and reposeful. Studying his friend, John Bull noticed the absence of any symptoms of excitement, nervousness, or anxiety. There was no moistening of lips, no working of jaw muscles, no change of posture, no quickening of speech. It was the same old Buck, large, lazy, and lethargic, with the same humorous eye, the same measured drawl, the same quaint turn of speech. In striking contrast with the immobility of the American, was the obvious excitement of the Cockney.

"It'll be an 'Ellova fight," he kept on saying. "Gawdstreuth, it'll be an 'Ellova fight," and bitterly regretted the self-denying ordinance which he had passed upon himself to the effect that no liquor should wet his lips till all was o'er. . . .

Luigi Rivoli, followed as usual by Malvin, Toutou Boil-the-Cat, Borges, Hirsch and Bauer, strode into the Café. He was accustomed to attracting attention and to the proud consciousness of nudges, glances and whisperings wherever he went. Not for nothing is one the strongest and most dangerous man in the Foreign Legion. But to-night he was aware of more than usual interest as silence fell upon the abnormally large gathering in Carmelita's Café. He at once ascribed it to the widespread interest in the public challenge he had received from John Bull to a *duel à l'outrance* and the rumour that the Englishman had as publicly withdrawn it. He felt that fresh lustre had been added to his brilliant name. . . . Carmelita *had* been useful there, and had delivered him from a very real danger, positively from the fangs of a mad dog. Very useful. What a pity it was that he could not marry Madame, and run Carmelita. Might she not be brought to consent to some such arrangement? Not even when she found she could have him in no other way? . . . Never!

Absolutamente . . . Curse her. . . . Well, anyhow, there were a few more francs, dinners, and bottles of Chianti. One must take what one can, while one can—and after all the Canteen was worth ten Cafés. Madame had been very kind tonight and would give her final answer to-morrow.

That had been a subtle idea of his, telling her that, unless she married him, she should marry no one, and remain a widow all the days of her life, for he'd break the back of any man who so much as looked at her. That had given the old sow something to think about. Ha! Ha! . . .

As he entered, John Bull was just saying to the Bucking Bronco, "Don't do it, Buck. I know all about that

> 'Thrice-armed is he who hath his quarrel just,
> But four times is he who gets his blow in fust.'

But thrice is quite enough, believe me, old chap. You've no need to descend to such a trick as hitting him unawares, by way of starting the fight."

"Is this my night ter howl, John, or yourn? Whose funeral is it?"

"Fight him by his own methods if you like, Buck—but don't put yourself in the wrong for a start. . . . You'll win all right, or I shall cease to believe in Eternal Justice of Things."

It had been the purpose of the Bucking Bronco to lessen the odds against himself, to some extent, by intimating his desire to fight, with a shattering blow which should begin, and, at the same time, half win the battle.

Rivoli approached.

Ha! There was that cursed Englishman, was he? Well, since he had given his promise to Carmelita and was debarred from a duel, he should repeat his apology of last night before this large assembly. Moreover, he would now be free to handle this English dog—to beat and torture and torment him like a new recruit. Bull's hands would be tied as far as weapons were concerned by his promise to Carmelita. . . . The dog was leaning against the flap of the bar which he would have to raise to pass through to his dinner. Should he take him by the ears and rub his face in the liquor-slops on the bar, or should he merely put him on the ground and wipe his feet on him? Better not perhaps, there was that thrice-accursed American *scelerato* and that indestructible young devil Rupert, who had smitten his jaw and ribs so vilely, and wanted to fight again directly he had left hospital and *salle de police*. The Devil smite all Englishmen. . . . His wrath boiled over, his arm shot out and he seized John Bull by the collar, shook him, and slung him from his path.

And then the Heavens fell.

With his open, horny palm, the Bucking Bronco smote the Italian as cruelly stinging a slap as ever human face received. But for his friend's recent behest, he would have struck with his closed fist, and the Italian would have entered the fight, if not with a broken jaw, at least with a very badly "rattled" head.

"*Ponk!*" observed 'Erb, dancing from foot to foot in excitement and glee.

"Ah—h—h!" breathed Carmelita.

The Italian recovered his balance and gathered himself for a spring.

"No you don't," shouted Rupert, and the three Englishmen simultaneously threw themselves in front of him, at the same time calling on the spectators to make a ring.

In a moment, headed by Tant-de-Soif, the Englishmen's friends commenced pulling chairs, tables and benches to the walls of the big room. Old Tant-de-Soif had never received a sou or a drink from the bully, though many and many a blow and bitter humiliation. Long he had served and long he had hated. He felt that a great hour had struck.

The scores and scores of willing hands assisting, the room was quickly cleared.

"This American would die, it appears, poor madman," observed M. Malvin ingratiatingly to Carmelita.

"I do not think he will die," replied the girl. "But I think that anyone who interferes with him will do so."

The eyes of the good M. Malvin narrowed. Lay the wind in that quarter? The excellent Luigi was found out, was he? Well, there might be a successor. . . .

Meantime the Italian had removed and methodically folded his tunic and canvas shirt. A broad belt sustained his baggy red breeches.

So it had come, had it? Well, so much the better. This American had been the fly in the ointment of his comfort too long. Why had he not strangled the insolent, or broken his back long ago? He would break him now, once and for all—maim him for life if he could; at least make a serious hospital case of him.

Bidding Malvin mount guard over his discarded garments, Rivoli stepped forth into the middle of the large cleared space, flexing and slapping his muscles. Having done so, he looked round the crowded sides of the room for the usual applause. To his surprise none followed. He gazed about him again. Was this a selected audience? It was certainly not the audience he would have selected for himself. It appeared to consist mostly of *miserabile* whom he had frequently had to punish for insubordination and defiance of his orders. They should have a demonstration, that evening, of the danger of defying Luigi Rivoli.

As the American stepped forward John Bull

caught his sleeve. "Take off your tunic, Buck," he said in surprise.

"Take off nix," replied the American.

"But he'll get a better hold on you," remonstrated his friend.

"I should worry," was the cryptic reply, as the speaker unbuttoned the upper part of his tunic and pushed his collar well away from his neck at the back.

" 'E'll cop 'old of 'im wiv that coller, an' bleed'n well strangle 'im," said 'Erb to Rupert.

"Fancy that now, sonny," said the Bucking Bronco, with an exaggerated air of surprise, and stepped into the arena.

Complete silence fell upon the room as the two antagonists faced each other.

Nom de nom de bon Dieu de Dieu! Why had not le Légionnaire Bouckaing Bronceau stripped? Was it sheer bravado? How could he, or any other living man, afford to add to the already overwhelming risks when fighting the great Luigi Rivoli? . . .

The Bucking Bronco got his "blow in fust" after all, and, as his friend had prophesied, was glad that it had not been a "foul poke"—taking his opponent unawares.

"Come hither, dog, and let me snap thy spine," growled the Italian as the Bucking Bronco faced him. As he spoke, he thrust his right hand forward, as though to seize the American in a wrestling-hold. With a swift snatch the latter grabbed the extended hand, gave a powerful jerking tug and released it before his enemy could free it and fasten upon him in turn. The violent pull upon his arm swung the Italian half left and before he could recover his balance and regain his position, the Bucking Bronco had let drive at the side of his face with all his weight and strength. It was a terrific blow and caught Rivoli on the right cheek-bone, laying the side of his face open.

Only those who have seen—or experienced—it, know the effect of skilled blows struck by hands unhampered by boxing gloves.

The Italian reeled and, like the skilled master of ringcraft that he was, the Bucking Bronco gave him no time in which to recover. With a leap he again put all his strength, weight, and skill behind a slashing right-hander on his enemy's face, and, as he raised his arms, a left-hander on his ribs. Had any of these three blows found the Italian's "point" or "mark," it is more than probable that the fight would have been decided. As it was, Rivoli was only shaken—and exasperated to the point of madness. . . .

Wait till he got his arms round the man! . . . Corpo di Bacco! But wait! Let him wait till he got his hand on that collar that the rash fool had left undone and sticking out so temptingly!

Ducking swiftly under a fourth blow, he essayed to fling his arms round the American's waist. As the mighty arms shot out for the deadly embrace, the Bucking Bronco's knee flew up with terrific force, to smash the face so temptingly passed above it. Like a flash the face swerved to the left, the knee missed it, and the American's leg was instantly seized as in a vice.

The spectators held their breath. Was this the end? Rivoli had him! Could there be any hope for him?

There could. This was "rough-housin'"—and at "rough-housin'" the Bucking Bronco had had few equals. He suddenly thought of one of *the* fights of his life—at 'Frisco, with the bucko mate of a hell-ship on which he had made a trip as fo'c's'le-hand, from the Klondyke. The mate had done his best to kill him at sea, and the Bucking Bronco had "laid for him" ashore as the mate quitted the ship. It had been "some" fight and the mate had collared his leg in just the same way. He would try the method that had then been successful. . . . He seized the Italian's neck with both huge hands, and, with all his strength, started to throttle him—his thumbs on the back of his opponent's neck, his fingers crushing relentlessly into his throat. Of course Rivoli would throw him—that was to be expected—but that would not free Rivoli's throat. Not by any manner of means. With a fair and square two-handed hold on the skunk's throat, it would be no small thing to get that throat free again while there was any life left in its proprietor. . . .

With a heave and a thrust, the Italian threw the Bucking Bronco heavily and fell heavily upon him. The latter tightened his grip and saw his enemy going black in the face. . . . Swiftly Rivoli changed his hold. While keeping one arm round the American's leg, at the knee, he seized his foot with the other hand and pressed it backward with all his gigantic strength. As the leg bent back, he pressed his other arm more tightly into the back of the knee. In a moment the leg must snap like a carrot, and the American knew it—and also that he would be lame for life if his knee-joint were thus rent asunder. It was useless to hope that Rivoli would suffocate before the leg broke. . . . Nor would a dead Rivoli be a sufficient compensation for perpetual lameness. Never to walk nor ride nor fight. . . . A lame husband for Carmelita. . . . Loosing his hold on his antagonist's throat, he punched him a paralysing blow on the muscle of the arm that was bending his leg back, and then seized the same arm by the wrist with both hands, and freed his foot. . . . A deadlock. . . . They glared into each other's eyes, mutually impotent, and then, by tacit mutual consent, released holds, rose, and confronted each other afresh.

So far, honours were decidedly with the American, and a loud spontaneous cheer arose from the spectators. "Vive le Bouckaing Bronceau!" was the general sentiment.

Carmelita sat like a statue on her high chair—lifeless save for her terrible eyes. Though her lips did not move, she prayed with all the fervour of her ardent nature.

Breathing heavily, the antagonists faced each other like a pair of half-crouching tigers. . . . Suddenly Rivoli kicked. Not the horizontal kick of *la savate* in which the leg is drawn up to the chest and the foot shot out sideways and parallel with the floor, so that the sole strikes the object flatly—but in the ordinary manner, the foot rising from the ground, to strike with the toe. The Bucking Bronco raised his right foot and crossed his right leg over his left, so that the Italian's rising shin met his own while the rising foot met nothing at all. Had the kick been delivered fully, the leg would have broken as the shin was suddenly arrested while the foot met nothing. (This is the deadliest defence there is against a kicker, other than a savatist.) But so fine was the poise and skill of the professional acrobat, that, in full flight, he arrested the kick ere it struck the parrying leg with full violence. He did not escape scot-free from this venture, however, for, even as he raised his leg in defence, the Bucking Bronco shot forth his right hand with one of the terrible punches for which Rivoli was beginning to entertain a wholesome respect. He saved his leg, but received a blow on the right eye which he knew must, before long, cause it to close completely. He saw red, lost his temper and became as an infuriated bull. As he had done under like circumstances with the

Légionnaire Rupert, he rushed at his opponent with a roar, casting aside wisdom and prudence in the madness of his desire to get his enemy in his arms. He expected to receive a blow in the face as he sprang, and was prepared to dodge it by averting his head. With an agility surprising in so big a man, the Bucking Bronco ducked below the Italian's outstretched arms and, covering his face with his bent left arm, drove at his antagonist's "mark" with a blow like the kick of a horse. The gasping groan with which the wind was driven out of Rivoli's body was music to the Bucking Bronco's ears. He knew that, for some seconds, his foe, be he the strongest man alive, was at his mercy. Springing erect he punched with left and right at his doubled-up and gasping enemy, his arms working like piston-rods and his fists falling like sledge-hammers. The cheering became continuous as Rivoli shrank and staggered before that rain of terrific blows. Suddenly he recovered, drew a deep breath and flung his arms fairly round the Bucking Bronco's waist.

Corpo di Bacco! He had got him! . . .

Clasping his hands behind the American, he settled his head comfortably down into that wily man's neck, and bided his time. He had got him. . . . He would rest and wait until his breathing was more normal. He would then tire the *scelerato* down . . . tire him down . . . and then . . .

This was his programme, but it was not that of the Bucking Bronco, or not in its entirety. He realised that "Loojey had the bulge on him." For the moment it was "Loojey's night ter howl." He would take a rest and permit Loojey to support him, also he would feign exhaustion and distress. It was a pity that it was his right arm that was imprisoned in the bear-hug of the wrestler. However, nothing much could happen so long as he kept his back convex.

Seconds, which seemed like long minutes, passed.

Suddenly the Italian made a powerful effort to draw him closer and decrease the convexity of his arched back. He resisted the constriction with all his strength, but realised that he had been drawn slightly inward.

Again a tremendous tensing of mighty muscles, again a tremendous heave in opposition, and again he was a little nearer.

The process was repeated. Soon the line of his back would be concave instead of convex. That would be the beginning of the end. Once he bent over backward there would be no hope; he would finally drop from the Italian's grasp with a sprained or broken back, to receive shattering kicks in the face, ribs and stomach, before Rivoli jumped upon him with both feet and twenty stone weight. For a moment he half regretted having so stringently prohibited any sort or kind of interference in the fight, whatever happened, short of Rivoli's producing a weapon. But only for a moment. He would not owe his life to the intervention of others, after having promised Carmelita to beat him up and bring him grovelling to her feet. He had been winning so far. . . . He *would* win. . . . As the Italian again put all his force into an inward-drawing hug, the American, for a fraction of a second, resisted with all his strength and then suddenly did precisely the opposite. Shooting his feet between the straddled legs of his adversary, he flung his left arm around his head, threw all his weight on to it and brought himself and Rivoli crashing heavily to the ground. As the arms of the latter burst asunder, the Bucking Bronco had time to seize his head and bang it twice, violently, upon the stone floor.

Both scrambled to their feet.

It had been a near thing. He must not get into that rib-crushing hug again, for the trick would not avail twice. Like a springing lion, Rivoli was on him. Ducking, he presented the top of his head to the charge and felt the Italian grip his collar. With an inarticulate cry of glee he braced his feet and with tremendous force and speed revolved his head and shoulders round and round in a small circle, the centre and axis of which was Rivoli's hand and forearm. The first lightning-like revolution entangled the tightly-gripping hand, the second twisted and wrenched the wrist and arm, the third completed the terrible work of mangling disintegration. In three seconds the bones, tendons, ligaments, and tissue of Rivoli's right hand and wrist were broken, wrenched and torn. The bones of the forearm were broken, the elbow and shoulder-joints were dislocated. Tearing himself free, the American sprang erect and struck the roaring, white-faced Italian between the eyes and then drove him before him, staggering backward under a ceaseless rain of violent punches. Drove him back and back, even as the bully put his uninjured left hand behind him for the dagger concealed in the hip pocket of his baggy trousers, and sent him reeling, stumbling and half-falling straight into the middle of his silent knot of jackals, Malvin, Borges, Hirsch, Bauer, and Tou-tou Boil-the-Cat. Against these he fell. Malvin was seen to put out his hands to stop him, Borges and Hirsch closed in on him to catch him, Bauer pressed against Malvin, Tou-tou Boil-the-Cat stooped with a swift movement. With a grunt Rivoli collapsed, his knees gave way and, in the middle of the dense throng, he slipped to the ground. As the Bucking Bronco thrust in, and the crowd pressed back, Rivoli lay on his face in the cleared space, a knife in his left hand, another in his back.

He never moved nor spoke again, but M. Toutou Boil-the-Cat did both.

As he left the Café he licked his lips, smiled and murmured: *"Je m'en ai souvenu."*

CHAPTER XI

GREATER LOVE . . .

At the bottom of the alley, le bon Légionnaire Tou-tou Boil-the-Cat encountered Sergeant Legros. . . . A bright idea! . . . Stepping up to the worthy Sergeant, he saluted, and informed him that, passing the notorious Café de la Légion, a minute since, he had heard a terrible *tohuwa-bohu* and, looking in, had seen a crowd of excited Legionaries fighting with knives and side-arms. He had not entered, but from the door had seen at least one dead man upon the ground.

The worthy Sergeant's face lit up as he smacked his lips with joy. Ah, ha! here were punishments. . . . Here were crimes. . . . Here were victims for *salle de police* and *cellules*. . . . Fodder for the *peloton des hommes punis* and the Zephyrs. . . . Here was distinction for that keen disciplinarian, Sergeant Legros.

"*V'la quelqu'un pour la boîte,*" quoth he, and betook himself to the Café at the *pas gymnastique.*

§2

At the sight of the knife buried in the broad naked back of the Italian, the silence of horror fell upon the stupefied crowd.

Nombril de Belzébuth! How had it happened?

Sacré nom de nom de bon Dieu de Dieu de Dieu de sort! Who had done it? Certainly not le Légionnaire Bouckaing Bronceau. Never for one second had the Légionnaire Rivoli's back been toward him. Never for one instant had there been a knife in the American's hand. Yet there lay the great Luigi Rivoli stabbed to the heart. There was the knife in his back. *Dame!*

Men's mouths hung open stupidly, as they stared wide-eyed. Gradually it grew clear and obvious. Of course—he had been knocked backwards into that group of his jackals, Malvin, Borges, Hirsch and Bauer, and one of them, who hated him, had been so excited and uplifted by the sight of his defeat that he had turned upon him. Yes, he had been stabbed by one of those four.

"Malvin did it. I saw him," ejaculated Tant-de-Soif. He honestly thought he had—or thought he thought so. "God bless him," he added solemnly.

He had many a score to settle with M. Malvin, but he could afford to give him generous praise—since he was booked for the firing-party beside the open grave, or five years *rabiau* in Biribi. It is not every day that one's most hated enemies destroy each other. . . .

"Wal! I allow thet's torn it," opined the Bucking Bronco as he surveyed his dead enemy.

Carmelita came from behind the bar and down the room. What was happening? Why had the fight stopped? She saw the huddled heap that had been Rivoli. . . . She saw the knife—and thought she understood. This was as things should be. This was how justice and vengeance were executed in her own beloved Naples. Il Signor Americano was worthy to be a Neapolitan, worthy to inherit and transmit *vendetta*. How cruelly she had misjudged him in thinking him a barbarian. . . .

"*Payé*," she cried, turning in disgust from the body, and threw her arms round the Bucking Bronco's neck, as the Sergeant burst in at the door. Sergeant Legros was in his element. Not only was there here a grand harvest of military criminals for his reaping, but here was vengeance—

and vengeance and cruelty were the favourite food of the soul of Sergeant Legros. Here was a grand opportunity for vengeance on the Italian trollop who had, when he was a private Legionary, not only rejected his importunities with scorn, but had soundly smacked his face withal. Striding forward, as soon as he had roared, *"Attention!"* he seized Carmelita roughly by the arm and shook her violently, with a shout of: "To your kennel, *prostituée*." Whereupon the Bucking Bronco felled his superior officer to the ground with a smashing blow upon the jaw, thereby establishing an indisputable claim to life-servitude in the terrible Penal Battalions.

Among the vices of vile Sergeant Legros, physical cowardice found no place. Staggering to his feet, he spat out a tooth, wiped the blood from his face, drew his sword-bayonet, and rushed at the American intending to kill him forthwith, in "self-defence." At the best of times Sergeant Legros looked, and was, a dangerous person—but the blow had made him a savage, homicidal maniac. The Bucking Bronco was dazed and astonished at what he had done. Circumstances had been too strong for him. He had naturally been in an abnormal state at the end of such a fight, and in no condition to think and act calmly when his adored Carmelita was insulted and assaulted. . . . What had he done? This meant death or penal servitude from the General Court Martial at Oran. He had lost her in the moment of winning her, and he dropped his hands as the Sergeant flew at him with the sword-bayonet poised to strike. No—he would fight. . . . He would make his get-away. . . . He would skin out and Carmelita should join him. . . . He would fight. . . . Too late! . . . The bayonet was at his throat. . . . Crash! . . . Good old Johnny! . . . That had been a near call. As the maddened Legros was in the act to thrust, Legionary John Bull had struck him on the side of the head with all his strength, sending him staggering, and had leapt upon him to secure the bayonet as they went crashing to the ground. As they struggled, Legionary Rupert set his foot heavily on the Sergeant's wrist and wrenched the bayonet from his hand.

The problem of Sir Montague Merline's future was settled and the hour for Reginald Rupert's desertion had struck.

An ominous growl had rumbled round the room at the brutal words and action of the detested Legros, and an audible gasp of consternation had followed the Bucking Bronco's blow. Sacré Dieu! Here were doings of which ignorance would be bliss—and there was a rush to the door, headed by Messieurs Malvin, Borges, Hirsch and Bauer.

Several Legionaries, as though rooted to the spot by a fearful fascination, or by the hope of seeing Legros share the fate of Rivoli, had stood their ground until John Bull struck him and Rupert snatched the bayonet as though to kill him. Then, with two exceptions, this remainder fled. These two were Tant-de-Soif and the Dutchman, Hans Djoolte; the former, absolutely unable to think of flight and the establishment of an *alibi* while the man who had made his life a hell was fighting for his own life; the latter, clear of conscience, honestly innocent and wholly unafraid. Staring round-eyed, they saw Sergeant Legros mightily heave his body upward, his head pinned to the ground by 'Erb 'Iggins, his throat clutched by Légionnaire Jean Boule, his right hand held down by Légionnaire Rupert. Again he made a tremendous effort, emitted a hideous bellowing sound and then collapsed and lay curiously still.

Meanwhile, Carmelita had closed and fastened the doors and shutters of the Café and was turning out the lamps. Within half a minute of the entrance of the Sergeant, the Café was closed and in semi-darkness.

"The bloomin' ol' fox is shammin' dead," panted 'Erb, and removed his own belt. " 'Eave 'im up and shove this rahnd 'is elbers while 'e's a-playin' 'possum. Shove yourn rahnd 'is legs, Buck," he added.

While still lying perfectly supine, the Sergeant was trussed like a fowl.

"Naow we gotter hit the high places. We gotter vamoose some," opined the Bucking Bronco, as the four arose, their task completed. They looked at each other in consternation. Circumstances had been too much for them. Fate and forces outside themselves had whirled them along in a spate of mischance, and cast them up, stranded and gasping. Entering the place with every innocent and praiseworthy intention, they now stood under the shadow of the gallows and the gaol. With them in that room was a murdered man, and an assaulted, battered and outraged superior. . . .

The croaking voice of Tant-de-Soif broke the silence. "*Pour vous*," quoth he, "*il n'y a plus que l'Enfer.*"

"Shut up, you ugly old crow," replied Reginald Rupert, "and clear out. . . . Look here, what are you going to do about it? What are you going to say?"

"I?" enquired Tant-de-Soif. "Le Légionnaire Djoolte and I have seen each other in the Bar de Madagascar off the Rue de Daya the whole evening. We have been here *peaudezébie*. Is it not, my Djoolte? Eh, *mon salop*?"

But the sturdy Dutch boy was of a different moral fibre.

"I have not been in the Bar de Madagascar," replied he, in halting Legion French. "I have been in le Café de la Légion the whole evening and seen all that happened."

" 'E's a-seekin' sorrer. 'E wants a fick ear," put in 'Erb in his own vernacular.

"If my evidence is demanded, I saw a fair fight between the Légionnaire Bouckaing Bronceau and le Légionnaire Luigi Rivoli. I then saw le Légionnaire Luigi Rivoli fall dead, having been stabbed by either le Légionnaire Malvin or le Légionnaire Bauer, if it were not le Légionnaire Hirsch, or le Légionnaire Borges. I believe Malvin stabbed him while these three held him, but I do not know. I then saw le Sergent Legros enter and assault and abuse Mam'zelle Carmelita. I then saw him fall as though someone had struck him and he then attempted to murder le Légionnaire Bronco with his Rosalie. I then saw some Légionnaires tie him up. . . . That is the evidence that I shall give if I give any at all. I may refuse to answer, but I shall tell no lies."

"That is all right," said the Bucking Bronco. "Naow yew git up an' yew git—an' yew too, Tant-de-Soif, and tell the b'ys ter help Carmelita any they can, ef Legros gits 'er inter trouble an' gits 'er Caffy shut. . . . An' when yew gits the Gospel truth orf yure chest, Fatty, yew kin say, honest Injun, as haow I tol' yew, thet me an' John Bull was a-goin' on pump ter Merocker, an' Mounseers Rupert an' 'Erb was a-goin' fer ter do likewise ter Toonis. Naow git," and the two were hustled out of the Café.

"Now," said John Bull, taking command, "we've got to be quick, as it's just possible the news of what's happened may reach the picket and you may be looked for before you're missing. First thing is Carmelita, second thing's money, and third thing's plan of campaign. . . . Is Carmelita in any danger over this?"

"Don't see why she should be," said Rupert. "It's not her fault that there was a fight in her Café. It has never been in any sense a 'disorderly house,' and what happened, merely happened here."

"Yep," agreed the Bucking Bronco. "But I'm plum' anxious. I'm sure tellin' yew, I don't like ter make my gitaway an' leave her hyar. But we can't take a gal on pump."

"Arx the young lidy," suggested 'Erb, and with one consent they went to the bar, leaning on which Carmelita was sobbing painfully. The strain and agony of the last twenty-four hours had been too much and she had broken down. As they passed the two silent bodies, 'Erb stopped and bent over Sergeant Legros, remarking: "Knows 'ow ter lie doggo, don't 'e—the ol' cunnin'-chops?" He fell silent a moment, and then in a very different voice ejaculated, "Gawdstreuth 'e's *mort*, 'e is. 'E's *tué*."

John Bull and Reginald Rupert looked at each other, and then turned back quietly to where the Sergeant was lying.

"Cerebral hæmorrhage," suggested John Bull. "I struck him on the side of the head."

" 'Eart failure," suggested 'Erb. "I set on 'is 'ead till 'is 'eart stopped, blimey!"

"Apple Plexy, I opine," put in the Bucking Bronco. "All comes o' gittin' excited, don't it?"

"He certainly made himself perfectly miserable when I took his bayonet away," admitted Legionary Rupert.

"Anyhow, it's a fair swingin' job nah, wotever it was afore," said 'Erb. Whatever the cause and whosesoever the hand, Sergeant Legros was undoubtedly dead. They removed the belts, straightened his limbs, closed his eyes and 'Erb placed the dead man's képi over the face, bursting as he did so into semi-hysterical song—

"Ours is a 'appy little 'ome,
I wisht I was a kipper on the foam,
There's no carpet on the door,
There's no knocker on the floor,
Oo! Ours *is* a 'appy little 'ome."

"Shut that damned row," said Legionary Rupert.

"Carmelita, honey," said the Bucking Bronco, stroking the hair of the weeping girl. "Yew got the brains. Wot'll we do? Shall we stop an' look arter ye? Will yew come on pump with us? Will yew ketch the nine-fifteen ter Oran? Yew could light out fer the railroad *de*-pot right now—or will yew stick it out here, an' see ef they takes away yure licence? They couldn't do nuthin' more. . . . Give it a name, little gal—we've gotter hike quick, ef we ain't a-goin' ter stay."

Carmelita controlled herself with an effort and dried her eyes. Not for nothing had her life been what it had.

"You must all go at once," she said unhesitatingly. "Take Signor Rupert's money and make for Mendoza's in the Ghetto. He'll sell you mufti and food. Change, and then run, all night, along the railway. Lie up all day, and then run all night again. Then take different trains at different wayside stations, one by one, and avoid each other like poison in Oran; and leave by different boats on different days. I shall stay here. After trying for some hours to revive Legros, I shall send for the picket. You will be far from Sidi then. I shall give the Police all information as to the fight, and as to the murder of *that*, by Malvin; and shall conceal nothing of Legros' murderous attempt upon the Légionnaire Bouckaing Bronceau and of his death by *apoplessia*. . . . They will see he has no wound. . . . This will give weight and truth to my evidence to the effect that it was a fair, clean fight and that no blame attaches to le Légionnaire Bouckaing Bronceau. . . . Where am I to blame? . . . No, you can leave me without fear. Also will I give evidence to having heard you plotting to make the promenade in different directions and to avoid the railway and Oran. . . ."

The Bucking Bronco was overcome with admiration.

"Ain't that horse-sense?" he ejaculated.

Laying her hands upon his shoulders, Carmelita looked him in the eyes.

"And when you write to me to join you also, dear Americano, I will come," she said. "I, Carmelita, have said it. . . . Now that *that* is dead, I shall be able to save some money. Write to me when you are safe, and I will join you wherever you are—whether it be Napoli or Inghilterra or America."

"God bless ye, little gal," growled the American, folding her in his arms, and for the first time of his life being on the verge of an exhibition of weakness. "We'll make our gitaway all right, an' we couldn't be no use ter yew in prison hyar. . . . I'll earn or steal some money ter send yer, Carmelita, honey."

"I can help you there," put in Legionary Rupert.

"You and your loose cash are the *deus ex machina*, Rupert, my boy," said John Bull. . . . "But for you, the Russians would hardly have got away so easily, and now a few pounds will make all the difference between life and death to Buck and Carmelita, not to mention yourself and 'Erb."

"I am very fortunate," said Rupert, gracefully.

"By the way, how much have we left Carmelita?" he added.

"Exactly seven hundred francs, Monsieur," she replied. "Monsieur drew one thousand, he will remember, and the Russians after all, needed only three hundred in addition to their own roubles."

"What are you going to do, 'Erb?" asked John Bull. "You haven't committed yourself very deeply you know. Legros can't give evidence against you and I doubt whether Tant-de-Soif or Djoolte will. . . . I don't suppose any of the others noticed you, but there's a risk—and ten years of Dartmoor would be preferable to six months in the Penal Battalions. What shall you do?"

"Bung orf," replied 'Erb. "I'm fair fed full wiv Hafrica. Wot price the Ol' Kent Road on a Sat'day night!"

"Then seven hundred francs will be most ample for three of you, to get mufti, railway tickets and tramp-steamer passages from Oran to Hamburg."

"Why three?" asked Rupert.

"You, Buck and 'Erb," replied John Bull.

"Oh, I see. You have money for your own needs?" observed Rupert in some surprise.

"I'm not going," announced John Bull.

"*What?*" exclaimed four voices simultaneously, three in English and one in French.

"I'm not going," he reiterated, "for several reasons. . . . To begin with, I've nowhere to go. Secondly, I don't want to go. Thirdly, I did not kill Legros," and, as an inducement to the Bucking Bronco to agree with his wishes, he added, "and fourthly, I may be able to be of some service to Carmelita if only by supporting her testimony with my evidence at the trial—supposing that I am arrested."

"Come off it, old chap," said Rupert. "There are a hundred men whose testimony will support

Carmelita's."

"Wot's bitin' yew naow, John?" asked the Bucking Bronco. "Yew know it's a plum' sure thing as haow it'll come out thet yew slugged Legros in the year-'ole when we man-handled him. Won't that be enuff ter give yew five-spot in Biribi?"

"Yus. Wot cher givin' us, Ole Cock?" expostulated 'Erb. "Wot price them blokes Malvin, an' Bower, an' Borjis, an' 'Ersh? Fink they'll shut their 'eads? An' wot price that bloomin' psalm-smitin', Bible-puncher of a George Washington of a Joolt? Wot price ole Tarntderswoff? Git 'im in front of a court martial an' 'e wouldn't jabber, would 'e? Not arf, 'e wouldn't. I *don't* fink."

"And don't talk tosh, my dear chap, about having nowhere to go, please," said Rupert. "You're coming home with me of course. My mother will *love* to have you."

"Thanks awfully, but I'm afraid I can't go to England," was the reply. "I must . . ."

"*Garn*," interrupted 'Erb. "I'm wanted meself, but I'm a-goin' ter chawnst it. No need ter 'ang abaht Scotland Yard. . . . I knows lots o' quiet juggers. 'Sides, better go where it's a risk o' bein' pinched than stop where it's a dead cert. . . . Nuvver fing. You ain't goin' ter be put away fer wot you done, Gawd-knows-'ow-many years ago. That's all blowed over, long ago. Why you've bin 'ere pretty nigh fifteen year, ain't yer? Talk sinse, Ole Cock—ain't yer jest said yer'd raver do a ten stretch in Portland than 'arf a one in Biribi?"

John Bull and Reginald Rupert smiled at each other.

"Thanks awfully, Rupert," said the former, "but I can't go to England." Turning to the Cockney he added, "You're a good sort, Herbert, my laddie—but I'm staying here."

"Shucks," observed the American with an air of

finality, and turning to Carmelita requested her to fetch the nuggets, the spondulicks, the dope—in short, the wad. Carmelita disappeared into her little room and returned in a few moments with a roll of notes.

"Well, good-bye, my dear old chap," said John Bull, taking the American's hand. "You understand all I can't say, don't you? . . . Good-bye."

"Nuthin' doin', John," was the answer.

"Hurry him off, Carmelita, we've wasted quite time enough," said John Bull, turning to the girl. "If he doesn't go now and do his best for himself, he doesn't love you. Do clear him out. It's death or penal servitude if he's caught. He struck Legros before Legros even threatened him—and Legros is dead."

"You hear what Signor Jean Boule says. Are you going?" said Carmelita, turning to the American.

"No, my gal. I ain't," was the prompt reply. "How can I, Carmelita? . . . I'm his pal. . . . Hev' I got ter choose between yew an' him?"

"Of course you have," put in John Bull. "Stay here and you will never see her again. It won't be a choice between me and her then; it'll be between death and penal servitude."

The Bucking Bronco took Carmelita's face between his hands.

"Little gal," he said, "I didn't reckon there was no such thing as 'love,' outside books, ontil I saw yew. Life wasn't worth a red cent ontil yew came hyar. Then every time I gits inter my bunk, I thinks over agin every word I'd said ter yew thet night, an' every word yew'd said ter me. An' every mornin' when I gits up, I ses, 'I shall see Carmelita ter-night,' an' nuthin' didn't jar me so long as that was all right. An' when I knowed yew wasn't fer mine, because yew loved Loojey Rivoli, then I ses,

'*Hell!*' An' I didn't shoot 'im up because I see how much yew loved him. An' I put up with him when he uster git fresh, because ef I'd beat 'im up yew'd hev druv me away from the Caffy, an' life was jest Hell, 'cause I knowed 'e was a low-lifer reptile an' yew'd never believe it. . . . An' now yew've found 'im out, an' he's gorn, an' yure *mine*—an' it's too late. . . . Will yew think I don't love yew, little gal? . . . Don't tell me ter go or I might sneak off an' leave John in the lurch."

"You can't help me, Buck," put in John Bull. "I shall be all right. Who'll you benefit by walking into gaol?"

The American looked appealingly at the girl, and his face was more haggard and anxious than when he was fighting for his life.

"This is my answer, Signor Bouckaing Bronceau," spake Carmelita. "Had you gone without Signor Jean Boule, I should not have followed you. Now I have heard you speak, I trust you for ever. Had you deserted your friend in trouble, you would have deserted me in trouble. If Signor Jean Boule will not go, then you must stay, for he struck Legros to save your life, as you struck him to avenge me. Would *I* run away while you paid for that blow? . . ."

Carmelita then turned with feminine wiles upon John Bull.

"Since Signor Jean Boule will not go on pump," she continued, "you must stay and be shot, or sent to penal servitude, and I must be left to starve in the gutter."

Sir Montague Merline came to the conclusion that after all the problem of his immediate future was *not* settled.

"Very well," said he, "come on. We'll cut over to Mendoza's and go to earth. As soon as he has rigged us out, we'll get clear of Sidi."

(He could always give himself up when they had to separate and he could help them no more. Yes, that was it. He would pretend that he had changed his mind and when they had to separate he would pretend that he was going to continue his journey. He would return and give himself up. Having told the exact truth with regard to his share in the matter, he would take his chance and face whatever followed.)

"*A rivederci*, Carmelita," said he and kissed her.

"*Mille grazie*, Signor," replied Carmelita. "*Buon viaggio*," and wept afresh.

"So-long, Miss," said 'Erb. "Are we dahn'arted? *Naow!*"

Carmelita smiled through her tears at the quaint English *ribaldo*, and brought confusion on Reginald Rupert by the warmth of her thanks for his actual and promised financial help. . . .

"We'd better go separately to Mendoza's," said John Bull. "Buck had better come last. I'll go first and bargain with the old devil. We shan't be missed until the morning, but we needn't exactly obtrude ourselves on people."

He went out, followed a few minutes later by Rupert and 'Erb.

Left alone with Carmelita, the Bucking Bronco picked her up in his arms and held her like a baby, as with haggard face and hoarse voice he tried to tell her of his love and of his misery in having to choose between losing her and leaving her. Having arranged with her that he should write to her in the name of Jules Lebrun from an address which would not be in France or any of her colonies, the Bucking Bronco allowed himself to be driven from the back door of the Café. Carmelita's last words were—

"Good-bye, *amato*. When you send for me I shall come, and you need not wait until you can send me money."

§3

The good Monsieur Mendoza, discovered in a dirty unsavoury room, at the top of a broken winding staircase of a modestly unobtrusive, windowless house, in a dirty unsavoury slum of the Ghetto, was exceedingly surprised to learn that le Légionnaire Jean Boule had come to *him*, of all people in the world, for assistance in deserting.

The surprise of le bon Monsieur Mendoza was in itself surprising, in view of the fact that the facilitation of desertion was his profession. Still, there it was, manifest upon his expressive and filthy countenance, not to mention his expressive and filthy hands, which waggled, palms upward, beside his shrugged shoulders, as he gave vent to his pained astonishment, not to say indignation, at the Legionary's suggestion. . . . He was not that sort of man. . . . Besides, how did he know that Monsieur le Légionnaire had enough? . . .

John Bull explained patiently to le bon Monsieur Mendoza, of whose little ways he knew a good deal, that he had come to him because he was subterraneously famous in the Legion as the fairy god-papa who could, with a wave of his wand, convert a uniformed Légionnaire into a most convincing civilian. Further, that he was known to be wholly reliable and incorruptibly honest in his dealings with those who could afford to be his god-sons.

All of which was perfectly true.

(Monsieur Mendoza did not display a gilt-lettered board upon the wall of his house, bearing any such inscription as "*Haroun Mendoza, Desertion Agent. Costumier to Poumpistes and All who make the Promenade. Desertions arranged with promptitude and despatch. Perfect Disguises a Speciality. Foreign Money Changed. Healthy Itineraries mapped out. Second-hand Uniforms disposed of. H.M.'s Agents and Interpreters meet All Trains at Oran; and Best Berths secured on all Steamers. Convincing Labelled Luggage Supplied. Special Terms for Parties. . . .*" nor advertise in the *Echo d'Oran*, for it would have been as unnecessary as unwise. . . .)

All very well and all very interesting, parried Monsieur Mendoza, but while compliments garlic no *caldo*, shekels undoubtedly make the mule to go. Had le bon Légionnaire shekels?

No, he had not, but they would very shortly arrive.

"And how many shekels will arrive?" enquired the good Monsieur Mendoza.

"Sufficient unto the purpose," was the answer, and then the bargaining began. For the sum of fifty francs the Jew would provide one Legionary with a satisfactory suit of clothes. The hat, boots, linen and tie consistent with each particular suit would cost from thirty to forty francs extra. . . . Say, roughly, a hundred francs for food and complete outfit, per individual. The attention of the worthy Israelite was here directed to the incontrovertible fact that he was dealing, not with the Rothschild brothers, but with four Legionaries of modest ambition and slender purse. To which, M. Mendoza replied that he who supped with the Devil required not only a long, but a golden spoon. In the end, it was agreed that, for the sum of three hundred francs, four complete outfits should be provided.

The next thing was the production and exhibition of the promised disguises. Would M. Mendoza display them forthwith, that they might be selected by the time that the other clients arrived?

"*Si, si,*" said M. Mendoza. "*Ciertamente. Con placer.*" It was no desire of M. Mendoza that any client should be expected *comprar a ciegas*—to buy a pig in a poke. No, *de ningun modo.* . . .

Shuffling into an inner room, the old gentleman returned, a few minutes later, laden with a huge bundle of second-hand clothing.

"Will you travel as a party—say two tourists and their servants? Or as a party of bourgeoisie interested in the wine trade? Or—say worthy artisans or working men returning to Marseilles? . . . What do you say to some walnut-juice and haiks—wild men from the *Tanezrafet*? One of you a Negro, perhaps (pebbles in the nostrils), carrying an *angareb* and a bundle. I could let you have some *hashish.* . . . I could also arrange for camels —it's eighty miles to Oran, you know. . . . Say, three francs a day, per camel, and *bakshish* for the men. . . . Not *meharis* of course, but you'll be relying more on disguise than speed, for your escape. . . ."

"No," interrupted John Bull. "It only means more trouble turning into Europeans again at Oran. We want to be four obvious civilians, of the sort who could, without exciting suspicion, take the train at a wayside station."

"What nationalities are you?" enquired the Jew.

"English," was the reply.

"Then take my advice and don't pretend to be French," said the other, and added, "Are any of the others gentlemen?"

Sir Montague Merline smiled.

"One," he said.

"Then you and that other had better go as what you are—English gentlemen. If you are questioned, do not speak too good French, but get red in the face and say, 'Goddam' . . . Yes, I think one of you might have a green veil round his hat. . . .

the others might be horsey or seamen. . . . Swiss waiters. . . . Music-hall artistes. . . . Or German touts, bagmen or spies. . . . Father Abraham! That's an idea! To get deported as a German spy! Ha, ha!" There was a knock at the door. . . .

"*Escuche!*" he whispered with an air of mystery, and added, "*Quien esta ahi?*"

"It's the Lord Mayor o' Lunnon, Ole Cock," announced 'Erb as he entered. "Come fer a new set of robes an' a pearly 'at."

"That one can go either as a dismissed groom, making his way back to England, or an out-of-work Swiss waiter," declared Mendoza, as his artist eye and ear took in the details of 'Erb's personality.

A great actor and actor manager had been lost in le bon M. Mendoza, and he enjoyed the work of adapting disguises according to the possibilities of his clients, almost as much as he enjoyed wrangling and bargaining for their last sous. A greedy and grasping old scoundrel, no doubt, but once you entrusted yourself to M. Mendoza you could rely upon his performing his part of the bargain with zeal, honesty, and secrecy.

The two Legionaries divested themselves of their uniforms and put on the clothes handed to them.

Another knock, and Rupert came in.

"Hallo, Willie Clarkson," said he to Mendoza, who courteously replied with a "*Buenas tardes, señor.*"

"That one will be an English caballero," he observed.

"Thought I should never get here," said Rupert. "Got into the wrong rabbit-warren," and took off his tunic.

The Jew did not "place" the Bucking Bronco immediately upon his entrance, but studied him carefully, for some minutes, before announcing that he had better shave off his moustache and be a Spanish fisherman, muleteer, or sailor. If questioned, he might tell some tale, in execrable French, of a wife or daughter kidnapped at Barcelona and traced to a Tlemcen brothel. He should rave and be violent and more than a little drunk. . . .

And could the worthy M. Mendoza supply a couple of good revolvers with ammunition?

"*Si, si,*" said M. Mendoza. "*Ciertamente. Con placer.* A most excellent one of very large calibre and with twenty-eight rounds of ammunition for forty francs, and another of smaller calibre and longer barrel, but with, unfortunately, only eleven rounds, for thirty-five francs. . . ."

"Keep your right hand in your pocket, each of you," said M. Mendoza as they parted, "or you'll respectfully salute the first Sergeant you meet. . . ."

§4

The two Englishmen, in light summer suits, one wearing white buckskin boots, the other light brown ones, both carrying gloves and light canes, attracted no second glance of attention as they strolled along the boulevard, nor would anyone have suspected the vehement beating of their hearts as they passed the Guard at the gate in the fortification walls.

Similarly innocent of appearance, was an ordinary-looking and humble little person who shuffled along, round-shouldered, shrilly whistling "Viens Poupoule, viens Poupoule, viens."

Nor more calculated to arouse suspicion in the breast of the most observant Guard, was the big, slouching, blue-jowled Spaniard, who rolled along with his *béret* over one eye, and his cigarrillo pendent from the corner of his mouth. The distance separating these from the two English gentlemen lessened as the latter, leaving the main promenades, passed through a suburb and, turning to the right, followed a quiet country road, which led to a rail-way station.

Making a wide détour and avoiding the station, the four, marching parallel with the railway line, headed north for Oran.

So far, so good. They were clear of Sidi-bel-Abbès and they were free. Free, but in the greatest danger. The next thing was to get clear of Africa and from beneath the shadow of the tri-couleur.

"*Free!*" said Rupert, as the other two joined him and John Bull, and drew a long, deep breath, as of relief.

"Not a bit of it, Rupert," said John Bull. "It's merely a case of a good beginning and a sporting chance."

"Anyhow, well begun's half done, Old Thing. I feel like a boy let out of school," and he began to sing—

> "Si tu veux
>   Faire mon bonheur,
>   Marguerite, Marguerite,
>   Si tu veux
>   Faire mon bonheur,
>   Marguerite, donne-moi ton cœur,

You'll have to sing that, Buck, and put 'Carmelita' for 'Marguerite,' " he added.

"Business first," interrupted John Bull. "This is the programme. We'll go steady all night at the 'quick' and the 'double' alternately, and five minutes' rest to the hour. If we can't do thirty miles by daylight, we're no Legionaries. Sleep all day to-morrow, in the shadow of a boulder, or trees. . . . By the way, we mustn't fetch up too near Les Imberts or we might be seen by some-body while we're asleep. Les Imberts is about thirty miles from Sidi, I believe. To-morrow night, we'll do another thirty miles and that'll bring us to Wady-el-hotoma. From there I vote we go indepen-dently by different trains. . . ."

"That's it," agreed Rupert. "United for defence—separated for concealment. We'd better hang to-gether as far as Wady-what-is-it, in case a Goum patrol overtakes us."

"Why not bung orf from this 'ere Lace Imbear?" enquired 'Erb. "Better'n doin' a kip in the desert, and paddin' the 'oof another bloomin' night. I'm a bloomin' gennelman naow, Ole Cock. I ain't a lousy Legendary."

"Far too risky," replied John Bull. "We should look silly if Corporal Martel and a guard of men from our own *chambrée* were on the next train, shouldn't we? Whichever of us went into the station would be pinched. The later we hit the line the better, though on the other hand we can't hang about too long. We're between the Devil and the Deep Sea—station-guards and mounted pa-trols."

It occurred to the Bucking Bronco that his own best "lay" would be an application of the art of "holding her down." In other words, waiting outside Sidi-bel-Abbès railway station until the night train pulled out, and jumping on to her in the darkness and "decking her"—in other words, climbing on to the roof and lying flat. As a past-master in "beating an overland," he could do this without the slightest difficulty, leaving the train as it slowed down into stations and making a détour to pick it up again as it left. Before daylight he could leave the train altogether and book as a passenger from the next station (since John strongly advised against walking into Oran by road, as that was the way a penniless Legionary might be expected to arrive). By that means he would arrive at Oran before they were missed at roll-call in the morning. Should he, by any chance, be seen and "ditched" by what he called the "brakemen" and "train-crew," he would merely have "to hit the grit," and wait for the next train. Yes, that's what he would do if he were alone—but the four of them couldn't do it, even if they possessed the necessary nerve, skill and endurance—and he wasn't going to leave them.

"Come on, boys, *en avant, marche*," said John Bull, and they started on their thirty-mile run, keeping a sharp look-out for patrols, and halting for a second to listen for the sound of hoofs each time they changed from the *pas gymnastique* to the quick march. Galloping hoofs would mean a patrol of Arab gens-d'armes, the natural enemies of the *poumpiste*, the villains who make a handsome bonus on their pay by hunting white men down like mad dogs and shooting them, as such, if they resist. (It is not for nothing that the twenty-five francs reward is paid for the return of a deserter "*dead* or alive.")

On through the night struggled the little band, keeping as far from the railway as was possible without losing its guidance. When a train rolled by in the distance, the dry mouth of the Bucking Bronco almost watered, as he imagined himself "holding her down," "decking her," "riding the blind," or perhaps doing the journey safely and comfortably in a "side-door Pullman" (or goods-waggon).

Before daylight, the utterly weary and footsore travellers threw themselves down to sleep in the middle of a collection of huge boulders that looked as though they had been emptied out upon the plain from a giant sack. During the night they had passed near many villages and had made many détours to avoid others which lay near the line, as well as farms and country houses, surrounded by their fig, orange and citron trees, their groves of date-palms, and their gardens. For miles they had travelled over sandy desert, and for miles through patches of cultivation, vineyards and well-tilled fields. They had met no one and had heard nothing more alarming than the barking of dogs. Now they had reached an utterly desert spot, and it had seemed to the leader of the party to be as safe a place as they would find in which to sleep away the day. It was not too near road, path, building, or cultivation, so far as he could tell, and about a mile from the railway. The cluster of great rocks would hide them from view of any possible wayfarer on foot, horseback, or camel, and would also shelter them from the rays of the sun. He judged that they were some two or three miles from Les Imberts station, and four or five from the village of that name.

The next trouble would be water. They'd probably want water pretty badly before they got it. Perhaps it would rain. That would give them water, but would hardly improve the chances of himself and Rupert as convincing tourists. Thank Heaven they had a spare clean collar each, anyhow. Good old Mendoza. What an artist he was! . . .

John Bull fell asleep.

§5

"Look, my brothers! Behold!" cried "Goum" Hassan ibn Marbuk, an hour later, as he reined in his horse and pointed to where the footprints of four men left a track and turned off into the desert. "Franzwazi—they wear boots. It is they. Allah be praised. A hundred francs for us, and death for four Roumis. Let us kill the dogs."

Turning his horse from the road, he cantered along the trail of the footsteps, followed by his two companions.

"Allah be praised!" he cried again. "But our Kismet is good. Had it been but five minutes earlier it would have been too dark to notice them."

"The footprints lead into that el Ahagger," he added later, pointing to the group of great boulders.

The three men drew their revolvers and rode in among the rocks. The leading Arab gave a cry of joy and covered Rupert, who was nearest to him. As the Arab shouted, John Bull awoke and, even as he opened his eyes, yelled *"Aux armes!"* at the top of his voice. (He had shouted those words and heard them shouted, off and on, for fifteen years.) As he cried out, Hassan ibn Marbuk changed his aim from Rupert to John Bull and fired. The report of the revolver was instantly followed by three others in the quickest succession. John Bull's cry had awakened the Bucking Bronco and that wary man had slept with his "gun" in his hand. A second after Hassan ibn Marbuk fired, the Bucking Bronco shot him through the head, and then with lightning rapidity and apparently without aim, fired at the other two "Goums" who were behind their leader. Not for nothing had the Bucking Bronco been, for a time, trick pistol-shot in a Wild West show. Hassan ibn Marbuk fell from his saddle, the second Arab hung over his horse's neck, and the third, after a convulsive start, drooped and slowly bent backward, until he lay over the high crupper of his saddle.

"Arabs ain't no derned good with guns,"

remarked the Bucking Bronco, as he rose to his feet, though it must, in justice, be admitted that the leading Arab had decidedly screened the view, and hampered the activity of the other two as he emerged from the little gully between two mighty rocks.

"Gawd luvvus," said 'Erb, sitting up and rubbing his eyes. "Done in three coppers in a bloomin' lump!"

The Bucking Bronco secured the horses.

"I say," said Rupert, who was bending over Sir Montague Merline, "Bull's badly hit."

"Ketch holt, quick," cried the Bucking Bronco, holding out to 'Erb the three reins which he had drawn over the horses' heads. He threw himself down beside his friend and swore softly, as his experienced eye recognised the unmistakable signs.

"Is he dying?" whispered Rupert.

"His number's up," groaned the American.

"Done in by a copper!" marvelled 'Erb, and, putting his arm across his face, he leaned against the nearest horse and sobbed. . . . He was a child-like person, and, without knowing it, had come to centre all his powers of affection on John Bull.

The dying man opened his eyes. "Got it where the chicken got the axe," he whispered. "Good-bye, Buck. . . . See you in the . . . Happy Hunting Grounds . . . I hope."

The Bucking Bronco looked at Rupert.

"Carmelita put thisyer brandy in my pocket, Rupert," he said producing a medicine bottle. "Shall I dope him?"

He coughed and swallowed, his mouth and chin twitched and worked, and tears trickled down his face.

"Can't do much harm," said Rupert, and took the bottle from the American's shaking hand.

The brandy revived the mortally wounded man.

"Good-bye, Rupert," he said. "I advise you to go straight down to Les Imberts station . . . and take the next train. . . . There will be a patrol . . . after this patrol . . . before long. You can't lie up here for long now. . . . Buck might take a horse and gallop for it. . . . Lie up somewhere else. . . . And ride to Oran to-night. . . . 'Erb should go as Rupert's servant . . . or by a different train. . . . Remember Mendoza's tips."

The stertorous, wheezy breathing was painfully interrupted by a paroxysm of coughing.

"Much pain, old chap?" asked the white-faced Rupert, as he wiped the blood from his friend's lips.

"No," whispered Sir Montague Merline. "I am dead . . . up to . . . the heart. . . . Expanding bullet. . . . Lungs . . . and spine . . . I . . . expect . . . Shan't be . . . long."

"Anything I can do—any message or anything?" asked Rupert.

The dying man closed his eyes.

The Bucking Bronco was frankly blubbering. Turning to the dead "Goum" who had shot his friend, he swore horribly, and deplored that the man was dead and beyond the reach of his further vengeance. He fell instantly silent as his stricken friend spoke again.

"If you . . . get . . . to Eng . . . land, Rupert . . . will . . . you go . . . to . . . my wife? She's Lady . . ." he whispered.

"Yes—Lady . . . *who?*" asked Rupert eagerly.

"NO," continued the dying man, in a stronger voice, as he opened his eyes. "I never . . . had . . . a . . . wife."

Silence again.

"Why *Marguerite* . . . My . . . darling . . . girl. *Darling* . . . at . . . last. *Marguerite.*"

Sir Montague Merline's problem was solved, and the last of his wages paid. . . .

§6

The Honourable Reginald Rupert Huntingten never forgot the hour that followed. The three broken-hearted men buried their friend in a shallow, sandy grave and piled a cairn of rocks and stones above the spot. It gave them a feeling akin to pleasure to realise that every minute devoted to this labour of love, lessened their chance of escape.

Their task accomplished, they shook hands and parted—the Bucking Bronco incapable of speech. Before he rode away, Huntingten thrust a piece of paper into his hand, upon which he had scribbled: "*R. R. Huntingten, Elham Old Hall, Elham, Kent,*" and said, "Wire me there. Or—better still, come—and we'll arrange about Carmelita."

The Bucking Bronco rode away in the cool of the morning.

Having settled by the toss of a coin whether he or 'Erb should attempt the next train, he gave that grief-stricken warrior the same address and invitation.

With a crushing hand-clasp they parted, and Huntingten, with a light and jaunty step, and a sore and heavy heart, set forth for the station of Les Imberts to put his nerve and fortune to the test.

EPILOGUE

"Well, good night, my own darling Boy," said the beautiful Lady Huntingten, as she lit her candle from that of her son, by the table in the hall. "Don't keep Father up all night, if he and General Strong come to your bedroom."

"Good night, dearest," replied he, kissing her fondly.

Setting down her candlestick, she took him by the lapels of his coat as though loth to let him out of her sight and part with him, even for the night.

"Oh, but it is good to have you again, darling," she murmured, gazing long at his bronzed and weather-beaten face. "You won't go off again for a long, long time, will you? And we must keep your promise to that wholly delightful 'Erb, if it's humanly possible. But I really cannot picture him as a discreet and silent-footed valet. . . . I simply loved him and the Bucking Bronco. I don't know which is the more precious and priceless. . . . I do so wonder whether he'll be happy with his Carmelita. . . . I shall love seeing her."

"Yes, 'Erb and Buck are great birds," replied her son, "but poor old John Bull was the chap."

"Poor man, how awful—with freedom in sight. . . . You knew nothing of his story?" she asked.

"Absolutely nothing, dearest. All I know about him is that he was one of the very best. Funny thing, y' know, Mother—I simply lived with that chap, night and day, for a year, and know no more about him than just that. That, and his marks— and by Jove, he'd got some. . . . Simply a mass of scars, beginning with the crown of his head, where was a hole you could have laid your thumb in.

Been about a bit, too; fought in China, Madagascar, West Africa, the Sahara and Morocco, in the Legion. Certainly been in the British Army—in Africa, too. I fancy he'd been a sailor as well—anyhow he'd been in Japan and got the loveliest bit of tattooing I ever set eyes on. Wonderful colours—snake winding round his wrist and up his forearm. Thing looked alive though it had been done for over thirty years. Nagasaki, I think he said. . . ." He yawned hugely. "But here I am rambling on about a person you never saw, and keeping you up," he added. He bent to kiss his mother again.

"Mother!—*darling!* Don't you feel well? Here, I'll get you a little brandy."

Lady Huntingten was clutching at the edge of the table, and staring at her son, white-lipped. Her face looked drawn and suddenly old.

"No, no," she said. "Come back. I—sometimes— a little . . ." and she sat down on the oak settle beside the table.

"The heat . . ." she continued incoherently. "There, I'm all right now. Tell me some more about this—John Bull. . . . He *is* dead? . . . You buried him yourself, you said."

"Yes, poor old chap, it was awful."

"And he gave you no messages for his people? He did not tell you his real name?"

"No. Nothing. He's taken his story with him. The last words he said were 'Will you go and tell my wife, Lady . . .' and there he pulled himself up, and said he never had a wife. But he had, I'm sure —and he called to her by her Christian name. As he died, he cried out, '*At last—my darling—*' "

"*Marguerite,*" whispered Lady Huntingten.

SOWING GLORY

THE MEMOIRS OF "MARY AMBREE"
THE ENGLISH WOMAN-LEGIONARY

Edited by
PERCIVAL CHRISTOPHER WREN

"Partout où nous avons passé,
　Partout où nous sommes tombés.
　Nous avons semé de la gloire!"

"Wheresoever we've passed by,
　Wheresoever we may lie,
　We have sown our glory."
　　　　　　　(*Song of the Legion*)

*"When captains couragious, whom death could
    not daunte,
Did march to the siege of the citty of Gaunt,
They mustred their souldiers by two and by
    three,
And the formost in battle was Mary Ambree."*
                    Old English Ballad (1584).

DEDICATED

BY PERMISSION

TO

THE BRAVEST MAN AND GREATEST
GENTLEMAN

I HAVE EVER MET

HIS MOST CATHOLIC MAJESTY ALFONSO XIII

THE KING OF SPAIN

"Here's a health unto his Majesty,
  With a fa la la!
Confusion to his enemies,
  With a fa la la!
And he that will not drink his health,
I wish him neither wit nor wealth,
But a good stout rope to hang himself!—
  With a fa la la!" etc.
Cavalier Song, 1667.

The characters in this book are not fictitious, though, in many cases, the names have been changed

EDITOR'S PREFACE

Some time ago, I received from Belgium a letter signed "Mary Ambree"—a fairly obvious *nom de plume*—in which the writer stated that she had served for five years in the ranks of the French Foreign Legion as an ordinary *légionnaire*; and that, for part of this time, she had kept a diary, and had since written her memoirs of the remaining part.

The object of her letter was to ask whether I would edit her memoir-diary and arrange for its publication, provided I found it of sufficient interest and felt convinced that the document was genuine.

The writer of this letter, modestly, but quite truthfully, confessed that she had no gift for writing, and that her account of her life in the Legion was so dull, condensed, dry and uninteresting, that it was unfit for publication.

Would I read the diary and either undertake the task of editing it, or else return it to her without showing it to anyone else; and would I treat her letter, and the whole affair, as absolutely private and confidential—her strongest desire being to preserve her anonymity?

I agreed; and found the diary to be as terse and dry as a ship's log, the merest bare summary of each day's doings, some of them days of the most hectic, with pale patches that should have been purple, or at least scarlet—of the colour of the blood of the brave.

As a précis-writer "Mary Ambree" would excel.

Of one thing I was at once convinced, and that was the complete authenticity of the diary and memoirs—so far as they purported to be those of a *légionnaire.* Of this there could be no doubt whatsoever.

By the time I had finished my study of the document, I was equally convinced that the writer was a woman, and I have since been quite assured of the fact.

I wrote to "Mary Ambree," giving my opinion that she was right in thinking that her outline MS. was unpublishable in its present crude colourlessness, its bare poverty; and that the only possible thing for her to do, was to have it completely rewritten—her facts providing the skeleton for a flesh-and-blood body, articulate, moving and alive.

Observing that, quite frequently, people who "do things" cannot write, while many people who write don't "do things," I suggested that she should find one of the latter and collaborate with him or her to produce a really full and graphic story of a woman's courage and fortitude. Wherewith I returned the intriguing but heart-breakingly inadequate MS., and forgot the matter.

Some weeks later I received another letter from "Mary Ambree," explaining that she could not collaborate with anyone, and asking if I would rewrite her MS. myself, as I was "obviously the proper person to do so"—her only stipulation being that no attempt should be made to lift the veil of her anonymity, and that I would do nothing, and write nothing, that would be in any way likely to lead to the discovery of her identity.

I replied that I should be delighted to attempt to make her brief bald notes and jottings into a book.

One would probably have denied one's intuitions and rejected all evidence, documentary and other, but for knowledge of the fact that many women *have* served as soldiers, with great success and high credit—one, at least, in a Spahi cavalry regiment (the famous Fraulein Eberhardt, who rose to the rank of Squadron Sergeant-Major, was decorated for bravery, and was not known to be a woman until she was killed in battle). An even more remarkable case than "Mary Ambree's" is one of which the King of Spain told me, and of which he vouched for the historical truth—that of a Spanish nun who, fleeing from her convent, enlisted in the Spanish Foreign Legion and fought long and bravely for her King and her Country.

In this book, then, the words are the words of the Editor, but the actual facts, incidents, adventures, memories, descriptions, tales and stories, are those of "Mary Ambree"; and the *dramatis personæ* are the living (and the dead) men who were her comrades in the ranks of the French Foreign Legion.

The various tales told by the *Légionnaires* are amplified and expanded from the outlines sketched, and the notes made, by the diarist.

I feel it a very great honour to have been asked to introduce the modest and heroic "Mary Ambree" to those who read my books.

P. C. W.

NOTE

As this book goes to press, the following paragraph appears in *The Daily Telegraph* of June 19, 1931, under the heading *Paris Day by Day. From Our Own Correspondent*, Paris:—

"There is a strong suspicion that a woman has succeeded in enlisting in the Foreign Legion and has, so far, escaped detection.

"According to the notice from the Legion headquarters at Sidi-bel-Abbès, a watch is to be kept on all soldiers of the Legion at a forthcoming bathing parade, when everyone will have to pass under a shower bath.

"The authorities mean to be certain that no soldier shall take another's place. This happened once in the case of German twins, brother and sister, who joined the Legion in 1908. At the various medical examinations the male twin passed the inspection twice—once for himself and once for his sister, who remained in hiding while her brother impersonated her. It was not until the girl had served for six months as a soldier of the Legion, that the trick was discovered through the Commander's insistence on the complete roll-call for the shower-bath parade.

"Similar precautions are to be taken now, so that the regiment in which identities are cloaked in mystery shall, at least, be sure that its members are all males".

*   *   *   *   *

From this it would appear that the French Military Authorities at any rate do not consider it impossible for a woman to get into the French Foreign Legion.

BOOK I

". . . She added to the courage of the man, that intrepidity, properly feminine, that refuses to recognize obstacles, and attains victory through paradox."

JEAN-RICHARD BLOCH.

"And, being also a trained maker of books, White, as he read, was more and more distressed that an accumulation so interesting should be so entirely unshaped for publication. 'But this will never make a book,' said White with a note of personal grievance. His hasty promise had bound him, it seemed, to a task he now found impossible. He would have to work upon it tremendously; and even then he did not see how it could be done.

"This collection of papers was not a story, not an essay, not a confession, not a diary. It was— nothing definable. It went into no conceivable covers. It was just, White decided, a proliferation. A vast proliferation. It wanted even a title. . . . At the end only its ideals of fearlessness and generosity remained."

H. G. WELLS, *The Research Magnificent.*

CHAPTER I

About Terence Hogan.

I call him Terence Hogan because his family's name has been prominent in Irish history for hundreds of years, though whether it is Norman or Irish I need not specify.

You'd know his family name if you heard it.

I cannot remember the time when there was no Terence Hogan in my life, for he was my father's friend as well as my brothers', coming about half-way between them in point of age.

My earliest memories of him centre round our house, then in Ireland, and his "playing horses" with me and the boys, whom I can see now, putting a racing saddle on his back and girthing it round him as he went down on the lawn on all fours, to give me a ride.

It does not seem much later that I myself was riding to hounds, and trying to follow him on a chubby pony.

Symbolical. I have followed Terence Hogan all my life.

When I was passing through the inevitable school-girl stage of calf-love and sloppiness, Terence Hogan was my impeccable hero, my king —who could do no wrong. As I grew out of that chrysalis stage—not that I ever became a butterfly, good God—I realized slowly and reluctantly that my king could, and did, do a great deal of wrong.

It is terribly difficult for me to give a clear idea of Terence Hogan's character. Perhaps my account of his actions will best do that, for it is only with the passage of the years that it has become really clear to me.

It is enough to say that, like most of us, he has his good points and his weak spots, and that the latter have been his undoing, his ruin—for no one can say that Terence has made a success of life.

In those old Curragh days—when life went so well with him and all of us, Terence Hogan was beautiful. To me, absolutely beautiful, with his Irish blue eyes, blue-black hair and sunburnt face. He was lean and tall, a perfect horseman, and perfect dancer.

When he came to our house, and he came almost daily, the sun shone. I am not musical, but I knew what musical people get out of music when I heard his voice.

When my father decided that I had run wild with the boys long enough, and it was time I was turned into a girl, it was like receiving sentence of death to hear that I was to go to the Belgian convent where my mother (who died when I was born) had been educated.

I was to go to a Belgian convent to be finished. I, who had never been begun.

I was not of the weeping sort—I had never cried in my life—but I went so completely off my oats that even Terence Hogan noticed it. When he realized what was the matter with me, he laughed. Had he not done so, I should not have gone to the convent. As it was, I departed in a rage, without saying good-bye to him. I further punished him by not writing to him, and he punished me a thousand times more—I hope more than he knew—when he revealed the fact of his complete unawareness.

It was while I was at the convent that the crash came. Had the holidays not been close at hand, I should either have earned expulsion, or not waited to be expelled.

My father was then stationed at the Curragh,

and so was one of my brothers, the other two being at Sandhurst.

"What's this about Terry? Where is he?" were my first words to my brother, as he met me on the platform, on my arrival.

"Sloped."

"Where?"

"Dunno."

"What's he done?"

"Sent in his papers."

"Why?"

"Had to."

"*Will* you tell me?" I cried, almost stamping with rage and anxiety.

"I am, aren't I? He was allowed to resign his commission."

"Cards?" I asked. For somewhere at the back of my mind floated the memory of a remark I had overheard, or that one of the boys had overheard, about Terence Hogan being "almost too good a card-player."

"No. . . . Horses. . . . Mess funds. . . . Big cheque on a bigger overdraft."

"Did everybody help him?"

"Yes. It would have been a bad business if they hadn't. . . . Prosecution and all that."

I felt stunned.

"I wouldn't have believed it of old Terry," said my brother, as we drove off from the little station.

I can see it now.

"I don't," I said, clenching my teeth.

"True though. . . . He'd struck a bad patch. . . . Elbow too."

From this last remark I gathered that Terence Hogan had been drinking again. There were times when he did, for a shorter or longer period.

Nothing much, and nothing to cause too

unfavourable comment—but on mess nights; at hunt balls; dinner parties; dances; or even lunch-eons, people were apt to say next day—though usually with a smile:

"Terence Hogan had been out in the sun a bit, hadn't he?"

That sort of thing.

I myself had quite frequently seen Terence Hogan the better for champagne, but never the worse, except once.

It was the year before the crash, when we had the hunt ball at our house, and my first time home from the con-vent.

Things got definitely merry toward morning. I went to bed about four and fell asleep at once.

Terence, who was staying with us, burst into my room some time later and, gathering me up into his arms, bed-clothes and all, begged me never to consent to marry him, whatever he might say or do. He kissed me long and hard, and in a manner somehow different.

I had a few moments of bewilderment, and then shattered the romance by hitting him violently in the eye when I realized that he was simply drunk.
. . .

I don't know whether Terence Hogan has had much experience of being thrown out on his ear, before or since, but it certainly happened to him that night—or morning—and there was a flight of stairs included in his downfall. . . .

"Real elbow, Bob?" I asked.

"Lifting it all day—and night. . . . Bad patch altogether. . . . Went all to pieces."

"Oh, I *wish* I had been at home," I wailed.

"You? What could *you* have done?" asked Bob.

And I had the sense to hold my peace.

But Terence was gone. Ruined. Broke. Cashiered but for the kindness and forbearance of his Colonel. . . . Missing funds replaced by brother officers. . . . Swindled bookies paid, and their mouths closed.

How could he? How was it possible? I remembered tales I had heard about his father, and grandfather—the latter a drunken, card-sharping, duelling rascal, who was reputed to sleep six nights a week in his hunting-kit and boots.

I was utterly miserable, the more so because there was so little I could say when his name cropped up, and so little I could do to help him.

No one knew what had become of him, and I got no answer to the endless letters I wrote to the places that had been his haunts.

*   *   *   *   *

About myself.

I ought to have been a boy.

The whole story of my life turns upon that fact, and it has to be borne in mind by anyone sufficiently interested to read that story, if my doings are to be understood, or even believed.

I was an enormous baby, and a huge sturdily-built child, gruff-voiced, tough and hardy.

Partly because I was so like a boy, and partly because we almost lived on horse-back, I was dressed exactly as my brothers were, my hair was cut as theirs was, and in no way was the wind tempered to the shorn lamb. Not that there was anything lamb-like about my appearance, character or conduct. I really believe that when my father gave the matter a thought at all, he was under the impression that he had four sons, by no means the least troublesome of whom was the youngest.

Nor, I am perfectly certain, could any visitor—and we had a good many, hunting, shooting, fishing—have picked out the girl from his host's four offspring, who could all ride, shoot, hunt and throw a fly, as well as any of the guests.

Nevertheless, the sex problem arose in my untutored mind at a comparatively early age, for there was one thing which my brothers would not do—and definitely would not do *because* I was a girl.

They would not teach me to box, nor box with me when I had taught myself—as I endeavoured and contrived, to do with book and ball and gloves. Nor would any one of them take me seriously when I challenged him, nor defend himself other than raggingly and laughingly when I attacked him.

It was the same with other boys, my brothers' friends, and with Terence Hogan.

I was a girl; and, simply *because* I was a girl, and for no other reason, I was to be debarred from this form of sport.

It struck me as most unfair, and sowed the seeds, in my young bosom, of those feelings which later developed into the strong, if somewhat original, views, and line, that I took on the subject of woman's suffrage.

I could have understood it, and have accepted the position, if the reason given by my brothers and friends—entirely supported by my father—had been that I was not strong enough, or not active enough; or that I had any beauty to be marred by pursuit of this sport.

Nothing of the sort, particularly the last.

The sole reason was that I was a girl—little as anyone might have supposed it. And this brought me fairly and squarely up against the idiotic, indefensible, and, to me, incredible, fact of inequality and disability based wholly and solely upon sex and nothing else.

Riding to hounds, I was quite at liberty to break every bone in my body, or to shift, change or remove any feature of my face; but receive a thump at boxing—no.

I was a girl, and girls must not box.

One would have thought God and Moses had said so.

Anyhow, it was about the only boy's pursuit that I did not follow. And at the rest, I was as good a man as any of them.

So, like a boy, I rode and ran and climbed, quarrelled, ragged and wrestled with the others, lived in sweater and breeches, fished, shot, cubbed, rode to hounds, and adored Terence Hogan with all my heart and soul.

Life at the Belgian Convent was the most utterly complete and absolutely terrible contrast that could be imagined. It was so different and so dreadful, that I think the abject misery into which the new life plunged me, helped me in my other misery, separation from Terence.

I am not saying a word against the Convent or the Sisters; but I could say some very pungent words against the cruelty of suddenly plunging an untrammelled, care-free, open-air boy (as practically I was) into a girls' school—a girls' school of definitely repressive discipline.

Every excellent rule was, to me, a mere petty restriction, a wanton and foolish interference with natural and proper freedom. . . . It would have been bad enough for any ordinary girl. For me it was plain and simple prison. . . . And, oh, how I was homesick. Homesick for Terence Hogan.

It seemed that I could do nothing right—that I was wrong from head to foot. Wrong in thought and word and deed; wrong in mind, body and soul.

Oh, how I hated it, and myself, and all that I had to do and be and wear.

For the first time in my life I had to wear girl's clothes, and behave as a girl should.

"And why on earth should there be special and separate girl-behaviour?" I asked. "Surely right, proper and natural good behaviour is good behaviour for boy or girl? Why this damnable 'girl-behaviour'?"

The nuns endeavoured to teach me the answer to my question—and unconsciously and unintentionally strengthened my equality-complex, and raised again, and in a different form, the question of why girls mayn't do this and mayn't do that, simply *because* they are girls, and for no other reason.

The dear kind Sisters, endeavouring to turn me from a young savage into a young lady, turned me into a young rebel.

For a time I entertained the idiotic idea of refusing to remain at school, after Terence Hogan's crash and disappearance, so that I could devote my life to searching for him.

However, there are limits even to the folly of a silly school-girl; and, partly because I hadn't the vaguest idea of where to begin, or the faintest notion of where he might be, I bottled up my grief and woe, and returned to the Convent. Possibly the decided views of my father, who could be a pretty sharp martinet on the rare occasions when he put his foot down, had something to do with it—and, just possibly, my bitter disappointment in Terence was getting the better of my youthful hero-worship.

Had I not gone back to the Convent, it is

probable that I should never have joined the Foreign Legion, for I spent the next holidays at a French château belonging to the family of a school-friend, Amélie de R——, and here I met René, her brother.

He, too, was home for the vacation from the military college of St. Cyr, and his extremely polite superciliousness changed very quickly to something quite different when he found that I was at least as good a horseman, fisherman and shot as he was himself. Also that when he condescended to put on mask and fencing-jacket, he had to go all out to beat me with foil and sabre.

I was something new in the way of *jeunes filles* to René, and, on the night before Amélie and I returned to school, he very formally declared his love for me!

As I was a good deal bigger than he was, and he called me his little dove, it struck me as being terribly funny, and the emotion with which I obviously struggled was laughter.

Thank heaven René did not discover this, and accepted my plea of a previous entanglement and a broken heart.

He was a dear, and I wouldn't have hurt his feelings for the world, but by then I had no more use whatever for what I termed sloppy boy-and-girl-business.

We parted the best of friends, and met again on the same footing.

At last the apparently impossible happened, and the time came for me to leave school and return home.

I felt like a prisoner released from gaol.

"Well, young woman?" said my father at the station, but,

"Good-morning, my lad," said he next morning,

when I appeared at breakfast, dressed as I had always dressed at home.

Oh, it was good to be back again, and I had rootled amongst the kit of my absent brothers, and fitted myself out with all the clothes improper to my sex, years and station.

I took up life where I had left it, but not quite as I had left it. I missed Terence badly. Missed him everywhere and at every turn.

It may have been this, or it may have been the spoken and unspoken criticism of our local old women of both sexes, that saved me from being the wholly thoughtless and unintelligent hoyden that I appeared.

I thought a lot about poor Terence and I thought a lot about what seemed to me the idiotic and impudent claim of men, to dictate *de haut en bas* to women, simply because they were women. My crude and callow view was "Let the best man win," so to speak, quite irrespective of sex, and let there be at least equality of opportunity for both— absolute equality of opportunity.

Where was the sense or defensibility of the attitude,

"You can perhaps do this far better than a man, but, simply *because* you are a woman, you shall not be allowed to try."

But for the suffragettes, I should probably have become a suffragette.

I went to London, attended meetings, heard all that the leaders had to say, and decided that I liked neither them nor their methods.

What was not childish beyond belief was malevolent beyond decency, I thought; and it seemed to me that the programme of these leaders was less calculated to prove their equality with men than with monkeys—of a peculiarly mischievous and destructive species.

Particularly did I feel this in the case of a young woman, very prominent among them; and, having told her so quite frankly and bluntly, I found that I fell so low in her opinion and in the esteem of the executive, that I could be of no further use to the party.

I returned home, suffered the jeers of my father and brothers, in silence, and sought about for ways in which I could quietly but plainly demonstrate that women are, in most ways, the equals of men, and, in all ways, deserving of an opportunity to show their equality.

Then came the Great War, and for women the Great Opportunity. Thanks to the influence of my father and of one or two powerful friends, I was one of the first women to get to France and into the danger zone. There I remained, throughout the war, and never left France and Belgium once, except for a special course in lorry-driving and running repairs.

By the end of the time, I was as strong, hardy and tough as the average soldier—by which I mean old soldier. Old Contemptible, in fact. I was tall, broad, lean, hard as nails, weather-beaten, close-cropped and no beauty.

Nor had four years of dirt, oil and manual labour improved my never-delicate hands—now as big, strong, and capable as a man's.

I am not going to write my Great War experiences here, except in so far as they concern Terence Hogan, who came into my life again, and with whom I had several encounters.

CHAPTER II

My third leave in Paris. Father killed: brothers killed.

A detached, homeless, brotherless orphan, to whom leave was something of a mockery, and everything of a necessity.

The same hotel. I had stayed there in happier days with Amélie and René de R——, when he met us in Paris on our way from school to their chateau.

Lonely misery at the little table in the corner, whence I could see the whole of the dining-room.

Occasional stares, meaning glances, leers, raised eye-brows, winks and ogling, from young officers of half a dozen nationalities, and a score of services; young men who, I thought, might have been better employed, for obviously there was not a man of them straight from the Front, as I was.

I was more than their equal, anyway—in physique, experience and war record. . . .

And suddenly I was aware of a man stopping instead of passing my table, standing and staring. I raised my eyes with a savage scowl and,

"Terry!" I said.

"Hallo, Jacq," said Terence Hogan. ". . . Er . . . Can I feed at your table?"

"Yes."

And that was how I recovered Terence.

He was looking splendid. Clean-cut, clear-eyed, lean and hard. He was an officer, one pip, and his uniform was worn, mended, and stained. Just what an officer's uniform should be in war-time.

Hogan was evidently straight from the Front. I looked again. A good regiment. One of the best.

And I gave Terence my hand and a grip that told him all I wanted him to know—or part of it, at any rate.

I was glad of my uniform too—worn, mended and stained like his. It set us apart together, and it helped me to play the man.

Terence Hogan—rehabilitated. Back on the bough. Terence Hogan with his head high, the bit in his teeth, and the hunt up.

He must run straight now.

How handsome he looked. Better looking than ever. His cropped blue-back hair and clipped moustache. . . . His dark-blue Irish eyes, his glowing healthy cheeks, clear skin, small gleaming teeth, firm mouth and jutting chin.

It was one of the most glorious moments of my life, to see Terry sitting there, happy, laughing, on terms with Life again.

And then he drank his large whisky and small soda at a draught, and poured himself out another.

Being straight from the Front myself, I could understand that.

During dinner he told me about his regiment, brother-officers, and experiences since getting his commission.

After dinner we sat in the lounge and he told me of how he'd enlisted directly war broke out. He had been promoted Sergeant in three months, recommended for a commission in 1915, and sent home for training. It must, of course, have been obvious from the first that Terence Hogan had already been a soldier when he enlisted: and his experience as a cavalry officer must have been of enormous help to him when in training for an infantry commission.

I could not help being conscious that Terry skated over a good deal of thin ice, and he made no reference to his crash and disappearance, or his subsequent doings, up to the time of his enlistment.

Naturally I forbore to question him, and there were large omissions, assumptions, blanks, and tolerances.

Nor did I reproach him with his unkindness, his lack of faith amounting to cruelty, in never writing to me or sending me a single word or message.

But I then and there made him definitely and seriously promise and swear that he would keep in touch with me, letting me know of his progress, welfare, and where-abouts; and that he would promptly and truthfully answer any letter of mine that he might receive.

He promised, with the ring of sincerity in his voice.

Side by side, on that dingy red plush settee, we sat, hands in pockets, cigarettes in mouths, apparently quite cold and detached, beneath the curious eyes of the numerous and variegated patrons of the hotel.

"Thanks, Jacq, old chap," said Terence at length. "You've done me a world of good."

"Nonsense," I replied, as gruffly as I could. "You were always my best, kindest and truest friend—from the time I could toddle—and I owe you a debt I can never repay."

"Bilge," said Terry. "You staying here?"

"Yes. Another nine nights."

"Shall I move in here?"

"Splendid. . . ."

Terence Hogan kept his promise. Wrote about as frequently and regularly as could be expected in the circumstances of war, and we contrived to meet at Amiens.

Terence was then a Captain. Had won the M.C., and looked five years older than when I had seen him last. He wasn't wearing too well, though he still looked hard and fit and splendid . . . at any rate, when I first caught sight of him.

But he drank half a bottle of whisky with dinner, and confessed to about a hundred cigarettes a day. How I wished the cursed war would end. . . .

Then, after an interval that seemed like years, we contrived to make our leave coincide, and met again, in Paris, at the same hotel.

Terence Hogan was a Major—and a drunkard.

He behaved well enough in that respect while he was with me, for what else he ever was, Terry was definitely a gentleman. But the signs were plain and, by that time, after nearly four years of varied and amazing war-experience, I knew them too well to be mistaken.

It was heart-breaking. . . .

He was happy enough. And it was obvious from what a brother-officer, Major L——, said to me about him, that there was nothing wrong—yet. Obviously Terence Hogan was immensely popular in his battalion, and certain of promotion to Colonel at the next vacancy.

But there it was. Hogan drank: and perhaps it was all the worse that, though he drank, he did not get drunk.

At dinner, on our last night, after cocktails, we had two bottles of champagne, of which I drank one glass; and a bottle of port, of which I drank half a glass. Terence had brandy liqueurs and, after dinner, as we again sat in the lounge, he drank several brandies and sodas.

At bedtime he was, in speech and movement, as sober as a judge—and might have been drinking water the whole evening. But his eyes were glazed and his face suffused. His hands trembled.

I don't pretend to be wise or clever but, during that fortnight, I used all the wisdom, cleverness and tact that I possessed, to help him. I knew the folly and hopelessness of exacting from him any definite promise. But I did all that love prompted me to say and do. . . .

I made a bargain with him—and kept my side of it. . . . But the best that I could hope for was that the war would end in time.

The war that was killing the world, mowing men down by millions, and bringing ruin, degradation and destruction to half the nations, must end in time—for me to save Terence Hogan from himself.

It didn't end in time.

One day I got a letter from Major L——, who had promised to let me know if "anything happened" to Hogan.

Something had happened.

But he wasn't wounded, maimed, or killed.

It was something much better—or worse—according to one's point of view.

It must have been an extremely difficult letter for Major L—— to write, and he had done it very nicely.

Terence Hogan had gone—again without waiting for the formality of a court-martial. But this time, I gathered, he had simply fled. He had escaped, in fact. Major L—— was reticent, and, to this day, I do not know the full details of the story.

Evidently it was pretty bad. . . . Drunkenness. . . . A horrible fiasco in consequence, involving the needless sacrifice of lives, with the failure of an important little raid and night-operation. . . . A righteously incensed General, insulted.

*   *   *   *   *

Terence in hiding—again.

Terence Hogan who had come back. . . . Who had made good. . . . And who would, as it transpired, have been a Colonel in a matter of days.

The unutterable fool . . . the silly damned fool.

But who had any right to talk like that of any man who had done four years in the trenches?

Poor Terence Hogan.

For a time I was divided between rage and pity.

But I hadn't driven many more ambulance-loads of mangled men; gasping, groaning, screaming, or apparently dead, before the rage died and the pity grew.

What Terence had seen and heard and faced for over a thousand awful days and more awful nights!

Let those who did four years of it, without cracking, cast the first stone.

I suppose it was quite a good thing for me that the hardest of hard work filled the whole of my time not given to the snatching of hasty meals and brief broken slumber. I did not realize until then how Hogan's reappearance in my life had filled the gap left by the deaths of my father and brothers and of every friend that I'd had or made.

Surrounded and crowded to the point of suffocation, I walked alone. And then two things happened; two things which seemed to me to be of about equal importance.

The Armistice came. And I got a letter from Hogan.

I wired to the address that he gave, and implored him to await my letter and to keep in touch.

For, in his letter to me, Terence had tried to give me some idea of the self-loathing that he felt;

of his utter ashamedness; and of how the worst thing to him about the whole business was the thought of what he must appear to me.

He said that every time he thought of me, and I was never out of his thoughts, he hated himself afresh and the more. After what I had done for him—and what he had promised to do for me.

It was a letter of the deepest self-abasement, the humblest apology, and farewell.

Now that the war was over, he was going to emerge from his hiding-place and join the French Foreign Legion, where he would find death, oblivion—or another chance.

He answered my wire and letter, and agreed to wait and meet me as soon as I was demobilized.

Apparently he did not wish to do this, but felt that he owed it to me to do as I ordered. So he expressed it.

I then wrote to René, and in the end, after a terrible amount of arguing, persuading and wrangling, I got my way.

René's attitude was:

"Mad as ever, and I ought not to help you. But the prank won't last long, and you're quite able to look after yourself."

Terence Hogan's attitude was:

"It's madness. Lunacy. Sheer impossibility. And I ought not to agree to it. But I can't help myself—and anyhow you'll be found out at the very beginning, and I don't see what they can do to you."

And then:

"A woman couldn't possibly do it."

And that would have put the lid on it, had it not been there already.

CHAPTER III

Whatever I forget, I shall always remember the hour I spent at the *Gare de Lyons* waiting for my two men. Both must come, or my scheme fell to the ground and I should be robbed of my great adventure and of my plan to help Terry. I was sorry to realize that I felt less sure of him than of René, who, I knew, would come.

I walked up and down, glancing, from time to time, at the clock. I sat on the grimy seats and watched the *va et vient* of the big terminus. I wondered which of the many soldiers were going, as I hoped I was, to Africa.

I listened to family conversations; saw heart-rending partings; stood aside and watched myself watching.

Suddenly I saw Hogan; looking shabby, a little seedy, a little hang-dog. Unmistakably a man of breeding; but, I had to admit—deteriorated since last I saw him.

"Evening, Terry," said I, as he came toward the steps leading up to the refreshment-room, at the bottom of which I was standing.

"Good Lord . . . Jacq! . . . Smart gent's suiting . . . hat and stick complete. . . . S'pose I was expecting to meet a girl. . . . So you're coming as far as Marseilles with me, are you?"

"Yes," I said. "Farther—if René turns up."

"Shall we go and get a drink meanwhile?" said Hogan.

"We shall not," I said.

Terence Hogan was as steady, coherent, and sober as a judge, and also completely drunk.

"Nice of you to see me off, Jacq," he said. "Is

René coming as far as Marseilles too? Nice, obliging, attentive feller, what?"

"Yes," I said. "One of the best. What they call a gentleman."

"He'll love meeting *me*, then," observed Hogan.

"That's why he's coming," I countered. "Got your papers?"

"Yes, and damn little else!"

I caught sight of René approaching our rendezvous. Fine, dependable René. Thoroughbred.

He too seemed surprised when I hailed him.

"*Mon Dieu!* . . . You'll succeed yet—I'm afraid," he smiled, as he grasped my hand. "Anyhow, you'll get as far as Sidi, Saïda, or Sousse, anyway, I do believe. . . .

"There you are," he added, handing me an envelope, "and don't forget your name is X——. Nor forget to practise the signature. Nor that someone will be arrested as a deserter unless you present those papers at Fort St. Jean within two days."

"Did you go through the bureau and pass the doctor yourself, René?" I asked. "Or did you send someone else?"

"Never you mind, *mon cher* Monsieur X——. *Someone* went through the little mill and emerged with those papers."

He was staring hard at Hogan who elaborately pretended that he was not there—or perchance that we two were not.

"This is my friend—er—Terry," said I. "He also proposes to trail a pike for *Madame la République.*"

Raising his hat a little, René bowed slightly, very cold and unsmiling.

Terence Hogan returned an off-hand semi-military salute.

"Will you gentlemen give me the very great

pleasure of dining with me?" said René. "There is plenty of time. They give one an edible meal here, and have some drinkable wine."

"I should love to, René," said I.

"Right-o," said Terence.

And René led the way up into the excellent restaurant of the *Gare de Lyons*.

"Got your ticket?" René asked me, as we went up the steps, his arm through mine. "Or are you going to start your lunacy from here, and travel on the military pass?"

"*Wagon-lit!*" I replied. "I'll begin roughing it when I have to."

It was an uncomfortable meal, in spite of Rene's social tact, suavity and skill. Terence Hogan was difficult. The two men disliked each other, and I fancy that each would have liked to say to the other,

"You ought to be ashamed of yourself to be helping this girl to attempt such a mad prank."

René kept up the assumption that I should be returning again in a week or two, at most; and made me promise that I would write or wire in time for him to come and see me as I passed through Paris on my way home.

"And for you, Monsieur," said he courteously to Hogan, raising his glass, "I hope promotion, decoration, a commission . . . a career . . ."

"Er—thanks," said Hogan.

René came down to the train with us, and as we stood at the door of our *wagon-lit*,

"Good-bye—ah—old chap," he said, wrung my hand warmly, forbore to embrace me, raised his hat to include Terence, and left us.

I watched René until his smart, soldierly figure was lost in the crowd. . . .

As gentlemen, Terence Hogan and I travelled in comfort to Marseilles.

*   *   *   *   *

On leaving our compartment in the morning, we were aware of another train, from a third-class carriage of which tumbled a heterogeneous collection of unwashed, unshaven, and definitely travel-stained men of the poorest sort, who were being, not so much welcomed as unenthusiastically accepted, by a couple of non-commissioned officers.

"Our future brothers-in-arms," said Hogan, eyeing the dirty and dishevelled mob with distaste.

"Look here, we're not going to march through the streets with that crew," he said.

"No," I agreed. "We'll follow at a respectful distance and see where they go. And either slip in behind them, or present ourselves for admission later."

"A lot later," growled Terence. "This particular army of two is going to march on a full stomach. Let's go to the pub down the *Cannebière*, the *Noailles* or *Louvre* or something, and have a last decent meal. Anyone can tell us where this Fort St. Jean place is."

"Right," I agreed, visualizing a last decent bath also.

We had baths. We had *déjeuner*. We had afternoon tea of a sort. We had dinner. We sat in the lounge and smoked.

Terence Hogan had his thoughts and certainly I had mine.

"We need not go in until to-morrow morning, of course," said Terence.

"No," I answered. "We need not. Once we're there . . . we're there."

"Yes," replied Terry slowly. "And while we're here . . . we're here . . ."

We stayed the night . . . Terry and I . . .

CHAPTER IV

Next morning, Hogan and I made our way to Fort St. Jean, whither he had been directed by the staff-sergeant at the *Bureau de Recruitement* in Paris.

This clearing-house for the African Army Corps proved to be a sea-girt mediæval fortress, gloomy, damp, and forbidding.

The Sergeant of the Guard seemed surprised when we announced that we were recruits for the Legion and produced the grey enlistment papers attesting the fact. From being quite polite, he became quite rude, when he grasped the fact that we really were what we professed to be, and not what we appeared to be.

As we were well-dressed, well-nourished, and well-spoken, it was quite obvious that the police must be close behind us. At any rate, he looked out across the draw-bridge, appeared surprised to find that we were not pursued, and bade us hurry inside while yet we might.

We had arrived, it appeared, at an auspicious moment.

Monsieur l'Adjudant was in the very act of receiving new arrivals. An orderly, curtly and somewhat contemptuously, bade us follow him. We did. Along the darkest, dreariest, dampest tunnels of passages that I have ever traversed, to a dirty little office that was the local *Bureau de la Légion*.

And here, at the very outset, I very nearly came to a bad end, by making the worst of bad beginnings.

In point of fact, I came exceedingly close to

committing a crime which might have got me five years' imprisonment, as a preliminary to my five years' soldiering.

Being brusquely ushered into this office, we beheld a most important-looking man, seated at a table, and we rightly assumed that he was an *adjudant* of the Legion.

By the way, a French *adjudant* is not to be confused with an English adjutant, for the former is invariably a non-commissioned officer, whereas the latter, of course, is always an officer.

After this person had glanced at my documents, he bawled at me to sign my name to another one, and, in order to do so, I placed my attaché-case on the table.

A red rag to a bull . . .

It was as though I had laid a vast red sheet right beneath the nose of the most dyspeptic and violent bull that ever needed the attentions of a ministering matador.

The gentle creature sprang to his feet, with what I can only describe as a terrific roar.

No, I can describe it better and maintain the metaphor. It was a paralysing bellow.

With empurpled face, swelling veins, suffused eyes, quivering moustache, bared teeth (and incidentally with his hands) he seized the offending attaché-case and hurled it with tremendous violence and accurate aim through the open doorway and against the wall of the corridor, where it burst asunder, to the mild surprise and moderate enrichment of one, Bassompierre, a passing orderly.

The officer and gentleman, then shaking his quivering fist beneath my contemptuous nose, exploded with such an eruption of invective and insult, that I actually brought my right hand from its place, thumb in line with the seam of the trousers, with the full and firm intention of smacking his beastly face; but, almost before I had moved, I found my wrist in the iron grip of Terence Hogan's red right hand. No, left hand. At the same moment, Terence became surprisingly fluent in apologizing to *Monsieur l'adjudant* for my manners, my ignorance, and my very existence.

He then stated clearly that I was a fool, like all Englishmen; but that he was an Irishman, come to join for the love he bore beautiful France and her lovely Foreign Legion.

And all was well. I was allowed to live.

But to this day, I'm still a little scared when I think of how near I came to smacking the face of that temperamental officer, and qualifying for a long sojourn in a French prison or penal battalion.

From all I've heard—and I've heard a good deal—French prisons and French penal battalions are splendid places to keep out of.

Terence was extremely angry with me afterwards—in the spirit in which a quite-devoted mother will severely slap her child when safely restored to her from almost beneath the wheels of a passing steam-roller, in front of which it has not crossed but sat down.

Hogan particularly insisted that he was thoroughly ashamed of me; that I ought to know better; that nobody would think I'd been in the Army; and that I must not be "undisciplined"—not only because it is thoroughly bad form, but inevitably quite fatal.

Having escaped unscathed from the lion's den —or bull's boudoir—we found ourselves free to see the sights and smell the odours of Fort St. Jean.

Among the sights was the astonishingly motley crowd of our future comrades-in-arms, which included some undeniably disreputable human wreckage.

Hogan and I, being the most prosperous-looking of the lot, were the objects of a certain amount of speculation and some questioning on the subject of our reasons for joining the Legion.

As I soon discovered, this is one of the things which are absolutely not done in the Legion. But we were not properly in the Legion, as yet.

A mild and pleasant-looking young German, who might have kept a *delicatessen* shop in Munich, or daily have breathed his soul into a trombone, cheerily, cheerily, beerily, beerily, in the noonday sun and a German band, came up to me and said:

"Hullo, Englishmans, vhy you join zis Legion, *hein?*"

And by reason of my reply, with sudden and inexplicable memories of holiday-task *Lycidas,*

"Bitter constraint and sad occasion dear,"

he, not to be outdone in friendly politeness, pleasantly reciprocated by thereafter invariably addressing me as "dear" likewise.

He was a nice little thing, rejoicing in the appropriate name of Hans Petsel which I inevitably rendered as Pet Hansel.

I was surprised to find that quite the majority of these men, German, Russian, Belgian, Italian, Austrian, Swiss and French, spoke English, some only a few words, some quite accurately.

Hogan had but one reply when asked why he had joined the Legion:

"Fond of fishing" . . . a hard saying which, with an even harder and somewhat menacing stare, discouraged curiosity.

By a kind of natural selection, mutual attraction, like going to like, or deep calling to deep, Hogan soon got *en rapport* with an extremely tough-looking person whom he, with a worthy Anglo-Saxon broad-mindedness and charity to all "foreigners," indicated to me as an obvious fellow "white man." What he called the Latins, the Argentines and the Greeks, I don't know, but he offered to bet much more than he possessed that the tough-looking person was a white man.

He proved to be an American sailor (who had also served in the United States Corps of Marines), our afterwards-admired and well-beloved "Abraham the Sailor."

What his name was, I don't know to this day, but when he said out of a corner of his grim mouth, and with a certain look in his hard eye, that he was Abraham the Sailor, why, Abraham the Sailor he certainly was.

I don't think any sensible man would have contradicted him had he said he was Sindbad the Sailor.

Within a few minutes Abraham the Sailor was one of us.

A less attractive member of this strange exotic crowd was an amazing person who, though by no means white as the lily, was beautifully muscled from head to foot. That he was proud of being a perfect Apollo-Hercules work of art was evinced by the fact that he went about stripped to the waist and wearing only a pair of brief and ragged running-shorts, and ornate and sharp-toed, but cracked and laceless shoes.

Abraham declared at once that the man was a sailor.

As the fellow was sitting down, and thus not displaying a sea-roll or shell-back walk, I asked Abraham how he knew.

He replied:

"By the cut of his jib."

And when I replied that the man's jib appeared

to be cut like those of most of us, Abraham, tolerant of my stupidity, ignorance and lack of perception, said:

"Dust your brains, and look how he holds his hands."

And sure enough, a sailor he was—a deserter from the Brazilian Navy and, judging from his habits, manners and customs, I imagine that Navy will survive the loss. A real ruffian and brute; a disgusting, decadent and degraded beast.

Early he displayed desires not merely for prominence, but for pre-eminence, until Abraham, observing that the Dago was getting too fresh, "looked at him," as he called it—in other words, thrust his face close to that of the noisy foreigner, protruded his colossal chin, and expressed his feelings by means of a most murderous scowl.

The Brazilian flinched and wilted as Abraham, with a swift movement, suddenly raised a mighty fist and—scratched his own head, smiling benignly.

"You go chase yourself," he said. "When we want 'the March of the Men of Garlic' we'll ask for it."

The crowd laughed at the Brazilian's swift deflation, and Abraham the Sailor, had he so desired, could have become cock of the walk.

Another person, of a very different type, was a delightful Swede who called himself Gustavus Adolphus, a most merry creature, fair-haired, blue-eyed, and so clean-looking, who appeared to find food for laughter in the most unexpected places.

His English was almost perfect and so—as far as I could judge—were his French and German.

What could have brought such a man, young, gifted, educated, obviously quite happy and apparently affluent, to the French Foreign Legion? His own account that, in an absent-minded moment, he had married a famous opera-singer and come to the Legion for a little peace, I did not accept.

I was convinced it was nothing criminal, anyhow. He was too ingenuous, joyous and comical a person. Perhaps he gently but firmly pressed the Mayor's top-hat down over the Mayor's fine eyes and ears at the moment that he declared the Municipal Wash-house now open, or something of that sort. I could quite imagine him doing it.

I remember that one thing I could not help noticing was the curious and interesting fact, that by far the longest and the loudest grumblings at our accommodation in Fort St. Jean, came from those who were quite obviously accustomed to the rudest and roughest of provision, environment, and circumstance.

Certainly the accommodation was vile. We were herded into a long dark room, furnished only with un-washed tables, rough benches, and an almost unbearable stench. The battered metal mugs supplied to us were rusty on the outside, and foul with dirt and grease within.

A kind of stew was brought into this beastly place in buckets, and I have seen pails of hog-wash that looked more appetizing.

Gustavus Adolphus announced that on leaving he should ask for the Visitors' Complaint Book.

"What's wrong with the eats, Bo?" growled Abraham the Sailor. "It's hot and plentiful, and what I say is, a bellyful's a bellyful, look at it how you may."

"Exactly," replied Gustavus Adolphus. "That precisely will be my complaint. We have to look at it in rusty and greasy pots, whereas the authorities should supply nice pig-troughs so that we can get down to it on all fours and eat it correctly and comfortably. Good food should be properly served, and I shall tell them so."

As we sat at the filthy tables, enjoying our stew —and it was really quite nourishing—a detachment of Senegalese arrived and joined us.

These negroes showed no signs of racial prejudice, drew no colour line at all, and ate with us as amicably as though we were their equals.

It may perhaps have been because it was the rush season, or Great White Sales time, or a crisis in the franc, or a fall or two of the Government, but whatever the cause, there were no beds in this dining-bed-sitting-dungeon.

We were, however, given a blanket each, and these blankets, though rough and coarse, did not scratch—for we wore our clothes.

It was we who scratched.

*   *   *   *   *

I have had quite a few unforgettable nights in my life, and this one takes high place among them.

I slept not at all. I did not weep. Once I smiled.

It was when I thought of the superhumanly good Sœur Paul de la Croix, Mother Superior of the Convent.

Her opinion of me had never been exalted, but I do not think that her most pessimistic view of my ill-omened future ever envisaged me as sleeping on the floor of a bare and filthy room with nineteen assorted men. . . . No.

*   *   *   *   *

During our second day in Fort St. Jean, we were guarded from the *ennui* of monotony and boredom in a variety of ways.

In the first place, we were all rendered

practically bald by an enthusiastic barber and a most efficient clipping-machine.

This didn't improve the appearance of any one of us in the slightest degree, but it did, as the barber pointed out, render us easy of identification by the police, should any of us be so ungrateful and foolish as to desire to depart from Fort St. Jean and the Foreign Legion.

Other games and pastimes provided for our benefit were potato-peeling, floor-sweeping, gutter-cleaning and generally playing a lovely game of pretending to be Municipal dustmen, scavengers, and sweepers—all very good exercise as Hogan observed; and all useful practical vocational-training, in the opinion of Gustavus Adolphus.

Thus early did we learn, that in any place where a unit of the Foreign Legion is to be found, all heavy, dirty and disagreeable work is freely relegated to it, with the warm approval of the other troops, whether French or native.

It was on the next day, I think, that a fresh batch of recruits arrived, and that Hogan, Abraham the Sailor and I, critically looking them over from the height of one-day seniority, simultaneously discovered another "white man."

He was a very big man indeed, tall, broad-shouldered and with a drilled back. A pair of piercing light-blue eyes literally shone in his sunburnt face, on either side of a fine, high-bridged nose, beneath which a big moustache curled above a great jutting chin.

He proved to be an Australian.

Hogan had encountered Australians during the war, and had formed a high opinion of, and developed a vast admiration for, them. He addressed this man as "Digger," and Digger he remained to us to the end of the chapter.

He was one of the whitest, staunchest, truest

men I ever met, and I was terribly sorry for him when I knew his story.

*   *   *   *   *

We were more than thankful to leave Fort St. Jean even for the steerage deck of an ancient packet, of which Abraham the Sailor formed a very low opinion.

Here we were given one small blanket, a "quart" pot and a tin cup wherewith to face the world and the vicissitudes of life.

The food was no worse than that to which we had by now become more or less accustomed, and the iron deck was no harder nor colder than other iron decks.

The blue Mediterranean was a leaden grey; the glorious southern sky almost black; the balmy breezes of the Côte d'Azur a howling bitter wind; and the sea, in the Gulf of Lyons, extremely rough. Personally, I am a good sailor and, at this time, if at no other, I was in a position of superiority to Terry and Digger who, poor souls, are not. I was terribly sorry for them and very proud of myself, as I swaggered about with Abraham the Sailor.

But at the dawn of a most glorious morning we sighted the port of Oran in Algeria, a truly lovely scene with its marvellous background of the mighty Atlas mountains, their peaks glowing and warming from pink to red in the light of the rising sun. Tier above tier, the white flat-roofed houses, rising from the water's edge, climbed up the cliffs, and at that hour, at any rate, Oran was unforgettably lovely.

I forgot myself and my incredible and weird position, with its daunting, if unknown, dangers and possibilities, as I gazed—and wondered whether Oran would look as lovely at sunset from the deck of a departing ship; a ship that was taking me back to safety and sanity and the humdrum life; to Paris and to London, to my friend René and—nice womanliness and good conduct. . . .

I was brought swiftly to earth by the sound of sharp orders to fall in.

We were quickly marched off, past a crowd of dirty Arab beggars on the wharf, through the town, to the Zouave Barracks, about a mile and a half from the docks.

Personally I was quite exhilarated by the sight of colourful Arab costumes, various French uniforms, the gardens, bazaars, cafés, novel street-scenes and the sounds of voices speaking in Spanish, French and Arabic.

On arrival at the Zouave Barracks, our heterogeneous and somewhat forlorn company of scallywags was allotted a barrack-room and given a meal of stew and bread.

How those poor fellows ate, after their two days' fast—and more than fast—and they certainly made up for lost time and lost meals.

What interested me more than food was the question of a bath. I'd have given a large sum of money for half an hour in an English bathroom, with unlimited hot water, a huge cake of soap, a loofah, bath salts, and all the trimmings. But the best I could procure, by bribery and corruption, was one of which the water was cold, though clean, the soap strongly disinfectant, and the towel a not-unreasonably dirty duster.

We were a filthy gang, but only Terence Hogan, Abraham the Sailor, Digger, Gustavus Adolphus and my Pet Hansel availed themselves in turn of the opportunity of a bath and, one after the other, they returned looking, as I told them, quite different, if not greatly improved in appearance.

We were indeed a mouldy gang. Freely and frankly I confess that most of us were freely and frankly verminous. And whereas to some it was apparently a normal condition, to others it was not; and the latter were divided into those who had reached that state and disliked it, and those who had not—and greatly feared lest they might do so.

Personally I intensely dislike being verminous. Abraham the Sailor said it would break his heart, for never had he sunk so low; while Digger was completely indifferent and unaffected. He said that he had been so often and so entirely "crumby" during the war, that he had got rather fond of "cooties."

Hogan remarked that it would be a new experience and he welcomed all experiences.

My little Pet Hansel seriously pointed out to me that Nature, the Great Mother of us all, cared as much for the life and well-being of each separate louse as she did for that of a man; and we had no less reason to suppose that we were created for the benefit of lice than to suppose that they were created for the annoyance of man. Nature, so careless of the individual, so careful of the type . . .

I interrupted him to point out that this was just where I differed from Mother Nature—and squashed several of the type.

I'm afraid that life on the road to the Legion was already making me rather coarse—or perhaps coarser. But I've always been rather inclined to call a spade precisely what it is, and felt little urge to tie bows of pink ribbon on it.

*   *   *   *   *

Having eaten and rested, and some of us

having washed, we were marched back, down by the docks, to a small Barrack belonging to the First Regiment of the Foreign Legion, and here received by some decrepit and wine-sodden old soldiers.

Old soldiers never die, they only fade away; and these time-expired pensioners of the Legion were definitely faded.

I can honestly say that the Barrack Room allotted to us in this ancient building was no dirtier or nastier than the one we occupied in Fort St. Jean. Fortunately our sojourn here below was brief, and in the evening, in charge of a smart Sergeant and a couple of Corporals, we entrained for Sidi-bel-Abbès.

The Sergeant was a Russian who had been to school in England, a pleasant and kindly person who accepted a present from me and allowed me to travel in his compartment. With this unusual man, I had a long and most interesting talk about the Legion, though I must admit that, once I was in uniform, he never spoke to me again, for I was then less than the dust beneath his feet.

Like so many Russians, he was a fatalist, and his philosophy of life was *laisser faire* and *mektoub rebib*—what is written is written and what will be will be.

When I asked him if he didn't believe that Heaven helps those who help themselves, he replied to the effect that neither Heaven, nor the person who apparently helps himself, actually does help him, since obviously everything was ordained before the beginning of time, and not God himself can change it by a hair's-breadth.

"Do you believe that God knows and sees the future?" he exploded, when I smiled at that.

And when I replied that of course I did, he crushed me with a triumphant:

"Then if it *is* the future and He knows it, how can He alter it, my good ass?"

And the answer was a melon, which I immediately bought for him as the train stopped at the thousandth way-side station.

He burrowed into a great slice of it, even unto his ears, and, watching him in mute amazement, I wrestled with the thought that this too had been ordained before the beginning of Time. . . .

At the station of Sidi-bel-Abbès we were met by a large armed party. We fell in, in two ranks, on the platform, and marched off to the Depôt, surrounded by a guard, quite fifty in number, with fixed bayonets.

Abraham the Sailor expressed his wonder as to whether we were free men voluntarily joining the Army of France, or convicted criminals about to be imprisoned.

"We haven't done nothing wrong, have we, Digger?" he asked.

"Yes, chum," replied the Australian. "Too right we have. We've come here."

After half an hour of this somewhat degrading march, we arrived at the famous Barracks of the Legion and were at once allotted to rooms.

We were each given a real bed with two blankets; and, as, half-dressed, I most thankfully tumbled into mine, I could scarcely believe that it was only a week since I'd slept in one.

My first "hardship" was having to sleep always in a vest and pants, as everybody else did, but I soon grew accustomed to the practice.

*   *   *   *   *

Réveillé sounded at four-thirty next morning, and, a few minutes later, milkless and unsweetened coffee was brought round in a big jug.

The inner man fared better than the outer, as it was impossible for one to wash so much as one's face, no water ever being turned on until nine o'clock.

Doubtless the French military authorities argue, with that sound logic for which they are famous, that, though a man cannot drill, march, and work for several hours with a perfectly empty interior, he can quite well do so with a perfectly filthy exterior.

That first day, though not precisely a crowded hour of glorious life, was quite hectic, what with being inspected, examined, enrolled and "issued with" kit.

Though fully prepared to rough it in every way, to take the bitter with the sweet, if any; to be blessed in expecting little; to be tough with the tough and stiff with the stiff, I confess to a feeling of horrified and shrinking disgust when I found that the clothing issued to me was second-hand, much worn, and very dirty.

With the underclothing one could deal, but I could not help spending a little time in speculating upon the person, or persons rather, who had previously worn my two suits, overcoat and old boots.

Somehow I formed a wholly unfavourable opinion of each one of those persons, and I hated them, the uniforms and myself.

Then came the Rubicon, and I knew that I should either cross it or be turned back in disgrace and in the unfortunate position of having provided the authorities with a peculiar and perplexing problem. If all went as it usually did, I should get by, and, after that, I should be comparatively safe—unless I were laid low with some dire illness, or were wounded in battle.

But what I was doing had been successfully done before, I knew, and I did not see why it should not be done again, especially by a girl equipped with my unusual size, physique, voice and strength.

If a German girl could enlist in the Spahis; become *Soldat Première Classe*; be promoted to Corporal for general merit; be decorated for bravery; be promoted to Sergeant, and again decorated; and never be suspected of being a woman until she was mortally wounded in battle, I saw no reason why an English girl who had roughed it behind the lines in the Great War should not succeed, in however less a degree.

But fancy that woman drilling a troop of cavalry at the trot, the canter, and the gallop. What a voice she must have had!

As it turned out, I crossed the Rubicon with the utmost ease, and was not caught as René had foretold. Having put on our uniforms, we were taken to the Bureau of the *Médecin-Major* for medical examination, and it proved to be the merest formality, all of us (except myself, whom René had impersonated in Paris) having been most thoroughly vetted before being accepted at the Recruiting Station as *bon pour le service*.

So far as I was concerned, all that the doctor did was to glance at me, perfunctorily pull down one of my eyelids, look at my teeth, and give me a word of peculiarly unnecessary advice.

From the Bureau of the *Médecin-Major*, we were marched to another, where we all gave unverified, and probably unveracious, information as to our respective nationalities, professions, army service, and so forth. Good soldiers were two a penny in those days, from all the armies of Europe, and France wanted every one that she could get, for trouble was brewing—and not only in Morocco and Syria.

I, with perfect truth, and for some reason curiously comforted by that grain of truth, stated that I had served with the British Army for four years. The Orderly Clerk who took down our facts and fictions looked at my hands and then at my face, shrugged his shoulders and was moved to remark:

"God help you. . . . Why did you do it?"

For one awful moment I thought that the wretch had singled me out from the others and had his suspicions as to my sex, but I soon realized it was only his pretty way.

To Abraham the Sailor, he observed:

"There are fools, there are sacred fools, there are unnameable fools, and there are fools who join the Legion."

To Terence Hogan, his comment was, as he entered the necessary particulars:

"You look intelligent. I wonder why you chose this form of suicide."

To Digger:

"And so you would die for France, eh? . . . You will."

A pleasing and philosophic person who sees, in all its marvellous variety, an endless procession of the genus *homo* alleged *sapiens*, and has a very low opinion of it.

All the afternoon, Digger, Abraham the Sailor, Hogan and I, like the other recruits, wrestled in the Barrack Room with our new, but old, weapons, kit, accoutrements and clothing, helped by a fatigue of *légionnaires* of the Depôt Company detailed to show us the ropes.

My friends being old soldiers, and I being fairly quick-witted and deft-handed, we made good progress at *paquetage*-building and, after the second and last meal of the day—stew and bread—we decided that we had, like Caesar, done enough for honour, or at least for the avoidance of punishment or rebuke.

So we set forth, arrayed in dead men's clothes, and appropriately beheld some dead men before the evening was finished.

Being stalwart fellows, we filled the uniforms pretty well, and successfully passed the Sergeant of the Guard at the big gates of the Parade Ground.

The orthodox sights were remarkably flat, stale, and unprofitable, this being, in truth, a dull provincial town, containing nothing of interest except the Legion itself.

However, concealing all signs of boredom and gloom, and assuming what I hoped to be an air of gay hilarity, I accompanied my friends from tenth-rate café to eleventh-rate café and tasted an assortment of strange beverages ranging, so far as my companions were concerned, from good wine to bad beer and whisky, and so far as I was concerned, from nauseating but non-alcoholic *syrops* to more nauseating coffee—after I had had one glass of quite decent red wine, a sort of Algerian claret.

It wasn't until later that we knew where to get real coffee, made by Arabs for Arab customers.

What did interest me upon this Via Dolorosa of drink and mild debauchery, was the marvellous medley of, to me, quite novel human types.

I should have loved to sit on a seat in the open air outside one of the cafés, and watch them all go by.

Soldier and civilian; European and African; male and female, in endless variety. But if "Order is Heaven's first law," and should be man's, the silly creatures' second law appears to be that, if you are out to enjoy yourself, you must visit beastly interiors, breathe beastly atmosphere, drink beastly drinks, and smoke beastly tobacco amongst beastly people.

Terence said he was reminded of the pursuit termed gin-crawling, and of the days when, home on a "drop of leave," he was wont to go from night-club to night-club and haunt to haunt. Terence Hogan was drinking quite as much as was good for him, and a little over.

Digger affirmed, probably with truth, that he preferred the Strand, and that the worst dive in Sydney had got a better bar than the best one here; while Abraham the Sailor complained that all that was wrong with the place was that it wasn't any good, and that there was nothing wrong with the drink except that it wasn't fit to drink.

When my cup was full, my last cup of coffee empty, and I could hold no more and bear this wild Life of Pleasure no longer, I suggested a walk. One of the *légionnaires* who had helped us with our kit, and whom we were now treating, offered to take us to a place called the *Village Nègre*—the native quarter.

Arrived at this part of the town, we heard sounds of devilry by night, and found a high-class—or low-class—row in progress outside a house in front of which was an armed guard or picket of the Legion.

I was absolutely amazed.

So far as one could discover, it was an actual battle, a triangular battle wherein Arabs armed with knives or heavy cudgels fought Spaniards armed with revolvers, knives or brickbats; and assorted soldiers armed with fists—a regular dog-fight. Free for all, and all on to all. Spaniards fought Arabs and soldiers; soldiers fought Arabs and Spaniards; Arabs fought Spaniards and soldiers. Now and again a man fell, in answer to a pistol shot; or one of a wrestling writhing pair collapsed and lay on the ground, while the other rose, wiped his knife and recovered his breath.

The picket looked on, interested but impartial, and awaited reinforcements.

"Say," quoted the market-merry Terence, " 'Is this a private fight, or can anyone join in?' Come on, boys."

And he would have dashed headlong into the *mêlée*, doubtless followed by Digger and Abraham, had not the *légionnaire* who had brought us cried:

"Look out, let's run for it,"—and we heard the feet of the awaited reinforcements arriving at the double.

By devious ways the *légionnaire* led us swiftly thence, observing that it was about to become an unhealthy spot for innocent men.

*   *   *   *   *

Terry grew joyous. Uplifted. Beginning to find himself already. We stopped for a drink, and a big *légionnaire* made a disparaging remark about *bleus*.

"Faith, how I love me enemies!" whooped Terry. "Without them there'd be no foightin'. God bless 'em all."

And with that he sailed into the big soldier and knocked him down.

"He has the light of bottle in his eye," said Terence. "He has drink taken."

And as the man did not rise, Terry struck a Spahi who had laughed.

"Come on, me bhoy," he roared.

"I've no quarrel with you," said the Spahi.

"Quarrel," shouted Terry. "We don't want to *quarrel,* we only want to foight."

I tried to drag him away, and a young lady tried to detain him.

"Me dear," said Terry, cupping her chin in his hand, "do you know the difference between a good girl and a bad one?"

"Not I," laughed the charmer.

"Faith I'm sure ye don't," said Terry solemnly, "so I'll tell ye. Good girls get taken in—and bad girls get taken out."

CHAPTER V

On getting back to Barracks between eight and nine I realized that I was extraordinarily tired in mind, body and soul—more tired than I had ever been when ambulance-driving or lorry-driving in France. So, seeing nothing to prevent, I simply removed my tunic and trousers and got into bed without waiting for roll-call.

This ceremony is performed by the Company Orderly Sergeant for the week, who, with the Sergeant-Major or Adjudant, passes through every room and obtains a slip from the room Corporal showing the number of men present.

At the close of the inspection, the slips are handed in at the Company Orderly Room, and the names of absentees are sent along to the Guard Room at the main gate. The Sergeant of the Guard checks the names of the men as they return, retaining in cells for the night those who are late.

In the morning, these men are handed over to the Company Orderly Sergeant, who treats them as guilty of something, unless they can prove themselves innocent of everything.

After drill and roll-call on the following morning, we were detailed off for various fatigues. All recruits come to this Company to begin their training, and the majority of the full privates forming the Company are in "permanent employment" in Sidi-bel-Abbès. Seasoned troops returning from the Sahara, Morocco, Madagascar, Cochin China and elsewhere are also stationed there temporarily, so it's a Company much of whose personnel is continually changing, with the perhaps not unnatural result that its officers and N.C.O.'s are, as a rule, wholly indifferent to the men's welfare.

After midday *soupe* on this second day, we recruits were called out by the Sergeant, a score or so at a time, and marched off to the Company's Stores. Each Company has its own Store, the French army system differing from that of the English army—with its General Store and the Quartermaster in charge.

Here we received the remainder of our equipment, and were then sent back to our respective Barrack Rooms to await further orders; and here it was that Silver (or Silva) the Brazilian sailor sinned, and I suffered.

The Sergeant suddenly ordered out the recruits from my Barrack Room for inspection, giving us instructions to fall in in front of the Bureau of our own Company, for a kit inspection by the Company Orderly Sergeant. All that we now possessed in the world was to be taken with us, so that the Company Orderly Sergeant might see that our kit tallied exactly with the account thereof which was written on the slip issued to him.

Why are men-folk such fussers?

Standing on my left in the rank, the Brazilian, evidently in a state of some perturbation, was volubly explaining, in execrable French, to the man on his left, Gustavus Adolphus, that he had most certainly been robbed by some filthy brigand, or had, even more probably, dropped it on his way from the Company's Store to the Barrack Room.

"It" was evidently a cleaning-brush as, instead of the four which he should have possessed, I perceived but three among the kit laid out before him.

Gustavus Adolphus bade him get forthwith to

his knees and pray—pray hard, pray like Hell—for assuredly he would be court-martialled, and then given thirty days' solitary confinement.

The Brazilian did not pray. He cursed, and all but wept.

Abraham the Sailor, on my right, was just asking me the French for, "Won't you have a bottle of wine, Corporal?" when the Company Orderly Sergeant appeared, and on a terrific bawl of "*Garde a vous. . . . Fixe*" . . . we stood to extreme attention while he walked slowly along the line, his practised eye taking in the details of each man's kit as it lay spread out on the ground at his feet.

As he halted in front of me, and eyed that valuable portion of the property of *Madame la République* temporarily entrusted to my care, I stared stonily at his cap, fearing nothing in my conscious rectitude and perfect correctness.

Imagine my horror and dismay at the pricking of this bubble, as the man first emitted a yelp of bitter anguish and then uttered a howl of uncontrollable rage.

"Where's your fourth brush, *salaud?*" he roared, or words to that effect; for so inarticulate was he, either by reason of the violence of his emotion, or the fact of his being a German, that I did not, at first, understand what he said.

Once again he bawled the question, and I could only dumbly gaze upon his empurpled countenance, swollen and suffused with rage and hate, in my bewilderment and terror.

Suddenly he seized me by the front of my tunic, rocked me violently to and fro, flung me from him, and then, pointing to the ground, directed my wandering gaze upon my kit—the kit which I knew to be all present and correct.

"*Salaud! Vaurien! Dummkopf!* Where is your

fourth brush?"

And I really thought he was going to strike me—for my four brushes were now but three. I had committed a heinous and horrible offence. I had treacherously robbed good kind *Madame la République*.

Salaud indeed! Miserable miscreant, vile scoundrel, *sale cochon*, low criminal, base bandit, ungrateful mean hound that I was, I had robbed *Madame la République* of a little cleaning-brush well worth threepence when it was new.

Conceive and visualize that heartrending scene if you can. Words failed me, as why should they not? The bristles of but three brushes grew where those of four had grown before.

Instinctively I glanced at the kit of the Silver descendant of Christopher Columbus or stout Cortez or somebody. At the feet of that traveller lay four good brushes, and on his face was a look of modest virtue and smug satisfaction.

"Abandoned bastard of a small yellow dog," bawled the Company Orderly Sergeant. "What have you done with the fourth brush?"

And it was obvious to me that his wrath and horror were supplemented by a bitter personal hate.

"Shall I tell you, escaped convict? Shall I tell you, sewer-rat? You've sold it for a cup of wine."

"Or a mess of pottage," said I in English, being a younger and even sillier fool in those days than I am now.

The Sergeant did not accept what he apparently thought to be my excuse, but he fell silent. His mouth closed grimly, and he passed on to Abraham the Sailor, Digger and Terence Hogan, all well accustomed to show-down inspections, and with a portentous nod in my direction, dismissed the parade.

The incident was closed, but would be re-opened elsewhere when I should hear something to my disadvantage.

Later I was brought up before the Captain of the Company and given eight days' *salle de police* for stealing and selling part of my equipment—to wit one button-brush—with a severe reprimand and the information that only the fact of my being a recruit saved me from a punishment worthy of my crime.

And then Terry, speaking perfect French and exhibiting perfect charm of manner, went straight-way to the Company Sergeant-Major and told him exactly what had happened, taking his most solemn oath that he'd seen my left-hand man remove a brush from my kit and put it with his own, while I was talking to my right-hand man, a moment before the Company Orderly Sergeant came out of the Bureau.

He also begged to state that the two men he had brought with him as witnesses, had both heard the real culprit complaining that he had lost a brush.

The Company Sergeant-Major bore my troubles bravely, merely remarking with a shrug of his shoulders that, since the Captain had given me eight days' *salle de police*, eight days' *salle de police* I'd got, and adding that it was French Army law that a man could always appeal against his sentence after he'd served it.

On Hogan politely inquiring what good that would be, the Company Sergeant-Major replied:

"None whatever; so why do it?"

Whether that wily and experienced army-diplomat, Terence Hogan, spoke with a tongue of gold (in francs) as well as in perfect French, I don't know, but I have my suspicions. For when the Corporal came to our Barrack Room that evening to march off any men who were condemned to *salle de police*, and I meekly surrendered myself to him, he bade me hop it, and held out the hand of friendship—and expectation.

Into this ready receptacle I slipped a couple of francs, and the interesting ceremony was eight times repeated. In this manner were the law and my eight-days' *salle de police* fulfilled and satisfied.

I have forgotten to mention that when I returned from receiving sentence from the Captain in the Orderly Room, I went in search of the Brazilian, intending to remonstrate with him and to say that I thought his conduct unsocial. Like most women, I can bear almost anything better than injustice, and I was very angry with the miserable petty thief.

When I found him in his Barrack Room, I discovered that he was unwell, uncommunicative, and disinclined to receive visitors. Also that his face consisted largely of one eye and a bruise.

Returning to my own *caserne*, where my friends were cleaning their kit, I noticed that one of Digger's knuckles looked a little damaged.

"You been fighting?" I asked.

"Me, chum?" replied Digger in great surprise. "Fighting? Fighting with that Dago, Silver? Why, I just went up to him and said, 'Excusin' me, Mr. Dago Sapolio,' I said, 'would you be so *very* kind as to be so good and so obligin' as to hand me one of those brushes,' I said. . . . And with that he shakes his head in a contrary manner and makes an insulting and provoking gesture, calculated to create a breach of the peace. Well, I didn't want to do that, of course, so I merely took the brush, gave him a push in the eye, and came quietly away—not wishing to be involved in any unseemly and disgraceful fracass in accordance with military regulations. . . . 'Nuff said. . . ."

*   *   *   *   *

The days that followed were a vain repetition, not as the heathen do, of routine drill and fatigues.

Daily one learnt the things that one must do in the Legion and, possibly more important, the things that one must not do—things both official and unofficial, things public and private, so to speak.

One of the most important of the latter, is the very rigid piece of etiquette that no *légionnaire* should ever crudely and bluntly inquire of another as to why he joined the Legion. To break this rule is the worst of bad taste and bad manners, and may lead to bad trouble.

I suppose the reason for this is the undeniable fact that a certain proportion of the soldiers of the Legion does undoubtedly consist of men who have left their country for their country's good. Some of these are criminals; some social outcasts; some hiding from the police, with or without good reason; some political offenders; some deserters from the armies of their respective countries; some eccentrics, cranks and perverts; some self-condemned to punishment for sins of which the law takes no cognizance.

And the remainder are just poor men out of work, mostly trained soldiers unfitted for any other profession.

"Single men in Barracks—most remarkable like you," in fact.

Don't, for one moment, entertain the idea that the French Foreign Legion is a rogues' refuge, a robbers' roost, and a home for escaped criminals. Very far from it.

On the whole, and allowing for the fact that a few "wanted" people hide here, this glorious regiment is not so very different from any other, and contains a large proportion of admirable and excellent people who are fond of change and adventure; rolling stones who don't want to gather any moss but who do want to see life; worthy and quite harmless social misfits; keen professional soldiers; ordinary failures who've come to grief through no criminal fault of their own; and quite a lot of perfectly commonplace out-of-works who simply joined because it was so long since the last meal.

Anyhow, a most amusing and intriguing crowd, with here and there an intensely interesting case.

And I soon, to some extent, forgot myself and my troubles in observing these cases. I make no secret of the fact that I prefer men to women, and would always rather be with men than with women. I don't mean that I am a freak, a pervert, or in any way abnormal; but that, owing to my upbringing, physique, and the circumstances of my life, I am naturally and incurably mannish.

There are certain manly virtues, and especial womanly virtues. I happen to prefer the manly ones. There are recognized masculine vices and faults, and undeniable feminine failings and short-comings. I happen to dislike the former less than the latter, and I always have got on, and always shall get on, better with men than with women.

Doubtless it is this fact that makes most women dislike me, and find me brusque, abrupt, gauche, clumsy and unsympathetic.

None the less, my creed is "Equal opportunity for men and women."

And also I must admit that, though I have little or no criminal inclination and tendency myself, I have not the proper condemnatory attitude toward criminals.

I've known quite a number of criminals and quite a number of widely respected and justly admired good men, and I find them very much alike—except that the criminals are so much more interesting, amusing, enterprising and alive. When I say criminal, I mean a man who's done something wrong, something for which the police want to catch him and shut him up, or cut his silly head off. I do not mean the depraved bestial creature that is a mere predatory brute. A lethal chamber is the place for that.

I came across a good example of this criminal of non-criminal mind and nature, one night when I was on guard.

A man in a very advanced state of intoxication was brought in at about three o'clock, and thrown into a cell. The Corporal, a German who had been either a baker or a waiter (I forget which) in London before the war, told me that the fellow, a confirmed drunkard, was an ex-captain of one of our Guard Regiments—I need not name the Battalion—and that whilst on leave from his unit, he had gone to Monte Carlo with all the money that he could raise and an infallible system for breaking the Bank. As soon as he had lost the lot, he had begged, borrowed and in a sense stolen (for he had a big hotel bill unpaid) every penny that he could scrape together by selling all his effects and wiring home to such relations, friends and acquaintances as he thought might be foolish enough to entrust him with some more.

He then promptly returned to the Casino and lost this as well.

Absolutely ruined, penniless, and in a slough of debt from which he could never escape, he bolted, joined the French Foreign Legion—and here he was.

I made it my business to get to know him, and found him a charming and cultured gentleman, no more a criminal than I am, but deliberately, steadily and purposefully drinking himself to death.

I felt terribly sorry for him, for though not forty years of age, he was an absolute wreck.

Fancy coming straight from the Officers' Mess of a Regiment of His Majesty's Foot Guards to be a private soldier in the French Foreign Legion, cut off from everyone and everything and every habit that made life worth living. . . .

I heard some time afterwards that, one day when the Battalion was out on manœuvres, he did what he hadn't done until then—got incapably drunk when on duty; and that, by way of punishment, he was dragged along the street and into the Barracks by his feet, and later was discharged by a Medical Board as unfit, after repeated attacks of delirium tremens.

Doubtless this poor soul died in some foul rat-infested gutter-hole in a Sidi-bel-Abbès slum. I never knew his name, of course, but his case has remained in my mind as one of the most tragic that I've known, and I have come across more than a few real tragedies; also a good many comedies—and dramas innumerable.

There are, of course, some very nasty people in the Legion, but so there are in all regiments, and in any other large collection of men.

There is good in them, though. There is good in everybody. Even in Silva and the "White Slave" ruffian they call Matthieu le Maquereau—both of whom have courage, self-reliance and determination, if nothing else.

But on the whole, the Legion average level is neither lower nor higher than that of the average regiment of professional soldiers. . . . Undeniably its peaks are higher and its depths lower, for it is a unique cosmopolitan assembly, representing every stratum of the society of every nation.

*　　*　　*　　*　　*

At the end of some months of routine drill and intensive training, our Company was transferred to Saïda, making the journey partly by road and partly by rail.

We marched under active-service conditions, but on a good military road, and on the whole, I preferred the marching to being jammed immovable into a tiny compartment, in which oven-like box we had as much space as sardines have in their tin.

I far preferred Saïda to Sidi-bel-Abbès, and was very glad we went there.

Terry was beginning to get stale in Sidi. The novelty had worn off and he had learned all they had to teach. Although he had not once been drunk—really drunk—he was drinking far too much and not always of good sound wine. The fact was, he was bored; mentally idle, stunted and thwarted; suffering from repression and lack of self-expression.

At the daily deadening grind he was like a racehorse at cart-horse work, and his evening escapades and follies were but reaction. . . .

Saïda is the real Algeria, whereas Sidi-bel-Abbès is provincial France. Saïda is Arab, high, fresh, comparatively clean and free from Sidi's low-class European and half-breed Europeanised population. It is not one quarter as big as Sidi, and one sees only Arabs and soldiers. It is really picturesque and most interesting, and I loved wandering with Terence in the unspoilt bazaars, alleys and arcades among the shops and booths kept by Jews, Moors, Riffians and Algerian Arabs.

I saw scores of things that I wanted to buy, but one of the things a *légionnaire* cannot do, is to accumulate possessions.

But as I was determined to have a souvenir of our stay in Saïda, I bought a tiny charm from a vast dumb negro. It was a little silver hand, and when I showed it to Père Cocteau, an old *légionnaire* who was with us, he roared with laughter.

"Do you know what you've got there, my boy?" he said, slapping his thigh. "A sure and certain charm against barrenness! Ha! Ha! Ho! Ho! It will have its work cut out to make a *légionnaire* produce a baby . . . I'll be its godfather . . ."

It appeared that I had indeed purchased "a silver Hand of Fat'ma", the Mussulman charm against sterility in women! . . . H'm. . . .

Saïda was good for Terry and daily he improved, as he found more to interest him. In point of fact he began to take too much interest in the Ouled-Naïls and their wonderful dances.

Granted that the scene in front of the Moorish Bath where they dance at night is more like a stage scene than any ever seen in a theatre, that the music of the *raita*, flute, *derbukha* and tom-tom was wonderful, the dancing equally wonderful, the audience, representative of all Africa, even more wonderful—the whole thing, in fact, a page of the *Arabian Nights* come to life—enough may be more than a feast; and a game's a game, fun's fun, a joke's a joke, and fair's fair. . . .

It was not long before I knew what Terry knew, and what Terry knew that I knew—that these Ouled-Naïl dancing-girls, albeit very different from the European-contaminated frauds of Biskra and the tourist towns, have, nevertheless, another profession beside that of dancing.

*　　*　　*　　*　　*

So when the order came for us to return to Sidi-bel-Abbès, it was not with wholly unmixed regret that I heard it.

Are all strong men weak too? Terry *is* so fine and brave and strong—and so weak . . .

CHAPTER VI

Looking back, the succeeding months of intensive training and gradually increasing marching exercise at Sidi, really seem a very brief space of time. Life was too full for thought; and work was so hard, and sleep so deep, that the time passed swiftly.

Nevertheless, I was very thankful when, a sudden order arriving for five hundred men to march immediately for a destination unknown, I was included. Since I was worthy of inclusion in the draft, Abraham the Sailor, Digger and Terence Hogan naturally were, for they were all old soldiers.

Hogan had been a British officer in a crack regiment and had risen from the ranks to be a Major too; Digger had been at Gallipoli in an Australian regiment; and Abraham the Sailor (who had really been a sailor as well) had served in Haiti and the Philippines, in the United States Marine Corps. . . .

We marched out of Barracks at nine o'clock one morning, headed by the band of the Legion playing the Regimental March, and we must have done nearly fifty kilometres before we bivouacked.

I shall never forget my first forced march under real active-service conditions. It was truly hard, and most terribly monotonous.

On we went, day after day; and, before long, this changed to night after night, the heat being terrific, and cases of collapse from heat-stroke numerous.

Nor is night-marching and day-resting quite as good an arrangement as it sounds, for, after marching throughout the entire night, most of us found it almost impossible to sleep during the day, owing to lack of shade, to extreme fatigue, and to great heat. There is such a thing as being too tired to sleep, and we discovered it.

I was terribly anxious as to my powers of endurance, and most thankful to find that, while far from being as good as the best, I was certainly better than the worst. I probably owed something to having a greater spur to endeavour than any man in that column had, and some-thing to my keenness in training and exercise, and to my abstemious, careful way of life in Sidi-bel-Abbès.

I got a horrid shock one moonlight night, though, for unfortunately, something put Kipling's poem "Boots" into my head, and nothing would get it out again until, at last, I found myself reciting aloud:

> "*Boots—boots—boots—boots, movin' up and down again!*"

It was a real fright and I passed through moments or minutes of desperate terror, for I knew I was going mad—mad or hysterical. I could not stop reciting, and my voice was getting louder and louder, a dreadful accompaniment to the endless steady shuffle of those boots, boots, *boots*, BOOTS. . . .

Suddenly the whistle blew. We halted, and fell down where we were—and the spell was broken.

Curiously enough, it is still one of my few real fears, that the spirit of that terrible poem will seize upon me one day toward the end of a long march and get the better of me.

A woman's nerves, and nerve, are different from those of a man. I know that some of my comrades fear things of which I am not in the least afraid.

On the other hand, I fear certain things which would make them laugh. Bats, for example. And big cockroaches, even more than bats. Snakes, curiously enough, I don't fear in the least. Nor bullets.

But I was in deadly fear on that "Boots" night; and I think that the dread of becoming hysterical helped me physically, perhaps. I was much more afraid of my fright than I was of the endless kilometres of the road.

It was an awful physical strain, though; for, in addition to being overworked, we were under-nourished. Apparently there simply was not time to feed us properly on that forced march.

After all, war is war.

Macaroni, covered with grease, was our staple diet, and at nightfall we would continue our march as hungry as we were tired. In the light of dawn, the poor fellows were really a pathetic sight, with their haggard grey faces, stamped with an expression of suffering and fatigue, showing the strain they were undergoing, carrying from sixty to seventy pounds of kit, hour after hour and day after day, on inadequate and insufficient food and water.

But I'd seen worse things in France—remnants of battalions marching from the line to rest-billets; and I had worked for longer hours under conditions that were harrowing mentally, as well as almost impossible physically.

On we went, and I don't think we left anyone behind us, for no *légionnaire* falls out sick, so long as it's humanly possible for him to keep on his feet. It simply is not done—partly for reasons of regimental pride and *esprit de corps*, and partly because falling out is, in point of fact, just about the one thing worse than keeping on.

And when we had at length about reached the

limits of human endurance we also reached our objective, a kind of mushroom garrison-town, and went into camp.

*　　*　　*　　*　　*

Here, any of us who had had dreams of martial glory and visions of warfare leading to quick distinction, promotion, and decoration, were doomed to disappointment.

What the mighty hurry had been about I do not know, but presumably our arrival enabled the authorities to send away an equal number of better-trained and more seasoned troops than we were.

On arrival, we were allowed to rest for a whole day, and, on the next, we were marched to some newly-constructed Barracks and allotted to different rooms. I was delighted to find that in No. 3 *chambrée* I was still with Digger, Hogan and Abraham the Sailor, as well as Pet Hansel, Gustavus Adolphus and several other *légionnaires* who had been in our Section at Sidi-bel-Abbès.

*　　*　　*　　*　　*

And now fell a bolt from the blue which, but for good luck, good judgment and good wangling, would have knocked me out of the Legion.

We received notice that on the morrow we should be inoculated against typhoid, and, by all accounts, we should not only be made very ill, but should have an unpleasant time in the process of inoculation.

According to the old soldiers, a kind of garden-squirt would be thrust into each man's side and about a pint of noxious fluid injected. To enable the Butcher to get at us, we should parade naked, or at best, stripped to the waist.

I was in despair.

Having surmounted all obstacles and arrived at the very outset of a campaign, it seemed hard indeed to be discovered now and ignominiously ejected; to leave Terry; to fail; to be a laughing-stock. . . .

I thought of my dead father and brothers and their jeers at my equality-of-women claims and assertions:—

"Huh! Wait till women can be soldiers and sailors. . . ."

"I suppose we're to have women M.P.'s to make wars that men will have to fight . . . ?"

"Time enough to give women a vote when we can give them a rifle. . . ."

Once again I learnt the power of money in the Legion, and used my money to good purpose.

Of the four men whom, under Père Cocteau's guidance, I corrupted, one lived by corruption and the other three in the hope of being corrupted.

I shall not say enough to risk getting anybody into trouble, or to render more difficult such evasion for another. But a corporal, a sergeant, an orderly clerk and an *infirmier* benefited by my evasion.

I need hardly say *Monsieur le Médecin-Major* knew nothing about it. Those who did, quite understood anyone who could afford to do so paying to escape the extremely crude, rough, and sickening performance, with its unpleasant consequences.

For a couple of days, everybody was ill, some very ill with high fever; and all parades and fatigues were cancelled.

I took advantage of the fact that everyone lay in bed, to have two glorious days of utter rest.

I groaned as loudly as anybody and only raised

my head to take coffee and *soupe* when they were brought round by the unfortunate room-orderly, disgruntled and grumbling, who was as sick as anybody. I felt shame, but had to maintain the pretence.

*   *   *   *   *

The following week we were allowed what to us seemed quite a slack time, and then intensive training began again.

We were formed into two companies of two hundred and fifty each, and though I then thought life was hard, monotonous, wearisome, and uninteresting, I've often looked back to it as by no means one of the worst of our times in the Legion. It wasn't very long before we had to put up with conditions that were very much harder.

Our daily routine consisted of being roused at four-thirty, given a mug of coffee at four-forty-five, and then falling-in for inspection by an officer.

This was a most boring and wearisome business, a long and stupid stand-easy, during which one neither worked nor played; neither drilled nor rested; but merely stood and talked in undertones and waited for something to happen. Why it was impossible for us to get on with our drill and training, and get it over, until an officer had looked at us, I don't know.

This part of the day's routine annoyed Hogan almost unbearably and to the point of mutiny, though Digger and Abraham the Sailor were quite philosophical about it, Abraham observing that he'd sooner stand than walk and sooner walk than run. What he did "allow" was, that since we stood-at-ease for any length of time up to half an hour, we ought to be allowed to sit-at-ease or indeed lie-at-ease.

What surprised me, and shocked Terence Hogan, was that officers would often stroll over to parade, smoking, wearing slacks and unauthorized foot-gear and without their belts.

No one can deny that, splendid soldiers and brave men as they are, French officers are, generally speaking, much less smart than those of the British Army.

However, the N.C.O.'s saw to it that there was no slackness on our part. After the useless and perfunctory "inspection," we were marched off by Companies to the training-ground, which was any of the surrounding country that was still desert, scrub and stone-strewn sand.

A good deal of the land round the village was cultivated by the natives, and there were quite large vineyards, of which each of the tiny vines, a foot or so high, bore several pounds of grapes—of which more anon.

The morning's training work lasted for about four hours, each Section consisting of three Sergeants, six Corporals and forty men, exercising under its own officer.

On returning to Barracks, the Orders for the Day were read out in French and at once translated into German and Russian, that fact indicating the preponderance of those two nationalities in the Company. But for Hogan, I am not sure that Abraham the Sailor and Digger would have gathered very much from any one of the three efforts, nor I absolutely everything, from the quickly-gabbled French.

After this, water was turned on, and those who felt they needed it, had a bath. At ten-thirty the bugles played the ever-popular *soupe* call.

The marvellous thing was, that time and custom did not stale its infinite lack of variety, and that one enjoyed this stew as much, and as little, on the thousandth occasion of devouring it as upon the first.

Some humorist at the War Office had once laid it down that every French soldier should get two hundred and twenty-five grammes of meat, including bone and fat. (How infinitely annoying to the excellent *piou-piou* if he were sitting down to only two hundred and twenty-five grammes of meat, including bone and fat!)

With this two hundred and twenty-five grammes of meat, including bone and fat, were cooked either rice, lentils, beans, split peas, or macaroni. Upon memorable occasions, green vegetables took the place of the above dry facts. By the time the two hundred and twenty-five grammes of meat, including bone and fat, had been augmented by an unspecified number of grains of rice, lentils, or whatever it might be, and the whole was cooked, it somehow reduced itself to well under one hundred grammes of that stew which the French call *soupe*.

What, of course, the War Office humorist did not insist upon, was the precise proportion of bone or fat, or both, that should appear in each two hundred and twenty-five grammes. . . .

Soldiers are born grumblers (or are they made grumblers?) and there is probably little or no truth in the statement made, twice daily, in every *chambrée*, camp and bivouac, that the invariable composition of the sacred two hundred and twenty-five grammes of meat, including bone and fat, is two hundred and twenty-four grammes of bone and one of fat.

Anyhow, it was evidently sufficient, for the troops did wonders on it, and kept healthy.

We each had also about a pound (a *livre*) of bread a day, and, three times a week, a glass of red wine. When bread was unprocurable, its place was taken by biscuits, and then more than sufficient unto the day were the weevils thereof.

After we had consumed each our two hundred and twenty-five grammes of meat, including bone and fat, came *siesta*.

This sounds lazy, or as though a paternal Government had grown grand-paternal.

It was nothing of the sort, however. It was compulsory and, but for the order, cases of heat-stroke and sun-stroke would have been what are sometimes known as "too numerous to mention." The heat, out of doors, between eleven and three, was so great that every man, on pain of punishment, had to be in his Barrack Room between those hours.

From three to six followed lectures, theoretical instruction, and small classes, instructed by N.C.O.'s, in parts-of-the-rifle, care of arms, aiming-drill, and similar more or less sedentary military amusements.

At 6 p.m. came what was either lunch or dinner, according to whether you regarded the ten-thirty meal as breakfast or lunch. Anyhow, it was the second, and last, meal of the day, and whatever the first was, the second was like unto it, there being no variation whatsoever.

How I did miss my tea, at first. From four till five I was possessed and obsessed by a positive craving, painful in the extreme. Let some good teetotallers, pussy-foots, temperance preachers, and all those who would withhold from others those things which they themselves do not like, let them, I say, suddenly and completely give up their tea. I should then respect them even more than I do now.

Until the craving died down to mere longing, I think I would have sunk to any depth, done any evil deed, given anything I possessed, for a large cup of good English tea, properly made; teapot thoroughly warmed; a big spoonful for each person and two for the pot; the water poured on in the same second that the kettle boiled; all that water immediately poured off into the hot-water jug; and the teapot then a quarter filled and allowed to stand for exactly three minutes before being filled and the whole infusion poured off into another hot teapot. Milk and one lump of sugar, and a coffee-spoonful of thick cream into the cup first. . . .

When poor old Thirsty-face and Cocteau the Cannibal sat side by side and wept for want of wine, I would go and sit beside them and weep for want of tea.

They thought it was for wine that I wept, and respected my grief. . . .

After 6 p.m. lunch or dinner, the evening was our own, to spend as we pleased in any form of equipment-cleaning, clothes-washing or similar military domestic delights.

And even here it was to be seen that the abominations of the capitalistic system reared their hideous heads; for any man who had the money—a *sou* for a week's boot-cleaning and a franc for a fortnight's entire fatigues, bed, *paquetage*, washing, cleaning and polishing— could pay another to do his work for him while he strolled forth to take the air, if he couldn't afford to take anything better.

The down-trodden, exploited and face-ground proletariat who stayed behind and sweated while their bourgeois brethren strutted forth in idleness and clean white uniform, thus amassed the wherewithal themselves to become capitalists upon the morrow. Personally, I joined the ranks of the capitalists on every possible occasion, and undeniably I received the heartfelt thanks and blessings of whatever member of the exploited and expropriated proletariat got the job. They positively brought their faces to be ground. . . .

But when one did thus shirk one's duty and become an unprofitable servant, if a profitable comrade, there wasn't really much to do in the village A—— el-H——. Not even in the West End. I remember that wine was then a franc per litre, but as a franc was five days' pay, a *légionnaire* couldn't exactly bathe in wine on his salary alone.

I have a modest income of my own, and I frankly and shamelessly admit that I never got more pleasure from my money than I did in giving an occasional glass of wine to a man who loved it and couldn't afford it.

"Suppose this mug of good red wine is to him what a cup of tea would be to me," thought I; and stood drinks as freely and frequently as I could afford to do.

Obviously I was born wicked. Hell-doomed from the cradle. So how avoid my fate—or why try to, for that matter?

Personally, I never drank more than one glass of wine and that generally with a meal. I simply could not afford to. (I don't mean financially-speaking, of course.) The temptation was too great for me ever to toy with it. Wine loosens the tongue, and weakens inhibitions. Without becoming intoxicated and allowing a sea of wine to sap the foundations of one's protective walls of reticence and reserve, or even becoming what the farmers at home used to call "market merry," one might become—chatty.

I'm not a chatty person at the best of times, but I might become one at the worst, if I were fool enough to get "full" enough.

I did not contemplate the possibility of getting drunk and casting myself upon the broad bosom of Digger, or Abraham the Sailor, and sobbing forth my shameful secret; but I did, in my dark hours, visualize the possibility of being careless; saying a word too much; for an instant lowering my guard and giving myself away to the sharp eye of a comrade; or of taking the wrong line—the mothering line—with some poor devil who told me all his troubles, as most of them did, sooner or later.

And always there was Terence Hogan and his little weakness to remember. . . .

So I drank very little, and gave away a hundred times more wine than I drank, and though it honestly never occurred to me to do this in order to buy popularity, it undoubtedly helped to make me popular, and this greatly smoothed the somewhat thorny and stony path of my interestingly violent life.

*   *   *   *   *

And speaking of popularity, I wondered whether there can be such a thing as unconscious sex-appeal—I mean whether a man can be attracted to a woman as a woman, without knowing that she is one.

It seems to me quite possible, for, time after time, I incurred the affection—I can use no better phrase—of men with whom there was no other reason for my popularity. I mean men to whom I had not given wine, help, or the means of earning money. . . . Men whom I scarcely knew and to whom I had hardly spoken. Nice, decent men, I mean.

They would come and ask me to be their *copain*[54]—a great honour and compliment. I can

---

[54] Chum; pal; mate; special close friend.

think of no reason for this curious popularity but entirely unconscious, unrecognized sex appeal.

Among such men who sought my company I do not of course include Silva or Matthieu, both of whom insulted me by suggested friendship.

Silva astounded me by coming to me one day and making a suggestion which at first I did not even begin to understand as he gabbled his Portuguese-French into my English ear.

When I got some glimmering of what he was jibbering about, I said.

"Go and explain the idea to my *copain* Hogan. . . ."

"And why?"

"Only that he will explain my ideas to you—more clearly than I can do. He will also remove your seven vital organs, and put them back in different places."

Matthieu le Maquereau, an Argentine who has lived in Paris, or a Parisian who has lived in Buenos Aires, speaks excellent English, as well as French, Arabic and Spanish, and his proposal of close friendship was made in a few ill-chosen words devoid of ambiguity.

His understanding of English being perfect, I merely remarked that as the mere sight of him always made me sick, he'd better go while the going was good . . . go to Hell in fact. . . .

When this creature has had a couple of bottles of wine, he tells of the days when he was a gentleman and always wore patent-leather shoes and white waistcoats.

Apparently he was foreign representative and partner in a good commercial house in Buenos Aires—girls being the commerce and trade always brisk.

Sometimes he would explain his fall from being a gentleman to being a soldier by blaming the

Paris police; and sometimes by blaming his partner, a Spanish-American lady of remarkable psychic and clairvoyante powers—an infallible prophetess, seer and fortune-teller.

Apparently it was her disturbing practice to assure him from time to time that he would be killed by a woman—this fate being foretold for him by her crystal, the cards, and the lines of his hand.

Presumably there were times when the gentleman felt safer in the Legion than in the company of the girls whom he had inveigled to Buenos Aires. . . .

*   *   *   *   *

With the best will in the world, one couldn't spend much in this place, and it always seemed to me that if one daily bought the entire stock of every shop, the owner would still be heading fast for bankruptcy.

There was, however, a canteen in the Barracks, and at the canteen there was an arrangement whereby *légionnaires* could purchase various articles of use and ornament, necessity and luxury, on credit.

Madame la République did not stand to lose by this system, for a *légionnaire's* credit was limited by the amount of bonus due to him. This was two hundred and fifty francs if, and when, he got it. Two hundred and fifty francs was once the equivalent of ten pounds. It has also been the equivalent of one pound. So, what with one thing and another, the "bonus" partook of some of the qualities of the will-o'-the-wisp—lightness, brightness, fickleness and illusiveness. Particularly illusiveness.

Nevertheless, when Abraham the Sailor heard

of the credit arrangement, he took thought for its morrow. He gave it, indeed, his close personal attention. He walked apart, withdrawn, and wrapt in thought. And he sure thought something up.

And it appeared that, though in the credit system there was no danger to *Madame la République*, there was some to Captain B——, who had the honour of being our Commanding Officer.

Doubtless Abraham the Sailor was as guileless as he looked; doubtless it was an accident that a new Canteen Corporal was appointed, who knew not Abraham and was under the impression that Abraham came to him with a clean *livret*—soldier's book. It must have been by accident that Abraham had lost the old one, and it must have been owing to Abraham's faulty French that the Corporal understood that a bonus was very nearly due to Abraham, and that he might thus well be given credit to the extent of two hundred and fifty francs.

But as the debt of Abraham the Sailor increased and multiplied and grew ever bigger, the Canteen Corporal went to the Company Bureau to inquire as to why this *légionnaire's* bonus had not arrived. . . .

He learned that Abraham's hopes of a bonus were about as justifiable as his hopes of Heaven, and about as likely to be realized.

In horror and alarm, he had Abraham the Optimist haled before the Captain, and, as the latter gentleman spoke English well, Abraham was doubtless able to explain how the unfortunate mistake had arisen.

But the wine was drunk, the cigarettes were smoked, the food eaten, the soap dissolved . . . everything consumed beyond return.

Captain B—— was a just man, one who would not punish the innocent, or confuse mere mistake with intentional crime. And what decent and fair-minded person could doubt Abraham the Sailor when, almost with tears in his eyes—but not quite —he declared that he had been given to understand, or at any rate had understood, that he only got a halfpenny a day because he received a bonus of two hundred and fifty francs a month?

Abraham's misapprehension was corrected, his pay stopped, and the money refunded to the Canteen by his reluctant Captain.

But as Abraham pointed out, the stoppage of a halfpenny a day, more or less, is scarcely noticeable and is neither here nor there—whereas a couple of hundred francs' worth of assorted goods is quite noticeable and much better here than there. And, anyway, we should be off to the Front before long, where money wouldn't matter.

It was just after this unfortunate mistake, due to the Canteen Corporal's stupidity, or to the system, or to the confusion of tongues caused by the building of the Tower of Babel, or, conceivably, to Abraham's innocence, that that guileless man heard of the local sport known as grape-shooting. He explained that though grape-shot is an obsolete form of ammunition and that one does not shoot grapes, there nevertheless was an excellent form of sport that went by that name, and was free to all who cared to indulge in it.

The game was played at night, and by two opposing sides, and any number might take part. We four Anglo-Saxons, for example, could make up a side, and play against one, two or more of an opposing side. These would consist of Arab watchmen, employed by the *propriétaire de vignes* who owned the vineyards that more or less surrounded the town.

These Arab watchmen were armed with shotguns, and it was considered unsporting for them to use buckshot—and it was against the rules (and the law) for them to have rifles.

The game was, on our side, to see how many pounds of grapes we could get without being shot; and, on their side, to see how many times we could be shot without getting any grapes.

It was really most thrilling on dark nights, and much more thrilling for me than for the others. If one of them got peppered with a charge of Number Fives or Number Sixes, as he fled for his life, that was that. He'd only got to ask a pal to take them out with the point of a knife.

But it might have been extremely awkward for me, and I didn't at all like the idea of having my career as a *légionnaire* cut short for a few bunches of grapes, especially as we could buy them at almost nothing a pound. So I was more discreet than valorous, and better at "keeping *cave*" than at raiding.

However, it was good fun and reminded me of the games we used to play as kids in the shrubbery at dusk: "Robbers and Thieves," "Hide-and-Seek," "Save-All," *et cetera*.

*   *   *   *   *

It gave me infinite joy to see how Terry flourished here. He seemed quite happy, keen, content and cheerful. He drank a good deal, but only good wine; and when he had a real drinking-bout it seemed to do him no harm, and I was able to keep him out of trouble.

Thank Heaven, since he *must* drink, he "carries his wine like a gentleman."

CHAPTER VII

It was at this place, I remember, that I came across one of those astounding incidents, or rather, facts, that have to be personally experienced to be believed.

I had been "walking-out" alone, one evening, and had gone farther than usual. Coming to a halt, and standing silent and still, watching the glorious sunset, my mind, such as it is, far away, I was suddenly brought to earth and to reality by the sound of a woman's voice singing an *English* song. . . . I knew the air and could hear the English words. . . .

The voice came from a wretched, and more or less temporary hovel, built of a sort of enclosure of reeds and plaited palm-leaf about a dirty tent. Without thinking, I marched to the entrance of this little compound, and called out something in English.

A woman came out of the tent and, seeing me in *légionnaire's* uniform, bade me begone—the sooner the better. She spoke in French.

"I say," I said in English, "was that you singing? Are you an Englishwoman? I am . . . English."

"English?" she cried. "English? How I'd love to have a talk to you. I'd give anything to. . . . But you must go. . . . Please go quickly. . . . My husband will be coming soon."

"A Frenchman?" I asked, turning to go.

"No, an Arab. . . . A farmer. . . ."

"An *Arab?*" I said.

"Yes. I was a nurse. . . . I nursed him. He was in the French Army. I fell in love with him. I used to be a great one for those Sheikh novels."

Good God! . . . Poor soul. . . . What could one say or do?

"Have you any children?" I asked, as I backed slowly away.

"Yes, a little girl. As it's only a girl, he let me take it to the Roman Catholic Sisters."

"Can I bring you anything? . . . Send you anything? . . . Write to you?"

"Oh, no, no, and *please* don't come this way again. . . . My husband. . . . Go away," she cried loudly, and pulled a rickety door of palm-leaf matting on a wooden frame across the entrance to the little compound.

I turned on my heel and went my way, saddened.

What a tragedy! What an unthinkable life for a girl, even if she came from the poorest sort of English home. I suppose she had contrived to get to France towards the end of the war, as a Waac or something of the sort.

Her Sheikh!

And yet I suppose she wasn't so much worse off than some of those English girls who marry young Indian students of the baser sort, in England, under the impression that they are as soulfully and romantically gentle as they look, and that they are the authentic Rajahs that they profess to be.

Poor soul. I never went that way again, nor said anything about her to the others. Her life would have been the harder—and her death the earlier— had her Arab husband discovered that she was in any sort of communication with French soldiers.

*   *   *   *   *

It was at this same place too, I remember, that

Terence Hogan and I made contact with a fellow-countryman who, with his detachment, was passing through—a meeting brief, but long enough. This individual told us an extraordinary story which, being about himself, was presumably true.

Being enamoured of a military career, he had enlisted in the British Army in 1913 and was sent with his regiment to France in August, 1914, being still under twenty years of age, which may possibly be taken into account by those who sit in judgment upon him.

So far as I can remember his actual words, he told us his story as follows:

"Well, I don't care who hears me say it, I'm not afraid of fighting. I don't mind fighting at all. Rifle or bayonet, or bombing, anything you like. I don't mind sitting in a trench and shooting and being shot at, and I don't mind going over the top, and I don't mind a blooming good bayonet-charge; and if we could have kept on going forward, or only stood our ground, I should have been all-right. But that Retreat from Mons fair got on my nerves.

"I could have stood the marching—any amount of marching—if we'd been going the other way. But that retreating all day and all night, and never stopping except to turn round and fight until we were shelled out of it, did for me altogether, and I began to look out for a chance to get out of it.

"I wasn't afraid of being killed and I wasn't afraid of being wounded, and I think I'd have preferred either of them to being captured by the Germans. We believed all sorts of funny tales in those days about what they did to prisoners . . . all lies. . . . But we didn't know it then.

"And although I didn't much mind being killed and didn't much mind being wounded, I hated the idea of what one or two young recruits did during the war when they couldn't stand it any longer.

. . . Accidentally wounding yourself on purpose. Funny thing, although I was looking out for a chance to desert, I couldn't do that self-wounding business. Seemed a dirty trick to me, somehow.

"And it wasn't that I was afraid to do it—afraid of the pain, I mean—because I'm not afraid of that sort of thing at all. It was just that marching got on my nerves . . . marching the wrong way. . . . Doing a bunk from those Germans. . . .

"Well, before I'd seen my chance, the Retreat came to an end, and we turned about and began the Battle of the Marne. But my nerve had gone: I was so blooming tired. . . .

"My battalion was in the thick of it, and I got that weary and that hungry, and what with the marching and fighting and want of sleep, we were about all in. I was, anyhow. And, one time, after we'd been advancing by rushes, or what was supposed to be rushes, I felt too blooming tired and weary to get up. There was any number of wounded and dead lying about, and as the man on each side of me was killed, I reckoned I'd be dead for a bit, too. And when the others had to scramble up and make another rush, I just lay still where I was. And in about two ticks I was sound asleep, battle or no battle. . . . Sound asleep I was. . . .

"First thing I knew was a couple of stretcher-bearers pulling me over on to me back.

" ' 'E's a stiff-un, too, Bert,' one of them said. ' They're all three dead.'

" 'No, 'e ain't, yer fool,' said the other. ' 'E's opened 'is blinkin' eyes.'

" 'Where did yer cop it, mate?' he asked.

" 'Something hit me in the leg,' I said.

" 'Reckon you can walk or crawl?' he asked. 'You can 'ave a ride in the stretcher down to the Dressing Station if you can't 'op, 'obble, roll, bowl or jump.'

" 'I'll 'ave a try,' I said, wanting to get rid of them, and off I went, dot-and-carry-one.

"I reckoned those two stretcher-bearers would have turned unkind if I'd let them carry me back— and they'd found out that I was no more hit than they were.

"When they were out of sight I took out my field-dressing and bandaged one of my legs, and by the time I'd carried the joke that far, I wished I might stop a real packet.

"But d'you think anybody ever got hit who wanted to? No fear.

"So I went hobbling along till I came to the Dressing Station and found such a crowd there of all sorts of wounded that if I'd been bleeding to death, I should have died long before my turn came.

" 'Blooming bad arrangement, I call it,' I said to a bloke who was sitting there holding tight on to his wounded arm.

" 'Yus, mate,' he said. ' They ought to 'ave early doors.'

" 'Or more doctors,' said another fellow who'd got his head bandaged up after a fashion. 'I shall lodge a complaint, if I misses my train and gets 'ome late for tea.'

"Then I just lay back on the ground and had another sleep, and when an R.A.M.C. chap woke me up, I told him my leg had already been dressed, though I didn't mention that I'd dressed it myself.

"Then when he told the M.O. that I'd been done, and they started to help me into an Ambulance Car with a lot more, I didn't raise any objection. . . . I was too tired, see?

"That Ambulance Car was driven right straight away to Calais and down to the Docks, and I slept pretty nearly the whole way.

"I found they'd tied a label on to me, saying what my wound was, and as I saw that some of the others were marked 'Serious,' and heard them saying that all marked 'Serious' would be taken straight to England, I thought I might as well try my luck and be 'Serious' too.

"So while we were all waiting, lying in a shed at Calais Docks, I got a pencil out of my pocket, and when I thought nobody was looking, I took off the label and wrote 'Serious' on it.

"As it happened, there was a Hospital Boat in, or perhaps it was because there was a Hospital Boat in that the Ambulances had gone straight to the Docks.

"Anyhow, I just lay back and shut me eyes, and the Orderlies from the Hospital Boat carried me on board, straight away!

"As soon as I was dumped, I took my label off, screwed it up and threw it away. And when a Nurse came, I said:

" 'I suppose there must have been a mistake somewhere, because I wasn't wounded, but ill. Awful pain in my inside.'

"She looked wise and asked me if anything had been said about appendicitis, or anything. I said I didn't know, only that I was very ill.

"The Nurse said anyhow it was too late now, and I'd have to go on to England and be operated on there.

"Then she went away and brought another label, marked 'Internal,' and when the Hospital Train, that we were put into at Dover, got to London, I was taken to Hospital.

"There I swung the lead and managed to get a week in bed, anyhow. But after another week I was discharged fit, and given a paper and a railway-warrant and told to report to the Depôt of my Regiment.

"But somehow I thought not. I'd had enough of marching.

"So I went home and told 'em a tale, had a good time, and then went and joined the R.A.M.C. They work just as hard and get just as much danger, but there's not so much blooming drill and marching, and there's more cushy jobs; and I finished out the War and took my discharge all regular and in order. . . .

"What do you think of that?"

"I prefer not to think of it," replied Terence Hogan.

CHAPTER VIII

From this place we went to B—— which is quite a biggish town—a garrison town in fact, being right on the frontier of Morocco, and a halting-place for troops entering and leaving that distressful country.

We were here for a week, and, as there was no drill, we might have had a restful and peaceful time in this attractive—or so it seemed to us after A—— el-H—— —metropolis, but for the fact that we were much troubled by non-commissioned officers in the matter of the issue of new rifles, ammunition, special campaign-kit, cooking utensils, and so forth.

However, we contrived to explore the town pretty thoroughly and to get into, and out of, various forms of trouble. One noticed here that the climate was changing, the nights being definitely colder.

From B—— we had one of the most miserable train journeys that I have ever experienced, tedious, monotonous and slow, on a military train and an eighteen-inch gauge line, in open trucks—not even the boxes of *huit chevaux ou quarante hommes* type.

Along we went at fifteen miles an hour, cold, cramped, uncomfortable, and thoroughly miserable. I think C—— was our first halt, nothing but a military post occupied by a company of Senegalese.

I remember wondering if they felt the cold as much as I did.

We spent the next day in getting from there to D——, a little Arab village with two alleged

"Europe" shops, where we spent the night in an earth bivouac and an appalling smell. Without reluctance or regret, we left here at two in the morning, and got to A—— B—— at four in the afternoon, and went into camp beside another battalion of the Legion.

I suffered a curious home-sick feeling here, not for home but for Switzerland, a country that I love. I suppose it was the bracing cold and the sight of the Atlas Mountains, thickly covered with snow.

Oh, the glorious colouring of the sunrise and the sunset pictures painted on that illimitable canvas of virgin snow. It made my heart ache. And, oh, the washing of my clothes, between those sunrises and sunsets, in illimitable cold water. It made my back ache.

From A—— B—— we marched, and did not halt until we reached T——, a distance of about forty kilometres, say five-and-twenty miles, a pretty good step with the kit we were carrying.

Thence, next day, we marched on to G——, and it interested me to notice that the population was entirely Spanish, although the place was in French Morocco and had been captured from the Arabs only six months earlier.

Trade follows the flag. In this case it appeared to be entirely Spanish trade.

Cavalryman Terence Hogan, who is not fond of marching, had been grumbling all the way from A—— B——, but at this place, G——, he became less plaintive and more thoughtful when he saw a battalion of the Legion working precisely as navvies do at home, building roads and bridges. These men were soldiers, enlisted, uniformed, and paid as such; but for months past they had been nothing but hard-driven, unskilled manual labourers, digging, stone-breaking, carrying, building and road-making.

Except that they were "free" men following the honourable profession of arms, they might just as well have been road-gangs of convicts, so far as their drill and all-day occupation went.

Our turn was to come.

From G—— we did a record march, my record, at any rate, and I hope to God I shall never break it. Sixty kilometres with a sixty-pound pack. *Some* hike, as Abraham the Sailor said. Thirty-seven miles.

Old Cocteau—also called The Cannibal—aroused my admiration, and my wonder too, on this march, for when Terence Hogan and I were staggering along deaf, dumb, and nearly blind, whacked to the wide and, speaking for myself, feeling positively sick with weariness, this old man, or old devil, broke into song.

In quite a strong voice, almost in tune, and with almost recognizable words, he sang "Tipperary," a song he must often have heard in France.

It was out of bravado, doubtless, that he did it, and it shamed me, for one. Terence too, I think, for he visibly pulled himself together.

And the sad but undeniable fact is that old Aristide Cocteau, who says he's sixty and looks more, is something of a drunkard. He has the very profoundest contempt for a moderate drinker like myself, and no feelings whatsoever towards a teetotaller—no more than I have toward a Martian or a Lost Atlantisian—and, according to the old rogue's own account of himself, the more red wine he drinks, the better he can march; the more he marches, the better can he drink red wine. And thus his life rolls on in an unvicious circle.

Anyhow, for the thirty-seventh mile of that awful march, Cocteau the Cannibal sang. . . .

Where we halted we fell, and where we fell we

lay.

Someone may have done something in the matter of making a perimeter camp, fetching water and fuel, pitching *tentes d'abri* and posting sentries. If so, it was not I. I know nothing of what happened that night from the moment I fell down to the moment when Digger and Abraham the Sailor pulled me on to my feet and held me upright.

One ache from head to foot, too stiff and sore and lame and weary to move, as I thought. But "a hair of the dog" proved good medicine once again, and youth and hard training triumphed, and when "March" was the order, I got going and kept going, until we reached H——, a big military post on a plateau, where a couple of Sections of our Battalion were left behind with the —th Company of the —th Regiment, one of which Sections, by the mercy of Heaven, was ours.

Here life began to be quite interesting, for we were on the fringe of war. It was quite thrilling to learn that there was quite a possibility of an attack upon the post; that the place was occasionally sniped at night; that three foolish men, who had disobeyed the order placing the native village out of bounds, had been killed there; that a Sergeant had been shot the other evening within a few yards of the main gate of the Barrack; and that at sunset the huge iron gates were closed, and all sentries were mounted inside the *poste*.

Here we had our first taste of road-making, and for a whole month we laboured with pick and shovel, and with hand and shoulder at stone-carrying, making a strategic road from H—— to J—— for the quicker bringing of supplies or reinforcements.

One day as we sweated, working like niggers—

but as no Senegalese ever worked—at road-building, I said to Hogan:

"Which do you prefer, Terry, labouring as a navvy or marching as a soldier? Or don't you know which you really like better?"

"I *do* know, my lad," he replied, "and I'll tell you. When I'm marching like a soldier I wish I were a navvy; and when I'm road-digging like a navvy I wish I were a soldier."

Personally, I would rather be over-navvied than over-marched. When one is using pick or shovel, one can, at any rate, straighten oneself up from time to time, look around, give one's belt a hitch up, spit upon one's hands, heave a sigh, and get down to it again. But when one is marching, well—one marches.

But I confess that after picking-and-shovelling, hefting great stones, and carrying them like a beast of burden, stone-breaking, quarrying, and all the rest of it, I was entirely in sympathy with Hogan, who asked whether he'd enlisted to fight for a halfpenny a day, or to be a common labourer at a hundredth part of a common labourer's wages and less than a hundredth part of his freedom and his little comforts.

"Keep my hand from picking and shovelling," prayed Terence Hogan.

We stayed here at H——, road-making, for a month, and then marched again, reaching K—— the first night and M——, where there was an aviation camp, the next.

Here we found the rest of our Company and, next day, marched thirty miles, made a perimeter camp, and from there started building a road back from that camp to H——. It took us a month of constant hard labour before this road joined up with the one we'd already made from H——.

CHAPTER IX

I remember very clearly the morning that we marched again, soldiers once more, for M——. It was most bitterly cold. Terence, with casual friendliness, produced a most intriguing and attractive-looking bottle and presented it to me.

"Many happy returns of the day," he said.

"But my good Terry," I objected, accepting the bottle nevertheless, "it isn't my birthday to-day."

"No? You surprise me," said he. "Anyhow, have a drop in your coffee, my son," he returned kindly. "The finest cognac. Forty years old."

I felt that I stood at the cross-roads—a turning-point in my life; to fall or not to fall?

Was I, against all my principles, practice, precepts and belief, to drink brandy before breakfast?

But how very very good it would be in the hot strong black milkless coffee. And even though one put in quite a good drop, one would hardly taste it—and so would not be pandering to one's lower instincts, baser passions, and more degraded tastes. But how it would warm one and hearten one up, before starting on the day's march on an empty tummy.

Besides, how ungracious a response to Terence Hogan's generous kindliness, to ride the high horse of one's moral superiority.

" 'The only thing I cannot resist is temptation,' " quoted I. "Thank you so much, Terry," and I drew the cork. "Give us your mug," I continued.

"You first, my dear chap," demurred Terence.

And I poured some into my coffee.

It was cold water.

It was also April the First.

There are times when I love Terence Hogan less than I do at other times.

Perhaps, or rather doubtless, this is why I remember that particular day so well.

We marched out of camp at ten in the morning and halted for breakfast between twelve and one, three-quarters of an hour, exactly, being allowed for the meal and subsequent rest. This sounds quite reasonable—not to say excessive and likely to develop a sybaritic and voluptuous laziness. It doesn't sound so good, however, when one mentions that, in this three-quarters of an hour, fuel had to be gathered, fires made, the meal cooked, served, and eaten. In fact, I should say that the *rassemblement* bugle found the majority of us chewing for dear life.

On this particular occasion no wood whatsoever could be found anywhere. Not even the Legion non-com. can make a fatigue produce wood from a place where there is no wood.

The fires were accordingly made with grass, more or less dry, so the extent and nature of the cooking may be imagined.

The day, badly begun, grew worse; for, as we fell in, it began to snow, and the snow-storm grew steadily heavier and continued for the whole of the day, and, by the time we reached our objective, K——, the place was almost buried beyond discovery. The snow was certainly five feet deep.

Chilled to the bone, with blue numbed hands and faces, wet through, with sodden boots, tired to death and profoundly miserable, we were put into absolutely unheated unfurnished wooden huts.

An hour or so later we were each given hot coffee and a blanket, and clear instructions to spend the remainder of the day in "drying ourselves"!

Digger respectfully approached our room Corporal with the request that a piece of rope, stout cord, or strong wire, might be issued to the Section.

"What for?" asked the Corporal.

"To dry ourselves," answered Digger.

And I think that Corporal Iminoff—a not noticeably intelligent man—is still wondering what he meant.

And this day that had begun badly and grown worse, finished with the worst of all.

While I was sitting cross-legged on the floor, trying to keep warm and to "dry myself " by the expenditure of much energy about the cleaning of my rifle and equipment, Sergeant Pflügge kicked open the door, called us to attention and, in his stentorian voice, bawled, as though we were half a mile away:

"Any professional cook here?"

No answer.

"Anyone here who can cook, at all?"

No answer.

Allah had willed it that I should be standing nearest to Sergeant Pflügge.

"Here, can you cook?" said he to me personally.

"No, Sergeant," I promptly and truthfully replied.

"Know nothing whatsoever about cooking?"

"Absolutely nothing whatsoever, Sergeant."

"Good. Then you are appointed a Company Cook, and will report for duty to-morrow. And," he added, turning away, "see that thou cookest well, thou species of floating dog's-body."

Well, well. I couldn't cook much worse than any of the other incumbents of the office, and, should I fail to give satisfaction, Pflügge, the cook-maker, could also unmake; and, having raised me up, could cast me down again.

Anyhow, it would mean that I, at any rate, would be among those who always had enough to eat. . . .

Orders having gone forth that the Company should now be very strenuously trained for open warfare in the most intensive as well as extensive manner, it mattered not that the country around Midelt varied from deep snow, by way of freezing slush, to thick mud. As everyone pointed out to everyone else, we couldn't have done all this confounded creeping, lying flat on our faces, crawling and belly-crouching, when we were on dry ground, could we? It would have been a pity to do it otherwise than under conditions the foulest conceivable for such exercises.

However, all good things come to an end, and after a month of cold, wet, muddy misery that nearly brought me to the end of my tether, we suddenly marched off to Z——, and did the march of fifty kilometres in the day.

Here we made a camp and, marching out from it each day at dawn, occupied the surrounding heights through-out the day.

And, at this, although it involved much arduous climbing, we did not grumble, for daily convoys of ammunition-lorries passed, on their way to K—— from the railway at A—— B——, and it was quite likely that a surprise attack might be made upon them at any time.

It is curious how the mental attitude affects fatigue. It is twice as tiring to march stolidly from a place to a place, than it is to go out and march an equal or a greater distance with the hope and the chance of good sport.

And, at this time, we certainly classed a fight as sport—what Terence Hogan described as an afternoon's nice gentlemanly war as it was in the old days aforetime, without gas, barrages, liquid fire and other caddish abominations.

*   *   *   *   *

Our Company Commander, Captain B——, left us here, to our great regret. He was very popular because he was just, strict, ruthless, and yet pleasant and humorous; a fine, competent, experienced soldier, whose men would follow him anywhere.

His successor, Captain Z——, who, according to old Père Cocteau, "wasn't a real Legion officer at all, but who had come from some miserable Line Regiment," made a mistake, immediately upon arrival, by ordering a double ration of wine as well as of food for everybody; and by making a speech in which he said he was proud to lead us and was going to take the greatest interest in our welfare.

"I know that sort," grumbled Père Cocteau, after the parade. "Thinks he can buy the respect of *légionnaires* with a gallon of *soupe* and a bottle of wine. Personally, I should have thought better of the man if he'd doubled all punishments for a week."

"There's one place, and only one, where you'll never grumble," observed Old Thirsty-face, "and that's Heaven."

But Père Cocteau, scorning to fall into so crude and obvious a trap, held his peace.

He proved quite right in his estimate of Captain Z——, for, after that first day, he left absolutely everything to the non-commissioned officers, and was, like many other officers, patently and entirely indifferent to the welfare and comfort of his men.

This sort of thing does not matter so much in Algeria as it does in Morocco.

In Algeria, as elsewhere in the French Army, a

'*commission*', consisting of a President and five officers, manages the feeding of the Battalion. Contractors and tradesmen submit tenders to the '*commission*', which decides which of these people shall provide the various food-stuffs to the troops —meat, rice, lentils, beans, macaroni, flour, wine, etc. Thus there is no fear or possibility of peculation or swindling of any sort, at the source of supply. That only begins when the food has reached the store and cook-house.

On active service, the system is different. The Officer commanding the Company, himself purchases the food and drink for the Company, and here is seen the first great difference between the keen and conscientious officer such as Captain B—— and a slack careless Company Officer such as Captain Z——.

Like so many officers who were brave and competent enough as tacticians and fighters, Captain Z—— took no interest in the internal economy of his Company and, as usual again, left the feeding of the men entirely to the Quartermaster-Sergeant.

In nine cases out of ten, this means that from fifteen to twenty-five per cent. of the money paid out to the Quartermaster-Sergeant for messing-costs, remains in that good man's pockets, and the *légionnaires'* food and drink suffer proportionately in quality and quantity.

We estimated, and I think fairly accurately and justly, that Quartermaster-Sergeant Weidmann now began to make about five hundred francs in each two thousand that was paid out to him by Captain Z——.

It was at about this time that we observed a very famous fête of the Legion, celebrating one of the innumerable glorious deeds of the Regiment— the fête of the Day of Camaron.

On this day in 1863, Père Cocteau told us, a Company of the Legion, sixty strong, with three officers, were the advance-guard to a convoy. They were suddenly attacked by a whole Brigade of Mexican cavalry, and forming square, they fought the Mexicans off with bullet and bayonet, moving on from time to time, until they reached a *hacienda* called Camaron.

This they put as quickly as possible into a state of defence, and repulsed repeated attacks by the dismounted cavalry, until two Regiments of Mexican Infantry arrived, and the Mexican Commander, advancing under a white flag, ordered the garrison instantly to surrender.

His reply was a burst of Homeric laughter from the Immortal Sixty.

"Why on earth should two to three thousand Mexicans imagine that sixty *légionnaires* should surrender to them?"

True they had no water, the heat was terrible, and they hadn't very much ammunition.

The Mexican General retired and the battle was resumed.

The infantry repeatedly charged up to the doors and windows of the *hacienda* while the cavalry kept up a heavy fire.

After six hours' incessant fighting, from eight in the morning until two in the afternoon, the flag of truce again appeared, and the Garrison was summoned to surrender.

A man went out to meet the Mexican Commander and stated the terms on which the Garrison would do so.

"We will surrender this place," said he, "inasmuch as we do not want it, on condition that the Garrison be allowed to retain their arms, and march out with flags flying, drums beating, and all the honours of war. Also that they further be allowed to march away and go wherever they wish. Also that every care and attention be shown to the wounded. Also that the dead be buried with military honours."

The Mexican General agreed—for he had already lost hundreds and hundreds of his men, and wished to lose no more—and the *légionnaire* turned about and marched back into the *hacienda*.

A little later he marched out again with his rifle slung, a flag sticking up above his pack, and a drum slung in front of him.

On this he beat a resounding roll as he marched, in full sight of the remnants of two Battalions of Infantry and two Regiments of Cavalry, to where the Mexican General sat his horse.

"When is the Garrison going to march out?" asked the General.

"*I* am the Garrison," replied the *légionnaire*.

He was—and of the Sixty, only he and four dying men remained alive.

The officer commanding these men was Captain Danjou. He had already lost a hand in the Crimean War and had an artificial one. This hand is still preserved in the *Salle d'Honneur* of the Legion at Sidi-bel-Abbès.

Surely Danjou and his sixty at Camaron are worthy to rank with Leonidas and his three hundred at Thermopylae, especially when one remembers that the Sixty were not patriots dying for the Fatherland, but "mercenaries" earning their pay?

Nor was this act of "Honour and Fidelity" (the motto on the flag of the Legion) a mere piece of futile glorious heroism. It was an invaluable act of devotion, for, while the Sixty engaged the Brigade, the convoy of provisions that they were guarding got safely through to where it was badly needed.

*   *   *   *   *

Thus does the Legion serve France.
How does France serve the Legion?

*   *   *   *   *

"God bless our brave brothers in arms. God rest their noble souls," prayed Old Thirsty-face, as we sat in cheerful conversation after our special Camaron fête dinner.

"But indeed yes, a thousand times yes," agreed Père Cocteau, "for they brought great honour to the glorious flag of France."

"Oh, quite so," assented Old Thirsty-face. "But what I mean to shay is, they brought me this glorious bo'll wine. God rest those gallant gen'l-men."

*   *   *   *   *

Shortly after, we paraded to march off from Z—— and Captain Z—— improved the occasion and made a speech.

I do not wish to do him an injustice, and I keep in mind the fact that the French regard the oratorical word and the apt gesture to be as essential to the proper rounding off of heroic deeds, as they regard sauce to be necessary to fish or meat, and wine to be appropriate to the rounding off of a noble meal.

The English take a different view, leaving the brave deed (to the French way of thinking) unhonoured, unsung, unadorned, bare, cold—an opportunity wasted, a dish unseasoned.

No English Tommy falls on the stricken field

with a cry of "I die that England may live."

And no British General kisses him upon both cheeks, or upon either cheek, in recognition of the fact that he died that England might live—or even that he as good as died that England might as good as live. . . .

The French are more graceful and more gracious than ourselves in these *petits soins*, less lumpish and self-conscious; more articulate and artistic. But *chacun a son goût.* . . .

Anyhow, Captain Z—— made us a speech, and did it in style. He told us that now, not only were we going to march in real earnest, but we were going to fight, and fight in real earnest.

"You will march always," he cried, with pardonable hyperbole. "Always you will march. When you can no longer march upon your feet, you will march upon your hands and knees. And when you can no longer march upon your hands and knees, you will march upon your bellies. But always you will march, and always I shall be at the head. You will march always, and I shall be at the head always."

I might mention that at the Battle of El K—— he was noticeably not always at the head, but markedly always in the rear.

And so obvious was his preference for leading from behind and allowing the Company to follow in front, that he was relieved of his command.

Probably he was ill and war-weary, for there are no braver officers in the world than the French.

CHAPTER X

The march took us to a big concentration camp for troops of all arms, near J——; and, after a few days of real hard labour at intensive training and kit preparation, the whole force marched out, bivouacked, and, at dawn the next morning, began the attack upon E——.

I don't know why, but, for me, the whole affair fell flat, and scarcely differed, save for noise, from a long and tiring day at manœuvres.

There was too much going on and it covered too much country.

The real reason why it was very much less thrilling than I had anticipated, was the fact that our Battalion formed the flank guard, and its duties were mainly confined to marching and climbing, and the exchange of a few long-range shots with enemy patrols.

Personally, I did not fire my rifle at all, and was quite thankful for that small mercy.

It is one thing to be part of a vast organization for the Spread of Civilization, a cog in the great machine of Progress, an insignificant member of the great Band of Pioneers who open up new lands; to be, in short, one of those who, according to Monsieur André Maurois, are fulfilling to the utmost their duties as practical educators, are inheriting the mission of the Roman Legions, and who, in addition to serving France, are serving Civilization.

It is quite another thing to take a pot-shot, with intent to kill, at a man with whom one has no quarrel, and against whom one bears no possible sort of grudge. . . .

It was sunset before the tide of battle ceased to flow, and the troops halted and consolidated their position.

We had been on the move from 4.30 a.m. until 6.30 p.m. and, during the whole of that time, had received a piece of bread and two sardines.

I suppose such things must be at every famous victory.

But I did hear the opinion expressed that the Commissariat might have done us better, in view of the fact that we were so near our base; and Digger, Abraham the Sailor, and Terence Hogan, drew comparisons and contrasts between the Supply-and-Transport Services of their present and former Regiments.

When Père Cocteau inquired, as we stood making three mouthfuls of our bread and sardines, as to what Digger thought he wanted in the way of rations on Active Service, Digger told him.

"Beef?" ejaculated Cocteau. "Bacon? Tea? Plum-and-Apple Jam? . . . No coffee? No wine? But, *mon Dieu*, how disgusting! Were there no mutinies?"

"No," Digger assured him. "There wasn't. But there's goin' to be some if I've got to march and fight on two sardines an' a slice of bread."

"Reminiscent of another five thousand—fed with five loaves and two small fishes," murmured Terence Hogan. "*Hors d'œuvres*, in fact," he growled, "entirely *hors* and no *œuvres*."

However, all that remained to be done before we got our proper and usual meal of *soupe*, was about two and a half hours' real hard work in consolidating our own Battalion position.

The moment we had piled arms and dumped our *sacs*, we all had to set to work building a dry wall right round the camp; and by about nine o'clock at night the work was finished, the little *tentes d'abri* pitched, fuel collected and fires lit, *soupe* kettles boiling, the wall completed, the guard mounted, and sentries posted.

This was one of the days that I shall always remember, and more particularly the evening. I suppose the day sticks in my memory because it was my first day in action as a soldier, however lacking in thrills the day had been; and I suppose that the details of that night are impressed upon my mind because it was my first bivouac, as a soldier on active service, in a camp that was sniped and might at any moment be rushed.

I had been in infinitely greater danger in Flanders when driving an ambulance so near to the line that twice my car was struck by shrapnel, and when once I was myself wounded by a shell splinter; though probably there was more danger in the actual driving of a car on a pitch-black night of pouring rain and howling wind, along a road covered with the greasiest mud, and punctuated with great shell-holes filled with water.

It was then that I knew real heart-clutching fear; fear of failure in my duty; fear of a weakening and breaking of moral fibre, leading to collapse; and fear for my car-loads of maimed mangled shattered men . . . one of whom, one night, insane with pain or through damage to the brain, screamed the whole time, like a wounded horse; howled like a dog. . . .

Those nights when I was a non-combatant were nights of pure fear; but this night was a night of exhilaration, with no real fear at all. It was, in fact, a jolly night. Possibly the exhilaration and gaiety, so far as I personally was concerned, may have had their origin in taut nerves, a little over-strain; but nothing, I think, remotely connected with hysteria.

Fond as I was of my comrades, I positively loved them all that night and saw them at their best.

It was a story-book night, a night recaptured from childhood games when we—I and my brothers and boy friends of theirs (myself as much a boy as any of them), diversely and strangely dressed, armed and accoutred—lit a bonfire and watched the firelight playing on the toy tent; posted sentries; cooked horrible messes; used passwords; started up when an alarm was given; clutched our weapons and gazed out into the gloom; repelled attacks and fought to the last cartridge. . . .

And here we were, doing just the same things, though perhaps not quite so sternly and seriously as in childhood.

True, we could not stop our game and go indoors when tired of it. The enemy was real, but otherwise the difference was small. There was the bonfire, there was the horrible mess cooked over it, there were the boys with their weapons, their uniforms, their passwords, and their posted sentries peering out into the night, and the firelight playing on the little tent near by . . . myself as much a boy as any of them.

No, there wasn't so much difference, after all. We were only bigger children, playing the game more thoroughly and more roughly.

"Men are but children of a larger growth." These men were children, surely enough. . . . Men *are* children—bless them. . . . As I looked at our Section round the fire I realized that I was probably the youngest of them all—and far, far, the oldest.

And just for a moment Fear, whose cold hand had, in Flanders, so often crushed my heart in its cruel icy grip, did perhaps lay a finger-tip upon it, for a second, as I thought of what might happen to Terence, Digger, or Abraham the Sailor . . . or to Gustavus Adolphus, Père Cocteau, Old Thirsty-face, "Baron" Trenck, Bilenski, Pigou, Fabricius, Demenko, Lapone, Moronoff, and the rest of them.

As to myself—whenever I found I was beginning to think of that half-wit and her possible fate, I resolutely switched off, comforting myself with the thought that Death I did not fear in the least. If I were wounded, and likely to be captured by the Moors, I had my little automatic; and if I were wounded, taken to hospital and discovered for the cheat I was, the worst that could follow would be that I should have failed in my foolish under-taking. . . .

But as I have said, the cold finger touched but for a second, and moved on, and for me it was a happy night.

Although they had marched and climbed from earliest morning till late evening, hungry and weary and some of them in action; and had then done three hours of heavy labour at stone-carrying and wall-building, the *légionnaires* were merry. Having eaten their poor meal of stew and bread, they sat and lay around the fires singing, laughing, jesting, story-telling and talking.

It gave me a real and pleasurable thrill to be there among them, one of them. I think I was as proud to be there, accepted by them and liked by them, as I have ever in my mis-spent life been proud of anything.

Life was, for once, living up to its promise; the play was as good as the posters, and in starlight and firelight Reality took on the hues of bright Illusion.

I heard many wonderful songs, some too wonderful for uncensored quotation, and too truly witty to be Bowdlerized; and I heard some good tales and some good talk. I love the tales and talk of these men and, in my remarkably retentive memory, I "collect" scraps of conversation as some people collect postage-stamps.

A conversation, between men from various ends of the earth, on some subject utterly new to me, interests and often thrills me in, I suppose, the kind of way that a Roman arch or a Norman keep or a Tudor house does an American discovering England.

A man who strolled over to our fire from another Company told us that the left flank of our line had "run right into it" and suffered heavy casualties, the worse because their reserve troops, a section of Senegalese *tirailleurs*, young soldiers who had never been under fire before, had panicked, turned and bolted, taking with them the machine-gun, just at the moment when they were signalled to advance to reinforce the thinned and broken line of *légionnaires*, pinned down and held at that point by weight of fire and vastly superior numbers.

He also said that a mob of Arab friendlies called *Partisans*, a tribe of about a thousand strong under their own Kaid, had come up in time to take part in the battle, and had certainly loosed off an inordinate amount of ammunition.

Whether they'd hit anybody and, if so, whether that body had been friend or foe, had not been ascertained. . . .

To make this stage-scene and stage-play yet more life-like or stage-like, I don't know which, there was a sudden bang, quite close to our fire, and a cry of "*Aux armes.*" A sentry had fired his rifle and shouted the alarm.

Wonderful is the power and the value of drill—

drill that in time turns men into automata.

Without the slightest hesitation or confusion, the singing laughing camp of relaxed ungirt care-free men became, in an incredibly short space of time, a silent square of alert soldiers, every man kneeling in his place at the wall, rifle at the ready, and prepared for whatever might befall. Ready for salvo-fire, volley upon volley at a swarming foe, or to leap the wall and charge with bayonets fixed.

Again, as I knelt between Digger and Abraham the Sailor, I felt thrilled and exhilarated, with no sense of fear, and waited for what might happen. . . .

What did happen was precisely nothing.

An over-anxious nervous and cautious sentry, taking no risks, had fired at nothing, unless it were a wandering donkey or dog, and given an alarm which was but the baseless and futile expression of his own.

Nothing happening, the *Dismiss* order was given, and we returned to our camp fires, cursing the sentry. However, many more sentries were cursed later and even more heartily, for it was a night of constant alarms, all false, that brought us rushing from our snug billets and *tentes d'abri*, a thousand men turned out for one miserable sniper or rifle-thief.

Disgusted as we all were, I felt considerable sympathy with the sentries, and was sorry for them.

On a dark night, in the midst of extremely elusive grey-clad enemies who can move as silently and unobtrusively as cats, it is, as I was soon to learn, a horrible responsibility to have to make swift and sudden choice.

Shall one fire one's rifle, yell *"Aux armes"* and rouse a sleeping battalion for nothing at all; or shall one refrain and, suddenly, too late, realize that an irresistible avalanche of fanatical foemen is upon one, and, a few seconds later, will be slashing and stabbing sleeping men; and then shooting, slashing, and stabbing sleepy bewildered waking men, as they roll from their blankets?

*　　*　　*　　*　　*

For a fortnight our Battalion occupied this spot; nor did we rest on our laurels, if any. We turned once more from soldiers into navvies, masons, heavy-weight lifters and skilled and unskilled labourers generally, but all at the same halfpenny a day.

I could not help thinking of certain "gentlemen in England," and the wages that they struck against, as I toiled to earn my own halfpenny.

First of all, we heightened (if there be a verb to heighten—and I certainly shouldn't convey my meaning correctly if I said "raised") the wall that we had made on the previous night.

When this was of the required height, stoutness, and strength, with a proper gate, so that we were reasonably safe from sudden rush attack, a number of men were told off to build a *poste*—a small block-house, combined barrack and fortress in one, a kind of strong point which would be permanently garrisoned and held by a small force when we passed on.

This was the routine in carrying out the system of penetrating new country. The troops moved forward, not leaving behind them a road as yet, but a line of *postes*, each holding a small but efficient garrison.

Some were sufficiently large to need a garrison of two Companies; some to need one Company; others so small as to require only a Section; each *poste* being commanded by an officer or a senior non-commissioned officer, according to size.

As the force advanced, the *postes* first constructed were occupied by *Tirailleurs Algeriens* or Senegalese, the relieved *légionnaires* marching on once more. But wherever a *poste* was considered open to attack, it would be held by *légionnaires*.

At the end of a fortnight, my Company marched off with the rest, leaving behind us a really strong well-garrisoned and well-provided *poste*.

One would have thought that a contractor with a thousand skilled men—and every sort and kind of up-to-date method, tool, appliance and facility— had been at work there for a month. I was amazed at what the soldiers had done with stones and entrenching tools, and the improvisation of everything necessary for the building of a fort.

CHAPTER XI

"Slavery! Absolute unredeemed slavery!" growled Hermann, as he joined our circle round the camp-fire one night, and flung himself down.

"Not white slavery, anyhow," observed Terence Hogan, as he glanced at Hermann's peculiarly filthy face and hands.

Apparently he had been on a cooking-pot cleaning fatigue. But so had I.

"Slavery!" grunted old Cocteau. "I wish it was. . . . Slavery. . . . Huh! . . . No such luck. . . . I wish to God I could be sold into slavery to-morrow."

"Not in Morocco, you don't," sneered Matthieu le Maquereau.

"Don't I? . . . What do you know about slavery in Morocco or anywhere else? . . . Come to that, you *are* a slave in Morocco."

"No, no," objected the solemn and serious Hermann. "Our life is hard, but we are not slaves. We are soldiers."

"That's what I complain of," grunted Cocteau.

"Slavery is the blackest blot upon the page of human history," observed Hermann sententiously. "Think of the happy innocent village. . . . The raid. . . . The groans and cries and lamentations. The ghastly . . ."

"I know! I know!" interrupted Père Cocteau. "I've heard it all. Seen it all. Do you suppose I was known in the *Marsouins* as Cocteau the Slaver, Cocteau the Pirate, Cocteau the Cannibal, for nothing?"

"Tell us," I suggested, passing my mug to the grizzled, shrivelled old soldier who, from boyhood, had, with very brief intervals, served France in the

Colonial Infantry; the Line, the Legion; throughout the Great War; and now again in the Legion. Old Cocteau was always worth hearing when he could be got to talk, for, in nearly forty years of assorted service, he had seen and done some strange things. His bronzed face, seamed and lined till it resembled sun-cracked clay, from which twinkled bright grey eyes and gleaming teeth, creased yet further as, smiling, he accepted my cup, drained it, and wiped his beard with the cuff of his sleeve.

"Slavery? . . . Yes. . . . I've been a slaver, and did very well while it lasted; did well out of the 'mules' . . . the black ivory, you know. . . . As I may have mentioned. . . ."

"Not at all," sneered Matthieu le Maquereau.

". . . I was once a Sergeant. That was when I was in the *Marsouins*. A Sergeant, do I say? I was a King. At Obek that was, in French Somaliland, after they'd moved the government to Djibouti. I was the only white man at Obek and I ruled that palm-leaf city like old what's-his-name rules where-is-it."

"Are you alluding to Il Duce Mussolini, who governs Italy?" asked Guiseppe Lapone.

"Or Mustapha Kemal Pasha, who now speaks for the Unspeakable Turk?" suggested Terence Hogan.

"Or Trotski the Troubadour, who rumbles for Russia," murmured Abraham.

"Yes. All of these," agreed Cocteau. "But the person to whom I was really alluding is my late cousin of Abyssinia, old What's-his-name."

"Menelik, *alias* the Jujube of Judah," supplied Abraham the Sailor. "Go on, Cocktail, and don't interrupt yourself so much."

"Well, there was I at Obek, Sergeant of Colonial Infantry and Chief Collector of Customs, Post-master-General, Consul-General, Commander-in-

Chief, Senior Naval Officer, *Commissaire*, and a lot of other things—besides being the only white man. . . . There I was alone, and *mon Dieu* wasn't I alone! I was so lonely that I almost took to drink. That is to say, I nearly sat up all night to drink, as well as drinking all day."

"What did you drink?" asked his old *copain*, Thirsty-face, licking his dry lips.

"Palm-wine," replied Cocteau. "It's more palm than wine, but you can get drunk on it if you are a really first-class drinker. And you can help the drink by chewing *qat*. That's a green leaf grown in Abyssinia, that the Somalis chew. Myself, I prefer opium, morphia, cocaine, *kief, hashish, bhang, charas, kola* . . . any of those things. But when you can't get something good and wholesome, *qat* does very well. . . . So I lived on palm-wine, *qat*, and tobacco; and the more *qat* I chewed, the more palm-wine I seemed to need. And the more palm-wine I drank, the more *qat* I chewed. And what with these, and the funny things I smoked, the larger grew my mind, and I understood lots of things that I'd never understood before.

"Domestic happiness, *par exemple*.

"As a misogynist I had been in error.

"I married.

"A Shankalla girl. Marrying is their profession. It almost became mine.

"For, on the first Monday in every month, at midday exactly, I fired the noon-day gun and married a Shankalla girl. There's nothing like regular habits.

"I became a philosopher. Matrimony is conducive to philosophy, and broadens the mind. So my outlook grew wider than ever, and when old Sheikh el Lokhum—that means The Shark . . ."

"Sheikhy the Shark!" murmured Hermann.

"Or Sharkey the Sheikh!" added Abraham the

Sailor.

". . . came to see me, to give himself the pleasure of gazing upon my face, as he told me, I let him gaze. . . . For nothing. . . .

"And when he'd done gazing, I waited to hear what he'd come for. . . . For something.

"He'd come to make me a rich man, and a great Chief. Wasn't that kind of him? I told him I was already pretty rich (a franc a day) and certainly a great man. The greatest man in all . . . er . . . Obek. But he wanted me to make a franc a minute instead of a franc a day, and to be a Captain of Industry instead of Sergeant of Infantry."

"What industry?" I asked.

"The *bogul* industry. . . . You know . . . 'mules.' . . . Well, what with the heat—for Obek is the very hottest place in the world, let me tell you—and the *qat;* and the palm-wine; and some funny stuff in bottles, left in bond in the Custom House; and the amusing things I smoked, I suddenly saw matters with the eye of Sheikh Omar el Lokhum.

"He was right. Undoubtedly he was right.

"France had abandoned me at Obek. For a time, anyhow. And gone about her own affairs. I would abandon France. For a time, at any rate. And go about my affairs, and make a large fortune and be a Captain of Industry . . .

"So I took off my uniform, dressed myself in butter, which is the best protection there is against the sun and the moon; and, taking my rifle and a haversack full of cartridges, set off with Sheikh Omar el Lokhum."

"Did he take anything too?" inquired Matthieu.

"Certainly. I am a man of my word. He took everything he wanted. Some old, but quite serviceable rifles, stored in the Custom House for export. Chassepot, Gras, Lebel, Mauser. All sorts. Quite a nice lot of cartridges; any amount of assorted stores; and whatever he and his Danakil *askari* could get out of the citizens of Obek in the way of rice, dates, dried fish, *durrah*, and other little odds and ends with which they could persuade them to part."

"I guess old Sharkey the Sheikh was some persuader too," murmured Abraham the Sailor, with no note of strong condemnation in his voice.

"You wore a few boots, I suppose, Cockie?" asked Digger.

"Two, to be exact. I have my pride, and no desire to be taken for a native. So I wore boots at one end and a *képi* and *couvre-nuque* at the other, and connected them with a complete suit of butter. Sheikh Omar wanted me to go in full uniform, to lend colour to his statement that the Governor of French Somaliland had gone into partnership in slave-raiding, with him. But I have always declined to have anything to do with faked prospectuses and bogus company-promoting."

"What did he want you for, at all, Cannibal?" inquired Matthieu le Maquereau.

"He desired that I should be associated with his ventures for several reasons. He enjoyed intelligent conversation and the things I let him remove from the Customs shed. He had a great respect and liking for me and for the cartridges and rifles that were in my charge."

"What were they doing in the Customs at all?" asked Thirsty-face. "I thought there was nothing but liquor and tobacco in Custom Houses."

"Which shows you are an ignorant old man, as I have had occasion to remark before," was the reply. "They were imported by an intelligent and enterprising syndicate of French gentlemen, from Liège, at a franc a piece. . . . Old-fashioned weapons but in perfect condition. . . . These gentlemen had to put them in bond and pay a small duty on them. Then they took them out of bond and sold them to Arab merchants, at exactly a thousand per cent, profit. And the Arab merchants loaded up their *dhows* with them, and sailed away to sell them to the enemies of England, Germany, Italy, Portugal and others. But that wasn't the fault of the intelligent French gentlemen, was it?"

"What enemies of England?" asked Digger.

"Well, according to the correspondence on the subject, of which I in my official capacity was cognizant, they took them to Muscat in the Persian Gulf, and there made a big depôt and market, whence they were bought by other Arab gentlemen who took them across to the coast of Persia and sold them to the real consumers, so to speak—gentlemen from Afghanistan, and the Indian border. . . . Of course, the English (who are always fighting on that border), although they are great believers in Free Trade for themselves, didn't like free trade in rifles for their enemies; and so their Foreign Office made polite and friendly over-tures to the *Quai d'Orsai.*

"Our little Obek and Djibouti were quite in the lime-light for a time. Of course, the *Quai d'Orsai* was shocked to its depths—and they're pretty deep, let me tell you, *moi qui parle* who have mixed in high matters, held high office, and been involved in international concerns. Shocked to its depths, and deeply sympathetic it was—especially with the intelligent French gentlemen who had made the arms-trade so extremely flourishing an affair, who had made French Somaliland a real asset to France, and who had been a thorn in the side of the English for twenty years.

"And the *Quai d'Orsai* acted promptly. No more arms whatsoever were to be imported into French Somaliland save to Djibouti, and any that came there were to be seized—and placed in bond. Nor was anyone ever to be allowed to take them out of bond, for any destination save Obek only.

"Well, who'd want to take arms to a wretched, deserted and abandoned spot like Obek, where there was nobody at all but Danakils and me? Just me and Danakils.

"And yet they did, you know . . . They did. They took the trouble to ship them from the Djibouti Custom House to Obek in thousands; and I, of course, promptly put them in the Custom House and locked them up, and that was that."

"Well, how did they get out of there?" asked Terence Hogan.

"Oh well . . . I, of course, had instructions to let the owner of any rifles remove his property as soon as he paid duty. Of course, he might want to take them by caravan into Abyssinia, and nobody had any objection to that. But if they wanted to load up *dhows* again with them, and clear the port, then they found they were up against trouble. . . . They were up against the *Quai d'Orsai* and me. . . . For what did I do? I immediately confiscated their papers, and bade them leave the port of Obek immediately. Yes, I drove them forth. Pariahs of the sea. Lost dogs. Absolutely without any papers of any sort or kind. And what is more, I made my Government *dhow* see them safe off the premises, escort them to the very limit of French waters, abandon them to their fate—to sail for some destination unknown. . . . Unknown to us, that is."

"And where did they go?" I asked.

"Same old place. And sold the same old rifles in the same old markets at the same old price."

"*Perfide Albion!*" murmured Terence Hogan. "But what about this ghastly raid that you say you took part in?"

"Well, I keep trying to tell you, don't I? It is one

of those horrors that should not be concealed, however lacerating to the feelings of the hearer. The whole civilized world should hear of it.

"Well, off we went. Sheikh Omar el Lokhum and I and his band of slavers—Danakil and other Somali *askaris*—and marched nearly all night to his *zariba* camp, where he kept his camels and details. There we had a feast."

"What did you have, Cocteau the Cannibal?" asked big Hermann, whom food interested even more than it did most of us.

Poor Hermann. He lived in a state of chronic hunger. His huge frame always seemed to ask for more than it could get.

"Have? Let's see now. There were curds; porridge; pan-cakes, of fried *durrah*; rice pudding, made with mutton gravy; jolly good dates—better than you ever see over this side; little lumps of boiled meat stuck on skewers . . ."

"What sort of meat?" asked Hermann.

"Oh, just meat. Any old meat. Goat; camel; dog; what not."

"Baby?" asked Matthieu le Maquereau.

"Baby what?"

"Well, one calls you 'Cannibal' . . ."

"Offensiveness, rudeness and vulgarity recoil upon the offensive, the rude and the vulgar," observed Cocteau. "Some animal may have applied the word to me; but if any blasted poodle faced, yellow livered, mangy headed, knock kneed, pigeon toed, blear eyed, pot bellied, bat eared, lop sided misbegotten child of his uncle wished to insult me, he cannot do it. . . . He is not of such stature. . . . Insults, as I have remarked, injure the insulter, and not the insulted. Not that I am insulted . . . the incident occurred years later, and has been grossly exaggerated and the story absurdly distorted. Utterly false, in fact. Besides, I

433

did not know what was in that delicious stew—until afterwards. . . .

"Well, if that spotted dog can cease from barking for a moment, I will resume. We feasted, I say, and drank."

"What did you drink, Cocktail?" inquired Thirsty-face, whom drink interested.

Poor Thirsty-face. . . . He lived in a state of chronic thirst. His shrivelled frame always seemed to ask for more than it could get.

"Nothing that would appeal to you, drunkard," Cocteau rebuked his aged friend. "*Kishir* is a most excellent and warming drink for cold nights, and it could be devilishly cold on wet nights up on the plateau. Made by boiling coffee-pods, and flavouring the brew with cloves, pepper, nutmeg, and various other excellent and aromatic spices. Most warming and enheartening."

"Sounds pretty foul," observed Hogan.

"A splendid cordial and drink, in one. And probably a valuable stimulant, though non-alcoholic, just as *qat*, *kola*, opium and . . . er . . ."

"The Demon Rum," suggested Abraham the Sailor. "Splendid. How far are we from the blood-bespattered slave raid?"

"And after the feast we sat and smoked."

"What did you smoke?" I asked, not to be out-done.

"A water-pipe," replied Cocteau gravely. "Passed round from mouth to mouth. A large earthenware cup full of glowing charcoal and native tobacco-leaves, stuck in a calabash full of water. You draw the smoke *et cetera* up a hollow wooden walking-stick, with a bone handle. Then you praise Allah, and spit . . . and exchange compliments. I told Sheikh Omar in Arabic, in Danakil, in Abyssinian, and various other dialects that I know well, that he was a scholar and a gentleman, and one worthy to be my friend. . . . And in French, I told him that he was a low bastard, a thief, a rogue, a swindler, a smuggler, a slaver, and a terrible scoundrel, adding that I was his brother-in-law (and that's a shocking insult, you know) and also his favourite wife's favourite lover, and that if I should so far demean myself as to spit in his eye, it would be a great honour to him. . . . All of which pleased him very much, and he endeavoured to outdo me in compliment and praise. But as he could only speak to me in Arabic, Danakil, Abyssinian and similar languages that I know well, I was one up on him.

"Next day we started on our long *safari* to the Ethiopian highlands and the Shankalla country."

"What, your wives' home town?" said Abraham the Sailor. "You must have had a lot of little loving messages to give and take. 'Well, good-bye, dear. My love to Mother, and thank her for the rabbit,' " he murmured.

". . . and one night, one night that I shall never forget, we came, treading softly in single file, to the outskirts of a sleeping village. We had parked our camels afar off, that no sound might betray our presence. We lay down where we were, and as we were, stuffed our mouths with tobacco-leaves and *qat*—a custom of the country—and chewed ourselves to sleep. Within half a kilometre of us, many slept their last sleep on earth as free men and women. . . .

"And before break of day, we arose, made a hasty meal of parched *durrah*, and, at the first streak of dawn, marched into the still-sleeping village. As the sun peeped above the eastern hills, it saw us in position right in the middle of the market square . . . ready . . . waiting."

Cocteau the Cannibal paused. And a silence fell upon the group, each man visualizing the scene that followed.

"I would rather not speak of that day," he resumed. "I, Aristide Cocteau, who have soldiered so long and seen so much. I, who have fought in seven campaigns, nineteen battles, and skirmishes innumerable; been wounded eight times, and spent, in all, eleven months in hospital . . ."

"And eleven years in cells," murmured Thirsty-face.

". . . even I do not care to remember, and to talk about, that day. But never, never shall I forget the wailing, the weeping, the shrieking, and the groaning, of men, of women, of youths and maidens, aye, and of little children, as we left that stricken place. The dreadful sounds pursued us. . . . They pursue me still. . . . In my sleep I hear them yet, those cries of anguish."

"You didn't kill those you didn't take, then?" inquired Matthieu le Maquereau.

"Kill them? Nobody was killed."

"All merely wounded?"

"Wounded? Nobody was wounded."

"From whom, then, proceeded the shrieks, the screams, the cries, the groans that pursued you?" I asked.

"From those whom we refused to take with us."

"*Eh?*"

"Well, we couldn't take them all, could we? Sheikh Omar hadn't unlimited capital wherewith to feed an unlimited number on their way to the coast, and to keep them plump, healthy and in fine fettle. Besides, there was the question of *bakshish* to every wretched Chief through whose country the slave caravan had to pass. It was a *per capita* business, of course; and the more slaves we took, the more we had to pay. Besides, how could the old people, the too-young, the halt, lame, blind and diseased, expect us to take them?

Where would our profit be? They could hardly expect us to give them a joy-walk, from their wretched village to the seaside, for nothing, could they? . . . And then give them a pleasure-cruise over to Arabia and Persia after that? . . . No. We weren't philanthropists, and it was up to them to make their own way in life. The only ones for whom we could guarantee soft jobs in good Arab and Persian families were those who'd do us credit —and bring us a profit."

Père Cocteau drank deeply and gazed, reminiscent, into the fire.

"Well, at times it looked to me as though Sheikh Omar had had to cut his overhead expenses too fine, and had come on the expedition with an insufficient force of *askaris.*

"Each *askar*, besides being a splendid fighting man, powerful, tireless and ruthless, was also a trained and experienced slaver, a skilled workman at his job. But even so, it seemed to me that it was a well-nigh impossible task to keep our band of slaves as originally selected.

"From the moment we had finished our task of picking them out and herding them together within the ring of *askaris*, it was one constant struggle to keep the others off.

"Every minute or so, a family, headed by some stalwart son, would dash at our flock, seize upon some member of it and, while the family ran him off by the arms and the scruff of the neck, the son would take his place, and stand there trying to look as though he had been selected from the first.

"The same with the girls.

"The family possessing some eligible but un-selected daughter, would suddenly and swiftly swoop upon the chosen people and dash away again, bearing with them some protesting shriek-ing maiden, and leaving their own daughter smugly smiling in her place.

"It was a din, *and* a struggle. . . .

"No more slaving for me, I thought. I'd sooner go elephant-catching. The heat, the noise, the dust, the shoving and pushing and wrangling and screaming and shouting!

"It would have been bad enough if there had only been men. But you have to realize, *mes amis*, that there were women in it. You, who have perhaps seen a summer sale in a great Paris emporium, have no idea, no ghost of an idea. . . . I, a man of affairs, accustomed to direction and management—had I not been practically Governor of Obek when I was the only white man there— was disgusted at the lack of method, the absence of organization.

"Shouting in his ear, to be heard above the din,

" 'My friend,' I said, 'You should bring a book of printed passes, with a blank for the name of each person selected; or a bag of arm-brassards, each with a brass-plate bearing a number.'

"But Sheikh Omar, smiling sadly, shook his head.

" 'They sell them, my friend. Sell them to the highest bidder. The affair becomes a damned ticket-auction, a stock exchange, a *bourse*, instead of a slave-raid. No. There's no easy money in this,' and again he cracked his great whip at a violently active, desperately earnest band—father, mother, uncles, aunts, sisters and brothers, who were trying to substitute their own hopeful for one of his best slaves . . .

"Yes, *mes amis*, that is one of the days that will remain for ever in my memory; one of the experiences that I shall never forget. Of course, looking back to that day of unspeakable horrors, it is really impossible to say which was the worst. But I *think* that perhaps the most dreadful thing of all is the memory of those poor souls, both youths and maidens, who followed us for a whole day, begging, imploring, holding out hands of entreaty, and even still trying to insert themselves into the slave-gang under the very eyes of the *askari* who, rifle in one hand and whip in the other, had all they could do to beat them off.

"However, *tout passe, tout casse, tout lasse.*

"The worst day comes to an end and, in time, we were alone; with our caravan of *bogul* 'mules,' our black ivory; and well on our long march down to the coast.

"And you can imagine what a caravan it was; how big and how costly; seeing that we'd got to feed all these Shankallas on fresh goats'-milk, the best fresh dates, and the finest rice, all well cooked and plentiful. Think of the number of men we had to employ, in addition to the *askari*, to construct huts for the slaves to sleep in, at night."

"Couldn't the slaves have built huts for themselves?" asked Hermann.

"Doubtless they could. But do you think they would? No. They knew that they were our property, and that we'd jolly well got to look after our property. . . . I tell you, they're a high-stomached lot, those slaves."

"Besides," murmured Terence Hogan, "were they not his 'honoured guests'? Would that be your idea of hospitality in Germany, Hermann?"

"We have no slaves in Germany," said Hermann. "Nor were there ever slaves in any German colony."

"No, you Germans are a selfish and a callous race," agreed Cocteau. . . . "Well, as I was saying, it was an expensive, as well as a troublesome, business; for we had to pay our way pretty nearly right down to the coast, and give *bakshish* to every rascally petty chieftain whose frontier we crossed.

"At last we got back to the Danakil country, and were all right. Sheikh Omar's customers, wealthy Arab traders, came and very quickly bought up the whole of our stock and took them, in small parties, down to the coast at Tajura, Medehr, Roheita, Zeila, Id, and Obek. Here they embarked them at once on their *dhows*, and set sail for Arabia and Persia. I went with one lot to Jeddah and on up to Mecca, in disguise."

"But did the authorities never take them red-handed? Catch them with the slaves in their possession, I mean?" asked Hermann.

"What slaves?"

"Slaves you were talking about."

"The Shankallas and Gallalos who'd come down with us? They weren't slaves now. They were seamen. Sailors who formed part of the crews of the *dhows*. If any French gun-boat had seized one of the *dhows* and said that the Shankallas were slaves, they would have told them they were liars."

"Who would?"

"The Shankallas and Gallalos would."

"But what about the women?" objected Hermann.

"Why, they were the daughters of the crew, of course. To every man a daughter," said Cocteau.

"In fact, each skipper had taken his little daughter to bear him companee," observed Hogan.

"Quite so. The joy-walk had now become a pleasure-cruise."

"But what happened when they got to Arabia?" asked Hermann, still not satisfied.

"Sold in the open market-place," said Cocteau. "Fifty to eighty pounds for a man, and forty to sixty pounds for a girl. A healthy child, twenty to thirty pounds. Prices varying according to individual merits, and also according to the relative conditions of supply and demand, of which the latter was always greater than the former. Yes, bidding was always brisk."

"Then they *were* slaves. It was absolute slavery," said Hermann triumphantly.

"It has just dawned upon our comrade that I'm telling you about a slave-raid, and how I won the honourable title of The Slaver," observed Cocteau.

"Slavery is the foulest blot on the page of civilization. It is the most . . ." began Hermann.

"Someone's been pulling your leg, Hermann," interrupted Cocteau. . . . "How I envied those slaves."

"What became of them, really?" I asked.

"Well, they became the absolute property of the men who bought them; and, as property, were taken jolly good care of. Does a man buy a valuable horse to chuck bricks at it? Or hang it up by the tail, for his amusement? If the slave had any intelligence at all, he became, in time, his master's confidential servant, major-domo, responsible head of the household; combined treasurer, secretary, and manager of his master's affairs and property.

"Not being Arabs, but strangers in a strange land, without other ties, temptations and family cares and responsibilities of their own, they are, almost invariably, absolutely trustworthy and trusted. Very frequently they rise to excellent positions; and in any case, are better off in every way than they would have been as free men in their own starving country."

"I don't believe a word of it," stubbornly replied the bewildered Hermann.

"No? Did you ever read your Bible, Hermann? . . . Yes? And did you ever hear of the young man of the name of Joseph? One has a sort of dim recollection that he was sold from poverty and hunger to Arab slave-dealers—and by his own thoughtful and kind-hearted brothers—and that the Arab slave-dealers, in precisely the manner I have described to you, sold him in the open market-place in Egypt.

"Also, unless one is mistaken, this slave became not only his master's private secretary . . . a Monsieur Potiphar was the name—yes, and there was also a Madame Potiphar one recollects . . . but actually rose to be Chancellor of the Exchequer, or Minister of the Interior, or something of the sort, and, having improved the shining hour to the extent of making a corner in wheat, died rich and respected, a very typical Jewish gentleman."

"All very fine," grumbled Hermann. "But what about those women slaves, sold in the open market-place by your Arab slave-dealers?"

"All went into *harims*, my dear Hermann," was the reply.

"Ha! White slavery in fact . . ."

"No. Black."

"They became the concubines of these rich Arabs who bought them. Slave mothers of slave children."

"Wrong again, my good Hermann. The beloved mothers of perfectly free children. Legitimate as you are, and a damn sight freer. . . . Contrast their lives of ease, dignity and pleasure—well fed, well housed and beautifully clothed—with those of working-class women in Europe. Contrast them with the lives they would have led as the hungry and well-beaten wives of Shankalla warriors, in their own starving country. Slavery, I tell you, is the finest . . ."

"*Blagueur!*" said I.

"Don't call him a blackguard, chum," expostulated Digger. "He's dinkum, all right."

"Sure," agreed Abraham. "Old man Cocktail is the best and biggest old liar in the Legion; an' that's saying something. I cert'nly hand it to Cock."

"What happened to you afterwards, Cocteau?" I asked. "Does the *Quai d'Orsai* still think you are Governor of Obek and governing same?"

"No," replied Cocteau. "My absence was discovered owing to the fact that the annual letter did not arrive from me, and that I was not present to take delivery of pay and rations when brought by the local Government gunboat.

"There was Cocteau's uniform, neatly folded on his desk in the Custom House, but where was Cocteau? . . . Gone!"

"Then there was trouble, I bet," said Thirsty-face.

"Yes. They were plunged in mourning. Despondency and alarm prevailed. Pessimism spread. Some feared that I had gone swimming, and been devoured by sharks. Others, logical-minded men, pointed out that I should not have gone swimming in my boots.

"Some feared that I had been taken by wild beasts. Others, also logically-minded, objected that practically no known wild beast removes and folds the clothing of its victim before devouring him. Nor do many, even of the most savage, devour the boots of their prey.

"Someone suggested that, retaining my *képi* and my boots, and removing the rest of my uniform I, having gone mad—through overwork and cares of State—had run round and round in circles, in the sun, until I had succumbed. To this, people of the *type* Hermann, replied that the theory, excellent in other respects, did not account for the absence of any trace of my corpse.

"And in the end, the theory that I had marched off, in boots and *képi*, with Sheikh Omar el Lokhum and his men, was accepted, in view of the fact that everybody in Obek stated that this was precisely what had happened.

"So the authorities, prone as ever to think evil, premature and presumptuous, posted me as absent without leave; and, basing their action upon the childish and untenable theory that I had disappeared just about one second before the discovery of my disappearance—whereas I had been gone for months—they let that sentence stand for five days, whereafter they posted me as a deserter.

"Aren't the ways of such people incalculable, illogical, incredible? What connection is traceable between the premises and the conclusion; between the simple fact that Sergeant Aristide Cocteau had gone slave-raiding and—desertion.

"If the Governor of French Somaliland went lion-hunting (a thing he would never be so foolish as to do, of course), would they post him as a deserter, if he were away from the official arm-chair for more than five days? So when, returning to Obek, I saw the miserable Corporal Delarue, promoted to my place, sitting in the seat of the mighty, I spread my arms abroad, struck a noble gesture and cried, 'Cocteau is here.'

"But that miserable and mannerless *cochon*, yawning, merely replied,

" 'Is he? Then put the bastard under arrest, and keep him there until the boat comes from Djibouti. They're going to shoot him or give him ten years, or something, for desertion.'

"So having kicked the impudent Corporal Delarue twice round the office and once down the steps, I resumed my chair and duties.

"However, when the Government boat came into Obek it really seemed that Delarue's idiotic story had something in it, and that it behoved me to go down to Djibouti and put the fear of God and

Sergeant Cocteau into whomsoever was at the bottom of this amazing business.

"Well, believe me or believe me not, *mes amis*, they stuck to it. Oh, they stuck to it. They stuck to it all right.

"And when, at the end of an impassioned speech to that miserable Court of Alleged Justice, I said,

" 'And is it thus that France rewards her servants? Is it for this that the *Commissaire* of Obek risks his life in investigating the truth of rumours concerning slavery? Is it for this—to be brought to trial and impeachment—that the Governor-in-the-sight-of-God of Obek risks his life by actually himself going into the interior to get first-hand information on the subject?'

"As well talk to a stone wall. Better—a stone wall can't answer back.

"I was condemned. And the sentence made my blood boil."

"How many years did you get?" I asked.

"Years! I got thirty days, and reduced to the ranks!

"How's that for logic, I ask you? Was I not either a criminal and a deserter who should have been shot; or else an unusually efficient and enterprising official who should have been decorated, promoted and rewarded?

"But, no. Oh no! I was neither a criminal to be sent to prison, nor a zealous investigator to be sent to a wider sphere of influence and activity. Can you conceive such muddled thinking? Thirty days and reduced to the ranks for being absent from my post for six months and allowing the Custom House to be looted. Thirty days and reduced to the ranks for obtaining first-hand information on all the ramifications of the slave-trade at the risk of my life.

" '*Monsieur le President*,' said I to the old fool who pronounced the sentence at the Court-Martial, 'is it supposed to be a reward or a punishment?'

" 'It is the merciful, lenient and nominal punishment inflicted upon a soldier suffering from *cafard*,' was the answer.

" 'Well, *Monsieur le President*,' I replied with dignity, 'if that is the sentence for suffering from *cafard*, hadn't the Court better give me three more merciful, lenient and nominal sentences also, while they are about it—for I confess that, besides *cafard*, I am also suffering from chicken-pox, mumps, and the itch.'

"And that's how I came to be reduced to the ranks, and to herd with people like Matthieu le Maquereau," concluded Père Cocteau. "I, who went to Mecca and am a Hadji."

"Slavery," began Hermann, "is the most shameful and disgraceful institution that ever blackened the face of civilization. I say slavery should be abolished. . . ."

"Say it to the Sergeant-Major, will you?" begged Cocteau. . . . "And tell him that we all agree."

*　　*　　*　　*　　*

I was still a Company Cook and my kit was even larger and heavier than that of the other *légionnaires*, as cooks have (and badly need) extra clothes in which to cook and receive the inevitable baptism of grease, as well as stains of smoke, soot, and dirt from cooking-vessels.

Luckily my charm of manner, or the gift of wine or food that I didn't want, had brought down upon me the friendship of an amazing Spanish muleteer, a man named Ramon Valago, with the biggest mouth, biggest ears, smallest nose, and smallest eyes I've ever seen. Wonderful to relate, being a muleteer by trade, profession, vocation or calling, he was actually put on to mule-driving in the army; and being a mule-driver, he could, and did, put my spare kit on to a mule.

And on this day, I remember, I sinned—and, learned once again the truth of the warning proverb, "Be sure your sins will find you out."

In point of fact, it was the Quartermaster-Sergeant who nearly found me out.

Now since I was taking advantage of the friendly mule-driver—or of the friendly mule—I decided to do the thing properly. Accordingly, I abandoned my cooking-clothes and my khaki uniform trousers, and wore my blue uniform trousers (as they were warmest and I was of the coldest), knowing that when we made a halt I should have no need to change into my cooking-costume, as rations were carried by each man, and nothing had to be cooked.

But I had reckoned without the deep, ineradicable, and fervent—nay fanatical—love of the French official, civil or military, for red tape. The hearts of these worthy men are the very hearths and homes of the red-tape worm.

Sergeant Pflügge saw me.

"*Gott in Himmel*," he gasped, "and who gave *you* permission, oh species of most mangy goat, to array yourself thus fantastically in fancy dress?"

"I am a Company cook, *mon Sergent*, and I . . ."

"I did not ask what you are, illegitimate offspring of an ever-ashamed and eternally regretful hyena. . . . I can see for myself what you are, species of maggot that wriggles in dead and decaying mules."

I thought of my mule, and stood like a statue, at attention, staring, as per regulation, "at an imaginary point, ten metres beyond the Sergeant's left ear and quarter of a metre to the right of it."

"I can see *what* you are, and I can see how you're dressed. Let me ever again catch you wearing anything but the kit of the day, and we'll see how you'll enjoy eight days' 'detention on the march.' . . . Ever tried 'detention on the march'? . . . No? . . . Well, if you do, God have mercy on you, for I'll have none. . . . You ever disobey me again—and I've caught you at this game before—and I'll hound you into the Lunatic Asylum where you belong."

How I would have liked to have said:

"You putty-nosed, red-whiskered, fat-necked, bullet-headed old liar."

For it was an absolute lie, and he knew it, that he'd *ever* had occasion to find fault with my uniform or my conduct.

Instead of that, I said to myself instead of to him:

"You hopeless helpless fool and idiot. Those precious khaki trousers are six or seven miles away, wandering along on the back of a thrice-accursed mule, in charge of its thrice-accursed bat-eared, shark-mouthed muleteer."

Seven miles away! And Sergeant Pflügge not likely to be much more than seven yards away, when we marched on the morrow.

I was in a fix; a very awkward and unpleasant position indeed. I'd seen a man doing 'detention on the march' during a halt . . . bound more or less spread-eagled to a great wagon-wheel, with the big hub sticking into the small of his back in such a way as to render the position very painful, and its prolongation, for hours, positive torture. Added to this, the man's face was turned to the sun and covered with flies and insects which he could not brush away.

No. Something must be done, and I promptly called a meeting of my comrades. Each one of them promptly offered to change with me, and Terence Hogan, of course, firmly insisted. I was touched by their kindness, but naturally I absolutely refused to consider anything of the sort.

Nor could I give consideration to the suggestion of Gustavus Adolphus that we all contribute one pint of coffee and make a united endeavour to dye those blue trousers brown.

"Consider, my little ones," said I, "though this change a criminal blue to a beautiful khaki (which I gravely doubt) I feel sure it will not change the material."

Suddenly Père Cocteau, that resourceful man, who had not soldiered for forty years for nothing, cried that he "had it."

"*Pigou!*" he cried.

"And what is it that it is that this Pigou can do?" I asked.

"None other is he than batman to *le bon Sergent Pflügge* himself. I go to find him. He owes me a little money and a lot of gratitude."

"Gee!" observed Abraham the Sailor to me, in the vernacular. "I've certainly heard of giving your buddy your last cent, your last crust, or the shirt off your back—but the trousers off your legs. . . ."

Cocteau returned later, jubilant and triumphant, with something in khaki tightly rolled beneath his arm.

"It is I," he crowed. "I, Aristide Cocteau, who can produce khaki trousers from the empty air."

"Are they from the empty batman of the Sergeant, too?" I asked.

"From the Sergeant himself," replied Cocteau, closing one eye and placing his right forefinger with some firmness against the side of his already asymmetrical nose.

"From the Sergeant, with his love. A Present from Morocco," I said. "Didn't he send any other kind message with it—or them?"

"He did not," replied Cocteau. "Be serious, *mon enfant*, for *le bon Dieu* knows it'll be a serious matter for some of us, if that crapulous camel of a Sergeant Pflügge ever finds out that he has lent you his trousers."

"Tell me what happened, *mon père*," I demanded, aghast. "A nice thing if I were to bring upon us the wrath of *ce bon* Sergeant Pflügge, on private and personal grounds. . . . He'd go mad and bite us. . . ."

"What happened?" replied Cocteau. "Why, I went to the little pig Pigou and said:

" 'Oh pig, pay me instantly the twenty francs you owe me.'

" 'Ask me for twenty thousand, my beloved friend,' said he, 'for I could as easily find them.'

"And he spread his arms abroad in a gesture of desolation and despair.

" 'Then forget them. Wipe them from your memory. Cancel the debt,' I cried, as he embraced me and kissed me on the right cheek.

" '. . . and lend me a pair of trousers,' I added, as he kissed me on the left one.

" 'Lend you my trousers, dear friend?' he exclaimed. 'But of a certainty. For how long?'

" 'For but a day or two,' quoth I, 'until the transport is with us once again.'

" 'For a day or two,' ejaculated the little Pigou, turning pale. 'How then? What is it that you say, my friend? Would you have me for a day or two to run about without my trousers? Am I to make a whole army blush?'

" 'And are you not the Sergeant's batman?' I asked him sternly, 'and do you tell me that you are the miserable servant of a man so miserable that he has but one pair of trousers?'

" 'By no means. Think not such thoughts,' begged the little Pigou. 'The Sergeant has indeed a spare pair, a beautiful pair, a new pair, a Sunday pair, a courting pair—but did he see me in them, he'd have me out of them with but a single kick.'

" 'And who, species of a blow-fly, who, pray, asked you to presume to dare to wear the Sergeant's breeches?'

" 'I do not understand, my dear friend.'

" 'Who wants you to understand, my species of a Pigou? Go instantly and fetch me the Sergeant's Sunday trousers.'

"I tell you, *mon enfant*, that pale perspiring Pigou almost wept. But at length, fear of losing the friendship of Père Cocteau and twenty francs, all in one terrible *coup*, prevailed, and *voilà!* Behold the Sunday trousers of Sergeant Pflügge."

I went "a little mean at my stomach" as Abraham the Sailor says.

This really was the horns of a dilemma . . . the Devil and the Deep Sea . . . Scylla and Charybdis.

If I marched forth at dawn in my blue breeches I should certainly be a candidate for eight days' "detention on the march"; and if I marched out at dawn, wearing Sergeant Pflügge's khaki breeches, Heaven alone knew for what hideous punishment I should be liable.

"Oh, what a tangled web we weave
When first we practise to deceive."

I practised hard.

In the darkness of my bivouac I changed, and then practised auto-suggestion by walking about and saying to myself:

"You are not wearing Sergeant Pflügge's breeches; and, every day, in every way, they fit you better and better" . . . until I began to think that really I was not—and kept looking to see, thus making myself conspicuous.

"Splendid, my little one," praised Père Cocteau. "Truly of a *chic*. One would say you had been born in them. Go find *cet animal* of a Pflügge and dance before him. Say, 'Behold my trousers so beautiful. Do you not wish that they were yours?'

"But," he continued, *"pour l'amour de Dieu* be careful of them—for the sake of *le petit Pigou*. Do not sit nor kneel nor lie down in them, my child, and sprinkle them but sparingly with coffee, wine and *soupe*. Remember that not only are the trousers of the Sergeant Pflügge in your hands, but the honour, nay, the very life, of the little Pigou."

Next morning, réveillé found me, outwardly, as I should be, but inwardly a quaking and craven creature.

We fell in, and, a minute later, Sergeant Pflügge bore down upon us, obviously in his usual early morning condition of liverish ill-temper.

Would he forget me?

Not he. . . .

One swift glance he gave, as he passed in front of me, and I could have sworn that a look of disappointment clouded his unpleasing face.

And then, to my amazement, he suddenly rasped an order which I did not remember to have heard him give before:

"All Company cooks will march in front."

I wondered whether this were merely an excellent idea for having cooks on the next camping-ground before the Company arrived, by making us out-march the others; or whether it had some sinister connection with myself and my—or rather his—trousers.

We marched.

I was then left-hand man of the leading section of threes, and, beside me, for twenty mortal miles, marched Sergeant Pflügge. For twenty miles his weekday trousers marched beside his Sunday trousers, and he did not know it; and it was the longest twenty miles I ever marched.

That night I took time from my much-needed hours of sleep to discover my muleteer friend, Valago; and the excellent Père Cocteau paid another visit to the little Pigou.

"It is done. The Pigou breathes again, my child," he said, on his return; and, giving his broad chest a thump, added:

"Always turn to your *bon papa* Cocteau when in trouble."

I endeavoured to thank Père Cocteau.

"Enough, enough, my cabbage. Say no more," he begged.

"Except that I feel I owe you twenty francs," I added.

"You really feel you owe me twenty francs, my child?" smiled Père Cocteau. "Ah well . . ."

I was positively thankful to feel the full weight of my entire kit on my back, as we marched next day; although it weighed more than seventy pounds.

CHAPTER XII

A few days later we made another attack at El G——. Our Battalion was right-flank guard again, but we had our share of the fighting and, for half an hour, had a really hot time of it. We had deployed, and were advancing in open order, my Company being on the extreme right, when a sudden burst of rifle-fire broke out from a perfectly invisible enemy on the hill-side in front of us.

We got the signal to lie down; and a Section, widely extended, skirmished forward, scouting ahead of us.

There was soon a brisk exchange of fire. The scouts had evidently run into a body of the enemy and located them.

We got the order to rise and advance, and a minute later, we were ordered to close on the centre and rush a kind of hollow plateau or crater, straight ahead of us.

Up we went, and as we appeared over the nearer lip of the crater, a horde of grey-clad Arabs swarmed over the opposite one and fled.

By the time we had crossed the crater and lined the opposite side, these men had absolutely disappeared, gone to ground behind rocks and in the gullies, dry stream-beds or *wadis* in which this country is so rich.

While we halted, peering through the shimmering heat-haze that danced over the stony ground before us, there was again a sudden outburst of rifle-fire on our front and right flank.

It was evidently a crude form of trap, and the enemy had, at any rate for the moment, got us where they wanted us, and probably with the range carefully paced out by each man, from where we were to the rock or the *nullah* whence he was shooting.

The bullets came thick and fast, knocking up sand all round us and among us, ricocheting off rocks and stones, sometimes striking a rock with a vicious smack, and occasionally a man, with a dull thud, a horrid sound to me—one of the beastliest that one can hear.

I was more than glad to find that I was not in the least afraid but, on the other hand, was ashamed to discover that I was trembling violently. This was certainly not due to fear, because I felt no fear, nor was it "nerves," using the word to express a state of being nervous. It was, I honestly think, pure excitement and a condition one may describe as "keyed-up-ness."

At first it was so bad that I couldn't hold my rifle still, and, though I have won a good many pots at shooting—and once entertained idiotic and conceited dreams of having a try for the King's Prize at Bisley—I certainly couldn't have hit anything then. However, everybody was much too busy attending to their own affairs to take any notice of me.

At the end of what seemed to me an eternity, but which I discovered to be about an hour, the enemy's fire slackened, and presently stopped, as they drew off from their position across the narrow valley. Presumably our rapid and heavy fire had decided them not to assault the plateau or crater place that we were holding.

At first we had had fire orders, from Captain Z——:

"Prepare for salvo-fire at five hundred metres . . . *Fire!*" . . . time after time, and we had fired our wonderfully crisp clean volleys as one man, and so far as I could see, *at* one man, a remarkably courageous person who stood on a rock, "hurling defiance," and encouraging his followers.

After that, we got the order *à volontiers* for independent fire, which nearly always seems to me infinitely more sensible than the other.

In the "salvo" or volley-firing, everybody is thinking far more of the volley than of its effect; much more concerned to press the trigger at the exact moment than to hit the object.

Moreover, if the word-of-command is withheld too long, one's rifle inevitably begins to sway or wobble as one breathes; whereas with the *à volontiers* fire, you can get down to it in comfort, rest your rifle, wait till there's something to shoot at, and then shoot at it.

When the "Cease fire" whistle was blown, we lay in an irregular line along the edge of the plateau, behind whatever head-cover Heaven had vouchsafed to us, and awaited events.

Personally, I lay perfectly flat for awhile, with my head on my arms, feeling more tired after that hour's firing than I should have done after a twenty-mile march.

Captain Z—— suddenly appeared from somewhere and walked up and down behind us, occasionally scanning the opposite hill-side through his field-glasses. After he had passed, I heard Digger ask Abraham the Sailor if he'd noticed the position whence the Captain gave his orders.

"Too right, I did," replied Digger, and Terence Hogan irreverently imitated the Captain's voice and brave words:

" 'And ever I shall be at your head.' "

In point of fact, he had promptly got behind a large rock, the moment we came under fire, and, with an occasional peep to left and right of it, but never over the top, had exercised fire-control for but a brief space.

"If it had been old Papa B——, he'd have been walking about smoking his cigarette, glancing at everybody's rifle-sights, and bestowing a friendly kick in the ribs on anyone idling and not paying strict attention to duty," observed Cocteau.

"Poor chap looks ill to me," I said. "He certainly looks very white."

"I think discretion is the better part of pallor, in his case," said Terence.

"Sort of thing you would think," I replied.

For Terence Hogan's epigrams and jests are sometimes more witty than kindly.

"He surely has gone pale in the features," agreed Abraham the Sailor. "Heap Big Chief Pale-face. He's certainly sick."

"Sick of being shot at, anyhow," growled Hogan, in whom I think the Regular Officer felt ashamed, both for, and of, Captain Z——.

Suddenly orders arrived by flag, helio, or field-telephone, for us to advance. We sprang up and, in open order and irregular line, descended into the valley, Captain Z—— well in our rear.

Up the hill-side, whence heavy fire had so recently been directed at us, we climbed, very much on the alert, not knowing at what moment a brawny wild-cat fanatic might spring, slashing wildly, from behind a rock; or a sudden heavy volley from above mow us down.

But nothing happened.

We gained the top unopposed, and found it to be another plateau or crater, somewhat similar to the one we had left, and considerably larger. Across this we advanced at the double, and reached the opposite side, some three or four hundred yards away, just in time to see a few scattered grey-clad objects dash from the base of the mountain into a *nullah* or *wadi*, and disappear round a bend of it before more than a few snap-shots could be fired at them.

Away on the left flank we could still hear the heavy firing that had been going on, more or less, since the action began. This now died down and, shortly after, orders came for us to consolidate our position—in other words, form an entrenched camp and hold on.

Once again began that back-breaking, nail-tearing, hand-scratching labour of carrying great stones, of the right size, shape, and flatness, to build the wall.

I found this work a much greater strain than marching. It's awful, carrying these great stones in both hands as a washerwoman would carry a basketful of wet clothes; and worse still, I think, carrying them on the shoulder as a butcher-boy does his tray of meat.

Corporal Minaud, a person of whom I was not inordinately fond, had a vile (and to his superiors, valuable) trick of turning the business into a heavy-weight-lifting competition; offering a litre of wine to the man who could lift and move the biggest and heaviest stone.

Egged on by the competitive spirit, in the hope of winning the wine, some of these poor fellows of the stronger sort would perform absolutely super-human feats of strength, achieving the almost impossible.

Behind the back of such a man—staggering along by inches, bent more than double, with cracking sinews and breaking blood-vessels—Cor-poral Minaud would nudge a brother non-commis-sioned officer and laugh at the poor fool shorten-ing his life that Corporal Minaud's duty might the sooner be done. I never heard of any of these Atlases getting their litre of wine. I think the competition always ended in a dead heat, with the prize reserved for next time.

That night the troops had their first glimpse of a different aspect of "savage" warfare.

Savage indeed.

On our left lay a Battalion of *Tirailleurs*. The left of this Battalion again lay at the edge of our flat-topped mountain, one of the El G—— range. From this edge, the mountain fell away sheer, in what was practically a precipice; and was either un-patrolled that night, or else was in charge of weary sentries who saw no point in staring into the Beyond, from which only a winged enemy could approach.

Doubtless they patrolled their part of the front of the plateau—from which the ground sloped gradually—as vigilantly as we did.

Anyhow, at the base of that precipice, on the *Tirailleurs'* flank, was a big Arab *ksar*, called Ait J——, and, during the night, the "simple villagers" became the wild fierce mountaineers that they really are; left their guns and ammunition safely hidden in the roof; and, each clad in oil and a long sharp knife, sallied forth, and, in perfect silence scaled the "unscaleable" precipice—up which they had no doubt a well-known and well-worn path.

Arrived at the summit, the first man stabbed the—probably sleeping—sentry dead, and cut his throat; and then the whole band, incredible as it may seem, crawled, silently as phantoms, among the sleeping *Tirailleurs*. Each one stabbed to the heart the first man he saw, cut his throat, took his rifle and ammunition and vanished. All this with-out a sound; without an alarm of any sort being raised.

In the morning, twenty-nine dead men were lying there, each in a pool of blood, his head half-severed from his shoulders.

Almost as soon as we heard the news, the order came for the *Tirailleurs* to move elsewhere, and for us to take up their position.

As it happened, our Section took over this position that had been the flank of the line of the *Tirailleurs*, and I saw some sights that made me feel almost sick—hardened as I was by my experiences in the Great War.

Everybody was filled with unbounded indignation, and called the Arabs all sorts of evil names, of which 'treacherous assassin' was about the mildest.

Having seen what I had, I was moved to agree with the most indignant, until Terence Hogan damped my fine frenzy with his quiet drawl.

"Did you ever hear of any merry lads in France called Ghurkas? They used to go out and collect heads for breakfast, or at any rate, before breakfast. It was called trench-raiding, as you may have heard. They used to bring back the heads because they were given to understand that the raids were made for identificatory purposes. They didn't seem to understand when they were told that shoulder-straps and caps were better for the purpose of identifying German Battalions. However, always wishful to oblige, they left the heads behind thereafter, and brought the caps."

"It's a beastly way of fighting," I said.

"Oh, don't be silly," replied Hogan. "Wouldn't you rather have your head neatly and artistically sliced off by a competent Ghurka than be gassed by a German chemist, until your lungs bubbled out in green foam?"

"War is foul and beastly, anyhow," I said.

"You've said it all, Bo," agreed Abraham the Sailor. "Let's go home."

"These Arabs are sacred assassins, pigs,

species of camels, matricides who eat their own children, owls, animals, politicians . . ." stated Cocteau. "I know them in all their filthy manifestations, Touareg, Bedouin, Riffian, Senussi, Berber, Dervish and What Not. . . . All alike. . . ."

"Well, if you ask me," observed Digger, as he cleaned his rifle, "I think they're dinkum sportsmen. Would a bunch of us dare walk into an Arab camp one night, odds a hundred to one, and bayonet twenty-nine of them and get away with it?"

"Sure. What's bitin' you all?" agreed Abraham the Sailor. "This is a war, isn't it? . . . I always thought all holds were allowed in war. . . . Butt, kick, bite, throttle, and gouge. Do you guys want the poor heathen to do it with a band and banners and torchlight procession, or what? You make me tired."

"You'd be more tired if it had been us posted here last night, and you'd got your throat slit by an Arab," remarked Matthieu le Maquereau.

"Sure I should," replied Abraham the Sailor, "and serve me damn right too. What was that outfit of *Tirailleurs* and their sentries up to, that such a thing could happen? You don't suppose they're going to get *us* that way, do you? And if they do, I hand it to 'em for better men than we are."

And of course he was right. We were making war on these people, invading their country, and killing them when and where they resisted. If we could kill them in the light of day with our superior weapons—grenades, machine-guns, aeroplane-bombs and high-explosive shells, why shouldn't they kill us by night with their inferior weapons?

Undeniably it was a horrible messy massacre; horrible by reason of its being done in silence and

461

darkness upon sleeping men. But war is war, and one can hardly expect the Arab and the Moor to acquiesce in the view that the law of "the greatest good of the greatest number" must prevail. Nor can they be expected to realize that, nowadays, vast sections of the earth's surface, potential granaries for the feeding of mankind, can no longer remain waste, useless, and vacant, so that a few semi-savage tribes may use them for a battle-ground. North America could not be left to the Red Indian; South America to the Carib; nor Australia to the Aborigine; and, regarded in the cold light of logic and of reason, the French, advancing in Morocco, were doing the same kind of service to Europe that the Romans did when conquering Britain.

The ethics of this "conquest for the good of civilization" theory, present a big problem which will no doubt be hotly debated as long as there are any large usable tracts of the world unused.

Anyhow, war is beastly, even when it is for the greatest good of the greatest number.

There wasn't very much sleep for us that night, in spite of the long day's heavy manual labour, and I can testify that, from time to time, there was at least one unauthorized sentry helping the regular sentries.

We were all—at any rate the young soldiers—a little on edge and over-anxious, not to say nervy, in spite of the fact that we had been told that the village or *ksar* at the foot of the precipice had been seized. We heard later that, when it was occupied, it was found to be quite ready for occupation, being absolutely deserted by every living thing. . . .

It may have been because there were so many of us patrolling to and fro, with our rifles at the ready, that there was no alarm the first night; or it may have been because the Arabs who had entered the camp, the night before, had come up from the village and could not get at the path now that the place was occupied by French troops. Anyhow, there was no alarm that night at all.

On the next night again there was no alarm, and much less amateur or, rather, unofficial, sentry work by imaginative men who could not sleep for thought of Arabs creeping up in the darkness. There was no "alarm" or challenge throughout the night, but there were both consternation and alarm in the morning when it was discovered that a rifle was missing.

There was no getting away from the fact that Matthieu le Maquereau had lain down, clutching his rifle with one hand and with the rifle partly under his body, and had awakened in the morning, undisturbed and unhurt, but with no rifle.

Even Sergeant Pflügge could hardly, in the circumstances, accuse him of having sold it for a bottle of wine. He did, however, suggest that the Arab had spared his life because he recognized in Matthieu a fellow swine-of-a-native, or a brother fiend-from-the-Pit.

That was really the amazing part of this alarming experience. Why on earth hadn't Matthieu been killed when his rifle was taken, as the twenty-nine *Tirailleurs* had been killed when theirs were stolen?

Père Cocteau's suggestion that Matthieu had promptly handed over his rifle to the Arab and given him something else as *bakshish* and ransom for his life, was well received and applauded, though not believed.

What probably happened was that a single rifle-thief had wriggled his way into camp, from some other direction, and with the single purpose of stealing a rifle and getting away with it.

Doubtless Matthieu had turned over in his sleep, and the Arab, lying motionless among the sleeping men, had seen him move and expose the rifle, and had there upon picked it up and crept away. On a moonless or cloudy night, an Arab apparently finds no difficulty whatever in crawling between sentries into a camp. There, when he is alone, he may or may not use his knife, but he knows he will never get out of the camp alive if he makes a sound.

When a party of them makes a raid at night, there is certain to be knife-work, as every man knows that many of them will get away in the confusion, and each hopes that he will be one of them.

That *Tirailleurs'* section must have been sleeping like logs, and the whole lot, sentries and all, must have been killed almost simultaneously, since not a sound was heard and no alarm given.

Orders were now issued that every man was to fasten his rifle tightly and strongly to his left wrist, in such a way that it would be impossible for the rifle to be stolen without its owner being awakened; but also in such a way that the rifle could be used at a moment's notice, without untying it.

Full information was also afforded on the subject of what would happen to any other man whose rifle was stolen from him. . . .

A pretty bad time followed, one of those periods of unbroken work by day and very broken sleep by night, that lead to epidemics and outbreaks of *cafard.*

This madness is temporary, but the tragedies are permanent.

A man whom a day of rest and a night of unbroken sleep would have saved; a man over-wrought, over-strained and over-driven; insufficiently fed; lacking sleep; devil-driven by his nerves, may suddenly, although quite sane, almost unconsciously, commit some act which may be his ruin, if not his death.

Or the result may be different. The spring may break and the sane man become, at any rate temporarily, a lunatic.

*　　*　　*　　*　　*

"I suppose officers never get *cafard*," I said.

"Huh! Why should they?" growled le Maquereau. "Haven't they everything that we lack? Wine, good food, rest, ease, leisure. . . ."

"Say a sense of responsibility that keeps them from worrying over trifles like . . ." began Terence Hogan.

"That's it," interrupted Abraham the Sailor. "It's like fleas."

"What on earth are you talking about?" I asked.

"Dogs," was the enlightening reply. ". . . and officers. Fleas keep a dog from brooding on being a dog. . . . And thinking about their responsibilities keeps officers from *cafard*, and so they never get it."

"They do get it though," asserted Père Cocteau.

"Never," interrupted Matthieu le Maquereau with a sneering laugh, "any more than they get empty bellies and dry throats, or lice or sore feet."

"They do get it," repeated Père Cocteau, ignoring le Maquereau, "and when they get it, things happen."

"Eh, Thirsty-face?" he added, turning to his *copain.*

"*Ah*," agreed Thirsty-face weightily.

"*Cafard?* An officer get *cafard?* Get drunk, more likely. When did an officer get *cafard?*" asked Matthieu.

"Did you never hear of Voulet?" replied Cocteau. "Surely even the sewer-rats of Paris, including yourself, heard of Voulet and Chanoine."

"That wasn't *cafard*. That was witchcraft," replied le Maquereau.

Old Thirsty-face laughed loudly.

"Witchcraft be damned. There's no such thing —not effective witchcraft, where white men are concerned," replied Cocteau.

"That was *cafard*, pure and simple," he continued. "Granted Tamarné was a witch to the extent that all fascinating women are witches, she didn't amount to anything much in the matter, and, but for *cafard*, she wouldn't have amounted to anything at all. . . .

"Besides, my good fool, suppose Tamarné did bewitch Voulet—in the sense of real black magic witchcraft—what about Chanoine, who never had anything to do with her at all? She didn't bewitch him too, did she? And if so, why didn't she bewitch J—— and Pallier and Henric, and make a proper job of it while she was about it?

"Witchcraft! You give me a pain in the stomach, species of talking camel. . . . It was a clear plain case of genuine officer-*cafard*."

"One observes that you know all about it— while the rest of the world merely thinks it does," sneered Matthieu.

"Of course I know all about it, my worthy camel. And perhaps you will close that irregular hole in your unfortunate face while you cock your deplorable ears and listen, when I tell you that my comrade Thirsty-face—whose little toe is worth more than the whole of your tribe—that he was none other than Chanoine's own Sergeant!"

The Frenchmen present stared open-mouthed, almost incredulous, at Old Thirsty-face. Obviously here was something interesting, something remarkable.

"Yes, I was Sergeant L—— of the Spahis in those days," smiled Old Thirsty-face, and saluted —saluted either the present company or the Sergeant L—— whom once he had been.

"Tell us," I begged.

"Cocteau will tell you," replied Thirsty-face, "and will share equally with me the litre of wine which you will provide."

It was evidently an old-standing and satisfactory arrangement.

"Cocteau tells the story better than I can," he continued, "and I can correct him if he makes a mistake in the facts."

And there I heard, in the presence of one of the actors in that amazing and almost incredible drama, what I have no doubt is the absolutely true tale of the *affaire* Voulet-Chanoine, an incident of French Colonial history which, but for its coinciding with the *affaire* Dreyfus, would have been as famous as that extraordinary case itself.

"It must be twenty years ago now," mused Père Cocteau, ". . . and Old Thirsty-face and I were the two youngest and smartest Sergeants in the French Army; Thirsty-face assisting in the pacification of Africa on the West, and I on the East.

"Yes, in 1900 or so, General Chanoine was Secretary of State for War, and Thirsty-face and I were Sergeants; he in the Spahis and I in the *Marsouins*, the Colonial Infantry. . . .

"Well, General Chanoine, besides being Minister for War, was also father of Captain Chanoine; and Captain Chanoine, let me tell you, was a young man with a very brilliant future behind him. Like all sons of prominent and successful generals and politicians, he was brave, skilful, reliable, and in every way a brilliant soldier. So was his great friend and brother-in-arms, Captain

Voulet.

"Being the son of the Minister for War, Cha-noine was not only brilliant but lucky. Oppor-tunities came his way. They do, somehow, come the way of the sons of distinguished generals and statesmen. Quite right, too. . . .

"They came his way, and he made the most of them. He and Voulet—with the help of Thirsty-face —conducted the Moussi campaign. They put up a very fine show, and were thanked and decorated.

"They had certainly made the most of their opportunities up to that time; and then they went and spoilt it all by making too much of the next one.

"That was the Lake Tchad affair.

"Papa Chanoine at the War Office thought it was time that his brilliant son had another chance to distinguish himself.

"So he put into the head of the President of the Republic, Monsieur Dupuy, the bright idea that a Mission should be sent, peacefully to penetrate the country from Lake Tchad to the Niger; to give a glimpse of the Blessings of Civilization to the poor ignorant natives; smell the flowers; pat the ani-mals; stick up a pole with a flag on top of it; and see whether there were any wicked English, or wickeder Germans, straying that way from Sokoto or Cameroun.

"Just a nice picnicking peaceful Mission, you understand, with four or five picked officers; two or three picked Sergeants; a score or so of Spahis for a bodyguard; a thousand or so porters to carry the food, water and what-nots; and a company of *Tirailleurs* to look after the porters, and argue with the Bedouin, the Touareg, and the Hoggar rob-bers. . . .

"And who so fitting to conduct this Mission as the brilliant son of the distinguished Minister of

War?

"So off went the Column, headed by Captain Chanoine and Captain Voulet, with Captain J——[55] and Médecin-Major Henric, and Lieutenant Pallier, with twenty Spahis riding behind them, and two picked French Sergeants . . ."

"Bouthier was the other," observed Old Thirsty-face.

". . . and two hundred and fifty *Tirailleurs* under native officers. And the only transport for these two hundred and eighty soldiers was a thousand porters; so, as you will perceive, progress was not rapid.

"Well, they jogged along when they felt like it, and they camped when they felt like it. And all sorts of Chiefs and Sheikhs and Kaids and Sultans and things came and had a good look at them, and brought them good presents, too—owing to the presence of the two hundred and fifty *Tirailleurs* and the troop of Spahis.

"And all sorts of common people came too; not only Bedouin and Touareg and Hoggar robbers and every kind of Arab, but a fine variety of assorted black people; Negroes whom the Arabs ruled and robbed and exploited."

"And that was where Tamarné came in," observed Old Thirsty-face. "She came to the camp one evening with her brothers; a Touareg girl from the Hoggar mountains; daughter of a very powerful and important Chief. Like a lovely bronze statue. Voulet always had an eye for a fine lass; and as for Tamarné, she fell in love with him on sight. . . . Love at first sight. . . .

"You know these Touareg girls are entirely different from the Arab lasses; just the opposite in fact, in some respects. There is no veil and *harim*

---

[55] Still alive. Now a distinguished General.—*Ed.*

469

nonsense about them. . . . On the contrary, they make the running.

"If a Touareg girl sees a youth whom she fancies, she makes no secret of the matter, and he knows it just about as soon as she does. If his tribe is encamped within a ride of hers, she thinks nothing of setting off on a racing camel at sunset and returning at sunrise, having spent the whole night in riding hard, save such time as she could spend with her lover. . . .

"As a matter of fact, it's the girl who proposes marriage, if, after thorough investigation of the young man's attractions, mental, moral, social and physical, she thinks a spot of matrimony is desirable.

"Yes, they're splendid girls those Touareg maidens, and every bit as good as the men, both in peace and war, for they fight like fiends. . . . Clever too. . . . Cleverer than the men. . . . They write poetry. God knows why—but they do.

"And Tamarné was as good as the best, full of ideas and ambition, as well as of courage and of love—for Voulet.

"That was all the witchcraft there was to it—passionate love and boundless ambition."

"This becomes quite an oration in effect," sneered Matthieu le Maquereau.

"Listen!" hissed Demenko the Cossack. "Interrupt again, and by the living God, I'll put my bayonet through your throat."

Le Maquereau spat, and half-drew his bayonet —but only half.

"That's all the 'witchcraft' there was to it," repeated Père Cocteau. "A splendid girl; a chief's daughter; who began by riding into the camp at night, and ended by staying there altogether.

"Witchcraft be damned. It was *cafard* and nothing else. Pure *cafard*, I say. . . . Voulet and

Chanoine had both been too long in the desert; what with the Moussi campaign and this Lake Tchad-Niger Expedition. . . . It began with Voulet, and he very soon infected his *copain*, Chanoine. Yes, it began with Voulet, and, to people who knew —people like Thirsty-face, *par exemple*—it was plain simple *cafard*."

"Simple *cafard*," agreed Old Thirsty-face, nodding his head sagaciously.

"What did he do?" asked Terence Hogan. "At the beginning, I mean."

"What were the first signs, *mon vieux*?" asked Cocteau of Old Thirsty-face.

"His head swelled," replied the old soldier. "His ideas got big. Captain Frog thought he was General Ox."

"He gave himself local rank of General, didn't he?" asked Cocteau.

"At first," was the reply. "And everybody had to call him 'General.' . . . Then he made Chanoine a Colonel; and of course, that started trouble of a mild kind. . . . Then he began behaving more and more queerly. He used to go and stand on a sand-dune with his hands behind his back, and 'brood.' Then he'd stick his right hand inside his tunic and strike an attitude. . . ."

"Like Napoleon," nodded Gustavus Adolphus.

"Like Napoleon in effect," agreed Thirsty-face. "And he got more and more like him, too. He would parade the *Tirailleurs* and walk up and down the ranks, now and again pinching the ear of a favourite N.C.O. Oh, it was *cafard* all-right, for he would do the maddest things. Little things; but such as only a madman would do. He'd sit down and write a long official letter to an officer in the next tent, and I would have to take it and wait for a written reply. And judging by the officer's face, J——, or Pallier, or Peteau, or Henric—the letter would be unintelligible. They were mightily puzzled, I can tell you, and upset and worried too.

"And whatever queer order he gave, they had to obey it, because up to this time he'd done nothing too impossible—given them no real grounds for taking so terrible a step as mutiny—but go on, Cocteau."

"And all this time, Chanoine supported him," resumed Père Cocteau. "And that, of course, made it all the harder for the others to do anything. They would have been in a nice position if Voulet had recovered from his *cafard*, and he and Chanoine had turned up at Dakar or Kayes or Dasso or somewhere, perfectly sane and sober, and said that the rest had refused to obey orders, mutinied and wrecked the Mission!

"It would have been ruin and imprisonment for them, if nothing worse; so they carried on. But, as Thirsty-face can tell you, they were in a terrible state of anxiety, as things went from bad to worse, and Voulet, with Chanoine abetting him, got more and more Napoleonic. He began to make speeches to the native N.C.O.'s and tell them that, provided they observed absolute obedience and perfect discipline, they would all before long be wealthy and powerful, each of them a great sheikh and ruling chief."

"Napoleonic Generals, in fact," observed 'Baron' Trenck.

"Exactly. And some of the native N.C.O.'s were mightily pleased, and some were mightily puzzled. . . . And one or two of the most puzzled ones told everything to their white Officers.

"Then, as so often happens in cases of *cafard*, Voulet suddenly blew up.

"One morning he paraded the force and announced that it was time for them to throw off their disguise as a pacific Mission. They were really a punitive expedition, he said, and their job was to strike terror into the hearts of all peoples dwelling between Lake Tchad and the Niger River. In fact, conquest was their business; conquest plain and brutal, naked and unashamed.

"He then called a council of officers, and, with all the skill and cunning of the mad, he sketched his plan of campaign, and described the strategy and tactics that he had devised for the war he was about to open.

"The officers were aghast. This was the very first that they'd heard of any 'conquest,' or punitive expedition. Who was to be punished? And for what? And if the authorities had had any intention or idea of fighting, why this pitiful handful of men? A mere half-troop of Spahis and a company of *Tirailleurs*—an Officer's Escort. . . .

"Anyhow—there he was, their superior officer and their leader, giving them their orders and instructions, with complete correctness and apparent sanity.

"And there was Chanoine, taking his place as Second-in-Command, supporting Voulet in every way, and behaving as though everything were quite in order, quite normal, and quite official.

"The officers felt that something was wrong—that everything was wrong—but that their hands were tied; tied by the bonds of discipline and loyalty; and by the fact that, if they took action, the native troops would probably refuse to obey; refuse to follow them, as against Voulet; and that the Mission, divided against itself, would perish of internecine strife, thirst, and the attacks of savages and robber tribes. . . .

"Then Voulet, ably seconded by Chanoine, began his war—and, after a sanguinary onslaught upon an unsuspecting tribe, announced that this was the first battle of a great campaign—a campaign that was not to extend French influence at all, but to carve out a great kingdom *for Emperor Voulet!*

"Yes—that was the form that Voulet's *cafard* took. . . . He was going to found a great Saharan Empire, and he was going to be Emperor Voulet I, sole, arbitrary, and untrammelled ruler of millions of square miles of country, and of its teeming millions of people.

"Chanoine was to be his principal vassal King, and everyone who threw in his lot with them was to be a great Ruler, with no one in the world to question his doings or interfere with him, except Voulet himself.

"This sounded very good to most of the native N.C.O.'s . . . and not so good to others—especially those who knew something of the might and majesty of France. They listened to all that Voulet had to say, and they talked all night among themselves and to their two hundred and fifty men—upon whom, after all, depended the success or failure of the Conquest of the Sahara.

"Yes, the native N.C.O.'s were puzzled and intrigued, I can tell you.

"But imagine the feelings of the white officers! Imagine their awful position. Before Voulet declared himself, it was mutiny, court-martial, and probably death, to have disobeyed him.

"To carry on, obeying Voulet's orders, after he had declared himself, was aiding and abetting him in what amounted to making war on France.

"And, mark you, even now that he had declared himself for what he was—a madman, a rebel and a traitor—although their course was clear, it wasn't so easy to follow. . . . It was one thing to decide upon the correct course for honourable French officers to pursue, but it was quite another thing to pursue it. Voulet held all the cards. So long as the native N.C.O.'s and troops obeyed him, he was exactly what he called himself, Emperor—of that part of Africa.

"If Voulet had chosen to order their arrest, they would have been arrested. Had he court-martialled them and ordered them to be shot, they would have been shot.

"And another thing.

"In the middle of the Sahara, you can't march off into the blue with a biscuit in your pocket and a quart of water in your *bidon*—and march a thousand miles or so. You want a caravan. *And* don't forget, even if they'd been able to bring water from the ground like Moses, and have rations brought to them by ravens like Elijah, even so, what about the Touareg? How far do you suppose those Assassins would have allowed a small party to march?

"They'd have hunted them to death in a week or less.

"No. Those officers were up a gum-tree if ever men were; and it looked as though they had the choice of sticking to Voulet and becoming outlaws, outcasts, and enemies of their country; of defying Voulet and being shot by him; or of marching off to certain death by thirst and Touareg bullets and knives.

"And all because *Monsieur le Capitaine* Voulet had got *cafard*, and had infected his old pal Chanoine with the same disease. For it is infectious, mind you. *Cafard's* as bad as panic. It spreads like wild-fire among those who are ripe for it— which Chanoine was.

"Just plain officer-*cafard* and no damn-nonsense about 'witchcraft.' Not but what Tamarné backed him up, and was more than useful. She was for it, naturally; and could quite see herself as Empress of the Sahara, the power behind the throne.

"And, of course, she was useful to Voulet beyond words. She knew all the ins and outs of the local politics, and could tell Voulet exactly who was who, and what was what. It goes without saying that her tribe stood in solid with Voulet's force, and brought all their pals along as well—and the first thing they did was to see that all their enemies got it in the neck, for a start. And what with Voulet's own disciplined force, and the enormous and ever-growing army of 'friendlies' or *partisans*, there was endless dirty work at every cross-roads they came to.

"Then Lieutenant Peteau decided that he'd chance what seemed to him the least of the three evils; and pushed off with one or two native N.C.O.'s who loved him. They persuaded a *peloton* of *Tirailleurs* to follow them, and, somehow or other, this little force, or a few of them, got to some *poste* or other and reported."

"They got to Kai," said Thirsty-face, "and reported to Colonel Klobbe."

"Yes," continued Cocteau, "and Colonel Klobbe, having sent in his report, got orders to follow up the Mission at once, take command, hold an inquiry, act accordingly, and carry on. . . .

"Off went poor old Klobbe, full of beans, very much obliged to Voulet for playing the goat and giving him this chance of distinguishing himself.

"Off he went, as I say, into the desert—and was never seen nor heard of again.

"Except by Voulet.

"As it happened, Colonel Klobbe, a couple of months after leaving Kai, ran straight into Voulet and his *Tirailleurs*, operating with a big force of 'friendlies' against some tribes who hadn't yet realized that he was Emperor Voulet of the Sahara and their Paramount Overlord. . . .

"You were there, *mon vieux*, and saw exactly what happened. Tell us."

Old Thirsty-face drew the back of his hand across his mouth, and nervously stroked his beard.

"It was the middle of July," he said, "and so hot that we breathed fire. . . . The rocks were hotter than the sun itself. . . . We were just breaking bivouac to return to the temporary Base Camp, where the other officers and the rest of the Force were, and suddenly the sentry reported that a small column was approaching.

"At first Voulet thought it was the rest of his own Force, and began to curse. Then, through his glasses, he saw that this was a different lot and, as they drew near, that they were headed by a French Colonel. . . . Then he knew that the new Emperor of the Sahara had got to reckon with France. He gave orders for his *Tirailleurs* to stand-to; and, as Colonel Klobbe rode within hail, Voulet bawled '*Halt!*'

"Old Klobbe stuck his fist on his hip, and rode straight on.

" '*Halt!*' cried Voulet again. '*Halt!* . . . or I'll fire.'

"Klobbe came straight on. He was a brave man, for he must have heard Voulet's order to the *Tirailleurs* to prepare for a volley.

" '*Halt!*' cried Voulet for the third time; and a few moments later he shouted '*Fire!*'

"The *Tirailleurs* fired a ragged volley, and I should think most of them aimed to miss; for even they must have been puzzled.

"Anyhow poor old Klobbe had time to clap his hand to his chest and shout '*Vive la France!*' before he toppled over, with five wounds. . . . I tell you I didn't like it and wished myself well out of it."

Thirsty-face removed his *képi* and gazed into its

interior.

"Poor old Klobbe," he murmured. "He smoked very nice Turkish cigarettes—and I had the burying of him."

"Well, the fat was in the fire all right then," said Cocteau.

"And the other officers felt that they'd better follow Peteau's example, and clear out. The senior of them, Captain J——, had, on the whole, been opposed to Peteau's going, feeling that they ought to stick with the Mission in the hope of eventually getting more and more of the men over to their side. . . ."

"What I don't understand," put in Terence Hogan, "is why they couldn't have staged a sort of *coup d'état*, put Voulet and Chanoine under arrest, and carried on."

"The reason why they didn't, and couldn't, do that," replied Cocteau, "was that the black troops and N.C.O.'s had been won over by Voulet at the very beginning—some dazzled and debauched by promises, others hood-winked and fooled, others charmed by the tune he played, and the rest too utterly densely stupid to think at all, or do anything but obey their own officers. . . . Also Tamarné talked to them. Every night. . . ."

"Well—but—what became of Klobbe's column?" persisted Terence Hogan.

"He only rode up with a small native escort," answered Thirsty-face. "They were buried near Klobbe. Chanoine himself went over and brought Klobbe's caravan to our Base Camp."

"And what did the other officers do now?" asked Terence Hogan. "Klobbe's death must have brought things to a head."

"You are right, *mon ami*. Things were different now, and so Voulet found. Returning to the Base Camp that night, he called a Council of all the officers and non-commissioned officers in the whole force, and made a fine speech. What did he say, Thirsty-face?"

" 'I have burnt my boats,' " replied the old soldier, speaking as though he were reciting an oft-told tale which he knew by heart.

" 'I have burnt my boats,' he said. 'There is, now, no going back for any of us. Here, to-day, the blood of the emissary of France has set the seal upon the charter of my new Empire of the Sahara. For those who follow me and obey me, I guarantee wealth, power, glory and fame. For those who refuse and disobey my commands—death. . . .

" 'Within a few months, nay, weeks, I shall be master of a far, far greater country than France; sole Lord and Paramount Chief of a country bigger than Europe. . . . France will be glad to treat with me; proud to enter into alliance with me; Emperor Voulet I of the Saharan Empire. . . .'

"And a lot more hot air like that, ending up with the unpleasant words, 'At sunset to-night, each of you shall declare himself—whether he be for me or against me. *But*—he who is not for me is against me; and he who is against me shall die.' "

"And that put the officers in a nice hole," Cocteau took up the story. "It was bad enough for our comrade here; but it was ten times worse for them. A Sergeant can always slip back to the ranks—ahem!—if he feels like it; or his superiors feel like it for him. But there's no slipping back for an Officer. . . .

"Well—Captain J—— was equal to the occasion.

"He made a speech too, pointing out that this was a very big step for him and his colleagues to take; and that Emperor Voulet ought to give them at least until sunrise on the next day to think matters over; make up their minds; and give him their decision. . . .

"Of course, he wanted the night to himself, and the hours of darkness in which to act.

"Voulet agreed, and the moment he went into his tent, Captain J—— and the others got to work, and soon found that two of the senior N.C.O.'s were really loyal at heart and were prepared to follow him and the other officers, if they broke away from Voulet. Each of these Sergeants could bring an *escouade* of men, all more or less related to himself, who would do precisely what their N.C.O.'s told them.

"Anyhow that gave Captain J—— and the others about thirty-five good reliable men; and, in the middle of the night, they crept from the camp, fell in, and marched off—leaving Voulet and Chanoine to get on with their Empire-building."

"What became of them?" I asked curiously.

"What, Captain J—— and the others? They reached Dakar eventually, and told the tale," replied Thirsty-face.

"Next morning," continued Père Cocteau, "when he learned what had happened in the night, Voulet made another fine speech, pretending that what had happened was a jolly good job. He said it was a proper purge, and he was now rid of all cowards and weaklings and those who had neither the sense nor the guts to be loyal to Emperor Voulet I.

"Every one of the N.C.O.'s who had remained behind was soon to be a General or a Prince, or both. . . . Yes, every Sergeant Koko and Corporal Kiki was to be a Prince of the Holy Saharan Empire. It was a very fine speech and a most enthusiastic meeting.

"And as soon as it was over, the N.C.O.'s held another meeting—a little less enthusiastic this time. What began to worry them was the fact that their two senior Sergeant-majors had gone off with all the white officers, except Voulet and Chanoine; and there, *mes amis*, was where our brave Old Thirsty-face came in.

"He had not marched off with Captain J——'s party, for he had seen where he could be even more useful, and do even more good, than by setting the example of leaving the *cafard*-stricken Voulet. . . .

"Also, he hoped against hope that Voulet's *cafard* might leave him.

"Anyhow, our friend busied himself among those *Tirailleurs*, and talked common sense to such of them as would listen. With a hint here and a laugh there, he managed to throw a lot of cold water on the scheme, and struck a fine note by asking when they thought they'd see their homes and wives and families—away in French territory —again.

"And it wasn't very long before there were two parties at that very meeting, one of which was definitely beginning to take the sensible view, and see the hopeless idiocy of the idea of starting an Empire on two hundred men, a few rounds of ammunition, and the help of some robber tribes.

"Mind you, Thirsty-face couldn't get up and make a speech. He didn't want a bullet through his head. And he couldn't openly show himself as working against his Commanding Officer—the first rebel in the new Empire.

"No. He just asked questions of the *Tirailleur* N.C.O.'s and men.

"And each question seemed to have a very nasty answer. And they grew more and more thoughtful about it. So much so that, that night, about a half of the remaining N.C.O.'s got their men together and marched off in the direction of

Zinder. One of the sentries who saw them go, thought the matter over for a few hours and, when he was relieved, reported what he'd seen.

"When the news reached Voulet, he went a little madder, and promptly sent Captain Chanoine off in pursuit, with most of the remaining troops.

"Chanoine, by a forced march, came up with the retreating force next day, and the senior N.C.O. served Chanoine just as Voulet had served Colonel Klobbe. He brought his men into action, opened fire, and Chanoine was shot down. The N.C.O. then called on Chanoine's men to lay down their arms—which they did; and, after a speech from him, joined up with his party.

"Meanwhile, Voulet, imagining that Chanoine would soon be back with the 'party of rebels,' conceived the bright idea of pursuing Captain J——'s party on the road to Dakar.

"And off he went, with the remainder of the *Tirailleurs.*

"He had no difficulty, of course, in the matter of 'intelligence,' as all the tribes around were taking the deepest interest in the affair—and by nightfall he was led straight to the spot where Captain J—— and his force were encamped.

"And then happened the event which, I maintain, absolutely proved that what Voulet was suffering from was *cafard.* . . .

"And no damned 'witchcraft' nonsense about it," added Cocteau, eyeing Matthieu le Maquereau with severity.

"Halting his men he walked toward the nearest camp-fire.

"A sentry challenged him.

" *'Halte! Qui va là?'*

"And by way of reply Voulet actually drew his revolver and fired at the man.

"What's that but plain madness. An officer—

correctly challenged by what was, after all, one of his own men—shooting at him for doing his duty.

"What with the darkness and the position of the sentry, who was standing partly behind a bush, Voulet missed, and the sentry, very properly, after such an answer to his challenge, threw up his rifle and fired.

"Voulet fell dead.

"And if that wasn't an instance of officer-*cafard*, I should like to know what it was.

"When a soldier gets *cafard*, he only kills himself or, at worst, himself and his enemy.

"But when an officer gets it, things happen.

"In this case, Voulet's *cafard* caused the death of at least three officers, scores of soldiers, and hundreds, if not thousands of Hoggar Arabs, Touareg, and harmless black tribesmen.

"And, worst of all, it lost our friend here his stripes—and, from being the rising young Sergeant L——, he became Old Thirsty-face, the deplorable wreck who now disgraces our *escouade*."

"I thought he was the Virtuous Apprentice, the White-haired Boy, who did his duty and saved the situation," objected Terence Hogan.

"You're right, Comrade. I saved the honour of France, and ended the Voulet-Chanoine Insurrection, or Empire, or whatever it was. . . . So they arrested me for being behind Voulet when he fell in the act of making war upon the troops of *Madame la République!*"

"Well, didn't the native N.C.O.'s give evidence that you'd used your influence on the right side; even if you had stayed by Voulet and the rebels?" pursued Hogan.

"I don't know that they were invited to express any opinion in the matter," said Thirsty-face. "*Que voulez-vous? C'est l'armée.* When Voulet fell, we who were with him were told to lay down our arms and surrender, or we'd all be shot down. . . .

"Yes, all the thanks I got for saving France was punishment, and I was so annoyed about it that I went for a walk."

"Deserted?" I asked.

"Well—no. No more than Cocteau the Cannibal did, when he went investigating the conditions of the slave-trade. . . . I just went exploring on my own account; and when I reached Kai, to present my report and account of my investigations, discoveries and opinions, they gave me sixty days' cells for being 'absent without leave.' "

"Absent how long?" asked Hermann.

"Oh, a few months, more or less. . . . So I joined the Legion. . . . And serve them right," concluded Thirsty-face.

"Serve who right—the Legion or the authorities?" asked Matthieu.

"Both," said Cocteau.

"What a tragedy," I mused.

"*L'affaire* Thirsty-face; or *l'affaire* Voulet?" inquired Terence.

"Which do you think?" I replied. . . . "Voulet."

"*Que Voulet-vous*—in fact," murmured Terence Hogan shamelessly, and broke the spell.

CHAPTER XIII

Just in time, orders came for action; and men who had been very nearly mad with the monotony, hardship, and general misery, now went mad with joy. Like boys from school, or even more like prisoners from gaol, we marched out and played our part in quite a battle, a general attack on a place called El K——. This place had been very unsuccessfully attacked before, the Arabs being in an extremely strong and inaccessible position, and fighting with desperate courage.

The new attack was successful, but at very considerable cost, nineteen officers being killed. I witnessed the death of one of them myself, a brave and handsome young man, an artillery officer, I think.

We had been advancing in open order, and had been ordered to halt and line the bank of a shallow water-course that crossed our direction. Apparently there was some misunderstanding as to direction, and, suddenly, an armoured-car came lurching and bumping along the very rough track by which we had advanced.

Suddenly it stopped quite near us, and this young officer jumped out and, regardless of the fact that he and his car at once became a target for Arab sharp-shooters, he stood alternately consulting a map and gazing to our left front through his glasses. Evidently he had seen what he was seeking; for, suddenly, he turned and called to Sergeant Pflügge, who had gone along to the flank of the Section to be near him if wanted.

. . .

"Where's your Officer?"

They were the last words he ever spoke.

A bullet struck him almost as he uttered them and he fell on his face. Coughing blood and unable to speak, he raised himself on one hand and, with the other, pointed half-left, looked at Pflügge and made an urgent sign for him to advance.

That was enough for Sergeant Pflügge who, if he were a beast, was as brave as any beast that ever fought.

"Come on, *salauds*," he roared. "Another rush. *En avant*," and, springing to his feet, dashed forward, half-left, until we reached another dry water-course, where he signalled to us to halt and take cover again.

As we lay here, keeping up independent fire whenever we could see, or thought we could see, an object to aim at, Captain Z—— came along, and I heard him say in an angry tone to Pflügge:

"What the devil do you think you're doing? Who the devil do you think you are? Who the devil told *you* to give the order to advance?"

"Officer from armoured-car, sir," replied Pflügge. "He said:

" 'Tell your officer, the orders are to advance immediately half-left.'

"Then he said:

" 'No, stop. Go forward yourself at once, with as many men as you can get.' And as I obeyed his orders, he fell. . . ."

A good lie—well told.

We heard cheering on our right, and saw another Company rushing forward into line with us. The firing grew heavier, and the Arabs on the hill-side below El K—— actually began to advance to attack their attackers.

Soon one could see them plainly enough, as they dashed from rock to rock, looking like an army of suddenly-awakened men in dirty grey dressing-gowns and bedroom slippers.

Again the firing increased, as another Company came up on our left, and our line was steadily lengthened, strengthened, and reinforced.

I found that my excitement was changing and improving, if not decreasing. I was thrilled and undoubtedly still excited. The thrills, though not wholly pleasurable, were certainly not painful.

Looking round as I loaded my rifle, I saw Terence firing methodically and steadily, sitting comfortably with crossed legs, elbows on knees; Digger, lying flat, was snap-shooting and, I should think, getting results, for he was a wonderful shot; Abraham the Sailor, methodically chewing something, appeared to be waiting, as he leant against a rock, for something worth shooting at. . . .

Then suddenly I saw an amazing thing, a battalion, or mob, of *Partisans*—Arab "friendlies" bribed, armed, and organized by the French— advanced from the rear and passed through our line in the direction of the enemy. There was a lull in the firing as they passed through us, not only on our part, for obvious reasons, but on the part of the enemy. . . . I should rather have expected them to have redoubled their fire upon these people, whom surely they must regard as treacherous renegades. . . .

Having advanced one or two hundred metres, the *Partisans* suddenly halted, wheeled about, and, before we realized what was happening, poured in a heavy and accurate fire upon us, their "allies"—and then swiftly melted away, vanished from sight, behind rocks, boulders and bushes.

But this abominable, though courageous, act of treachery probably did the Arabs more harm than good, and may have contributed largely to the French victory of El K——. Disgusted and enraged, the whole line, apparently by common consent, rose and dashed forward, fixing bayonets as they ran, without waiting for the order *"Baïonnettes au canon!"*

Like all Arabs, dreading the bayonet far more than the bullet, the *Partisans* rose and fled, very many being shot and some bayoneted as they did so.

In their headlong retreat, pursued by *légionnaires*, they carried the other Arabs back with them. It became a "soldiers' battle." The Arabs were kept on the run and, by sunset, were in full flight. The position and the village of El K—— were taken. Our job was done and all objectives gained.

For myself, I cannot claim that I had taken part in a bayonet-charge nor, I am thankful to say, been under the hideous necessity of using my bayonet. As a matter of fact, there was no real bayonet-charge, and the cold steel was used but little—only here and there, where some desperately courageous tribesman stood his ground, firing from behind his rock until he was rushed. It was really a very rapid advance and equally quick retreat, rather than a charge, at the best.

Personally, I jogged along, dropping down and firing, from time to time; and, if I did not actually keep behind Terence Hogan, Digger and Abraham the Sailor, I took most particular care not to get in front of them.

Anybody else, who wanted glory or the thrill of a hand-to-hand combat with a stalwart tribesman, active as a cat and brave as a lion, was very welcome to it.

For myself, I was only too thankful to find that I was no more out of breath than other people; and that I could put up a sufficiently good show, in the eyes of my comrades. Not mine to attract attention by my valour, but thankfully to escape it by my prudence.

When the last Arab had disappeared and the last shot been fired, we set about, hungry and weary as we were, to make camp.

I was glad to learn, when we at length sat down to eat, that our Company had got off lightly, though some of the others had suffered quite severely.

"All very well," observed Père Cocteau, "but I hear we have lost nine mules. . . . That, let me tell you, is the equivalent of fifty-four *légionnaires*."

"How do you mean?" I asked. "Brain-power?"

"No, young man. Let me tell you that a *légionnaire* is estimated by the French Government as worth five hundred francs. . . . Some are, no doubt. . . . But a good mule actually costs three thousand francs in Morocco. So, if you get a pencil and work it out, you'll find that a mule is worth six *légionnaires*. . . . Some are, no doubt. . . . Anyhow, it's a lot easier to get six more *légionnaires* than to get one more mule. That is why, as a patriot, I am disturbed at the news of this heavy butcher's bill among mules."

It was at this camp that I was discharged with ignominy from my post as assistant-cook, an ex-baker named Horst having been discovered and installed.

We spent about three weeks in fortifying El K——; and, for over a couple of years, the wretched place was in a state of semi-siege, with constant casualties.

However, all was peaceful for the moment; and the whole Brigade or *groupe mobile*, went into camp on a plateau, close by, to rest and re-fit, and to observe the great fête of the Anniversary of the French Republic.

Wherever they may be, on this date, all French

soldiers take holiday, and make merry. Even Colonial coloured troops and foreigners who wear the French uniform are encouraged to celebrate on this day.

The Legion needs little encouragement, and, I must say, the military authorities are amazingly lenient, and, on this occasion, look with a blind eye upon some fairly outrageous breaches of discipline. For once in the year, an N.C.O. is wiser to exercise tact instead of strictness, and to consider, within limits, discretion the better part of discipline.

*　　*　　*　　*　　*

In view of the fact that in the French Army so very little is done for the amusement of the troops, the Authorities can well afford to have two or three such holidays in the year. The only pity is that the swing of the pendulum is so sudden and violent that it swings too far; and, by commencing at rosy dawn and continuing to dewy eve, the pampered *légionnaire* usually has, ere night-fall, forgotten not only his troubles, but his manners and everything else.

On this, our second experience of a fête-day in the Legion, *Madame la République* did us not only well, but over-well. In spite of the fact that we were on active service, more or less surrounded by a daring and desperate foe, and Heaven knows how many miles from our base in enemy-country, we ate, drank and made merry, feasted, sang, danced and sported; revelled and rioted to our hearts' content and our stomachs' dolour.

The day began amazingly, when, at six o'clock réveillé, we were given, not the usual black *jus*, but real *café au lait* . . . ambrosia . . . coffee with hot milk and sugar. Not only this, but cakes . . .

perfectly good cakes of the rock variety, but with nothing rock-like about them from the famished *légionnaires'* point of view.

Having sat around at our ease, like the gentlemen of leisure that, positively for this day only, we were, we received, at nine-thirty, a noble *petit déjeuner* in the shape of a quarter-litre of white wine, three sardines, and half a loaf of bread.

There may, of course, be found, here and there, people who do not hanker for white wine, sardines, and bread at nine-thirty in the morning; people who would despise these viands; people, even, who would reject them. But if such exist, they are not under-fed *légionnaires* on active service.

At eleven o'clock we received our usual ration of *soupe* and bread, and I personally saw no-one do other than welcome it.

At one o'clock came the *pièce de résistance* of the feasting—a five-course banquet that was a real credit to the commissariat department, with half a litre of red wine, followed by *café noir*.

This was all most delightful, and my lower nature, bless it, rose up and revelled, and enjoyed itself most thoroughly. So did those of my comrades—for a time.

But only for a time.

For, sad to say, as the afternoon wore on, gaiety flagged somewhat; and it became quite apparent that this high living and plain thinking was too much and too sudden for half-starved and long under-nourished men accustomed to a *menu* as lacking in variety as it was in bulk.

However, as Père Cocteau pointed out, sorrows exist but to be drowned; and black care exists only to be painted red. Moreover, as our feast-day also happened to be a pay-day, the wherewithal for the drowning was available; and, in addition to the free issue of wine, each man was able to buy a couple of litres at the field canteen. As this amount is equal to three and a half pints, it is not surprising that, by the end of the afternoon, all of us were merry and few of us were bright.

At six o'clock a small incident marred the end of this perfect day, when Sergeant Pflügge ordered Hans Petsel to go on sentry-duty.

Petsel, pot-valiant and full of wine and foolishness, not only refused but discovered an unsuspected vein of ribaldry and back-chat.

In German, he told Sergeant Pflügge not only what he thought of him, but what the whole Company thought of him, and, after hurling at him a well-chosen selection of epithets, hurled his quart mug as well.

With a bound like that of a tiger, Sergeant Pflügge was on him, and, with a smashing blow, knocked the young fool head over heels.

"Hi! Damn your eyes! Stop that!" shouted Terence Hogan, springing to his feet as Pflügge commenced to kick the prostrate lad.

Promptly I flung my thirteen stone upon Hogan, tripped him up, hung about his neck, and generally grappled with him, while endeavouring convincingly to ask him whether he really wanted two years' hard labour for interfering with an N.C.O. in the execution of his duty.

"Duty?" bawled Hogan. "It isn't the foul swine's duty to . . ."

"Shut up, you blasted fool," I shouted at him, and tried to shove my *képi* into his mouth while I yelled to Digger and Abraham the Sailor to come and sit on his head.

Père Cocteau, drunker than any of them, obligingly lay down across Terence Hogan's legs, and warned him that he, Cocteau, would be very ill if shaken.

Abraham and Digger, in reasonable possession of their faculties, saw to it that Hogan should have other matters to occupy his attention until Pflügge had finished with Petsel, and had had him flung, insensible, into a tent. . . .

Terence was not drunk on three or four bottles of assorted wine, but was distinctly quarrelsome and in a dangerous mood.

One of his many virtues is a burning hatred of cruelty, injustice and oppression; and at that moment he would have thrashed Pflügge within an inch of his life, regardless of the fact that it might have been beyond the inch of his own, and would certainly have been within measurable distance of Hell—in a Penal Battalion—after a couple of years in prison with hard labour.

"He'd no right to hit him on the fête-day," he kept grumbling.

"He didn't, Bo! He hit him on the jaw-bone," guffawed Abraham the Sailor.

"I say Pflügge had no right to hit him with his fist—on a holiday," repeated Terence Hogan.

"Well, Petsel had no right to hit him with a quart pot on a holiday," I pointed out.

"True, *mon enfant*. It isn't so much of a holiday as all that," agreed Père Cocteau with sweet reasonableness.

"He hammered the poor little beggar senseless," growled Hogan. "Let me get up."

"Well, what of it?" expostulated Abraham. "He had his whang at the Sergeant, didn't he? Isn't that well worth being beaten-up for? He can always say, 'See that guy Pflügge over there? Well, I bunged a quart pot in his eye.' "

" 'Not Heaven itself can take away the wallop I gave yesterday,' " I misquoted, and Terence had to grin.

"Another little drink won't do us any harm," he

said.

"I'll have Petsel's," he added, "as I did try to stand up for him."

Harmony was restored, but not for long, and the next trouble was really serious.

Having been eating and drinking almost continuously all day long, we now received the usual evening *soupe* meal, and another free wine issue; and, after this, some merry fool suggested going over to a big canteen, near the Sixty— —the *Tirailleurs'* camp—on the strength of some foolish legend that something was procurable there that was not available in our own canteen. What it could be, Heaven knew, unless it were some different form of trouble.

Just as I was trying my noblest to exercise the restraining and peculiarly irritating influence of the sober upon the drunk, another fool arrived with the news that there were ladies on view in that identical canteen. Truly it would appear that things were procurable there that were not available in our own canteen.

A different form of trouble indeed. . . .

With one accord my foolish comrades rose to their feet and trooped forth, with whoops, cat-calls, ribald jests and Homeric laughter, in the direction of the *Tirailleurs'* camp, our numbers being constantly augmented as we rioted along.

It was true.

Actually, in this canteen, there was a number of Arab women and several Spanish and non-descript half-caste girls of the camp-follower type —the sort of people who suddenly appear out of the blue, at the gates of desert outposts, and announce that they have come to call.

In this case *les légionnaires* had come to call, and were by no means hospitably welcomed by the

Tirailleurs, if they were by the ladies.

Before long, as was inevitable, somebody hit somebody.

Someone else hit the hitter, and the first phase of a camp free-fight opened. A dozen individual fist-fights were ended and swept away by surging mob-rushes from side to side.

"*Attaboy!*" yelled Abraham the Sailor, leaping joyously upon a huge *Tirailleur.*

"Yoicks. Tally-ho!" bawled Terence Hogan, dashing into the fray; while Digger took a run, a jump on to a table, and literally a dive, that hurled him into a struggling surging mass of seething fighting humanity.

I grabbed a bottle by the neck and, with an eye on Hogan, kept as near the fray as I thought safe.

The first phase of camp rough-housing is all very well, and leads to nothing more than harmless if painful cuts, bruises and contusions.

But on a sacred and holy fête-day, with everybody drunk, a row is pretty sure to reach the second phase, and is likely enough to continue into the third.

Suddenly some fool or drunken maniac drew a knife and stabbed. Another, a pistol, and fired— and the second phase was on.

It was now a real fight, with weapons . . . a fight that would lead to broken heads and limbs, severe and dangerous wounds, considerable bloodshed and a number of deaths.

The girls fled shrieking, and canteen orderlies did their best to defend, pack, and remove their goods, as the maddened drunken soldiery used bottles as clubs and missiles; knocked the bottoms off bottles and used them as daggers; tore up benches and used them as clubs; while those who had knives and pistols used them without thought or mercy.

The rough-house had become a desperate and bloody battle, and with cries of *"La Légion! La Légion!"*, *"A moi, la Légion!"*, *"Vive la Légion!"*, *légionnaires* followed their usual tactics—got together in a compact body and fought as though they were on a veritable battlefield, and the *Tirailleurs* were the Arab foe.

An armed guard from the Legion arrived at the double and turned the tide of battle in favour of their comrades, while the Sergeant of the Guard bawled to the fighting *légionnaires* to break off and make a bolt for their camp.

More *Tirailleurs* came running to the assistance of their comrades, scores and scores of them, and the fight increased and spread.

Suddenly a bugle blew. There was a cry of *"Machine-guns!"* . . . a burst of fire—in the air above the heads of the rioters, and the third phase was on.

The French use no kid-glove methods on occasions like these. Everybody knew that the next burst of fire—and that in short order—would be turned on the rioters who, after the warning bugle and burst of fire, would be treated as mutineers.

"Come on, Terry," I yelled. "Come on, Digger," and again set a good example of prompt and headlong flight, dragging Terence and Digger with me.

"Right here is where we get off, I guess," panted Abraham the Sailor, and we turned and fled, followed by the rest of our comrades.

The *Tirailleurs* melted away into the darkness, the guards and machine-gunners marched off, and that was that.

"Yes," said I to Père Cocteau, as we licked our wounds, "all very fine. But suppose the Arabs had chosen to-day for a serious attack in force?"

"Pooh, my little one," replied the old soldier, "*Monsieur Budoo l'Arbi* is a brave-enough lad, I grant you; but he knows better than to interfere with *La Légion* on a fête-day. . . . Why, if he'd dared to attack to-day, *les légionnaires* would have been so annoyed they'd have got up and hunted him out of it with their belts. They'd have chased him half-way home, kicking his backside as he ran. . . . Attack on a fête-day, indeed! . . ."

And so ended that particular fête-day.

And at a minute past midnight, the Day being well and truly over, an order came, from the G.O.C. himself, that we should instantly get up and pack; march away a couple of miles; and make another camp—which would take us more than half the night to do.

Thus would the wicked *Légionnaire* learn not to fight in camp with the innocent *Tirailleur*.

CHAPTER XIV

But the lesson was not finished.

Scarcely was camp made, tents pitched, perimeter line made defensible, and ourselves ready to drop with fatigue, and only awaiting permission to do so, when orders were received to abandon camp and parade for a march and attack.

Few had the heart and strength even to curse. But under the lash of the Sergeants' tongues and the drive of their energy and power, the bustle recommenced. Tents were pulled down, blankets rolled, kit packed; and at four in the morning we fell in, about as sore-headed, sad-stomached, heavy-livered a band of wretched halfpenny heroes as ever paraded for a night march.

Presumably, some great brain—thinking in Battalions and Brigades, poring over a map and listening to the sifted wisdom of his Intelligence Department—had some good reason for starting us forth empty-bellied, heavy-headed, and sleepless. But to us, thinking only in individuals and squads, and quite devoid of intelligence, the reason seemed far to seek, and not good when found. Doubtless it was connected with the fact that our Battalion was again detailed as Advance Guard, and had to be on the march, and in position, while the rest of the Brigade slept off the effects of the fête-day.

Incidentally, this post-of-honour Advance Guard business is all very well on paper, and in high-falutin' speeches, and for the Colonel and Officers . . . and we always pretended it was very nice and delightful too. But personally I haven't the very slightest doubt that when the honour was announced at three in the morning, the only genuine and solid joy was felt by the Colonel and one or two senior officers who hoped to be Colonels.

We vile *légionnaires* positively preferred another three hours' sleep, daylight-marching, and fewer casualties, by far.

Alas! Had we been offered the post of rearguard and reserve, with comparative peace, retrenchment and reform, prosperity, and safety, we would have accepted it with alacrity and three loud cheers.

Nevertheless, when appointed Advance Guard, *les légionnaires* curse like troopers, grumble like soldiers, march like cavalry, and fight like tigers.

In an amazingly short time after the receipt of orders, we moved off, in absolute darkness, along no sort of road or even track or path, down a rocky hill-side and across a boulder-strewn plain, the going being most difficult and dangerous and —in spite of care and precaution—extremely noisy.

I stumbled along—in theory, between Digger and Abraham the Sailor with Terence Hogan just in front—but, in practice, we were a broken-ranked rabble rather than a Battalion marching in column.

When I was just thinking that I had about touched Misery's lowest level, and had never before felt so profoundly wretched and disgruntled with fatigue, sleeplessness, hunger, thirst and cold, it was suddenly borne in upon me that I was wrong. There was yet a deeper depth and, to the sounds of loud splashing in front of me, I tottered down its shingly slope—into beastly cold water which came nearly up to my waist. I gasped with the cold.

I could have wept.

I could have thrown myself down and drowned.

. . . How beautiful just to lie down and drown and end my troubles. . . . And as the thought occurred to me, I realized with the utmost horror that, if I slipped and fell, I *should* drown, weighed down with my heavy kit.

Heavens, how carefully I watched my step, and prayed that no clumsy lout might barge into me and upset my balance.

The water shallowed, and fell to below my knees, and, with the thought that I was safe, came the remembrance that I had not filled my *bidon* before marching out. Two quarts of water add a dreadful extra weight, and the temptation to march without it and, if water be short, to trust in Heaven, chance, and one's comrades, is a terribly strong one.

It occurred to me that I'd better take this opportunity and fill my *bidon* now, as it was quite likely that, doing Advance Guard, we might be stuck up on some peak or plateau all day in the sun. Under those conditions it is unfair, even if it be possible, to cadge water from a comrade who needs it himself, and has taken the trouble to carry it.

Suddenly I was grabbed and almost knocked down, as the voice of Sergeant Pflügge roared,

"Get on there, *salaud*. What the devil are you stopping for? Filling your water-bottle! I'll teach you to leave camp with an empty water-bottle and try to stop on the march. I'll get you thirty days' field-punishment, you . . . Who are you? You . . ."

Modestly concealing my identity, I splashed forward like a demented hippopotamus, and again mingled with my comrades. Had I been caught and punished it would have served me right, for I had deliberately committed a military crime, or else been guilty of great and inexcusable careless-ness, in leaving camp with an empty water-bottle.

In the desert or the mountains, water is apt to be a *légionnaire's* greatest and truest treasure, with a price, if not beyond rubies, at any rate beyond five francs a drink, which I have known a man unsuccessfully offer.

The standing order was that every man should carry enough for his own drinking and cooking purposes—at least two litres—and if in a waterless bivouac he could not contribute his litre to the cooking-pot, he couldn't expect to share the evening meal.

Later, that day, I was so thankful for the water I had obtained before Pflügge caught me, that I was never guilty of that particular folly again.

On we went, with the additional joy of soaked clothing and sodden boots, making our way as best we could, with frequent halts for the closing up of the straggling column, which at times must have been strung out over a mile.

By-and-bye, one last burden was laid upon us, for we began to climb, and soon found that we were slowly and painfully making our way up a very steep mountain-side. As day began to dawn, and the light strengthened, we were urged and driven the more, it being highly desirable, if not absolutely necessary, that we should be at the top of this mountain, and in position, before broad daylight discovered us to the enemy.

At length, distressed and panting, we reached the top, a wide plateau which we had to cross. Even here our progress was slow and difficult, so broken was the ground, rock-strewn, and intersected by deep *wadis*.

"How're you making it, kid?" asked Abraham the Sailor, as we halted, and I bumped into him.

"I'm dead," said I. "Ought to have been buried hours ago."

"Stick it, son," said Digger. "It's only a few

years now before we get our discharge."

Terence Hogan gave his short side-way nod of the head, which was his expression of approval, and which never failed to hearten me and give me pleasure. . . .

As soon as we were all up, the column was formed into line, and we advanced in open order to the far side of the plateau, where, on the signal to halt, we not only obeyed with soldierly promptitude, but, almost as one man fell to the ground, and lay with out-flung limbs, resting our weary bodies against the packs strapped to our backs.

Personally, I had closed my eyes and instantly fallen asleep, when I was almost immediately awakened by a tremendous hullaballoo. Shots were fired, whistles blown, orders bawled, and with tremendous shouts of,

"*Aux armes! Aux armes!*" "*Baïonnettes au canon!*" "*Charge!*" officers and N.C.O.'s dashed forward down the slope.

The Arabs were on us.

Feeling that I could not possibly move, and that nothing and nobody could get me up, I rolled over, got on to my hands and knees, and staggered to my feet. Everyone else was doing, or had done, the same, and a moment later, in a heavy lumbering tottering stumble, we charged down the hill-side.

We ran because, at that angle, running was easier than walking. On the level we should have walked, and uphill we should have crawled, if we could have progressed at all.

Beside me, Père Cocteau, charging, found breath repeatedly to bawl strange words in Arabic.

"Pig's fat!" he yelled. "Pig's fat! I have pig's fat on my bayonet."

A splendid idea! I would certainly explain to any Arab, who tarried long enough to give me the opportunity, that I too had pig's fat on my bayonet. The fattiest fat from the piggiest pig in Africa. . . .

Whether by reason of their Mussulman horror of pork in all its manifestations; their comprehensible terror of our horrible faces; or their well-founded dislike of the long lean French bayonet, the Arabs fled, almost without firing a shot, and certainly without striking a blow.

And, within half an hour, we were back on the edge of the plateau whence we had charged.

Speaking for myself, I received the order which was then issued—to strengthen the position by digging in, or piling stones—in the spirit of:

"*Certainly!* . . . If I am more use to you dead than alive, kill me by all means. Who am I that I should ever require rest? Who am I that I should be treated like a human being? . . . Oh, *certainly* . . ."

I remember scratching a shallow hole, placing two or three biggish stones in front of it, and then lying down, just to see if it were high enough to pass as cover within the meaning of the Act when Pflügge or an officer should come along. . . .

The next thing I knew was the receiving of a kick from someone and scrambling to my feet.

Captain Z—— passed and nodded approval of my contribution to the "strengthening of the position."

This surprised me, until a glance showed that my hole was a foot deeper and my wall a foot higher and thicker than when I had lain down. I had slept for two hours and someone had laboured while I slumbered.

"Thanks, Terry," said I, as we sat down again.

"Whaffor?" grunted Terence, settling himself to sleep.

"Building me a cubby-hole," said I, with allusion to the days when he was sole architect and builder of my cubby-holes, wigwams, camps, and robber-caves, in the wood behind our house.

"Abraham," he grunted.

"Thanks, Abraham," I called. "God bless our home."

"Digger," growled Abraham.

"Thanks, Digger," I amended.

"Hogan," replied Digger.

"Gang of liars!" I remarked.

And we slept.

*   *   *   *   *

But not for long.

Firing broke out suddenly on both flanks and, in a moment, we were alert and ready, rifle in hand, awaiting the attack which appeared to be developing.

Our position was not a particularly good one because, although we lined the edge of a plateau from which the ground fell fairly steeply away, this ground, up to within anything from twenty to fifty yards of our line, was fairly thickly covered with bushes and small trees of the white oak species—a form of Moroccan flora that the *légionnaire* knows too well, as he often gets a meal of its acorns fried in fat, accompanied by coffee made from the same dainty, baked hard and ground into a powder. . . .

Down into these bushes I stared, the nearest being some thirty yards away and, suddenly, I had an adventure that happened too suddenly for me to be frightened—or else I was too frightened for the adventure to give me any sort of a shock.

As I say, I was staring hard, and thinking of other things—a beautiful meal, with Terence Hogan, at my beloved restaurant in Paris—when suddenly, or not suddenly, the bush at which I was staring slowly parted, opened, and a face appeared. Partly owing, I suppose, to sleepiness and the light-headedness which comes with hunger and fatigue, I merely stared at this face vacantly, one eye, as it were, upon my rose-lit restaurant table, and the other upon the face, which really conveyed but little to my mind. . . . Anyhow, the face would be at another table, and we needn't look at it; and I was in the act of commencing a yawn, when it began to occur to me that it was indeed an extremely ugly face, a face hateful and full of hatred. The face of a most evil-looking and horrible ruffian. . . .

The bush moved again slightly, close to the face, the face was half-obscured, there was a terrific bang and my *képi* spun from my head. Had I not been crouching, half-lying, half-kneeling, with only my eyes above the big stone, over which I was looking, my story would have finished here.

Instinctively I thrust my rifle forward, and, let me confess it, without the slightest compassion or repugnance, returned the shot. Almost simultaneously Terence Hogan fired, and I heard him utter winged words—and, as I turned and reached to recover my cap, I realized that he was swearing at me. I quite understood. . . .

Heavy fire broke out all along the line of bushes below and in front of us; and it seemed a good thing to me that the Arabs had to shoot upward, though at the same time I am not sure that some of us did not have to expose ourselves more than they.

An Arab shooting from behind a bush was practically invisible, whereas a *légionnaire* had to expose at least part of his head when firing. However, the bushes were no protection against bullets, and our fire was heavy. Suddenly the scrub, bushes, and undergrowth in front of us seemed to spring into life, and, almost before one realized it, there was a swift determined rush of big active grey-clad men, who, as they sprinted, brandished long knives in their right hands—their form of a bayonet-charge.

It was a near thing. They were in great force, and had they got among us and broken our thin line, there would have been a murderous hand-to-hand *mêlée* and possibly the loss of the position—which might have spoilt the G.O.C.'s plans completely, and endangered the marching Brigade of which we were the Advance Guard.

There was no time for any orders. Every man fired for dear life and, as the Arabs fell, recoiled, and fled back to the cover of the bushes, snapped his bayonet on to his rifle, and fired at the bushes themselves.

Before long, the *"Cease fire"* was ordered and, instead of the independent fire, *à volontiers*, orders were given for "salvo" fire; and, crash after crash, heavy volleys swept the bushes with daunting sound and deadly effect. A very few of these silenced the Arab fire completely, and, by the time our *"Cease fire"* bugle blew again, there was not a sound or a sign of any enemy in front of our position. . . .

Orders reached our C.O. and it was forward again for the Advance Guard, our instructions being to capture without fail, and hold at any cost, the top of the mountain which we could see to our right front.

That, once occupied and strongly held, the Brigade could deploy in safety on the plain below, and make its big attack on the key-position, on the gaining of which everything depended.

I might here remark that one excellent feature of French Army training is the endeavour made to give all ranks a clear understanding of the why and the wherefore of what is expected of them. Even the rank-and-file generally know, not only exactly what their unit is going to do, but why it is going to do it.

As opposed to the You're-not-here-to-think; you're here-to-obey school, with its "Theirs not to reason why, theirs but to do and die" motto, the French Army takes the infinitely wiser view that the better the soldier understands what he is doing, the better he is likely to do it. Not only is he more interested, and given something to think about, other than his own troubles, but he is also far more likely to do the right thing when deprived of leadership.

The Colonel gets his orders and explains them with the utmost clearness to his officers, each of whom endeavours to explain them with equal clarity to his Sergeants. And the Sergeants see that each man in his *peloton* understands them too.

Another virtue of this admirable plan is seen in the fact that so frequently a Sergeant can carry on almost as efficiently as did his fallen officer, a Corporal replace the Sergeant, and the senior soldier the Corporal. It is this system that places a Field-Marshal's *bâton* in the knapsack of every soldier (where it usually stays).

So, when the French soldier and, indeed, the foreign *légionnaire* falls, he has the satisfaction of knowing not only that he Dies that France may Live, but that he is doing it in the manner most likely to achieve that desirable end—together with his own.

With no soldierly promptitude nor the slightest alacrity, we rose to our feet to abandon each the little home that, in the sweat of his brow, he had so painfully got together. No labour of love. He had cursed every stone and every spadeful; but now he left that little nest with heavy heart and affection's deep regret.

"And me just about to plant a wind-break, and run a boundary-fence round it," grumbled Digger.

"And the roses round the door made me want mother a darned sight more," averred Abraham, spitting lovingly into the parapeted hole that he had dug for himself. . . .

It seemed to me an extraordinarily dangerous proceeding, this launching of the Battalion into the oak scrub, a thin and straggling line that might bump blindly into the worst sort of trouble at any moment. Presumably it was the only thing to be done in the circumstances, and quite possibly the O.C. had satisfied himself that the Arabs had fled, though I did not see any scouts go out to skirmish ahead of us.

However, all was well, and we reached the bottom of the mountain-side and the clear open country without casualties.

I was surprised to see no Arab wounded in the bushes, and, remarking on this to Père Cocteau, as we sat waiting and resting at the bottom of the hill, he told me that the tribesmen had the very greatest objection to letting their dead or wounded fall into the hands of the Infidel. The wounded, they believed, would be taken away and given food and drugs of the most defiling description, forcibly converted by baptism to Christianity, and then put to death. The dead, they believed, would be either burnt in such manner that their souls could never enter Paradise, or else buried with defiling ritual and accompaniments that would have the same effect.

"And they take their revenge on our dead and wounded," continued Père Cocteau, "so don't get wounded—or dead—*mon enfant*. Not that it is wholly in a spirit of vengeance and of nastiness that they do these unsocial things. One must be just. To understand all is to forgive all. Not that I effectively forgive any Arab but a dead Arab. . . ."

Père Cocteau drank and wiped his lips with the back of his hand.

"But being a man of experience, knowledge, and enlightenment, I can tell you that religion—what we call superstition, for any other religion than one's own is superstition, of course—plays a considerable part. . . . You see, they think, poor heathen, that unless a dead enemy has been properly *halalled*—his throat decently cut—his spirit, his ghost, will return and haunt those who killed him. . . .

"Well, naturally, they don't want that added to their troubles. They've enough already, what with lice, wives, heat, cold, drought, floods, dust, mud —and the French . . . so they just take ordinary sensible precautions for their own protection.

". . . And that's why you'll find that our dead, killed by rifle-fire, have been mutilated with knives, and our wounded tortured in curious ways. . . ."

"They overdo it a bit," observed Terence Hogan. ". . . Get a bit ritualistic. . . . Let symbolism smother the spiritual idea, and all that."

"You are right, *mon ami*," agreed Cocteau. "Cutting a wounded man's throat, lest he die and haunt them, is all very well; and quite as logical as our imprisoning a debtor so that he shall have no chance to work and pay his debts. But there is no earthly need to treat him as though he were a chicken to be cooked, or a rabbit, and then stuff him with *alfa*-grass. . . . No. That is, as you say, making not only a virtue but a pleasure of necessity, *n'est ce pas?*

"Still, there is a religious basis, I maintain, even when glowing charcoal is used instead of *alfa*-grass for stuffing an Infidel."

"Heh! Close your tripe-traps, you jabbering apes," growled the fatherly voice of Sergeant Pflügge, "and fall in."

A few minutes later, we got the order to advance, and, in open order, our line began its slow progress across a wide level boulder-strewn rocky plain toward our objective, the mountain that was the key-position in the general scheme.

For a time, it was simply a slow march in extended order at the "trail," everyone carefully scanning the terrain ahead, as it was more than probable that the big force of Arabs that had so suddenly rushed our position and vanished from the woods beneath it, was somewhere ensconced between us and the next mountain-top.

In fact, there was no reason to suppose that they were not merely the skirmishers of an army, invisible, but near, awaiting our approach. The way in which a tribesman can conceal himself is simply marvellous, and the way in which a big force can materialize before one's eyes, as though from nowhere, is something that must be seen to be believed. Every greyish rock and greyish bush suddenly produces a grey-clad Arab, hitherto invisible; indeed, the boulders themselves seem to turn into Arabs, as a motion-less amorphous grey hump suddenly comes to life and fires a rifle.

It is aimed fire too, from the best of rifles. There is no banging off of gas-pipe guns, with a view to making plenty of self-heartening and enemy discouraging noise, as is the case with many more negroid and less civilized savage tribesmen. Nor is there anything in the nature of that "powder-play," *lab-el-baroda*, which is a feature of the spectacular but comparatively bloodless battles between the Moorish tribesmen themselves.

These mountaineers must very closely resemble the Pathan tribesmen of the North-West Frontier of India, and there are no braver or tougher foemen. Ammunition, being scarce and valuable, is not wasted; and the standard of marksmanship is about as high as any in the world. . . .

Suddenly a shot rang out . . . another and another . . . and in a minute we were under a heavy and increasing fire from, so far as I was concerned, a completely invisible enemy.

Being near a large and convenient boulder, I promptly got behind it and took a brief rest in safety.

Our line continued to advance, and unwillingly I left my rock and scuttled to another. On we went, bullets striking the ground and rocks; whizzing and whistling as they ricocheted from the stones; the Sergeants, well ahead of us, looking to left and right and rear with partly encouraging, partly menacing, shouts of:

"Come on, *salauds! En avant!* Come on, you sacred dogs! . . . Keep up!"

Brave splendid men, the backbone of the Legion—and the *bête-noire* of the *légionnaire*.

We quickened our pace, and the steady extended order march became more of a rock-to-rock and bush-to-bush skirmish.

Although several bullets had come quite near me, I still hadn't seen a single Arab. . . .

Again I scurried to a boulder sufficiently in my line of march to warrant my visiting it for a minute's breathing-space and safety.

A man of our section, named Fabricius, arriving at the same moment, said:

"Got any . . ." and fell down.

I thought he had stumbled, but he slumped

over on to his side, stretched his arms and legs (as one does, yawning, before getting out of bed), quivered convulsively, and then relaxed.

I ought to have gone straight on, I know. . . . Whether I stooped behind that rock in compassion or in cowardice I do not know; but I knelt down and turned my comrade over. Apparently he had been hit twice, in the face and the chest—and was dead.

Poor old Fabricius. . . .

I had always called him "Consul"; his name sounded so Roman; and I remembered being somewhat horrified when Terence Hogan assured me that Fabricius imagined that the name was suggested by that of a chimpanzee or orang-outang, more famous in England than any Roman.

I put his cap over his poor shattered face, thanking God that it was not Terence.

I was also glad for the thousandth time, that my experiences in France had been what they had been, and that I had seen the sights that I had seen. Had I not been inured to horror and to hardship during those terrible years, I could not have carried on. . . .

"Come on, *salauds! En avant!* . . . Come on, you holy tripe-hounds. . . . Get a move on!"

And I hurried forward, hunching my shoulders and bowing my head as one does in rain. It certainly wasn't raining bullets, but the fire was getting hotter and heavier as we drew nearer and nearer to the enemy.

This couldn't go on much longer. . . .

What would happen when we reached them?

How I did hope they would run away before it came to hand-to-hand fighting. I felt that any Arab —whose drill and training included the manœuvre of running away—was a silly fool not to do so in circumstances such as these; and I also felt that these Arabs were not going to be silly fools.

Suddenly we got orders to close-in by sections; the advance-formation was turned into attack-formation; and we got down to serious business. Sections fired volleys while their neighbour sections rushed forward, and those sections fired volleys while the others rushed up into line with them.

There was a great expenditure of ammunition, quick progress, and a notable slackening of enemy fire. Evidently they were retreating, for, after a few hundred yards of this, the whole line advanced at the *pas gymnastique* to the high bank of a deep and wide *nullah*, or rather dry river-bed.

From the edge of this, we could see across the lower opposite bank to the rising ground beyond, and there we could see, for the first time in this action, our mobile and elusive enemy—in full retreat.

Anyhow, the hand-to-hand business was postponed, and I prayed that these wise men might continue in their wisdom and their flight, even though it might be a case of *reculer pour mieux sauter.*

Along the top of this bank we lay, firing volleys to speed the parting host, and then independent fire, *à volontiers*, that the damage we were doing might not be merely moral.

"Like shooting at sand-fleas with a pea-shooter," observed Hogan, taking a snap-shot. "Or at lepping-mad March hares, with a Lebel rifle."

And indeed, the retreat of that Arab *harka* was masterly beyond praise; a huge mob vanishing among the rocks, boulders, and bushes of the mountain-side. The face of the mountain absorbed them, just as sand absorbs water.

"Yoicks! Gone away!" laughed Terence. "Hope

the Old Man puts us on to them before they've time to go to earth. We don't want to have to keep on digging them out."

There wasn't much fear. No colonel of a Foreign Legion Battalion had much to learn about Arab warfare; and we were working, as a Battalion, under the Colonel's eye.

And it was "up and away" while the Arabs were still retreating before our heavy fire.

Scrambling down the steep bank, we halted in the river-bed, assembling and straightening our long line; clambered up the opposite bank: advanced quickly under the thin dropping fire of a most informal rear-guard; and started to climb. . . .

And climb . . .

And climb. . . .

Never, as long as I live, shall I forget it.

There were times, I freely admit, when I longed to be shot down, just for the ineffable joy of being down and staying down.

There were times, I shamefully confess, when I was sorely tempted to *lie* down, feigning a wound and hoping to escape, or deceive, the eye of the N.C.O.'s, those men of iron who found not only breath to climb, but breath to shout. . . .

"Come on, *salauds*! *En avant!* Shake a leg, you sacred hounds. Up with you! Come on!"

And the faster we staggered on, the steeper grew the hill-side. For once in my life I was utterly, hopelessly, brave under fire. I simply did not care.

I imagine that a man pursued by an elephant would reck but little of an attack by a flea that bit him as he fled. To me, in that hideous hour of agony, Arabs were as fleas, and wounds as flea-bites, while with straining lungs, whooping breath, and bursting heart, I laboured up that awful slope, sideways, on the edges of the soles of my boots, openly and unashamedly using my rifle as an alpenstock, a crutch, and a walking-stick.

I saw the forms of bolting Arabs. . . .

I saw men fall. . . .

I knew that men above me, and not far in front of me, were shooting at point-blank range. . . .

I did not care.

I was past caring for anything, in that dreadful heat, climbing that mountain of scorching rock; my cracked lips, parched tongue, my whole mouth, like dried bone; my eyeballs bursting in my head; and the knowledge that, with another step, I should vomit my soul up. . . .

And just before I fell, we got the signal to halt.

I dropped to the ground, rolled over that I might rest against my pack and get the sun off my back, and lay gasping like a fish upon a river-bank.

And what . . . *what?*

"*Baïonnettes au canon* . . . *!* Prepare to charge!"

It was utterly inconceivable. What raving lunatic thought that we . . .

"Come on, *salauds! En avant!* Up with you! *Now* come on . . . *Cha-a-a-arge!*"

And the incredible N.C.O.'s actually sprang up, actually dashed forward . . . and actually expected us to follow them.

"Come on, Pup," croaked Digger, and wondering at myself, I rolled over, got to my hands and knees, picked up my rifle, climbed to my feet, and crawled forward.

Blindly I stumbled over a body . . . put my foot on a face . . . fell on a stinking blood-drenched Arab . . . and was sick.

Oh God! I was being given all I'd ever asked for in the way of "equal opportunity with men."

Damn these men. . . . Why should they have stouter hearts and stronger limbs, better wind, and more endurance, than women. . . .

Why should they be so tough, so bloody-minded, that they could not only bear, but positively grin and bear, things that . . .

Like a jack-in-the-box, a great bearded man, fierce, savage, terrible, a wild beast in human shape, sprang up from behind a bush and literally leapt at me, a long curved knife in his hand.

At the moment I was holding my bayoneted rifle at the "charge," but my finger was round the trigger. My gun went off, and involuntarily I shut my eyes. In the act of opening them, I was swept from my feet as the man's falling body came crashing against my legs.

I was down, and oh, the temptation to stay down.

For a moment I thought I was wounded, and then realized that I'd merely been knocked down and had banged my face and nose with extreme violence upon a stone, or the butt of my own rifle, as I fell.

It was rather a horrible moment, in which I seemed to be drowning in this hideous welter of suffering, noise, danger and superhuman effort. . . .

Suppose I had been wounded.

Somehow the hum, whistle and whine of bullets had not brought the likelihood home to my mind with anything like the force and reality with which this savage's curved gleaming knife had done. Under fire, one had realized there was a possibility; during the making or repelling of attacks this had almost seemed a probability; at this moment, with the huge tribesman dead at my side, it became a certainty.

What would happen to me if I were wounded, and it was discovered that I was a woman? Was it conceivable that the doctor would take the "chivalrous line" and hold his tongue—and then the other kind of "chivalrous" line and attempt a form of blackmail?

No; absurd. Most unlikely.

What line would the authorities take? Should I be immediately returned to Sidi and deported as an extremely undesirable "foreign body" which had found its way into the machinery of the Legion? Would the Colonel take a sporting view and say, "*Bien, mon enfant!* If you wish to fight for France, why shouldn't you?"

No; absurd. Most unlikely.

The Colonel would take the view—very naturally and correctly—that the position of a woman, known to be a woman, would be quite impossible and untenable in the ranks of the Legion.

Or, on the other hand, having had another look at me, and grasped the fact that I had stood the training, marching, and fighting, might he not, splendid soldier and fighting-man that he was, let me—the daughter, sister and companion of soldiers—carry on, if I could show that it was possible?

As far as that aspect of the matter was concerned, I could take pretty good care of myself, and anything I couldn't do in that line, Terence Hogan, Digger and Abraham could do for me.

What a shock to Abraham and Digger. How would they react to it?

Like the white men they were, of course.

Anyhow, I wasn't wounded.

I contrived to get to my feet again, more shaken, distressed, than ever I had been before, or was to be again, for many a long day.

"Come on, *salauds! En avant!* Who's going to be

on top first? Come on, you creaking cripples, curse you!"

And scrambling, stumbling, climbing, crawling, clutching at bushes, rushing up and slithering back, we got to the top.

Had the Arabs charged then, really charged home with the sword, knife, and clubbed rifle, they could, and would, have swept us back, back over the edge and down the mountain-side in rout and defeat.

For, although *légionnaires*, we were also human beings, and to human endurance there is a limit.

Once over the edge and on to the level—this mountain-top also being a small plateau—the ragged line, almost as one man, simply fell down.

Here and there, one stouter hearted or stronger lunged than the rest, remained standing and made some pretence of shooting at retreating Arabs.

A few knelt and fired.

Some fired sitting, others lying. But for a few minutes quite the majority simply lay whooping and struggling for breath.

Beside me Hans Petsel, on his knees, elbows, and face, gasped:

"*Ich bin ganz todt!* . . . *Ich bin ganz todt.* . . ."[56] and though, thereafter, the sound of his whistling, laboured breathing contradicted him, he certainly looked as though he was about to die. . . .

It takes long in the telling, but in point of fact, laden like mules, and tired as pedlars' donkeys, we had literally run up the side of the mountain—yelling, shooting and fighting, in time that appropriately-clad mountaineer athletes might envy.

Gradually we recovered, and, that we had

---

[56] I am quite dead.

minutes of grace in which to recover, was doubtless due to the fact that even Officers and Sergeants were, for the moment, physically defeated and quite speechless.

And then it was:

"Come on, *salauds! En avant!* Show a leg. . . . Rise and shine. Out of it! *En avant,*" once again.

And with rifles at the ready we swept across the plateau.

*　　*　　*　　*　　*

I suppose that, at about this point, such numbed faculties as remained to me must have ceased to function; for I remember practically nothing more of that day.

I know that the heat was terrible; that practically every man had drunk all his water; and that we were suffering really badly.

Apparently it was now that Digger saved the lives of Terence Hogan, Abraham and myself by producing the astonishing quantity of water that, thanks to his wisdom, economy, and self-denial, still remained in his *bidon.*

It was always a point of honour with Digger to drink less than anybody else (except when wassailing), and he affected to despise those who complained of thirst.

"You don't know what thirst is," he would smile.

Undoubtedly Digger had known what thirst was, when prospecting in Australia, and upon two more particular occasions; once when he was lost in the bush; and once when, after a terrible journey, he reached a water-hole to find it baked clay.

I have a clear recollection, anyhow, that the small plateau being completely cleared of the enemy, we bivouacked; for I can recall the agony of protest with which I heard the always-hateful order:

"*Aux murailles!*" ("Build the wall!")

follow the always-welcome one of:

"*Sac a terre!*" ("Down with your knapsacks!")

I suppose I took my part in carrying stones for the wall—doubtless the smallest I dared bring—and doubtless I carried on like a Robot, a mindless automaton, until the blessed moment came when I could legitimately relax and sink into oblivion.

Quite possibly I lay like a log while my comrades did my share of the work, as well as their own.

Quite possibly, too, I was to all appearances entirely normal—or as normal as I ever am; but there is a blank in my memory between that "*Aux murailles*" order and a sudden dawn cry, probably heard the next morning, of "*Aux armes! Aux armes!*" and the firing of sentries' rifles.

Having waited until we had finished the wall—such as it was—the Arabs attacked the position in great strength and with the greatest determination.

Every *légionnaire* rushed straight from his bivouac to his *créneau* (loop-hole) and opened fire. . . . Véry lights were fired, and a number of bombs thrown. . . . Scarcely awake, and still almost too weary to care whether I were wounded or not, I still remember the feeling of thankfulness which filled my heart.

It may seem a curious time and place—cold and hungry dawn on a mountain-top, with a vast horde of brawny tribesmen intent on massacre and torture—for the entertainment of sentiments of gratitude; but I was, nevertheless, profoundly grateful.

I was grateful to the Arabs for coming to us

instead of making it necessary for us to go to them. How much more desirable that they, bred and born mountaineers, and encumbered by no impedimenta whatsoever, should bound up the mountain-side while, for a change, we sat waiting at the top, discouraging their efforts.

Also I was thankful that, whether I myself had made it or not, I had got a beautiful little *créneau* through which I could fire without standing up. It wasn't so much the danger attaching to standing up that I considered, as the fatigue; for I had reached such a point of utter weariness that nothing else mattered.

I was yet further grateful to these good tribes-men for waiting till dawn and giving us a complete night's rest before they attacked; and something visible to shoot at when they did do so.

This attack looked quite bad enough—for we were completely surrounded and overwhelmingly outnumbered—but how infinitely worse it would have been had they assembled on the plateau in complete darkness, beyond the range of the sentries' vision and hearing, and then made a sudden rush, in one vast wave, with nothing but a few sentries and a three-foot wall between them and the sleeping camp.

As it was, we had but to fire swiftly and steadily to repel rush after rush.

Every now and then, with undisciplined valour, a mob would arise up from among the bushes, and charge with the speed, straightness and de-termination of hurdlers running a race. As they ran they fell. It was as though the hurdler had caught his foot upon the obstacle, and taken a toss.

Now and then, a few stout runners would almost reach the winning-post, but bullet or bomb would halt them in their stride, and they would come crashing down within a few yards of their goal. Now and again one would actually reach it, miraculously untouched, or carrying bullets which, in his frenzy, he ignored.

One such man . . .

His face scarcely that of a human being . . .

Rushing at me? . . .

I cannot fire in time . . .

At me . . .

Yes . . .

He reaches the wall and leaps . . . Abraham lunges . . . The Arab, stones from the wall, and Abraham, all come down together . . .

I swing sideways and dare not fire . . . Abraham scrambles to his feet, and, putting one foot against the Arab's chest, hauls on his rifle and withdraws the bayonet, apparently with great effort.

It is not a "dripping" bayonet; but it is a bent one . . . Abraham does not shoot the Arab, as he is obviously dead. . . .

He apostrophizes him unkindly—for knocking down the wall . . .

Swiftly he kneels in the gap and gets off a burst of rapid fire . . .

Digger stands beside him, with a *sac* full of bombs, as he rebuilds the wall. . . .

As it grows lighter, the attacks on our wall become less numerous, and the general firing heavier.

Danger, if any there be—danger of defeat, I mean—threatens from the side facing the open plateau.

Our side, close to the plateau-edge, gives less cover to the enemy, and little scope for sudden attack from cover. Judging from the incessant rifle-fire and constant crashing of bombs, the fighting on the opposite wall is desperate.

Things on our side of the fort grow quieter.

Suddenly Captain Z—— runs crouching along behind us, giving orders to Sergeants; and two Sections are rushed across to strengthen the other long side of the camp.

"Come on, *salauds!* . . . Across the garden. . . . *Houp là.* . . . Jump to it, you fleas . . ."

We were none too soon. The ground was strewn with our dead, inside the wall, and heaped with Arab dead without it.

As we arrived, a bugle was blown, the Colonel himself took fire-control, and ordered *salvo.*

Volley after volley was fired, with the regularity and precision of rifle-range practice, and had its usual depressing and deterrent effect upon the enemy. Groups gathering for rushes melted away; and rushes that did develop were broken and stopped, as the clustered charging tribesmen fell in heaps, and ragged rushing lines fell in swathes. . . .

This phase of the battle ended in a last great charge, when I imagine that every Arab on that side of the plateau rose up at a given signal, and the survivors of the *harka* charged as one man. . . .

We had just fired a volley.

Does it say something for the discipline of the Legion that—as this huge line, five or six deep, rushed headlong over the narrow open space between the bushes and the wall—not a single shot was fired? Not one weary, excited, frightened, or wounded man pressed the trigger of his rifle; and when the word *"Fire!"* rang out, there were no ragged edges to that close-range volley.

Again, *"Fire!"*

Again, *"Fire!"*

And when the order, *"A volontiers!"* was given, the independent-firing was brief, and aimed only at the swiftly-retreating survivors and a few desperate heroes determined to enter Paradise anointed with the blood of an Infidel. . . .

"*Cease fire! . . .*"

An incredible silence.

Terence Hogan surveys the battle-field and mutters to himself. I catch the words:

> " '*As the lean locked ranks rush roaring down to die.*' "

As we lay imagining things—for my own part, the longest and coolest of drinks—and almost praying for the issue of a coffee-ration, we suddenly heard the booming of artillery.

"That listens good, don't it?" observed Abraham the Sailor.

"Attaboy! . . . Spill another earful. . . . Good old Seventy-fives. . . . I wonder if that's the Boss, attending to this bunch, eh, Cocteau?"

"For myself, I hear nothing," replied Père Cocteau loftily. . . . "Ah, yes. . . . The faint popping of some miserable little mountain-battery or other. . . . No, the General is not paying the faintest attention to the little outpost skirmish, up here. He says to himself,

" 'I don't know what's happening up there, and I don't care. What I do know is that there's a Battalion of the Legion, Colonel R——, and Père Cocteau. . . .'

"He dismisses us from his mind, and gets on with the big battle, seeing to it that his artillery backs up, and heartens up, those who need it—the 6-th *Tirailleurs* and such-like. . . .

"Oh no, *mes enfants*, the General's getting on with the war. Though I grant you the sound of those popguns may have something to do with our present peace. . . .

"The effect of Artillery, *mes enfants*, is purely

moral.

"And that is curious. . . . For they are most immoral men, *ces artilleurs*. . . .

"One pinched my girl. . . . When was it? . . . Belfort. . . . in '97. . . .

"Why don't those goat-grandfathered food-spoilers bring us a *soupe* ration? . . ."

The sound of artillery-fire increased and personally I forgave "*ces artilleurs*" any immorality of which they might have been guilty.

Sergeant Pflügge, indefatigable man of iron, standing near us, unbent.

"A nice appetizer before breakfast—if there is any—eh, Cocteau, my lad?" he observed. "It would seem that *Messieurs les Arbis* want this position as much as the General does."

"Then let them have it, *mon Sergent*," replied Cocteau. "For myself, I have no use for it."

Apparently the General wanted it more than the Arabs did, and they hearkened to his voice— the guns.

There were no more attacks that day, and scouts reported that the plateau and the mountain-sides were clear of the enemy.

*   *   *   *   *

To our joy we learned that, so far as our Battalion was concerned, it was a case of "*Nous y sommes, nous y restons.*" The position that we had won was apparently of both great and permanent importance, and must be held at any cost. Orders came that it must be strongly fortified and strongly held. The decree went forth that we were to build real walls, ten feet high and four feet wide. These would surround the miserable little three-foot *murailles* that we had set up on the previous day. When the walls were finished, a regular fort would be built inside, with watch-tower, keep, officers' quarters, barrack-rooms, store-house, *et cetera* . . . a nice outpost, with cells complete.

By the mercy and grace (purchased) of Corporal Eicholtz and the kindness of my comrades, I did a great deal more sentry-go than manual labour, during this period of building, when my Battalion, save for one Company, ceased to be soldiers and became navvies, bricklayers' labourers (the bricks being huge stones) and masons.

It is an amazing fact that, in addition, of course, to unskilled labourers—which all have to be at times—the Legion can always produce representatives of any skilled trade, craft, or profession, and produce artisans of any required type.

Orders having been issued that the walls and buildings of this post should be solid and permanent—what the English Army calls *pucca*—real builders had to be discovered, suitable kinds of stone selected and burnt for the making of lime, cement prepared, and crude pug-mills established for the making of mortar.

For a day or two the tide of battle surged about us on the plain below, while, behind the protecting and warning screen of one Company, we worked like beavers.

One day, when our Company was on this duty, I had a wonderful view of a splendid attack made by another Battalion upon a strongly-held village below us, and to our left front—doubtless the village from which our recent opponents had come, and to which they had retired.

In extended order, the Battalion advanced with fixed bayonets until, in a wide-open space devoid of cover, it was held up and then driven back by a very heavy fire.

Withdrawn, and re-formed, they attacked again; and, again, in the same bare open belt, came under so withering a fire that, a second time, the line was halted, broken, and driven back to cover—again leaving scores and scores of motionless or writhing figures upon the ground. Here and there I could see a poor fellow crawling, or dragging himself painfully back, while bullets made the sandy gravelly soil seem to dance around him like water beneath hail.

A heavy rifle-duel ensued, volley upon volley answering the enemy's independent fire.

A third time, with Officers and Sergeants leading, the line advanced; and again it recoiled, not in flight, but to cover, whence it could again endeavour to lessen the enemy's determined resistance, by means of salvo fire.

Suddenly the volleys ceased. The line rose up and advanced once more—with the same result. It seemed to me that a third of the Battalion must by now be lying dotted about on the bullet-swept plain.

Five times was the attack in this form repeated. . . .

Evidently orders were now received that the place must be taken at all costs.

The sixth attack was a bayonet-charge straight from cover across the open belt and up to the village wall, men falling right and left in scores. There was a minute of even heavier firing, and then, almost suddenly, comparative silence, as the Arabs turned and fled before the swift on-rush and the long gleaming dreaded bayonets.

It was a glorious charge and the most marvellously dramatic and thrilling sight I have ever witnessed. . . .

For a while the top of the mountain was like a

vast builders'-yard, and by the time building oper-
ations were finished, and the plateau cleared of
trees, bushes and scrub, it was like—what the
General wanted—a very strong military post, a
point d'appui and future guardian of the lines of
communications.

Two drawbacks it had: lack of water, and an
undesirable neighbour—a curious crag in the form
of a pinnacle—that commanded it, at a range of
about a kilometre. However, there was a brook at
the bottom of the hill; and a permanent post (poor
devils) was established on the crag. . . .

Scarcely had we settled down to routine life in
the new *poste*, when a rumour reached us,
brought by a visiting patrol—a rumour which
proved to be true—that the objective of the *groupe
mobile* was attained, and that there would be no
further advance that year. This meant that the
greater part of the Brigade would retire, and its
units disperse to their respective headquarters.

Who would remain to garrison the *postes* and
hold the occupied country?

"The Legion, of course," said the old soldiers,
"or part of it, at any rate."

And, one day, orders came that half our
Battalion was to garrison the fort we had built,
while the other half went to M— to rest and refit.

Wild excitement. . . .

Terrible anxiety. . . .

Which half would go?

Ours.

And, one glorious morning, glorious in every
sense of the word, we marched out and away to
M— ragged; almost barefoot; lacking most
necessities, except our weapons; lean, haggard; a
tatterdemalion half-battalion of scarecrows. But
real soldiers, a unit equal to any in the world in

fighting spirit and fighting ability. . . .

At M—— we rested, refitted—and deteriorated in every possible way.

BOOK II

CHAPTER I

"A man can't do that," said Digger at length, shifting his Lebel from his right shoulder to his left. He always carried it gripped by the muzzle. It seemed to hurt him to march with the butt-plate in the palm of his hand.

"Tell me again," I said huffily, for it was the first time he had spoken to me this day.

"Too right, he can't," he growled.

I looked up at his lovely face, apparently carved from oak, in which, as I have said, shone two of the brightest and bluest eyes I have ever seen on either side of an aristocratic nose, a gentleman's nose. Not that Digger was a "gentleman," though he was one of the finest gentlemen God ever made.

"Say, Digger . . ." I tried. But he wouldn't turn those wonderful eyes of his to mine, and I couldn't see his mouth. None of us had ever seen Digger's mouth, by reason of his big moustache. But his chin looked more than ever like the toe of a very square-toed boot.

One couldn't read his face, a real poker-face, but I was certainly in disgrace with Digger. Shifting my own rifle, I took a cigarette from my *képi* and offered it to Terence Hogan.

"Ah! Thank you, no," declined Hogan, loftily.

"Hoighty," I replied, "and to that, my lad, you may add, Toighty!"

Terence Hogan emitted his sniff superior, a rather crushing brief comment that he makes when occasion requires.

I never met anybody who could say so much, with one sniff, as Terence. It is the sniff eloquent; and an amazingly telling remark, crushing, snubbing, aggravating, humiliating, exasperating, and guaranteed promptly to put you in your place —and Terence Hogan in his, far above you.

I looked at the face of Terence, and decided that our months in M—— had done him no good at all. He looked dissipated. I told him so. . . .

Unlike Digger, he was showing what he thought of me quite plainly, and I gathered that he thought very little. Preferred not to think of me at all, in fact.

Yes, Terence was certainly registering disgust, and he was quite good at it. In fact, I think it is his best register, for he often looks as though he has got an unpleasant smell under his nose. In the Legion, of course, one frequently has. . . .

It is terribly interesting to note the things that Terence, being a "gentleman," cannot do; and the things which Digger, not being a gentleman, can do: and contrariwise, the things that Digger, though not a "gentleman," would never dream of doing, while Terence Hogan sees no harm in them, and does them too.

Although good friends and my friends, they have extraordinarily little sympathy with each other's point of view, and rarely meet on common ground.

They met on common ground to-day, and I was that common clay.

Two minds usually without a single thought— as I pointed out to them—were now two minds with but a single thought: my utter, incredible caddishness.

And, incidentally, Abraham the Sailor, marching in front of me, entirely agreed with them. His very back expressed disapproval.

So here were these three Anglo-Saxons, my comrades, and, up to last night, at any rate, my dear friends, united in their complete condemnation of me, as well as of my dreadful deed of last night.

And to each of them it clearly was a truly dreadful deed, unthinkable, impossible; in fact, the thing a man can't do.

In the eyes of Terence I had behaved as no *légionnaire* should. As to the others—I had smacked a woman's face!

Good and hard, with all my strength. With the utmost satisfaction and all my might, I had smacked a woman's face.

What a wonderful and a fundamental thing is the point of view! It is at the bottom of all *odium theologicum* and the beginning of all wars, and the cause of most quarrels. From my friends' point of view I had been an unspeakable cad, and done an unbelievably dreadful thing. From my own point of view, I had done a righteous act.

Incidentally I had thoroughly enjoyed the doing of it, and would like to do it again. . . .

Abraham the Sailor and Terence Hogan had decided that, this being our last night in M——, our last night in a civilized spot—civilization being measured by cafés, bars, dance-halls, and similar haunts and homes of "pleasure"—our last night under a roof, and near tables, chairs and decent food; and quite probably one of our last nights on earth, we ought to make the most of it.

Digger agreed with them and said that we must get out somehow, and celebrate.

In point of fact, getting out proved simple enough, and I soon began to wish that celebrating had not proved simpler still.

Abraham the Sailor had got money, as usual; and, as always, was unhappy in its company. Abraham the Sailor viewed a nail in his boot and a franc in his pocket with equal abhorrence.

"The sky's the limit," said he.

"And the ocean's my limit," said Hogan.

"Leave me one of the Seven Seas," requested Digger, and,

"You shall have the Great Australian Bite," said I wittily, "and have it first. Never drink on an empty stomach."

"What do you know about drinking, you miserable water-baby?" was the reply. "Is a herring-gutted, slop-swilling, bilge-lapping, swipes-swigging teetotaller going to tell me how to drink?" asked Digger.

"Aw, can it. . . . The Kid wasn't telling you how to drink . . . he was telling you how not to drink. And who better fitted than a guy that does as much at not-drinking as he don't? Good advice, too. We're going to hear how the best-looking eats tastes in this burg," said Abraham the Sailor; and, without the ghost of a smile on his tough, grim, clean-shaven face, added:

"You reckon you can fight a lot of bottles and I reckon I can beat you to it, and then Terence Hogan could put us to bed and settle down to some honest drinking; but I tell you the Kid's got us all beat. Bravest of the lot. Why, without turning a hair, that Kid would drink off things we three'd shrink from. Things that'd make our hair curl or get right up and lie down the other way if it was as stiff as yourn. God-awful things, pink and green and blue, like a goddam chemist's shop."

"Lemonade," said Hogan.

"Orangeade," said Digger.

"Raspberryade," groaned Hogan.

"Sure," agreed Abraham, "and gooseberryade, first-aid or hand-grenade. I seen that Kid drink things like he was weary of life. He's that tough he'd pour out a tumbler of castor-oil and drink yer health in it, rather than touch the every-day stuff that's good enough fer sissies like us. . . ."

And so talking we tramped from camp into M——, through the marvellous old Moorish gate, down the brilliantly lighted *boulevard*, into a dark and narrow alley, and so to *L'Homme Qui Rit*.

L'Homme Qui Rit was full, as usual, and of its usual *clientèle;* soldiers of every regiment of the XIX Army Corps; fat and greasy citizens of the Levant, or rather ex-citizens, for, from being Levantine scum, they were rapidly burgeoning and blossoming into plump and prosperous Frenchmen; Moroccan Jews, who not long ago cringed and crept about their *mellas*, in fear and danger of their lives, and who now set their feet firmly and squarely upon the earth, or rather their latter ends firmly and squarely upon their own motorcars; Spaniards, who had hitched their sumperter-waggons to the martial star, or in little shops made wealth from others' poverty; Arabs, aloof, contemptuous but appreciative of infidel amenities, pleasures, vices and diversions; "lesser breeds without the law," but somehow definitely and obviously the mental, moral, and physical superiors of the wretched half-breeds, and many of the full-breeds, within the law; cosmopolitan scoundrels from half the countries of Europe, interested in the liquor-trade and the girl-traffic, whose faces, clothes, diamonds and jewellery always filled me with the Christian and charitable desire to see them hanged by the neck till they were nearly dead, and then hanged again till they were quite. . . .

If any argument were needed that War is a foul and fearful thing (save war to extend the productive area of the earth; or war in defence of hearth and home) one might be found in the nature of the creatures that profit by it—rats and carrion crows in Europe; vultures, wolves, jackals and hyenas in other parts.

And here were the human rats and carrion crows, the foul two-legged wolves, jackals and hyenas, fattening and battening on the brave men who bore the heat and burden of the day; the cold and misery of the night; the agony of wounds; maiming; blindness; and death in battle—for the poorest pittance, clothes to cover them, a roof to shelter them, sufficient food to keep them alive, and a penny a day to put by for old age. . . .

So it was without a twinge of regret for their rudeness that I lent my countenance, such as it is, to the act and deed of Digger and Abraham the Sailor.

For, seeing that all the little iron tables crowded round the dancing-floor were full, Digger laid his hand upon the shoulder of a Turkish-looking person whose large, fat yellow face would have looked the cleaner, if not the better, for a shave, and said "Farewell" to him in a perfectly friendly manner.

Abraham the Sailor, quick in the up-take, placed his hand beneath the chin of one of the Turk's companions, a hook-nosed swarthy oily-haired nut, clad in the height, or depth, of local fashion, and bade him "Good night."

Terence Hogan, always polite, thanked the third member of this party—a weedy youth who looked as though he lived on absinthe and cigarettes—for his chair, and jerked it from beneath him.

I, rarely polite, and seldom delicate in my sense of humour, took advantage of the fact that the fourth man was maintaining his balance by means of his feet beneath the centre of the table, while, tilting his chair backwards, he picked his teeth with abandon.

It needed but a touch of my heavy hand to disturb his unstable equilibrium. With a wild cry, a clutching hand and bitten fingers, he fell heavily backwards.

Picking up his chair and offering him my commiseration and my thanks, I seated myself upon it.

My movements had not been slow, and yet I was the last of our party to be seated. Our predecessors, though men of weight and (now) standing, decided that they had done with the table for that evening—a decision to which they were undoubtedly helped by the kindly faces and encouraging gestures of Digger and Abraham the Sailor.

My only regret was that they had gone so meekly, for my friends are really wonderful in a rough-house, and the departed were of those with whom I would fain have seen them rough.

"What shall we start on?" asked Terry, rising and bowing once more to the scowling but retreating gang.

"Wine," said I. "Start on it, stay with it, and finish on it. You'll leave your little cot at four tomorrow morning, and you'll march best part of forty miles before you curl up again."

"We'll start on the flower-water, anyhow," decided Digger, as a Berber Arab waiter, in dirty white, came for our order.

"Flower-water" was our name for a very decent white wine sold at *L'Homme Qui Rit*, and we called it that, because it was always dispensed in a curious huge decanter shaped like a flower-vase, and having no stopper.

The bulbous base of each of these curious vessels was a great flat-bottomed ball of glass which must have held about a gallon of wine, and the neck was a thick glass tube, about three feet long. The way in which Madame and her satellites at the bar could pour out a glass of wine from one of these receptacles, without spilling a drop, was an unfailing source of wonder and admiration to me; for the mouth of the decanter was never within a foot of the glass, and the thin stream of wine gushed forth with the force of a jet from a fountain.

"Thanks, Digger," I nodded, for I knew that he, with his fundamental kindness and innate consideration for others (which is of the essence of gentlemanliness), had said this because he knew that I should drink only one glass of wine, and that I preferred this Algerian Sauterne.

It was a pity that Abraham the Sailor was host, because, being the soul of hospitality, he felt he must flog the all-too-willing horses, and see that no drinking-trough was empty—always excepting mine, for he knew that, in no circumstances whatsoever, would I have more than one glass. I dare not. The temptation is too strong on days that I am so weary that I am a living ache, and am far too tired to sleep.

It is no virtue on my part, for often I envy my comrades who can find in wine—oblivion.

And so we began on flower-water, and when flower-water palled, it was succeeded by *pinard*, and when Abraham the Sailor felt it was time to begin drinking, he ordered a bottle of cognac, which kept off the worst pangs of thirst until *l'heure de l'absinthe* arrived.

"Absinthe makes the heart grow fonder," murmured Terence Hogan during a brief lull in our intellectual conversation. "Fonder of other things. Beer's the only true drink. Let's start a movement—toward the bar—for Brighter Beer for British Boys."

"Let the beer come to us, if you want to waste your time drinking French beer. We don't want to lose our table," objected Digger.

"Sure," agreed Abraham the Sailor. "Why—a table and a chair is home. Why leave home?"

"Especially when it has all the comforts," he added, as a passing girl put her arm about his neck, kissed him, and slid on to his knee.

"I am so thirsty, *chéri*," stated the creature, shaking her mop of brassy curls, and stretching her vermilion mouth into a grin.

I hated the sight of her; and it made me feel sick to see Abraham kiss and cuddle her.

"Sure you are, Sweetie," he replied. "You're thirsty as two camels; an' nothing will quench it but sweet champagne—opened outside, and brought in without the cork. I'll fall for it. Tell 'em to bring it in that same bottle with a bit of gold foil on, it's an old friend of mine."

"*Comment?*" interrupted the girl, and beckoned a waiter.

"Yes. We'll 'come on,' " agreed Abraham the Sailor.

And the girl promptly ordered five bottles of champagne.

"*Five?*" objected Abraham. "Have a heart, Cutie. We'll have fifty. . . . Only we'll have 'em one at a time. So we'll start with two."

And a minute later, with wry faces, these three asses were tasting the filthy muck, which was probably concocted on the premises.

"Just like Mother makes," observed Abraham, "only she calls it near-beer, an' makes it with nettles and ginger."

"I thought you were thirsty!" I said to the girl.

"So I am," she answered. "Wouldn't you like to give me a viski-soda?"

"No," I said, as disagreeably as I felt. "Drink the

champagne. Serve you right."

"What's biting you, son?" inquired Abraham.

"You," I replied. "Letting yourself be fooled and robbed by a thing like that . . . the beastly little bitch."

This, as I intended, stirred my sentimental friends to the depths of their noble beings.

Was she not a woman?

Hadn't she a hard row to hoe?

Hadn't she a mother somewhere, and possibly a blue-eyed child?

And hadn't she been started on the downward path by some villain of a man whom she had trusted?

Tears of alcohol and sentiment stood in Digger's eyes as he thought of it.

Tighter she was clasped to Abraham's bosom while he stroked her arm murmuring:

"Poor kid! Poor little kid!"

Even Terence Hogan took the line of,

"Damn it all; a woman is a woman whatever else she may be, what!"

There wasn't much sentiment about Hogan, but there was a lot of white wine, red wine, cognac, beer, and bad champagne.

I said how right they were! "Too right," as Digger would say. I fully agreed with their statements.

I agreed that she was undoubtedly a woman—of sorts; that she certainly had a hard roe; that probably she'd had a mother—conceivably a father too; that undoubtedly she had been put upon evil ways by a villain, probably with a waxed moustache, a high collar, a large gardenia button-hole and a crush hat—and that probably she herself had made him a villain; also that she probably had a che-ild—several, and all grievously afflicted.

To their credit, or their discredit, my friends stood up for the woman, and defended her so eloquently that she spat venomously—invective and saliva.

Being restrained, and yet further comforted, by the indignant, drunk—and amorous—Abraham, she flung her arms about his neck, collapsed upon his shoulder and whispered in his ear.

It was time to get these fools home, and it was up to me.

"What about moving on?" I suggested, draining my glass, my first and last of the evening.

"Sure," agreed Abraham. "I'll . . . I'll overtake you."

Then he got to his feet, the girl hanging on to his arm.

"You're coming with us, Abraham," I said.

"Sure, Boy," grinned Abraham sheepishly. "I'll be right along. Be back in camp 'most soon as you are."

I looked at Digger. He wasn't drunk, but very definitely "having drink taken."

"Let's run him out, Digger," I said. "Come on, Terry."

Digger yawned and endeavoured to focus me with his bright blue eyes.

"Fac' is," he said, "fac' *is*—you're what-is-it!"

"Quite so," drawled Terence Hogan. "Digger, with his inevitable selection of the *mot juste*, has—er—said it all. You're what-is-it. . . . And if I might presume to paint the lily, to gild refined gold, and cast perfume upon the violet, I would add to it—You're also . . . what-you-may-call. . . . Do I make myself clear?"

"Very," I answered. "You're clearly drunk."

Abraham was searching in his *képi* and pockets for more money; and the girl was helping in the search, her left arm round his waist, and her left hand secretly in his pocket; while her right openly assisted Abraham's fumblings inside his tunic.

"Mind you're not robbed by that whore—as well as poisoned," I said venomously. "She's picking your pocket."

This time, my sentimental gentleman literally stood up for the lady, and the girl, thus jerked to her feet, snatched up a glass of champagne and, with a filthy oath, threw it straight at me. Then, leaning across the table, with her face as close to mine as she could thrust it, she screamed a torrent of abuse and abominable suggestion.

So I smacked her face.

With all the strength of an arm in fine muscular training, and a hand well-hardened by pick, shovel and rifle, I smacked the horrible face of that beastly harpy, and put into it all the force of my indignation and hatred of her and all her sisterhood who poison and degrade clean men.

And I had the double satisfaction of an act of self-expression combined with the furtherance of my plan, for Goldilocks had played into my hands —or my right hand—inasmuch as pandemonium broke loose at once, beginning at our table, and spreading throughout the room.

The girl seized an empty champagne bottle, and Abraham seized her.

An indignantly chivalrous Spahi smote Abraham from behind. Digger knocked him down. His friends sprang upon Digger; and Terence Hogan with a joyous whoop and an iron chair, sprang to his assistance, while Madame, big, strong and ugly as a big, strong and ugly man, rushed from the bar, bawling for the picket, the police, and the help of God.

It was a glorious shemozzle, of the knock-down and drag-out variety, and, when Hogan was knocked down, I dragged him out, and then helped him to drag out Digger, which was difficult as he had a Zouave in one hand and a *Tirailleur* in the other.

Abraham the Sailor needed no dragging out. He burst forth from the café with a large wilted civilian and a vague but persistent idea of holding him to ransom. Who he thought was going to ransom him did not transpire, and he released him on my assuring him that, judging by the look of the creature, the only money we should get would be a reward for removing him.

And so to bed.

The minds of my three companions being still full of pleasant reminiscence of the delightful rough-house, and the general joyous doings of the evening as seen through a roseate hue of wine, my own conduct was forgotten, and the homeward march unmarred by recrimination.

But to-day I am in disgrace.

All is remembered, and the transfiguring mists of wine have turned, alas, to the miasma of bile. Things are seen for what they are, through a yellow glass clearly.

I am seen for what I am, my deed for what it was, and I am in disgrace.

"A man can't do a thing like that!" they are all agreed.

No. A girl can, though.

*   *   *   *   *

In what is commonly known as "due course," we reached our destination, the mountain, in the assault of which I had so nearly died; the plateau drenched with the blood of so many of my comrades; and the Fort which we had helped to build.

The joy of our other half-battalion, which we had come to relieve, was something to remember, but not to attempt to describe. So was the gloom with which we took over.

They had sat in this wretched fort for weeks and weeks—each week, as Bilenski the giant Russian said, a month. . . .

"Yes, *mon petit*," agreed Cocteau. "And we may be here for months, each month a year."

We were there for months, each month a century.

CHAPTER II

I take an insatiable delight in hearing these men talk. They represent the whole world and every social grade in the world—almost every trade, profession, calling and vocation in the world, from prince to priest, from fiddler to financier, from osteopath to orchid-hunter, from crook to diplomat—although the best-represented profession is that of arms.

I love to sit quiet and listen to their conversations, arguments, wranglings, points of view, and stories.

Particularly their stories.

I like to divide these into three categories.

Those which, without any sort of proof, I know to be true; that I feel in my bones must be true.

Those which are obviously untrue, and that one intuitively rejects and refuses to believe.

And thirdly—and these I think I like the best—those that leave one wondering, inasmuch as they may very well be true, though possibly they are not.

I note one thing; and that is, the longer I live and the more I see and hear, the fewer stories I relegate to the class of the obviously untrue, and the readier I am to accept the dictum that nothing is impossible.

I may mention here that I do not include in "stories" the kind of yarns told by men like Cocteau for the benefit of people like Hermann; stories which, begun in good faith as round unvarnished tales, gradually become masses of embroidery (is this a mixed metaphor?) under the overwhelming temptation offered by the foolish questions of that large class of people who are at once incredulous and gullible.

Excellent specimens from these three classes of stories are, of the first kind, Cocteau's Voulet-Chanoine story, which I believe to be absolutely true in every detail; and, of the second, Cocteau's slave-raiding yarn, of which the grains of truth were literally well hidden in chaff.

Of the third class is the following.

It interested me deeply, by reason of the personality of the teller; the way in which it was told; and the admirable setting of the tale—or rather of the telling—moonlight and firelight; the ring of silent men; the curiously varying types of faces—of boys of twenty, of men of sixty, of the gross, the refined, the stupid, the intellectual, the ugly, the handsome, the clean-shaven, the bearded, the Teutonic, the Slavonic, the Latin. . . .

"Well, a promise is a promise," said Demenko, the Cossack, a charming and blood-thirsty savage, of delightful manners. "And a man who can't keep a promise can't keep anything. . . . Or shouldn't be allowed to."

"Yes, quite so. Generally speaking," agreed the handsome sad-faced man, nationality doubtful, known as "Baron" Trenck, "but a promise can land you in a terrible hole sometimes."

"A promise is a promise," dogmatized Demenko.

"Yes, and life is life," replied Trenck, as I will call him. "And very dear when it comes to selling it. Dear even to a *légionnaire*. I had a queer experience once. . . . A choice between keeping my promise and losing my life."

"You are still alive, one perceives," remarked Demenko, who spent his young life in looking for trouble and seeking sorrow.

"Yes," agreed Trenck. "I am still alive, as you

brilliantly observe."

"What's the story, Baron?" I asked, partly in the hope of getting it, and partly to stop these two idiots from squabbling.

"You wouldn't believe it if I told you," he replied. "Still less would the intelligent Demenko."

"What does that matter?" I asked.

Trenck shrugged his shoulders.

"True," he said. "What does it matter whether it is—true. I myself sometimes wonder whether it is true."

" 'What is truth?' said Pontius Pilate, being another liar himself, no doubt," remarked Demenko.

"Do you want a clout on the ear, Vodky?" inquired Digger, turning threateningly upon Demenko.

"Yes," bristled the Cossack, who was about half Digger's size.

"Well, wait till Baron Trenck's told us the tale and I'll give you two," replied Digger.

"And I'll give you a lift in the seat of your pants, Demenko," promised Abraham the Sailor.

"Come on, Baron," I said.

"Oh, it's nothing. A thing that happened to me when I was in—er—another place."

"Let us call it Vienna, Baron Trenck," said Matthieu le Maquereau.

"Certainly, if it pleases you," replied Trenck. "I was a cavalry—offi . . . a cavalry—man in those days . . . and—er—life went very well. . . .

"There was a man in my Regiment whom I—er —knew very well, without his being particularly a friend of mine. . . . You know how it is—a man whom you see almost daily and speak to quite often—both on duty and off . . . at the cafés, balls, race-courses, opera, and so on. . . . Let us call him . . ."

"Tzigan," suggested Matthieu.

Trenck's short laugh was contemptuous.

"Thank you," he said.

"Well, during the War, the gentleman whom we are to call Tzigan did me a most comradely kindness. In fact, he saved my life at some risk to his own . . . one of those deeds that, done in daylight, in the proper circumstances, and under the proper eye, are rewarded by a piece of ribbon of the appropriate colour, at the end of which dangles some cross or medal that soldiers respect. . . .

"But this was done at night, in darkness, in No-Man's Land—and in rain and mud and cold, and the misery that so damps the fires of courage. . . . I think it was as much gratitude for getting me in, out of the deadly wet and cold in which I was lying, half-buried in mud, as it was for saving my life, that made me seek him out when I was on my feet again, and attempt to thank him—and add to my thanks my promise that, should he ever be in need of help, there was literally nothing in the world that I would not do for him.

"Shortly after that, came one of the great battles of the War, and the end of the first day of it saw nine-tenths of my Regiment dead, dying, or wounded on the ground.

"Tzigan and I were among the wounded, and for both of us the War was over. We were not taken to the same hospital—and I never set eyes on Tzigan again till he strode up to me as I was sitting on my cot cleaning my equipment. . . .

"And where do you think that was, Monsieur Well-informed Maquereau?" Trenck interrupted himself to ask.

Matthieu smiled, if the baring of sharp teeth by a wry elongation of parted lips can be called a smile.

"In Colomb Bechar, in Southern Algeria! A spot which some of you may know," continued Trenck.

"In front of the *légionnaire* Trenck stood the *légionnaire* Tzigan. . . . He had recently arrived at Colomb Bechar, and had just heard, from a fellow-countryman, of my presence in the Legion and in Colomb Bechar.

"I sprang to my feet and wrung his hand, for I am one of those fools in whom the sentiments of gratitude and loyalty die hard. This man, a mere acquaintance, as I have already said, had, without hope or thought of distinction or reward, gone out of his way to save my life at the gravest risk to his own.

" 'Good God! Fancy our meeting here. Well! Well! I suppose this means that things have gone ill with you, too,' I said, for before the Great Collapse he had been a wealthy man. And as I looked him in the eyes I saw that things had indeed gone ill with him.

"That magnificent man who would have been an ornament to any regiment in Europe, looked wretched, miserable and hunted. He looked desperate. And he who had been the bravest of the brave, the coolest and the stoutest of heart, had obviously got 'nerves.'

" 'Come out with me,' he said. 'I want to talk. . . . Be quick.'

"Hurriedly I dressed for walking-out, and, in a minute or two, we left the *caserne*.

" 'What about a bottle of wine?' I suggested, turning in the direction of the canteen.

" 'No, no! . . . I mustn't. . . . I simply daren't drink until night,' he said. 'Come where we can talk privately.'

" 'Will you do something for me?' he said as soon as we were seated.

" 'Absolutely anything,' I replied. 'There is nothing I would not be glad to do for you . . . as I once told you. . . .'

"He laughed a little bitterly.

" 'You appear to be the man you were,' he said. 'Well . . . I'm not. I've gone a very long way down a very steep hill. I'll tell you. . . . In hospital at—er—' "

Trenck paused for a second.

"Buda-Pesth?" suggested Matthieu quietly.

"If you like, M'sieu le Maquereau," agreed Trenck.

" '. . . I fell in love with my nurse, in the approved fashion. Nothing remarkable in that. But when I was discharged from hospital, what do you think I did?' asked Tzigan.

" 'Ran away with her,' I suggested.

" 'Yes, and married her,' replied Tzigan. 'What do you think of that?'

" 'I never met her, my friend,' I said.

" 'Huh!' sneered Tzigan. 'I'm not so sure of that! It wasn't long before I found a good many people had—er—met her before. When she put off her nurse's uniform, she put off a good deal more of her *façade* . . . and I learnt quite a lot. . . . Well, well! The War had a lot to answer for, and I am something of a philosopher.

" 'Not long after the end of our honeymoon, I had to go to . . .' "

"Vienna," murmured Matthieu.

" '. . . and was caught up in the maelstrom of the troubles. The criminal gutter-scum—that is always the filthy froth on the surface of such maelstroms—was on top, and, after some desperate fighting, one had to go into hiding. It was weeks before I could get back to my place in the country, and to my wife.

" 'The house was still there.

" 'But my wife wasn't. She had gone.' "

Matthieu le Maquereau sniggered.

" '. . . and what I think shocked me even more than her revealed wantonness, was her vulgarity—in removing everything of value. Not merely the jewellery that I had given her, but my own too; as well as money and securities and everything that was both valuable and portable.

" 'I took it rather hard, for I really did fall in love with her in that hospital, and there she had seemed such an angel of light, such a sister of mercy, a gracious and ministering presence, whose very aura was healing and soothing. . . .' "

Trenck fell silent.

"Poor old Tzigan," he resumed. "One could see that he had suffered. So this was why he was in the Legion?"

Trenck paused in contemplative reminiscence.

"But there was worse to come," he resumed.

" 'I held out for a time,' continued Tzigan," he said. " 'Clung hard to my self-respect and proper pride. But gradually my grip weakened. I began drinking to excess. At first to bring sleep and, before long, to bring forgetfulness, to drown care, to drown thought, to drown memory. And as I deteriorated and self-respect vanished, I began to go down-hill faster and faster; and, by the end of the year, I was a dissipated and riotous drunkard, a gambler, a loose-liver whose days were spent in hoggish idleness and nights in debauchery.

" 'I became a frequenter of night-clubs; some, fashionable and frequented by people of good social standing, if doubtful taste; some, shady resorts of people of doubtful social standing and doubtful morals; others, mere dens and dives frequented by people about whose social standing and morals there was no doubt at all. Places that were practically brothels.

" 'And one night, sitting in a dance-hall in which, for most of the time, the lights were kept so discreetly dim that the place was almost in darkness, I suddenly saw my wife. The lights went up as usual to indicate that closing-time was near —and there she was, dancing gaily in the arms of a typical habitué of such haunts.

" 'A minute later the lights were lowered again. She had not seen me. What was to be done? Nothing at all—by me. I found that I was trembling from head to foot. I felt faint and ill. I thought that I was actually going to faint dead away, there on that corner settee. I pulled myself together, drank some more of my cognac, and sat with my hand across my face until the place was empty and the weary waiters invited me to go.

" 'I returned to my room, drank neat brandy all night—and it had no more effect upon me than so much milk—and gradually I turned from the sick and shaken creature that I had become at sight of her, into a savage beast, a morose brute, desperate and dangerous.

" 'All day I brooded, and at night I returned to that same dance-hall. She might be there again, or she might not. If she were, so much the worse for her. If she were not, so much the better for me.

" 'And do you know what I had in my pocket— er—Trenck?' he asked.

" 'I had your knife.

" 'The knife with your name and crest engraved upon its beautiful blade.

" 'The knife you gave me as a little souvenir of the night in No-Man's Land.

" 'Do you remember, Trenck, that I wouldn't accept your watch that had been given to your great-grandfather by his Emperor? And that I accepted your lovely knife instead, since you insisted on its being something personal.'

"I did remember that knife," mused Trenck. "A very beautiful thing that I had bought as a *souvenir de visite* in Madrid; a lovely knife with a gold-inlaid metal handle and a beautiful damascened Toledo blade, on which I had had my name and crest inscribed.

" 'It had been mine so long,' continued Tzigan, 'that I had forgotten it ever had been yours. When I say forgotten, I mean that the memory was not ever-present with me. I swear to God it was not, on that night. . . . It was just a pocket clasp-knife. . . . *My* knife, with five or six inches of beautiful blue blade. . . .

" 'She came all right. . . . Came with the man who had been her partner of the night before; but she danced most of the time with another man. . . . A man with whom her partner seemed to have an understanding.

" 'From my dark corner, where a square pillar and a potted palm further concealed me, I watched.

" 'Several times she passed quite near where I sat.

" 'I poured out a tumbler of brandy and drank it neat.

" 'I opened the knife, rose to my feet, stood on the more shadowed side of the pillar, and, next time she passed (her back turned to me) I struck. . . .

" 'The blade sank into the side of her neck until my hand once again, and for the last time, touched her flesh.

" 'And then, stepping back behind the pillar, I made my way, in the dim obscurity, round the crowded dance-hall to the door. . . .

" 'There had been a faint cry, a sharp:

" ' "What's that? What's up?" in a man's voice.

" 'Apparently some confusion in that corner of the room, and a laugh.

" 'I heard a woman call,

" ' "Look out, she's fallen down," and a man, the one who had laughed, I think, said,

" ' "Disgraceful. . . . This Night Club champagne, I mean."

" 'Then there was crowding, confusion, a growing babel of voices, and, as I quietly walked out of the place, a piercing scream. I imagine the lights went up then.

" 'It was not until I got back to my room that I realized two facts.

" 'One was that a man, who took his hat and coat from the cloak-room just after I did, was the man who had brought my wife to the dance.

" 'And the other fact was that I had left my knife buried to the handle in the woman's neck.

" 'In a desperate state of mind, with mingled feelings of disgust, remorse, horror, self-loathing and fear, especially fear, arrant coward fear—for my nerves were utterly shattered by war strain, wounds and debauchery, I fled next day.

" 'Fled from the very shadow of the gallows, which seemed to pursue me.

" 'Like so many ruined and broken ex-soldiers of the Great War, I joined the Legion for a living, a hiding-place and a refuge. . . .

" 'Trenck, a month ago I was in Saïda; and, in a café in Saïda, I picked up a copy of *La Dépêche Algérienne*, or it may have been *L'Écho d'Oran*, when my eye fell upon a heading that made my heart stop and my stomach seem to sink.

" 'It was to the effect that *you*, the husband of the girl who had been murdered in the Montezuma

Night Club; you, the owner of the knife that had been left buried in her neck, were believed to have joined the French Foreign Legion—and that representations had been made in the proper quarters regarding assistance in your identification, arrest and extradition!'

" 'Good God!' I said. 'Zita? You married Zita? You murdered Zita?'

"Tzigan rose to his feet, a look of the utmost horror on his face.

" 'She was your wife, Trenck?' he stammered. 'The police were right?'

" 'Zita?' I repeated. 'What are we talking about? . . . What are we saying?' . . .

" 'Look, Trenck, my friend,' said Tzigan, seating himself, and seizing my hand that lay upon the table, 'the blade buried in the woman's neck bore your name and crest. The police supposed that the murdered woman was the divorced wife of the man whose name and crest it was.'

" 'I remember now . . . I heard that she was nursing,' I said dully. 'Yes, she would be a ministering angel, a gracious presence and a healing touch to any man—except her husband.'

" 'And Zita was your wife before I married her!' Tzigan whispered.

"And added bitterly, 'Comrades in arms, indeed, you and I, my friend.'

" 'Do you know, Trenck, in a way, that helps me a little. It makes what I am about to do a little easier. . . . Somehow. . . .' he said.

"I stared at him in silence, my mind confused and whirling.

" 'It helps me, my friend, a little . . . to ask you to keep your promise. Trenck, I am shattered. I'm all in. I couldn't bear it. I saved your life. . . . Save mine. . . . Time after time, you've said it to me that

you would do anything, *anything*, for me; anything
that it was in your power to do. You said that your
life was mine, for I had saved you and your life
belonged to me. . . . Now save me.'

" 'But of course,' I said. 'How?' . . . for I was still
bewildered.

" 'By keeping your mouth shut.'

" 'But of course,' I said. 'What else should I do?
Why should I go out of my way to denounce you?'

" 'Don't you see. . . . Don't you understand? . . .
Your wife. . . . Your knife. With your name and
crest on the blade. Even the newspapers know
that the police have traced you to the Foreign
Legion. You may be arrested at any minute.'

" 'And then?' I said.

" 'Then—don't say to whom you gave your
knife.' "

" 'Don't say to whom I gave my knife,' I mused
aloud. 'No, I will not say to whom I gave my knife.'

"Tzigan seized my hand and wrung it.

" 'Save yourself, my friend,' he said, 'but save
me too. . . . I can't face it. . . . Nerves. . . . My
nerve has gone. D'you know, I can only get sleep
by drinking myself insensible.' "

"About a week later, his Company was moved
on, and thereafter I began to think less and less
about my dangerous position. We were worked so
hard that one scarcely had time to think—you
know what it is when orders have come, and you
may move at any minute—and I was too tired at
night to lie awake and think. Thank God, I, unlike
Tzigan, have never been denied the gift of sleep.

"I wasn't much worried about it all, really; for
in any case it was more likely than not, that I
shouldn't return from the campaign. I've always
inclined to be something of a fatalist. . . .

"The evening before the Battalion marched, I was arrested in the Barrack Room and taken straight to a cell. When I pretended the greatest surprise and incredulous consternation, I was told to hold my tongue until I was asked to speak, which would be soon enough.

"It certainly was not soon enough for me. Next day I was sent under armed escort to Sidi-bel-Abbès and, as I entered the familiar gates, the Sergeant of the Guard greeted me with the kindly words:

" 'Who's this? The woman-stabber? We'll soon show you whether you murderous gutter-rats can defile the ranks of the Legion.'

"I was handed over to the Authorities and taken straight to the Military Prison. Although I had not been asked a single question by anybody, much less received any sort or kind of pretence of a trial, I had been brought as a criminal, under escort, to Sidi-bel-Abbès, and was now marched as a criminal to the gaol.

"Here, I was taken to a cell which was a little longer than I was, when I lay down; a little higher than I was, when I stood up; and a little wider than I was, as I stood and faced the door. In this cell, there was no window whatsoever, the walls being entirely unbroken by aperture of any kind. In the iron door was a grating, six inches square.

"There was no bed in this cell, but I was given a blanket which was not big, not thick, not clean and not uninhabited. The sole furniture of that cell was myself and the blanket, and I was not allowed to leave the cell for any purpose whatsoever.

"About twenty-four hours later, a Corporal and two armed warders came for me and conducted me to an office-room, at a table in which sat an officer of the rank of Captain.

"He asked me but one question.

" 'Were you, before you joined the Legion, in the R—— H—— Regiment of the A—— Army?' he asked.

"I answered promptly in the affirmative. There was no point in denying this—apart from the fact that they obviously already knew it.

"That was all. I was taken back to my cell and there I spent thirty days in solitary confinement. I was allowed out of my cell to wash my clothes once a week; and, as I was not allowed sufficient time in which to dry them, I had to put them on again while still wet. I used to snatch an opportunity of washing my face on these occasions, but I was given only one bath of cold water, without soap, in the month. I received food twice a day, half the army ration, and of poorer quality.

"By the time I was taken from this cell, I was contemplating suicide, and I think I should have killed myself but for the fact that I was really too tired. It's an awful business, committing suicide when you have nothing with which to do it. I had neither boot-laces, braces, knife, fork nor spoon. Men in those cells have gnawed their wrists and bled to death. Others have battered their heads against the wall until they died; but by the time I was feeling properly suicidal, I was, as I say, really too tired.

"Living in darkness, I had turned an ugly yellow colour; and was a miserable sore-skinned bag of bones—and, after that first day, I had spoken to no-one, and no-one had spoken to me.

"When on the thirty-first day I was ordered out of the cell, and told that I was to be handed over to *gendarmes* who were to take me under escort to Paris, I was so glad to go that, even had I known for certain that I should there receive a death sentence, I should still have welcomed the chance to leave that cell.

"As I emerged into daylight, I cannot have looked a credit to that model prison, for I was taken to the baths, thence to the barber's cell, and from there to the Quarter-master's stores. Washed, shaven, clipped and dressed, I must have looked much more worth the trouble of shooting or hanging; and I must have been pleasant company for the three *gendarmes* whose duty it was to escort me to Paris.

"After that dreadful interminable month, and the dreadful silence unbroken by a single word from my dumb guards, life on the journey from Sidi-bel-Abbès to Paris was positively gay. There were sunlight and blue sky, air that moved and smelt sweet, palm-trees, occasional flowers, children, people going about their business, and, at night, the stars. And then the sea . . . the open sea, after that cell. . . .

"And these *gendarmes* were not dumb. In comparison with the prison guards they were really rather kindly men, who would civilly answer a question, and treat one as though it were a fact that he had not even been tried for any offence, much less convicted of the worst possible.

"Once on the journey, when the train stopped—at Dijon, I think it was—the brigadier of the *gendarmes* gave me a large glass of wine. . . .

"Arrived in Paris, I was taken to a civil prison and put into a cell where there were already three other prisoners, people of markedly unpleasant type and characteristics. No less than two months did I spend in this prison before I was taken before a civil judge, on a charge of murdering my wife Zita in the Montezuma dance-hall in—er—Vienna.

"That two months in the civil prison was sheer pleasure, rest-cure, joy, after the month I had had in the military prison at Sidi-bel-Abbès.

"My trial was brief.

"The knife. Did I recognize it?

"Certainly.

"It was mine?

"Undoubtedly.

"The name inscribed upon it was my own name?

"Undeniably.

"The crest upon the blade. That was the crest of my family?

"It was.

"The murdered woman, Zita. She was my divorced wife?

"The christian-name of my divorced wife was assuredly Zita.

"This photograph. Was it that of my divorced wife?

"Certainly.

"Ah!

"And where pray was I on the night of June 13th, 19—?

"Merciful God, where was I? Tzigan had given me no dates. Where was I at that time? Merciful God, where was I?

"Ha-ha! Ha-ha! Oh, how *drôle*. How I laughed.

"Had the prisoner gone mad?

"Where was I on that night?

" 'I was in the barracks at Sidi-bel-Abbès in Algeria, in the depôt company of the French Foreign Legion, Monsieur le Juge.'

"And so I was able to prove, without the slightest difficulty.

"I was discharged without a stain on my

character—though with an indelible stain upon my soul.

"But I had kept my promise. . . .

"I was taken back to Sidi-bel-Abbès and then sent to rejoin my company.

"So, as Tovarish Demenko has observed, one perceives that I am still alive. . . ."

*   *   *   *   *

No, I reserve judgment on "Baron" Trenck's story. I don't disbelieve it, but somehow I can't quite accept "Tzigan" (though I suppose there are such people), and none of the protagonists is English. By which I mean that one must not judge everybody from an English stand-point.

But, bless me, after all, aren't bad Englishmen as bad as anybody else? . . . Yes, but somehow it's a different kind of badness . . . I don't know.

And come to think of it, that beast Matthieu le Maquereau knew something about Trenck and Tzigan. Quite probably he knew Zita too.

CHAPTER III

"Wine, Women, and Song," play a very large part in that rather small commodity the *légionnaire's* spare time—if time be a commodity—when he is at a *depôt*. He drinks the good red Algerian wine (much of which finds its way to British dinner-tables under the name of Claret, Burgundy and Bordeaux, product of France. It is certainly one of the products of France and it goes to England via Bordeaux, so *que voulez vous?*) whenever he can get it, and he thinks of it when he is unable to get it.

Half a litre is issued to him on alternate days when this is possible; and he can buy it marvellously cheaply in the canteen on pay-day, or when finances permit. Taken in moderate quantities, it is good for him—cheering and sustaining—and its brightening mental effect must have a further favourable physical effect. And, should any staunch teetotaller disagree, let him try it under the *légionnaire's* conditions of diet and circumstance. And when the *légionnaire* exceeds as, alas, he so frequently does, good wine is a better medium for intoxication than bad spirit or synthetic beer.

As to Women, the attitude of the *légionnaires* is as various as their respective nationality, age, social stratum, and experience. Many of them know practically nothing at all about women, and many know a great deal too much. Quite a number of men are in the Legion on account of women; a good many because they could not marry the woman whom they loved; a good many because they did marry her.

I can never quite understand the reasoning of any young man who—because his *fiancée* played him false, or turned him down, or because some girl could not, or would not, return his love—promptly says:

"Ha! I will join the French Foreign Legion."

I should imagine that the young woman in the case would reply, or at any rate mutter, *sotto voce:*

"Splendid. That disposes of you for five years, if not for good."

I suppose what really is at the back of the young man's mind is the feeling:

"Yes, and when I lie on the battle-field, cold and calm in death, with my handsome face bathed in the pale light of the desert moon—you'll be sorry. Too late you will regret—" whatever it was she ought to regret.

However, the fact remains, many and many a fine recruit comes to the Legion under these unhappy, if romantic, auspices. So many, that there was at one time a *médecin-major* who never examined a recruit for the Legion without remarking:

"Ah! You want to enlist, do you? Some woman brought you to this. But for a woman, you would not be asking to go to a life of the greatest danger and the hardest labour for a *sou* a day."

Should the recruit truthfully or untruthfully, as he thought, stoutly deny this, the *médecin-major* would crush him with his perennial little joke:

"Oh? So you never had a mother, eh?"

Anyhow, save for the confirmed misogynists like Cocteau the Cannibal, or a morose old brute like Moronoff, or a bitter cynic like Trenck, most *légionnaires*, celibates of circumstance, talked and thought a very great deal about women.

And I am quite sure the average man dreamed of some impossibly-lovely and complaisant *houri* who would, one day, fall in love with him as he rescued her from the burning *hareem* of some old Bluebeard of a Kaid whose castle or *kasbah* or *ksar* his Company was attacking.

Actually there was a legendary admired hero of whom we had all heard, and whom we envied from the bottoms of our hearts, who had married an extremely lovely and wealthy Moorish lady, the daughter or sister of some great Kaid upon whom he had imposed himself as a French officer and gentleman; or whose service he had entered as organizer-instructor, and had finally become commander, of his troops.

About this interesting and romantic gentleman I could never get actual accurate and convincing details, but just as everybody knows someone who has seen a ghost, so everyone knew someone who had known him.

Doubtless the tales one heard were much exaggerated, but that some such person did some such thing, I am quite sure.

With regard to Song—and, in spite of his hard life the *légionnaire* does sing—on the march and in the canteen, it is a pity that no one has ever made a complete and comprehensive collection of the songs particular and peculiar to the Legion. Should this ever be done, the reader must not be particular, for the songs *are* peculiar.

The music of these songs is interesting, largely German in origin, and they make splendid march-tunes. Some are classic, as old as the Legion, and some are products of the Great War. Some are exclusive to the Legion, as they deal with the idiosyncrasies, traits, appearance, deeds, and frequently the morals and manners, of officers of note, such as General Brigeaud.

I think an officer regards it as a mark and proof of his popularity, when his men sing about him by name—a doubtful compliment, however, for the words of the song are generally very far from being complimentary—such as (in free translation):

"Good Colonel de Minorca,
Mon Dieu, he is a corker!
From hearth and home he had to roam
For pinching the General's porker."

But this would be but the beginning, and infinitely the least libellous, of twenty such verses, dealing faithfully and unfaithfully with his private life and morals—to which the Colonel would grimly listen as he rode at the head of the column.

A curious custom, the tolerance of which is a strange concomitant of the most rigid, most repressive, military discipline in the world.

*   *   *   *   *

We had had some Wine to-night, we had had some Song, and now Women were on the *tapis*.

Men spoke of them according to their kind; and exhibited their kind in the way in which they spoke of them.

Old Père Cocteau, Cocteau the Pirate and Cannibal, as usual grunted his disapproval of woman in every manifestation and aspect. When asked his own personal experience—the experience upon which he based his unvarying attitude and opinion—he positively spat his disapproval.

Of himself, with regard to Woman, and the reason why he would have no relations with women, nor approve of any of his friends doing so, he would never speak; though he was full of wise saws and modern instances of how mischief is never wrought by a man's want of thought, still less by his want of heart—in regard to women.

"Women!" he growled. "You and your women! How many times have I told you . . ."

"Tell us again, Cannibal," begged Gustavus Adolphus. "I told you I joined the Legion for the sake of peace . . ."

"Wisest thing you ever did," grumbled Cocteau. "Not that a man's safe, even then. Look at Boulanger."

"The General?" I asked.

"No, the Sergeant," replied Cocteau.

"I don't want to look at any Sergeant," observed Abraham the Sailor.

"Well, you can't look at Sergeant Boulanger, anyhow, although I recommended you to do so. . . . I spoke meta-meta-metaphysorically. You can't actually look at him, more's the pity. . . . Not at the moment, you can't."

"Why, where is he?" I asked.

"In Hell," replied Cocteau. "And sent there by a woman."

"Tell us," I begged.

"Tell you? Why should one give oneself the trouble to tell this band of camels the sad story of the finest Sergeant who ever added lustre to the immortal glory of our Regiment . . . I, who have been a Sergeant and done the same myself . . . added lustre, I mean. . . . I tell you, it was an even worse tragedy than mine. . . . And yet I know not. . . . Boulanger would have preferred death to dishonour and reduction to the ranks. Dishonour such as is bringing my grey hairs in sorrow to a hero's grave."

"What about Boulanger's grave?" interrupted Matthieu le Maquereau.

"Species of a pink and spotted dog, I am telling you, am I not?" snarled Cocteau, turning upon Matthieu, whom he detested—as did most of us.

"Spill the story, Cocktail," requested Abraham

the Sailor. "If that Bedouin's bastard utters again, I'll bust him one on the dome."

Both Cocteau and Matthieu understood the speaker's meaning if not his words.

"It was in Sidi-bel-Abbès, and *le bon Dieu* Himself only knows how long ago; and I, Aristide Cocteau, who have been *le Sergent* Cocteau of the *Infanterie Coloniale*, was a recruit of the Legion. . . . There, I used to see something that puzzled me.

"A poor woman, accompanied by either two or three little children, each bearing a tin can, was in the habit of coming daily at noon to the Barrack gates. Like all good women and good children in Improving Stories for the Young—as this is for you—they were spotlessly clean, and their poor rags were washed and mended with the utmost care. And as such people do in such stories, they looked pale and wan—and hungry, *mon Dieu*, how hungry!

"On arrival at the Main Guard, the woman would present a card to the Sergeant of the Guard who, having scrutinized it carefully, would detail a man to conduct her and the children to the cookhouse. At the cook-house door, a cook would slap a ration of *soupe* into each of the cans, topped by a hunk of bread.

"Well, you know what our *rata* is apt to be at times, but the woman and children—those poor ones—eyed it wolfishly, looked at it like old Thirsty-face would eye a bucket of wine.

"I am, by nature, kindly and tender-hearted, unlike you savage sons of village vultures, and it made my heart ache to see the hungry stare in the hollow eyes of those *misérables*. The hollow cheeks, pale faces . . ."

Abraham the Sailor emitted a deep groan, while

Digger wagged a mournful head and appeared about to weep.

"Ah! Of a pathos pathetic!" continued Cocteau rebukingly. "I tell you, *mes amis*, so heartrending was that little band, that woman and those infants, that the heart of many a hard and callous *légionnaire* was so softened that voluntarily he thrust upon them some portion of his own rations —that he could not possibly eat, or otherwise dispose of, himself.

"Now I am not a naturally curious man. . . ."

"I think you're a damn curious man," interrupted his friend, Thirsty-face, politely suppressing a hiccup.

". . . but I confess that my natural and proper curiosity was aroused by this phenomenon. The Legion is not primarily a philanthropic organization, and I had never hitherto heard of it giving anything away. So I was moved to make inquiries. I learned from an employed pensioner that this woman took care of these children, who were the family of a married *légionnaire*. A halfpenny a day does not go far in this direction.

"Apparently in those days it was the custom to issue a ration of food, once a day, to the family of any married *légionnaire*, if the family was present in Sidi-bel-Abbès and he was absent from it on duty."

"Kind of 'married on the strength,' " murmured Terence Hogan.

"On the strength of a pint of stew?" asked Digger.

". . . I don't imagine that the custom proved a severe strain on the resources of *Madame la République* because, as one has mentioned before, those who do not come to the Legion because the Beloved will not marry them, come because the Beloved has married them and the Legion offers a refuge from family life.

"And you can imagine how many of the rest, having joined the Legion as bachelors, desire to set up house-keeping on a halfpenny a day, or can find anyone willing to share it. No. The established *légionnaire* does not marry much. But this man did."

"What man?" asked Moranoff.

"The man we're talking about, my good fool. We, or rather I, am talking about Sergeant Boulanger.

"He was indeed a fine man, a man with a sense of duty, a patriot and a hero, spiritual descendant of Marshal Ney, the 'Bravest of the Brave.'

"He was an Alsatian, but when his time came for him to be called up for the German Army, he fled into France and joined the Legion (long before the War) so that, at the end of his service in our Regiment, he could claim the French citizenship for which this would make him eligible.

"You see, *mes amis*, Boulanger had a French soul as well as a French name; and not only did he not desire to remain the German that he was born in Alsace, but he hated the Germans. Saving your presence, my dear Petsel, he loathed them. And when war broke out, he demanded to go to France to fight, and refused to remain with the German *légionnaires* who were kept in Algeria, Morocco, Madagascar and Cochin China.

"And this, although he had fallen desperately in love with a woman in Sidi-bel-Abbès, had actually married her, and was the father of a family.

"Yes, he had fallen madly in love, which I suppose is not remarkable in a sentimental young German-bred Alsatian. . . . And he had married, which is remarkable in a *légionnaire*. Also remarkable in a woman of Sidi-bel-Abbès. Those ladies fortunately know but too well what are the pay and prospects of a *légionnaire*.

"But this Boulanger was handsome . . . hand-some . . . as handsome . . . as . . ."

"Me?" inquired Abraham the Sailor.

"Me?" asked Digger.

"Well, the handsomest man that ever came to the Legion," continued Cocteau, ignoring these suggestions.

"He was much over six feet tall, his hair was of the golden colour and curled, his eyes were blue and big. . . . Well, anyhow, he was the handsomest man imaginable; and being as fair as the fairest of Northerners, he fell in love with a Spanish girl, who was dark even for a Southern Spaniard. All you scoundrels know the type. Great brown eyes and long black eyelashes. Thick black eyebrows, face the colour of an apricot kissed by the sun, and that blue-black patent-leather hair. . . .

"She served and danced in the Café Valencia . . . Kissed by the sun? Yes, and by every son of a gun of a *légionnaire* and Spahi, and everything else in uniform, that had got a franc or two.

"And Monsieur Thor-and-Odin Lohengrin Bou-langer married this Spanish trollop, and still more remarkably, the Spanish trollop married Lohen-grin.

"Why should she?

"Heaven alone knows. As a rule, Heaven alone knows why a woman does anything. I suppose she was tired of the life she led in old Diego Ramon's café, and wanted a rest. And Boulanger must have had a little money, for he brought all that he'd got with him, when he joined the Legion, and banked it at the *Crédit Lyonnais* in Sidi-bel-Abbès.

"Anyhow, on what he had, and his Sergeant's pay, he married this woman and set her up in a room in the Spanish quarter. And there he spent every hour of the day or night, when he was not on duty. He had been in several campaigns and picked up a couple of decorations, and they were glad enough to have him as Sergeant-Instructor with the *depôt* Battalion.

"Then came sudden trouble in Morocco. Trouble that spread like wild-fire—and Boulanger had to go. The place for a twice-decorated and be-medalled Sergeant of that type was the firing-line, and not the barrack-square.

"Boulanger kissed his wife and the two babies and tore himself from the beloved woman who was about again to become a mother. I should not like to have been present at that parting, for this poor Boulanger was one of those strange men who love but once. Oh, there are such men. It is a form of madness akin to that of a man who might say:

" 'This indeed is a perfect bottle of wine. I will never drink another.' "

"Send him 'Sylum," murmured Thirsty-face and hic-cupped heartily.

"Well, he went. Marched out one fine morning, leaving behind him the woman he loved, the children he adored. With the woman he left his heart and, incidentally, all his worldly possessions. All the money that he had in the bank, his pay, and everything that he could beg, borrow and scrape together. Should it be necessary, she could, of course, work again after her baby was born.

"But Sergeant Boulanger most earnestly hoped that this would not be necessary; for he detested the thought of his wife serving drinks in the café, and doing her Spanish dances for the diversion of the habitués of the Café Valencia.

"Well . . . once again, Sergeant Boulanger came home from the wars, and not only with another medal, but with another decoration. For he had not merely the courage of the lion combined with the tenacity of the bull-dog, but also the sagacity of the elephant. He could think, as well as do; and he would hang on to what he had done. What better type to be in charge of a *poste*, surrounded and cut off, with dwindling rations and deteriorating *morale?* No wonder they decorated him for the third time.

"And so he came back—certain of promotion to *Adjudant*, and much more than likely to go on to a commission. Yes . . . with just a little luck and the continuance of his impeccable conduct, initiative and ability, he might well hope to retire from the army and settle down in France as *M'sieu le Lieutenant* Frederic Boulanger.

"One can imagine how, the moment his duty was done, he rushed off to his home in the Rue Christophe, his fine chest seeming too small to contain the great heart that beat so wildly.

"He hurried, he ran . . . to his home.

"There was no home.

"The occupant of his room had never heard of a Madame Boulanger having lived there.

"A neighbour, however, who had lived in the same house for years, knew all about Madame Boulanger. One figures to oneself that this good woman had no love for the departed Madame Boulanger.

"She told the unhappy husband, then almost too stricken and bewildered to understand, all about Madame Boulanger. And one doubts not that the tale lost little in the telling.

"Madame Boulanger? Oh, la, la! That one! Madame All-the-town rather. And the poor little ones, *les pauvres misérables*. That fine Madame Boulanger had left them as a pariah bitch would not leave its pups . . . abandoned them as no back-yard cat would abandon its kittens. . . . And her husband? That fine Sergeant. . . . *What*, was *Monsieur* the husband himself, come back from the war? *Monsieur le Sergent Boulanger! Mon Dieu!* The poor man!

"One sees her, that *méchante*, getting her own back on Madame Boulanger, and killing the husband where he stood, for I think *le Sergent* Boulanger died there, listening to that woman's tale.

"One imagines him asking, 'Where is she now?' and being told, 'Who knows . . . ? And not she herself knows where she'll be to-morrow night.'

" 'And my children?'

" 'God knows. . . . The gutter. . . . When the landlord turned them out, one took one, and one took another, until the mother should come for them, or the father return. . . . But one grows tired of other folks' children, look you, especially when one's own are clamouring, and times are hard.'

" 'Could you not tell me where one of them is?'

" 'Not I. Haven't set eyes on one of them for months.'

" 'Is there anybody who might be able to tell me where they are?'

" '*Le bon Dieu.*'

"One imagines poor stricken Boulanger . . . pale . . . he trembles . . . his flat back and square shoulders sag and droop.

" 'What am I to do?' he whispers.

" 'Find that *putain* and wring her neck,' says the woman.

"And Boulanger turns away.

"And, mark you, Boulanger was a deeply religious man. One notices such in the Legion. . . . And a staunch Roman Catholic for whom there was no divorce.

"It seems he spent the whole of that night in searching the slums of Sidi-bel-Abbès, going from *maison tolerée* to *bouge;* from wine-shop to café; from dance-hall to dive; from lodging-house to haunt . . . trying to trace his children and his wife.

"Well for him, that night, that he was the man he was, and a smart and model Sergeant of the Legion.

"Well for him also in the morning, having overstayed his pass and missed parade, that his record was what it was.

"The next night the same; and the next the same.

"And when his Officer sent for him, instead of telling him the whole story, he answered as a man is apt to answer who has been on his feet for a week, without sleep and almost without food.

"And soon the poor fellow, unable to eat, turned to the good red wine—as we all do—to be food and drink to him, both. To keep him going just a little longer . . . just until he could find his children.

"And it played him false—as it plays us all false. Is not Wine bracketed with Woman? Yes, we turn to wine for comfort as we turn to women, and it plays us false as women play us false. Wine is a mocker . . ."

"Turn from it, and give me your ration!" cried Thirsty-face.

"Peace, pig," replied Cocteau.

"Wine is a mocker, and it mocked this poor Boulanger. He went down-hill with amazing speed, as all must do who literally live on wine. And, *mes amis*, within a month, this tragic heroic victim of Fate, the sport and mockery of the ironic gods; brave, reticent and self-respecting; his life devoted to a noble quest, degenerated into the victim of the bottle; the sport and mockery of Arab gutter-snipes; a maudlin nuisance who, at night, wandered about drunk, self-pitying, almost incapable of making himself understood by those whom he accosted, to ask whether they had seen his wife and children.

"And one night, forgetting his rank and his sorrows, he drank with a gang of bad-type *légionnaires* in a low pot-house—each one a *mauvais sujet;* men whom he had often punished, and to any one of whom, a month ago, he'd have given eight days' *salle de police* if he'd had the amazing impudence to dream of so much as suggesting the offer of a bottle of wine to Sergeant Boulanger.

"And these rascals, in their element at such work, jumped at this devil-sent opportunity of ruining a Sergeant—especially the particular Sergeant who had tried to make soldiers of them. They mixed his drinks, poured rice-spirit, sawdust gin, and similar poisons into his wine; got him fighting-drunk, fought him and battered him until his mother would hardly have known him; flung him in the gutter; rolled him in every kind of filth; knocked him insensible, and then, taking him back to Barracks, respectfully delivered him up to the Sergeant of the Guard, as men who had done their duty for the credit of their Regiment.

"He was tried for behaviour unbecoming to a Non-Commissioned Officer of the Legion, and, in view of his splendid record and unblemished character, the case was treated as one of *cafard*, and he received the mild sentence of severe reprimand and reduction to the rank of Corporal.

"The very next night that he was out, he got drunk on his own accord, and, lurching in at the gates, assaulted a Corporal for not saluting him. He then struck the Sergeant of the Guard in the face, and began to rave and shout, kick and struggle, like—what he then undoubtedly was—a lunatic.

"This time the sentence was sharper. He was reduced not only to the ranks, but to the rank of a second-class *légionnaire*, and given fifty-two days' imprisonment.

"He came out from that sentence a thin, bent, yellow-faced man, and as changed in mind and spirit as he was in body. As he recovered some of his former strength, he bore himself well, and became the model soldier of the second class. But he scarcely ever spoke, and he seemed at times to have been stricken dumb.

"But he did his duty perfectly, and the Sergeants who had been his friends, and the Corporals who had feared and admired him, now respected his misery. And this was rendered easier by his irreproachable conduct.

"Now you, *mes amis*, may think he had been through his worst hell, but I tell you, I who know, that it was only just beginning.

"Who, but the man who has been through it, can understand, can imagine, what it is to serve in Hell after ruling in Heaven. For that is the comparative difference. . . . Who, but the man that has been through it, can grasp what it means to be ordered instead of ordering; to be shouted at instead of shouting; to perform the most menial and filthy fatigues, instead of directing somebody else to see that they are done . . . to sweep the room; to peel potatoes; to fetch and carry at the double; to be for guard, and go on sentry; to drill with recruits; and to be of actually lower rank than the first-class soldiers who have, for years, been one's respectful and obedient servants, leapt at one's word, and trembled at one's frown. . . . To live with them night and day; their butt, their sport, the overthrown and fallen god; to be ridiculed and rolled in the mud.

"That was his real Hell, *mes amis*. That life as a soldier of the second class, among the men whom he had ruled as a despot.

"A soldier of the second class! He, who for years had been saluted by such, as well as by soldiers of the first class, and by Corporals. . . . You cannot imagine his life. . . . But I can . . ."

"Having to herd with swine like us?" interrupted Matthieu le Maquereau.

"Exactly. Thank you. Having to herd with swine like you. You personally, I mean.

"And without such alleviation as a Sergeant's pay could bring. We know how much wine a halfpenny a day brings. And, add to his other miseries, the thought that he had for ever lost his Sergeant's pension; lost it on the very eve of gaining it—a pension earned by such bitter years of sweat and blood—small enough, God knows, but sufficient to keep him from starvation in his old age.

"Do you wonder that he brooded, that broken man, who had lost wife, children, position, pension, everything?

"Captain Lamartine, who had known him for years, and thought highly of him, was desolated. Time after time, he sent for him and bade him pull himself together, make an effort; and try, at any rate, to become a soldier of the first class. There was neither time nor hope for him to regain his rank of Sergeant.

"On the last occasion that the Captain sent for him, he said he wished to ask a favour. He promised that if the Captain would grant it, he would never never again give him cause for complaint and dissatisfaction. What he wanted was an all-night pass for the night of November the First. . . . That had been his wedding-day and he wished, from a certain spot, to see the sun rise on that day."

" 'I have a rendezvous with Death,' " murmured Terence Hogan.

"I know all this because old Frontrelles, the Orderly-Clerk, was present, and told me all about it.

"And thus, *mes amis*, it is I, I who speak, Aristide Cocteau, who can tell *you* all about it.

"That morning at six o'clock Frontrelles had to go, as usual, to his Captain's house, and, on the way along the ramparts, met *ce pauvre* Boulanger —and apparently he was Sergeant Boulanger once again.

"He was in full uniform, his medals and decorations flashing and gleaming in the rays of the rising sun, gold Sergeant's chevrons pinned to his cuffs, his *képi* carefully adjusted as a smart soldier should wear it, slightly toward the left ear, somewhat pulled down in the front and the peak well bent in the middle. The only thing wrong about his dress was that he was only wearing one puttee.

"The other was partly about his neck and partly about the branch of the tree from which he had hanged himself.

"He had preferred to die as a Sergeant than to live as a *légionnaire*.

"*Chacun a son goût*. Me, I would rather live as a *légionnaire* than die as a Sergeant.

" 'I stood and stared in horror,' said Frontrelles. 'There was nothing to be done for Boulanger. He must have been dead for quite an hour. Doubtless he had died at sunrise, and had I been able to get his body down, it would probably have cost me quite a lot of time and trouble to prove that I hadn't murdered him.

" 'However, one or two people came along; an Arab, a Jew, a Spaniard, until there was a small crowd staring at what had been the finest Sergeant in the Foreign Legion. I sent a boy running for the police. The sooner this poor fellow ceased to be the centre of a gaping crowd the better I should feel. And I needed to feel better—

for the sight of poor Boulanger. . . .

" 'But he was a *légionnaire*, and I was another, and I must stand by him until an ambulance came to remove him.'

"The crowd grew larger, and, before long, there were women and children among them; and the whole crew of ghouls seemed to gloat over the spectacle of a dead *légionnaire*.

"Some Arab women of the lowest class gathered close and, but for Frontrelles, would doubtless have removed the dead man's boots.

"Some of the loafing scum of Sidi-bel-Abbès came along; and one wag, pushing his way through, stepped into the little space about the corpse and exercised his wit. Having raised a laugh he took poor Boulanger's right hand and shook it, with a vulgar jest.

"I do not practise *le boxe* as a sport, *mes amis*, but believe me, I know where and how to hit a man when I am fighting to save my life—or to lose his. Could but I have hit that man—I doubt if he would have recovered yet.

"It was over two hours before the military ambulance arrived. Boulanger was cut down, placed on the ambulance, and wheeled back to barracks.

"And who do you think was standing waiting at the barrack-gates as his body, decently covered, thank God, was wheeled through them?"

"Not his wife?" said I.

"No. The worthy woman who had for so long lived in the house in which Sergeant and Madame Boulanger had made their nest in the Rue Christophe. Yes. And with her, Boulanger's three children. She had come upon one of them, the oldest one, slaving for some wretched stall-owning tradesman, and through her, had found out where the others were.

"Captain Lamartine ordered that the dead man's rations should be given to this woman and the children, for so long as they chose to come for them. Whether he paid for them himself I do not know."

Père Cocteau, removing his *képi*, sought in its unattractive interior for a cigarette. He found one —like himself—battered, war-worn and weary, but still entirely *bon pour le service.*

"And from my story, you young soldiers who talk about women, may draw a moral. . . ."

"Surely," agreed Abraham the Sailor. "Don't marry the highest kicker in the lowest café in Sidi-bel-Abbès. . . . I don't see no other moral."

*   *   *   *   *

Sergeant Pflügge is a man who speaks most evilly of us to our faces, but apparently speaks well of us, or of some of us, behind our backs.

Terence Hogan and I were sent for, this morning, and informed by Lieutenant V——, now commanding this *poste*, that we were to take charge of the Store Room, the dry-food *magasin*, be responsible for it and for all issues from it, in the absence of the Sergeant; and to be the Store Room guard by night and by day. We should have to issue, on indent, the necessary food and wine to the *légionnaires* who would be sent in, twice a week, from the various small out-lying *postes*, for their supplies.

Lieutenant V——, something of a dandy and a fine gentleman, eyed us speculatively as, with pursed lips and folded arms, he leant back in his chair.

"I hear well of you both, *mes enfants*," he said, "and expect well of you. No drunkenness. . . . No selling of stores. . . . No trouble with accounts. . . .

No complaints that short rations are issued. . . . And, mind, never both absent from the Store Room at the same time."

We stood at attention, like statues, and at appropriate moments murmured the appropriate replies.

"*Bien*," said Lieutenant V——. "*Rompez*," and as we saluted and turned to go, added, looking at Terence Hogan,

"An Officer—er—formerly?"

"*Oui, mon Commandant.*"

"And you?" he asked, looking at me.

"Er—I was not in the ranks, *mon Commandant*," I replied quite truthfully.

"Well, I shall hope to see you both Sergeants some day," smiled Lieutenant V——.

Outside his quarters, Sergeant Pflügge brought us back to earth.

"Meanwhile, my budding Field-Marshals, hop like Hell and get your kit—and jump to it. Transfer your beds to the Store Room, and sleep there."

"*Bien, mon Sergent*," we both replied.

"God bless our Home," observed Terence as we finished rigging up some blankets across a corner of the Store Room, cutting off a space, and making a tiny room within the room.

"God bless our cubby-hole," I endorsed.

" 'Tis but a tiny cottage," squeaked Terence in a high falsetto. "But Lurv will make it Heavern."

I looked at the earth floor, the rough stone walls of the corner and the blankets which formed the third wall of this triangular heaven.

" 'Stone walls do not a prison make, nor iron bars a cage,' " continued Terry, "but they make a damn good beginning. I suppose we lock ourselves in every night . . . ?"

*   *   *   *   *

I'm sorry for Sergeant Marcovitz, a reasonably honest man in a position of unreasonable difficulty for an honest man.

As Sergeant Store-keeper he is practically compelled to play the dishonest grocer; and I am glad that the evil that I do is done at his command, the burden of my sins on his conscience.

When he tells me to water the wine, it is my duty to water the wine.

When he tells me to damp the sugar, it is my duty to damp the sugar.

Water is an even more useful commodity than I had realized. Twenty litres of water poured into a wine-barrel containing five hundred and eighty litres of wine, bring the cubical contents up to six hundred litres, which is the right amount—and ten kilogrammes of water poured on to two hundred and ninety kilogrammes of sugar bring the weight up to three hundred kilogrammes, which is the right amount.

The trouble is that the convoys that bring the food-stuffs up from the Base to this distributing centre, invariably bring less than they profess to bring, and give us short measure and short weight.

The fault is not ours. We do but pass it on.

Quite probably the commissariat people at the Base, themselves receive short measure and do but pass it on. If so, perhaps the Head-quarters whence it comes to the Base, suffers in like manner and from the same complaint. Where is the seat of the original sin, and who is the original sinner?

"A contractor, doubtless," answered Hogan. "And I would fain take a running kick at the seat of the Original Sin. . . . He sits around a groaning board in Paris, with lovely ladies; and I sit around a groaning stomach with . . ." And he eyed me in grim silence.

We get two terribly busy days each week, when the grumbling *légionnaires* come for their dry goods and wine, and—judging others by themselves, as we tell them—firmly refuse to believe that, in the heat, the wood of the six-hundred-litre wine-barrels shrinks a trifle, and inevitably causes a small leakage.

"*Sans doute! Sans doute!* . . . Leaks down your dirty necks. . . ."

"Anybody seen a rubber tube lying about?"

"No. It's down at the bottom of the wine-cask."

"They don't use a rubber tube, you fool. They stick their heads in. Smell his hair."

"What do you call this? . . . Oh! Sugar is it? I thought it was molasses or porridge."

Sergeant Marcovitz arrives, bustling.

"Did I hear a remark out of you? . . . Something of a wit, eh? . . . I'll take your name, or the name your mother guessed at. . . .

"Name of a name of a hairy little serpent! Get out of this, you bald-faced bat-eared bandicoot . . . before I have a word with you. . . ."

Nevertheless the days that Terry and I spent as grocer's-assistants were very happy ones.

*   *   *   *   *

Something has got to be done about Matthieu le Maquereau.

He provided me with a hideous experience to-day, and brought me very suddenly and clearly face to face with the fact which, by day, I am apt actually to forget—that I am a woman.

I don't mean that I think he has guessed or

discovered my secret, but he put me in a position in which I had literally to play the man.

One of the things I have always feared, and hitherto have managed to avoid, is anything in the nature of a fight—fisticuffs, I mean, private and personal combat with a fellow-soldier.

Such fights between sober men are comparatively rare in the Legion, and if any trouble of that sort ever blew up, Terence Hogan was always at hand and would butt in.

Similarly with Digger and Abraham the Sailor. They took the line, from the first, that I was a young and foolish lad, and, as one of their outfit, was not going to be hazed by any bully.

I was alone in the Store Room and Matthieu came to the door.

"What about a litre of *pinard?*" he growled.

"Cash," I replied tersely.

Matthieu swore abominably and spat disgustingly—into the Store Room.

"Filthy brute," I said.

He came into the Store Room.

"Outside," I ordered. "You've no right to come in here."

Matthieu crossed to where I was standing behind a kind of desk-counter—a couple of planks across a couple of barrels.

Somebody shouted outside, and he dashed, swift and lithe as a cat, to the door, and looked round.

Back he came, vaulted my barrier, and suddenly aimed a swift tremendous blow straight at my face.

Absolutely instinctively I flinched—and, so violently, that the flinch was either a duck or a dodge, I don't know which. But with all his strength and all the weight of his body behind the blow, Matthieu struck the stone-wall beside my head, with his bare fist.

I shan't forget in a hurry his shouted oath of pain—nor the look on his contorted face as, nursing his gashed and shattered hand, he literally danced in agony.

"Now will you get out," I said, "before I . . ."

"*Ah-h-h,*" gasped Matthieu. . . . "And you wait till I come back."

I told Terence exactly what had happened, as soon as he returned with the pails of water that he had gone to fetch.

We decided that we must certainly not follow the proper course and report him to Sergeant Marcovitz—that sort of thing would not be according to Legion code at all.

"I'll beat him up," said Hogan, "the foul sewer-rat. . . . Disperse his features. . . ."

"All very well," said I, "but it will look funny if you start doing my fighting for me. Matthieu will say that his quarrel is with me, and that he's going to quarrel with me if he wants to."

"You need not come into it at all. As soon as his hand's all right, I can go and push his face, for coming into the Store Room at all."

"Well, that won't make him love me any better, will it, my good Terry? If he's got it in for me, as apparently he has, your beating him up won't alter the fact. . . . I can't tell you how I hate the idea of 'mixing it' with a creature like Matthieu. . . . Or fighting anybody at all. . . . Don't so much mind an Arab with a rifle and a long knife. . . . But I couldn't bear being thumped by Matthieu. . . . It was a jolly shame not to let me learn to box. . . . I'm every bit as strong and tough as that animal. . . ."

"Well, what's to be done?" mused Terence.

"What do you suggest? About yourself, I mean. Personally, I'm going to beat him up, good and plenty, for my own amusement and satisfaction."

"Yes, and he'll knife you when you're asleep," said I.

"Not he," denied Terence Hogan. "And I shall tell him that every time he comes near the Store Room, I'll wallop his soul out. . . . That'll keep him away from you when you're here alone; and if he started anything when the rest of us were about . . . but he wouldn't."

"If he catches me alone and sets about me, I shall shoot him," said I, patting my pocket where rested, as always, my small automatic. "And then there'll be a hell of a mess. . . . Court-martial, I suppose, and perhaps prison. . . . Damn the reptile."

Terence strode up and down the Store Room, hands in pockets, head on chest, in deep thought.

"I'd sooner that, than that he gave you a hiding, Jacq," he said at length. "They fight ugly, those scum . . . *Savate*, and all that; and kick you when you're down. Kick you insensible, and gouge your eyes out. . . ."

"Well, if it came to mere rough-and-tumble—he might do the tumble. It's the boxing. . . . And judging by the way he slammed at me, he might be a pro," said I.

"And judging by the way you ducked and let him punch the wall . . ."

"Yes. But it was only by the grace of God that the wall was there. Suppose it hadn't been? Next time he'll see there isn't a wall for miles. I'm not afraid of him, Terry, any more than you're afraid of a dead frog. But I hate the idea of struggling with him, like you'd hate a dead frog in your coffee. . . . I'd love to fight a duel with him—with pistols or army sabres."

"The only form of duel that gutter-snipe has heard of is knife-throwing," opined Terence.

We sat in silence.

"Look here, Jacq," said Hogan, at length. "Suppose I kill him."

"What do you mean?" I asked. "Fighting?"

"I mean what I say. Suppose I kill him. I'm absolutely ready, willing, and able—if you think the only alternatives are your getting a hiding from him, or shooting him in self-defence, and risking a prison sentence for homicide or murder."

"And what about you?" I asked. "Wouldn't you get a prison sentence?"

"Better I than you," said Terence. . . .

Sergeant Marcovitz came into the hut, and instantly we became industrious apprentices.

*   *   *   *   *

I have an idea that perhaps I shall not be troubled again by Matthieu le Maquereau, after all.

It was a queer amusing sickening business.

I, in sole charge of the Store Room, was yawning my head off, and wondering where on earth the flies came from. Presumably, like certain two-legged insects, they came up with the convoys. . . .

Sergeant Marcovitz had taken Terence Hogan with him, to bear witness before Lieutenant V——, that a Corporal from Poste Danjou had said his wine issue was watery, or his sugar sandy; or that he had sneezed in a manner prejudicial to discipline, or something of the sort.

A footstep crunched without, and the big spare figure of Abraham the Sailor cut off the sun-light.

"Say, Kid," quoth he, "have a heart. . . . Gee! If I was bar-tender to this saloon, it'd be drinks on me for all the boys, whenever they . . ."

"Not it. You'd have drunk the lot before they

could get here," said I, as Abraham produced his mug and a vast grin.

"Only borrowing, Buddy. I'll bring it back when I draw my ration."

"Sure," said I, mocking him, and producing a private bottle from which I half filled the mug.

Again footsteps crunched outside.

Silently and swiftly as a leaping shadow, that large man, Abraham, disappeared behind the concealing blanket of our sleeping-quarters, as—not Sergeant Marcovitz—but Matthieu le Maquereau, with a swift glance round, came into the room.

"Get out," said I. "Go on. Get to hell out of this."

Matthieu strode forward, and, fists on hips, stood and stared me out. His face was perfectly beastly with its heavy frown, evil eyes, and leering jeering mouth—its whole expression a threatening snarl.

"I've come to pay," he said.

"For something you've stolen?" I asked.

"For this," he said, holding up his right hand, and tensing and crouching for a spring at me.

"Pay *me*, Bo!" said a voice, and Matthieu's spring was never made. He jumped instead.

"So! . . . One understands. . . . Ha-ha! . . . A little love affair! . . . Pay *you*? . . . And what do you pay *this* bastard?" he snarled at Abraham—and pointed at me.

Abraham made two long strides and a long arm toward Matthieu, who ducked, dodged, backed into a corner, and whipped out his ugly knife. In the corner, protected on either side by the walls, he stood with the knife extended before him, as one holds a foil.

"You look out," he said. "Don't you butt in—if you want to keep your health."

"Looks like one of them goddam tarantulas, don't he, Kid?" said Abraham consideringly, and planted himself before Matthieu, feet apart and arms akimbo.

"Just like a goddam tarantula."

"Only uglier," he added.

"You look out," warned Matthieu. "I'm dangerous. I'm tough."

Abraham chuckled.

"He's tough!" he guffawed. "He's *tough!*"

And the chuckle and guffaw became a roar of laughter.

"*Tough!* Him! Wouldn't that jar you!"

Matthieu caused the knife to dart in and out, in the direction of Abraham's stomach.

"Why, you poor fish," continued Abraham. "You dunno what 'tough' means. What you ever done tough?"

"I'll stick your throat and I'll slit your belly and . . ."

"I arst you what you ever done tough?"

"I've cut a man's ear off—and eaten it."

"W-e-ell now; say," drawled Abraham, "that's only telling me yer favourite eats. I said, 'What you done *tough?*' "

"You watch out," warned Matthieu, edging forward.

"Why, I believe you shave with a razor," jeered Abraham.

"And *you*, pray?"

"Me? I shave every mawnin' with a burnin' candle, and wipe off with emery paper. Then I wash in sand. I blow me hair straight with me automatic and part it with me bayonet. But I don't allow I'm *tough*. . . .

"Nope. A mad dog ran at me and bit me in my home town. Bit me in the leg as well as the home town.

" 'Waal,' thinks I, 'pore mad dog's out of his mind. . . . Married very likely. . . . Won't take advantage of a pore dumb animal. . . .' So I also goes down on all fours and bites back at him . . . bites him in his home town . . . bites him right where he lives. . . . Dog dies while I'm chewing the piece. . . . But I don't allow I'm *tough* . . ."

I laughed.

Matthieu bared his teeth and edged a trifle nearer to Abraham.

"Say, you ain't going to bite me in the stomach, are you?" continued Abraham.

"Rattlesnake tried it on me, way back in Arizona. . . . Broke all his front teeth on my bare arm—but I don't allow I'm *tough*. . . . I had that rattler quite a while. . . . Tied a handle to him and used him for beating mules. . . . Called him Clarence. . . . Ongrateful beast. . . . Tried to run away one night, taking my handle with him. . . . After that I just nacherly slep' on him. . . . Couldn't trust him. . . . But he throve on it. . . . Throve? Why he grew as long as—oh—as long as . . .

"*Ah-h-h* . . ."

Like lightning, Abraham's hand, extended to show the length attained by Clarence, smacked down on Matthieu's wrist, closed on it and at the same time jerked it, and him, violently forward.

The two hands, the one held below the other, described a swift full-arm circle between the two men, slowed, stopped, slowly began to move again. . . . There was a screaming oath from Matthieu, and the knife fell to the ground.

Abraham kicked it across the floor.

"*Now*, Bo," said he, releasing Matthieu, "put 'em up."

"My wrist's broken," snarled Matthieu, backing again to the corner.

"Then put one up," snapped Abraham, no

longer bantering, and put one hand behind him.

"Come on, my tough bird,"—and Abraham smote.

"Get up," ordered Abraham later. "Get up and show us some tough."

"I've had enough," whimpered Matthieu.

"Enough for whom? Not for me, you haven't. Get up, you tough knife-thrower. . . . You won't? . . . We-ell, you can have the rest lying down then. . . ."

"Say, Kid. . . . Guess I'd better drag this outside and dump it somewhere. This *poste* oughta have an incinerator. I'll just . . ."

Swift footsteps, and up march Sergeant Marcovitz and Terence Hogan, to meet Abraham the Sailor dragging the unconscious Matthieu from the Store Room.

"Hell's Bells! What's this?"

Abraham springs to attention, and salutes.

"Unauthorized man in the Store Room, *mon Sergent*. . . . Assistant store-keeper just thrown him out. I was taking him away."

"You are seeking promotion, one would say," observes Sergeant Marcovitz dryly.

*   *   *   *   *

Leaving Hogan on guard this evening, I went for a stroll round, and then joined some of our Section who were yarning round a fire.

Cocteau, Thirsty-face, Petsel, Gustavus Adolphus, Demenko, Moronoff, Pigou, Digger, Trenck, Bilenski, Marbeveld, Matthieu, Abraham the Sailor, and Treshnev.

Digger, I notice eyeing me appraisingly and speculatively from time to time. I wonder why.

I think I understand when suddenly, *à propos* of nothing whatsoever, he turns to Matthieu.

"Say you," he growls, "I've got *le cafard*, and I want a fight."

"I'm not interested," observes Matthieu, but puts his hand behind him and under his tunic.

"It's going to interest you though," says Digger. "And we aren't going to play about with knives, or loaves of bread, or belts, or sausages, or *képis*. . . . I want a fist fight—and a bellyful at that. And I want it with you and nobody else. . . . See?"

Matthieu sees.

CHAPTER IV

Life is very sudden in the Legion.

One day, Terence and I are ensconced in our cosy, draughty, smelly, stuffy little home like two mice in a cheese—incidentally it smelt strongly of cheese—and the next we are out in the cold world.

A bugle blows. Orders are issued, and the fever of packing-up breaks out.

Another Company will take over to-day, and we are for the hard high road; or for the hard and high—and no road.

We march . . .

We march . . .

We march . . .

. . . A tiny rivulet of men that flows into a little stream of men, that in time joins a river of men; and again we are part of a *groupe mobile* which flows forward, more or less peacefully penetrating; and then again breaks up, as does a river into a many-streamed delta ere it spreads into the ocean.

One day, the Great Directing Mind behind, poring over maps and listening to the sifted and collated intelligence of its Intelligence, calls a halt, makes a number of tiny dots upon one of its maps, and decrees that upon each dot *les légionnaires* shall construct a *poste*.

Two Companies, of which ours is one, receive orders to construct eight *postes*, each capable of containing twenty-five men; and stores of dry goods and wine, sufficient to last those twenty-five men for six months. . . .

Six months!

To the sound of the faint far-off booming of guns (Oh the brave music of a *distant* gun), we get to work once more, clear spaces of encumbering trees and shrubs, build outer walls of dry stones, and then set about the interior construction of one more brief abiding place, which we name *Poste V——* after our Lieutenant, alas! no longer with us.

I thank God that our twenty-five include Terence Hogan, Digger, Abraham the Sailor, Père Cocteau and Thirsty-face; and am glad that Pet Hansel, Gustavus Adolphus, and Baron Trenck are with us, and that Matthieu le Maquereau has gone.

Less pleasing are the facts; first, that our Commandant is *l'Adjudant* Sartene, a Corsican with fourteen years' Legion service, brave as a lion; hard as the rocks; cruel, ruthless and violent as any feral beast: and, secondly, that we have lost Sergeant Pflügge whose bark, after all, is worse than his bite, and have in his place Sergeant Bartak, a Bulgarian whom nobody likes, and another Sergeant and two Corporals who are strangers to us: thirdly—for we old soldiers know, and have an eye for these things—that the *poste* is badly sited and difficult to defend, while our nearest water is much too far away. Nevertheless, here it has to be.

However, we have four mules, each of whom carries two barrels, each of which holds sixty litres. So they bring some four hundred and eighty litres of water each time they go to the stream. Incidentally, the four muleteers have to walk nearly twenty miles a day, for they make two journeys every morning and two in the afternoon.

As *Adjudant* Sartene considers that an escort of six men is necessary for the defence of the twelve thousand francs' worth of mule committed to his charge and care, ten men have to be detailed for water-fatigue, leaving only eight Balbuses (or should it be Balbi?) for the building of walls.

Now when eight men set to work to build a fort, if two are masons, one mixes the mortar-mud (a sack of lime to a ton of earth and a great deal of our precious water), one cooks for the *sous-officiers*, one for the men, and one stands sentry, there remain just exactly two—to select and carry from ever-increasing distances, all the tons of great stones of which the place is built.

It is slow work, in spite of the fact that the stone-carriers are the two giants, Bilenski and Moronoff, by this time, I should think, World's Champion Weight-Lifters, and about as powerful a pair as you'd find in a year's search.

Although all work like slaves—probably a great deal harder than any slaves ever did work—it soon becomes quite clear, even to *l'Adjudant* Sartene, that even *l'Adjudant* Sartene cannot get the *poste* completed in the time decreed. Not Sartene himself can get out of men more than is in them.

As the decree cannot of course be altered by a hair's breadth, or by an hour's time, and as the men cannot do more than it is possible for men to do, it looks as though something has to happen.

It has been my good fortune, combined with my good powers of ingratiation with Corporal Sevlije-vo, to be on escort-duty, and to remain with him and two others of the escort at a strategic spot, the position of which holds the double merit of halving the distance that we have to march, and of being in full view of the water-party and out of sight of *Adjudant* Sartene.

I don't fancy that Corporal Sevlijevo has boast-ed at all to *l'Adjudant* Sartene of his brilliance in discovering this spot and its great tactical value and assets. Nor do I think that it would be in a happy hour for him that Sartene discovered the fact that only half the escort goes to the water.

However, the Corporal's conduct shows that he possesses definite military gifts, and that he has grasped certain military principles, such as the wisdom of conserving, as far as possible, the energies of himself and those under his command.

*   *   *   *   *

I said it looked as though something had got to happen.

Sartene has had the bright idea of weakening the escort by half, and now three patient pedestrians have joined the world's workers, poor Digger and Abraham being among them.

With six men carrying stones, the work goes on —(I had almost said, more merrily)—more quickly. God grant that I be not ordered to carry stones, mix mortar, or blossom overnight into a skilled bricklayer or mason.

*   *   *   *   *

Lieutenant V—— rode in to-day on a tour of inspection.

I was delighted to see him, and I verily believe that, in spite of everything, including sunburn and grime, I flushed with pleasure when he spoke to me.

L'Adjudant Sartene's batman announces the glorious news that Lieutenant V——, realizing the heavy handicap under which we (as compared with the other seven *postes*) work, in view of our distance from water, has promised Sartene that he will send us six more men.

*   *   *   *   *

Not so good. Matthieu le Maquereau is one of the six.

* * * * *

I have had mixed good and bad luck to-day—great excitement and a bullet-wound.

The latter is really only a trifle, a messy graze across the left fore-arm, but a near and rather nerve-shaking squeak, inasmuch as the bullet must have passed across my left side within an inch or two of my heart.

An inch or two nearer and it would have ended my career as a man—and as a woman.

As it happened, and quite by chance, Corporal Sevlijevo's labour-saving device, of hiding half-way between the *poste* and the water, proved amazingly successful. Like other great soldiers, he is evidently lucky as well as brilliant and brave; for, to his ill-concealed surprise, he discovered that we had ambushed an ambush!

As the muleteers and their escort—now restored to their former number—marched on toward the water, leaving us in our little private *poste*, I, on sentry, and dutifully following their movements, with watchful eye, was amazed to see a number of grey-clad forms emerge from behind some rocks, and creep, crouching, to where they would be able to shoot our comrades down as they worked at filling the water-casks and loading the mules. Doubtless they were going to creep as near as possible, shoot down the unsuspecting escort and muleteers, and disappear as swiftly and suddenly as they came—with the mules.

"*Hsst!*"

Without stopping to point, I knelt and took aim.

"*Wait. . . . Volley,*" whispered the Corporal.

And a few moments later our four rifles banged as one. . . .

Again. . . .

And by that time, the escort were all down behind boulders, and snap-shooting at the running Arabs, while the muleteers dragged, beat, and bucketed their precious animals to cover.

"Rapid independent. . . . And as fast as you like!" shouted Corporal Sevlijevo, and we proceeded to sound as numerous as we could.

The Arabs, disconcerted, between two fires, and with their well-meant plans entirely upset, went home—inconspicuously.

One rebel against *Kismet*, probably their leader, moved either with the laudable desire to cover the retreat of his comrades, or more probably by ordinary bad temper, stood bravely forth and took no less than three carefully aimed shots at us, before Demenko brought him down.

One of the three shots hit Demenko's private boulder within an inch of his face; the second ricocheted between him and me; and the third, as I raised my rifle to fire, went through my left sleeve, passed across the top of my fore-arm, and between my upper arm and my side.

As a wound it is nothing, but as a sore into which a dirty coat-sleeve has been well rubbed, it may be quite nasty, in view of the present total lack of any antiseptic.

* * * * *

My arm is rather ugly to-day and I am definitely seedy, but it has given me a brief respite from labour, though not from usefulness. Not while *l'Adjudant* Sartene commands the *poste!*

I am excused manual labour and water-fatigue escort, but am doing a kind of perpetual sentry-go.

I have to do sentry throughout the whole day, and again, four hours at night—twelve hours and four hours—sixteen out of the twenty-four!

I must form a union and complain that I have to work sixteen hours a day for threepence-half-penny a week.

*   *   *   *   *

The others are really much worse off than I am, for we have six sentries on duty at night, in addition to their appalling hard labour by day.

On the other hand, they do get three hours' *siesta* during the worst of the heat, while I am not supposed to be relieved for a minute during the twelve hours—not even being relieved when I eat my food.

Let workers, who think this is not "work," try it for themselves, with the lives of five-and-twenty comrades perhaps dependent on their watchfulness.

*   *   *   *   *

Everyone is getting nervy, jumpy, and bad-tempered under the strain of continuous over-work in such heat. Particularly *Adjudant* Sartene, who has the responsibility not only of getting the *poste* finished to time, but of keeping it as a *poste* in being, meanwhile.

I had a taste of his quality this afternoon.

Either the day had achieved the impossible in being hotter than usual, or I was feeling the heat more, in spite of my arm and my general health being much better.

Necessity is the mother of invention. I had been ingenious, and, by means of four sticks and a piece of sacking, had contrived to rig up a quite useful, if not ornamental, protection for my head and shade for my eyes.

I was very pleased with it. My pleasure was marred only by the thought that I hadn't had the sense to do something of the sort before.

Not only was there actual shade, but a, possibly quite imaginary, sense of coolness; and I could undoubtedly see better, or at any rate see with less eye-strain and headache.

Excellent. . . .

And round the corner came *Monsieur l'Adjudant* Sartene.

He stopped. He gaped. His dark red face became purple.

"Ten verminous million vermilion vermin!" he roared. "Entrails of a frog! What is this? You scrofulous son of Satan's sister, what d'you think you're doing? What is it that it is that I seem to behold? . . . What shall I see next? You trussed up *en crapaudine?* . . . Delights of howling hell, is it thus that they do sentry-go in the British Army?"

"No, *mon Commandant,*" I replied. "They do not go on sentry for twelve continuous hours in the British Army."

I could have bitten my tongue out.

Sartene stuck his face close to mine.

"You shall be relieved," he said. "Stone-carrying for you, to-morrow! . . . Tear that sacred bird's-nest down!"

*   *   *   *   *

When I told Terence Hogan all about it, he told *me* all about it. Ticked me off proper, as they say in the British Army.

However, absolutely nothing has come of it. Either because Sartene with all his worry, work and anxiety has forgotten the incident, or else, and more likely, because he is too good a soldier to risk the crocking-up of one of his all-too-few men.

* * * * *

Strain and jumpiness increase, and men who go on the water and fire-wood fatigues try to look all ways at once, and, on leaving the *poste*, openly wonder whether they will come back alive.

A patrol brought news this morning that the next *poste* but one to ours had barely beaten off a sudden, violent and determined attack at dawn. Being close to water, and thus having more men on building-work, they were in better position to stand attack.

I wonder what would have happened had it been our unfinished *poste*.

Probably on account of this news, we have all been put on to ground-clearing fatigue, as, before building-operations commenced, the shrubs and trees had only been cleared away over a space of about a hundred yards square. It would be terribly easy for quite a large force to surround the *poste* under complete cover.

CHAPTER V

Thank God the *poste* is practically finished and we are once again merely soldiers—on active service under the hardest conditions. We feel like gentlemen of leisure.

Adjudant Sartene, though not less anxious, has a change of anxiety—that of finding us enough to do. He need not worry, for he is quite successful.

Nevertheless, the strain is lessened, the tension relaxed; and the Arabs can come when they like. The next trouble, I suppose, will be monotony; the monotony that breeds *cafard*. The day will come when an assault would be wholly welcome.

Meantime, *siesta*, normal sentry-go, ordinary routine, brushwood-clearing parties, water-and-firewood fatigues. . . .

The barrack building is seventy-five feet long, fifteen feet high, and divided into a number of rooms—the *Adjudant's* quarters; the Sergeant's quarters; the *Sous-officiers'* kitchen; the men's kitchen; and the caserne, some forty feet long, in which we sleep.

God bless our Home.

*　　*　　*　　*　　*

"There!" said Rideau, as he brought me an attractive-looking little steak, beautifully browned on either side, and a piece of bread. "You won't get a more tender, juicy little *plat* in Paris."

Rideau, one of the six men sent to us by Lieutenant V——, is a professional cook, and we in this *poste* like to think that Lieutenant V—— sent him to us for that reason.

I could not leave my post, so ate—and enjoyed —my picnic meal right heartily. One is always hungry in the Legion. I was particularly hungry this morning and the meat was particularly good.

Rideau squatted near while I ate, laughing and talking. He is a great fat Belgian, whose avoirdupois no amount of hard-labour and hard-living seems able to reduce. There may be some connection between his condition and the fact that he is a cook. Possibly also, some connection between his popularity and the fact that he is a cook.

To be just, he would be popular, in any case, if only because he is always cheerful, generally laughing, and frequently engaged upon some buffoonery or other.

When I had finished, I thanked him heartily for his kindness, and congratulated him sincerely upon his cooking.

"You enjoyed it? *Bon*," said Rideau. "Sweet and tender, eh?"

"Like a *poussin*," I said. "A tender spring-chicken, beautifully grilled. What was it?"

"You really enjoyed it?"

"Best thing I've tasted for months. Loved it. What was it?"

"*Dog!*" was the reply. "Just village dog."

Rideau glanced at my face, burst into one of his thunderous roars of laughter, and departed convulsed with merriment, his vast body shaking from head to foot.

Legion humour. . . .

The next person I saw was Père Cocteau.

Hearing my tale he was filled with a burning indignation.

"The *salaud*," he said. "The *cochon*. The unspeakable son of an unguessable father—he never gave me any."

A fact of Natural History new to me. *Légionnaires* eat dogs. Sometimes.

*   *   *   *   *

I shall be very glad indeed when we are ordered to move in and occupy the Barracks, for it's jolly cold at night. Snow has fallen twice already; and, being November, we are getting more than sufficient rain. Our tents, three and a half feet high, are utterly inadequate for such conditions.

Père Cocteau and the other old soldiers have made braziers from old tin cans, and these are kept alight day and night, so that one can at least warm one's hands.

I had not realized when coming to soldier in Africa that I was going to suffer from cold as well as from heat. Cold has its compensations though, for the last convoy brought us a new delight, and we are now pampered with an issue of what the men call *Schnappes*. It is supposed to be a sort of gin, but, though admired and approved by the old soldiers, Terence Hogan says it is "rum" gin.

It is very comforting, anyway.

*   *   *   *   *

Last night, it was most bitterly cold, and, to us proud and pampered soldiery—albeit to our great surprise—was issued what a generous broad mind could call mulled claret. It was red wine and hot water, anyhow, and I for one, counted my many blessings.

It may have been the good wine that led to some good talk and good stories.

*   *   *   *   *

An extremely rare—indeed a rather remarkably rare—event occurred in a neighbouring *poste* yesterday.

A non-commissioned officer was murdered, presumably by one of his men.

One hears a good deal of grumbling, and a great many threats, in the case of some particularly brutal and vindictive non-commissioned officers, and such remarks as:

"Yes. Wait till the next time we go into action, and see whether that species of a pickled camel's head isn't shot from behind—if I have a chance to get behind him."

But it is very rarely that anything comes of this sort of talk. Now and again, a man suffering from *cafard*, after months of semi-starvation, overwork, bad insufficient water, terrific heat and terrible monotony, runs amok and kills the first non-commissioned officer he can find.

Occasionally a man, goaded to desperation by a bullying non-commissioned officer who has a down on him, loses control for one second, and, in that second, drives his bayonet through the heart of the man who has driven him mad.

But apart from a concerted mutiny, incidental to which is the elimination of the non-commissioned officers, it is quite a rare thing for a man deliberately to conceive, plan, and, in cold blood, carry out the murder of one.

But, according to the patrol that has come over from the next *poste*, this is precisely what has happened.

"Quite a thrilling piece of news," observed Terence Hogan, as we sat at morning *soupe*. "A bright spot in the monotony of our young lives. Something new to talk about. Doubtless this Sergeant Kazanski was born to that end."

"How do they know it wasn't an Arab?" I asked.

"Well, I heard the Corporal from over there telling Corporal Clement that Sergeant Kazanski was found dead in his blankets, suffering from a fearful thump on the head. Somebody had come and given him a tap with a tent-peg mallet," said Thirsty-face.

"Now you will agree with me," he continued sententiously, "that comparatively few Arabs carry a three-foot tent-mallet. They prefer a magazine rifle for long range, and a twelve-inch knife for short. . . . Nor would one say that it was the custom of Arabs who, at the risk of their lives, have managed to creep in the middle of the night into a Legion *poste,* to break into the padlocked store-room in search of the Company tent-mallet, which may not be there."

"You've cert'nly slobbered a bibful, Bo," observed Abraham the Sailor, who, like most of us, understands French better than he talks it.

"And having administered his little tap on the thin skull of Sergeant Kazanski, why did he then hurry away? . . . Was it to put the cat out? I ask you. . . . To feed the canary? . . . To put Fido on the chain? . . . Or to feed the chickens? . . . Why did he steal nothing, disturb nothing? Having the ability and skill to get the tent-mallet from the store-room, all in the dark, why not a few bombs, a box of ammunition, a rifle or two? Why did he crack no one else's egg with his little mallet? Away with him. Bah! Away with him, this Arab, this figment of the wine-heated imagination of the miserable Cannibal Cocteau."

"Decrepit toothless ancient, I have not spoken," cried Père Cocteau indignantly.

"Speak now, then," was the reply. "It is all thou art fit for."

"The aged camel is right, for once," Père

Cocteau complied. "And since it is clear to him, it must be clearer than the daylight. . . . Of course, it was done by a *légionnaire*. An Arab would have knifed him, and a few other sleepers as well.

"Also he would have taken at least one rifle and stabbed at least one sentry. The man who killed Kazanski was a *légionnaire*, a fool and a bungler."

"Anyhow, he had sense enough not to do it with a Legion bayonet," objected Matthieu le Maquereau.

"Thank you. I was about to remark that he *hadn't* the sense to do it with a Legion bayonet, and make it look like Arab work. He used the tent-peg mallet, because he hadn't the sense to see that a stab is a stab, whether inflicted by a long thin bayonet, or a long thin knife."

"And pray how would you have done it?" sneered Matthieu.

"I would not presume to think that I had anything to teach *you* in that line," observed old Père Cocteau. "Because you, my friend, are . . ."

"But you feel quite certain it was a *légionnaire*?" I interrupted hastily, for when annoyed, the fearless Père Cocteau is apt to say things very hard to forgive—when said in front of others.

"Yes, *mon enfant*," he replied. "Sergeant Kazanski was deliberately murdered, in cold blood, by one of his own men; and that, let me tell you, is a thing so unusual that I, with all my long experience, have only personally once before come across such a case in the French Army.

"A curious case that. . . . Very curious . . ." he mused provocatively, as the bugle sounded.

I scented a story, and determined to get it at the first opportunity.

*   *   *   *   *

How all normal-minded people do love a good murder. I really think the general health of this *poste* has been better since the patrol brought in the news of the really rather mysterious death of Sergeant Kazanski. Everybody seems to take a greater interest in life, as well as in death; and an interest in life is the one thing needful here.

Men who, one would think, haven't exercised their intelligence since they left school, are now full of ingenious theories and ideas on the subject of the who and the how and the why of the murder.

I wonder if our own dear *Adjudant* Sartene is at all uncomfortable. He must know that he has one or two thoroughly dangerous enemies in this Section. Men who'd kill him as soon as look at him if they had a safe chance. Matthieu le Maquereau, for example.

The talk round the fire was good to-night again, and old Père Cocteau excelled himself.

"There's nothing new under the sun," he observed.

"Not even that remark," sneered Matthieu.

Père Cocteau ignored this, with cold dignity.

"Nothing new. *Cette affaire* Kazanski is quite *routine*, quite in order, given the circumstances. Same causes, same effects. . . . It reminds me of the *affaire* Wehlaner.

"A curious case that. . . . Very curious. . . . At Fort Taflet. . . . The sort of experience one remembers, *mes enfants*.

"Do you know that I, Père Cocteau of the Line and the Colonial Infantry and the Foreign Legion, I, began to think I was seeing things, and to believe in ghosts."

"Plenty of wine at Fort Taflet, one imagines," smiled Hogan.

"There was no wine at Fort Taflet, when this occurred," rebuked Cocteau, ". . . for we had drunk it all.

"That may have had something to do with the trouble, for we had then been ten months on six months' rations. I forget why. Either the tribes were out between us and our base, a hundred and twenty miles away; or else the General had fallen in love again and forgotten us; or the Quartermaster-General's Acting Assistant Deputy-Adjudant's Staff-Sergeant's clerk had filed us with the mule indents or receipted laundry bills. . . . Or perhaps the relevant document had blown out of the window and been eaten by the Quartermaster-General's Acting Assistant Deputy-Adjudant's Staff-Sergeant's clerk's wife's goat.

"As I say, we know not. What we do know is that at Fort Taflet, which was nothing but a dilapidated little block-house, half-buried in sand, there were twenty-five good *légionnaires*, three bad Corporals and a worse Sergeant.

"Believe me, you young soldiers who have only seen such gentle creatures as Sergeant Pflügge, meek and mild, docile as a little child, this Sergeant Wehlaner was such as you have never dreamt of in your worst Legion night-mare.

"He was a Prussian born and bred—in Prussia. He was a Prussian, polished and perfected in the Prussian Army. And, *mes amis*, he had been a Prussian Sergeant on his native heath. And to crown the career of that noble work of God and man, he was now a Sergeant in the Foreign Legion.

"As he frequently told us, he had 'left' the Prussian Army because he had himself killed a recruit after having been the cause of seventeen others hanging themselves—and he had come to the Foreign Legion because there a good Sergeant was under no necessity to 'leave' if he should kill a man, or be the cause of seven times seventeen hanging themselves.

"Speaking as one who has himself been a Sergeant, one says that this Wehlaner was an excellent and most efficient non-commissioned officer. A real disciplinarian whose men really feared him as they feared neither their Colonel nor their God. The flap of his holster was always open, and his hand was generally on the butt of his revolver; and every man in Fort Taflet knew that *ce bon Sergent* Wehlaner would shoot him dead as soon as look at him, if he so much as blinked an eyelid in an improper manner."

"But wouldn't that be plain, ordinary, punishable murder?" I objected.

"No, my child, it would be self-defence, prompt, commendable and leading to promotion."

"But the other *légionnaires?* Wouldn't they give evidence?"

"*Sans doute*—if invited to do so . . . and be punished for a gang of rascally perjured liars, whose evidence was in total conflict with that of the good Sergeant and the Corporals. The rascals would hang together, and the Officer holding the inquiry—if any—would say they ought to be hung together."

"But might not there be an honest Corporal among them?" I still objected.

"All Corporals are honest, my innocent," rebuked Père Cocteau, "and they all want to become Sergeants.

"Anyhow—there we were, baked to death, drilled to death, worked to death, and hounded to death, by Sergeant Wehlaner who, to give him his due, knew that our only hope, and the hope of keeping Fort Taflet in existence, with the French flag flying over it, was to keep us at it until we were too tired to do anything but sleep.

"How we hated that man! How we cursed him! And how we obeyed him! There was not a better-disciplined, better-drilled, smarter or finer fighting unit in the whole French Army than that Section at Fort Taflet.

"And then suddenly things blew up.

"There was an explosion of *cafard* that would have blown us all to the Devil, and sent us, a band of murderous mutineers, marching out into the blue, except for the fact that, just at this very time, an old bird who owned the nearest oasis, and who had been sitting on the fence for a long time, came down on the wrong side of it. Started plundering the caravans that had to go through his oasis to get water; threw in his lot with Sheikh Abou-ben-Ibrahim, who was also looking for trouble; and actually let some of his playful young bucks take some pot-shots at some of our patrols.

"Sergeant Wehlaner sent him a couple of friendlies, with orders to come in at once, bring in the culprits, and as big a peace-offering, in the way of sheep, goats, dates and so forth, as he hoped might save his bacon. The old Sheikh—I have forgotten his name—neither came nor sent the peace-offering. All he sent in was the heads of the two friendlies, and they were quite spoilt—no ears, no eyes, lips, tongues nor noses, and no doubt the unfortunate friendlies had parted with these useful and ornamental appendages before they parted with their heads.

"How were they returned?

"Just thrown over the wall, in the middle of the night, by some gentleman who then took a pot-shot at the sentry and got him too. Sergeant Wehlaner told the sentry that if he recovered he'd wish to God he hadn't."

I visualized those heads, and felt a little sick.

Glancing round at the others I found no reflection in their grim faces of any of the queasiness that I was feeling.

Heads! Without eyes, lips, nose, ears and tongues. Should I ever be in a place where such things happened? And yet how quickly I had recovered from the sight of that huge pile of arms, legs, hands, feet, that lay outside the casualty-clearing-station that awful night at Passchendaele. I had seen it as I swung my ambulance about, been suddenly and violently sick, and forgotten it by the time my ambulance was loaded with its dreadful freight. But mutilated heads! Ugh!

Thirsty-face yawned loudly.

"This is dull, *mon* Cocteau," he said. "We know all about Arabs. What was this explosion that so unfortunately did not blow you to the Devil?"

"Would that you had been there, old drunkard. Sergeant Wehlaner might have made a man even of you. . . .

"Now the first curious thing about this curious *affaire* Wehlaner was that, one day, I went into the Sergeant's room on some duty or other, and, to my infinite amazement I, who was even then almost beyond amazement at anything whatsoever, saw one of my comrades shaking his fist under the nose of Sergeant Wehlaner and bawling at him at the top of his voice—bawling what seemed to me to be accusations, curses, and threats!

"When I say 'seemed to me,' I mean that he was yelling in the barbarous language, or patois, or dialect, or whatever it is that Germans talk."

"We talk in German," said Hermann reproachfully, in his gentle voice.

"That's it. . . . In German. . . . It was a chap

named Müller—or more likely not named Müller, really—and positively foaming at the mouth. And what he was saying was evidently something worth hearing, so far as Sergeant Wehlaner was concerned; for though, as usual, he'd got a firm grip on the butt of his revolver, and looked as pleasant as a wolf in a trap, he was listening.

"Oh yes, he was letting *ce bon* Müller say his little piece—so far as he could for spluttering, stuttering, stammering, waving his fists and foaming in German.

"Every moment I expected Wehlaner to shoot him dead. I had an awful feeling that the moment Müller stopped he'd do it. And suddenly he said a word, the name of some place in Prussia, I suppose, that brought in a flash to my mind something that Müller had once told us about his having served with Wehlaner in the German Army; or it may have been that they both came from the same town.

"Anyhow, I was just remembering that these two Germans had known each other before they joined the Legion, when poor old Müller suddenly dried up and turned to me as though his life did not hang by a thread, and said to me in French, with tears in his silly eyes:

" 'It was he that stole her from me. . . . He ruined her. . . . And caused her death. . . .'

"I tell you, my friends, I stood to attention like a statue and wished I was one. I stood there, eyes front, little fingers against the seam of the trousers, palms outward, head up, and stared like hell at nothing; fairly radiating deafness, dumbness, blindness, and the complete idiocy.

"Never did anyone give a finer rendering of the rôle of a person who wished it to be noticed that he was not there.

" 'He has her photograph here, here, *here*, I tell

you. . . . It fell out of the inner pocket of that coat as I polished the buttons. . . . I tell you that man, that dog, that . . .'

"*Bam!* Wehlaner's great fist caught him on the point of the jaw, knocking him head over heels, clear through the doorway of the hut.

"Then Wehlaner let a roar like a lion that has sat down on something, and everybody in Fort Taflet jumped. In about two minutes Müller's hands were bound behind his back, his feet tied together, and then drawn up behind him and tied to his hands. And when he came to, he found himself *en crapaudine.* . . . None of you has ever seen that punishment, I suppose. . . .

"Now that's a painful position if you are kneeling on the ground and leaning back squatting on your heels. You'd find five minutes of it about four too much, if you were kneeling on a cushion in a nice cool shady place. But what about when you fall over on your side, and begin to struggle, and your heart begins to hurt you, and you can't get your breath properly, and your neck swells, and your eyes begin to bulge, and the agony of cramp in your shoulders and arms and thighs makes you scream, and you froth at the mouth and begin to go mad. . . .

"And then suppose, *mes amis*, that instead of being in this nice cool place, you are lying in the dust, with your face to the sun, in such heat that to touch a stone or a rifle-barrel is to burn the hand?

"And what about the flies when your face is sticky with sweat. The flies that cover your face like a mask; crawling into your eyes, and ears, and mouth? And what about the big ants that come and bite? And what about when the five minutes have become ten, and twenty, and an hour, and five hours, and ten hours, *hein?*

"That's what happened to Müller. And though we growled together in corners and in our barrack hut, what could we do? Who could trust whom? And if we shot Wehlaner as he deserved, and the Corporals, what could we do then? Stay there till the relief came, and be tried and shot—or sent to twenty years of the most terrible life that human beings have ever endured. . . . Guiana, Cayenne, Devil's Island, the 'Dry Guillotine' . . .

"Or march out of Fort Taflet and die of thirst. The lucky ones who didn't die slowly under the Arab knife. . . .

"Müller was alive at Retreat, though quite unconscious, and when he came round again, found himself in a perfectly dark, unventilated cell and a temperature of about a hundred and twenty. He must have kept on finding himself, for he was there for twenty-eight days, and that, as you may have noticed, is a month.

"When he came out he was queer—permanently queer, I mean.

"As you young soldiers may or may not know, there is a class of old *légionnaires*—men who've done a lifetime of soldiering before they join the Legion and do fifteen years more—who are permanently queer. They get *le cafard* once too often, and get it for keeps. It is the sun and the Sergeants; the wine and the absinthe; the hardship, marching and monotony; the dreadful experiences in the tiny outposts away down in the real desert, far away south of Morocco and south of Algeria. By the time they're relieved, especially if the relief is a few months late, they're all mad . . . especially if the Officer or Sergeant-major goes mad first."

"One imagines that you had many such experiences, *mon vieux*," sneered Matthieu.

"Before you were born in a Paris sewer," replied Cocteau.

"Well, as I was saying," he continued, "*ce pauvre* Müller came out of that black hole with a fine dose of *cafard*. He could talk of nothing but the photograph of his girl, or his wife, or whatever she was, that Wehlaner had got in his pocket; and was for ever wanting to thrash out the question as to whether, possibly, Wehlaner had himself written the inscription on the photograph, and deliberately put a wrong date. . . .

" 'Surely no woman could be so base as to have given that particular photograph, their own betrothal photograph, to another man, and written such a message on it, the very week after they were married?

" 'Wehlaner must have stolen the photograph and written the inscription. . . . But the handwriting was Greta's. There could be no doubt of that,' and so forth. . . .

"And at all sorts of times, by day and night, poor old Müller would suddenly bawl out:

" 'Wehlaner wrote it.'

"Once he shouted it out on parade, and got another ten days in the dark—which did not improve his condition or his state of mind. And, the night after he came out, he was on sentry, and suddenly challenged somebody.

"It was a bright moonlight night and I was lying awake (on my cot in the *chambrée*) for it was far too hot to sleep, when suddenly I heard Müller bawl:

" '*Halte!* . . . *Qui va là?* . . . *Halte!*'

"*Bang.*

"Well, the Guard turned out, and so did the rest of us, in half no time, wondering why no other sentry had fired, and Müller hadn't given the alarm and hadn't bawled:

" '*Aux armes!*'

"There was old Müller facing *inwards*.

"He hadn't fired at anyone approaching the Fort at all, but at someone inside the place.

"He seemed sane enough in his talk, and swore that 'something white' had approached across the square. He had challenged it, and twice ordered it to halt, and then done his duty and fired.

" 'A good bit of shooting, eh?' sneered Sergeant Wehlaner. 'Can't hit a man at ten paces, in full moonlight now, eh?'

" 'It wasn't a man.'

" 'What was it, then, you miserable fool?' demanded Wehlaner.

" 'A ghost,' replied Müller. 'The ghost of a woman . . .'

" 'A *woman?*' cried Wehlaner.

" 'Yes,' replied Müller. 'A woman. *The* woman.'

"That, of course, got Müller another spell of the quiet life, with not so much as a ray of light to disturb his peace; and, while he was safe and sound in that cell, of which Wehlaner had the key, another sentry, Schledel, one night also suddenly challenged and fired without giving the alarm. The Orderly Corporal and Guard were on the spot almost before the bullet was out of the rifle; and anybody else, who wasn't out as soon as the Guard, had only stopped to pull his boots on.

"What had he challenged and fired at?

"Something white.

"Something what white? A white camel or a white mouse or a white poodle or a white elephant, or what?

"Something white. Someone white. It might have been a woman—the ghost of a woman.

"I thought Sergeant Wehlaner would have shot him, then and there.

" 'Oh! So you've seen the ghost of a woman, too, have you?' he said in the tone of voice that always meant the worst kind of trouble. 'We'll find out in the morning how much that shambling camel, Müller, gave you to see the ghost of a woman. I'll teach you to go firing off your rifle here in the middle of the night. Corporal, put this man under arrest and bring him up before me after parade in the morning.' . . .

"But Schledel stuck to it. Someone or something, man, woman or ghost, had come gliding towards him, and he had done his duty, as he had been taught it—challenged twice and then fired.

" 'Yes, but ten thousand thumping thundering devils from the cellars of Hell, where was it? . . . Where was the body? . . . If he shot something at zero, point-blank, at a few paces, where in the name of Satan's Sister was the body? How could anybody—a child—a great-grand-mother—a *pekin* of either sex—miss at ten yards?'

" 'I did not miss, *mon Sergent*,' declared Schledel, once again.

" 'Then ten thousand *teufels*, where's the body?'

" 'There was no body. It was a ghost.'

"So Schledel got a packet for firing off his rifle at nothing, and another one for missing it, and a third for conspiring with Müller to play imbecile tricks about seeing ghosts.

"Now the curious part of it was that Schledel swore to us, whom he'd no earthly reason to deceive, that what he'd said was absolutely true. . . . He had suddenly woken up to find himself leaning against the wall, sound asleep, as he put it—had pulled himself together, started to walk his beat, seen something white coming towards him, challenged, and fired.

"It wasn't until his rifle banged that he was properly awake; and whatever he fired at suddenly 'went small and disappeared.' I asked him whether it flew away or disappeared into the ground, or ran for its life like a Christian. But he could only say that it vanished, disappeared.

" 'In fact,' I said, 'ducked as you threw up your rifle, and dodged behind the store-shed.'

" 'Have it your own way,' said Schledel. 'But let me have a shot at you at ten paces to-night, will you, and see how much ducking and dodging you'll do.'

"When Müller and Schledel were both out of the cells, they compared notes, of course, and both agreed that 'the ghost' had a terribly white face.

" 'As white as china,' said Müller.

" 'That's right,' said Schledel, 'as white as chalk.'

"And it really seemed to us that it wasn't any sort of a put-up job between them.

"You see, if Müller had been trying to play some ghost-trick on Sergeant Wehlaner, and had got Schledel to help him—and carry on the good work while Müller was in cells—why didn't he tell the rest of us about it?

"We'd have jumped at it. We'd have helped him fast enough. We'd all have seen ghosts. We'd have provided a ghost. . . .

"Well, after that, everything went as merry as a funeral bell for a few days, and we continued to bear the unbearable while everybody got madder and madder; and then, one night, I, I who speak, Aristide Cocteau, joined the ghost-seers, and the company of Wehlaner's more especial pets.

"I was doing my duty to my Country, my Regiment and my comrades, in the style that I always do."

"You mean you went to sleep?" asked Matthieu.

". . . and walked my beat in a smart and soldierly manner, with an eye and a half on the desert outside, and with half an eye on the square inside the Fort. And when I rested, I took care to lean against nothing. I was interested in this queer *affaire* Müller and Schledel, and had my own theory on the subject. If anything did happen—which I did not anticipate—I did not intend to be asleep at that moment. . . .

"Now believe me, or believe me not, according to your own truthfulness, my friends. I was standing still, standing at ease, wide awake, and not even leaning on my rifle, when, just as I was in the middle of a great and satisfying yawn, I was suddenly frozen—mind and body. My yawn stopped in the middle, and there I stood with my mouth wide open, as well as my eyes and ears, while a cold shiver ran up my spine.

"I, Aristide Cocteau, forty years a soldier, admit it. For something white, something that might have been the ghost of a woman, passed rapidly across the space between the low one-storied barrack-building and Sergeant Wehlaner's hut. As it either vanished or passed behind the hut, it looked up to where I was standing, and its face was of a terrible whiteness—white as my two comrades had said—like china or chalk.

"And then Cocteau was himself again.

"My mouth snapped shut. I threw up my rifle and waited for the ghost to reappear on the other side of the hut. There I stood, like a statue in bronze. The Statue of *le Légionnaire* Aristide Cocteau, by Monsieur Rodin."

"Epstein . . . surely," murmured Terence unkindly.

"There I stood, my unwavering rifle pointing like an accusing finger, the finger of Death, at the spot where this apparition must come into sight again. . . . Thus I stood."

Père Cocteau fell silent.

"I might be standing there now," he continued,

"as far as the ghost was concerned. It never came from behind the hut at all. After a while, how long I could not tell you, I brought my rifle down to the ready and stood like a . . ."

"Another mud effigy," observed Matthieu.

". . . like a tiger about to spring . . . tense . . . watchful . . . prepared instantly to throw up my rifle and fire with unerring aim. . . ."

"And then, by and by, I had to relax and rest the butt of my rifle on the ground, for nothing appeared, absolutely nothing happened.

"To me nothing, that is. . . .

"Something happened to the other sentry though, on the opposite side of the Fort, poor old Mosso.

"When the relief came, they found him lying down.

" '*Mon Dieu*, the dog's asleep,' said Corporal Draque, and fetched him a kick in the ribs fit to wake the dead. It didn't wake Mosso though. He was too dead.

"I was sorry for Mosso—but I was sorry for me too. For of course Sergeant Wehlaner took the view that I must have been asleep when it happened, or I should have seen and heard something.

" 'I did see something, *mon Sergent*,' I swore, standing to attention, between my guards—for I was under arrest—with Corporal Draque standing by, to give any false evidence that would cook my goose or please Sergeant Wehlaner, who wanted a scapegoat.

" 'Oh, you did see something, did you, species of a debauched and mangy sheep? And what did you see, with your eyes shut and your nose snoring?"

" 'The ghost, *mon Sergent*,' I replied.

"Wehlaner, who was sitting at his table, sprang to his feet with a roar, snatched his revolver from its holster, and pointed it straight at my face.

" 'Say that again, you lying dog,' he shouted, 'and I'll blow your face off.'

"That being no satisfactory inducement, I did not say it again. I stood silent, looking past Wehlaner's head.

" 'Tell me exactly what you saw,' he growled, putting the revolver back in its holster, 'and unless you want twelve hours' *en crapaudine* and a week's solitary—without water—speak the truth.'

"I spoke the truth. As always. And by the time I'd done, Wehlaner's jaw was beginning to fall, for he had to believe I'd seen a white-faced, white-clad ghost of a woman. . . . For poor old Müller's sake, I stuck to it that it *was* a woman. . . . And so it might have been for all I'd seen of it.

"Suddenly Wehlaner pulled himself together.

" 'Ghost of a woman, you braying jackass, you idiot son of Ananias! . . . And did this "ghost of a woman" kill Mosso? Does a ghost stab a sentry to the heart and take his rifle?'

" 'No, *mon Sergent*,' said I. 'Nor have Arabs dead-white faces, and vanish when . . .'

" '*Vanish?*' bawled Wehlaner. 'You shall vanish, my imbecile pigeon. You shall vanish into the cells, and see if you can see any ghosts there. . . . Ten days' solitary for a start. . . . Perhaps that'll teach you not to sleep on sentry while your comrades are murdered. . . .'

"Well, when I was restored to the bosom of my sorrowing Section, I found that, in my absence, if not owing to my absence, things had gone from very bad to much worse.

"Mutiny was brewing.

"Wehlaner was insane; the Corporals, afraid of him, were still more afraid of their men; and with two or three exceptions, the *cafard*-stricken

Section were as insane as Wehlaner, or worse.

"Wehlaner spent the whole of his time in dishing out punishments to everybody; the Corporals spent their time superintending the punishments —with their revolvers in their hands; and the men spent all their time in doing the punishments.

"In the daytime, that is to say.

"At night, the men who were not in punishment-cells or on guard, spent their time in plotting—some arguing that to kill Wehlaner would be to jump out of the frying-pan into the fire; and others, the majority, objecting that we were already in the fire, would be better off in prison, and that we owed it to ourselves, as men, to punish Wehlaner.

"An undesirable little man from Paris—he might have been Matthieu le Maquereau's own brother—was the ring-leader. Very eloquent he was. He showed us how it could be done in such a way that no particular individual could be identified as the—er—executioner.

"His plan was that Wehlaner should be 'removed' one night, and that none of us should know anything about it. Also that an anonymous letter should be placed on the table in the Corporals' hut, pointing out that an Arab, or Arabs, had evidently killed Sergeant Wehlaner and that we sincerely hoped that no such fate would overtake the Corporals. That, in fact, we were sure it would not, if they agreed with us that the lamented death of Sergeant Wehlaner was caused by the knife of an Arab.

"Some were for this and some were against it, though all agreed that something had got to be done; and while they were still wrangling—and somebody producing some mad new scheme as soon as everybody had agreed on some other mad scheme—something was done.

"It was done by poor old Müller too, though I'll swear he was as innocent as—young Hermann here, he being just such another.

"He put 'paid' to Wehlaner's account all right, and it seemed to me like what they call poetic justice, though personally I've never come across either. Either poets or justice, I mean.

"Still, it was a curious and interesting end, in that unspeakable desert outpost, to a story that must have begun in some German village, where their Greta probably still lives—and has forgotten them both by this time, I daresay—very happily, with yet a third fool.

"Wehlaner was having more and more sentries posted, and so posted that nothing could happen to one of them without another seeing it.

"Things were quietening down a bit, until, one night, I was posted over the store-house, in sight of the sentry at the south-west corner of the parapet walk.

"I was just beginning to think that my two hours hadn't much longer to run, when, in the perfect stillness and silence, I heard the slight but unmistakable sound of a sharp movement.

"Now, as we all know, a sentry, especially toward the end of his spell of duty, doesn't make any swift and sudden movement whatever, except for some very good reason.

"I turned and glanced up, and, sure enough, the sentry had sprung into the 'ready' position and thrown up his rifle, prepared to shoot.

"Like lightning I did the same—in the same direction.

"There was the ghost, and in a second or two it would emerge from shadow into the faint moonlight that fell across the door of the hut.

"Then several things happened almost simultaneously. Wehlaner threw open the hut door just as the ghost was crossing it. . . . The sentry fired and Wehlaner fell. . . .

"I fired and the ghost fell. . . .

"We had both scored a bull's-eye this time, all right.

"Then the sentry threw a fit, and when everybody came running, there were three men on the ground. . . .

"Our good Sergeant Wehlaner, shot through the chest and evidently pretty close to the heart. . . .

"An Arab—in a white garment; no turban; and with his face completely whitened with clay or white-wash—shot through the head. . . .

"And the sentry, groaning and writhing and foaming at the mouth.

"And who do you think the sentry was?

"Müller.

"And when they'd dumped Wehlaner on his cot and brought Müller up before him, old Müller went on like the prophets Jeremiah, Isaiah, Nebuchadnezzar and Emile Zola rolled into one.

"He pointed his shaking finger in Wehlaner's grey face and shouted:

" *'Greta! Greta!* It was Greta killed you, after all. . . . I saw her. . . . I saw her ghost. . . . She pointed and bade me fire; and I did. . . . I never saw you at all. . . . But Greta did! . . . Greta did! . . . She came for you. . . . She came to . . .'

"Müller stopped—for Wehlaner's jaw dropped, and he died."

CHAPTER VI

Joy.

L'Adjudant Sartene has been transferred or gone on leave, and Lieutenant V—— has taken his place. Long may he remain, for he is a good officer—experienced, cool, competent, firm, hard and just—and that is all we ask.

It was time he came, for *le Sergent* Bartak, a Bulgarian, though not a hard and bullying brute, is a depraved and vicious beast, which is infinitely worse.

Compared with him, Sergeant Pflügge, seen in retrospect, seems a gentle angel of light.

I gather from what the men say, that Bartak's vice is distinctively Bulgarian, and nobody in the *poste* felt that *Adjudant* Sartene would hold any sort of impartial inquiry if there were real trouble between Bartak and a victim.

It is that sense (or certainty) of injustice that is at the root of the hideous tragedies which lie beneath the bald notifications stating that '*le légionnaire* X—— is sentenced to death—or a long period of penal servitude—for striking *le Sergent* Y——. . . .'

We feel now that the mere presence of Lieutenant V—— will prevent trouble; and that if it does not do so, the trouble will be investigated, and be dealt with impartially.

A great cloud has been lifted from the mind of Hans Petsel, the chubby little German in whom *le Sergent* Bartak was beginning to interest himself unduly.

Also from that of Hermann, who was one of the six men that Lieutenant V—— sent back here.

Hermann hates Bartak and his vice so fiercely that he is afraid he will murder the loathsome fellow.

*　　*　　*　　*　　*

Lieutenant V——'s first order was that we should occupy the Barracks, finished or not.

He is a real good sort. Never interferes unnecessarily; never worries, chivvies and hounds men merely for the sake of doing it; and does his best, by a kindly word in season, thought for our welfare, and by his own example, to keep us cheerful.

What we fail to realize is how lonely he must be.

There is a photograph of a very lovely girl on the table in his room.

He must long to hear her voice sometimes.

Most of the men utterly refuse to accept the idea of officers having an excuse for suffering from *le cafard*. Personally, I should say that Lieutenant V——, of all men in this *poste*, would have most cause, reason, and excuse for getting it; being as he is, so utterly isolated, indeed insulated.

I should imagine that there are times when he would give all he possesses for an ordinary chat with a man of his own class and position.

As it is, from week's end to week's end, he is dumb, save for the issuing of orders; deaf, save for the hearing of reports; while he is absolutely devoid of mental and physical recreation.

Nous autres—we have our troubles, God knows, but we have our little pleasures and can nightly gather round the fire and *talk*.

*　　*　　*　　*　　*

I don't think I am what you would call a

credulous person. Quite the reverse, I imagine. And yet, when old Père Cocteau gives me his word that he is speaking the truth, somehow I believe him. Which, of course, may but be a tribute to his convincing way of telling a story.

Anyway, I believe a story that he told last night. Believed it then, I mean. I don't know that I do now, when I come to set it down.

The conversation still ran on the subject of ghosts.

I had been sceptical and remarked that, surely, if there were one place in the world where ghosts, if there be such things, would appear, it would be a battle-field where men had died sudden and violent deaths, cut off in the midst of their sins, desires and activities—and shovelled into a hole in the ground on which they fell; or a lonely outpost, such a place as this for example, where they brooded and suffered and went mad, and died by bullet, knife, disease, or their own hand.

And yet who ever heard of a genuine ghost on a battle-field or in an outpost?

Père Cocteau smiled and looked across at his *copain*.

"Eh, Thirsty-face?" said he.

"I suppose you are both going to pretend that you saw the ghost of a dead man—after seeing the ghost of a dozen empty bottles, eh?" I chaffed.

"No, *mon enfant*," was the solemn reply. "I am not going to pretend anything. Least of all that I have seen something I have never seen. . . .

". . . I, *moi qui parle*, Père Aristide Cocteau, have seen too much that is strange to have any desire or need to invent. I'll tell you about this extraordinary affair, if you like."

"Fact or fairy-tale, *mon père?*" I asked.

"The simple truth. It will leap to the eye as obvious truth, when I tell it. . . . When we both tell

it—Old Thirsty-face and I—for we were both in it.
. . .

"Yes—there are two halves to the story, and they fit together like the two portions of a broken biscuit. Not that Thirsty-face can tell a tale, the poor dumb animal, but his 'statement,' bald as that of a *gendarme* in a police-court, will suffice to show that I am telling you the truth."

Old Thirsty-face wagged his head in confirmatory nods.

"Ah!" he agreed, and added: "It's a story worth a litre of *pinard* at the least."

"Well, it occurred in those days, happier for myself and for France, when I was a Sergeant again, a Sergeant of the Legion, this time; and, as *le bon Dieu* for His own inscrutable purposes willed it, I, Aristide Cocteau, was in sole command of the outpost known as Fort Vigaud.

"I do not say this would have been the case but for the fact that *Adjudant* Zolle had pulled the trigger of his revolver when its muzzle was in his mouth; and Sergeant-Major Baerlin, out on patrol, had been for ever lost, together with six better men than himself, in a sandstorm.

"Anyhow, there was I in temporary but sole command of Fort Vigaud, with four Corporals and thirty-seven good men. . . .

"It wasn't what you'd call a gay life. Not a bit like Paris. Not a bit like this, even; where we see a convoy once a fortnight, and get news of the great world—such as that Captain Blanc has stopped a bullet with his big paunch; or that the tribesmen have captured a cartload of onions. . . .

"No, there was no news at all, and nothing happened. When I say nothing happened, I am forgetting that the sun rose every morning and set every evening; but nothing else happened, except that I kept my scoundrelly *légionnaires* so busy that they had scarcely time to grumble; barely time to scratch themselves; and no time to hatch plots.

"Mind you, I wasn't harsh or tyrannical like some of these slave-drivers of Sergeants—like Sartene *par exemple*—I merely kept them on the run from réveillé to 'lights out'!

"And when there was really nothing else to do, I had a truly enormous hole dug in the middle of the parade-ground, and then had it filled in again.

"Of course, this was all very well for *les légionnaires* and the Corporals who had to drive them to it, but it wasn't so good for me. I had too little to do, and too much time in which to think.

"Positively, in a few weeks I began to wish they'd send an Officer or even an *Adjudant* or a Sergeant-Major, to give me something to do.

"You must understand there was no *village nègre*; no *douar*; no nomad camp; no anything; *rien du tout*.

"There wasn't a human being nearer than the garrison of Fort Gherdieh, and that was fifty kilometres away to our left flank. Just such another God-forsaken, man-forgotten, desert-hell-hole as our own; and the next nearest was the oasis and town of Oued-el-Kebir, a hundred and eighty kilometres behind us, which was the Base, where there were a company of ours, a battalion of Senegalese, and some Batt. d'Af's.

"Nowhere to go. Nothing to do. And if, just to keep them from getting fat, one took *les légionnaires* for a promenade out into the desert, which was all soft loose shifting dunes, there was always the chance, if not the probability, of losing ourselves and dying of thirst, or of being buried alive in a sandstorm.

"And hot! You little ones have never felt heat.

You don't know what it is.

"Whatever you touched burnt you like the top of a stove, and at night everybody slept naked on the roof of the Barrack huts.

"Some of the mad ones were very funny. Oh, very amusing.

"I think the funniest, perhaps, was Hoorne, who thought he was a crab, and could only move sideways. You will conceive that it caused a certain amount of confusion in the ranks, when on the word 'March!' everybody stepped forwards and Hoorne stepped sideways.

"His Corporal thought he was shamming mad, until I said:

" 'All-right. Let him step sideways into the cells, and be a hermit crab.'

"But when I looked in through the hole and saw him waving his legs in the air while he fed himself with both claws at once, I decided that anyway he was better where he was. That sort of thing spreads, and may *le bon Général Dieu* punish me if I lie, but I began to feel a bit like a crab myself. I caught myself wishing I knew what sort of noise crabs make, and I'd have made it too.

"And then, *mes amis*, I began to see things. *Moi*—the Commandant of that Fort, upon whom the honour of France and those forty-one worthless lives depended.

"After 'Retreat,' and the hauling down of the flag at sunset, I went into my hut, flung my *képi* on the table, sat down, and wondered how many times more I could bear to do just those things.

"I buried my face in my hands and groaned. . . .

"And, when I looked up, I tell you I looked hard, and rubbed my eyes, and looked again.

"For there, standing on the other side of my table, not ten feet away from me, as plain as any one of you, and *le bon Dieu* knows you're plain enough—was a man whom I did not know.

"He was an absolute stranger. Neither one of my garrison, nor a man whom I had ever seen before.

" 'How the devil has he got here?' I wondered. 'He can't have crossed the desert alone. Why was there no "*Alerte!*" when his party was sighted? . . .'

"But then, again, 'How did he get into this room?' I asked myself. 'For he wasn't here when I entered, and the door certainly hasn't been opened since I sat down.'

"And in the same second that these thoughts flashed through my mind, I realized that he was an *Adjudant*, and, springing to my feet, I saluted.

" '*Pardon, mon Adjudant,*' I said, and stared at him.

"He was a rather queer-looking chap; tall and thin; with a gaunt, narrow face; a longish nose, that had been broken and turned slightly to one side; a forked beard; and, more noticeable than any of these things, a damaged eye. I wondered whether he could see out of it. It was half-closed, and like his nose, turned to one side.

"There was a big scar above it, and I observed as I stared at him, that this was the same scar that crossed his nose. He'd had a frightful whack at some time or other.

"And while I stared at him, he stared at me—and, he being my superior officer, I waited for him to speak first.

"Well, he didn't speak first; nor yet second.

"He merely gazed at me with the utmost intentness, as though he had so much to say that he couldn't say it.

"Well, that was his affair. I'd done the correct thing—apologized for not seeing him, and stood to attention. . . . And the next move was up to him.

"By and by I grew aware of three things.

"First, that this was getting uncomfortable; second, that if he didn't soon say something I should have to, or else seem impudent; and, thirdly, that he was no longer there.

"What do you think of that, *mes amis*. I tell you I sat down on that chair quicker than I had got up, and that had been quicker than lightning. . . .

"I was the most puzzled man in the French Army, and that is saying something. . . .

"And then, for a little while, I felt rather queer. I had seen an *Adjudant* of the Legion—complete to the last button, a real man, mark you, scar, damaged eye and all—where there was no *Adjudant* of the Legion.

"He had appeared in my room, and he had disappeared in my room. . . .

"I was seeing things. . . .

"I, Aristide Cocteau, sober-drinking, hard-working, respected and responsible Sergeant of the Legion. . . . Seeing things. . . .

"Was I also to become a crab, and wave six legs in the air while I fed myself with my claws?

"No.

"Springing to my feet, I threw open my door and let a roar that roused four Corporals and thirty-seven men, a large assortment of whom came running.

" 'Why wasn't I called?' I bawled at Corporal Anton, when he stood at the salute in front of me.

" 'For what, *mon Sergent?*' he asked, obviously puzzled. 'I don't understand.'

"And it occurred to me that if I were going to see things, or become a crab, the less that was known about it in Fort Vigaud the better for the health and discipline of that salubrious spot.

" 'Weren't the gates opened just now?' I bawled.

" 'But no, *mon Sergent*. Why? . . .'

" 'I thought I heard something out there,' I said, realizing that I must be careful.

" 'No, *mon Sergent.* Nothing. . . . Brunelli was bawling in the cells that he wanted a litre of wine and a roast chicken. . . . But I went in and—er—soothed him. . . .'

"I went the rounds. Then I paraded every man in the *poste*, and, while they stood at attention, I made a tour of inspection of the whole place. I don't know why, nor what I expected to find. But I just felt like it. I was very upset. . . . There was a man in the *poste* whose face I had never seen before—and I didn't like his habits. . . . He came and went too suddenly for my comfort. . . . And I was both puzzled and worried.

"Well, wouldn't our Commandant here be puzzled, if he suddenly saw a stranger in his room this evening; a superior officer whom he didn't know, and who vanished while he stared at him—and no miserable herring-gutted ghost that he could see through, either, but a proper man, with a forked beard, a scar, a swivel-eye and two decorations? Wouldn't he?

"Next day I should think *les légionnaires* must have thought I'd got news that we were going to be attacked; or else that I'd got *le cafard* in a funny form, for I kept them fairly on the jump.

"Of course I'd heard of *légionnaires* dressing up and playing tricks, often enough. I expect even you youngsters have heard of Meier and Rosenbach who went 'on pump,' and came back a few days later, correctly dressed as Pomeranian Grenadiers of the Eighteenth Century? Rosenbach had been a tailor, and they'd cut their uniforms about until they'd got them pretty correct. The Guard nearly fainted when they saw two of Frederick the Great's men marching up to the gate.

". . . But as I kept telling myself, if some rogue —who'd been an actor, say—could make his face up so that I didn't recognize him, and had faked up an *Adjudant's* badges of rank, how could he suddenly appear in my hut like that? And, what was more interesting, how could he suddenly *dis*-appear, while I was staring at him?

"But then, as I told myself again, people don't appear and disappear before your eyes like that. It's all nonsense. I must be going dotty. A plain case of *le cafard*, and I must watch myself. No playing crabs for me—with a Fort and forty-one men on my hands.

"Nevertheless I left no stone unturned, though there were precious few stones to turn in Fort Vigaud. And when I gazed upon the foolish faces of those four Corporals, and those thirty-seven rascally *légionnaires*, I knew in my bones that not one of them, be he the cleverest actor from Paris, could have got himself up to look like the man who had appeared to me in my room.

"After giving them all such a busy day that three of them found themselves in cells for think-ing it was too busy, I followed my regular routine and after the '*au drapeau*' salute, I went into my room as usual.

"Closing the door, I seated myself in my chair and looked round the room. No chance of anyone hiding there, and stepping out from concealment, to play a trick on me. There was nothing in that room but myself; the chair and the table; a small locked box containing papers; a pair of camel-bags; my bed, under which I could see; and the shelf above it, upon which were folded my spare uniforms. Nothing in the room but just that, and my *bidon*, *musette*, and so on, hanging from nails.

"There couldn't be a dog hidden in the room, much less a man.

"And there he was.

"He was standing exactly where he had stood the night before, an *Adjudant* of the Legion, with a scarred face, damaged left eye, forked beard, and two decorations. And with the same curious look or expression on his face—anxious and troubled— something like a dumb man with a frightful lot to say.

"I am not good at words, but there is one that expresses it. How shall I say? . . . Yearning? . . . Yes . . . that, perhaps, is as good as another.

"Well, there was I, and there was *Monsieur l'Adjudant*, and from sheer force of habit—or is it instinct—I sprang to my feet, saluted, and stood at attention.

" '*Bon soir, mon Adjudant*,' I said respectfully, and then I felt foolish and very cold, and a little afraid.

"For, stare at him as I might; examine him as I would, he was not one of my men dressed up. He was an *Adjudant* of the Legion in a place where there was no *Adjudant* of the Legion—not within fifty miles. And supposing, just supposing, there had been a visiting patrol, an Inspecting Officer, or new man come to take over command, would he have come alone across two hundred kilometres of desert?

"Would no sentry have uttered a sound? Would he have been admitted silently to the fort? Would he have appeared before me suddenly, through a closed door or a barred window high up in the wall?

"No.

"And there he stood.

"And there I stood.

"I tried to speak again, but somehow do you

638

know, *mes amis*, I was not very fluent . . . nor very ready-witted.

" 'Has *Monsieur l'Adjudant* come to take over command?' I stammered, when I couldn't bear the staring silence any longer.

"He made no reply.

"Taking my eyes from his face for a moment, I drew my chair to one side.

" 'Will you be seated, *mon Adjudant?*' I said, and looked up to discover that he wouldn't, for he was no longer there. . . .

"Now how would you feel, *mes enfants*, if, looking down, at this moment, you perceived that you had no feet, that your legs ended at the knees? Difficult to describe, *hein?* Well, that's how I felt. And it certainly is difficult to describe. . . .

"However, I was out of that room in a flash, and round that *poste* at the gallop. It would have been a dark and dismal day for any man I'd seen wearing a crooked nose, scarred face, swivel eye and a forked beard—not to mention an *adjudant's* uniform.

"It would very probably have been his last day too. But I found no such person.

"I found four inefficient Corporals and thirty-seven worthless *légionnaires*, of whom five were in the cells—one of them, Hoorne, crawling on as many of his six legs as would function, while with his claws he sought for food upon his ocean bed.

"No, this vanishing-*Adjudant* performance was no trick of a *cafard*-stricken *légionnaire*, even had such a thing been possible. . . .

"And then an idea occurred to me—a reasonably foolish one, I admit.

"Supposing they'd sent a new Commanding Officer—an *Adjudant*—from the base at Oued-el-Kebir, and, on the way, what with a touch of the sun and a shortage of water—he had got a little more than a touch of *le cafard* himself?

"Or, while one was about it, suppose he'd been lost for a week or two in the sand-dunes, and had gone hopelessly and incurably mad, as some folk do in those circumstances.

"And suppose he'd arrived at *siesta*-time, when I and everybody else except the sentries, were lying down asleep; and had ridden up to the sentry, at the gate, and, as his superior officer, had ordered him to admit him and say nothing.

"And then suppose he was hiding in the Fort, and spying on my conduct as temporary Commandant.

" 'Yes,' said I, 'and suppose my grandmother were the Minister for War, what an improvement there would be, not only in my prospects, but in the general management of the military affairs of France!'

"Suppose and suppose. . . .

"And even admitting that this theory of a *cafard*-stricken *Adjudant* was for one moment tenable, how could he appear and disappear like a thrice-accursed jack-in-the-box?

"And I shrugged my shoulders, and told myself that if he appeared to me again, I'd see whether a bullet from my revolver would do him any good.

"And then,

" 'Yes, Aristide Cocteau,' said I to myself, 'yes, and a pretty state of affairs that will be, won't it? When the acting-Commandant of Fort Vigaud not only sees things, but starts shooting them up! . . . They'd say, at Head-quarters, that what I saw was pink rats, the illegitimate offspring of my brain and absinthe. And reduce me to the ranks once more.

"No, that would not do. I must face the fact and face it alone—that I was haunted. Haunted by the ghost of some dead *Adjudant* who had died of his wounds in that very room. Or more likely, been murdered there by his own men. . . .

"But was I, alone, being haunted by him? Might not some of the others have seen this apparition? I must find out. Shouldn't I look a fool though, saying to that fat-headed calf of a Corporal Metzner:

" 'Er—by the way, Corporal, have you noticed the ghost of an *Adjudant* of the Legion promenading himself, at all? Among other things he wears a forked beard, a scar, one eye, and two decorations.'

"Wouldn't the news go round pretty quickly that Sergeant Cocteau had got *le cafard?*

"No. A better idea. I wouldn't do that. I'd ask each of the Corporals, casually, if he knew *Adjudant* Somebody who was killed here in Fort Vigaud. I'd pretend I'd forgotten his name for the moment, but knew him so well that I could describe him quite fully. Then, if one of them had seen this ghost he would surely say so.

"Yes, undoubtedly he would say:

" 'Why that description tallies exactly with a man I thought I saw last night. . . .'

"Well . . . the next night . . . straight from parade I went to my room. . . . I sat and waited; staring straight in front of me.

"I was conscious of something slightly to one side of my line of vision.

"I turned my head, and there he was.

"There he was.

"This time I did not rise to my feet and salute. I stared at him.

" 'Well,' I said, 'who are you and what do you want?'

"He stared at me and said nothing.

"I stared at him and felt as though the hair were rising on my head, and I broke out into a cold perspiration.

" 'Here,' I shouted to keep my courage up. 'What the devil are you doing here? Who are you?'

"Rising to my feet, full of frightened bluster, I knocked my chair over, thrust the table to one side, and strode toward him. I would seize him by the throat, shake him, choke an answer out of him.

"I raised my clutching hands.

"He was not there.

"At that moment there was a heavy knock on my door. It opened, and Corporal Zeeberg entered, saluted, and stood at attention. If he felt any surprise at seeing my chair overturned and my table askew, he did not show it.

" 'Well?' said I; and he gave me some report or message. As he turned to go, I called him back.

" 'Corporal,' said I, 'you're an old soldier. Did you ever know *Adjudant* . . . What's his name . . . ? I've got it on the tip of my tongue . . . I shall forget my own name next . . . a man with a forked beard, terrible scar across his face and a swivel-eye—who was killed here in Fort Vigaud?'

"Zeeberg thought a moment.

" 'No, *mon Sergent*,' he replied. 'I never heard of him.'

" 'Ask Alvez, Popoulos and Metzner if they knew him.'

"Zeeberg saluted and went out, returning a few minutes later to say that none of the Corporals knew a *Sous-officier* answering to that description; nor indeed had they heard of an *Adjudant* being killed in Fort Vigaud.

" 'It's of no consequence,' said I, adding as he went:

" 'By the way . . . we've got several *vieux moustaches* here. Tell each of the Corporals to find out whether any man of his section remembers the name of the *Adjudant* who was killed here.'

And I briefly repeated the description.

"I can't tell you why I did this. I didn't know then, and I don't know now, but I had a sort of feeling that if I could establish that such a man had lived and died here in Fort Vigaud, it wouldn't be so bad. I should feel better about it. I should lose some of this dreadful fear that I was going mad. . . .

"After all, people do see ghosts, and if it was a ghost—all right! I'm not afraid of ghosts. I'm not afraid of man, beast, devil—or ghost. . . . And I told myself that this was why I was so anxious to establish the fact that *Adjudant* Somebody had been killed in that room, and that I was seeing his ghost. I didn't mind seeing anything—provided it was really there.

"So I argued to myself in explanation of my conduct.

"And yet, do you know, *mes amis*, it wasn't that at all.

"It was a sort of *urgency*. A sort of curious compulsion that drove me to make these inquiries. I *had* to find out.

"And by-and-bye, just as I had finished my *soupe*, back came Corporal Zeeberg, bringing with him an old rascal named, or known as, Tomaso.

" 'Well?' said I, as they saluted and stood at attention.

" '*Pardon, mon Sergent*,' said Corporal Zeeberg, 'this man says that, although he knows of no *Adjudant* having been killed here, he does know, for an absolute fact, that *l'Adjudant* Pierrefond, under whom he was serving last year, answers to the description you gave me. He is a tall thin man, with a scar that goes across his forehead and face —he got it at Fez from an Arab sword—a forked beard, a swivel-eye and a broken crooked nose. He has the *Croix de Guerre* and *Médaille militaire*.

" '*L'Adjudant* Pierrefond, did you say?'

" '*Oui, mon Sergent.*'

" '*Bien.* . . . *Rompez!*'

"And when they had gone, I again sat and stared. This time at nothing, and doubtless with my mouth open.

"*L'Adjudant Pierrefond!* . . . who had won the *Médaille militaire* as well as the *Croix de Guerre* in the Fez campaign!

"*He was commanding at Fort Gherdieh.*

"And *l'Adjudant* Pierrefond, commanding at Gherdieh, fifty kilometres on our left flank, had appeared to me, on three consecutive evenings, at sunset!

"I flung open the door.

" 'Sound the *Rassemblement!*' I bawled. 'Every man on parade *en tenue de campagne*, in nine minutes.'

" 'Corporal Zeeberg!' I yelled. 'Two hundred rounds a man, two days' rations, and a full *bidon!*'

"I was going to give my merry men a little walk. If they were finding life a bit monotonous, they should have a break in the monotony. . . .

"Fifty kilometres. . . .

"They should do that little promenade in eight hours . . . nine perhaps. We could get there at dawn—and shouldn't I look a species of camel-faced fool if I got there and found that *l'Adjudant* Pierrefond had gone long ago, or were dead; and that all was merry and bright at Fort Gherdieh.

"And what particular species of camel should I resemble if, while I was away, a wandering band of Touareg captured and destroyed Fort Vigaud?

"But I did not pause for more than a moment. I felt in my bones that something was wrong at Fort Gherdieh, and here was my chance to strike a blow for France, and two for Sergeant Cocteau.

"As I came on parade, nine minutes later, and my rascals sprang to attention, I could see that they were already different men. Gone were all signs of gloom, boredom, misery and *cafard*. I would take thirty, and leave seven in charge of the fort.

" 'Bring me the prisoners from the cells,' said I to Corporal Anton.

"Five dirty and miserable objects fell in, outside the prison hut.

" 'Ho, you scum of the earth!' said I, addressing them. 'The Company marches out and the Fort will be attacked to-night. Can you hold it if I leave it in your charge, a man to each wall and one in reserve?'

"At those words they grew visibly taller and their shoulders broader. They stood up and became men.

" 'Ho! You, Hoorne. Are you still a crab? If so, get back into that cell.'

" '*Non, mon Sergent.* I am a soldier,' grinned Hoorne.

" 'Three paces forward; *March!*' said I. 'About turn. Three paces forward; *March.* . . . About turn.'

"Hoorne obeyed, and moved as a good *légionnaire* should, and not like a crab, in the least.

"There was no stepping sideways now.

" '*Bien,*' said I. 'Corporal Anton, you and these five will be the garrison of Fort Vigaud, and hold it until I return.'

"Anton saluted, but his face fell. Nearly fell off.

"We marched all night, and when I say 'marched,' I mean that I set the pace at ten minutes to the kilometre, with ten minutes' rest after every five kilometres. They could keep that up indefinitely, and it would bring them about where

I wanted them by dawn.

"When I saw, by my watch, that dawn wasn't far off, I extended them over a front of about three hundred yards, and let them lie down, eat a biscuit, drink and sleep.

"In due course, as usually happens, the sun peeped over the edge of the eastern horizon to see what was doing; and there, just a bit nearer than I thought, and a bit to the left flank of where I expected to see it, was Fort Gherdieh.

"And, *mes enfants*, while I stood and examined the place through my glasses, and wondered whether I hadn't better about-turn and go back again, what did I hear?

"What I had often heard before, but never with the same feelings. A shot. . . . Another shot. . . . And some ragged independent firing.

"*Figurez-vous, mes enfants.* . . . Imagine it. . . . Think of it. Fort Gherdieh was besieged, and I, Sergeant Aristide Cocteau, Acting-Commandant of Fort Vigaud, had come to its relief—and arrived in the nick of time.

"I scarcely needed to give any orders.

"At the first shot, every one of my beauties rolled over on to his belly, took up his rifle and looked at me.

"I got to the middle of the line, signalled to them to rise up, crouch low, and get into the valley between us and the next sand-dune.

"Over the top of that I peeped; and over the top of it we all went a minute later.

"And then the next . . . and the next . . . until we were within range, and I could see exactly what the game was. They had captured the oasis and had camped there, thus cutting Fort Gherdieh off from its water-supply, and were conducting a leisurely siege of the place, leaving thirst to do the real fighting.

"I soon saw my obvious plan of campaign.

"With a signal, I got my braves back down into the sand-valley behind them, turned them from line into file, and led them round to where we had the little oasis, the enemy base, between us and the Fort.

"Once again we advanced, closing in on the centre a little, as we did so, until we lined a sand-dune, not three hundred metres from their camp.

"And then we had them. . . . But yes, *mes enfants*, we had them. Those who were not out enjoying their morning sport, shooting at the Fort, were watering camels, cleaning weapons, cooking, reading *La Vie Touaregienne*, or what not.

"And oh, the joy of that first volley!

"Did they jump? . . . Did they run? . . . Did we fire three more volleys, and then carry on à *volontiers?*

"And did Fort Gherdieh wake up?

"Believe me, by the time I blew the '*Cease fire,*' and gave the order, '*Baïonnettes au canon!*', and the garrison of the Fort had done the same, and thrown open the gates for a sortie, there wasn't much to bayonet.

"Not that the garrison could have done a lot in the way of a charge.

"There wasn't a quarter of them who could do more than lie against a loop-hole and pull a trigger. . . . I don't want ever again to see men in the state that they were in. Those who could walk threw discipline to the winds, and made a staggering rush to the oasis and water. . . . Mad. . . . Yes—but mad. . . .

"And there he was.

"Standing in the gate unable to speak for his swollen tongue, but gesticulating, threatening them with his revolver, and striking at them as they ran out—there he was. . . .

"A tall thin man, with a scar across his face, crooked nose, swivel-eye, forked beard; and wearing the bronze *Croix de Guerre* and the gilt-and-silver *Médaille militaire.*

"Just as he had stood in my room at Fort Vigaud, there stood *l'Adjudant* Pierrefond, in the gateway of Fort Gherdieh.

"Marching up to him, I saluted, stood to attention, and then pulled forward my *bidon* and held it out for him to drink.

"Without speaking he stared at me.

" 'I am glad that I was in time, *mon Adjudant,*' said I.

"He moved cracked and blackened lips in an attempt to reply, but could not do so.

"Taking the *bidon* he drank . . . washed his mouth, moistened his lips . . . and drank again.

" '*Bien,*' he croaked.

"And then:

" 'What made you come?'

" 'You came for me,' I said.

" 'When?'

" 'At sunset last night . . . and the night before . . . and the night before that.'

" ' Ha! . . .'

"It was a curious sound . . . part laugh, part exclamation, part cry—a cry of triumph, of belief confirmed.

" 'At sunset!' he croaked. 'At sunset! . . . Each of the last three nights. . . . At sunset! . . . Ha!'

"He was queer. Evidently still feeling the strain, and very naturally.

"The Arabs had been there ten days, and there had been precious little water in the Fort when they made their first rush; and that, it seemed, had been a pretty near thing.

"Oh, yes. They were for it, undoubtedly . . . that

very day, if I had not turned up.

"Those who could still stand were going to stagger out that night, with fixed bayonets, and get to the water or die. They'd have died of course, shot down like lame dogs.

"Pierrefond had sent two men off, the first night, to get to Fort Vigaud for help; and their heads had been thrown over the wall within an hour of their starting.

"No less than three men had volunteered, the next three nights, and each had come back in the same way, or rather, part of him had. There were still men who would have tried it, but Pierrefond couldn't afford to waste any more like that.

"And slowly, except when it happened quickly, they all went mad. It being the hottest time of the year, of course.

"Well . . . we cleaned up the mess; shot the Arab wounded and prisoners—and felt that shooting was too good for them, after we had seen the mutilated remains of our comrades whom they'd tortured to death before they had thrown their heads over the wall—buried the dead; did what we could for our own wounded; and then I agreed to take over all duties in Fort Gherdieh while the garrison slept for twenty-four hours.

"When *l'Adjudant* Pierrefond had seen everything in order, and all *klim bim*, he also went to his cot, and fell asleep before he was fairly on it.

"And then I had a chance of a talk with this aged species of a demented goat that has earned for itself the dishonourable title of Old Thirsty-face —and I heard the other end of the story."

Thirsty-face smiled, nodded his head, and took another pull at his *bidon*, the contents of which were evidently not water.

". . . Bad. . . . After about a week, very bad," he said. "Not a drop of water in the place . . . half of us wounded . . . the other half mad with thirst. Not but what the wounded were the thirstiest of the lot. Croaking *'Water! Water!'* all day and all night, like frogs. . . .

"On the eighth morning, a Dervish, the dirty Father of all Holy Old Men, stood up on the nearest sand-dune, called on Allah to come and have a look, held up a great fat skin full of water, and then poured it all out on to the sand . . . yelling and dancing, and flinging all this lovely water about, in front of men who would have given a litre of blood for a teaspoonful of it . . . the damned dirty dancing dervish. . . .

"Anyhow, *I* stopped his dancing.

"The heat waves off the sand were shimmering so badly that it was chancey shooting, and we were very short of ammunition. . . . But I got him. . . . I got him all right. . . . And he spilt more than water. . . . I set him dancing on his back. . . ."

"Yes. . . . Yes. . . . Yes. . . . You're a wonderful shot when you're sober," interrupted Cocteau. "But what about *l'Adjudant* Pierrefond, when he went mad?"

"Well, I'm coming to that," grumbled Old Thirsty-face. "I was just coming."

"Yes. So's Christmas," agreed Cocteau. "Probably you'll arrive together."

"Well, as I was saying," continued Père Cocteau. "Old Father Christmas here, told me all about everything, it still being fresh in what we must call his mind. He spoke a bit quicker in those days.

"After about a week of it, *Adjudant* Pierrefond had got queer. Queer in the head. Not *cafard*, you understand. No one gets that when there's any fighting about. But queer as a man may, who has not slept or drunk for a week, and scarcely eaten, either. For he was a good officer, this Pierrefond. He did not put himself on the same water and food ration as the men. He put himself on one half of it from the very first. Isn't that so, Thirsty-face?"

"*Vraiment!* He did so," nodded Old Thirsty-face. "For an *Adjudant* he was a good man. He'd have been a better one if he'd kept more water in the Fort, though.

"But then," he added, "he'd nothing else to keep it in. And there had been no Arabs along that way for years. . . ."

"So what with his quarter-ration of water," continued Cocteau, "no sleep and little food—not to mention the anxiety of his responsibility for the Fort—it isn't remarkable that *l'Adjudant* Pierrefond did get a bit queer. According to Old Thirsty-face's tale, he got eccentric, imagined things and behaved strangely.

"*Par exemple.* Going the rounds he'd ask the sentry if he'd seen anything, and being told 'Nothing,' he'd say,

" 'Never mind, *mon enfant*, watch well, and you'll see French troops coming. Watch and pray. Watch, for the night cometh when no man can work.'

"Isn't that so, Thirsty-face?"

"*Vraiment.* He did so. He told the sentries to watch and pray! . . . Pray! *Les légionnaires.* . . . Pray! . . . He, he, he!" chuckled Thirsty-face. "Watch and pray! Watch and curse, more likely. . . ."

"Then on the eighth evening," continued Cocteau, "he paraded all the garrison that were still on their feet, and addressed them.

" 'The Arabs are now calling on Allah!' he said. 'It is the hour of their *ashä* prayer. With perfect faith and complete belief, they call on Allah. They pray to Him to help them to defeat us. I shall now go and pray to God, also with perfect faith and complete belief. I shall pray to Him to help us to defeat them. Remember that Fort Vigaud is but fifty kilometres away, and that nothing is impossible to God. On the word *"Rompez,"* let every man go away and pray, confessing his sins. For myself, I shall go into my room and pray, with all my heart and soul and strength, that God will send us help from Fort Vigaud. God is greater than Allah: and Fort Vigaud is but a night's march away. *Rompez.*'

"Well, that looked bad. And the *Sous-officiers* began to wonder what they should do if the *Adjudant* went off his head.

"Meanwhile *les légionnaires* undoubtedly confessed some remarkable sins to each other, and certainly brought forth some unique prayers. Probably more would have been heard had there been more water, for no man can do himself justice when his tongue and lips are so dry that you can hear the one tap against the other.

"All next day, those who could hold a rifle and pull a trigger carried on, and stood to their *créneaux* and embrasures from before dawn to after sunset, hoping for a quick bullet through the head.

"And again that evening, *l'Adjudant* Pierrefond paraded the survivors as the Arabs drew off, and made another speech.

"He told them that they must be of good heart for relief would surely come from Fort Vigaud. All that was wrong was lack of . . .

" 'Water,' suddenly croaked Old Thirsty-face from the ranks."

"*Vraiment!* I did so," nodded the old soldier, grinning proudly. "I knew he couldn't put a good soldier in the cells just then; and he couldn't cut down the wine-rations I hadn't got. So I thought I'd remind him to talk sense," and Old Thirsty-face chuckled reminiscently.

"And what happened then?" prompted Cocteau. "Go on. Tell us."

"Pierrefond looked at me," said Thirsty-face.

" 'Yes,' he said, 'poor village idiot. And why are we short of water? Because we lack faith. But I take the blame myself. I am responsible, and I speak for you all when I pray to God. My faith was weak. I now go to pray with a faith complete and perfect. Help *will* come from Fort Vigaud. *Rompez!*' "

"Well," continued Père Cocteau, as the old man drank again and lapsed into contemplative silence, "they stuck it out another day; a few more being killed and wounded, and a few more collapsing insensible with heat and thirst. . . . And, as always, Pierrefond was everywhere at once, setting an example, encouraging the men with fine promises, and telling them to make the most of that day, for it was the last one of the siege.

"And as the sun sank below the horizon that evening, he paraded the remnants of the garrison for the third time. . . . What happened that time, Thirsty-face?"

"Young Zozo Butt-the-Goat, the one they called Scorpion, took a pace to the front and presented arms.

" 'What's this?' snapped Pierrefond, pulling out his revolver.

" 'May I speak, *mon Officier*, for my comrades? We've got to drink or die. We may as well die fighting for water in that oasis, as wait and die here.'

" 'And you wish to make a sortie and rush the well, my brave one?' replied Pierrefond in a kind gentle croak.

" 'We do, *mon Commandant*,' said Scorpion, looking very fierce and brave and clever.

" 'Well, you won't do it, my pudding-headed pot-bellied flatulent fool. One pace backward march or I'll have you *en crapaudine* for the night,' answered Pierrefond, neither kind nor gentle.

" 'Now that that cockroach has finished singing, listen to me,' Pierrefond went on. 'There will be no marching out from here, because I intend to have no marching *in*—by Arabs. I am not concerned with the fate of five *sous*' worth of scum like you. But I *am* concerned with the fate of Fort Gherdieh. And when the Arabs get in here, it'll be because you're all dead at your posts. Not because you're outside playing with the water.'

"Then he changed his tune.

" 'But now you've said your foolish say, through the mouth of the silliest of you, I'll tell you something.

" 'We shall be relieved to-morrow. . . .

" 'Yes, you may cheer if you wish. . . .'

"And, putting our *képis* on our bayonets, we waved them above our heads, and tried to cheer old Pierrefond. It was the funniest noise you ever heard. More like a pond full of frogs than a Section of *légionnaires*. It was such a funny noise that we laughed.

"Then Pierrefond called us to attention again.

" 'Yes,' he said, 'To-morrow we shall be relieved. I know it. The night before last I prayed, with Hope. Last night I prayed, with Faith. This evening I shall pray, with Certainty. Do you know what that means? It means that my prayers will be heard. "Ask and it shall be given unto you; seek and ye shall find; knock and it shall be opened unto you." . . . Provided that you have the Faith which moves mountains. Watch and pray; oh ye, of little faith. . . . I now go to pray for you. *I know that relief will come from Fort Vigaud.*

" '*Rompez.*'

"Just as he was in the act of croaking '*Rompez,*' Zozo Butt-the-Goat, the one they called Scorpion, takes a pace to the front again and presents arms, and of course we all wait to hear what he's got to say.

" '*Pardon, mon Adjudant,*' he croaks. 'Do you know this for certain?'

" 'For certain, *mon enfant,*' says Pierrefond, instead of knocking him down and having him trussed up.

" 'Then we can go to the oasis to-morrow?' croaks Scorpion.

" 'You shall,' says Pierrefond.

" 'We shall,' answers Scorpion. 'Whether relief comes or not. If they haven't come by sunrise, we are going to attack the oasis and either die or drink.'

"Pierrefond pulls out his revolver. This was insolence, defiance and rank mutiny.

" 'That's the end of Zozo Butt-the-Goat,' I thought, and wondered whether Pierrefond would have to shoot more than one. It wouldn't be me anyhow, for Pierrefond was right and Zozo was wrong. But Pierrefond, having raised the revolver, suddenly put it back in the holster.

" 'You shall,' he said quietly. 'Such is my Faith, my Certainty. God is greater than Allah.'

"And he went off to his hut."

"Well, *mon enfant,*" said Cocteau to me, "you ask if I have seen the ghost of a dead man. What is my answer?

"No.

"Never have I seen the ghost of a dead man.

"But I have seen the ghost of a live one.

"A queer story," he mused. "The queerest part of it being that it is absolutely true."

"What became of this *Adjudant* Pierrefond?" I asked. "Did he get a commission?"

"No, *mon enfant*," was the reply. "He got a *biretta* and *soutane* instead. Took his discharge and became a priest. What would have been regarded as *cafard* in the Legion, was religious fervour in the Church."

"I should think he's a very splendid man," I said, ". . . the ideal Military Chaplain."

"Quite so, *mon enfant. Vous avez raison.* How right you are. It is a pity he's not here."

"And you, Père Cocteau? Was that the time you won the *Médaille militaire?*" I asked.

"One of the times, *mon enfant*," replied Père Cocteau modestly.

A queer yarn; and not the least queer thing about it is the fact that I implicitly believed every word as I heard it. . . . On mature reflection I'm not so sure. . . . I don't know at all—don't know what to make of it.

Terence Hogan, on the other hand, is quite annoyed with me that I cast the faintest doubt upon it, or entertain unworthy suspicions. But then he is a firm believer in telepathy and the power to project the astral form, given sufficient faith and urgency.

Abraham the Sailor allows that Cocteau has cert'nly put over a new one on him; and leaves it at that.

Digger reckons he's a great and good old liar.

Gottenberger doesn't see anything remarkable about it. Quite obviously Cocteau's visitant was Pierrefond's *doppelganger*. Apparently a quite common phenomenon in his part of the world.

Hermann likewise sees nothing remarkable

about it. It was a clear Answer to Prayer, such as any religious-minded man, of true faith, might expect. Why do we pray, if we don't expect our prayers to be answered?

And one way and another, I found my comrades' reactions to the story nearly as interesting as the story itself.

CHAPTER VII

Invasion. . . .

Silent; insidious; complete.

Rats.

Scarcely have we settled into our barracks, when the *poste* is invaded by rats.

It is amazing.

Terence Hogan addresses me, for the moment, as Hatto, Top-Hatto, and Bishop. Apparently he learnt the glum and grim poem at school, for he is over-fond of quoting from it in a sepulchral croaking voice.

As it happens, I am able to annoy him by out-quoting him every time; as, among the very few poems I do know, is the *Pied Piper of Hamelin*, which appealed to me greatly as a child—perhaps because we were so fond of ratting.

" 'Rats!' " I reply. " 'They fought the dogs and killed the cats, and bit the babies in the cradles, and ate the cheeses out of the vats, and licked the soup from the cooks' own ladles; split open the kegs of salted sprats, made nests inside the *légionnaires'* hats, and even spoiled the soldiers' chats by drowning their speaking—with shrieking and squeaking in fifty different sharps and flats.' "

Then Terence Hogan gives me another dose of Bishop Hatto—it being his humour to pretend that it is in search of me that the rats are sent by an outraged Deity.

"Rats . . ." I am able to counter. "It's you they've come for, Terry. 'Because your muttering grew to a grumbling, and your grumbling grew to a mighty rumbling, into the *poste* the rats came tumbling.

" 'Great rats, small rats, lean rats, brawny
    rats,
    Brown rats, black rats, grey rats, tawny
      rats,
    Grave old plodders, gay young friskers,
    Fathers, mothers, uncles, cousins,
    Cocking tails and pricking whiskers,
    Families by tens and dozens,
    Brothers, sisters, husbands, wives,
    Hunting Hogan for their lives.' "

The men say that, Heaven knows, the rats were dreadful enough in the trenches in France and Flanders, but absolutely nothing at all compared with what we have to put up with in *Poste* V——.

They aren't troublesome to us, personally, during the day-time, whatever they may be to the cooks; but the moment we lie down they get up. No sooner are we in bed than they arrive. We hear them come and, before long, feel them too, as they run across us.

First of all they ransack the room for food, rushing up the walls, dancing upon the shelves above our heads, bounding from shelf to shelf, and frequently falling upon the face of the man below.

Hermann takes his spare food into bed with him, and sleeps curled round it. The rats follow, and also curl round it. When Hermann turns, they turn. And when, in the morning, he arises, so do they.

Abraham the Sailor, truthful ever, swears that he saw one sitting on Père Cocteau's forehead, washing itself. Père Cocteau began to snore; and the rat, putting its hand to its ear, appeared to listen. It then beckoned with the other hand, as it called to a lady-friend who was exploring Hermann's ear. She joined him and the two, burrowing into Cocteau's beard, made a nest and started house-keeping.

"A lie," murmured Père Cocteau. "It is notorious that wine-bibbers are apt to see rats anywhere. One of your rats was named D. and the other T."

"Oh, D.T. was it?" said Abraham. "Then excusin' the question, what's this?"

And, from the depths of Père Cocteau's beard he, something of a conjurer, produces a small and very dead rat.

"One of the children, I presoom," observes Abraham.

And Cocteau uses a Word.

*   *   *   *   *

The earnest, simple and serious Hermann has once again added to the gaiety of nations, or to that of their representatives in this *poste*.

Yesterday his brain creaked, rumbled, groaned, and was delivered of an idea.

The association of ideas. Rats. A rat-trap. Splendid.

We begged him to take great care of the young idea. . . . Nurse it. . . . Nourish it. . . . Exercise it. . . . And in every way develop its growth.

What did we mean? A set of sniggering *dumm-kopfs*. Wasn't a rat-trap a good idea?

A grand idea. Original; brilliant; valuable. Could he not draw a plan and elevation . . . with book of the words? And directions A, B, C, D, showing us how to make it; and the rats how to use it?

No, he would not. But to any person who was not a half-wit, he would describe his idea of a practicable rat-trap.

"*You*'re not a half-wit, old son," Abraham

assured him.

And on receiving Hermann's grateful smile, he added:

"Not nearly half. . . ."

"He's not two-faced either," Abraham averred, and marred the testimonial by adding, *sotto voce*:

"If he were, surely to God he'd use the other one. . . ."

Nevertheless, we humoured Hermann to the top of his bent, and under his instruction built a rat-trap fit for the most heroic rats to live in.

As we pointed out, it was no mere trap, it was a Home.

This Rats' Home was a biggish and stout box, furnished with a front door and windows. The front door was for the rats to go in; the windows (wired) were for us to look in. As Hermann rightly said, we must be able to see whether there was a rat inside or not.

The front door, unlike most, drew up, in outside grooves, after the manner of a portcullis. From a nail in the middle of the top of the front door, a string proceeded, by way of a hole in the middle of the roof, into the interior of the house. At the end of the string, a piece of cheese, toasted and tempting, dangled in the middle of the Home. Simplicity itself.

To set the trap, you got your piece of string, tied the piece of cheese to one end of it, inserted your hand through the front door, threaded the other end of the string through the hole in the roof, and then brought it down and tied it to the nail at the top of the front door.

"But, you addled innocent," pointed out Abraham the Sailor, "if the front door's shut, the rat can't get in; and if the front door's open, and a rat goes in and pulls the string—the harder he pulls, the more the door will rise."

We all roared with laughter, for it was obviously so.

Hermann laid a vast forefinger against his nose, and smiled with cunning delight.

"*Ach, so!* That is where you are not such clever little *dummkopfs* as you think. That is where the trick comes in. That is the so-simple but so-clever whole point of the invention. . . . Look. . . . You tie a bow in the string, my funny ones. The rat seizes the cheese and pulls the string, the bow comes untied and the front door falls behind him!"

Again we roared with laughter.

In solemn earnestness, his inventor's pride elevating his spirit far above hurt from our ribald foolishness and mockery, Hermann tied his bow, set his trap—and caught a rat.

We had not been in bed five minutes before that amazing front door fell with a sharp tap!

A rat, ingenious even beyond the cunning of his brethren, had caught himself; had seen the eligibility of the Home, gone inside, untied the bow, and taken possession.

With one howl of glee, the Section, headed by Hermann, bounded from its beds, rushed to the trap and laughed itself silly.

Helplessly we rolled, laughing, at Hermann, the rat-trap—and the rat.

The trap had worked once, if it never worked again.

"Good old Hermann!" cried Terence Hogan, slapping him on the back. "Chuck the beggar out, and catch another."

"He must be put to death," said Hermann.

Loud cheers.

"You wouldn't hang him without fair trial, would you?" expostulated Digger.

"Rats are vermin, and must be exterminated,"

stated Hermann, solemn, didactic and Teutonic. "Nor shall I hang it."

"What shall you do?" asked Abraham, "this *poste* not having no electric chair. . . . Shoot it?"

The suggestion was acclaimed.

"Get Hermann's rifle," called somebody.

"Don't be foolish," expostulated Hermann. "I shall . . . I shall . . ."

"Make faces at it," suggested Terence Hogan.

"I shall . . . I shall . . . I must get it out first," Hermann decided.

"And then?" we asked.

Hermann pondered a while. The rat explored the Home.

"I shall kill it quickly and mercifully . . . with my bayonet," he said.

"Bayonet it! At the charge!"

"Not on the carpet of the Home, surely?"

"No, on the door-step."

With a whoop of joy, Gustavus brought Hermann's bayonet.

Hermann opened the door of the Home, and the rat ran away.

Marvellous Hermann.

*   *   *   *   *

Hermann told me his story to-day. I like Hermann. He is one of the very large number of men for whom the Foreign Legion is about the last place they should have come to.

Very big and very strong, and as mild and gentle as a child, like so many giants are.

He reminds me of the popular conception of the typical German before the hate-campaign was worked up against England. Musical, thoughtful, kind, law-abiding and sentimental. Conscientious too, for he "felt he could not honestly and truly be my friend," until he had told me something—made a confession.

We were squatting side by side, after midday *soupe*, in the shadow of the wood-stack we were building.

"What does it matter to me what you've done?" I said, trying to choke him off, for I hate confessions and sob-stuff.

"I *must* tell you about it," he said simply. "I have your friendship under false pretences.

"I'm a murderer. I committed a deliberate murder. I killed a sleeping man. I'm a deserter too, though I don't think I am a coward. . . . War's all wrong, you know. Any war. War made me a murderer and a deserter."

"You'd fight to defend your own country, I suppose!" I said.

"Oh, well, yes. That isn't war. That's—defending your country."

"Well, why did you join the Legion then, if you don't like war?" I asked.

"I'll tell you.

"I'm a Thuringian. I was born in the Forest. How happily I could have lived all my life, and died an old man in that Forest, happy and with a clear conscience. I was never meant to be a soldier. I've got an absolute hatred of blood. As a boy; in fact, always; I could stand pain as well as anybody, and I was quite good at difficult and dangerous mountaineering and rock-climbing. But I simply could not shoot a bird or a hare.

"Not so much out of tender-heartedness you know, but fear and hatred of seeing its blood, and getting it on my hands.

"I was very strong and fond of all forms of athletics. They wanted me to box because I was so very big and strong, and a good athlete. But I could never have done that. I should have been sick if I had made a man's nose bleed, or he mine.

"When Russia and France threatened Germany; and England and Italy, joining them, made a wall of steel about us, I was only fifteen, and did not dream that the War could possibly affect me personally. I was sure that justice and right would quickly triumph, and Germany would repel her foes who had attacked her."

"Especially the Belgians, I should think!" I remarked.

"They had but to realize that we were fighting for our lives, and let us pass, and not a hair of one of their heads need have been injured."

"That's all," I said . . . I, who had served in Belgium and seen something of that passing!

"Do you imagine . . . Can't you understand that . . ." I began, and then stopped. What was the good?

"I was wrong, of course," continued Hermann, "and on my seventeenth birthday I had to go. I cannot tell you what I suffered. I love my Country. I would die for my Country. If my life would have been of the slightest use to the Fatherland, I would have given it as willingly as I would have given a *pfennig*. But the thoughts of wounds and blood I could not bear; and I knew that I should desert. How I prayed that the War might end before I got to the Front, or that I might do all my service in some safe place. Not because I was a coward, you understand. . . .

"And where do you think I was sent?

"To Verdun.

"Verdun.

"Was my faith in the efficacy of prayer shaken, do you think? Yes . . . but not for long.

"Do you know, the very first night, I was sent out with a Sergeant and three other men, and we were surprised by a French patrol! The others were killed or wounded, and I was stunned with a rifle-butt or club, and was taken prisoner.

"It may be that we had run into a raiding-party, out to get a live German, as well as identification of opposing troops in their sector.

"Anyhow, I was kept alive and sent down the line to be questioned by the French Intelligence people. They were very clever, and I was very stupid. If they got anything out of me, it was indirectly and without my intending it.

"Much as I loathe soldiering and warfare and bloodshed, I love my Country and I would have told nothing under torture. Had they but known it though and brought in a bucket of blood . . ."

"Oh, shut up! . . ." I said.

"Well, I wasn't treated too badly, and they didn't keep me long in France. I was sent first to Marseilles and then, with hundreds of other prisoners, to Algeria. I shan't forget that journey from Verdun to Ain-el-Hadja. Perhaps you think you had an uncomfortable journey as a *légionnaire*. We travelled exactly like cattle in open trucks, exposed to pouring rain, sleet and snow, and then, like beasts penned in a cattle-ship. All of us sea-sick."

"Anyhow, you weren't torpedoed like English hospital ships were—full of wounded men, nurses and doctors," I interrupted. A girl acquaintance of mine, a V.A.D., had been thus murdered by some U-boat commander.

"*And* ammunition," said Hermann.

"Don't be such a fool," I growled. "Why should hospital ships carry ammunition to England *from* France, or from Egypt, or anywhere else?"

"That is what we were told," said Hermann.

I snorted.

"Well, we disembarked at Oran and marched to

Ain-el-Hadja, a small village of Spaniards and Arabs, with a military prison. They've turned it into a barracks now. It was really a barracks then, for a Company of the Legion occupied it. Mostly Germans who had been in the Legion when war broke out, and whom the French did not wish to send to fight against their own people.

"We prisoners-of-war were kept there for two years, road-building. It was a hard life, about as hard as life can be; but I was thankful to be there, for there was no bloodshed. No chain-gang of convicts ever worked harder than we did, or under much worse conditions. We knew what the Christian captives of the old corsairs went through, building roads and fortifications for them. . . ."

"I never heard that prisoners in Germany were exactly pampered," I observed. I knew of one boy who was lame for life for want of proper attention to a knee wound; one who died of pneumonia through semi-starvation and being housed worse than a pig; and of one, a splendid young public-school specimen, who became permanently insane.

"Did you ever hear of the fate of the prisoners of Kut?" I added.

"But they were taken by the Turks," said Hermann.

"Yes, by the Turks, your Allies," I pointed out. "Do you suppose that if the Turks had been *our* Allies, we should have allowed them to herd and drive and flog starving wounded and diseased German soldiers across a thousand miles of desert? After a fortune-of-war surrender and a promise that they should be treated as *'honoured guests'* . . . ? But get on with it." What was the good of wrangling.

"Well, war is war. . . . And everything you say supports my contention—that it is wholly indefensible and unutterably vile and wrong. Anyhow, we prisoners suffered terribly. That road from Ain-el-Hadja to Saïda—we German prisoners built every yard of it. . . . Yes, it was watered with our sweat and tears."

"Nasty," I said. "Pathetic. Didn't the guard weep, too?"

"And then the Armistice came at last; but they didn't set us free. Not when peace was signed. Instead of being liberated at once, we were invited to join the Legion! Many did; for a glass of wine; a chance to lay down pick and shovel; a change, any change, from the dreadful monotony of the last two years of hard labour; for freedom. The freedom of the Legion!

"Many Germans, many Austrians, some Bulgarians, Arabs and Turks accepted the invitation.

"I, and many others, refused. Mad as I was to escape from that serfdom, I could not bear the thought of going back to what to me was worse— military service, and service for the enemies of my Fatherland at that.

"What a simple *dummkopf* I was! Fancy thinking that the French would give fair play to Germans who were in their power. You know they hate us. They positively hate us. Why should they?"

"Conceivably something to do with 1870," I suggested.

"Why bear malice after a war? We bore none after 1870. . . . Anyhow, we who would not join the Legion were set free, free to go by train to Oran —and nowhere else. Well, at Oran we were turned loose and left to shift for ourselves.

"I at once set about finding a ship that was leaving Africa for anywhere in Europe. Once in Europe I could tramp to my home. . . . I might even find a ship that was going to Hamburg, or some other German port. Of course, I could not pay for a passage, but although I knew nothing of the sea, I was as strong as a horse, and would surely be worth my food on a tramp steamer, if only as a fireman.

"And what do you think happened?

"I was promptly arrested as a German spy, and put in prison without any sort of trial. That civil prison is an old fort, and contains some unbelievably horrible cells, filthy, damp and dark. Real dungeons. Will you believe me when I tell you that I was shut up in one of those cells for two days, without food or water."

"I will," I said. "But I also believe tales of much worse things that happened to innocent and harmless Belgian and French people, in the occupied area of Belgium and France during the War."

"Well, on the third day, the *sous-officier* came to my cell and told me that, black as the case was against me, I had a chance; for if I liked to sign on for the usual five years in the Legion, I should be released at once, given a good meal and sent to Sidi-bel-Abbès.

"Of course I refused, weak and starving though I was.

"I am not very good at saying what I think, but I believe I said it then. I was a prisoner-of-war. For two years I had had to work like a galley-slave and to carry stones like a beast of burden. The War was over, what right had the authorities to keep me as a prisoner now? Surely it would be easy enough to prove that my story was true, and to verify my statement that I'd been for two years at Ain-el-Hadja—that I'd been captured before Verdun.

"How then could I be a spy?

"The fellow smiled and made some remark to

the effect that some Germans, at any rate, might find that it had been easier to get into France than to get out again.

"I asked them if war was not war; and were not soldiers merely the machinery set in motion by Kaisers and Kings and Presidents. If he were run over by a wagon, would he blame a spoke of one of the wheels?

"It was all in vain, of course.

"I was merely wasting my breath.

"When he came again the next day, I was so hungry and so terribly thirsty that I think I would have signed my own death-sentence for a drink of water. For that, and a meal; and to escape from their dreadful dungeon, I gave in; signed the enlistment-form that he brought; and joined the Foreign Legion.

"Compared with my lot of the last two years, life at first seemed good, for my Company was almost entirely composed of Germans. But I am sorry to say—ashamed to say—that this did not turn out to be really a matter for self-congratulation. For the N.C.O.'s of that Company, although Germans to a man, were the most ruffianly bullies and brutes imaginable.

"The German N.C.O. is not exactly a gentle shepherd at home; and these Prussian pigs were ten times worse than the worst I ever came across in the German Army. They had far more power, of course, in the Legion, and they used it to the full; and without any check whatsoever from the French officers. It's a rotten system, this Legion one of giving N.C.O.'s the power to punish, especially when you put that power in the hands of a Prussian.

"You'd have thought German N.C.O.'s would have been reasonably decent to fellow-country-men, wouldn't you?"

"No," I replied.

"Well, you're right. They couldn't have treated any Belgian, Frenchman, or Russian, worse than they treated me. I don't know why, but they had a down on me, from the very first. *Schadenfreude.* I admit that I am naturally unsoldierly, and hate soldiering from the bottom of my heart. I'd sooner follow any other trade there is.

"I could do nothing right, and was bullied and hazed nearly to death.

"Then I made the mistake of appealing to my Officer, and discovered that I'd done about the worst thing I could do; for he showed his sense of discipline, if not of justice, by doubling every punishment that he found against my name in the *livre de punitions.*

"After that I was so continually being run in for every sort and kind of petty breach of discipline—for I never really did anything that I knew to be wrong—that it was not long before my name came so frequently beneath the Captain's eye that he remembered it. Nor was it long before they got tired of putting me in the *salle de police,* and giving me the maximum sentence short of prison.

"I was told that the next time I was punished, I should get a prison sentence.

"Naturally it was up to my chief enemy, Sergeant Potzner, to see that I got it.

"I was had up for being late on pass, dirty, drunk and resisting the guard.

"As you know, I am practically a teetotaller—but a Sergeant has only got to knock a man down and have him thrown in the cells and he's got him *and* witnesses to the assault—of the soldier upon the Sergeant.

"I got my sentence all right, and was transferred to the military prison. I don't know whether you know the military prison at Sidi-bel-Abbès?"

"Not yet," I said.

"Well, it's reckoned the show prison of the Legion, and to visitors it must seem quite a model House of Correction and place of detention. It's always beautifully clean, but believe me, it's a real whited sepulchre."

"All prisons are," said I, "only some are whiter than others."

"Well, this one's white enough. But some black deeds are done inside it. I was really shocked at what I saw. The place was constantly being inspected by the Authorities and other visitors; for no doubt some of the inspecting officers were genuinely anxious to satisfy themselves that all was as it should be.

"So it was, while they were there. They always found us sitting quietly in our cells, or engaged in such useful occupations as cutting and sawing wood. I only wish that an inspecting officer could have gone into each cell, and had a perfectly private talk with each prisoner."

"Or better still," I suggested, "had been man enough to get himself run in there, unknown to the prison Authorities, as an ordinary, genuine, military convict."

Hermann roared with laughter.

So his talk had done him that much good, at any rate. It was the first time I had heard him laugh. One does not hear a great deal of laughter in the Legion.

"Oh, that's a good one," he chuckled. "Oh, that's a fine idea, that is. Fancy old Colonel C—— finding himself chained up to a wall with his hands above his head; or pummelled almost to death in his cell by four warders at once! Fancy him calling out, 'Stop it! I'm Colonel C——' and them pummelling him all the harder!"

Hermann fell silent, visualizing the scene with

a beatific smile upon his foolish face.

"Well, personally," he went on, "I was so meek and quiet and well-behaved that I didn't have nearly as bad a time as some.

"I tell you, some of those convicts were regular devils, and one couldn't help admiring their awful courage; their unbreakable spirit.

"But what fools! As well might a naked man attack ten hungry lions.

"What could rebellion do, but increase their sufferings and end in the 'dry guillotine.'

"One's heart bled for them, although one could not but feel that they were fools . . . fools who asked for even more than they were getting.

"As I say, I was as meek as a mouse and as good as gold, and crept about attracting as little notice as I could, but my heart became hard, and daily I grew more and more embittered. Of one thing I was certain. On one point my mind was made up, if I died for it.

"I would not serve these French for a day longer than I could help. When I had served my three months' sentence, I would desert at the first opportunity.

"The very first week after I was released from prison, I did so. It is easy enough to get away.

"The difficulty is to stop away.

"Three nights of marching, and hiding by day, brought me safely to Oran; and on that same third night I watched my chance and crept on board a ship that was tied up to the quay, and lay down in one of its boats.

"How my heart jumped at every sound, and how my hopes rose when, in the course of the next morning, the ship put to sea. It was not until we were a good seven hours out of Oran that I was discovered, and brought before the Captain.

"He was, or pretended to be, a very violent man

in a very violent rage. I can see him now; with his red hair, clean-shaven red face, and great powerful hands and wrists.

"I found I was on an English tramp steamer, and that neither the Captain nor I could understand a word that the other said. It was quite evident to me, however, that he had the greatest objection to stowaways; they seemed to be his *bêtes noires*.

"After I had made my excuses and my appeal, in German and in French, and he had roared loudly at me in English and shaken his fist under my nose, he signed to the mate and boatswain and seaman who had found me in the boat, to throw me overboard!

"I was almost too amazed to struggle when these three burly Englishmen flung themselves upon me and rushed me to the side of the ship.

"Again the Captain roared and burst into laughter, and I was released while the sailor was sent below to fetch something or somebody. I wondered whether it were hand-cuffs or some instrument of torture."

"Rack, and thumbscrews, or gibbet complete with rope, I expect," I yawned, as poor Hermann fixed me with his earnest mild blue gaze.

"He returned in a minute or two with a small man in a filthy singlet and dungaree trousers, who spoke a certain amount of a kind of dock-side French.

"I told this cook's mate or engine-greaser, or whatever he was, that I was a German prisoner-of-war who had been wrongfully detained by the French, and was trying to make my way home; and that I threw myself on the mercy of the Captain, appealing to the famous sense of fair-play and sporting qualities of the English."

"Didn't you say you'd played for Germany?" I

asked.

"Played what?" inquired Hermann.

"Oh, cricket," I suggested.

"No. I have never played at cricket," was the solemn answer.

"What this man told the English Captain, I do not know; but the Captain bade him tell me that stowaways ought to be thrown overboard, and if we had not been so far out, he'd have put back and made me swim for it. As it was, I should have to leave the ship at the first port of call, and meanwhile work hard for any food I got.

"I was delighted. I could have embraced that rude and red-faced man.

"They treated me quite kindly in the fo'c's'le, called me 'Jerry' and 'Fritzie,' and I shared their tobacco, food, and clothes as though I'd been a brother Englishman."

"Yes," I said. "Without inquiring as to whether you'd served on a U-boat, and sunk such ships as theirs, and passenger-liners with women and children. . . . '*Spurlos versenken.*' "

"Well, didn't English submarines keep the blockade that starved our German women and children?" asked Hermann.

"You should have thought of that before you declared war," I replied. "Did you expect us to send food and raw materials and munitions into Germany? Or to stand by while so-called neutrals did it? . . . However, get on with the story."

"Well, they did put me ashore at the first port of call.

"And where d'you think that was?

"*Marseilles.*"

"Yes. Marseilles.

"I had stowed away at Oran, the rat-trap, so to speak, to be taken to Marseilles, the lion's den; where as you know, there actually is a *depôt* of the

Legion. When I saw that great *Chateau d'If* light-house, a cold fear seized me, and when, a little later, as I squatted upon the fo'c's'le, chipping rust, I saw the unmistakable harbour with the great Church of Notre Dame up above it, I could have wept."

"I expect you did, Hermann," I said, steeling my heart against pity. I will not be sloppy and sentimental.

"I tried to persuade myself that it might be some other place, until I saw that the huge advertisements were in French, and one of the crew, grinning at the splendid joke said:

" 'Marseilles . . . Frenchies . . . No *bon* for Jerry . . . Fritzie napoo, toot-de-sweet . . .' and similar barbarous gibberish.

"As soon as the ship was tied up, the Captain sent for me and the alleged interpreter, and told me he was going to hand me over to the police.

"I pleaded with him. I prayed to him with tears in my eyes that he would have mercy on me. I appealed again to his British sense of justice and fair-play. I took my solemn oath again to him, that I was an unfortunate prisoner-of-war, captured fighting for his country, and only trying to get back to it. And begged him to land me on any soil but that of France. I offered to work for him for a year, if he liked, without a *pfennig* of pay, if he would only land me in England or any other part of Europe that was not France, at the end of that time. I don't know how far the interpreter trans-lated my words correctly, but the Captain must have understood my beseeching signs, my extend-ed hands, my tears, my shrinking terror as the officer seized my arm to drag me away.

" 'No,' said the Captain, shaking his red head,

" 'Police . . . gaol . . . *Bang-bang* . . .' and then he made a quick motion with his hand around his neck, closed his eyes, put his head on one side, protruded his tongue, and made a hideous sound as though choking.

"I needed no interpreter to understand that I was to be gaoled and then probably either shot or hanged. Having finished his pantomime, this rough and red-faced Englishman picked up a bundle that lay beside the chair on which he was sitting, and threw it at me. It was an old blue suit, a cap, a shirt, collar and tie, socks and a pair of boots. He then gave me fifty francs from his own pocket and wished me good luck."

"What did he say?" I asked in some anxiety.

" 'Bong chance, Jerry!' he said. 'Ally-vous on and ally-vous off,' and then some more in English that I didn't understand."

"I wouldn't mind betting that what he said was, 'Now, hop it, Fritzie. Bung off. And good luck to you, old son,' " I hazarded in English.

"Yes, it sounded something like that," agreed Hermann, "but there was also the English soldier-word in it."

"Quite probably," I agreed, "for it is not unknown as a sailor-word."

"Well, I went back to the fo'c's'le and put on the clothes. I left the ship with some sailors and other hands, who had got shore leave. We went to a music-hall and then to a dance-hall; and, after that, from wine-shop to wine-shop, and café to café. While I was with these men, all obviously foreign seamen, I felt pretty safe. But after they had said 'Good-bye' to me, and gone back to the ship, I felt terribly lonely, anxious and nervous.

"You see, what troubled me even more than the German accent of my French, was my cropped hair. I had only been out of prison a little over a week, and a cropped head means something in France. However, I kept my cap pulled down as far over my head as possible.

"I crossed the road every time I saw a *gendarme*, and never did I see one approaching me without thinking that I was going to be arrested. It was a dreadful time. My fifty francs were dwindling fast and my clothes getting more and more dirty and dilapidated, as I never had a chance to take them off. Luckily the weather was warm and fine, and sleeping out was no hardship.

"One day, I got such an awful fright, as I turned a corner and almost ran into a Sergeant of the Legion, who seemed to eye me suspiciously, that I made up my mind, then and there, that I would leave Marseilles somehow, that very night.

"I decided that the most dangerous thing I could do would be to attempt to get away by train.

"The next most dangerous thing would be to attempt to tramp across France to Germany, or along the Corniche Road and try to get over the frontier into Italy.

"I had no papers of any sort, of course, not even forged ones. I had only a few francs, a cropped head and a German accent. And moreover, by now, my description was doubtless in the hands of the military authorities and of the police, as a deserter from the Legion.

"Nowhere, except in Marseilles itself, would a sharper look-out be kept than at railway-stations and frontier posts. The only way that remained, and the safest way, was to try my luck again by sea, and stow away on another ship.

"I hung about the docks, and a proper down-at-heel dock-loafer I must have looked too, until I saw a ship flying the blue-and-white flag that shows it is about to sail."

"The Blue Peter, I believe," I murmured.

"I watched her till night fell, and marched boldly on board, behind a small crowd of men, whether sailors or dock-labourers I did not know. I repeated my former tactics. It was not until, with a beating heart, I found myself crouching in perfect darkness in a boat that was slung out-board, that I realized that, while looking for the departure flag, I had not noticed the ship's own flag. I had a vague idea of seeing the French tricolour, but then every ship in the whole of Marseilles harbour was flying the French flag, of course, as usual, in compliment to the country.

"Anyhow, even suppose I were on a French ship, it was leaving Marseilles, and France; and Fate could hardly be feeling sufficiently merry as to have led me to a ship that was going back to Oran."

I yawned.

"You thrill me to the toes, Hermann," I said. "But I thought this was supposed to be a murder story."

"*Ja, ja*, it is. Do not be impatient. I am coming to it. Let me tell my story to you who understand."

"Story! It's a book already. Push along, Hans Andersen."

"Yes. I will be short. Where do you think that ship did go?"

"Don't say back to Oran, after all," I begged.

"No, my friend. Not Oran. *Algiers!* Poor silly fool that I was. I had walked straight on board a French tramp, that spent its miserable life plying between Marseilles and Algiers, as many do. I had done that."

"You would, Baron," I said.

"Baron?" he queried.

"Munchausen," I murmured.

"I swear to God I am telling you the absolute truth," he protested, "the whole truth, and nothing but the truth."

"The whole truth anyhow, Fritzie. Get on with

it."

"And there I was. On a French ship; in Algiers; where, as you know, there is a Company of the Legion. One piece of luck I had had. I had not been discovered under the tarpaulin or sail that lay across the thwarts of my boat, although, desperate with cramp, soreness and misery, I had been driven to sit up and stretch my limbs at night. Also I contrived to leave the ship at about four o'clock in the morning and get ashore unseen.

"You can imagine what I felt like, and how hungry and thirsty I was, having had nothing for three days but a piece of bread, three bananas, a franc's worth of chocolate and a bottle of water, which I had brought on board in my pockets.

"Well, I made my way as quickly as I could to the lowest part of the town, and slouched about until driven by hunger and the smell of coffee into a café. I have often wondered where I should be now if I had not at that moment been assailed by that glorious marvellous whiff of coffee-smell, from a side window of this café. It was irresistible and fatal. Like the song of the Sirens that led sailors to their doom."

"Lorelei in a coffee-pot!" I murmured, moved by Hermann's poetic fancy.

"*Ja*," he agreed, "exactly. It drew me in. I sat down and ordered all the things that I liked best, caring nothing if I spent my last franc on this beautiful meal.

"After I had ordered some lovely things that this sawdust-floored *casse-croûte* had apparently never heard of, I noticed that the waiter, a dirty squint-eyed non-descript dog, probably of about ten nationalities including town-Arab, went and drew the attention of the *patron* to me.

"They stood watching me, and talking, while I

ate; and then a gross ruffian, in a green baize apron, went and stood in the door-way while the *patron* came and, with much false politeness and many apologies, asked to see my money; and then tried to hold me in conversation.

"I said as little as possible, showed the man a twenty-franc note, and ate as much as I could; then asked for my bill, and got up to go. He took a long time to make out the bill. A suspiciously long time, and, getting more and more nervous, I went over to the hutch where the *patron* pretended to be busying himself.

"I did not wish to appear to be anxious to get away, and to look as though I was literally trying to escape.

" 'Never mind about the bill,' I said. 'I don't want to stop here all day. How much is it?'

" 'One moment, M'sieu. *One* moment,' said the man, with mocking politeness. 'No hurry. Let's see. You had?' and he slowly enumerated my rolls, coffee, slices of sausage and so on; and proceeded to ask whether I had had a number of things which he knew perfectly well I had not.

" 'Look here,' said I. 'What's the game? Tell me what I owe you, for I am going about my business.' "

" 'Oh, you'd try to run off without paying, would you?' he asked.

" 'Certainly not,' I replied. 'I, at any rate, am an honest man,' and I put my twenty-franc note down upon the desk in front of him.

" 'Ah, that's better,' said the rascal. 'Hello! What's this?' and looked across my shoulder toward the door.

"The waiter, the aproned door-keeper, and a couple of *gendarmes* were bearing down upon me. The scoundrel had sent out for the police to come and arrest an obvious German deserter from the

Legion—for the sake of the miserable reward he would get for denouncing me.

"And arrested I was. Taken to prison, handed over to the military authorities, and identified immediately, from the full description of my facial and physical appearance with which they had been furnished immediately after my flight.

"That very same night I left, under escort, by train—for Bel-Abbès and the very prison in which I had just served my three months' sentence.

"At Bel-Abbès I was tried by court-martial for desertion and loss of kit. My previous bad record of crime (alleged dirty buttons, slovenliness, insubordinate looks, and lateness for parade) was brought up against me, and the fact that I had already done a three-months' prison sentence.

"Obviously I was a hard case. A *mauvais sujet* and one of whom an example must be made. I was sentenced to six months' *travaux forcées*.

"At the end of that sentence, I was to return to the Legion to complete my five years of service, of which only the first three months before I went to the Sidi-bel-Abbès prison counted.

"Life in the model prison at Sidi-bel-Abbès had not been a bed of roses, but it was just about that compared with life as a convict at Tourit, where I was sent for my term of penal servitude. They call it *travaux forcées*, forced labour, and forced labour it was, and terribly hard labour.

"From sunrise to sunset we worked like slaves; and from sunset to sunrise we were herded together, several in one cell. Believe me, the bestial horrors of the night made me long for the incessant hard labour of the day, however terrible the heat, the thirst and the weariness.

"You see, I was still only a youth. I was decent-minded, and no more a criminal than the Pope of Rome; and these men with whom I had to live and work and eat and sleep, were criminals—genuine foul criminals of the worst sort; degraded human brutes, far lower in mentality and habits and utter beastliness than any beast that ever walked on four legs. I would a thousand times rather have spent the night locked in a cell with apes, or with any other animals, than with these human beings. We talk about the 'lower' animals! These creatures were lower than the lowest; and I had to live in the closest intimacy with them, hearing every word they said, and seeing every deed they did.

"And it was my fate to be in a room that was dominated and tyrannized by a very terrible monster, half-madman and half-fiend, known as The Fang.

"He was an apache and if ever a person was Voltaire's 'half-ape-and-half-tiger,' it was this Fang of the Devil.

"No tiger was ever more ferociously blood-thirsty; no ape ever more savagely mischievous and depraved. And, of course, he had his toadies, poor evil brutes who stood behind him that they might not find themselves in front of him—if you understand me.

"What a hell each of those 'rooms' was, when we were locked in for the night, and left to our own devices—be those what they might. And they ranged from enforced gambling and brutal horse-play to torture and murder. I wish every one of the smug citizens jointly responsible for the system could be made to spend just one night in that Inferno of stench, vice, villainy, cruelty, and every foulness of word and thought and deed.

"Frequently it was absolute Pandemonium—in fact, whenever The Fang thought fit to make it so.

"Everybody feared this savage, and all did their best to escape his notice, save the two or three who strove to win his favour by thinking of new

practical jokes, villainies, and robberies to per-
petrate upon the weakest, the new-comers, or
those sufficiently daring to be rebels.

"It was not long, of course, before I came
beneath his notice, and my offence apparently was
a look, the mere expression on my face—one of
utter incredulous disgust.

"It was about my third night in this terrible
place, just after I had flung myself down on my
plank bed to sleep, that pandemonium broke
loose. It could not be called a fight any more than
the attack of hounds upon a hare can be called a
fight. Apparently, The Fang and his gang were, for
some reason or no reason, killing a fellow-convict.
Perhaps he had something they wanted, or perhaps he had, during the day, done something to
which they took exception.

"Anyhow, after he had been repeatedly knocked
down and then kicked, to their hearts' content, by
The Fang and his swinish sycophants, he was
being held down by the scruff of his neck with his
face close to The Fang's filthy bare feet. Then with
a heavy blow or kick at each command, he was
ordered to lick them clean.

"He did it.

"And as I raised myself upon my elbow and
stared in amazed horror and disgust, The Fang, a
grin upon his evil face, looked up and caught my
eye, and noticed the expression of disgust and
indignation on my face. And then I was for it. The
Fang turned his gang's attention from their half-
demented and half-conscious victim to me.

"Here was fresh game. This might show good
sport and give them a fine run for their money.

"I resisted.

"I resisted with all the strength of mind and
body that was in me. . . . But they won. . . . I am
ashamed, to this day, to confess it. More ashamed

than I am of the murder—though that troubles me more, if you know what I mean. They triumphed, and before they had finished with me that night, I had done the same thing as the wretch whose actions had so disgusted me.

"And that was the beginning. Only the beginning. And things got progressively worse, for The Fang developed an apparently unquenchable personal hatred of me, as well as an insatiable lust for torturing me.

"I will tell you . . ."

Poor Hermann told me; but, on the whole, I do not think I will repeat it. Tough as one may wish to be, there are limits. A decent person must draw a line somewhere, and I draw it here.

"That was too much," he continued. "Something happened to my mind then; and my nature changed. I became a murderer that night; for murder is far more a matter of the intention and desire, than of an act. And to this day I do not know whether my motive was vengeance, despair, or self-protecting fear.

"Anyhow, I determined that I would kill The Fang—and I did it.

"One of the amazing things about this animal was the fact that he could, and did, procure wine or some other form of drink, in sufficient quantities for himself and his gang to have rousing midnight orgies, every now and then; and these were the times that the butts and victims of these brutes dreaded so much.

"If they were human hyenas when sober, imagine what they were when influenced by bad liquor. But there was one fact that I grasped, and that took on a mighty significance on the night when I became a murderer in intention.

"Their drunken orgies were followed by drunken sleep.

"Hitherto this had been my hour of respite and peace.

"The next one should be my hour of action. It came.

"When drunken row and violence was succeeded by drunken stupor, and obscene howlings gave way to the animal grunts and snores of heavy drunken sleep, I got up and, quietly, without haste or hurry, went to the partitioned corner of the room where were the iron buckets and our pile of tools.

"From these I carefully selected a pick, and silently removed it. It had a fine sharp point. It would do my business.

"Returning to my bed, I lit my candle. The dim light from the lamp that hung outside and sent its feeble rays through a hole, high up in the wall, was not sufficient for my purpose. I must not fail. . . . Not merely for fear of the terrible vengeance of The Fang and his band. . . . No. . . . No . . . I must not fail for fear that I should also fail in my task and mission—as the representative and avenger of outraged Man. . . .

"Mankind, Manhood, Man, had in me and these other victims, been degraded and debased.

"I must re-instate, re-habilitate, re-affirm. . . .

"Man must not lie beneath the Brute. I must not fail.

"Although I knew that more than one pair of eyes watched me, I walked with unhurried steps, my lighted candle in my left hand and my pick in my right, to where The Fang snored his last bestial sleep.

"Placing the candle where its light fell most usefully for my purpose, and ignoring the fact that two or three hitherto motionless forms stirred, heads were lifted, and men raised themselves on their elbows, I placed the point of the pick just at the spot where I intended that it should fall, swung it up—and struck with all my might—I, who had been using a pick for years, and who put the strength of despair and the weight of the sufferings of maltreated Mankind into the blow. . . .

"I then blew out my candle, quite methodically replaced the pick upon the pile of tools, returned to my bed, and, in a few moments, fell asleep—and slept better than I had done for years.

"Not a man in the room had moved from his bed or uttered a word.

"In the morning I awoke, feeling quite different, refreshed, satisfied, aware that a great cloud had lifted and dissipated. I had done a good deed. I was not a murderer. I was not a mere avenger. I was a saviour and a vindicator.

"In me, and through me, Man had triumphed over the Brute and if, in foolish misunderstanding of my righteous and necessary act, I were to be guillotined or shot, I did not care.

"The corpse of the Brute was discovered.

"An inquiry was held. It was cleverly decided that The Fang had met his death by being struck on the temple with a sharp instrument by some person or persons unknown. And the person remained unknown.

"Not a man in that room uttered a word; and though the room was collectively punished, I benefited by the one virtue those criminals possess. Nobody squealed. Not even the worst sycophant of The Fang's own gang.

"Also, to my amazement, I found that I had risen enormously in the estimation of my fellow-convicts—even of those who were almost as evil, brutal and aggressive as The Fang himself. No, it was not approval of a deed that rid them of a detestable foul tyrant. Not gratitude of any sort. It was merely that I was now a murderer and a member of the highest grade of their fraternity.

"Before, I was a worthless and unsullied wretch. Now I was a murderer—a valued and respected member of their society. Think of it. I, Carl Hermann, held, for the first time in his life, the respect, approbation and admiration of his fellows. . . . Because he had committed a murder. . . . Because he had murdered a sleeping man! And, as soon as I realized this, I changed again.

"I sank and sank in my own estimation. No longer was I the Vindicator, the just man armed with a mission and a noble cause.

"I was a murderer, a base murderer, who had slain a sleeping man. . . .

"Well. . . . Now I have told you. . . . Now you know what I am. . . . A murderer. . . . It is an ever-present load on my mind. . . . Do you think I am for ever damned?"

"No, Hermann. I prefer to believe in an Eternal Justice."

"I struck him while he slept . . ." muttered Hermann.

"That was a pity," I said.

"A *pity?*"

"Yes. He should have been wide awake, bound hand and foot—and made to watch you do it. . . ."

*　　*　　*　　*　　*

Matthieu le Maquereau deserted last night, while on sentry, taking his rifle and ammunition and a couple of bombs.

The general feeling is "good riddance to bad

rubbish" combined with great interest in the question as to whether he will get away, and what he will do.

CHAPTER VIII

"Water's a queer thing," mused Digger.

"Hark!" insisted Abraham the Sailor. "He's uttering wisdom and sounds."

"How does he know?" inquired Père Cocteau. "Has he ever tasted it?"

"Have you ever felt it?" countered Digger. "Except when we ford a stream. . . . It is a queer thing, though. We're giving our lives for it one day, and thanking God for a shelter from it the next."

"I'd sooner be short of food than short of water," observed Hermann. "Thirst's an awful thing."

"About the worst thing there is," I agreed, with painful reminiscence of some of our marches.

"Too right, chum," agreed Digger. "It is. . . . Not that you've ever been thirsty, though . . . nor anybody else here, either."

There was a laugh of derision, led by Père Cocteau, Thirsty-face, and Abraham the Sailor.

"Not one of you," re-affirmed Digger.

"Look," he continued. "Has any one of you fallen down dead of thirst? When I say dead, I mean so dead that a grave was dug for him. . . . I call a man thirsty when he goes mad; takes his clothes off; falls down and lies in the sun till he's one big blister; has his face so unrecognizable that his friends don't know him; and people who know the signs, say he's dead."

"Have you been as bad as that, Digger?" I asked.

"I have," he replied. "As bad as any human being could be, and recover. Real bad. . . .

"But the man with me was worse," he added,

and smiled grimly.

"Worse? He didn't recover then?"

"He did not."

"Tell us," I asked.

But Digger shook his head.

*   *   *   *   *

"I didn't want to tell that yarn in front of the crowd last night," said Digger, as he and I sat, side by side, in the moonlight, by the gate.

"No?" I said non-committally.

I'd never yet known Digger respond to a request for a story.

"No. . . .

"You got a wife, Jack?"

"Good Lord, no," I laughed.

"Got a girl at home p'raps?"

"No," I said, "and never likely to have."

"Ah . . . then I shan't give offence saying what I was going to. Some people that's got a good wife, or got a girl, won't hear a word against wives and sweethearts—and women. . . . Quite right too. . . . What's the sense? There are good women and middling women and bad women, same as there are good men, middling men, and bad men. . . . I got a bad one . . . that's all. . . .

"No call to pretend that all women are tarred with her brush.

"Still, there it is. . . . Real bad. . . . And you're apt to speak of them as you find them. . . .

"Then again, who made her bad? Any of us is liable to fall if we're tempted enough, aren't we? That's all it is—question of the size of the temptation. . . . And yet you wouldn't have thought Flash Hardmann was so much of a temptation . . . to a woman married to a decent chap. . . ."

I looked at the decent chap and wondered.

As fine a specimen of a man as you'd meet; very handsome, and to my knowledge and experience a proper white man; one of "Nature's gentlemen."

". . . Anyhow, he was temptation enough, and she went off with him, taking all I'd got . . ." continued Digger. "Not that that was much, but it was a few years' pretty hard going—after gold. . . .

"I suppose I was away a bit long that time, but I'd had to go four hundred miles on foot, and what with getting lost and one thing and another, I'd walked over a thousand miles before I got back to the town where I could get a lift to the sea and a boat home. . . .

"The place I went to didn't pan out so well, although it had caused a rush . . . and all the best claims had been pegged out before I got there. However, being there, I scratched around, gully and flat, shovelling gravel, or digging and sieving, and got a few nuggets. None as big as my head, but one or two as big as pigeons' eggs. . . . Sounds good p'raps, but have you any idea of the cost of living where water alone is from eighteenpence to half a crown a gallon?

"By and bye, I wasn't doing much more than making it. . . . Making a living for myself there, I mean, and I reckoned the best thing I could do was to cut my losses and go back—loss of time and trouble, I mean, and cruel hard labour. But that's all in the day's work, gold-chasing.

"Same time, nobody but the man who's done it knows how hard it is to go away while there's a chance—and there always is a chance. . . .

"Why on that very gold-field—and while I was there too—an old sun-downer who'd got nothing in the world but a pick an' a shovel an' a tin dish,

and hadn't earned enough tucker to keep him
healthy, for months past, picked up a nugget of
gold as big as his fist, and a good-sized fist too.
. . . Simply picked it up, lying around in the
gravelly dust where he was raking about. Place
called Dirty Flat. . . .

"Yes, it's hard to go; and before I cleared out, I
went on a wild-goose chase, through hearing some
men talk in Simpson's Hotel. . . . Hotel chiefly
canvas, boards and barrels. . . . Wonderful how
those Bush Hotels follow the diggers. They don't
p'raps make big fortunes like a gold-seeker here
and there does; but neither do they lie down and
die under a bush, of hunger and thirst . . . alone.
. . . No, they do pretty well.

"When I say I overheard men talking in Simpson's Bar, I mean just that . . . I heard them and
couldn't help it. It wasn't like cutting a slit in the
canvas and putting your ear to it to get information you can sell, like the damned touts, thieves,
sharks and pick-pockets that hang round gold-
camps. They were simply talking loud, as well as
talking big—and if anyone is distributing, free of
charge, something I particularly want, I accept it.

"Apparently they'd got wind of gold in a place
further out in the desert—whether from rapping
stone out that way or trying the gullies and flats
for alluvial themselves, I don't know, but they'd
got a specimen there that seemed to please them. I
heard one of them say:

" 'Why, the lump's only held together with gold.
. . . God-lumme, it almost *is* gold. . . .'

" 'Damn sight more gold than stone, anyway,'
said another.

"And I heard the words:

" 'Four saddle-bags and a camel-load anyhow.'
. . .

"Well, all this don't interest you . . . I'm

wanderin' on," Digger interrupted himself. "I was tellin' you about my wife and Flash Hardmann, wasn't I?"

"Something of the sort," I replied, yawning, knowing from experience that the slightest show of interest would, for some reason, make Digger shut up at once. A curious trait; but then Digger is a reticent and silent man, though why a show of interest should increase this, puzzles me.

Perhaps a life-long habit of guarding gold-seeker's secrets—and gold—has given him the habit of suspicion of anybody apparently interested in him and his doings.

"Still, this has a bearing on it . . ." he continued. "Anyhow, when I got back, my wife was gone, and all I could find out was that she'd been running round a bit with a man known as Flash Hardmann, who'd come just after I'd left. . . .

"Flash Hardmann . . . Flash Hardmann . . ." mused Digger.

"Millie. . . . Did I say she was a real lovely girl? You got to make allowances for that. . . . I always allow life's harder, more dangerous like, for a girl that's absolutely lovely. . . . Sort of girl people turn round in the street and stare after. . . . Lovely. . . .

"I struck a bad patch there, what with coming back empty-handed and finding Millie gone—and my savings too. . . . Not that that mattered much. . . . Still a man wants food and a roof, doesn't he?

"Nothing. . . . Cleaned out. . . . Broke. . . . Back at the beginning. . . ."

Digger fell silent, and I held my peace, almost held my breath.

". . . And I seemed to have lost even more than Millie and my hard-won gold. . . . I'd lost something more, if you understand me, chum. I mean: what was the *good* of anything? Who could you trust?

694

"No . . . I won't say I felt real friendly towards Flash Hardmann just then. . . .

"Well . . . I learnt what I could about Mr. Flash Hardmann; found out where he'd come from; and started after him. There was a chance, a good chance, that he'd gone back with Millie to where he'd come from. . . .

"He hadn't. But he was well known there, and I learnt a lot more about him. Learnt enough to look for him in places where he might be. And at last I ran him to earth.

"My oath! He was a world-beater! . . .

"Mr. Flash Hardmann! . . . When I first set eyes on him, he was breasting the bar in the Savoy Hotel. . . . Not your Savoy, Johnny. . . . Another bush-hotel. . . . The man was a giant. Six foot six if he was a penny. . . . Broad as a door, and thick as a tree. . . . Yes, he was a man all-right. Good-looking, too. No pink Pommy with a waxed moustache and spats. And I got thoughtful. . . .

"It was just simply no good me going up to him, slamming him on the jaw and being the avenging hero. *He*'d have done the avenging. . . .

"I don't say I wouldn't have slammed him on the jaw if I hadn't been serious. I was serious. I was going to get Mr. Flash Hardmann for keeps.

"Of course you'll say:

" 'Why didn't you walk up to him and shoot him and ask "How's that, Umpire?" ' . . .

" 'Course, that would have been very pleasing and agreeable no doubt; but I wasn't going to swing for Mr. Flash Hardmann. I don't like being hanged, and I reckoned Flash Hardmann had done me harm enough. . . .

"There was another thing too. . . . You will think I'm a damned old fool. . . . So I am. . . . But did I mention that Millie wasn't with him any longer? It seemed he had got rid of Millie. She wasn't there; and nobody there'd heard of Flash Hardmann having a wife, and he'd been there a long time. . . . You'll think I'm a damned old fool. . . . So I am. . . . For I'd have taken her back. . . . And, anyway, I wanted to know what had become of her, and whether she was all-right.

"Yes—I'd have taken Millie back if she'd have come.

"Well. . . . She wasn't there, and Flash Hardmann was; and Flash Hardmann had got to tell me what had become of Millie. He'd got to tell me that . . . and then I'd teach him something.

"I reckoned Millie'd be the last girl he'd serve that way.

"Did I say that I'd found out that Mr. Flash Hardmann was a great one for the girls? Millie wasn't his first, by quite a several. . . . No. . . .

"Well, Kid, I hadn't liked myself much those days I got home and found Millie gone, but I hated myself now—while I was making up to Flash Hardmann. I was going to do this job properly, thoroughly, make a success of it—and it was a nasty dirty job.

"I'd thought of a scheme, and it looked a good one. A part of it was getting to know Flash Hardmann, and getting Flash Hardmann to know me. . . . You remember that wild-goose chase I went on, after I heard those men talking in Simpson's Bar? . . .

"A long slow business, but never mind. . . . There was always the satisfaction of knowing I'd got Flash Hardmann on my hook. . . . A big fish . . . on a light rod. . . .

"Well. . . . All this don't interest you, Johnny. I'm yarning on . . ."

I gave Digger a cigarette.

"Thanks. . . . Well. . . . What I was saying. . . . He fell into my trap all-right; and a damned good one it was. . . . 'Gold . . . I knew a place. . . . Had been keeping the secret until I could get an outfit. . . . Couldn't trust anybody. . . . But now I'd got to know my new chum so well, I'd trust him and take him to the place—provided he put up the outfit—and we'd want, at the very least, two camels and a couple of brumbies, as well as a kit of picks and shovels, water-bags, billy-cans, buckets, frying-pans, sieves, ropes, tinned grub and stuff, and a camel water-tank.'

"Did I tell you Flash Hardmann was no bush-man? He was green. . . . He had knocked about mining-camps a lot, and had all sorts of irons in the fire—but he wasn't any swag-humping bush-man. . . . Better at robbing, claim-jumping, gold-smuggling, and buying stolen gold I reckon. . . .

"And whenever he'd successfully swindled anybody, he'd grin and say:

" 'Well! Well! . . . Business is business. . . . *Let the best man win.*'

"He was very fond indeed of saying '*Let the best man win,*' because he generally reckoned to be the best man—and he generally was.

"Not in the bush, though, as I said. He didn't know enough to make a certain fire with the last match: nor to take a billy off the fire without burning his hands and spilling priceless tea: nor to make a wind-break for his fire, in a breeze: nor how to look after a camel or a brumby . . . nor anything at all.

"A real shark in a camp or a town, in the bush he was like a shark in . . . treacle.

"Well—I bested the shark in his own waters. Got him on a string, just as he had had so many others on a string and ruined them.

"He was such a clever swindler that I'd made

up my mind that he should serve me well—while I served him right.

"I was going to *get* Mr. Flash Hardmann—and he was going to get me some gold. While he paid for what he had done, he was going to return my gold—and a bit more.

"Anyhow. . . . I was telling you about that wild-goose chase of mine—that time I heard the men talking in Simpson's Bar. . . . It was a wild-goose chase for me—but I reckoned there was a golden goose not far off. . . . A goose that'd lay a lot of golden eggs. . . . But I'd had to get back quick, before I died of starvation and thirst myself. What a man wanted there, was an outfit; camels; a travelling water-supply going along with him—so he wouldn't die when he came to dried-up water-holes. That's what would have happened to me on my wild-goose chase, if I'd held on.

"Well now, I was going to have the travelling water-supply, and everything else I wanted, to go in search of the gold that I knew was just there, or thereabouts.

"And you should have seen Mr. Flash Hardmann getting down to it! Getting down to the swindling of one more poor simpleton.

"Did he intend me to have one solitary ounce of that gold I was going to lead him to? Not one speck. Once Flash Hardmann, for the first time in his life, had got his hands on a genuine claim where he could make his fortune ten times over, without any more risky I.G.B. and gold-financing —that's buying gold from the illicit gold-buyers themselves and the gold-smugglers. . . . Of course, all this was before the Gold Producers' Association spoilt the market for the I.G.B.'s and swine like Flash Hardmann. . . .

"Well . . . all that don't interest you, Sonny. . . . But what I was going to say was, I got this outfit together, and Flash Hardmann paid for it.

"Then off we went to the place I told you about, where I heard the men talking in Simpson's Bar. . . .

"And when we got there I breathed freer, if you know what I mean. I felt I'd got him at last. And in Simpson's Bar, I'd sit and look at him while he chucked his weight about, and told everybody what a fine man he was.

" 'Yes,' I'd say to myself, 'you're a fine man, Flash Hardmann, but *let the best man win.*'

"When I'd made a few inquiries about one or two things, especially water-holes, I told Flash Hardmann it was time we pushed off.

"And off we went into the blue, starting in the middle of the night, after giving out for some days that we were going to have a look at an abandoned played-out gold-field that lay in quite a different direction. . . .

"Green? You wouldn't believe how green that smart know-all was, once I'd got him fairly out in the bush.

"And the things I told him. . . . I'd almost laugh when I heard them myself; and every hour I spent with the man, I hated him more than I did the hour before. . . .

"Flash Hardmann didn't like the desert a little bit; and real desert it soon was. The stunted trees grew poorer, and the scrub thin and dead-looking; then great stretches of porcupine-grass. Thank God they haven't got it here in Morocco . . . hardly grass at all—just a bunch of dry hard spikes with very sharp points, like so much knitting-needles . . . Spinifex, they call it; that's it. . . . The black-fellows make a kind of damper by grinding the seeds for the flour.

"Then we'd cross a regular sea-bed, dried up. A sort of place where you strike a dry water-hole and die. . . . The black-fellows can only live in those parts through knowing the *gnamma* holes—and nobody else but the black-fellows does know them. They're a sort of permanent natural well in solid rock.

"However. . . . In a few days we came to the place I was heading for, a spot where a number of bush-tracks crossed and where there was about the loneliest bush-hotel shanty in all Australia, and that's saying something.

"And wasn't that shanty-keeper surprised and pleased to see us!

"I told Flash Hardmann we'd stop there for a day or two, to rest the camels and brumbies.

"We did.

"And I'd sit and look at him as he drank his whisky and water cooled in a canvas bag, and I'd say '*Let the best man win.*' . . . And just as often as I could bring it in, I said it to him too. He got a bit tired of it.

"I enjoyed that last day or two—in a way. I'd been fond of Millie. . . . Fonder than I've told you . . . fonder than I could tell you . . . and I'd heard some pretty tales of this fine fellow. . . .

"Fact is, Johnny . . . I don't get angry easily and quickly; and I'm not what you'd call a vengeful man; but when I do—well, I do. . . .

"Slow to wrath. . . .

"Well, what I was saying. . . .

" 'Now, Hardmann,' I told him, one day, when we'd rested a spell, 'drink all the water you can hold, this morning. We're going to walk—and then some.'

" 'Why not ride?' he asked. 'Is this damned place of yours much further?'

" 'Ride?' I said. 'Take two camels and two horses and make a trail a blind beggar could follow on a dark night? Talk sense. I've brought you a bit of a roundabout way, and I guess no one has followed us. . . . They couldn't, over the dry lake, without an outfit and water-tanks. . . . And no one was going to get an outfit together to chase us, on spec.

" 'No . . . and no one's going to follow us from here neither. . . . It's a walk now . . . just a pleasant stroll . . .'

" '*Must* we walk?' he asked again.

" 'Yes,' I said. 'We'll have a walking-match, Hardmann. Just you and I . . . and "*Let the best man win.*" '

" 'I'm not so fond of walking that you'd notice it,' he grumbled.

" 'No?' I said. 'But I give you my word it's the last time you'll have to walk.' . . ."

"We-ell . . . did I tell you my idea was to leave the camels and horses with the shanty-keeper? I couldn't stomach the thought of their being sacrificed to Flash Hardmann, or I'd have ridden him right away out where probably no white man had ever been before. . . .

"Anyhow, without a word to the shanty-keeper, off we tramped before sun-rise, marching light.

"Lord! that man was green. . . . 'Should we carry our Winchesters in case of black-fellows?'

" 'Not on your life. . . . Quite enough to carry ourselves,' I told him.

" 'Shouldn't we carry water?' . . .

" 'Marching straight to a *gnamma*-hole. Water'd be there waiting for us.'

" 'Mightn't the *gnamma*-hole be dry?'

" 'They're never dry. . . . Can't dry. . . . Perpetual springs.'

"I don't believe he'd ever heard of one. . . .

"At the end of about ten miles, Hardmann said:

" 'I wish we'd brought some water.'

" 'Nonsense,' said I. 'You don't drink when you're marching. . . . Not on foot.'

"At the end of about fifteen, he suddenly said:

" 'Christ! I'm thirsty . . . I wish I hadn't listened to you. . . . It doesn't strike me you know as much as you think you do. . . .'

" 'I know more than you, anyhow,' I answered. 'About some things. . . . *Where's Millie B——?*'

"He stopped dead in his tracks and turned on me.

" 'What the hell do *you* know about Millie B——?'

" 'More than you do about humping a swag, Flash Hardmann,' I said. . . . 'Or you wouldn't be here without so much as a mouthful of water . . . let alone a billy-can, a bit of a damper and meat, or a fistful of flour. . . .'

" 'I thought this water-hole of yours was just a walk, out and back,' he said.

" 'Well, it is,' I agreed.

" 'It's a walk *out*, anyway,' I added. And I don't think he liked the way I laughed.

" 'What d'you mean by that?' he asked.

" 'Oh, come on, Flash Hardmann,' I said. '*Let the best man win.* I've got no more water than you have.'

"This seemed to reassure him a bit, but he was still mighty puzzled.

"Well, on we went, for about another five miles, and Hardmann suddenly stopped.

" 'I can't go much further, chum,' he said. 'I'm about done.'

" 'Well, you've got to,' I told him. 'A man who knows as much as you do, doesn't have to be told that he must push on till he reaches water.'

" 'How much further?' he asked.

" 'I'll be quite honest with you, Hardmann, and

702

tell you the absolute truth,' I replied. 'I don't know.'

" '*What? . . .*' he said. '*What? . . .*'

" 'I couldn't say exactly how far it is,' I told him. '*Where's Millie B——?*'

" 'In Hell for all I know. What's she got to do with it? . . . Look here . . . I'm going back.'

" 'Over twenty miles? You couldn't make it, Hardmann. Not forty miles in a day, this weather. . . . And could you find your way in the dark? . . . You couldn't find it in the daylight. . . . No. . . . Better keep on, Hardmann. You've got as much water as I have, and surely you're the best man, aren't you? *Let the best man win*, you know. . . .'

" 'How much further d'you suppose it is?' he croaked.

" 'Oh . . . somewhere between five and . . . and . . .'

" 'Five and what?'

" 'Oh, somewhere between five and fifty.'

" 'Between five and *fifty?*' he gasped. 'Look here, you, what's the game?'

" 'Walking-match,' I grinned. '*Let the best man win.*'

"Flash Hardmann stared at me, the most puzzled man in Australia.

" 'I don't get the big idea,' he said. 'We're after this gold, aren't we? Together, aren't we? . . .

" 'By God!' he added suddenly. 'You've *used* me. You got us here with my outfit . . . And now . . .'

" 'And now—I'm up the same tree as yourself, aren't I? . . . Come on, Flash Hardmann, *Let the best man win*. . . . But, first of all, *Where's Millie B——?*'

" 'If I'd brought a gun along . . .' he croaked, trying to moisten his lips.

" 'Quite so,' I croaked back at him, and managed to laugh. 'That's why we travelled light,

Hardmann. . . . No guns; no water; no tucker . . . you poor ignorant silly mug . . .'

" 'I'm going back,' he muttered.

" 'Well, so long,' I replied, and getting up, pushed on, as though I could walk for ever.

"I knew he'd follow me and, of course, he did.

"He felt pretty sure I was going to the water-hole. . . . In fact, he must have known I was. . . .

"Well . . . I'm talking, ain't I? . . . Anyway, the second day was like the first—stumbling on and lying down—mostly lying down.

"I fell asleep and dreamt of water and of Millie. Then I woke and got up and pushed on. Hard-mann saw me go.

"After a while I looked back. . . . Yes, there he was. . . . He was following all-right. . . . I went on for a spell and then stood and waited for him.

" 'Water!' he gasped, as he staggered up. 'I'm dying.'

"So was I, for that matter. Quite as dying as Flash Hardmann, for I'd played strictly fair by him . . . a thing I reckon he'd never done by any man, or woman either, in his life.

" 'What, The Great Flash Hardmann?' said I. 'Come on, Flash. *Let the best man win,*' and on I went.

"He followed. . . . But I could see he wouldn't follow very far, and I kept looking back. . . .

"By and by, at about sunset, I looked again, and saw that he had fallen.

"I turned back. He pointed to his black lips.

" 'Water,' he croaked again.

" 'Why, come on, Hardmann,' I said. '*Let the best man win.*'

"He shook his head. He was beaten.

" '*Where's Millie B——?*' I said. 'You tell me that, and I'll tell you something about . . . water.'

"He tried to moisten his lips. He didn't even know enough to keep a pebble in his mouth.

" 'I left her in C——,' he whispered.

" 'Got tired of her, and chucked her out, I suppose,' I managed to say.

"He nodded his head. . . . Then . . . '*Water*' . . .

" 'So you left Millie B—— in C——, eh? . . . Well now . . . I'll tell you all about the water. . . . *There isn't any.*'

"He pulled himself together. . . . Tried to get up. . . . Clutched his throat and pointed on.

" '*Water!*' . . .

" 'I don't know of any water-hole,' I said.

"His head fell on his arms, and I could see his jaws working.

" '*Now* I'm going back,' I said. 'Coming?'

"And I got on to my hands and knees and managed to get to my feet. . . . Do you know what Flash Hardmann did?

"He cried.

"Leastways that's what it looked and sounded like, and he got to his knees and put up his hands —like a damned praying mantis. I'd got a few more words left in me.

" '*Let the best man win,* Flash Hardmann,' I said. '*I'm Millie B——'s husband,*' and I staggered off—back along the trail we'd come."

Digger fell silent.

"Did he follow you?" I asked, as Digger gave no signs of continuing the tale.

"Yes," said Digger at length. "He followed me.

"Three times I looked back, and he was coming on, exactly like a drunken man. The fourth time I looked . . . he wasn't there. . . ."

"What happened to you? You must have been nearly as far gone, yourself?" I asked.

"Yes. . . . But it's the mind more than the body. . . . I had what held me up, and he had what thrust him down. . . . I had to find Millie. . . . He had Millie on his conscience, and he knew it by the time we parted. . . .

"What happened to me? . . . I dunno . . . rightly. . . . I went mad of course, and wandered. . . . And it seems I'd got to the point of taking my clothes off, when some black-fellows who'd followed our tracks found me. . . .

"They found Hardmann's body later.

"They decided I'd be more valuable alive than dead, gave me water, and took me back to the bush-hotel."

"Did you go after the gold?" I asked.

"No. I heard war had broken out, and I found I didn't care about using Hardmann's outfit after all.

"So I decided when I could move I'd go to C—— and look for Millie: and then enlist or not, according."

Silence.

"Did you find Millie?" I asked.

"Yes . . . 'Happily married' as they say . . . to another man."

Poor old Digger.

*   *   *   *   *

We had an alarm last night.

An astounding thing occurred, according to Old Thirsty-face who fired the shot that roused the post.

Père Cocteau rejects his story and bids him beware lest such foolishness leads him untimely to his ultimate bourne—a lunatic asylum.

Old Thirsty-face, however, stoutly affirms that he was *not* drunk at the time, neither was he asleep nor dreaming.

Personally, I believe his story, partly because he's neither the wit nor cause to invent such a tale.

According to this, he was standing in shadow, looking out over the wall, when suddenly, from somewhere outside, a voice began calling to him in French.

"Calling quietly" was the phrase Old Thirsty-face used.

Although it was a bright moonlight night, he could see no one.

"Sst!" went the voice. "Who's there? . . . Do you want a thousand francs, and a splendid time? . . . Freedom . . . Promotion . . . Women . . . Wine . . . Ease . . . Everything you want . . . eh? Come on down if you do. Come and join the Sultan, the Big Kaid, and be a nobleman instead of being a slave."

"Who are you?" inquired Old Thirsty-face.

"Friend . . . Old comrade . . . Once a two-sous *légionnaire*, now an officer in the Kaid's army."

"What? A deserter?"

"Yes. Easy as spitting. And now I'm rich and a gentleman."

"Then take that, gentleman," replied Thirsty-face, and fired his rifle, as he says, smack into the middle of the voice.

Apparently his story is accepted by Lieutenant V—— who has given strict orders that the excellent example set by Old Thirsty-face is always to be followed in such circumstances—from which we gather that this sort of thing has happened before, and may happen again.

At the inquiry, Old Thirsty-face maintained that he did not recognize the voice.

CHAPTER IX

I have distinguished myself at last, and done an amazing thing, though no one but Terry and I know how curious and remarkable it is, and I am asking myself the old, old question, which most people have cause to ask themselves at least once in their lifetime—pure, idle coincidence, or the sure inevitable hand of Fate?

I was in the middle of my two hours' sentry-go last night, thinking of nothing in particular, when suddenly I almost jumped out of my skin.

A voice suddenly called, in what was neither a stage whisper nor a low urgent shout.

"Hsst! Who's that? . . . Want a thousand francs . . . a couple of wives . . . a big income . . . Colonel's rank . . . freedom . . . ?"

"Who are you?" I called back.

A totally different voice replied and from a different place.

"A friend . . . Used to be a fool *légionnaire* . . . Now I'm a Kaid, and live like a lord. . . . Come on down, and I'll give you a thousand francs now. . . . If you can bring any others, they'll get a thousand each, and you another hundred each, for bringing them. . . . Come on."

I have splendid sight, and the moon was again full.

As I stared and stared, straining my eyes over the moonlit ground before the Fort, something moved.

Something as grey as the ground, and, like a shadow upon it, moved.

Resting my rifle, I took steady aim and fired, and distinctly saw two or three movements, as though large grey forms crept swiftly into the dark shadows among which they were but darker shadows.

I think I was under strong suspicion until sunrise this morning when my veracity and my marksmanship were both vindicated.

A man, clothed in a dirty hooded *burnous*, grey and dirty as the ground, lay dead a short distance from the wall.

As we approached the body, Père Cocteau who stooped and pulled aside the hood of the *burnous*, suddenly guffawed.

"Ho! Ho!" he cried. "Thought he was so absolutely certain he was going to be killed by a woman!"

Terry gave me a queer quick look.

It was Matthieu le Maquereau.

CHAPTER X

"Do you know what to-day is?" said I this morning to Terence, as we drank our *jus* at réveillé.

"Thursday . . ." he growled.

"Pay-day," he added, yawning. "About two-pence-half-penny in real money."

"It's something else," said I.

"My birthday?" he inquired, swirling the coffee round in his "quart" mug.

"No."

"Yours?"

"No."

"What then?"

"It's half-time, my son."

"What d'you mean?"

"To-day, Terry, we complete two-and-a-half-years' service in the Legion."

In the manner of a football-referee, Terence Hogan blew a long whistle.

"Half-time!" quoth he. "*Vive la France!*"

Available P. C. Wren Titles from Riner Publishing Company

The Collected Short Stories

Volume One: ISBN 9780985032609
Volume Two: ISBN 9780985032616
Volume Three: ISBN 9780985032623
Volume Four: ISBN 9780985032630
Volume Five: ISBN 9780985032647

The Collected Novels

Volume One: *The Geste Novels*
  Part A: ISBN 9780985032678
  Part B: ISBN 9780985032685
Volume Two: *The Sinbad Novels*
  Part A: ISBN 9780692639382
  Part B: ISBN 9780692639429
Volume Three: *The Foreign Legion Novels*
  Part A: ISBN 9780999074909
  Part B: ISBN 9780999074916
Volume Four: *The Earlier India Novels*
  Part A: ISBN 9780999074923
  Part B: ISBN 9780999074930
Volume Five: *The Later India Novels*
  Part A: ISBN 9780999074947
  Part B: ISBN 9780999074954
Volume Six: *The English Novels*
  Part A: ISBN 9780999074961
  Part B: ISBN 9780999074978
Volume Seven: *A Mixed Bag of Novels*
  Part A: ISBN 9780999074985
  Part B: ISBN 9780999074992

Further information can be found at
rinerpublishing.wordpress.com

www.ingramcontent.com/pod-product-compliance
Lightning Source LLC
Chambersburg PA
CBHW030737030726
47497CB00001B/14